# BATTLE CREEK

## THE 500 SONG
## ROCK & ROLL DAYDREAM

### AUGUST WANDERLUST

**Battle Creek**
*The 500 Song Rock and Roll Daydream*

© 2022, August Wanderlust.

Print ISBN: 978-1-66786-029-9

eBook ISBN: 978-1-66786-030-5

To those who let their imagination run wild to music.

Special thanks to everyone who helped me edit this mess.

Mom, Crystal, Spencer, Jeff E., Diane L.,

Beth L., Jared at Blueline Editing,

You all know who you are.

R.I.P. Oldies 97.3 KBSG FM, Seattle,

& the Skate King Roller Rink in Bellevue, Wa.

# CONTENTS

# AUTHOR'S STATEMENT

'Battle Creek' is a tale that was conceived to music, one song and one daydream induced by that song at a time, and so I feel the songs that helped in its creation are an essential part to the story. I have included space for them in this book without using any lyrics by simply listing the song title, performing artist, and version of the song by that artist (if applicable), where it is to be played. The **"Title" by Artist** followed by **"End Song"** will appear around text where the song is to be played. Any words or even blank space that is left between these two queues symbolize the time passage between the beginning and ending of the song(s). If the phrase **"to play over this scene"** appears after a given title, it means that song, as well as the ones immediately following it, are somehow playing in the background; whether they are coming out of the speakers in a nightclub, or simply playing in the minds of the readers or the characters. All other songs listed by their titles and artists alone are hypothetically being performed by the band 'Battle Creek,' the members of whom this story revolves around. The idea that Battle Creek wrote and performed these songs is, of course, total fiction for the sake of the story. All songs are copyrighted by their respective owners, who put all their blood, sweat, and tears into making them. Full song citation list at the end of the story.

I've used songs from the beginning of Rock and Roll in the 1950's, all the way to 2021, the year this novel was completed. This is because good music never gets old, and never fades away. I've only included awesome music in this book, and while bad things may happen in the story to the setting of these songs, nowhere in this book will any of them be used in a derogatory or mocking voice against the artists that created and/or performed them. This is meant to be a tribute to the greatest songs in the world, and to the people who wrote and performed them. I hope, if nothing else, this brings a bit of free advertising for the artists included. Especially for those who haven't been on the Top 40 charts in a long time. You all inspire me, and may these songs become known to, and loved by, the current generation, and all the future ones to come.

*Please pay for your music and help support your favorite artists.*

# CHAPTER 1

## (We're an American Band)

MEMPHIS, TENNESSEE. LATE AUGUST

| | |
|---|---|
| 1. | "Ring of Fire" by Johnny Cash |
| 2. | "Thousand Miles from Nowhere" by Dwight Yoakam |
| 3. | "Take Me Home, Country Roads" by John Denver |
| 4. | "Okie From Muskogee" by Merle Haggard |
| 5. | "Don't Rock the Jukebox" by Alan Jackson |

A thin haze of cigarette smoke hung in the air of the packed rustic tavern. Small wisps of it occasionally escaping between the cracks in the wall boards and out into the night. Most of the dim light inside stemmed from two mismatched bulbs on either side of the plywood stage, located at one end of the building. At the other end, bartenders turned out beer and mixed drinks in what was functionally darkness. The sound of bottles being set down on tables, mixed with the vague din of talking, sustained a low pulse of life in the room. But, between the crowds who showed up every night to drink, and the musicians who came and went off the stage, it gave the place enough of a soul to continue to stay open night after night.

The dim stage light cast an unusual appearance on all three of them as they sat at one of the old tables. The yellow-orange glow on Hal's hair and eyes made them look almost brown, even though both were ash grey, and had been since the day he was born. He had the hair of an old man even though he was barely past two decades in the world, though his face was certainly young enough to negate the color of his hair. Most who saw him assumed he had simply dyed it that color for some strange reason. His sideburns and the small goatee at the base of his chin were also grey. Observers would quietly marvel at the dedication it must take for someone to dye their facial hair to match what was on the top of their head. The grey didn't stop with his hair on this particular night. He was wearing a dark smoke grey button up shirt with stylish light grey jeans, and a pair of medium grey shoes. He had discovered the more grey he wore, the more of a spectacle he became to people. It was beautiful, sweet irony to him that he could make himself stand out more by wearing all monotone colors. He liked to think he was one of the few people on earth who had that ability. He didn't do this every day. He had a whole wardrobe of other colored button up shirts and jeans, but tonight felt like a good night to be stared at. He often wore a grey fedora hat to complete the look, however, it was hot out and the hat had been making him sweat. So, it had stayed back at the motel for their dinner outing.

The light on Ryan's arms gave all of his normally colorful tattoos an almost rusted tone; like old metal embellishments riveted to his flesh as opposed to skin ink. The light also played like streaked blonde highlights on the glossy hair gel holding up his black, fanned mohawk. It reflected brightly off his nose ring and the metallic plugs in his gauged, pierced ears, making him give off light like an earth-bound god in a romantic movie. Though he generally spent his time being an unholy terror. Uli was perhaps the least affected by the room. It simply turned his short hair from an acid-blonde to strawberry blonde, and made no difference to his black leather jacket or blue eyes, both of which were never under any circumstance willing to be anything other than black and blue. He was, however, casting a rather impressive shadow on the floor. Even though he was sitting down, he was still head and shoulders higher than Ryan and Hal. And so, he didn't lose any of the towering appearance that followed him wherever he went, and ducked down with him whenever he walked through a doorway.

"Does anyone else here think that this guy's actually not half bad?" Hal asked.

"God, Hal, you've got to be kidding me," Ryan replied.

"No, I'm serious."

"So am I. We've been to five high-end venues in as many days, and saw nothing promising at any of them. But now, as we sit here in a flea-pit tavern on open mic night, your interest is finally piqued by a guy wearing a dead animal on his head," Ryan said.

"Hey, we never set out to find the best dressed guitarist, and what I'm hearing right now is actual skill," Hal insisted.

"Great. Scouting at the redneck talent fair," Ryan mumbled as he took his fork and dove down into his steak, dunking the front spike of his black mohawk into a cup of barbeque sauce on the table as he leaned over. Hal cringed at the little strands of hair sticking out of it as Ryan straightened back up, and reached reluctantly across the table for the bottle of ketchup. "Besides, Hal, he's a country singer. He's not going to be up for your standard rock and roll band. Not to mention, most normal guitarists might get a little put-off by random bouts of German heavy metal."

"It is how you separate the boys from the men," Uli said, without looking up from his newspaper.

"Actually, Uli, I think it's how you separate us from any fans we might ever have," Ryan replied. Uli's two blue eyes appeared slightly over the top of the newspaper, glaring at Ryan.

"Uli, if looks could kill, yours would have done you in a long time ago," Ryan said.

"Just because you go everywhere with a mirror in front of your face does not mean everybody else does," Uli responded.

"At least I have a reflection," Ryan replied.

The two started to argue across the table, and Hal put his head in one hand and rubbed his eyes wearily as he turned his attention back to the short, stocky guitar player on the stage. He was sitting on a flimsy wood stool with the microphone well below his chin, so it wouldn't interfere with the harmonica in the homemade metal holster around his neck. Two big, thick, brown sideburns framed his face, and the light behind him illuminated the front tips of his fuzzy brown hair, which stood slightly up off his head like it was holding a static charge. The rest of his hair was hidden under a classic Davy Crockett-style raccoon skin cap, complete with a furry ringed tail hanging off the back. He was fairly muscular for his size, but with a tiny pudge of a gut sticking out over his khaki shorts. Visible only because his red, plaid flannel shirt had caught on one of the clasps of his guitar strap, and was pulled up a little bit; probably unbeknownst to him. The black sandals on his feet looked like they were nearly worn through the soles. The pick guard on his acoustic guitar was in much of the same condition; intact at its edges, but faded to what would soon be a hole at the center.

> End Songs 1 – 5

The song came to an end, and the audience clapped as well as a room full of drunk people could. The guitar player leaned over to the microphone. "Uh, thank you," he said, short and simple, before he started strumming his next song.

> 6.  "Achy Breaky Heart" by Billy Ray Cyrus

The deep, rich echoes of the guitar chords began to resonate throughout the room, and Hal listened to it for a few moments, deep in thought. "That guitar sounds pretty good considering it looks like it's about to fall to pieces, and this guy can hit those low notes. That would be useful for backup…"

"Hal, are you desperate!?" Ryan interrupted his own unfinished insult that was about to be sent Uli's way. "We don't want a country guitarist!"

"Well, why not!? If we added him, we'd probably have a complete collection. Between your punk rock, my pop rock, and Uli's heavy-metal rock opera… orchestra… stuff…" Hal hesitated while he composed the rest of his thought. "If we threw in a country guy, we could appeal to damn near everyone at least 25 percent of the time."

"And offend everyone else the other 75 percent of the time."

"Ryan!" Hal said sternly.

"WHAT?" Ryan defended.

"What is your deal tonight!?"

"How can you separate his deal tonight from the rest of the time?" Uli asked.

"What are you two, five!?" Hal said as he grabbed both of their forks, stabbed two buffalo wings, and stuffed them into their mouths. "Cram it!"

Uli chewed up his buffalo wing, swallowed it, then glared at Ryan. "Ryan, you should thank Hal, he is trying to feed your skinny, tattooed ass."

"He stuffed one into you too, stupid," Ryan said. A short pause followed until they noticed Hal staring at them in silent exasperation. Uli took back up his newspaper, and Ryan sat down and glanced around the room. The guitar player stood up and sang louder as he went into the final chorus, and the audience clapped and cheered furiously.

"You *really* want to try this guy in the band?" Ryan asked.

"Sure! Look at this!" Hal gestured at the audience. "Listen to this! This guy *knows* how to play the guitar, he's not just up there strumming random chords. He can work a crowd, he…"

"Hal, these people are drunk," Ryan interrupted.

"Hey, drunk people can be the toughest audience. You know that as well as I do," Hal said.

"Alright. Fine. Go ask him. He'll say no, and we can move on with our night," Ryan relented.

"I will, thank you," Hal replied.

End Song 6

The song came to an end, and the audience burst into applause. The manager of the tavern walked out onto the stage and took the microphone. "Ladies and gentlemen, let's hear it one more time for Ricky Raccoon!"

Applause erupted once again, even louder than before, and Hal cringed as Ryan suddenly looked back at him. "Okay. We're leaving," Ryan said, and started to get up. Hal caught him by the back of his shirt. "No… wait a…"

"Hal! No! This is the stupidest idea you've ever had. The guy's obviously some sort of weirdo."

"Exactly! He'll fit right in!" Hal insisted.

"I'm done with this shit," Ryan mumbled as he yanked his shirt free, and took a pack of cigarettes out of his pocket as he headed for the front door.

Ricky took a quick bow, then walked off the side of the stage. While the manager was busy introducing the next act, Hal took the opportunity to run backstage without being noticed. Uli followed closely behind. They found Ricky right around the corner, putting his guitar away in a case that looked like it was made entirely out of duct tape. They stopped a few feet from him, and Hal casually crossed his arms and leaned against the wall.

"Hey, you put on a really good one-man show."

The short country boy looked up at Hal, startled, but quickly developed a humble, toothy grin. "Uh… thank you," he said in a heavy Southern accent.

"Where'd you learn to play like that?"

"A neighbor," Ricky answered.

"Cool," Hal said, then there was a short pause. "Oh, uh, sorry. My name's Hal. Hal Hulsing. We're musicians too. In a garage band," he said as he nodded in Uli's direction, then held out an open hand to Ricky.

"Hi," Ricky said as he shook it.

"And this is my friend, Uli."

"Uli Von Wolff," Uli said as he reached a hand out to Ricky. Ricky took it as he slowly glanced upwards to look Uli in the eyes. Uli likewise had to look straight down to see Ricky's face. It was quite the sight to have Ricky's roughly 5'3 next to Uli's 6'5

"You local around here?" Hal asked.

"Oh, no. Ricky travels all over the country. Never in the same place for very long," Ricky answered. Uli looked over at Hal suspiciously, but Hal ignored him.

"Oh, sweet! Where are you from originally?"

"Ricky comes from a small town in Arkansas. Very, very small town," he emphasized.

"Nice! What's it called?"

"Battle Creek."

"You're… kidding…" Hal said.

"Um… no?" Ricky responded, clearly confused.

"It's that… I'm from Battle Creek, Michigan. That's the name of our band. Battle Creek," Hal said, his eyes lighting up. "What the hell are the chances of that?" he asked. Ricky smiled and shrugged awkwardly.

"So, uh, I know we just met you and this is crazy, but me and my band mates are one man short, and we're looking for a lead guitarist. I don't suppose you'd be interested in maybe playing a couple shows with us?"

Ricky stared at Hal blankly for a moment, then turned his gaze briefly to Uli before settling back on Hal again. "*What!?*"

Hal laughed. "Yeah, sorry. I know this is sort of sudden, but we've actually been travelling around searching for a skilled guitarist, and we're finding all the available ones aren't that good, and the good ones are already taken. But, you had this whole place captivated, and, I don't know, that was really entertaining and you seem like you have a lot of good talent, and that's sort of what we're looking for," Hal said. "You'd get your share of pay for the shows we do, of course, and you'd sort of live for free at my mom's house. At least at first, anyways."

Ricky pondered the two of them again silently. They didn't *look* like serial killers, or cult members who were searching for their next human sacrifice. If this was a legitimate offer, he could really use the money. It would also be a lot more stable than going from bar to bar looking for work on a nightly basis, and playing on street corners during the day with his guitar case open for passers-by to throw loose change in. If they were plotting on doing something bad to him, he could probably crack each of them over the head with his guitar before they knew what happened, and then get a running start. He could sprint faster than most people would assume from looking at him.

"Uh... okay?" Ricky answered.

"R...really!?" Hal said. Ricky nodded.

"Awesome! Okay, um, we were in town playing at a casino last night, but our base of operations is back home at my mom's house in Michigan. We were going to head back there in the morning. Do you have any other stuff somewhere to go get?"

"Nope," Ricky said as he lifted the duct tape case and grabbed a medium-sized army-green duffel bag next to it.

"Alright, well, it's a little early, but the train leaves at 9:00 a.m., so we were all going to go back and crash at the motel. I can't imagine you'd want to share a room with a bunch of strangers, so we could get you your own room for the night. Would that be okay?"

"Sure!" Ricky said. As they started to head for the exit, Uli leaned over to Hal and whispered: "You cannot tell me it is normal to talk about yourself in the third person in America."

"I've got a feeling about this, Uli. I mean, he's from a town called Battle Creek. If that's not a sign, I don't know what is," Hal whispered back.

"*God help us,*" Uli mumbled to himself as they walked through the front door. Ryan was standing outside, and he did a silent double take when he saw Ricky. "Oh, Ricky, this is Ryan, our drummer. Look, Ryan, he said yes! We finally have a guitarist! At least, on a trial basis. Isn't that great?" Hal asked, and Ryan's eyes widened as he puckered his lips around his cigarette like he was going to take the rest of it in with one breath. Ricky took a nervous step back towards the tavern. "I knew you'd be excited! Let's go," Hal said as he started walking quickly down the street. Uli and Ricky followed close after. Ryan spit out the stub of his cigarette in a frustrated huff, and then trudged at a length behind them.

The rhythm of the tracks made a steady back beat for the tune Ricky was strumming on his guitar. The sun was high in the sky, and the country fields flew by in one continuous, golden blur. The temperature outside was in the mid 90s, and the window was half open to let the breeze in as the train chugged along. They had only been awake for a few hours, however, the heat made it feel like late evening, and everyone was slumped back in their seats, half asleep. "So, the deal is…" Hal started to say in a drowsy voice, and Ricky stopped playing and put down his guitar, "…we have a once in a lifetime chance coming up in about a year from now to get discovered and get a foot in the door in the mainstream industry. But, we all agreed we needed a fourth man to be the designated guitarist to really make the band work."

"Hal's been our guitarist thus far, but he is also lead vocals, and he cannot play guitar and sing very well at the same time. Some sort of strange cognitive problem," Uli explained.

"What can I say, I'm not a multi-tasker," Hal said.

"We did finally get him to the point where he could walk and breathe simultaneously," Ryan mumbled, not looking up from his phone.

"Shut up," Hal laughed, then looked back to Ricky. "Now, the thing is, we're a sort of unusual group. By that, I mean we do an extremely wide variety of music. Everything from punk rock, to metal, to standard rock and roll. We've never actually dabbled in any country music, but I don't think there'd be an issue with throwing some of that in, as well. The main thing is, we need somebody that is willing and capable of playing a wide variety of styles, and is, perhaps, crazy enough to have some fun while doing it. So, how does that sound?" Hal asked.

"Ricky can do that!" Ricky answered, nodding his head enthusiastically.

Hal raised his hands in the air in a welcoming gesture. "Well, there we go, then!"

"So, what's the once-in-a-lifetime opportunity y'all have in a year?" Ricky asked.

"Oh, right. So, we managed to get a slot to play at the Timberstash Music Festival in New York. Ever heard of it?" Hal asked. Ricky shook his head no. "OK, so, it's a big deal for bands that haven't quite hit it big yet. Producers and talent scouts stake out there, and a few groups usually end up getting signed every year."

"Yes, and Hal got us a spot through a method we will call 'creative exaggeration,'" Uli said, his arms crossed.

"Hey, we're going to deliver everything I said we would, and we have a whole year to figure out how," Hal said confidently, leaning back in his seat. "So, total change of subject, where did you get that hat of yours?" Hal asked Ricky.

"Ricky's brothers made it for him, to go with his nickname."

"So, that's a real raccoon?" Hal asked.

"Yep. They wanted to shoot one to make it, but Ricky didn't want 'em to kill a poor little raccoon for a hat. But then we was headin' home one night in Dad's pickup, and one ran out in front of us an' got hit. There was no way we could'a saw it comin', so Ricky figured it was okay if they made a hat out of that one," Ricky explained.

"You're wearing roadkill..." Hal said slowly.

"Yes!" Ricky answered with great enthusiasm.

Uli and Ryan both observed him cautiously out of the corner of their eyes, and Ryan cringed in disgust.

"Okay then..." Hal said. "How did you get the nickname?"

"Ricky's mom gave it to him. Somethin' 'bout always creeping around in the woods at night."

"Ooo… kay…" Hal said uncertainly. "What's your real name?"

"Ricky Ransom."

"That's an awesome last name," Hal said.

"'Suppose…" Ricky answered as he picked his guitar up again and looked back out the window at the farmland going by. The train began to go around a curve, causing the sun to shine directly on his face, highlighting something else peculiar about him to Hal.

"Whoa! Does everyone in your family have eyes that color?" Hal asked. Uli and Ryan both looked at Ricky, and noticed for the first time that he had brilliant seafoam-green eyes. They were lighter in the middle, with a darker green ring around the edge of the iris. Ricky looked around at them embarrassed. "Uh, no. Just Ricky. Everybody else has brown eyes."

"That's weird. Are you sure…" Hal didn't get a chance to finish his question. "Yes, the mailman had brown eyes too," Ricky said. "Plus, Ricky looks a lot like his dad and most of his brothers. Just a freak of nature, 'spose," he said proudly.

"Most of your brothers?" Uli remarked in his thick German accent. "How many siblings do you have?"

"Fourteen."

"Fourteen!? Are you shitting me!?" Hal repeated in disbelief.

"Yep. Fourteen," Ricky confirmed.

"How is that even possible!?" Hal asked.

"Mom married Dad young, and they'd had at least one baby every year an' a half since then, plus a couple sets of twins..."

"Your parents are… busy people," Hal said with an uncomfortable laugh.

"Yup," Ricky agreed.

"What number are you?" Hal asked.

"Ricky is number four."

"So, you're towards the top of the food chain."

"Yeah. Starting about when Ricky was ten, he was dad number three and parent number six whenever any of the younger kids needed somethin', an' everybody older was already busy."

"I think I'm getting a clearer picture of why you left home now," Hal said, and Ricky shrugged his shoulders.

There were a few moments silence before Ricky looked at Hal and asked: "So… what's with the hair?"

Hal smiled as he took his hat off, better revealing the thick covering of grey. "All natural. Born with it, just like my mom. *Maybe he's born with it…*" he said in a high-pitched voice as he threw his head back and ran his fingers through the silver-grey strands.

"That's… interestin'," Ricky commented.

"Yeah, well, just a freak of nature I guess," Hal said.

Although he was clearly trying to seem at ease, something about Ricky's behavior had come across nervous and reserved up to that point. But he appeared to genuinely relax a little after Hal said that. "So… um, are all y'all from Michigan?" Ricky asked.

"No, just me," Hal answered. "Uli's from Dresden, Germany, and Ryan is from Seattle."

"How'd y'all meet?"

"Well, I was attending a music academy in New York, and Uli was in one of my classes," Hal said. Then Uli took over: "I wanted to travel and get away from my mother and father for a while. They are very prestigious business people back home, and they had always planned for me to take over the company for them someday. But, I wanted to be a musician. They were not pleased with my decision, and spent all the time that we were together trying to talk me away from the idea. So, I decided to leave."

"Oh, that's rough," Ricky said.

"Me and Uli actually ended up getting a lot of classes together as the year went on, and I finally convinced him to help me start a band, even though he thinks I'm a moron," Hal said, and Uli rolled his eyes. "Anyways, we started playing little lounges and casinos, and we actually had a bit of success. Then we heard about a big music festival in Seattle, so we decided to go and check it out. After we left the stage for the day, this gangly, tattooed asshole with a mohawk came over to tell Uli what a crappy drummer he is. I asked him if he thought he could do better, he said yeah, and has sort of been traveling with us ever since."

"I needed to get away from my parents too," Ryan said. "We've had problems for years. But now we all have Hal's mom to make us dinner and pester us to clean our rooms."

"Us?" Uli commented.

"Hal's mom is hot," Ryan added, and Hal lunged one hand across the table at him to try and hit him, but missed as Ryan jumped sideways into Uli. Uli shoved him forcefully back onto his side of the bench.

"Anyways, yeah… we'll crash at my mom's house for a while, while we look for some new gigs. She doesn't mind acquiring new sons," Hal said as he sat back into his chair.

"That's nice of her," Ricky said.

"Yeah, Mom's been really great to all of us."

"You guys got other jobs, or do you make enough from playin' to cover the bills?" Ricky asked.

"Combination of the two. Me and Uli worked as maintenance and sound setup at a nightclub in New York to get ourselves through school. When I moved back home, Uli came with, and we got hired for a while at a club in Detroit where I would also DJ occasionally. But, we ended up working there so much during the weekend that we couldn't get any offers for performances since we were working through prime party time. So, now I work as a waiter in a steak house downtown, though occasionally I still do some freelance DJ-ing as well. I also used to work for UPS during the winter months, but I don't know if I'm going to have enough time to do that this year. Uli works in the repairs department of an electronics store. Ryan works in a hardware store because, you know, it takes a tool to know a tool. And my mom is an assistant manager in a book store, so there's that. But we try and not take too much of her money since she's been so nice about not making us pay any rent. Each of us gets one utility bill to pay a month, and we all cover our own food and gas and call it even since she'd be paying the same amount on the mortgage even if we were gone. She's sort of letting us have a few years to experiment and hopefully find success before we call it a failed operation and have to go out and get real jobs," Hal explained.

"Well, Ricky can get a job to help since…"

"Whoa, hey, slow down. Sure, eventually that'd be great, but for now, we're the ones who asked you to come with us, so you're our guest. Give it a little time to make sure you can stand us before you start putting down any roots. We can be pretty annoying after a while," Hal said, and saw a small smile begin to form on the edges of Ricky's mouth, revealing the little gap between his two front teeth.

"Ricky shared a house with sixteen people and a single room with six other brothers. Ricky accepts your challenge."

They walked up a thin cement-step path to the front door of a little mint green craftsman house, dating sometime between 1900 and 1920. It was in decent shape for a house of its age, having been lovingly cared for by every family that ever lived there. It was one of the lucky ones. Many of the other homes in the neighborhood were not in such good condition. The door creaked and popped as it opened, and there was one resounding thud as a mountain of travel bags and instrument cases hit the hardwood floor inside. Frantic scuffling could suddenly be heard at the top of the stairwell. "Uh, oh…" Hal said, and a small grey cat came into view, tearing around the corner. It slipped on the top stair, and came tumbling head over paws down to the entryway where they were standing. *'Wreeeeeee'* it made a squeaking noise that sounded far more like a rusty hinge than a meow, and Hal reached down and quickly picked it up. "Slinky! You stupid cat! You're gonna break your neck someday doing that! MOM, WE'RE HOME!" Hal yelled into the house, and moments later, footsteps came running down the hall. A small, slender, pretty woman in her early 40s appeared at the top of the stairwell. She had on a white lace dress that came down barely past her knees, and silver-grey hair that was up in a short bob. Its lack of color didn't make her look a day past her age. She looked better than her age, actually. A beauty queen with a few small wrinkles. "Welcome back, everyone!"

"Hi, Mrs. H," Uli and Ryan said.

"And you brought company! Who's this? I thought you said you didn't have any luck on the recruiting?" she said as she started walking down the stairs.

"Yeah, well, you go through five nice clubs, find nothing, and then you crash at the end of the day at the right tavern on open mic night," Hal said.

"You know, life works like that all the time. And your name is?"

"Oh… uh, Ricky. Ricky Raccoon."

"Ricky… Raccoon?" she asked amidst a bubbly laugh. "Okay, well, it's good to meet you. I'm Cecilia Hulsing. Or Mrs. H, I guess," she said as she reached a hand out to him.

"Pleased to meet you, ma'am," Ricky said as he took off his hat. Slinky suddenly began to squirm and writhe in Hal's arms. Before he could put her down, she broke free and jumped off and landed on Ricky's shoulders. She started to purr vigorously as she curved around his neck and rubbed against his hair, and Ricky reached up and started petting the back of her head. "Hello, kitty."

"Goodness, Slinky approves of your new recruit," Cecilia said.

"I guess so," Hal said, baffled.

"Well, come on in, dinner's ready," Cecilia gestured towards the kitchen.

"Mom, you didn't have to do that," Hal said.

"Yes, I did. God only knows what garbage you've been eating over the last week. Somebody has to make sure you ingest a little real food here and there."

"You take such good care of us," Uli said.

"It's my job," Cecilia answered as they all walked through the living room and into the kitchen. Slinky was still riding on Ricky's shoulders as he filled his plate, and as he sat down at the table and started shoveling food into his mouth.

"A little hungry, were we?" Cecilia said as four chicken tenders and a large pile of rice disappeared in a matter of seconds.

"Ya. Haven't had much food money as of late. This is really, really good," Ricky said.

"Well, thank you, Ricky," she said, amused.

"Ricky has been living the nomadic musician life for a couple years," Hal said.

"My gosh, don't you have a home to go to?" Cecilia asked.

"No, Ricky has a home. Just decided to travel," Ricky answered.

"I can tell from that lovely accent of yours that you're from the South, but where exactly is home for you?"

"Small town in Arkansas, ma'am."

"I see. What's the name of the town?"

"Battle Creek."

"Really!? That's quite a coincidence! I'm sure Hal already told you what his band is called and what city you're in right now..."

"Yes, we already had that conversation," Hal confirmed.

"So, if it's a small town, probably not a lot to do there, huh?" Cecilia asked.

"No, ma'am."

"Not a lot of opportunity to get a good job either, I bet?"

"Nope," Ricky answered quickly. Right as he was about to take another spoonful of rice, Slinky's bushy grey tail, which had been resting draped over his shoulder, flicked up and hit him in the mouth. It left small clumps of little hairs on the spoon and a few on his face as well.

Cecilia jumped up and walked around the table. "Oh, dear. Here, let me take her…"

"No, no, it's okay…" Ricky said as he picked the hair out of the rice, then reached up and scratched Slinky's ears.

'*Wreee.*' The cat let out a quick squeak, and then started purring again.

"You seem to have such a draw with her," she said. Ricky shrugged. "No really, she never does this. I've never seen her hold still and ride around on anybody's shoulders before, let alone get up on them herself."

"Ricky and animals get along real good," Ricky said, and Cecilia raised one eyebrow at him.

"If you don't mind my asking, did you grow up on a farm?"

"Yes, ma'am. But not a livestock farm. Wheat farm."

"Oh, wow. I know farmers have such a rough go at it. Are they doing okay without your help?"

"Might be doing better," Ricky answered.

Hal jumped into the conversation. "Ricky has fourteen siblings, Mom."

"Oh, my God! Your poor mother!" Cecilia said.

"No, Mom's okay. It was her idea to have that many kids. Nobody really knows why, though," Ricky said.

"It must be even harder to feed that many mouths," Cecilia added.

"Yes, ma'am, it is. But we do hold the yearly record for fastest harvest in all ah' Battle Creek."

"Your family isn't at risk for losing the farm, are they?" Cecilia asked.

"Well, things got real bad for a while ah' few years back, and it looked like it was headin' that way. 'Cause, even though some of us was growin' up, there wasn't any other jobs around. But then grandpa died, and we got his estate and money, which wasn't that much, but Mom and Dad took a gamble with it and used all of it to send Rob, he's the oldest, to medical school. He graduated an' moved to Little Rock and got a practice there, and now he makes lots of money and sends enough of it home to keep the farm goin.'"

"Oh, good. That's good to hear," she said.

"Yeah. We got lucky with Rob. Rob's real smart. The rest of us ain't."

"Now, don't say that!" Cecilia said firmly, and Ricky suddenly straightened up in his chair. "Just because you don't want to pursue a heavy-hitting career doesn't make you any less intelligent than anybody else! Let me tell you something, I went to one of the highest-rated schools in the area growing up, and I'll bet you anything that plenty of my classmates are still in some dead-end, low-wage job that never took them anywhere. I knew one girl named Elizabeth who was a straight-A student, looked like a supermodel, got voted senior prom queen, the works. A year or two after we graduated, we both ended up working at the same café downtown. Despite how she was in school, at work she was pretty much useless. She was always late, and nobody wanted to work with her because she did more damage than good. She got fired fairly quickly after I started there. It was a night and day difference from what she used to be. Granted, she was a rather severe case. There are people who do okay in a controlled environment, but once they get out in the real world and have to make their own decisions, they completely fall apart." She put her hands on the table and looked straight at Ricky. "But you are a handsome young man who obviously has some incredible musical talent since you got invited by my son to come join this family. And, if you've been out in the world successfully taking care of yourself on a day-to-day basis, then you have a perfectly good brain in your head, and you're going to make something of yourself unlike a lot of people out there. Even the ones who have college degrees." Cecilia finished her speech, and Ricky looked down at his plate and turned a light shade of red. The table fell silent, and she stood up and looked at the clock. Boys, it's nice to have you all back home, but I'm going to bed early tonight so I can hit the farmer's market first thing in the morning before they run out of fresh fruit.

"Okay, Mom," Hal said, trying to keep a straight face.

"You are not going to sit and eat with us?" Uli asked.

"Oh, I already ate earlier. I didn't know when exactly you guys were going to show up, so I guessed later than sooner, to be safe."

"Ah. Well, it was excellent as usual, Mrs. H."

"Thank you, Uli. Put your dishes in the dishwasher when you're done, okay guys?"

"Yes, Mrs. H.," Ricky, Uli, and Ryan answered in perfect unity.

"I guess I'll see you all sometime around noon tomorrow, or whenever it is that you get up. Goodnight," Cecilia called as she headed back to the staircase.

"'Night, Mom," Hal called after her. After she disappeared upstairs into her room and shut the door, Hal, Uli, and Ryan all looked at Ricky and started chuckling quietly.

"You know…" Hal started to say, "…if you ever get the urge to look at her blankly and say '*Yes, mother*', she's used to it."

"She's… nice," Ricky said quietly.

"Yeah, she is. But there's more to Hal's mom than meets the eye," Ryan said as he got up and began scraping the remnants on his plate into the garbage. "Her dad was the scariest mob boss in all of Detroit twenty-something years ago. Mrs. H is a tough ex-mafia princess masquerading as an innocent house mom."

Ricky looked up, shocked.

"She never liked any of the mob stuff her dad did, but she does have a bit of his viciousness in her. You cross her, and she'll kick your ass while you look on helplessly in terror. The bruise will be sore for weeks," Ryan said.

"Yes, Ryan would be the foremost authority on Mrs. H's ass-kickings," Uli added.

"So… does your grandfather ever visit?" Ricky asked Hal, nervously.

"Oh, no, he was killed in a gun battle with the police when I was eleven," Hal answered.

"Oh... sorry..."

"Nah, don't worry about it. I didn't understand much about it when I was a little kid, because he was always nice to me. But, knowing now what he did back then, the city probably got a lot safer once he was gone. It's all in the past now, anyways," Hal said.

Ricky opened his mouth as if he was going to say something, but stopped and looked back down at his dinner. Hal had seen that face many times before and already knew what the question was. "Yes, my dad was in the mafia too. Except, he was in an opposing mob of my grandfather's. He was sent as a hit man to kidnap and kill my mom to get revenge on my grandfather for something he had done to their boss. But, after he had kidnapped her, they spent a few hours talking in an old warehouse, and by the end of the night he just couldn't bring himself to do it. They were so taken by each other that they ran off and tried to start a normal life together. Needless to say, my dad's boss found out about what happened and was not pleased one little bit. They managed to hide in Atlanta for a while, but were eventually tracked down. One day while they were walking home along a side street, a car drove up and some guys leaned out of it and grabbed my mom. Before my dad could even react, they shot him three times in the chest. That was the last she saw of him. She escaped a few hours later when the guard watching her dozed off, and went back to the spot on the road and found a big puddle of blood, but no body. Now, the classic way the mob would dispose of someone was to use cement to sink them to the bottom of the nearest lake or bay, so that's probably where he is. Mom didn't know at the time that she was pregnant, so Dad never even knew I existed. After she made her way back home and found out about me, she told her father that she wanted nothing more to do with the family business, and that he could either take care of the both of us, or he'd never see her again. So, I grew up going on weekend fishing trips with one of the most dangerous men in the country."

Ricky stared at him, speechless. Hal quickly changed the subject. "Anyways, like I said, it's all in the past. There's an empty room at the end of the hall upstairs. There's a bunch of storage crap in there right now that we'll have to clear out, but the bed should be accessible. Tomorrow you'll have to show us more of what you can do with that guitar of yours. I also have a spare electric one that you can use."

Ricky ate the rest of his dinner without a word, took his dishes to the sink, then went to pick up his bag, all the while staring vacantly ahead while he digested Hal's story. The cat never left his shoulders, and rode with him contently up the stairs and down the hall to the empty room.

Uli glanced in Hal's direction. "You like scaring people with your childhood, don't you, Hal?"

"Hey, Ryan started it! Plus, I figure I should get it all out of the way at once. It was going to happen at some point anyways. Why put it off?" Hal replied.

# CHAPTER 2

## (Bounce, Rock, Skate, Roll)

**The crack of noon the** next day found four hopeful musicians sitting in the living room of a modest craftsman house in the suburbs of Battle Creek, Michigan. The scene was a chaotic disarray of open luggage, dirty socks, empty soda cans, and half-eaten bags of potato chips.

"So, Ricky, have you ever played an electric guitar before?" Hal asked as he set a hinged case on the ground and pulled out a blue Fender Stratocaster.

"No, but kinda tried to play electric guitar-like stuff on a regular guitar."

"Well, let's see how well that practice translates onto the real thing," Hal said as he handed it to him, then tossed the cord over to Uli, who plugged it into an amplifier. Ricky turned a few of the knobs, flipped the pickup switch a few times, and strummed a chord or two. "Feel ready for heavy metal yet?" Hal asked.

Ricky made some final adjustments to the settings, then immediately began plucking a fast pattern starting at the top of the neck of the guitar, then moving gradually down. He continued the complicated riff to nearly the highest frets at the bottom of the neck, then began to work his way back up again. His fingers were moving so fast they were nearly a blur, and when he finished, the room faded back to silence without anyone saying a word. Ryan raised both eyebrows in disbelief.

"Uh, was that okay?" Ricky finally asked.

"Um, yeah. That should… that should be fine for what we're looking for," Hal answered, trying to sound indifferent. He continued: "Um, so, I figured today maybe we could spend some time getting you acquainted with our original songs, and with some of the classics we cover too. Maybe you'll already know some of them? Then, later, if you're up for it, we could have a little jam session, and see if we come up with anything new and good. Adding a new person in always helps."

"'Kay," Ricky said.

"I'm actually feeling jam session first today," Ryan said. "Just in that kind of mood."

"Alright. That's fine with me if it's okay with you two," Hal said, and Uli and Ricky both nodded.

"But first…" Ryan walked to the fridge and pulled out four bottles of beer, "…a bit of extra inspiration," he said as he handed them over to Uli, Hal, and Ricky.

"Oh, no thanks," Ricky said quietly. Ryan kept the bottle at the end of his outstretched arm in front of him.

"That's real funny, Ricky. You're kidding, right?" he said, then immediately realized from the uncomfortable look on Ricky's face that it wasn't a joke. "Oh, no. No, no, no. Don't tell me you don't drink," Ryan said.

"Uh… no…"

"Well, why not!?"

"Makes Ricky sick," Ricky said quietly.

"Just one. One won't make you sick."

"It does…"

"Ryan, leave him alone," Hal came to Ricky's aid.

"Hal, how the *hell* are we supposed to get along if the guitarist won't get shitfaced with us!? How are we supposed to compose anything decent if one of us is sober all the time? Don't you get what this means for the band if he won't drink!?"

"Uh, that y'all always have a designated driver and you can keep more of the beer for yourself?" Ricky interrupted. Hal and Uli struggled to keep a straight face while Ryan turned slowly to look back at Ricky. "There's something wrong with you."

"Prob'ly," Ricky answered.

"ANYWAYS…" Hal interrupted, "…does anybody have something new they've come up with to start us off? And the rest of us can try to improvise something to go along with it? Ryan, you're the one in the jamming mood, you got something?"

"Sure, why not," Ryan said as he popped the cap off the bottle and sat down at his drum set. "I'm in a fast mood today, so I hope the rest of you can keep up," he said as he started pounding a beat on his drums.

The squeak of the door opening a couple hours later was lost to the sound of music flowing from the living room. Cecilia set the bags of produce down in the entry and stood as a silent observer while pieces of a song came into existence. After a couple of minutes, she slipped unnoticed into the kitchen.

"Alright, let's see how far we can get this time," Hal said.

"Okay, here we go… 1, 2, 3!" Ryan shouted.

> 7.   "It's the End of the World as We Know It (And I Feel Fine)" by R. E. M.

The drumbeat exploded through the quiet room, quickly followed by Ricky's guitar and Uli's keyboard. It was a very fast paced song, and Hal sang his lines as quickly as he could without getting tongue-tied. Cecilia peeked out from around the corner and watched them again for a bit. Hal suddenly stopped singing when he noticed her, and the other three lost the rhythm one at a time and stopped as well.

End Song 7

"Oh, sorry guys, I didn't mean to interrupt you," Cecilia said.

"It's fine, I just wasn't expecting you there. When'd you get back?" Hal asked.

"About ten minutes ago. How long have you boys been at it?"

"Since noon."

"The creative juices are flowing freely, I see."

"Oh, yes," Hal said.

"Amongst other things…" Cecilia said, eyeing the empty bottles on the floor.

"We'll clean it all up," Hal said.

"I know," Cecilia said. "But this is your friendly reminder that you should consider putting something else in your stomachs besides beer. You want me to make you all lunch?"

"No, no, Mom. You made dinner last night. I'm the one who works in a restaurant. I'll make something," Hal said as he got up and made his way to the kitchen. "What do you want? Your choice."

"How about a Turkey sandwich and a bowl of tomato soup. Make some for you and your friends, too, to offset all the junk food."

"Coming up," Hal said as he began to grab supplies out of the fridge. Cecilia turned around with a smug smile on her face, and flashed a quick thumbs up to the rest of the room. They took a short break to eat, then went back to working on the song. They spent the rest of the afternoon making scattered progress on pieces of three different songs, and barely noticed the day had gone by until well after dark. By midnight, Ryan was passed out on the couch, and Ricky's fingers were sore and bleeding from the new steel guitar strings.

"Your fingers going to be okay, man?" Hal asked.

"Yeah. They'll heal," Ricky answered.

"I'm sorry, I wasn't really paying attention, but you should have said something before they got that bad. I didn't realize your acoustic guitar had nylon strings."

"It's fine. Didn't really wanna stop playing anyways."

"Alright, well, maybe we can just spend a few hours writing lyrics or something tomorrow before I have to go back to work on Sunday," Hal said, downing the last inch of the beer at the bottom of the bottle he was holding. "It'd be best to not keep re-opening the wounds every day."

"Yeah, prob'ly not," Ricky agreed.

"I'm going to bed," Uli mumbled.

"Me too," Hal said. He stood up abruptly and there was a loud pop. He paused for a moment before slowly bending backwards to stretch out his back. "Crap, that didn't feel like twelve hours until now."

"Should someone wake him up so he can go to bed?" Ricky asked, looking at Ryan.

"Nah. He behaves himself when he's asleep. Let's not ruin it," Hal said as he gathered up all his notes. Ricky set the guitar gently against the wall and reached down and flicked off the amp. Uli unplugged his keyboard and started to fold up the stand. Hal waited at the edge of the room until both of them finished, then turned off the light as they headed upstairs. "'Night all," he said at the top as they split to go to their separate rooms.

"'Night," they both answered back.

Hal woke up a few hours later feeling the effects of all the beer he drank and got up to stagger down the hall to the bathroom. The subtle thunk of the front door closing stopped him dead in his tracks. He quietly grabbed a thick wood baseball bat out of the closet, and glanced around the corner down the stairs just in time to see a figure wearing a raccoon hat jog out of sight around the street corner. His hopes sank. *Shit… shit, shit, shit…* He thought to himself. *Was it the incident with the beer? He seemed like everything was fine after that…* He walked halfway back down the hall and peered into Ricky's room. All his luggage was still half-unpacked on the floor. *He wouldn't leave without his stuff, right?* He looked back out the screen on the upper half of the metal door. *What the hell? Did I just imagine that?* He tried to recall the number of beers he had earlier, but kept losing count after four. Confused, he gave up and decided to figure it all out in the morning, and headed back down the hall towards the bathroom.

When he next awoke, the sun was beating down on his bed through the upper window. When he got up to close the blinds, he remembered what he had seen earlier that night, and ran silently towards the guest bedroom. He peered through the crack in the door, and saw Ricky sleeping on his stomach, with one dusty sandal hanging off his right foot. The cat was asleep on his back, curled into a fuzzy grey donut.

At breakfast, Hal glanced up again from his food at Ricky, who was starting to look a little more nervous each time it happened. "So... where exactly did you go last night at three in the morning?"

Cecilia peered over her shoulder from the stove, and Uli and Ryan halted their argument for a moment.

"Uh... for a walk..." Ricky answered.

"At three in the morning, in a city you've never been in before, after an exhausting day of songwriting?" Hal asked.

"Insomnia," Ricky said with a fake smile.

That was enough for Uli and Ryan, who went back to their fight. Hal remained unconvinced. Ricky tried to appear unbothered as he went back to his food. The phone rang, and Cecilia reached to pick it up, but found it was missing from the wall charger.

"Hal, where have you hidden the phone this time?" she asked.

Hal jumped up and tried to find the source of the ringing. He paused momentarily in the doorway to the living room, and then dove into the couch cushions. A quick beep, and he raised the phone to his ear.

"Hello?... Yeah, hi, Dave. What's up?...Well, that sucks... Really? I mean... absolutely... sure, we can do that... four fifteen?... Yes, we will... okay, thanks, Dave. See you then. Bye." He dropped the phone back into the couch. "Dave wants us to go play at the steak house again this coming Saturday."

"Cool," Ryan said, his look of approval suddenly sinking to suspicion. "Did his scheduled act die?"

"No, just a close relative of the lead singer."

"Well, that explains it," Ryan said.

"Hey, at least we've gone from 'Well, maybe next time' to back-up number one. I'd say that's a start, right?" Hal asked.

"Don't give yourself too much credit. Dave doesn't quite count since he's your boss. He probably feels sorry for us," Ryan said.

"No, I know Dave better than that. If he didn't want us playing there again, he'd straight up say so. He's a nice guy, but he doesn't do charity hearings for people he thinks suck."

"Maybe he's upgraded us to white noise, but I doubt it's anything beyond that," Ryan replied.

"Well, if that's the case, then he's going to be even more pleasantly surprised," Hal said as he looked over at Uli. "We can get a good set together by then, right?"

"Of course," Uli answered confidently.

"Yeah. Then, when he likes what he sees, we eventually become his main go-to, and use him as our reference for all the other restaurants in town," Hal said, and Ryan shook his head slowly.

"Hal, remember to put the phone back on the charger," Cecilia said as he came back into the kitchen.

"Don't worry, I'll get it in a minute, Mom."

She looked over at Uli doubtingly, but he was only able to offer up a sympathetic smile.

Later that afternoon, they had set up in the living room again to do more writing, but Hal finally had to admit defeat. "I've got nothing."

"Yeah, me either," Ryan agreed.

"We did so good yesterday…" Hal lamented.

"Yes, Hal. We wore ourselves out," Uli said.

"Yeah. I think we still need more time to recharge," Ryan commented as he reached down and picked up one of his drumsticks, then used it to pull and curl the front couple inches of his Mohawk. When he finished, he leaned over to check his work in the reflection on the TV screen.

"It looks fine, dear," Uli quipped.

"Thanks, Uli, that's sweet of you. I didn't know you felt that way."

"You know I try to make my feeling known to you any way I can," Uli replied.

"*Yeah, shove it up your ass,*" Ryan said under his breath, then said louder: "You know, we oughta take a break and go to the park. It's days like these that all the girls are half-naked and laying on towels."

"You do realize that it's illegal to get them completely naked in public, right?" Hal asked.

"Quit killing my fun, Hal," Ryan replied.

"Killing your fun brings me a lot of joy, Ryan."

"Fuck you, Hal."

"That's okay, Ryan, I think I'll pass on that."

"Shut up. So, you don't want to go girl watching?"

"I didn't say that," Hal said.

"Good. You had me worried there for a second," Ryan replied.

"You guys wanna take a break?" Hal asked Uli and Ricky, and they nodded. "Alright. HEY, MOM! We're going out, we'll be back later, okay?"

"Okay, don't work too hard…" Cecilia called back from the upper level.

It was another beautiful summer day in Battle Creek, and the sun was at the 5:00 p.m. position in the sky, casting long shadows under the trees in the park. Ryan joined in playing a volleyball game with a group of five girls in bikinis, while Ricky, Hal, and Uli laid on the grass under a large oak tree. Hal had been observing strange occurrences next to him for the last ten minutes, and he had finally had enough. "How are you doing that?" Hal asked.

"Doin' what?" Ricky answered.

"That!" Hal pointed at a little chickadee that swooped down and snatched a sunflower seed off Ricky's nose.

"Dunno. Ricky puts the seeds on his nose, and they come and get them," Ricky said.

"They wouldn't do that if it was me or Uli," Hal said.

"Here, try it," Ricky said, handing them a few seeds out of the bag. Hal and Uli took them and put them on their noses, then lay back motionless. They watched quietly as every bird in the park passed over them and took the seeds from Ricky's face.

"Seriously, what are you doing different from us to get them to do that?" Hal asked.

"Nothin'," Ricky insisted as he crushed up a potato chip, then held the pieces low to the ground in his outstretched hand. From out of nowhere, a chipmunk appeared, and ran up and started stuffing its cheeks with the flakes.

"You, sir, have the most serious case of animal magnetism that I have ever seen," Hal said.

Ricky chuckled a little to himself as he arranged ten seeds across his face, then shut his eyes and mouth tightly. Nine little songbirds and one blue jay descended upon him from out of the trees, and the seeds vanished in a matter of seconds. Uli and Hal stared in astonishment as Ricky sat up and picked a couple of down feathers out of his eyelashes.

"Do you, like, ever walk down the street and have problems with squirrels flying out of trees and sticking to your body as you pass?" Hal asked.

"Occasion'ly," Ricky answered.

Right then, Ryan sauntered up with one girl under each of his arms. "Hey guys, meet Amelia and Stacy."

"*Hiiiii,*" they both crooned.

"I was going to go back with them to their place for a while and play twister. You guys wanna come? They have friends."

Hal looked briefly at the girls, who were so covered in makeup it was hard to imagine what their real faces looked like, and whom he also had a feeling were wearing bras too large for them that were partially filled with something other than breasts. "That's okay..." he replied. "...I didn't get a lot of sleep last night. I'm not really in a partying mood."

Ryan looked at him suspiciously. "Fine, whatever. What about you two?"

"No, thank you, I require longer legs than that," Uli said, and Amelia and Stacy glared at him condescendingly.

"Just ignore him, it's his time of the month. Ricky?"

"Nah." Ricky shook his head.

"Fine, more fun for us three. See you losers later," Ryan called back as they strolled off.

"It is too bad we cannot volunteer Ryan as a test subject at The Center for Disease Control in the STD unit. It would probably lead to many great advances in medicine," Uli said. Hal laughed in agreement as he and Ricky got up and brushed the grass off of themselves. "We've still got four hours of daylight left. What do you guys wanna do now?" Hal asked.

"What are the options?" Uli asked.

"I dunno," Hal replied.

"There a roller rink 'round here?" Ricky spoke up.

"God, that's an idea. I haven't been skating in years," Hal said. "There's one about a half hour away."

"I've never tried it before," Uli admitted.

"Wanna give it a shot?" Hal asked.

"Sure," Uli answered, and Hal briefly had fun with the image of him slipping and falling helplessly all over the floor. They strolled leisurely down the street and back around the corner to the house. As they walked through the front door, Ricky ran upstairs and down the hall. He re-appeared a few seconds later holding two very beat up dark brown leather roller skates with black wheels.

"You're prepared," Hal said while he dug through a drawer and pulled out an old Ford key, then yelled out. "HI, MOM!"

"Ricky wants to see every state and skate at every rink in the country at least once."

"HI, HAL," was yelled back in their direction from down the hall upstairs.

"How many have you skated at so far?" Hal asked.

"Twenty-nine rinks in seven states."

"Jeez, you've been busy. You come from a family of busy people, don't you?"

"Mmm, hmm," Ricky replied as he bounded down the stairs four at a time.

"BYE, MOM!" Hal yelled again as they left.

"Uh… BYE, HAL."

As they headed across the yard towards the garage, a silver ball of fur suddenly fell out of the sky and landed on Ricky's head. Ricky dropped his skates, startled. Slinky purred contently while she curled around the back of his neck. "Hi, kitty…" Ricky rubbed her ears as he carefully bent over to pick up his skates.

"Ricky, seriously, you gotta leave the cat alone. She's supposed to stay inside." Hal carefully pried her off Ricky's shirt, and locked her back in the house. "God help us if we ever took you to the zoo." They walked over to a small, weathered, dark wood garage located across the alley on the street. Hal grabbed the handle on the garage door, then slowly pulled it up and shoved it over his head. The old tracks complained with a horrible screeching metal-on-metal grinding sound as it went, and two vehicles appeared out of the shadows. An old yellow van and a classic red Mustang rested in such close quarters, there was almost no room to walk in between them, or down the sides against the garage walls. Hal opened up one of the back utility doors on the van and climbed inside. Ricky started to follow, but Uli stopped him.

"He will back it out. This garage was only meant for one car and storage space, but because of those double doors on the back of the van, they can keep both cars in out of the rain and snow. Though to get the red car out, the van has to come out first."

The van chugged a few times before starting, and then a few seconds of smoke poured out of the tailpipe. As it backed out, Ricky saw it was an early 60's Ford Econoline. One of the old flat-front vans that had the engine located in the center of the body under a console in the passenger cabin. It was a brilliant shade of yellow and had a white pop-top camper roof as well as a white wheel cover over the spare tire on the back. Hal stopped it halfway down the driveway and let it idle, and Ricky stared at it for a few moments.

"Sexy, huh?" Hal said as he rolled down the window. "Meet the golden chariot of the Hulsing house."

"It's… a… Twinkie," Ricky stated slowly, and Hal and Uli burst out laughing. "It's even got the cream fillin'!" he added as he pointed at the wheel cover. Hal gestured towards the back of the van. "Look at the license plate."

Ricky walked around the back of the van and saw the custom Michigan plate:

### [TWINKIE]

"That's exactly what everybody says when they see it for the first time," Hal explained. "Tell you what though…" He shifted the van into park and got out. "The double doors on the back and side are great for loading large musical instruments." He opened both back doors, and there was enough room certainly to put a guitar case in lengthwise, if not an entire assembled drum set as well.

"Nice," Ricky agreed.

"It doesn't win any races, but it seats five plus all our equipment." Hal shut the doors firmly, then tugged at the handles a few times to make sure they latched. "Plus, it makes for a number of awful pickup lines," he said as he walked around the van and got back into the driver's seat. Uli and Ricky got in through the side doors. *"Hey ladies, wanna see my Twinkie? We can go for a ride..."* he said, and Uli cringed slightly and leaned over to Ricky.

"Sorry, Hal thinks he is funny sometimes when he's not," Uli whispered, and Ricky nodded slowly in agreement.

8.  "Stayin' Alive" by The Bee Gees *to play over this scene*

9.  "Starry Eyed Surprise" by Paul Oakenfold ft. Shifty Shellshock

10. "Uptown Funk" by Mark Ronson ft. Bruno Mars

11. "Play that Funky Music White Boy" by Wild Cherry

12. "Electric Avenue" by Eddy Grant

13. "Macarena" by Los Del Rio

14. "Respect" by Aretha Franklin

15. "Video Killed the Radio Star" by The Buggles

16. "Jump in the Line" by Harry Belafonte

17. "U Can't Touch This" by MC Hammer

18. "Saturday Night" by The Bay City Rollers

19. "Who Let the Dogs Out" by The Baha Men

20. "Whip It" by Devo

The rink was stuffed with people who came in to escape the late afternoon heat. The disco ball and floor lights cast a swirling, multi-color light show all throughout the cavernous building. A collection of retro songs set the mood, and the smell of fresh popcorn wafted out of the snack bar and across the floor. Uli spent most of the evening crawling along the wall, trying to keep his feet underneath him, while Hal found a pretty blond girl to skate with. Both of them watched out of the corner of their eyes as Ricky danced on his toes to the rhythm of the music in the center of the floor.

"Your friend is really good at this," she said to Hal.

"Yeah, he is, isn't he…" Hal replied.

She leaned her head against his chest while they skated backwards together and looked up at him through a set of seductive blue eyes.

"You're quite good yourself…"

End Songs 8 – 20

Two sets of feet hung off the end of Hal's bed at midnight as Ricky quietly crept by. Slinky followed him like a shadow down the stairs and out the back door. He dropped down onto a yellow lawn chair, and the cat did three circles, then laid down in his lap. He stroked her with one hand and rested his face on the other. Hal and Uli watched him for a few minutes from their windows, alerted by the quiet click of the back door. A few hours later, Ricky was asleep half under the covers with a small furry donut breathing slowly up and down on his back. The roar of an old van starting caused the little donut to stir momentarily, then it went right back to sleep. Ryan came up the stairs at a quarter past four, and gracefully tripped over the final step. On his spontaneous trip downwards, his desperate reach for the railing missed completely as he grabbed the frame of a large picture in the hall, which came off the wall and slammed into the back of his head.

"Good morning, Ryan," a pleasant voice gently offered from behind a closed door down the hall.

"Good morning, Mrs. H.," was the mumbled response from the hallway floor.

Uli cursed in his head as he looked at the clock and realized Hal's guess for when Ryan would get home had been closer, and he would be out another five bucks.

Saturday afternoon came, and Hal, Ricky, and Uli sat around the living room, waiting. "He should have been back twenty minutes ago," Uli said, impatiently.

"I know, just… give it a little longer. We can still probably get away with another fifteen minutes before we'll be in trouble," Hal said. Ricky was slowly strumming his old guitar while Slinky reclined on the couch next to him, batting at a loose string on his shirt sleeve.

"Here, wanna see another reason we named her Slinky?" Hal said as he took his keychain lanyard out of his pocket. Ricky put his guitar aside, and Hal held the lanyard over her face. "*Sliiiiinky…*" The cat immediately diverted her attention to the lanyard and grabbed it with both paws and sank her teeth into it. Hal tugged it gently a few times to make sure she had a firm hold, then began to slowly pull it back towards him. The cat's grip didn't loosen, however, while her upper half was dragged closer to Hal, her hind feet and tail stayed firmly planted next to Ricky; Her stomach seemingly growing longer with every inch he pulled. "She's like the Energizer Bunny, she just keeps going, and going, and going…" he explained.

"Longcat is long," Ricky agreed. The front door suddenly swung open, then slammed shut, and Slinky took off like lightning for a dark corner of the house to hide.

"Well, you decided to join us after all," Uli said as Ryan bounded up the stairs. He didn't even turn to look back at Uli as he headed down the hall.

"Look, I'm sorry, okay!? Somebody spilled a fuckton of tiny nails on aisle six right as I was about to leave, and the manager said I had to stay and help clean it up!" Ryan called back while taking off a red vest with a black name tag on it, and then disappearing into his room. He reappeared thirty seconds later wearing a completely different outfit. "Is all the equipment already in the van?"

"Yep," Hal answered as he stood up.

"Great, let's go. Of all the things I might be late for, you know I'm not late to drumming," Ryan said as he started back down the stairs. A minute later, the rusted door hinges screeched and shut, and the van pulled out of the driveway. "Is your mom coming?" Ryan asked.

"Yeah, she had to stay late at the store, but she promised she'd get there," Hal said. "It sucks trying to synchronize five different work schedules. I'm sorry we didn't get to practice more Wednesday, but Dave wasn't kidding when he called me in. When I got there, it really was a zoo. Apparently, the entire damn city decided it was a good night for a steak."

"I think that's a subcategory of Murphy's Law. If the universe can find an opportunity to use customers to screw with your schedule, it will take it. For example, sending a big bald guy to rupture a huge bag of nails when you're already late to your gig," Ryan said.

"Yeah, it's like they always know exactly when to strike," Hal agreed. "But I think we'll be okay. We were getting through everything fine on the first run before you had to leave, and if we get a little stuck somewhere, we can always BS it until we get back on track," he added.

"That's what I got my degree in," Ryan said confidently.

They drove six blocks through the city to the rear entrance of Dave's Steak House, then got out and started carrying in a mountain of instruments and sound equipment. An hour later, the lights flicked on, illuminating the small stage, and Hal stepped up to the microphone. "Good evening, beautiful people," he said, and the audience laughed a little. "My name is Hal, and I actually work here as a server on weeknights. But tonight, me and my friends are up here because Dave thinks we have a lot of potential as an up-and-coming local musical act... and because the scheduled entertainment had to cancel due to a family emergency." There was loud laughter and applause, and one enthusiastic YEAH from a random guy in the back. "So, we're just going to make some background noise while you all enjoy your food, and, yeah, we're Battle Creek. Thank you." Another round of applause, and Hal took a few steps back from the microphone, then glanced over at Ricky. "Ready?"

21. "Boys of Summer" by Don Henley

Ryan started in with a very gentle rhythm on his drums, then Ricky joined in picking a tune on the guitar. Uli joined in third playing a gentle melody on the keyboard. They played a long intro before Hal started to sing, and by the end of the first song, Cecilia was sitting at the closest table to the stage, adding as much as she could to the applause.

**End Song 21**

22. "You Can Do Magic" by America

23. "Life is a Highway" by Rascal Flatts

24. "Rock You Like a Hurricane" by The Scorpions

25. "Should I Stay or Should I Go" by The Clash

26. "I Want to Hold Your Hand" by The Beatles

27. "Free Fallin'" by Tom Petty

28. "All Summer Long" by Kid Rock

29. "Alive" by P.O.D.

30. "1985" by Bowling for Soup

31. "American Pie" by Don McLean

32. "16 Candles" by The Crests

33. "Friends in Low Places" by Garth Brooks

34. "Cemetery Gates" by Pantera

35. "Peaches" by The Presidents of the United States of America

36. "Absolutely (Story of a Girl)" by Nine Days

37. "Riptide" by Vance Joy

38. "Mr. Bojangles" by Nitty Gritty Dirt Band

39. "Talk Dirty to Me" by Poison

40. "What's My Age Again" by Blink 182

41. "Sunglasses at Night" by Cory Hart

When they had played in restaurants before, Hal noticed while the people may have been listening to every word, that they usually kept their eyes on their food and their company. But tonight, it seemed like the longer they played, the more the audience was actually watching *them*. Eating without looking down at their plates, and talking to their friends without making eye contact. He never wanted his band to only be a distraction in the background, even though he joked about it. That wasn't the point. He wanted to create an experience for people. And it may have been in his head, but when he looked out into the room, he felt like maybe for once he saw as many eyes as he did sides of heads.

End Songs 22 – 41

"Alright, we're going to end tonight with something that Uli, who is our own personal one-man symphony orchestra, composed on the piano. It blew us all away the first time we heard it, and we hope you'll like it too."

42. "Piano Man" by Billy Joel

Uli played a few light keys on the piano, spacing the notes out as a quick tease, then started in on a more even pattern as Ricky played accompaniment on the harmonica. With the intro setting the tone, Hal started to sing. Despite his often carefree and lighthearted attitude, he could sing with a heavily dramatic focus when he wanted to. With his eyes closed, he carefully wove the song's story to the room. As his mother watched him, it re-confirmed with her again why she wasn't pushing him harder to get a more serious job. He only ever seemed really, truly happy on stage, working magic on an audience. Uli stood up as he pressed down harder on the keys as they went into the final climax of the song. Hal sang like he could put any Broadway performer to shame, and Cecilia saw the delight in his eyes as they got their final applause of the night.

End Song 42

After the show, while they were packing their instruments back into the van, the evening kept replaying over and over again in his head. "So, Dave told me he thought we were really great tonight, and that we'd improved a lot. He even said he wants us back every other week or so, and he's recommending us to a buddy of his who has a bar across town," Hal said.

"Sweet!" Ryan's answer was half-muffled while he held a cigarette between his teeth.

"If this helps us start getting our name out there, we could be getting calls for bigger shows, like casinos and hotels, and..."

"Hal, yes, we had a good night, but calm down and try to focus on what's at hand," Ryan said.

"You really don't have any faith in us, do you?" Hal asked.

"Ryan has a point, somewhat," Uli said, and Hal turned to look at him. "Yes, I said it. We have to be smart about this, and not get ahead of ourselves."

"You get too damn excited over stuff that isn't happening yet," Ryan said.

"What's the point if we can't get excited about what could be?" Hal responded.

"I mean, just don't let it cloud things up! If we get some real leads we'll take them, but we can't just throw ourselves too quickly at anything. It'll make us fail on the business end of it if we look way too eager and overconfident for our own good," Ryan said.

"I'm not going to do anything to try and sink us. I'm just saying, why aim low?" Hal replied. He was starting to get annoyed.

"Hal, you can aim all you want, but if you go in too fast you'll end up messing something up anyways. Now look, I'm not going anywhere, I'm sorry to say I don't think Uli's going anywhere. Ricky, you think you wanna hang around with us for a while?" Ryan asked.

Ricky responded with an enthusiastic, "Yeah!"

"See? We've got time. Now, let us know what Dave's friend says about us playing at his place, and we'll go from there."

"Alright, alright," Hal relented, winding the cord loosely around his microphone. *One step at a time,* he thought as he set it down in its case, then smiled. *But even at that rate we're still going to make it to New York in a year...*

# CHAPTER 3

## (Takin' Care of Business)

LATE DECEMBER, 4 MONTHS LATER

---

43. "Tutti Frutti" by Little Richard *to play over this scene*

44. "Yakety Yak" by The Coasters

---

**The toast launched out of** the little toaster as it popped up, and Hal caught it mid-air before it hit the counter. After that, he unplugged the toaster and set the plug on the counter away from the wall. It had a short and would keep heating even after the timer went off. They should have retired it for a new one years ago, except the problem with new toasters was none of them had the spring that this one did. Plus, its polished metal body made it the best unbreakable mirror he had ever owned. He stuffed the toast in his mouth while pulling an old green vacuum cleaner out of the closet, then turned up a little red retro radio as high as it would go so he could hear it over the vacuum. He decided to begin with his mom's room upstairs, and drug the big vacuum up the staircase with the radio tucked under his arm. He picked up an electric blanket off the floor before vacuuming around her desk, and laid it gently down on her bed. It was her favorite little pet to keep warm with on cold winter evenings. He pushed and pulled the vacuum cleaner across the floor in time with the music, turning around as fast as he could with the beat whenever he reached a wall. Ryan and Uli liked to make fun of him for

44

dancing with the appliances whenever he was doing chores, but the music helped make the housework fly by so much quicker. Plus, nothing was going to bring him down today. Ricky decided to stay and had settled into living with them, they had been making steady progress on several original songs, and they were playing a big New Year's Eve show at a hotel the next night. He yanked the vacuum cleaner back towards him at the start of the next chorus, then heard a crack as the room suddenly went dim. "Dammit." He turned off the little orange table lamp, then unplugged it from the wall before carefully unscrewing what was left of the broken bulb. He opened the hall closet and started searching for a new bulb when Ryan stepped out of the bathroom into the hall.

End Songs 43 – 44

"Hey, Hal?" Ryan asked.

"Yeah?"

"You know that screwdriver you guys have with the really wide head?"

"Yeah…?"

"Where is it? A few of these corner tiles have really become one with the floor and I can't get them up."

"I think it's in the farthest right cabinet next to the dryer. That's the last place I remember it," Hal answered.

"Alright," Ryan said.

"I'm surprised you're having so much trouble with this. I mean, shouldn't you be an expert on bathroom floors by now?" Hal asked.

"Hey, I've woken up on some really nice kitchen floors and front lawns too!" Ryan yelled back as he went down the stairs to the main level, and then down the second flight of stairs to the basement.

"*To name a few…*" Uli mumbled from behind the closed door to his room, where he still had the innards of the family computer strewn about.

Hal had made the fatal mistake earlier in the day of starting a short conversation with Ryan, thinking, under reasonable suspicion, that his mom had already left for work. What he didn't know was she was still in the house, having traded the opening shift for the closing shift with the main manager on a last-minute request.

"I'm bored. Whatta you wanna do today?" Hal had asked. It was his day off. Ryan made the next mistake, running under the same suspicion. He also had the day off.

"I dunno... I was going to eat something then go back to bed." A few moments later, they noticed the shadowed figure of a woman standing in the doorway not far from where they were sitting. Even though she was in the dark, they immediately knew she was smiling.

*Take Out the Papers and the Trash, Get Caught up on Dishes, Do a Load of Laundry* and *Scrub the Litter Box* had already been crossed off the long list she left for them. Now, they were deep into to the more intensive things. Ryan was making progress on replacing the ancient, cracked tiles on the bathroom floor. Uli was fixing the computer, and Hal got full-housecleaning duty. He took a new 40-watt bulb out of its box, and carefully screwed it into the lamp socket. He flipped the switch, and the room filled with light at the same moment the front door opened. Ricky was home from his job. He kicked the snow off his sandals and bare toes at the base of the threshold before stepping inside, then heard Ryan start yelling from down in the basement:

"GODDAMMIT, WHERE ARE YOU, YOU LITTLE..."

Ricky went down the stairs, and found Ryan in the laundry room, grabbing handfuls of clothes off the floor and throwing them to the side. He leaned through the doorway behind him. "Whatcha' doin'?"

"I'm looking for the laundry weasel!" Ryan said loudly. Ricky pondered the statement silently for a few seconds. "You're... what?"

"THE LAUNDRY WEASEL. I'M LOOKING FOR THE LAUNDRY WEASEL!" Ryan repeated.

"Um… how do y'all know the laundry weasel is under the clothes?" Ricky asked.

"BECAUSE I CAN HEAR IT GIGGLING WHEN I'M WALKING AROUND IN HERE!"

Ricky said nothing more, and started to slowly back away towards the stairs. But just as he was about to go up, Hal and Uli started to come down. "RYAN! WHAT THE HELL ARE YOU YELLING AT!? Oh, hi, Ricky," Hal said as he caught sight of him. "Is he screaming at *you*?" Hal asked, and Ricky shook his head no. Ricky had an odd look of concern on his face, and Hal and Uli made their way to the bottom step and peered into the laundry room. "Oh God, you aren't hunting laundry weasels again are you?" Hal asked.

"Yes, I am, and I have no regrets," Ryan answered as he went back to sifting through the clothes. "Hal, Ricky's looking at me like I'm the weird one here. Will you *please* explain to him what the laundry weasel is?"

"Ryan, we've already had this conversation. Drugs are bad."

"You know what!? There's TWO weasels down here!" Ryan yelled and threw a shoe blindly in Hal's direction. "The laundry weasel is this stupid little one-dollar drugstore toy that a daughter of one of Mrs. H's customers gave to her. I'm actually not totally sure it's a weasel. It could be an otter, or something. But it's this little long fuzzy brown stuffed animal thing with tiny ears and whiskers, and when you squeeze it, it makes giggling, sneezing, and other sorts of noises. It got lost a while back, but I know it's in the laundry room because occasionally when I walk in here, it sets it off. Sometimes I won't hear it for a few months, and just when I've been led to believe the batteries finally died, I'll step on the layers of clothes just right so something shifts, and it's back. I should know to expect it by now, but it startles the shit out of me every time, and I'm going to find the little fucker and relocate him to the highest shelf in the house!"

"Okay, now tell us how you really feel about this Ryan," Hal said, and Ryan stopped again and pointed at him. "You should REALLY be the one doing this since you're in charge of the laundry. Which is why it got lost in here in the first place since you let the old clothes form into fossilized geo-logical layers on the floor instead of washing them or donating them! And I'm not going to..." *Ah, ahhh, AHH-CHOO! Tehehehehehehee!* Ryan stopped in the middle of his sentence, then stood up and started stomping around on the clothes. "WHERE ARE YOU... WHERE ARE YOU... WHERE ARE YOU...!?"

"You know, this kinda reminds me of a Weird Al song..." Hal said.

"YOU KNOW WHAT, HAL? YOU CAN... wait, holy hell, I've got it!" Ryan exclaimed.

"You found the damn thing?"

"No! We never did figure out a good DJ name for you..." Ryan said.

"No... we didn't..." Hal agreed.

"DJ Laundry Weasel! That should be the right amount of cheesiness and obscure innuendo to describe your musical tastes," Ryan said proudly, and Hal's face lit up at the suggestion. He looked down and around through the room like he was suddenly seeing into another world of inspiration, and watching it form in front of his eyes. He raised his fist up to his mouth, perhaps holding an invisible microphone, or maybe blocking the ideas from rushing out all at once. But then they heard him whisper it to himself: *"DJ Laundry Weasel..."* He smiled, and then after a short pause, said it again, louder and in an official manner: *"DJ... LAUNDRY... WEASEL..."* Completely lost in his own thoughts, he turned and walked by Uli and Ricky, then headed slowly back up the stairs.

Ryan dropped the fistful of clothes he had been holding and yelled: "THAT WAS A JOKE, YOU DUMBASS!" Hal ignored it, and they heard him ranting more to himself while the sound of his voice faded away upstairs.

"He has not looked that inspired in a long time," Uli noted. "Maybe he will try to rename us 'DJ Laundry Weasel and the Battle Creek Boys.'"

Ryan shut his eyes, and the look of pain on his face was undeniable. "Fuck... my... life," he said quietly.

The door opened again, and Cecilia stepped inside as fast as she could before pulling it shut to keep out the cold winter air.

"Hi, Mrs. H," Uli and Ricky said together.

"Hello, boys. Well, it was quite a day at the store, and I'm rather tired, so I was thinking maybe we could all go out for pizza tonight."

"Can we leave Hal here?" Ryan asked.

"No, sorry. Can't do that." She slipped her coat off and hung it on the rack. "I personally grew Hal and gave birth to him, so of all life forms in this house I feed, that puts him at the top of the list by default."

"I didn't say we weren't going to bring him something back, all I'm asking is can we leave him out of the actual getting-the-pizza part?"

"Ryan, dinner is a time of togetherness which must be embraced by all members of the family," she said cheerfully, and Ryan looked at her and frowned. "So, do I even want to know what…?"

"Hal's decided his DJ name is DJ Laundry Weasel," Ryan said.

"At Ryan's suggestion!" Uli added, excitedly.

"Yes, that's what I thought. I really should know better by now than to ask what goes on in this house while I'm not here. As long as there was also some cleaning and repairs involved," Cecilia said.

"Yes, the computer is all fixed now," Uli said.

"Oh my gosh! Really? You got it all done already? I thought you had work for most of the day?"

"I did, but Hal called earlier and left the message that you added the computer to the list, so I brought home the pieces I figured it needed. It didn't take too long to do once I had the right components."

"What was wrong with it?" Cecilia asked.

"The connection was fine, but your computer is so old it was having trouble running everything at once. I put in more RAM so it can keep up now," Uli said.

"Great. That's one less thing to worry about. If I had known it'd be that easy, I'd have had you do it a long time ago," Cecilia said.

"Well, it is taken care of now," Uli replied.

"Now, I can tell *you* probably just got back from work since I'm picking up the sweet aroma of rental skates from the Roller Dome," she said to Ricky, who brought his sleeve up to his nose and sniffed it briefly.

"Anyways, a working computer is definitely cause for pizza, so we're going to go out and enjoy a relaxing evening as a family as soon as Ricky gets out of the shower, and I shall address my son about his professional branding choices when we get back."

"Fine..." Ryan mumbled.

"Good," Cecilia said, and started up the stairs. "OH, DJ LAUNDRY WEASEL..." she called out, "...we're leaving for pizza in ten minutes!"

Hal scribbled intently on a napkin while they waited for their food to arrive. Cecilia couldn't quite see what he was writing from her side of the table. Lyrics, perhaps? Maybe musical notes, or chords? She hated to interrupt his concentration, but it was always difficult to get his attention at any other time besides when they were at a meal. "So, Dave wasn't mad you requested New Year's off?" she asked.

"Nah. I'm working New Year's Day, so he said New Year's Eve would be fine," Hal answered without looking up.

"You getting enough hours there?"

"Yeah. I mean, last week was a little off because of Christmas, but we'll be back to normal starting the day after tomorrow."

Cecilia looked over and saw Uli looking at her, concerned. She looked away quickly. He picked up on things quicker than the other three. Money had been a little tight since her shoulder surgery a few months earlier, though she had tried to not make it too obvious. As much as she didn't want to discourage him from spending time chasing his dreams, she at least wanted to make sure he was keeping up a steady schedule at the restaurant. She tried to lean forward to see any of what he was scribbling, but still couldn't quite make it out.

"So, I've got a plan!" Hal suddenly announced, sliding his napkin over to where Ryan could see. "If zombies ever attack, this is the perfect place to go. Days' worth of food, high brick walls with very few windows, and that thick metal door at the front."

"Yeah, what is with that door?" Ryan asked.

"I dunno. Mom, do you remember what this was before it was a pizza parlor?"

Cecilia took a moment to try and process the question. "I… don't remember," she said, closing her eyes and shaking her head.

"Eh, oh well. Probably a bank or something. Anyways…" Hal and Ryan chatted on, and she sighed. She didn't want to be the one to kill a dream, but it was also her job to keep a roof over their heads and ensure their ongoing survival. At the same time, she knew better than anyone, that somebody could either be making enough money to live comfortably or could have a life that let them comfortably be alive. She wasn't sure how much longer she'd be able to give him to figure it out himself before she'd have to intervene. She wasn't looking forward to the day. But for now, they still had a little more time, and the boys had more shows to do.

The next evening, they checked in with event staff at the back of the hotel.

"Battle Creek?"

"That's us," Hal replied.

Alright, you're on at ten. You'll have half an hour to set up after the group before you finishes.

"Thanks," Hal said, and turned to his band mates. "Well, you guys wanna hit the bar?"

"Yes, absolutely," Uli answered.

Hal watched Ricky squirm in a clean and pressed black collared button-up shirt as they headed toward the lounge. "It had to be done man, this is a nice establishment. They might frown upon us if you were wearing a torn red flannel shirt," Hal said.

"Ricky's shirt isn't that bad," Ricky answered.

"Yes, it is. Plus, you wear it almost every day. You should take my mom up on that offer to go buy some new clothes."

"Ricky's clothes are fine," Ricky insisted.

Hal sighed. "The world will keep spinning even if you go out and buy something on occasion. I know you had to settle for whatever you got back in that little town of yours, but I wouldn't call owning more than two shirts and two pants extravagant. Plus, if we ever have to play someplace really posh, I don't think any of Uli, Ryan's, or my suits are gonna fit you. We got really lucky with that old shirt."

Ricky continued to fidget.

"What'll it be, gentlemen?" the bartender asked.

"I'll take a glass of Pinot Noir," Hal said.

"The darkest beer you have," Uli answered.

"Bacardi and Cola for me," Ryan responded.

"Orange Juice…" Ricky mumbled while he tugged at his collar.

Smooth jazz music was playing in the background while Hal monitored the clock over the bar. Cecilia joined them at the counter twenty minutes later, and ordered a glass of white wine. "Look at you guys! You all look so handsome tonight. Especially you, Ricky. You should really let me buy you some new shirts that look like this one," she said while adjusting his collar. Ricky started to turn a little red.

"Well, we didn't get the spot of honor tonight, but we got second best. The group after us are the ones who get the countdown to midnight," Hal said.

"It's only the second-best spot if you think you won't do as well as the next group," Cecilia said, and Hal smiled. "Thanks, Mom."

"Don't forget that when you're up there," she added.

"I won't," he promised, looking down at his drink. "I called up a recording studio, and they said they'd be able to get us in in a few weeks."

"Oh, good! That's not as long as you thought it was going to be," Cecilia said.

"Nope," Hal agreed.

They sat and talked until 9:30 p.m., then made their way backstage. As they set up, a complex grid of wires began to form, connecting instruments to amplifiers and amplifiers to walls.

"Where's my drumsticks?" Ryan asked.

"They should be in the guitar case," Hal answered.

"Found 'em. Thanks."

"Ricky, your raccoon tail is stuck in the back of your shirt collar," Hal said.

"Notha' reason to not wear this shirt," Ricky grunted while he freed his tail.

"Is that everything?" Uli asked, looking around.

"I think so," Hal answered, then peered out between the curtains. "Everyone's still in their seats." A stage hand appeared a moment later. "You guys ready back there?"

"Yes! We're good to go," Hal said.

"Great. Go ahead and start, then. The less down time between acts, the better."

"OK," Hal said.

A booming voice came over the microphone. "How is everyone doing this fine evening?" the lounge manager asked, and there was a low rumble of applause. "That last group was the Turner Street Quartet. They came all the way out here from Chicago to play for you tonight." The audience applauded again. "This next group comes from only a few short hours away in Battle Creek, and that is oddly enough their name. So, please give a warm welcome to Michigan's next great band, Battle Creek!" The lights turned off behind the manager as he walked off the stage, and Hal approached the microphone.

"Good evening, beautiful people! Well, here I had a nice speech all written out, but this fine man here gave us such a good introduction, I think we'll just get straight to the music if that's okay with everyone," he said, and the audience clapped politely to let them know he had their approval.

---

45. "Clocks" by Coldplay

---

Uli started them with a haunting melody on the piano, then Ryan joined in with a strong drumbeat. As Hal started to sing, the room went still like a spell had been cast over them. It was exactly as he had hoped. It was a slightly slower song to start with, and they had argued about it being the one to open the show. But Hal insisted, and finally won out. It was New Year's Eve and they were at a nice hotel, so he felt something elegant and mesmerizing would be the way to start. He reminded them that they could speed up from there as they got later into the evening, but he was glad he was right about the start. Now that he had the audience's attention, he was going to take them for a little ride.

---

End Song 45

---

46. "Leave the Night On" by Sam Hunt

47. "Cum on Feel the Noize" by Quiet Riot

48. "Lifestyles of the Rich and the Famous" by Good Charlotte

49. "Rock this Town" by Stray Cats

50. "Boot Scootin' Boogie" by Brooks & Dunn

51. "We're Not Gonna Take It" by Twisted Sister

52. "In Too Deep" by Sum 41

53. "Semi-Charmed Life" by Third Eye Blind

54. "How Country Feels" by Randy Houser

55. "I Don't Mind the Pain" by Danzig

56. "American Jesus" by Bad Religion

57. "Strangers in the Night" by Frank Sinatra

58. "Head Over Boots" by Jon Pardi

59. "Bat Country" by Avenged Sevenfold

60. "Paradise City" by Guns N Roses

61. "Dancing in the Dark" by Bruce Springsteen

As lovely as one piece of music may be, listening to the same style too long will eventually cause all the songs to blend together and lose their appeal. At least, that was Hal's opinion. But throwing in different styles keeps each one unique, and their differences work to highlight each other's features. From the euphoria of an uplifting pop song, to the wild and fast city streets of punk, to the long, sunny backroads through the countryside, and finally down into the dark, eerie shadows of metal. Action, romance, drama, anger, and happiness all working together to make a complete story. That was the trick. Give them variety, keep them interested, make them wonder what will happen next, never wear them out on too much of one good thing. Hal held the microphone firmly as he sang out to them. They were his now for the next hour or so.

End Songs 46 – 61

The entire show went flawless, and they celebrated afterwards in the lounge until two in the morning; drinking and talking to guests. Hal and Ryan got quite drunk, and did nothing to hide it. Uli might have been drunk as well, but it was always harder to tell with him. His tolerance for alcohol was a lot higher than either of theirs, and he hadn't taken down anywhere near the amount of beer they had. But one small, potent mixture after another might have added up faster than he had anticipated. Because, while the other two only got louder and more exuberant as they drank, he had slowly gotten less talkative throughout the evening. Now, he was even sitting resting his head on one hand over the bar, looking somewhat withdrawn. Rarely did they see him out of his usual self-assured, bored manner, and that, more than anything, gave good reason to believe that tonight may have been one of the rare times he overdid it.

When they got home, Hal stumbled up the three short steps to the front door, but when he reached to open it, fell sideways instead and landed in the bushes next to the house. Uli had been walking right behind, and offered a hand down in what would prove to be a bad decision. Hal grabbed it a little too zealously, knocking Uli off balance and then yanking him down on top of him. Hal and Ryan spent so much time inebriated that they had developed their own style to suit it, and while Hal looked nearly at ease laughing in the entanglement, Uli had all the grace and poise of an upended giraffe stuck in a ditch. His long legs jutted awkwardly out of the shrubs, and kicked slowly in vain until Ricky grabbed both of them by the back of their coats and pulled them upright again.

"Thanks Ricky! We… might have died…" Hal laughed loudly.

"*Probably not, but you wouldn't have gotten very far without these,*" Cecilia said quietly as she pulled the keys out of her pocket and unlocked the door. Hal and Ryan landed on the couch in the living room, and started playing video games, a favorite pastime of theirs when they were really wasted. Uli quietly disappeared into his room. Ricky got an orange soda and sat down at the kitchen table. A purring cat appeared in his lap moments later.

"You're not going to play with them?" Cecilia teased.

"They ain't much competition right now," he answered.

"Oh, I know. And you don't really play video games much anyways, do you?" she asked as she sat down across from him.

"No. Didn't have any at home."

"I'm sorry to say that's hard to imagine being from around here," she said.

"Well, a few of Ricky's younger brothers got a hold of an old PlayStation thingy once, but the other siblings had broken it within a few hours," Ricky said.

"Yeah, I bet it was nearly impossible for anything fragile to survive in a house with that many kids. Hal was an unstoppable force when he was a lot younger. I can't even imagine fifteen of him in one house," she said, and then they heard a loud explosion and splattering noise from the living room, then a booming voice from the game said: *'DOUBLE KILL.'* Hal and Ryan started laughing hysterically.

"*Wait, where the hell did his arms go!?*" Hal shouted, then more laughing. The look on Cecilia's face perfectly summed up the sentiment of *Why yes, that's exactly what I was talking about. Thank you Hal for your perfect timing,* and she and Ricky briefly exchanged disgusted glances.

"To be perfectly honest, I'm actually kind of glad they keep making video games gorier and more graphic. I don't think many people completely appreciate what they do for society," she added, and Ricky looked at her confused. "When Hal has a bad night at work because he had to wait on a table of obnoxious guests or whatever might be the case, he comes home and starts a zombie apocalypse, then mows them down until he feels better. Back when I was a kid, when my dad got in a bad mood, he'd take it out on anyone standing close enough, and then sometimes real blood got spilled," she said, then paused to take a sip of her tea. "Now all the restless young people out there can get their fill of violence on a screen without doing any actual damage."

Ricky nodded a little bit. "Never thought of it that way," he admitted.

"I don't ever want Hal to turn into his grandfather, or his father either, I suppose. I'm glad he decided to start the band. It's a much nicer hobby. You guys did so well tonight." She smiled a little. "I hope you're all able to take this places, but if not, none of it will have been wasted time."

"You's really think we got a chance?" Ricky asked.

"Well, there's a lot of competition out there, but Hal hasn't changed that much since he was little, in the sense that once he decides he's going to do something, there's really no stopping him. I know he said if things went well tonight, that he was going to try and have the manager of the hotel try to put in a good word to any other business owners he knew. And by word-of-mouth, keep expanding possibilities any chance he gets."

"Yeah, we gonna keep tryin'..." Ricky said quietly.

"That's what it takes," she agreed as she stood up. "Sorry, but my staying up all night on New Year's days are behind me. I'm sure those two are going to pass out on the floor at some point. Goodnight, Ricky."

"'Nite Mrs. H." Ricky said, then turned around in his chair to watch Hal and Ryan play for a bit.

"Alright, everything's in place," Hal said to Ryan.

"It's not going to work..." Ryan insisted.

"It'll work, trust me. I've planned and studied it from every angle," Hal replied as his character on the screen grabbed a match out of his pocket and lit it up against a jagged rock. He threw it into a pile of wood crates as a massive army of the undead approached.

"Three... two... one... BOOM!" Hal yelled as a huge explosion lit up the screen. When the dust settled, Hal and Ryan stood victorious in front of a sea of mutilated zombies.

# CHAPTER 4

## (Oh, What a Night)

**The countryside spent the day** passing by in a hypnotizing pattern of power lines that swam up and down like fish if stared at long enough. But now as night was falling, the land faded away into the darkness, and the white and yellow stripes marking the lanes took over where the power lines had left off. They'd been in the van for about twelve hours at that point (including a few breaks to eat along the way), and Hal knew they were going to be turning the corner to the motel any minute now. He had agreed to take the last length of the trip as the driver since he usually had no trouble staying awake, but the road lines zipping by gave a strange feeling of dizziness. He tried to keep his eyes on the horizon. The breeze blowing past his ears made them feel like ice despite it being a warm August evening, but he couldn't roll the window back up due to the fumes the van produced. In the old Econoline vans, the centrally located engine rested between the driver and front passenger seats, under a console that looked like an enormous armrest to the untrained eye. While having the engine there made maintenance work a snap in bad weather, driving produced three main problems: fumes, heat, and noise. The fumes were the least noticeable after short exposure, but probably the worst of the three overall, and having the window down was a rule for long trips. His fingers were a little cold as well from the wind, and he exchanged one hand or the other from the wheel to near the console to warm them up. The heat was a blessing and a curse; a blessing in the winter, a curse in the summer, and for the times in between, it was bad during the day but comforting at night. At the moment, it felt pretty good. The noise was the most noticeable. For short trips it really wasn't an issue, but knowing they'd be listening to it for most of the entire day, they'd packed extra earplugs for everyone. Hal was the only one not wearing them now. The driver had to go without, for safety reasons. He figured his ears would probably be ringing all night, but he'd deal with it. That was another reason he took last shift, because as easy as it was for him to stay awake, once he had decided it was time, he also fell asleep the quickest.

Everyone else was asleep, or feigning sleep. Cecilia, Ryan, and Uli's heads were slumped to the side on the back headrests, and Ricky's against the front passenger door. While travelling, Ricky would often like to put his head outside the window like a dog. When asked, his official excuse was, he liked the feeling of the wind on his face. The front of his hair was still sticking straight on end, making him look like a cartoon character after having seen a ghost or have a bomb explode in his face. Having him along on these long trips was great for keeping the fighting down. When it had just been the three of them, it was anyone's guess if they were going to make it to their destination without a fistfight breaking out. But with Ricky there, not only did he work wonders for breaking up fights subtly, but Hal could swear the other two put effort into behaving better. Ricky was one of those people who nobody wanted to upset. Not for fear of him becoming angry, but rather, it just felt wrong somehow.

Hal saw a column of lights come into view as he topped the next hill, surrounded by grassy fields on every side. There it was. And he knew the stage was only half lit up compared to what it would look like tomorrow night. Driving by it immediately made him feel more awake. He knew Ryan and Uli were right about his tendency to get too excited about things, but he also knew it'd be impossible for him to get his hopes and dreams smashed if he didn't have them in the first place. A few more blocks down the road and the sign for the motel appeared. Perhaps he was going to have some trouble falling asleep tonight after all.

The sun sat on the final edge of the horizon, and the air was dense and sweet with barbeque smoke. After all the months spent in preparation, they finally sat backstage, waiting for the group ahead of them to finish. Ryan peered around the corner to the front. "Goddamn, there's a lot of people out there."

"Scared?" Uli asked.

"I bet that would make you happy," Ryan replied.

"Well, I'm scared. I'm not afraid to admit it, but I'm not going to let that affect anything," Hal said.

"Yeah, whatever Hal," Ryan said. "How 'bout you, Ricky? A few thousand people a little nerve-wracking for you?"

"Nah, this ain't that bad. They're all just sittin' out there. Try havin' yer septic tank back up when you live in a house with sixteen other people. THAT was scary," Ricky answered.

"Umm… okay. That puts it into perspective, I guess," Hal said.

The guitarist on stage jumped up and threw his arm down in one final power chord, and the crowd burst into applause as the lights on the stage dimmed.

"Our turn," Hal said.

They started setting up in the break, and had their first taste of facing down the audience in the dark. Hal found his mom standing off to the side, next to the stage. The security personnel would have found her a nice spot out front in the middle with nothing more than a simple request from him. But she insisted she wanted to watch from the side, to be less of a distraction. After everything was in place, the lights increased their glow to their full brilliance, and Hal took the microphone to do the introduction. "Good evening, beautiful people!" he yelled out to the crowd and was met with a wave of cheers. "Wow… thank you! We are Battle Creek, and we're about the most eclectic garage band you'll ever see. Throw a little punk rock, heavy metal, country western, and pop into a blender and hit 'go', and you get…" he looked over at Ricky, "…us."

62. "Time to Pretend" by MGMT

Ricky plucked the opening strings to the first song, and with each note a shot of adrenaline went through their veins. This was the largest crowd they had ever played to, and the fear of caving under pressure was ever-present. Hal hoped they could do their songs the same justice in front of a large crowd that they could do when it was just the four of them relaxing in the living room. Writing their own songs and performing them amongst themselves was fulfilling in itself, but to see other people's reactions was the ultimate reward. As he looked out into the audience where all eyes were on them, watching, waiting, anticipating, he felt something coming.

Uli turned around and played his part on the keyboard behind his back. He knew the keys by heart, and it was exciting to flirt with danger for the sake of becoming the master of it… and for the bragging rights. Ryan started the beat on his drums, and as Hal hit the baseline and leaned to the microphone, it was like the entire hillside rose up at once. Everyone was on their feet in unison, like he had summoned them straight up at his command. It was the sort of song that naturally created that kind of reaction; a strong introduction that gave little uncertainty that something more powerful was about to burst forth. He had to close his eyes for a second to take it all in, and to not let it tear away his concentration as he started to sing to them.

End Song 62

63. "Can I Play with Madness" by Iron Maiden

64. "First Date" by Blink 182

End Songs 63 – 64

Standing under the hot stage lights made it feel like he had a fever, the first song being the spark that set everything ablaze. Now as the third song came to an end, he dumped half of a bottle of water over his head and could feel the steam rising off his skin. "HOW ARE YOU ALL DOING OUT THERE!!??" he yelled out at the crowd, and as he listened to the roar that echoed back and saw the sea of hands rippling at his feet, he wanted so badly to immerse himself in it. He wanted to let that crowd wash over him and take him into its depths, and then, suddenly, he got an idea. Uli, Ryan, and himself had all voted three to one against Ricky that Ricky should do an entire guitar instrumental by himself to show off what he could do. While Uli and Ryan found ways to contribute back up music, Hal really had nothing to give, and had agreed to stand to the side and snap his fingers or something. On that note, he reasoned, they really wouldn't miss him for a few minutes.

65.  "Rebel Rouser" by Duane Eddy

After introducing Ricky, Hal slipped the microphone back into the stand, and started to take a few steps back. The first opening strings of the guitar made the world go in slow motion, the crowd becoming vaster with each pace. He stopped mid-step, and began counting down slowly in his head, to the part where Ryan would hit the beat on the drums. It was getting close, and he put one foot back in front of him, then again, and then again as he went into a short sprint. He didn't see the appalled look on Uli's face, or his mom clasp her hands over her mouth in wide-eyed terror. Nor did he hear the few quick notes Ricky missed, or Ryan mumbling 'You asshole…' to himself. But what he did hear was the excited screams of the people, the quick rush of air as he fell, and then the feeling of all the hands. The hands catching him, grabbing him, moving him, rolling him, holding him up, pulling him further out into their midst. As he struggled onto his back, he saw the stars above and heard the guitar as clear as the cloudless night, and he realized he was laughing. The sound of his own voice made him happy.

He spent a short eternity floating there, drifting like a god reveling in his own creation. The taste of victory was sweet. There was nothing he couldn't do. No, there is nothing *we* can't do, he glanced back at the stage and corrected himself. The three brothers he never had growing up. But fistfights and all, here they were, and he wouldn't trade it for anything. He thought about it more as the song began nearing its end. Then, like nothing special was happening, like he had done this plenty of times before, he looked down and pointed towards the stage and said loudly, "Back that way! Back that way now!" And the hands obliged as they turned him around and slowly moved him back towards the front. Once he had made it back to the stage, he crawled back up onto the platform, and lay on his back for a moment looking at the lights shining down on him. The guitar faded out while the song finished, and he got up and took the microphone again.

End Song 65

"I've never done a stage dive before," he admitted, and was met with waves of applause. "That was awesome, thank you. Alright, we have one more song before we leave you tonight. Again, we're Battle Creek, and thanks for an amazing night, New York!" Hal yelled out to the crowd as they began their final song.

66. "Cake by the Ocean" by DNCE

The last song went by too fast. He could barely even remember singing it afterwards. He was so caught up in singing that he wasn't thinking about it or recording it in his memory as he did. He had only blurry images of the crowd as he moved across the stage, minus one little kid who was dancing wildly right up front next to his parents. As brutally honest as kids often are, seeing one dancing excitedly like that with no real pattern, rhyme, or reason to his movements, literally dancing like no one was watching, was perhaps the best compliment they received that night. That one image stuck in his mind as they left the stage and started packing up for the night.

> End Song 66

Backstage, they pushed all the equipment into a cluster and stood and stared at each other overwhelmed.

"Hey, Hal?" Ryan asked.

"Yes?" Hal answered.

"The next time you want to do a stage dive…"

"…Yeah?" Hal asked.

"…TELL ME FIRST SO I CAN JOIN YOU, YOU SELFISH ASS!" Ryan yelled.

"Hey, hey! In my defense, I hadn't been planning to do one beforehand! It just sort of came to me in the spur of the moment," Hal said with the biggest smile.

"Uh, huh," Ryan mumbled.

"Have you done one before?" Hal asked.

"I've done a few dives in my time, yes," Ryan admitted as he took out a pack of cigarettes.

"Because, that was amazing."

"Well, duh."

"Yes, we need to talk about that…" Cecilia said sternly.

"You could break a bone," Uli added.

"Shut up, Uli. You know you want to try it someday," Ryan said.

"No, not really," Uli answered.

"Liar. Everybody should give it a try at least once before deciding they don't like it. Isn't that your motto, Mrs. H?" Ryan asked, and Cecilia shot him an annoyed stare.

"Hey, sorry for doing that during your song, Ricky," Hal apologized.

"It's okay…" Ricky answered.

"Wasn't trying to steal your thunder or anything…"

"It's alright," Ricky insisted.

"Still, I'm…"

"That was a spectacular show, gentlemen." A tall man in a navy suit suddenly interrupted them.

"Uh, thank you sir," Hal answered.

"My name is Darrin Jones, and I represent a record label that is always looking for new talent like yours." The man extended one hand to Hal, who took it eagerly. He looked down at Hal's hand, and Hal realized how sweaty he was and quickly retracted it.

"Oh, sorry… I sort of worked up a sweat out there."

Darrin laughed as he wiped his hand on his pants. "No problem at all. I should really be used to it by now. Anyways, I've been watching all of tonight's performances, and yours has absolutely been one of the best so far. So, I wanted to ask you, how serious are you about possibly turning your music into a career?"

"I… I mean… it would be the ultimate honor, a dream come true, and the culmination of everything I've been working towards for the last ten years?" Hal said.

Darrin looked at him for a second, then remarked: "Okay, fairly serious. What about the rest of you?"

"What he said," Ryan replied.

"It is a challenge I am ready to accept," Uli added.

"And you?" Darrin asked Ricky.

"Uh… sounds good?" Ricky said.

"Okay…" Darrin chuckled. "So, then, I'm wondering if you boys might be interested in coming down to one of our offices and chatting with us sometime."

"Sh… sure!" Hal said in disbelief.

"Excellent. So, here, tell me a little bit about yourselves. Where are you from?"

"Well, all over the place, actually. Uli is from Dresden, Germany, Ryan is from Seattle…" Hal gestured to the two of them. "And the other two of us are from Battle Creek but two different Battle Creeks. Michigan, and Arkansas."

"Wait, you and him are from two separate cities named Battle Creek? Darrin said as he looked from Hal to Ricky."

"That's right," Hal said.

"Well, that's unique. Did you name yourselves accordingly because of that?"

"Well, actually no. I grew up in Battle Creek, Michigan, and that's why we're called that. Ricky here was the last to join the group, and he was from Battle Creek, Arkansas, but we met him after we had already named ourselves Battle Creek."

"No kidding," Darrin said.

"Yeah, it was quite a coincidence," Hal said.

"Very cool. So, where are you living now?"

"Oh, at my house in Battle Creek, Michigan," Hal said.

"Great, hey, we have a studio in downtown Detroit. That's not too far, right?"

"No, I think we can handle that," Hal replied.

"Excellent, I've got a guy out there I'd like to hook you up with then. He can determine if you'll be a good fit with us. Then, if you decide you would like to sign with our company, he can assist with advertising and promotions.

He also does scheduling as well, so he can find you venues to play at so you are more freed up to focus on your music."

"So, he's an agent?" Ryan asked.

"Yes, exactly. His name is Jim Zimlan, and he's very good at what he does. Here's his card, I'll have him call you tomorrow so you can arrange to meet when you get back."

"Oh… uh, okay… that sounds great! Thanks, Darrin," Hal said.

"Absolutely, we look forward to working with you."

"Thanks, we… we look forward to it too!"

"You gentlemen have a good night." Darrin nodded and walked away, leaving Hal holding the card. Before he even had a chance to recover, a woman with a microphone followed by a cameraman suddenly appeared in front of him. "…and I think I see our second agent sighting of the night. This is Battle Creek, who just left the stage. One of the most energetic performances we've seen all night. So, first of all, you guys are my favorite band of the festival so far, and I'm not just saying that. Tell me, how do you feel your performance went?" she said as she put the microphone in front of Hal. It was the only time Ryan and Uli could ever remember seeing Hal rendered almost speechless. Almost.

"I think… it went fantastic!" Hal said, not having enough time to come up with anything more poetic.

"So, where are you guys from?" she asked and thrust the microphone back in his face just as quickly. "Uh, Battle Creek, Michigan, and…"

"Oh, duh. I guess that makes sense." She cut him off. "So, I saw you were just talking to one of the talent scouts. What do you think your chances are of getting a record deal out of this?" She put the microphone back to Hal.

"I'm definitely feeling hopeful!" he said.

"And what's your ultimate goal if that happens?"

"Uh, well, making a career out of music, touring the world, never being a slave to a desk job…"

"…living the dream?" she asked.

"Yes," Hal answered. "Living the dream," he repeated, looking down in disbelief at the business card in his hand.

Two days later, Hal was still pacing around the house in a daze. Mr. Zimlan had actually called them the day after as Darrin had said he would, and they had an appointment to meet with him the following day. Uli and Ryan were doing their best to humor Hal in his plotting about the future, though he was beginning to get really annoying.

"…Wonder if they're going to want us to put together an album right away, or…"

"Hal?" Ryan asked calmly.

"…start booking us to tour locally first, or…"

"Hal?"

"…if they pay for our hotel rooms, or if we sleep in a bus or something…"

"Hal?"

"…if we have to sign any contracts that will prevent us from…"

"HAL!?" Ryan yelled.

"WHAT!?" He snapped out of his daydream.

"Will you please shut up and come play Poker? Ricky's killing us over here," Ryan said, and Hal saw the enormous pile of candy Ricky had in front of him. Using candy for playing chips was a tradition Cecilia had started before he could even remember.

"Okay, okay." He went over and sat down.

"You know when you get excited you're like a little hyper squirrel on crack," Ryan said.

"You mean, like, a little hyper weasel?" Hal asked.

"I'm not answering that," Ryan said while he dealt a new hand. Hal picked up his cards and looked at them briefly before breaking out into a smile again. "Guys, we got the attention of an agent!"

"Yes, Hal, we got invited to talk to an agent, NOW PLACE YOUR BET!" Ryan grabbed a few candies off the top of Ricky's pile and dumped them down in front of him. Hal sighed and looked back down at his cards. Right as he put a few down on the table and started to draw two more from the pile, the doorbell rang.

"Who the hell is that? It's 10:00 p.m.," Ryan said.

"Hey, maybe it's opportunity knocking!" Hal said as he bounded up and headed for the door.

"I fucking give up." Ryan threw his cards down and got up to follow him to see who it was.

Uli set his cards down on the table and looked at Ricky. "Two pair," he announced triumphantly.

"Full house!" Ricky displayed his hand, then swiped all the remaining Jolly Ranchers from in front of Uli.

Ryan stopped at the edge of the corner between the living room and entryway, and Uli and Ricky joined him there a few moments later. They observed from a few feet back while Hal turned the lock and opened the door. Then, with one hand still on the doorknob as it stopped against the wall, he stood there motionless, a blank stare on his face as he gazed outside. Where he was standing, he was perfectly blocking their view of who was on the other side.

"What? Who is it?" Ryan asked. Hal didn't answer him, and they walked further out from the living room so they could see around him. Standing on the other side of the threshold was a near mirror image of Hal, only older. Himself in twenty years perhaps, a little bulkier, and with a short beard. He had on a dark navy button-up shirt with a black tie and matching dark navy pants, as well as a roughly matching navy fedora hat with a crisp black band around it.

"Hal, who's at the door?" Cecilia called from upstairs. Someone inhaled a sharp breath at the door, and then there was silence again. "Hal?" She appeared from her room rubbing her damp hair with a towel, and noticed the odd look on Uli, Ryan, and Ricky's faces as they looked up the stairs at her. "What? What happened!?" she asked as she walked quickly down the stairs. She looked out the door, then froze.

67. "Fast Car" by Tracy Chapman *to play over this scene*

They stared at each other for a few moments, both paralyzed with disbelief. A torrent of thoughts went racing through her mind. It was like watching a strobe light; alternating at super speed between the absolute certainty that it was him, and the opposing notion that there was no way it could be true. He took a few steps inside, and the towel around her neck dropped to the floor as she unwittingly moved back a couple paces. He stopped a little further than arm's length in front of her, and she scanned his face again, trying to settle on an answer. She'd spent many nights with someone who looked quite a bit like him. She'd be sitting in the passenger seat of an old black car while he drove them at reckless speed in a southeast direction to somewhere they had never been to, but were eager to find. It'd happened so many times, but they only ever made it there on the first attempt. Every time after that, they'd drive until her alarm went off, and she'd get up and look in the mirror and see her face slowly aging while his never did. Somehow, the knots in her stomach were saying this was the same man, though not quite as he had been burned into her memory. Seeing him now after that much time had passed, she had no idea what to do. What does one say to someone who has been dead for over twenty years? How did he find her? And why now, after so long? There was still the very strong possibility that she was going to wake up from this in a few moments, and then it all would be for nothing, yet again.

He took a small step closer, and slowly held out one hand. *"Cecilia... I..."* She looked at the hand for a moment, then started to raise hers. She didn't let their hands meet, and instead, reached out past his, towards his body. There was one way she'd know for sure. Her fingers touched down lightly against his chest, then moved across it. She could feel them easily through the shirt. One… two… three large, round pits. A single tear started to roll down her cheek.

End Song 67

Ryan got Ricky and Uli's attention, and nodded towards the door. They quietly snuck past the two of them, to where Hal was standing on the threshold. "Uh… we're going to go to the bar down the road for a while," Ryan said as they stepped out onto the front steps, and Hal nodded. They all stood there for a second, looking uncomfortable like someone should say something more, but it didn't happen. "Um, yeah… bye," Ryan finally said, then pulled the door shut.

"Well, that was… unexpected," Ryan said between sips.

"Indeed," Uli agreed.

"He must have seen her on TV at the festival. That girl interviewed us for quite a while. Or maybe he saw Hal. Or maybe he saw both of them," Ryan pondered while swirling the last few ice cubes around in his drink.

"That makes sense," Uli replied. Ricky had gone to the corner of the bar and was playing an old Pac Man game. They sat there for two hours killing time, until finally around midnight, Hal shuffled in and sat down next to them.

"Hey! I'm buying this guy a drink!" Ryan called down the counter at the bartender, then turned to Hal. "So…" he asked him, "…'sup?"

"Oh, you know…" Hal said, "…the usual."

"Right…" Ryan said. "…But, I mean…" Ryan started to say, then slowly raised his hand up into a cautious thumbs up, then turned it over into a thumbs down as he raised one eyebrow, then back to a thumbs up, waiting for a reply.

"I think… we're good," Hal said, nodding slowly. Ryan began to nod with him. "OK…"

"I mean… I think my life just changed? I'm still trying to wrap my head around it," Hal said.

"Shit, that's fair," Ryan agreed. "So, where has he been the last twenty five-ish years?"

"Okay, so, apparently the story is, after he got shot he got pulled into a different car from mom, and they started driving him to who knows where to get tortured for a bit before they finally finished him off. He was bleeding a lot, but somehow they had missed everything vital. He started faking like he was passing out from the blood loss in the back of the car while he tried to come up with a plan, but kept one eye open barely enough so he could see where they were out the window. They started getting into a more populated downtown area, and he realized they were coming up on a bridge over a river. He knew if he could somehow jump off the bridge, they probably wouldn't shoot at him because that would have drawn a lot of attention very quickly. So, he waited until they were on the bridge, then sprang into action and jumped out of the car and right over the edge.

"Holy shit! How fast were they going?" Ryan asked.

"Yeah! I asked the same thing. He said he wasn't sure, but they were getting into downtown so it probably wasn't over forty miles per hour. Forty isn't exactly anything to joke around with, but he was in that mode where he knew this was his last chance at survival, so he had enough adrenaline going to pull it off. Once he hit the water, he got himself under the bridge, and like he thought, no one came looking for him because there was too much traffic around and there would have been too many witnesses. He said he was just going to stay under there in the shadows for awhile before trying to go anywhere, but he apparently did black out from either the blood loss or the pain. He woke up in a hospital the next morning, so somebody found him at some point. His leg was in a cast, and it turns out he broke it jumping out of the car, but was still too pumped on the adrenaline rush to notice at the time. He stayed in the hospital for a few days, and when they released him, he got the hell out of town as fast as he could.

"He did not try to look for your mother again?" Uli asked.

"No. He didn't go looking for her because he was quite sure she would have already been dead at that point. You know, you see in movies and on TV someone taking on an entire army to save the person they love, but it doesn't work that way in the real world. He knew if he did find her alive and tried to do a one-man rescue mission against an entire mob, that would have just ended in him getting some sort of violent execution. That is, if he wasn't simply killed outright in the gun battle that would have broken out when they first saw him."

"Mmm. I see," Uli answered.

"Yeah, so, he got a rental car and just drove aimlessly for a few days, trying to figure out what to do. Eventually, he ended up in Oklahoma where he saw a sign for a trucking company advertising that they were hiring. He said that sign just sort of jumped out at him, and he got a motel room in the area for the night, and went in and applied the next morning after taking a sufficient dose of pain meds. He figured he could drive with the big boot on his leg, and it would be a way to sustain himself until the bullet wounds healed up. They hired him, and he ended up liking it so much that he decided to keep doing it even after he was better. He said he also realized it would be good because he wouldn't be in the same place for very long at any given time, so he would be hard to find if anyone decided to look for him to try and tie up any 'loose ends,'" Hal said as he made air quotes with his fingers.

"Would they have really followed him all the way to Oklahoma?" Uli asked.

"Some of those mob guys really knew how to hold a grudge, so yes, it could have been a possibility," Hal answered. "But, his plan worked, and he's been driving and living out of various trucks for the last twenty five-ish years. Some of those big rig trucks have something called a sleeper cabin, so the nicer ones are almost like mini-RVs with a bed, and sometimes a tiny kitchen and bathroom behind the driver's seat in the back of the cab. But, he saw Mom and us on TV at a truck stop in the middle of nowhere in Nevada, and couldn't believe his eyes and had to come see for himself. I had mentioned in the interview we were from Battle Creek, Michigan, of course, so he got himself here and then tracked us down locally, somehow."

"Fuck," Ryan said. "I guess he's going to stick around for awhile, then?"

"I'm assuming so. I doubt anyone's looking for him anymore, and he can really drive a truck from anywhere."

"Okay. And, you're good with this?" Ryan asked again, just to be sure.

"Yeah, I think so. Mom looked really happy. Not that she's been miserable, but I hadn't seen her like that in a long time. It was really… nice," Hal said.

Ryan raised both of his eyebrows in an unusually gentle, caring expression; especially for him. And, lacking any other words, Hal added: "Yeah…"

"Yeah…" Ryan agreed, and took the final sip of his drink. After a brief pause, he asked: "So… now what?"

"I… dunno," Hal answered.

"I mean, I sort of don't want to go back to your house tonight. Unless, you think it's alright?" Ryan asked.

"Well, it'd probably be alright. But I sort of don't want to go back either. Not 'til tomorrow," Hal replied.

"What are our other options?" Uli asked.

"Well, I doubt we have enough money for more than one hotel room, and I'm really not liking the idea of trying to fit all four of us in one bed if you know what I mean," Ryan said, and Hal snorted a laugh as he took a sip of his drink.

"Would Dave still be cleaning up at this hour?" Uli asked.

"I think so… why?" Hal asked.

"Maybe he would let us spend the night in his restaurant in the big reclining chairs in the lounge?"

"I doubt he'd be really excited about that idea, but we might be able to talk him into it," Hal said.

"How late is he usually there?" Ryan asked.

"Usually until at least one in the morning, sometimes longer," Hal replied. "To be safe though, we should probably head that way in about thirty minutes."

"Sounds like a plan," Ryan said, then swung around in his chair. "Hey, Ricky, we're leaving in half an hour! We're going to go see if Dave will let us spend the night in the restaurant."

"Okey, dokey!" Ricky replied, not looking away from the screen. He had gotten his initials on the high score board twice, and was trying for a third.

The next morning, Hal awoke to the blurred sight of a bulky, bald man in a long black apron standing over them. "*Wakey, wakey…*"

"Hmm. What?" Hal answered, half-asleep.

"It's an hour to opening time. Time to get up."

"Open an hour late today, Dave," Hal said, turning over in the chair.

"I'm sorry, Hal, I'm afraid I can't do that," Dave answered.

"Why not, Dave? What's the problem?"

"I think you know what the problem is just as well as I do."

"What are you talking about, Dave?"

"Would you two nerds shut up…" Ryan mumbled.

"You know, Ryan, if you'd like to stay a bit longer, I could always use help setting up the bread trays for later," Dave said.

"Unngggh," Ryan groaned.

"UP AND AT 'EM, BOY!" Dave threw a glass of ice water on Ryan, and Ryan jumped up and tripped over Ricky, then landed on Uli. Uli woke up and threw him off onto the floor. Ricky remained asleep.

"Okay, three out of four isn't bad I guess," Dave said, then nudged Ricky gently with the toe of his boot. "Is he okay?"

"Yeah, he's fine." Hal sat up. "This guy sleeps like the dead," he said, then started to shake him. "Ricky, we gotta get up." Hal shook him more. "Ricky…"

"Wait, wait. There's something I've always wanted to try," Ryan said, standing up off the floor. He sat on the arm of the recliner and leaned down and whispered next to Ricky's ear: "*Squirrell…*"

Ricky's forehead twitched, and he opened his eyes a crack and looked up. "Huh? Where?"

"Oh my God…" Hal mumbled. "Seriously?"

"Morning, buddy. Time to go," Ryan said with a proud smile, grabbing his shoulders and pulling him up.

"Thanks, Dave, we really appreciate it." Hal said as they headed for the door.

"Yeah, yeah. I'll see you tomorrow, Hal."

"Yep, see you then!" Hal called back as they dragged Ricky out the front door.

"Okay, we have three hours before we have to be at the studio to meet with the Jim guy," Hal said.

"Did they say we need our equipment?" Ryan asked.

"No, I think they're just going to talk to us first."

"When are we going to go back to your house?"

"Well, we need to go get the van to go to the meeting obviously, but maybe we go back into the house after we get back?"

"And let the awkwardness ensue?" Ryan asked.

"Yeah, pretty much," Hal agreed.

"Betcha your mom is in bed with your dad right now doing…"

"LALALA I CAN'T HEAR YOU!!!" Hal suddenly put his hands over his ears and ran down the sidewalk ahead of them.

"That was mean," Uli said to Ryan. Ryan stopped walking and stared at him, but Uli raised his fist and held it out in front of him, and Ryan smiled and bumped it with his, then they continued down the street.

They arrived at the office after the two-hour drive into Detroit. After waiting for about twenty minutes in the lobby, a middle-aged, slightly overweight man wearing a dark green business suit came through the doorway. He extended a hand to Hal. "Good morning. You guys must be Battle Creek. I'm Jim Zimlan."

"That's us, pleased to meet you." Hal took his hand while he examined the thin, Jedi-like ponytail that curved from around the back of Jim's head and rested over his shoulders, greeting them like a friendly pet snake.

"I watched the footage of your performance at the festival. That was quite the show you guys put on."

"Thank you," Hal said.

"Why don't you all come on into my office and have a seat."

"Sure," Hal replied.

"Anyways, your job today is to tell me about yourselves, and my job is to figure out how dedicated you are towards making a career out of music, and if this is the right organization to help you do that." Jim sat down behind his desk. "Because hopefully, you've already figured out this is not an easy industry to get into."

"Oh, we're aware," Hal said. "We've certainly been through the unglamorous side of it."

"Good. You're not totally clueless then," Jim said bluntly. "So, first of all, if you can introduce yourselves so I can learn your names and call you by them, and then we'll really start talking."

"Sure. So, I'm Hal. I'm the lead singer. I'm sort of the one who started the group. Well, me and Uli. Uli is the co-founder. Anyways, I was raised in

Battle Creek, which is where the name came from. Though our guitarist Ricky is from Battle Creek, Arkansas, which ended up being a huge coincidence since he's only been with us for a year."

"Huh. That's wild," Jim said. "So, how long have you been doing this?"

"Well, I've been trying to do this since I was probably thirteen, but in actual practice, me and Uli here really started forming the group and playing shows five years ago. Ryan and Ricky came in later, but they have their own histories in music before they joined up with us."

"Okay, actual practice, five years," Jim repeated to himself, writing it down on a notepad. "Okay, who's Uli? Him?" Jim looked in Uli's direction.

"Yes," Uli confirmed. "I am from Dresden, Germany, and I play piano, violin, trumpet, flute, and saxophone."

"Uli's our one-man orchestra," Hal said.

"How'd you two meet?" Jim asked.

"We met at a music academy in New York."

"You actually went to school for this?" Jim asked.

"Yes," Hal answered. "We both have a bachelor's in musical arts."

"No formal training," Jim said, making more notes on his notepad.

"Okay, and you?" Jim looked in Ryan's direction.

"I'm Ryan Summerfield, I'm from Seattle, and I play drums."

"God, you guys are from all over hell. Battle Creek, Germany, Seattle…"

"Arkansas," Ryan said, pointing in Ricky's direction.

"*Right… Arkansas,*" Jim repeated quietly, writing it down. "So, that makes you… Ricky?" Jim asked.

"Yes," Ricky answered.

Jim looked at him for a moment then gestured with his hands for him to continue. "And?"

"And what?" Ricky asked.

"And what about you?"

"Oh, Ricky plays guitar," Ricky answered. The two stared at each other for a moment.

"Okay…" Jim said, then pointed at Ricky's hat with his pen. "Is that thing real?"

"Yep," Ricky answered.

"Alrighty then. Moving on. So, you're all here because you want to get on the radio and go professional with this?"

Hal nodded eagerly.

"NOT EASY…" Jim said loudly, slamming his pen down into its holder, making all four of them jump. "But I can help. Hopefully," he added, in a quieter tone. "So, I'm assuming you already have recordings of your original songs?"

"Yes, we do," Hal answered.

Do you have an album put together? Or just the individual songs?"

"Well, right now it's only individual songs. But we certainly have enough to throw an album together immediately," Hal answered.

"Excellent," Jim said. "So, that can be our first project in between booking dates at local venues and beginning the upward battle of trying to get you some air time on the radio."

"OK…!" Hal said with a smile.

"Well, you've passed the first test. You seem reasonably dedicated to this."

"Sir, I've spent a huge chunk of my life working towards this. I've tried imagining myself doing something else, anything else as a career, and I can't. None of it would work. I'll keep pursuing this until we're successful, however long it takes, and even if the stress of trying ends up taking a couple years off my life. So, don't worry about the question of dedication," Hal said, and Jim considered him silently for a moment. "I want to entertain people. It's the only thing I've ever wanted to do. I know it's a lot of work, but it would be my dream to spend my life as a dedicated artiste."

"Ha! You're no artiste," Jim said.

"Now, wait a second…"

"You're a businessman. A businessman in the business of art, yes, but not an artiste. The artistes are the ones who show up here with papier-mâché animal heads on, telling us that they don't care about money, but that they have an important message from God that they must get to the people," Jim said.

Hal stared blankly at him for a moment. "Um… oh…"

"I like you, though. You've got guts. I think we'll make a good team," Jim said as he turned around to a filing cabinet behind him and pulled out a sizeable stack of documents and forms. "And thank you for not being an artiste," Jim said as he rotated back around in his chair and set the papers down on the desk.

"So, what I'm thinking is, before we do anything else, I'm going to give you this enormous stack of boring paperwork to read…" Jim pulled his glasses down a little as he looked at Hal. "…and I do suggest you read it…" He pushed his glasses back up. "…see if it all makes sense, sounds good to you, doesn't make you want to run screaming in the other direction, and then come back and maybe we can negotiate a contract of sorts. If we can reach an agreement in writing, then we start thinking about putting your album together and finding you places to play."

"Uh, okay, sounds good…" Hal replied.

"Betcha never thought you were going to get homework again," Jim said. "Anyways, have fun. Sorry to make you come out all this way for such a short meeting, but I got what I needed out of it, and paperwork has to happen before any play."

"As to be expected," Hal said. "We knew some of that would be involved."

"You're too positive about this," Jim said, looking at Hal suspiciously. "Keep that up and you're either going to get crushed by the harsh reality of the music industry, or you might be a huge success." Hal raised one eyebrow at him curiously. "Anyways, take notes. Bring questions. Seek understanding. I'm not trying to pull any moves here, but don't take my word for it. You can't trust anyone in this business except yourself."

Hal nodded again. "Alright… we will."

"You want to come back same time next week once you've read that mess?" Jim asked.

"Um, yeah. I mean, we'll have to figure out all our work schedules, but hopefully we'll all be able to get this time off again. If we don't, we can always call and reschedule right?" Hal asked.

"Yeah, we'll figure it out. Here, let me get you my card." Jim reached down and pulled one out of his desk to hand to Hal. "I'll see you next week… or at some point."

"Sir…" Hal started.

"Jim," Jim corrected him.

"Jim, thank you so much for meeting with us," Hal said as they got up and each took turns shaking hands with him again.

"My pleasure. Have a good rest of your afternoon."

"We will, you too!" Hal said as they went back out the office door.

The gears were clearly turning in Hal's head as he unlocked the van.

"I think that went well…" Ryan said.

"I think so too," Uli agreed.

"So, we go back to your house?" Ryan asked Hal.

"Yeah…" Hal answered, though the tone in his voice hinted at a twinge of uneasiness.

"Do you… not want to?" Ryan asked.

"No, we need to. It's not like we can keep avoiding it," Hal said, pulling the door shut and turning the keys in the ignition.

"Whoa, whoa, wait, I thought things were OK? I mean, I thought you were kind of excited about it last night? You spent two hours there before joining us at the bar," Ryan said.

"Well, I mean, Mom looked happy, and that was nice to see. But, I don't know, I've never known the guy. And to be honest, I'm starting to think I shouldn't have left Mom alone with him last night. That might not have been the best idea," Hal said.

"Dude…" Ryan said. "…it's *your mom*. I'm sure she kept a healthy dose of skepticism on hand last night. If your dad did try to do anything she didn't like, he probably *is* in a pair of cement shoes at the bottom of a lake now. Or at the very least, in the trunk of the Mustang for disposal later."

"I know, Mom can take care of herself, but… I don't know, it's been over twenty years. People change over time, and shouldn't he have long moved on from it by now? Even if he did see us, maybe he would have just said: 'Huh, look at that, she is alive,' to himself, and then go about his business?" Hal asked, and left the van in a tense silence.

"Maybe… he wanted to meet *you*?" Hal heard the sentence, but it was so slight he had to take a moment to figure out if it was something his subconscious had said in his head. He looked over at Ryan, who was looking straight at him, and realized he had said it. Hal had never heard Ryan say something that quietly.

"Why?" Hal asked.

"Well, I mean, finding out you have a kid will do that to some people," Ryan said.

Hal pondered this for a while as they drove. "OK, fine, he wanted to meet me. But now what? Is he suddenly my dad and I'm immediately his son? Is mom going to be mad if I don't know what to say to him at first?"

"Hal, when we get back do you want us to go somewhere else for a while? If I show up at work, I don't think my boss is going to be too mad about it," Ryan said.

"Yes, I can always go and sort the stock room," Uli added.

"No, no. Don't do that," Hal mumbled.

"Alright. I just wanted to check. If you'd rather have us there, fine. But can you at least let someone else drive the rest of the way home? You're sort of driving down the middle of the road," Ryan said, and Hal looked up to see the white lines right under the middle of the van, and he suddenly swerved back to the right side of the road. "Hal, pull over…" Ryan begged.

"I got it," Hal said sternly and drove the rest of the way home in silence.

They walked up the front steps to the house, and Hal knocked a long, loud pattern on the door, waited for a minute, then slowly opened it and stepped inside.

"HELLO!?" he yelled loudly into the house as they came in.

There was shuffling upstairs and then a door opening, and Cecilia appeared at the top of the stairs. "Hello! You're back! I was starting to get worried," she said. Ryan, Uli, and Ricky all saw Hal breathe a sigh of relief.

"We spent the night in the steak house," Hal said.

"Oh goodness, you didn't have to do that. You live here," Cecilia said, sounding flustered. Hal started to take a step up the stairs, but then they heard more footsteps, and when he glanced up again his mom wasn't alone. He stopped.

"Oh, boys, this is Harvey," Cecilia said politely.

Ricky, Uli and Ryan all answered "Hello" back.

"Hi," Harvey replied in a gruff voice.

"So, I was thinking tonight we could all go out and do something fun. Maybe go bowling and then find a nice place for dinner?" Cecilia said, sounding even more nervous. They'd never seen her like that before.

Uli, Ryan, and Ricky all nodded and said OK.

"And pick someplace nice. I'm buying," Harvey said. "And don't hold back. I mean, you three look okay, but this one definitely needs to gain some weight," he said as he looked at Hal, and Hal slowly raised his head to stare back at him. It wasn't quite an angry stare. Gritty, though not angry. Intrigued, even. The two of them sized each other up for a moment until Cecilia interrupted. "So, Hal, you had that meeting today with the agent, right? How'd that go?" she asked.

Actually, it went really well. We've got a bunch of paperwork to read over, then we're going back to meet again next week and talk more," Hal answered.

"Hal, that's great! Do you think they're going to sign you?"

"I mean, I don't know for sure. It's still early on. But he seemed interested in us, so I think it's a good possibility."

"Well, that's a good sign for sure! Here, let's get going and you tell us all about it over bowling," Cecilia said as she started trying to hustle them out the door.

As Harvey walked by, he looked at Hal out of the corner of his eyes and whispered, "*Chicken legs.*"

"*Target practice,*" Hal immediately whispered back, and strangely enough, he swore he could see a small smile form at the corner of Harvey's mouth as he passed through the doorway.

# CHAPTER 5

## (I Want to Rock and Roll All Night)

They'd signed a contract with an agent. It actually happened. There wasn't a lot of fuss or mess to it, either. After all their efforts to get to that point, it seemed so easy. But then, the real work was about to begin. While they'd already had recordings of most of their songs, Jim listened to them and said it'd be better to do them all over with better audio equipment. Perfection was the goal, and as always, perfection is elusive. They were up late once again in the recording studio.

"Alright, that was pretty good, but let's take it from the top again on three..."

"Jim, it's midnight. We've been at this for seven hours," Hal said wearily.

"Hey, if you actually want this to take you places, you have to make it the best you can. The recordings are your most precious commodity."

"Yeah, I know..." Hal said, yawning. "That's where the money is."

"Ha! You think you make money selling music?" Jim scoffed.

Hal looked at him confused. "Um... yeah?"

"Well, sorry, but no," Jim answered. "Maybe it was more true back in the day, but with all these rotten kids downloading it illegally and then dealing it out themselves, it's only one piece of your overall earnings. Yes, you make a little money from the honest ones that pay for it, but it's not where the real cash is at."

"So... where's the real..."

"In live performances," Jim interrupted. "And in merchandise sponsorships, and if you make it that far, paid interviews. No one source is going to provide your paycheck, it's a combination of everything, really."

"That's… depressing," Hal said.

"Isn't it, though?" Jim answered. "Money makes the world go round, but that's where people like me come in. It's hard to find success on your own if you don't already have a lot of cash put back to finance yourselves with. But we've got the systems all in place here so that you're basically plug and play, if you'll excuse the horrible pun."

"Pun excused," Hal mumbled.

"The plan is we get you signed to a smaller, local label to produce an EP. That will get us the cash to record, and then they'll take care of album production, retail shipment, radio campaigns, and so on. Now, while all that is going on, we find you places to play live wherever we can. You do your thing on stage and sell those EPs at the end of the shows, and throughout all that, we get the ball rolling on bigger things."

"Bigger things like…?" Ryan asked.

"Well, the ultimate goal is to establish yourselves enough that you get a deal with a much bigger label, though that takes a lot of work. Professional music is no slacker job. As a matter of fact, it isn't even a job at all. It's your life. You'll get to do some partying here and there, but nobody ever seems to talk about all the blood, sweat, and tears that go into it. That's what kills off a lot of young bands before anything ever really gets done. Though, the longer and harder you work at this, the quicker things are going to start happening," Jim explained.

"I know, I know," Hal said. "I'm just not sure I have anything left for tonight." He put his head in his hands and rubbed his eyes.

"Yeah, I'm about ready to fall off this chair," Ryan added from behind his drum set.

"At least you get to sit," Hal replied.

"Well, if you think you're at the point where you're going to fall asleep standing up we can call it a night. But, you'd be surprised to find that the one last run, the one that happens in the early hours of the morning after you've all given up, is that special one that comes out just right. I've seen it many times before."

"Uuungh," all four of them moaned.

"That's the spirit! Now again from the top… one, two, three!" Jim said loudly.

They recorded for another hour until one in the morning before they finally got to go home for the night.

The next day around noon, Ryan picked up the phone when Jim called, and he sounded less than enthused as he listened to what Jim had to say.

"Yes, we can come in tomorrow…" Ryan replied. At the same moment, Hal pitched a fastball to his dad in the back alley behind the house. Harvey hit it with a loud crack straight back into Hal's mitt. Ryan hung up the phone and leaned out the second story window. "He's trying to kill us, Hal!"

"Hmmm?" Hal looked up.

"Jim wants us in tomorrow to redo the chorus again. The man's trying to fucking kill us."

"Yeah, I know…" Hal said as he pitched another ball to his dad.

"And?" Ryan asked.

"AND?" Hal replied as he caught it back in his glove.

"Do you get the feeling we're never actually going to get to finish this thing?"

"No, we'll get there eventually," Hal assured him.

"We got that first single down in under a week, and Jim said at some point we were going to get it on the radio, but so far I've heard nothing. Seeing as we had an entire album's worth of songs already written and polished, we should have walked into that studio and put this thing together in no time. And with how much we've been nitpicked for every single second of every single recording, I feel like nothing's going to be good enough for the guy, and he's eventually going to drop us," Ryan complained.

"That doesn't make sense," Hal said as he pitched the next ball. "Jim doesn't make any money unless we do. And seeing how hard it is for new groups to get any attention for their work, I'm thinking he wants to make sure it's perfect before we try to sell it so that *he* hasn't wasted *his* time on the deal. He said it'd take a little time to try and get us some airplay, and that makes sense since the label has a lot of other material from other groups to try and promote. Honestly, the fact that he's pressing us as hard as he is actually makes me a little excited that he thinks we really might have a chance despite the competition."

"So, we're going to die of exhaustion for one EP?" Ryan asked.

"It's not the worst way to go," Harvey interjected. "Trust me, there's at least a hundred or so ways to go that are much more painful than exhaustion," he added.

"There, see? Sage advice," Hal agreed. "If you want to die from it that's your choice, but I'll be running that golden disc through my fingers at your funeral while me, Uli, and Ricky split your take from it," Hal said.

"Um… yeah, no," Ryan said.

"Good, because we should all be in this together, no matter what happens with it," Hal replied.

"Hal, you really ought to go start a motivational poster company and sell all this shit that goes through your brain," Ryan said.

"Yes, that's exactly what I want to do," Hal said as he pulled his glove off and turned to face Ryan. "Only, instead of making posters, we'll make these audio recordings, you see, and that way people can experience the words instead of just staring at them on a wall. And my plan is to get you, Ricky, and Uli to help me with the…"

"Yeah, yeah, yeah, okay, fine." Ryan stopped him. "So, are we gonna go see Zombies of Mass Destruction today, or what?"

"I'm planning on it. We've still got twenty minutes before it starts." Hal put his glove back on and began twisting the baseball again in his fingers.

"I like seeing the beginnings of my movies too you know, it kinda adds to the whole movie-watching experience," Ryan said.

"It takes ten minutes to get there, and the first twenty minutes are all previews anyways," Hal replied as he wound up the pitch and sent a curve ball barreling at his dad. Harvey jumped to the side and swung at it to keep it from hitting him, and the bat made another loud crack as he caught it with the tip, sending it flying over the fence next to them.

"Aww, shit," Harvey mumbled as it disappeared out of sight. A second later, there was a loud crash of glass breaking, and he tossed the bat into the bushes as him and Hal came sprinting into the house.

"You know, on second thought it might be fun to see what'll be coming out in a few months! Let's go!" Hal yelled as he made a break for the front door. Harvey disappeared down the hall giggling to himself while a woman outside started yelling at their house in Russian. Ryan, Uli, and Ricky quickly followed Hal to the van. They jumped in and took off down the street. "Well, I guess my dad can add one count of property damage to his fifteen outstanding warrants."

"He has how many!?" Uli yelled.

"Yeah, and those are just the one's he's been pegged for. Mom tells me he hasn't exactly been behaving himself for the last twenty-ish years; even while driving the truck."

"Jeez," Ryan said.

"Yeah. *Parents...*" Hal said as he flipped on the old radio and started surfing through the channels.

68. "The Way" by Fastball

*"Director of public re..."*

*"...or at $2.99..."*

*"...is available only at the concession..."*

*"...you know it..."*

*"...sir, there's no obliga..."*

"Wait, go back!" Ricky suddenly shouted, and Hal turned the knob back the other direction.

"There!" Ricky said, pointing at the old radio.

Hal focused the song out of the static, and they all stared at the radio in disbelief. He pulled over while they listened, and when the song ended, the DJ took over.

End Song 68

"Alright, that's new music there from a group called Battle Creek here on 106.1, KISS FM. New song, new group, I like it already. Already had a few requests for it since we first aired it this morning, so yeah. Battle Creek. Definitely a new band to watch. Coming up in about ten minutes we'll be announcing the winner of our..." Hal turned the radio back down and leaned back against his seat, and the van was so quiet they could hear themselves breathing.

"Cool!" Ricky said loudly, and as the other three turned to look at him, their faces hinted that it might have been the understatement of the year.

A few days later, on Sunday, Hal brought up the Top 40 website on his computer. Ryan, Ricky, and Uli leaned over his shoulders as he made his way to the page. "No one's going to pass out on me, right?" he asked.

"Just click the button Hal!" Ryan said.

The page loaded in what may have been a couple seconds, but after what felt like half an hour, the screaming and whooping down the hall brought a smile to Cecilia's face.

"THIRTY-NINE! THIRTY-NINE! WE DEBUTED IN THE TOP 40!" Hal yelled as he tripped over the threshold to the office and fell face first onto the hall floor.

The phone started to ring. Ryan and Uli jumped over him and bolted down the hall. Clothes and pizza boxes flew across the room in a frenzy until the ringing suddenly stopped and was followed by a calm "Hello?" from the kitchen. The other three peered around the corner, and saw Ricky had the phone.

"Yah, saw it. It's awesome!... mmmhmm… yep… oh yah, Hal tripped and fell on his face he was so excited… Yah, he's right here…" Ricky held the phone out to Hal, who grabbed it as quick as he could.

"THIRTY-NINE, JIM!" he yelled into the receiver and walked quickly back down the hall to the office.

"Like a kid on Christmas," Ryan said.

"Yep," Ricky agreed.

"Where was the phone, Ricky?" Uli asked.

"On the charger."

"How the hell did it get there?" Ryan asked.

The next day, they raised a round of beers with Jim in the studio, (except for Ricky, who had an orange soda), and discussed their next move. "Well, I was kind of hoping you wouldn't be listening to the radio so I would get to tell you myself, but here we are anyways," Jim said. "So, we're going to let this coast for a few weeks and see how far you go on the charts, and then we have a few options depending on what happens."

"Such as?" Hal asked.

"Well, if you top out in the thirties then go back down, we keep trying like we have been the last few months, but, either way, you have a foot in the door now."

"Okay," Hal said.

"If you make it up into the teens or higher, we really start going for it with the advertising and pushing you into the public eye. We'll be doing that anyway, but if we start going great guns with it, hopefully we get your EP to break wide open and then we really start having some fun."

"I like that option better. Let's go with that one," Hal said.

"Yeah, yeah. We can hope, but honestly, it's more likely you'll top out and we keep working on it for a while. But either way, we need to get this EP done and then start working on a full-on album. And we need to really get you out on the road more instead of just having you play locally."

"So, by 'on the road,' that would be pack-up-our-things-and-we-won't-be-home-for-weeks-or-months?" Hal asked.

"That's it, indeed. So, if you're serious about this, you gotta be prepared to leave your jobs and go day-to-day never knowing where you're going to wake up. And trust me, it's not a good way to live. Often, you'll be getting up at four or five in the morning to go meet with advertising reps, agents for different labels, etcetera. And then on the same day be playing somewhere late into the night. You'll realize you never knew the real meaning of being tired until you're out touring," Jim explained.

"If that's what it takes, then that's what we'll do," Hal said, and Jim saw Ricky, Uli, and Ryan look increasingly unsure.

"You really do want to be miserable, don't you?" Jim asked, and Hal nodded his head without a moment's hesitation. "Ha! Well, some people need to learn their lesson the hard way, I guess. So, keep in mind we're probably getting ahead of ourselves, but something to think about if you really do want to throw your lives away and start touring is there's a few ways you can go about it. Well, actually there's an endless number of different ways you can go about it. But the main two being either you go on tour alone and hop from one smaller venue to another. Or, if you really, *really* never want to have any freedom ever again, we can try to set you up as the opening act for a big-name artist and you go on tour at the mercy of their schedule."

"Well, I mean, which would you recommend?" Hal said.

"Neither, but if you insist, it's kind of a matter of picking your poison. You go on tour alone, the pace is a little slower, little less stressful, you have more options for how you want the tour to progress. On the other hand, playing small venues really doesn't get you anywhere quick because your music is only getting exposure to a few hundred people a night, if that. And chances are they're the sorts who showed up for any sort of show they could afford and really don't care who's playing. Now, if you go on the road with a big-name act, you could be playing for tens of thousands of people every other night. But you are completely bound to their touring agenda, and on top of that, you spend every night as the group that's stalling the audience from seeing the artists they actually paid their money to see. And, if your main group is running late setting up, the crowd can become a little hostile. So, like I said, it's all a matter of picking your poison."

"But, as long as we're good enough to entertain a large crowd for a while, then it sounds like being an opening act would be the best way to get exposure," Hal said.

Jim smiled and shook his head. "In a perfect world. You have time to think about it. For right now, we get you into the biggest smaller venues around the area that we can, and see what happens on the charts over the next few weeks."

"OK," Hal said.

"Oh, another question for you guys. Have you ever put any thought to whether you want to have a logo for yourselves?"

"Um, no… not really," Hal answered.

"I mean, plenty of bands go without one, or maybe just always have their name written in a unique script. But it's something to think about for when we get this album put together. Branding can be a powerful method of advertising. Also, be thinking of a title for the album."

"We can do that," Hal said.

"Great. Watch the charts, give your next few shows everything you've got, and let me know what you think," Jim said, raising his beer one more time.

"We will! And then we'll get ready to go out on the road," Hal said, raising his in return.

Over the next few weeks, in between work and playing shows, Hal would spend nearly all the rest of his free time sitting in front of the computer. He'd have at least one window open to the Hot 100 charts while working on logo sketches. Trying to make pictures or designs out of the letters B and C, or writing out the name in different fonts on the screen. It was something he could mess with for hours, but at the end of every day, he'd really gotten nowhere with it. *Could I do something with the first letters of our names? H, R, U, R. Hurr. No.* He flipped the eraser-smeared paper over to the other side. *Two Bs and two Cs arranged in a square?* He drew it out, and it was as predictable as he had imagined. He felt the back of his chair weigh down, and Uli appeared looking over his shoulder. "Still no progress?"

"No. I'm starting to see why a lot of bands go logo-less," Hal said.

"There is something you can try that my father would use on me," Uli said.

"What's that?" Hal asked.

"He called it the 'Von Wolff process.' Start with one small, obvious thought, and let it grow bigger slowly instead of thinking of many different thoughts at once."

"Oh… kay…"

"Here, I'll show you. First, what are you trying to do?" Uli asked, and Hal looked at him blankly. "The first answers are the obvious ones, but saying them out loud leads to better thoughts later. Now, what are you trying to do?"

"Make a logo," Hal answered.

"Why?"

"To… represent us as a band."

"For what purpose?"

"Uh… so that people will see our logo and know our work by that alone?"

"Okay, what would help them do that?"

"A simple, but very unique image?"

"Okay. Save that thought. Now, what is that simple, unique image going to be?" Uli asked.

"And there's our roadblock."

"No, no, not literally yet. What I really mean is what would that simple image need to do to be our logo?"

"It would… need to be something that represents us for what we do?"

"All of us as one?" Uli asked.

"Yeah, in a way. Though, if we could have something that represented all of us both at once and as four different parts of a whole, that would be best. Though I'm not sure that's even possible."

"So, four parts of a whole?" Uli repeated.

"Yeah…"

"Okay save that thought too. A unique image that has four parts of a whole. Now, for an image, four parts of a whole what?" Uli asked.

"I dunno," Hal answered.

"What would you want to see on a shirt? What is something that if you saw it on a shirt, you would want to wear it?"

"Well, something that probably had appeal beyond just being a shirt for some band."

"Would it be something more than words, then?"

"Yeah… probably not words or letters or a design with only either of those."

"So, an object?" Uli asked.

"Yes," Hal agreed.

"An object made out of four parts," Uli said.

"Yeah…" Hal said slowly.

"What kind of object?"

"Something that has four parts," Hal answered.

"Anything can be made into four pieces if cut with a sharp enough saw."

"I guess that's true…" Hal replied.

"I ask again, what kind of object? Describe it, though not literally," Uli insisted.

"Well, something eye-catching, something badass," Hal said.

"Like what? What would catch your eye?"

"Uh… a classic car, or a hot rod…" Hal mused, and Uli waited silently while more things came to him. "A sword… or weapon of some sort… a pretty girl… a lightning bolt…" Hal paused and looked at Uli.

"Okay, all good images, all could visually be made into different parts, but could any of these represent all of us?"

"Well… not really…"

"What do we all have in common, Hal?"

"Damn near nothing," Hal said.

"Except…" Uli prodded.

"We're a band…" Hal answered.

"And bands…"

"Make music." Hal replied.

"And music has…?"

"Players…" Hal said and then paused. "A vinyl record!" he suddenly said out loud. "All music ends up on a record or CD or in digital format… but a Vinyl record's got soul, and it's a big canvas to work on!"

"Okay. How would you draw a record to represent all of us?"

"I don't know. I mean, if we want to keep it 'simple' it could be a four-color record, kinda like a pie chart or something. Ricky's corner could be brown, like tanned leather and dry grass and brown ranch horses and all that good country stuff. Metal would be black, of course."

"Okay, but what is the color of punk and pop?"

"I dunno, punk could be, like, neon green, or red plaid, or something. But pop… I don't know…" Hal said, and then sighed. "Goddammit, Uli, I don't know."

"What about a guitar?" Uli said, and Hal suddenly looked up. "All rock and roll has guitars," Uli added.

"Yes… yes it does!" Hal said excited. "Four different guitars! An acoustic wood grain guitar, a black warlock guitar, a guitar with… that British Flag on it or something, and a nice straight-up single-color Fender guitar!"

"There are already shirts like that for sale that are not for bands," Uli said.

"Then WHAT, ULI!? You keep feeding me ideas here, then turn around and shoot them right back down! What do YOU think we should have, huh!?" Hal shouted.

Uli stood back up straight and started to walk out of the room. "Anything can be cut four ways with the right saw," he answered calmly as he turned the corner into the hall.

"YOU KNOW WHAT, ULI, I WAS TRYING TO WORK HERE!" Hal leaned out the door and yelled after him. "If you were bored and needed to fuck with someone's mind, I know Ryan is always up for a good fucking, and I bet…" Hal suddenly stopped as Uli stared at him in his usual bored gaze, and something suddenly clicked in his head. He quickly retreated back into the room and took up the pencil. An hour later, he went over and dropped the sketchpad down abruptly on the couch near where the other three were sitting. On it, they saw a drawing of a most unique guitar. The head and neck were a generic electric guitar assembly, but the top left quarter of the body was in the shape of a wood grain acoustic guitar. The top right quarter was part of a standard Fender Stratocaster. The Stratocaster piece flowed seamlessly downwards into a midnight black and sharply pointed warlock guitar. Then, on the other side of the lower half underneath the acoustic shape, was the rounded bottom of another standard electric guitar body that could easily have come from the same Stratocaster donor, except for the Union Jack flag sketched across its face.

"Holy shit!" Ryan exclaimed.

"You like it?" Hal asked.

"It's sick!" Ryan said.

"Yeah! It was Uli's idea."

"That's okay, it's still awesome! We actually need to have one of those made for Ricky to play on stage!" Ryan said, and Ricky nodded his head in agreement.

"That would be amazing, though it could be a while before we have enough money for that," Hal said.

"We gonna use this for the EP cover?" Ryan asked.

"I was kinda thinking that, but I figure we see how the photo shoot tomorrow goes first," Hal replied.

"You think we could actually get a photo more awesome than this for the cover?"

"Well, I'm not totally sure, but I drove by that really old abandoned warehouse down the road again today and got an idea…"

The next day around noon, Hal backed his mother's Red 1968 Mustang up to the rusted and warped chain link fence surrounding the old building and parked it at an angle so the photographer could get a good view of both. He rolled down the window of the car as he got out, and then shut the door firmly. "Gentlemen, ready to bring sexy back?" he asked the other three.

"Born ready," Ryan answered, spitting out a cigarette butt on the cracked pavement and rubbing it out with his shoe. They started to get into position before noticing Ricky was standing a few feet out of range of the camera, looking unsure.

"You alright?" Hal asked him.

Ricky nodded a little bit after a pause. "Do we have to?" he asked quietly.

"Um… yes?" Hal answered. "Why not?"

"Because…" Ricky mumbled.

"Because… you don't like having your picture taken?" Hal asked, annoyed.

"Yeah…" Ricky answered.

"Any specific reason?"

"Um… yeah…"

"…and that would be?"

"Ricky doesn't show up on film," he answered bluntly, and they could almost hear the sound of Hal's eyes rolling.

"Ricky, I don't know what in the hell…"

Hal was interrupted as a click sounded out next to him, and then Ricky was looking indignant at Ryan. Ryan looked at the screen of his cell phone for a second, then back up at him. "Just checking." He passed it to Hal to examine.

"Ricky, you know they haven't used film for quite a while. It's all digital now, and I'd say looking at this, you don't have anything to worry about anymore," Hal said with a smile, handing Ryan his phone back.

"Good thing, too," Ryan added. "Think about it, man. How the hell are millions of girls supposed to hang a poster of us up on their walls and fantasize about us while touching themselves if they don't have a picture of… well, us?" Ryan asked, and Ricky's eyes widened. At first it appeared to be a look of disgust, then he started turning red. It wasn't a furious red by any means, just the standard shading that he'd get with any past likewise suggestion from Ryan. He likely knew by now that it was his downfall, as he couldn't even look them in the eyes anymore when he felt his face getting warm. But Ryan couldn't help but notice he appeared like he was thinking, maybe even considering the thought, even though he was trying not to give anything away.

"Didn't think about that, did you?" Ryan finally said. "But hey, that's why you have us. By the way, I've made it a personal goal to get you laid once we hit the road."

Ricky's eyes were off the ground now, his face blank with shock.

"I know, I know," Ryan continued. "I don't usually go out of my way to help people like this, but that's part of being in a band. Watching out for each other's health and wellness. We know you'd do the same for us. And on that note…" Ryan and Hal grabbed Ricky by the shoulders and pulled him up to the hood of the car, holding him there between them. "…strike a pose, moron."

They sat around the studio table, staring at it. All of them around an old muscle car. A muscle car that had acquired a most unique rust spot on the hood since the photo shoot. A large, well-defined, vaguely multi-colored rust spot that looked strangely like a guitar, and a very strange guitar at that. Hal, Uli, and Ryan were standing confidently against the hood, with Ricky laying on top of the roof on his back. Ricky's head was hanging down over the windshield, his thumbs in his ears while the rest of his fingers were spread out wide, and his tongue sticking out at the camera. Across the top was written **Battle Creek**. And all of this encased in a clear plastic square.

"*You have your work cut out for you, Ryan,*" Uli said quietly while examining the image. Ryan didn't look like he disagreed with that assessment.

"Man… does anyone else feel like we just gave birth?" Hal asked without taking his gaze off the CD.

"If you ever say that again, I'm going to hit you," Ryan answered.

"Alright kids, ready for some news?" Jim asked as he walked back into the room holding a small packet of papers.

"More news? It's been nothing but news for the last few months," Hal said.

"Too much news?"

"Never."

"I'll ask one more time, are you guys really serious about wanting to tour as an opening act?"

"Yes," Hal answered for all four of them.

"Alright, I figured I'd give you one last chance to back out," Jim said.

"What? Did you find someone looking for an opening act?" Hal asked.

"Yes, I did. It's an older band that's had a really long career. They've been on a downswing for many years, and they're not sure if they're going to work on anything new in the future or not. But right now, they're going out for a thirty-city reunion tour mainly through mid-sized and a few smallerish-large venues for all the loyal fans they've held onto for all these years."

"Well, who is it? Maybe we've heard of them!" Hal asked eagerly.

"*Holy Hell*," Jim said, and Hal froze.

"That's hilarious Jim, now who is it really?" Ryan asked. Jim reached into his shirt pocket and pulled out a small pair of glasses, then held the paper right in front of his face and read very matter-of-factly, *"Ho... lee... Hell."* Then lowered the paper and looked at Ryan, hoping he was satisfied. Ryan didn't respond.

"Are you... serious?" Hal asked. Jim sighed and handed him the paper. Hal looked it over, then handed it to Ryan, and leaned back in his chair.

"Heard of them?" Jim asked.

"Oh, um, yeah... yeah, we've heard of them. Sort of," Hal answered.

"Indeed," Jim said suspiciously. "Anyways, their tour starts in March of next year. We should have your full album done by then, so you'll be ready to promote yourselves on the road. 'Til then, we promote the heck out of your little EP here wherever we can."

"OK," Hal answered.

"Alright, I'll make the call and commit you to this, and then from now to March your job is to simply get your affairs in order and give your workplaces notice. Because come tour day, that's the last your family and friends are going to be seeing of you for quite a while," Jim warned.

# CHAPTER 6

## (Playin' in a Traveling Band)

### MARCH

**Ryan and Hal were looking** in the box again. The same box Hal had pulled out of his closet the night they found out who they were touring with. It was full of old CDs and posters Hal had never wanted to get rid of. Things he had from when he was a lot younger. He and Ryan had spent that evening going through it and talking quietly in his room. Now they were going through it once more in the last hours before they officially had to leave to go on tour. It was weird to think that he was going out his front door today and wouldn't be coming back through it again for months. Cleaning up his room felt like he was prepping it to go into stasis; getting it ready to be frozen in time. When noon rolled around and they had to go, everything was as set as he knew he could get it. He and Ryan shoved the box back on the top shelf of his closet and shut the door.

All their equipment was in the back of the Twinkie, along with their suitcases. Cecilia was somewhat somber during the drive to the bus station, though never without a small smile on her face. When they got there, Hal barely knew what to say to her. He knew he'd have to leave home someday, but in his head he always secretly figured the music thing would never work out. He assumed he'd get a normal job and move two miles across town and still have dinner with her once a week on Sundays. He didn't want to get emotional, he knew he'd never live it down from Ryan and Uli if he did. Most of the time they meant no harm, though occasionally they took it too far. Neither of them really knew what it was like to have a parent who was a best friend. He set the last bag down on the bench and looked at her. She was standing next to Harvey, who had one arm around her shoulder. She still hadn't lost that smile. The greyhound bus was already loading up behind them, though they still had half an hour before it was supposed to leave.

"Well…" Hal said.

"You guys are going to do great on your tour, and I know you're going to get signed to something much bigger once people start hearing you out there," Cecilia said.

"Thanks, Mom," he replied, and hugged her for a good, long time.

"So, Hal, one last thing before you leave," she said as she stepped back one pace and looked up at him. He had stopped growing years ago, but it still surprised him to see how much taller than her he was. He wasn't exactly 'tall,' but his mom had always been a little on the short side. "Yeah, Mom?"

"I know you guys are going to be travelling all over, sleeping different places every night, living in the fast lane, and probably doing a lot of partying. So, there's something I want you to remember…"

*Well, this might make things easier…* Hal thought to himself. "Yes?" he asked.

"Hal, you know I want grandchildren someday, and I don't care if they're legitimate. After all, you weren't. Just let me know if one is on the way, and we'll work something out with the mother," she said, and Ryan, Uli, and Ricky burst out laughing. Hal stifled a laugh himself as one stray tear ran down his cheek. Cecilia reached up and wiped it away before anyone else saw.

"Good talk, Mom," he said as he leaned in and hugged her again. "Think you can take care of the Twinkie for me while we're gone?" Hal asked his dad as he gave him a quick hug.

"I'll change the cream filling every 3,000 miles," Harvey reassured him. After they had gotten all their luggage and instruments onto the bus and his parents had taken off in the van, the bus started moving towards the road.

Within a few minutes, they watched as Detroit slowly faded off into the distance behind them.

"Hey, there's the fresh meat!" They were greeted as they turned the corner into the room their host band was waiting in.

"In the flesh!" Hal said eagerly as him and Ryan both reached out a hand.

"Ha! That's the right attitude!" The lead singer jumped to his feet from the couch and shook their hands vigorously, as well as Ricky's and Uli's. "Name's Allen," he said, his long, black, wavy hair cascading over the ridge of his shoulders.

"Aww, I had one of these as a kid!" One of the guitarists quickly snatched Ricky's hat off his head and put it on.

"Hey, that's a good look for you, Tod!" the other guitarist said.

"Just don't try it with a live one," the drummer added.

"And why the hell not?" Tod asked.

"You might give it rabies, asshole," the drummer replied.

"I don't have rabies. I always use a condom," Tod said.

The other guitarist and drummer looked at each other skeptically out of the corners of their eyes.

"Anyways… if you don't already know, I'm Tod, and I play the guitar." Tod shook their hands now. Tod had thick black-rimmed glasses and short brown hair gelled up straight into short spikes, currently hidden under Ricky's hat.

"Gunder. Or just Gun. Also, guitar." Another one of the men reached out his hand. Gunder had shoulder-length blond dreadlocks back in a ponytail, and a large tan hemp necklace with a fossilized nautilus shell pendant on it. It was a necklace which he almost never took off.

"Donovan." The last man introduced himself. He was bald with muscular arms completely covered in tattoos. "Drummer."

"This is really an honor!" Hal said. "I'm Hal. I'm lead vocals."

"I'm Ryan, I'm drums."

"I am Uli, and I play piano or keyboard, violin, trumpet, and saxophone."

"Oh, wow," Gunder said.

"Uli is our one-man orchestra," Hal added, and then they all looked at Ricky.

"Oh, uh, Ricky. Ricky plays guitar," Ricky said.

"Ricky plays guitar, huh?" Donovan asked him.

"Yep," Ricky answered, smiling. "Ricky plays guitar."

"Ricky rocks a raccoon hat," Tod said, setting his hat back on his head.

"Ricky rocks way more than that," Hal added.

"Well, Ricky, Gun, and Tod should all have a jam session sometime," Gunder said, and Ricky nodded. "'Kay!"

"Hey, we can all do the jam thing on the road between gigs when we aren't tired," Allen said.

"I'm in!" Ryan answered.

"Yes! And you know, that's what I like about having a long-term opening act instead of a new group every two or three shows. Getting to know each other, getting that sense of comradery, doing jam-sessions and watching new ideas develop from it. I was so excited when our manager said he found us a group who wanted to be in it for the whole tour," Allen said, and Hal was nodding his head to every word. "Anyways, as you've already probably been informed, our first stop is Phoenix. A perfect city to bring to life the fiery revival of Holy Hell, and since this is your first tour of duty, I'm wondering if you want a tour of the tour buses?"

"Hell, yeah!" Hal said, and Allen gestured dramatically towards the door.

As they all got up to go, Ryan walked up to Donovan.

"Hey, is he always that..." Ryan looked in Allen's direction while he searched for the best word.

"*Upbeat?*" Donovan said quietly.

"Yeah," Ryan said.

"Yes," Donovan answered.

"Hal's the same way."

"Lead singers, man, I tell yah..." Donovan said.

"Maybe they'll keep each other busy," Ryan whispered.

"That'd be nice," Donovan answered. "I mean, Allen is an amazing human being. He's always there for you, he tries to see the good in any situation, he's been the glue that's held us together for all these years, but…" Donovan paused for a moment, then lowered his voice. "*That'd be nice.*" He said it again, and Ryan laughed a little as he took out a cigarette while they walked down the back steps.

"Ho-ley shit…" Hal was the first to get a look at the interior. It was a cavernous monster of a vehicle, to the point that it was hard to think of it as a vehicle at all instead of a narrow, mobile nightclub. The honey-colored wood floor was framed on either side with black leather benches, and color-changing rope lights lined the windows and arched across the ceiling. There was a small glass-top bar in the very center of the main aisle with long cabinets full of various bottles of liquor, four separate locking bedrooms, and a small hot tub in one of the bathrooms.

"Am I dead?" Ryan asked as he took it all in.

"No, no. They don't make 'em this nice in heaven," Allen said, looking around like it was the first time in a long while that he had really noticed it himself. They took a few minutes to look around and admire all the finishes, especially the collection of rock-and-roll themed kitchen utensils and appliances in the kitchenette area. All the large appliances had been painted to look like guitar amplifiers; the refrigerator, the dishwasher, the oven, and even the toaster was painted to look like a mini-amp. Containers on the countertop were full of instrument-themed spoons and utensils. Two wooden spoons ended in drumstick tips at the bottom of their handles, a metal spatula was in the shape of an electric guitar, the neck being the handle and the flipper part being the guitar body. Another wooden spoon had its head shaped like the body of an acoustic guitar. A pair of salad tongs was shaped like two long hand-held microphones. A barbeque fork ended in a hand shaped into metal horns; the pointer and pinky finger sticking up in two sharp spikes to plunge into a steak. Another handheld inverted V-shaped electric guitar had the body of a cheese grater. "That's the shredder," Allen said as Hal held up the grater, and uncontrollable smiles slowly overtook them as they started to giggle to themselves.

"Alright, I need the name and number of where to buy this stuff," Hal said. "I do a little cooking here and there."

"I'll get you a list. Though the appliances are standard name-brand models that were custom painted by a private artist. I'll see if I can find her website for you."

"God, this is incredible," Ryan said, putting his hands on either side of his forehead as he looked around. Like he had to hold his head steady as it tried to process the sheer amount of awesome that was surrounding them. Uli was silently admiring intricate Celtic knot work designs and skulls embossed into the back rests of the black leather seats. Ricky was keeping quiet as usual, though it was clear from the look on his face he was equally as stunned as the rest of them were.

"So, are we, I mean, are you and us, or…" Hal started to say.

"Well, unfortunately, no," Allen said. "This is ours, and that one out the back there is what you'll be travelling in." He pointed out the back window at a smaller, older camping RV parked behind them.

"Aw, man…" Ryan said.

"Well, I mean, that's what you'll be sleeping in between motels and such, but that doesn't mean you have to spend *all* your road time in there. We'll have plenty of those little jam sessions we were talking about together in the *House of Hell* here."

"I won't complain," Hal said.

"Most people don't," Allen laughed. "And some day you guys will earn one of these for yourselves, but you might want to go down and start getting acquainted with your little home away from home. It's always total chaos right before the tour caravan first leaves, and you'll want to get as settled as you can before that happens."

"Yeah, everyone was already running around like mad when we first came in," Hal said.

"Oh, yes, your road crew goes through a lot to make everything happen just right. They'll calm down once things fall into place, but I'd try and stay out of their way the next few days, and don't take it personally if they're a little short with you at first," Allen said.

"Can do," Hal answered.

"Excellent. Do it to it, then. Our adventure begins tomorrow," Allen said as they headed back out of the bus, and Hal thanked him again before they parted ways and went to get all their stuff together.

The bus ride the next day was short and painless, unlike the Greyhound trip from Detroit. It was only seventy miles from where they started in Arizona to Phoenix, and they arrived at the little motel where they were staying in no time. Their host band was staying at a much larger hotel where the security team could keep better control over things. They had two rooms for the four of them, and they split it into Hal and Uli in one room, and Ricky and Ryan in the other. Hal had apologized to Ricky quietly while they were unpacking, saying: "Sorry, man, but you're the only one who can stand him for that long." Ricky nodded in his usual way, and said it was okay. They only brought into the room the bare minimum that they'd need for the next few nights, since they were just going to pack it all up again when it was time to head out for the next city. Ryan brought in his toothbrush, a clean shirt and a pair of boxers before calling it good, then went and sat down on a plastic chair on the small back patio. He had one of his 'special' magazines with him that he kept under his mattress at Hal's house where Cecilia wouldn't find them. He started flipping through it.

"Hey, Ricky…" Ryan waved him over without taking his eyes off the pages. "C'mere. You gotta see the rack on this girl." Ricky sort of looked up from his luggage, his face already getting a little red at the suggestion. He stood there for a bit, watching Ryan, hoping he'd just keep flipping pages and forget about it. But Ryan glanced up at him impatiently, and knowing there was probably no way out of it, he walked over and stood about 6 feet behind him. "You must have pretty damn good eyes if you can see from back there," Ryan said sternly, and Ricky took a few steps closer. "Better. Now isn't this the nicest damn pair of boobs you've ever laid eyes on?" Ryan held the magazine up, and Ricky looked away embarrassed. Ryan reached up and put his hand on the back of Ricky's head, and turned it back to the magazine. "Dontcha wish those were real right in front of you so you could stick your face between them and rub it around a bit?"

"Um… well… they're… big…" Ricky said.

"Hmm?" Ryan mumbled.

"Hmm, what?" Ricky said, flustered.

"If you've ever seen a nicer pair than that, I'd love to hear about it."

"Uh…"

"Or are you more of an ass guy?" Ryan asked.

"What!?" Ricky answered.

"Does ass take priority over boobs?" Ryan asked. Ricky looked at him blankly. "Look man, you gotta give me some specs here so I can go shopping for you," Ryan explained.

"What are ya…?"

"Boobs, ass, or legs? I of course try to find a stunning example of all three, but I need to know what order to rank them. Next, I need to know taller, shorter, or about the same height as you, blond, black, brunette, or redhead, favorite eye color…"

"Is that all women are to you? Just things?" Ricky stammered out.

"Hey, I'm not mean to girls. I show them a good time. But do tell, what are they to you?" Ryan asked, and Ricky sort of shifted his weight nervously and rubbed his arm.

"Well… um…" That was all the further he got.

"I *know* you do like girls, Ricky. I saw those vintage magazines you were hiding in the junk in the closet of your room at Hal's house," Ryan said, and Ricky looked up again, doing his best to not to appear terrified. "And don't try to blame it on Hal or Uli. It might have otherwise been a pretty good alibi, except that I've seen everything they own since we sort of always traded stuff around. I knew all their hiding places too. And don't try to blame it on Cecilia either, because as hot as that would be, I don't think the universe is that amazing."

"Don't… don't know what you're…."

"Dude, vintage isn't their thing, but I could see it being yours. I could tell you what their things are, but I'm thinking maybe you don't want to know. So, are those something you got a hold of somehow back home, or did you buy them? Because if you did, there's nothing wrong with ladies who don't starve themselves to death, it's a more comfortable ride if you ask me. Getting stabbed by some chick's hipbone and having a bruise in the morning isn't cool. And there's certainly nothing wrong with those little sailor outfits and polka dot dresses they used to put on them." Ryan hooked the leg of another plastic chair on the deck with his foot and drug it over next to him. "So?"

"So… what?" Ricky asked, starting to panic.

"So… talk to me. About girls. Here, let's start over. Does this chick not have the best boobs you've ever seen, or what?"

"You shouldn't talk 'bout women that way…" Ricky said awkwardly, then marched back into the room and started pretending to be looking for something important in his luggage. He could feel Ryan's glare burning into the back of his head, but he kept his head down, hoping, praying he'd drop it. He heard Ryan shift a little in his chair.

"Make me a list, Ricky, and leave it somewhere I can find it. If you don't, I'm going to have to start making guesses, and it'd be a lot easier for the both of us if we didn't have to do it that way."

Ricky's fists clenched hard on the top shirt in the pile of his things. He didn't know if he was more mad or embarrassed, but a few moments later, the door to their room opened and Hal walked in. "Hey, let's go somewhere for dinner."

"We just got here half an hour ago!" Ryan said.

"And?" Hal asked.

"Well, are you paying for it? Because we're going to be living on fumes for quite a while, and the food in the RV fridge from the grocery store is a lot cheaper than eating out," Ryan said.

"It's our first night on tour! Don't you think that's cause to splurge a little?"

"I'll ask again, are you paying for it?"

"Sure," Hal relented.

"Yeah, you're right. We can live it up a little," Ryan said.

"Great," Hal mumbled. "You guys ready to go now?"

"Yes!" Ricky said eagerly.

"You know where we're going?" Ryan asked.

"No. I just figured we'd roam around Phoenix until we found something that looked good," Hal said, and then they set out. It only took them a few blocks to find a bar that they wanted to try. They sat down inside and ordered. It was karaoke night, and Ryan was hit with a moment of intuition. He was about to say something to Hal about not-even-thinking-about-it, but when he looked, Hal's seat was empty. He didn't even have to look at the stage to realize he was already too late.

69. "Don't Stop Believin'" by Journey

Hal tapped his foot in time with the music as he moved back and forth across the stage. He wasn't walking, nor was he quite dancing. Though while it was neither, it could have also been a combination of both. A small group of women began to form in front of the stage at his feet, clapping and whistling as he drew out the notes at the end of each chorus. He held the microphone tight in his fist and raised over his head, like he was trying to shake loose the last few drops of beer from a bottle. Ryan wondered if he was dancing like an idiot on purpose to be funny, or if he was trying to be serious and had no idea how stupid he looked. Certainly, that crowd that had formed had come to watch the spectacle, but with each round of applause and cheers, it was like they didn't really notice how stupid he looked either.

```
End Song 69
```

Hal sat back down triumphantly at the table after the song was over and took a long swig of his beer.

"What the hell was that?" Ryan asked.

"What the hell was what?" Hal asked after swallowing.

"That thing you were doing."

"What thing?"

"The thing you were doing all over the stage."

"Oh, you mean the little shuffle?"

"If that's what you call it."

"I dunno, it just sort of came to me."

"Well, I hope it doesn't follow you home."

"Huh?"

"That was the dumbest thing I've ever seen."

"To you maybe, but I liked it. You know what they say, dance like no one is watching."

"Yes, and that's exactly the problem, Hal. People *were* watching," Ryan said.

"Yeah, and they were enjoying it too."

"Maybe not in the way you intended."

"As long as they were having a good time, does it matter why?"

Ryan stared blankly at Hal, trying to think of a comeback, but Hal wasn't going to wait for him.

"Isn't that what being in a band is about? Letting your freak flag fly?" Hal added.

"Hal… there's many different varieties of 'freak,' and that phrase…" Ryan started to explain, but Hal cut him off.

"Nah, it's all the same," Hal replied. "You run whatever you've got up the flagpole, and the people who stop and salute, however many or few they may be, those are the people you run with."

"So, what you're saying is you're going to do that again while we're on stage," Ryan said, disgusted.

"And again, and again," Hal assured him before taking another drink.

"You are such an idiot."

"Yeah and look who's still drumming for me," Hal said with a smile.

The next evening, they found themselves with a little free time as they waited backstage until the clock hit nine. Everything was set up. It wasn't a terribly large venue; an old brick warehouse that had been turned into a downtown concert hall, but it was packed tight to the walls with people. At nine they stepped out. No one in the entire place knew who they were. But seeing any movement on the stage after some of these people had already been waiting inside for a few hours set off the first round of screams and applause.

"Good evening, beautiful people," Hal said, taking the microphone from the stand. "You wouldn't *believe* who I just saw backstage," he said, and then scanned the audience as the room fell silent. "*Holy Hell*," he whispered to the crowd, and there was an explosion of shouts and clapping. Once it started to die down, he kept going. "Well, we're *not* Holy Hell, but you know, nobody's perfect. I'm Hal, this is Ricky, that's Uli, and Ryan, and we're Battle Creek. Like Holy Hell, we play rock music, too, and it sounds a little something like this…"

70. "18 and Life" by Skid Row

71. "Devil Inside" by INXS

72. "Down with the Sickness" by Disturbed

73. "The Rock Show" by Blink 182

74. "Thunder Rolls" by Garth Brooks

75. "Burnin' for You" by Blue Oyster Cult

76. "Born to Be Wild" by Steppenwolf

77. "Psychosocial" by Slipknot

78. "Bottoms Up" by Brantley Gilbert

79. "Smells Like Teen Spirit" by Nirvana

80. "Dirty Deeds Done Dirt Cheap" by AC/DC

81. "Rock Out" by Motorhead

82. "Smooth Criminal" by Alien Ant Farm

83. "Smoke Rings in the Dark" by Gary Allan

84. "Eve of Destruction" by The Turtles

85. "Send Me an Angel" by Real Life

They had all been a little uneasy backstage, not knowing what to expect opening for someone else instead of playing for themselves. But as soon as they started to play, the audience was ready to go. It was only a few seconds until a group of people in the front were throwing their drinks on each other, and pulling strangers up above them and passing them around the room.

It seemed so incredibly easy compared to all the horror stories Jim had fed them. If this was going to be the standard reaction at the shows for the next six months, it made it feel like this whole opening thing might be kind of fun.

End Songs 70 – 85

"ARE YOU ALL READY TO RAISE SOME HELL!?" Hal yelled out at the end of their set, and the crowd yelled back and started chanting in unity. They stepped off the stage and sat to the side barely out of view as the main act made their entrance. Hal figured they must have played hundreds, if not thousands of shows in their career. He had occasionally wondered if it ever got old, if they ever got bored, or if it ever didn't seem worth it anymore. But when Allen grabbed the microphone and greeted their fans, the look in his eyes gave him the answer. He looked like a fallen angel in black leather as he sang, pulling his voice from an otherworldly power. He drew his energy from the screams of the crowd, converted it into something else within himself, then sang it back out again as a gift to them. Hal was mesmerized. He and the other three watched them the whole concert. They studied their every move. They didn't want to miss a single moment or lose a single lesson. Ryan was equally riveted. Neither of them thought they'd ever get this close to the stage at a Holy Hell concert.

After the show was over around midnight, they went to hit the city. They were tired, but Allen said it was tradition to go right after the concert on the first night of the tour. They knew an exclusive club in Phoenix that would be open for a few more hours. They had been there before, years ago. They always invited their opening act to join them.

> 86. "Jump Around" by House of Pain *to play over this scene*

They left one wild party and stepped straight through the club doors into another. Allen and crew were approached quickly by several women, so they parted ways with them for the night and headed towards the dance floor.

"You okay, man?" Hal asked Ricky, who was cringing and plugging his ears.

"It's loud."

"WHAT?" Hal shouted.

"IT'S LOUD!" Ricky answered.

"Don't worry, you'll get used to it. Come on, there's got to be five girls for every guy in here!" Ryan said.

"Nah, gonna go get somethin' to eat," Ricky said.

"Alright, but come join us when you're done, okay?" Hal said.

Ricky nodded, then headed for the bar.

"I don't get him," Ryan said.

"Hey, this is probably a pretty big shock to him. Maybe he's never been in a club like this before. Just give him a bit, he should come 'round," Hal said. The lights pulsated in rhythm with the music, and they took turns dancing with a group of girls, sometimes two at a time. Ricky sat down at the bar and ordered a plate of chicken strips, an orange soda, and a pair of earplugs.

> End Song 86

> 87. "We No Speak Americano" by Yolanda Be Cool Ft. D-Cup *to play over this scene*
> 88. "I Gotta Feeling" by The Black-Eyed Peas
> 89. "Around the World (LaLaLa)" by ATC

90. "Dynamite" by Taio Cruz

91. "Hips Don't Lie" by Shakira ft. Wyclef Jean

92. "Intergalactic" by The Beastie Boys

93. "Party in My Head" by September

94. "I've Been Thinking About You" by Londonbeat

95. "Single Ladies (Put a Ring on It)" by Beyoncé

96. "Bailamos" by Enrique Iglesias

97. "Insane in the Brain" by Cypress Hill

98. "Mr. Vain" by Culture Beat

99. "Krazy" by Pitbull ft. Lil' Jon

After the first hour, Hal decided Ricky had had enough time, and went across the floor up to the bar, only to find someone else in his seat. He scanned the club, but he was nowhere to be seen. After looking for him for about ten minutes, he gave up and headed back down to the others.

"He still won't come?" Uli asked.

"He's gone," Hal said.

"What? Where?" Uli asked.

"I dunno. Maybe he went back to the motel?"

Ryan walked up a moment later with a girl under each arm. The two women were a serious study in contrasts. One was tall, model-looking, with long blond hair. The other was probably the shortest girl in the club that night, though certainly no younger than the tall one. She had short layered brown hair, and a striking hourglass figure with a small-ish waist, but full, round hips and breasts. Despite this, neither Ryan, Hal, nor Uli could have said they were anything other than natural. "Hey, I thought you were going to make him get off his ass and come down and join us. Is he still sitting up there?" Ryan asked.

"Well, no. He's sort of disappeared," Hal answered.

"You're kidding, right?"

"Nope. I looked all over and I can't find him."

"I'mma kill him. I just spent the last hour getting him a date for the night," Ryan said, and Uli and Hal immediately looked over to the shorter girl.

"That's too bad he left. I'm always up for a guitarist, they're so talented with their fingers," she said, and Hal bit his lip to keep from laughing.

"Yeah, he's sort of shy," Ryan mumbled.

"Aww, that's sweet actually. If you do find him, come let me know. I'll be back on the other side of the center bar for at least another hour."

"Oh, you'll know the second we find him. Sorry about this," Ryan said.

"It's totally okay," the girl answered as she turned to leave.

Ryan looked back to Uli and Hal. "I figured maybe he'd appreciate not having to do his sightseeing while looking up the whole time," he said, and then there was a pause. "I'mma kill him," he repeated.

"I'm not sure he's a one-night-stand sort of guy," Hal said.

"That's the only chance there is on a tour!" Ryan said.

"Well, I mean… are there any cute girls on road crew? Or in light and sound?" Hal asked.

Ryan pondered it for a second. "I'll look."

"Yeah, give that a try," Hal said.

"Are you absolutely sure he's not in here, though?"

"Pretty sure, but I'll go look again. I suppose he could have been in the bathroom or something."

"Please," Ryan said, and the tall blond girl looked like she was starting to get bored.

> End Songs 87 – 99

Hal didn't find Ricky on the second attempt, nor the third or fourth that he made later in the night. Finally, they gave up and just decided to stay until they were nearly falling asleep. When they got back to the motel, Ricky wasn't there either. They were too tired to care and went to bed assuming he'd be back in the morning, which he was. Before Hal went to sleep, he looked at the clock and noticed how late they had stayed out. He realized his mom would probably be getting ready for work now since she was two time zones ahead of them. Despite how tired he was, something made him want to call her, and he started dialing on the motel phone.

"*Hello?*" Cecilia picked up after a few rings.

"Hi, Mom."

"*Hal! My gosh, you're up early.*"

"Um, yeah… up… early…" he said, barely coherent.

"*Lord, what was I thinking…?*" Cecilia said. "*Hal, how long have you been awake?*"

"Um, since 8:30 a.m.… yesterday… I think."

"*Okay, next question. Why? Or do I even want to know?*"

"We just played our first concert tonight… or… last night, and I wanted to call to tell you it was amazing."

"*Oh, Hal, you could have called me later after you had slept a bit.*"

"I know, but I didn't call you at all, uh, yesterday, and I said I would…"

"*Hal, you know I always love hearing from you, and you can tell me everything about how it went later today, but do me a favor and go to bed now, okay?*" she said, and it brought a smile to his face.

"Yes, Mom."

"*Good. Get some rest. I love you, Hal.*"

"I love you too, Mom. 'Night."

"*Goodnight, Hal,*" she said, and he reached over and hung up the phone on the side table, and then was asleep face down on the bed a few seconds later.

They had to get up and leave again in only a couple hours, but they slept most of the trip on the road. Hal woke up again in the late afternoon on one of the bench seats, and he laid there for a while watching the white clouds slowly drift by out the window above him. After the long night they had, he felt like now everything was going in slow motion, and they would probably wake up to a lot of long, boring road trips exactly like this one. The low crackling of the walkie-talkie the driver had, cut in and out; the voices of the other drivers making sure they were all going the right route and telling dirty jokes in between. His eyes began to wander away from the clouds, and around the room. Uli was sitting across from him on the other side of the aisle, his arms folded across his chest, his feet up on the bench, and his head resting back against the wall panel of the little kitchen unit. He looked a little too perfect to be asleep and was probably just resting after giving up on actually trying to sleep in the jostling RV. Hal then looked down the short hall to the back of the bus. In his haze, he found studying the cheap white cabinets and fake wood panel walls very interesting. Taking in the details of the interior that would be their temporary home until the mid-fall. He finally looked straight up, and then back a little over his head and saw a single, dirty foot hanging out of the elevated bed over the driver's cabin. Hal sat up, and saw Ricky with his hands behind his head, staring at the ceiling. "*Where did you go last night?*" he asked, and barely recognized his own voice for how hoarse it sounded.

Ricky looked over startled, to the sight of Hal cringing as he grabbed his throat. "Um… for a walk…" Ricky answered.

"You should not have done that Karaoke before the show," Uli said. He now had one eye open in Hal's direction.

"*That was only one song on top of the full set we did…*" Hal choked, getting up to see what he could find in the fridge.

"And we all had to yell in that club afterwards," Ryan said, out of sight somewhere at the other end of the RV.

"That settles it, you are not allowed to talk at all between shows, Hal," Uli said with a smirk.

"*Shove it,*" Hal said from behind the open fridge door. "*Dumb question, but does anyone have any tea?*"

"I do not," Uli said, and Ricky shook his head as well.

"*Shit.*"

"There are a couple honey packets in the right cabinet. Putting that in hot water might be the best we can do for you right now," Uli said.

"*Alright. I'll get some tea next time we do a food run.*" Hal put the honey in a cup of water, microwaved it for a minute, and sat back down with a spoon to stir it up. Ryan appeared from the back room and came up to the front where they were, looking around irritated.

"Did you find them?" Uli asked, his eyes closed again.

"No," Ryan answered.

"*What?*" Hal asked.

"My drumsticks. The nice ones. The ones I got signed at that concert… that one time… by that one guy…" Ryan said, still distracted.

"*Did you use them last night?*"

"Fuck yeah, I did."

"*Are they still at the hall?*"

"Shouldn't be. I thought I put them back in my bag."

"*Could they have fallen out?*"

"I… guess."

"The road crew probably picked them up if they did. They might be in the trucks with the other instruments," Uli said.

"*Yeah. We can call the hall, and if they didn't find them, they'll probably turn up when we set up the next show.*"

"Hey, Uli, your bag was right next to mine. Could they have tossed them in there if they fell out?"

"They are not in there," Uli answered.

"You already looked before you even knew I lost them?" Ryan asked.

"My bag was shut at the show."

"That doesn't mean they didn't find them on the floor and unzip it to put them in there, stupid." Ryan turned to go back down the hall.

"Do NOT touch my stuff!" Uli said sternly, and Ryan stopped.

"Uli, I bet your stuff loves it when I touch it…"

"YOU would not want me going through your luggage."

"Pshh. Go ahead. It's your nightmares," Ryan said, then started to walk again.

"I will look for them." Uli got up quickly and went past him to where their bags were piled. He rifled through the large black duffle bag for a minute or two before zipping it back up. "They are not here."

"Fine. Would it have been so hard to let me look? That way we wouldn't have interrupted your beauty sleep," Ryan said.

"I have old family photos and some valuable heirlooms in there," Uli said.

"I'm not gonna steal your stupid valuables," Ryan said, frustrated, and went back to look again through his own luggage. Uli went back to the front bench and sat back down.

"*Uli, Ryan's a whore, but I really don't think he's a thief,*" Hal said.

"I simply do not wish to have anyone touching my belongings besides me," Uli said and pulled his feet back up onto the bench and shut his eyes again. Hal sighed and stirred up the honey in his water that had settled to the bottom. Save from the clinking of the spoon on the glass, they sat there in silence again as the bus rambled on. Ricky had gone back to staring at the ceiling, lost in thought, like he was somehow watching clouds through the solid RV roof.

"*You alright?*" Hal asked.

"Yeah," Ricky answered quickly, without looking at him.

"*You just seem off. You feeling sick?*"

"No. Ricky just… has a melody stuck in his head," Ricky said.

"*Oh. You'll have to play it for us later. Maybe we can make something with it.*"

Hal was interrupted as Ryan burst back into the hallway. "I AM ULI, LORD OF DARKNESS!!!" he yelled, and Uli's eyes were wide open as he flung around in his seat. Ryan was in a long black leather trench coat with buttons on the front shaped like skulls, and sleeves that were lined up and down with short leather belts that adjusted the tightness around the arms. He was also wearing black platform boots with spikes on the toes and silver flames embroidered in the sides, and a black leather belt lined with spikes barely shorter than the ones on the boots. Ryan held up one arm and admired the coat. "Uli, you dick, you've been holding out on us. You…" Ryan started screaming as he looked up and saw Uli flying at him. He tried to dart into the small bathroom and pull the door shut, but Uli stopped it before he could get it latched. Uli grabbed him and pulled him violently back out.

"I said NOT to touch my stuff!"

"*Uli! Wait!*" Hal croaked as he grabbed his arms to try and get him to let go of Ryan. "OFF!" Uli shoved him back, but lost his grip on Ryan also, and Ryan ran to the front of the bus.

"IT'S NOT MY FAULT YOU'RE SECRETLY THE GOD OF HELLFIRE, WHAT'RE YOU TRYING TO KILL ME FOR!?" Ryan yelled. Uli cornered him again against the bench and grabbed him by the coat collar. Uli was so red in the face it didn't even look real. Ryan twisted his ankle in the tall boots trying to get away, and accidentally kicked Uli's feet out from under him so they both hit the floor. A small, round black case fell out of one of the coat pockets and rolled in front of Ryan's nose. He quickly snatched it. "Wait. Is this EYE SHADOW!?"

"GIVE ME THAT!" Uli reached for it, but Ryan threw it upwards. "RICKY! CATCH!" Ricky sat up just in time and caught it in both hands. "LOOK AND SEE IF IT'S EYESHADOW!" Ryan yelled.

"DO NOT! It is an old chain necklace! It is in pieces, and I do not want it to fall out and scatter all over the bus!" Uli yelled, and Ricky looked back and forth a few times from the small case to Uli, but then took the lid by the tip of his thumb and popped it up slowly. The red in Uli's face suddenly vanished and was replaced by an extreme pale, and Ryan's eyes were huge while he waited for the answer. Ricky seemed less than amazed as he examined its contents, but then slowly stuck his pinky finger into it and drew two black lines underneath his eyes like a football player would.

"HA!" Ryan burst out.

"You... YOU RAT!" Uli growled.

"No, raccoon…!" Ricky barely got the words out before Uli got up and grabbed one of his feet and pulled him down out of the loft bed. He landed with a loud thud on the floor next to Ryan. Hal ran towards them to try and prevent an imminent fight, but the scene quickly degraded into a kicking, screaming, punching, flailing mass of bodies.

The driver had remained entirely detached throughout the whole fight, as he most always did while trying to navigate. But after a few moments more of his usual low talking with the other drivers, they heard him say very monotone: "Hey, Earl, hold on a sec, will ya?" And then he turned around in his chair, and in a voice that could have demolished a small skyscraper, yelled: "SO HELP ME GOD IF YOU LITTLE BOYS DON'T SHUT THE FUCK UP AND SIT BACK DOWN I'M GOING TO PULL OVER AND YOU'LL BE WALKING THE REST OF THE WAY TO DENVER!" A few moments later, the bus was dead silent, and none of them were anywhere to be seen. The crackling on the walkie-talkie resumed with laughing from the other drivers. "*Haha! You tell 'em, Joe!*"

# CHAPTER 7

## (Stay-Just a Little Bit Longer)

### AUGUST

**Travelling was exhausting, like Jim** had promised, but it was a gratifying sort of exhausting. Every concert in every city was something different, so the comfort of knowing what to expect was scarce, but they were getting a lot of experience from touring. After the first few months or so, getting on stage in front of thousands of people was no big deal anymore. Allen and the other guys told them they were sounding better each time. Likely a combination of perfecting their timing by playing so often, and also losing any lingering stage fright they might have had. But, the one thing they discovered that was even better than gaining experience was collecting road stories. There was one night a very drunk woman jumped up onto the stage and grabbed Hal in the middle of a song and kissed him. "*Unfortunately, a kinda ugly chick,*" Ryan always made sure to add whenever they told the story. Or the time they were about to finish their last song and introduce their main hosts when 20-30 police officers burst into the building, and arrested a serial murderer for whom they got an anonymous tip would be at the concert that night. The strangest thing they saw, however, was when they were going 80 mph down a deserted country highway on their way to Reno. A deer somehow appeared out of nowhere (even though it was broad daylight, they were in the desert, and there was nothing for miles that it could have jumped out from behind), and they hit it at full speed. The driver and Uli both swore they saw it and that it *was* a deer. But when they stopped and got out, there was a huge dent and a little blood on the metal, however the deer was nowhere to be seen. Not dead or alive, nor on the road or to the side. Gone as fast as it had come, earning it the nickname: 'The Alien Deer.'

Ryan had still been unsuccessful at getting Ricky in bed with a girl, usually due to Ricky disappearing at the last second. The few times Ryan did corner him with a candidate, Ricky would make up an excuse like he felt sick to his stomach, or some other completely bogus reason to politely bow out. As far as the discovery of all the metal clothes Uli had been hiding in his bags, Gunder found out about the whole thing a week later, and went to ask him about it. Uli and Gunder became very good friends in the months that followed. Two of Gunder's grandparents were from Denmark, and his family had gone back there on vacation for a few weeks every summer, even after his grandparents had passed away. Because of that, Gunder shared many of the European viewpoints Uli had, as well as his love of metal, which made for easy conversation between them. Whenever they had spare time, they would sit and debate politics, world events, or anything else they could think of. It wasn't too long after they started hanging out that Uli appeared out of the dressing room before one of their shows wearing black shirt and slacks with the studded belt and boots, and a studded leather cuff they hadn't seen before. Despite all the spikes, Hal couldn't help but notice he looked more like he was preparing to lead a board meeting rather than play for a rock band. Uli walked by them without a word combing back his blond hair with a fine-tooth comb.

Things went well for a long time, despite all the drama that came with being in a travelling band. It wasn't until the beginning of August, when they only had a month and a half to go, that they started to get irritable when some little thing went wrong before a show. Even Hal caught himself wanting to yell at Uli or Ryan and pick fights with them. When Hal would go and sit with Allen to cool off after an argument, Allen would reassure him the fighting was normal as they neared the end of a tour. And that even he and his band mates would argue to the point where sometimes punches would be thrown over things that didn't even matter the next day. "The one thing you need to keep in mind through it all…" Allen would tell him, "…is to never let yourself lose respect for them as fellow artists and musicians. Even if the whole being buddies aspect seems to be falling apart, as long as you keep professional respect, it will never fall away entirely. And remember as well, that no band tours indefinitely. Breaks, and I mean breaks as in weeks, months, or occasionally years away from each other, are necessary to let all that animosity fade away before you're ready to start anew on another album, another tour, or whatever you might be trying to do again as a team."

Hal tried to keep everything Allen said in the back of his mind at all times, and he discovered adopting a "*Fine. Whatever. Okay.*" attitude and then just letting things go, really did help much more than trying to pursue a fight to the end. But while he'd developed a means for dealing with that aspect of touring, the other issue that came up was Ryan had started smoking weed with Tod and Donovan almost daily. At first it nearly seemed like a blessing, since it caused Ryan to chill out a bit. He hadn't started a fight with Uli for almost two weeks, and Hal was perfectly aware of how common a hobby it was, especially in the entertainment industry, and how most people would laugh at him for even suggesting it was a problem. But he'd had a rather bad experience with it in the past. Not from smoking any himself, but from watching it turn an old friend of his into a do-nothing loser. People would tell him his friend was an unusually bad case, or that it only does that to a small number of people, or that it really wasn't the weed at all and that 'he had a personality type that was naturally vulnerable to addition and slacking'. But in the event marijuana had any influence at all, why the hell would anyone take the risk in the first place? When Hal was still a kid, he and a boy named Cody who lived a few houses away spent almost every day after school together, as well as all through their summer vacations. Many sunny days had been spent re-arranging their elderly neighbor's lawn ornaments to irritate her, building their own skate board ramps to see how far they could launch themselves into the air, and drawing inappropriate images on their school's windows with silly string. But as they got older and Cody started smoking weed, it changed his entire personality. It wasn't immediate, it happened over a couple years, but ultimately, Cody wanted to go out less and less to do anything. He instead became insistent that if Hal wanted to hang out at all anymore, they could do so while smoking together in his basement and playing video games. The last time Hal saw Cody he was probably about fifteen, standing in the doorway to Cody's house, holding a cheap electric guitar by the neck. Cody came up the stairs from the basement.

"C'mon, let's go practice at my mom's house. We need more practice than we're getting if we're going to start playing actual shows," Hal said.

"Bring the drum set over here and we can practice here," Cody answered.

"I don't want to make your mom mad! You know she doesn't like us playing here and making noise," Hal insisted. He couldn't even believe he had to remind him of this.

"You know my mom's totally okay with us practicing in our house. Plus, she doesn't even get home for another two hours."

"Well, then we can practice without the amp plugged in. And I can drum on the bucket in the basement. If we can make it sound good that way, it'll sound really great when we can use the real drums and plug the guitar in," Cody replied.

"You want to practice with a bucket and an unplugged electric guitar?!" Hal said.

"Look, Hal, I'm trying to work with you here," Cody said.

"What the hell are you talking about? Work with me? I'm asking you to walk six houses down the road to practice at my house where we can be as loud as we want. What about that can't you do?" Hal asked.

"Alright, look, I'm not feelin' it today, okay?" Cody finally admitted.

"You haven't been 'feelin' it' for three weeks," Hal said. "Are you getting sick?"

"No," Cody said. "I'm just not feeling inspired as of late."

"*Gee, why's that,*" Hal said under his breath with his teeth clenched.

"What?"

"Nothing," Hal answered.

"Hey, it doesn't mean we can't hang out. Come on, I just got Monster Truck Zombie Massacre III," he said as he turned and started back down the stairs, motioning with one hand for Hal to join him. Hal watched him disappear into the basement, and he stood in the doorway for a bit, waiting to see if Cody would notice he wasn't following and come back. But after a while, he decided he had stood there long enough, and turned around and pulled the door shut behind him harder than he had intended. He marched back towards his house, kicking an empty soda can out of his way as hard as he could once he reached the sidewalk. He waited for days after that to see if Cody would show up so they could hang out, but he never came over again. Hal spent a lot of his time alone after that, practicing his guitar in his bedroom while listening to the new Holy Hell CD he'd just gotten. Last he had heard from a neighbor before they left for the tour, Cody was still unemployed living in his parent's house. Though he had been pushing to win a state disability pay case for some mysterious chronic stomach condition he had developed that was preventing him from keeping a job. That way, he could live off the state the rest of his life and never have to work.

The whole fiasco had made Hal wary of marijuana. Now that Ryan was smoking it, there was still the problem of what he could do about it. If he didn't say anything, Ryan would keep doing it, and likely make a habit of it even after their tour was done. If he *did* try to confront him about it, Ryan would probably get mad at him and tell him off, keep doing it, and then likely make a habit of it even after their tour was done.

"Yeah, I noticed that too..." Allen said when Hal finally decided to bring it up to him. "I'm sorry those two pulled him into it as well."

"I mean, has it changed them at all over the years?" Hal asked.

"Well, to be honest, I've never seen it do much to Don," Allen said. "He's been pretty consistent since the beginning. Tod has been acting a little off as of late, but he's going through a nasty divorce, so I'm not sure if that's what's on his mind. But he's probably been smoking more because of that, and the two things might be exasperating each other."

"But, it's never really affected Donovan?" Hal wanted to make sure he heard right.

"No, not really. I'll tell you, from what I've seen over the years in this industry, I think smoking weed is a bit of a Russian roulette game. Some people get shot through the head, and others don't. At the start, there's really no way to tell who that'll be. Though there can occasionally be an upside to it. I know Ryan is a bit of an irritation to you sometimes, so maybe it'll calm him down a bit."

"Oh, yeah, it has already. He hasn't started a fight with Uli for over a week," Hal replied.

"Yeah, the stuff does have that affect on a lot of people," Allen said.

"I dunno, I know this is stupid because I'm so sick of those two fighting, but…" Hal paused.

"That's how you know he's not being himself?" Allen asked.

"Yeah," Hal said.

"Well, it's up to you if you want to try and talk to him about it, or maybe just keep an eye on him for a bit. If you do start noticing anything else more drastic, let me know and I'll pull Tod and Don aside and have a word with them."

"Okay, I'll do that. Thank you, Allen," Hal replied.

As he started to head back to the RV, Allen stopped him. "You know…" Allen started to say, and Hal paused and turned around. "I think people like us are kind of rare." Hal looked at him curiously. "Not to sound like your middle school health teacher or anything, but that stuff really doesn't help anything. It makes you forget about your problems for a while. But, the truth is, by making yourself forget about the shit in your life and not dealing with it, sometimes you wake up in the morning and the shits piled higher since you lit up the night before."

"Seriously," Hal agreed.

"And it amazes me how many people don't figure that out, even in their adult years," Allen said. "To me, it's a sign of weakness."

"Yeah, I watched it turn a friend of mine into a complete loser years ago. I don't really want to watch that process happen again with Ryan."

"I don't blame you," Allen said. "And then there's the people who will insist they're not using it to hide from anything, and that it's for 'relaxation, meditation, and inspiration.' But that to me says they apparently can't be creative enough without its help, and I think that's a little sad. I mean, if you're comfortable with your inner weirdness, you know you can see strange visions and all the pretty colors on your own without the help of any drugs, am I right?" Allen asked, and Hal slowly smiled.

"I… I know exactly what you're talking about. I totally understand. I thought for the longest time that maybe I was the only one who thought like that."

"There's not many of us," Allen said with a grin. "And it's always a pleasure to meet another."

"Likewise," Hal said.

"We'll keep an eye on Ryan. Let me know if things take a turn for the worse, and then maybe we can come up with a plan."

"I will. Thanks, Allen," Hal said.

Hal ultimately decided not to say anything until they were done touring. They only had a few more shows to go at this point, and he didn't want to stir up the fighting again until they were settled back home. Late that evening, they pulled into the gravel parking lot of the next little motel. Hal stepped out with one small suitcase, and shut the door to the RV. It was late, and the single, glaring spotlight that lit the gravel lot from the roof of the one-story building was enough to cause an instant headache. It was making a horrible, high-pitched buzzing noise, and was being mobbed by a mass of moths and other insects; their movements making its light flicker and scatter in an unpleasant chaos. "I'll say it. I'm sort of looking forward to going home next month," Hal said as he drug his feet towards the room.

"I will second this," Uli said.

"But don't think for a second that I regret doing this. Because I don't," Hal added.

"I will second this," Uli repeated.

"Man, we couldn't have asked for a better host band," Ryan spoke up.

"Yeah, seriously! I know some of these famous bands out there are secretly assholes behind the scenes, but I think I'm a bigger fan now than ever," Hal agreed. "And they've been so patient with us. I don't think I could have been that nice. I'll bet they've dealt with a lot of openers over the years, and you'd think that would make them less tolerant," he added.

"Maybe if I ask nice enough they'll sign my drums," Ryan said, and while they were all starting to laugh, Ryan suddenly stopped in his tracks. "WHAT THE HELL...?!"

"WHAT!? What!?" Hal turned around and saw Ryan pointing at the RV behind them. Hal and Uli looked, but didn't see anything. "What!?" Hal asked again.

"Ricky!" Ryan said. Ricky had set his bag down to stuff a few more things in it before they went inside. He was still there in the shadow of the bus, bent over it trying to zip it up.

"Yes, that's definitely Ricky," Hal said sarcastically.

"His eyes were glowing!" Ryan shouted.

"Huh?" Hal asked wearily.

"His eyes were glowing! Like, like an animal in the headlights! Ricky, do that again!" Ryan called to him.

"*Do what?*" Ricky said in a low voice without looking up.

"That eye thingy!"

"*What eye thingy?*"

"Oh, just... look up stupid!"

"*Why?*"

"It's the light! The light was making your eyes glow!" Ryan said, and Hal sighed. Ryan had seemed more normal than usual all evening. He should have known it was too good to be true.

"Alright Ryan, you've obviously had a few too many, and didn't even share with us, so I think its bedtime now." Hal put his hand on Ryan's shoulder and tried to direct him to the motel door.

"No!" Ryan insisted. "Look!" He pointed back at Ricky, who still hadn't moved. "Ricky you little twerp! Will you look up already!?" Ryan yelled.

"*Why?*" Ricky asked again, irritated.

"Hey, Ricky, I know that damn light is really bright, but can you humor him for half a second so we can all go to bed?" Hal asked. Ricky stopped rifling through his bag and hung over it a moment or two like a brooding vulture. Then, with shameful hesitation, slowly turned to face them. As the light rolled across his eyes, a green shine rose out of them so brilliant that it nearly made the rest of his face fade back into the shadows, leaving two round, green orbs suspended in darkness.

"SEE!?" Ryan said much louder than he needed to.

"Okay…" Hal said after a pause, "… that's… sort of creepy."

"Sort of!?" Ryan asked.

"You know what though… we could use that in our shows…" Hal was already lost in thought with it, and as he was standing there studying him, Ricky was looking less and less shamed, and more and more confused.

"Hey, Hal, I don't think that's normal. Human eyes don't do that," Ryan insisted.

"No, I don't think Ricky's normal either, but I'm thinking you shouldn't be the one to judge. Isn't that right, Ricky?" Hal asked.

In the most timid voice he probably had, topped with a coating of his usual Southern accent, Ricky answered: "*Uh… raight?*"

"See?" Hal said, and started walking in the direction of the motel room. His cell phone began to ring. "God almighty, if it's not one thing it's another." He pulled it out of its case and looked at the screen. "Oh, it's Allen."

"Tell him whatever it is, we are too tired," Uli mumbled.

"Hey, Allen," Hal answered, and put the phone on loudspeaker.

"*Hi, Hal,*" Allen said, then they heard him take in a breath. "*Something's happened.*"

"What?"

"*We're in the ER of the community hospital right now, a few miles back down the road.*" They barely recognized Allen's voice, he didn't sound like himself.

"Wh... what happened?" Hal asked.

"*They just took Tod back. He wasn't breathing when we found him.*"

"Wh... what!? I mean..."

"*I don't know. I mean, when we found him... I realized he'd been wearing all long sleeves lately, and I never really noticed until tonight, but his arms are all covered in scratches and scars...*" He said the last few words in a whisper.

"Is it that hospital that was right off the highway?"

"*Yes.*"

"We'll be right there," Hal said.

"*Alright.*"

He hung up, and they got back into the RV so fast they left a few of their bags in the parking lot. When they got to the emergency room lobby, they ran in and found the receptionist. "We're here for Tod Williams. We're travelling with him and his friends." Hal said it quietly, in case anyone else in the waiting room was listening.

"Alright, we'll have security take you back," she said, and one of the hospital guards waiting by the desk scanned his card and opened the door to the back ward. He led them down the maze of hallways to one of the furthest rooms, and they turned the corner to see Allen, Gunder, and Donovan sitting quietly on a bench against the wall next to a closed door.

"Are these gentlemen with you?" the guard asked Allen, who nodded somberly, then he left them there. Gunder and Donovan looked up briefly at them before going back to staring vacantly at the floor. They sat down on the additional chairs in the hallway and waited with them. The muffled sound of voices seeping through the shut door was the only other sound besides the buzzing of the florescent lights lining the hall. All else was quiet. A single doctor came out of the room a while later and took them into another room and sat them down. It was a quarter past ten.

One by one, everyone except Hal and Allen went out to the waiting rooms. Allen volunteered to stay in the back for a few minutes more to help the doctors go through the saved numbers on Tod's phone to identify relatives and friends that should be called. He also said he'd take his things and make sure they got back to his family. He asked Hal if he wanted to stay and help him. Hal didn't know anything about Tod's relatives, but it sounded like it was a personal request. As they were sitting going through his wallet for anything else the doctors might need, Allen pulled a folded photo out from under a credit card and opened it. On it was a woman holding a young girl in her arms. The girl was two, maybe three years old, and was wearing a poofy white dress. The photo had been marked on with a pen. The woman had red horns drawn on, long dripping fangs, and a curving devil tail winding up from behind, and the young girl had a shiny gold halo above her, and little silver wings sprouting out of her back. Allen turned it, so Hal could see. "That's his ex-wife, Angela, and their daughter, Katie. Angela's probably not going to be too upset, as you can see, but…" He sighed. "…I wonder what she's going to tell Katie." Hal examined the photo silently. "Well, here we were just talking about you being worried about Ryan's drug habit when apparently I was the one who should have been paying more attention to my own guys," Allen said quietly.

"Hey, it's not your fault. We both thought they were just smoking weed, and that was it," Hal said.

"Yeah, but we were basically living together, so I should have saw the signs he was doing more than that. Apparently, I was oblivious."

"No! Allen, I mean, you're all so busy all the time. That's how touring is. And if someone's *trying* to hide something…"

"No, that's no excuse. It was right there in front of me the whole time," he responded. "It's so pointless. Shooting yourself full of poison for a little high. Not thinking about how many people you're going to hurt beyond yourself if you overdo it," Allen said wearily. "Tod wasn't exactly the sharpest tool in the shed, but he had the guts we were looking for after our original guitarist, Cliff, quit all those years ago. He was fifteen years younger than Gun, who had been the youngest up to that point. Gun and Don kept telling me he wouldn't be good enough, and to keep looking for someone else, but I didn't see how they could think that after we heard him play. 'Course, looking back at it, they probably knew he was good, but they wanted someone older so they wouldn't feel like they were having to babysit. I told them they were being a couple of sticks in the mud, and 'didn't we start out even younger than that,' and they finally relented and gradually took a liking to him. I knew they would, but… maybe they were right. Tod never really grew up. Though I suppose I shouldn't be one to say that, I still make plenty of my own stupid mistakes. I'm sorry, I'm rambling…"

"No, no it's fine. It all makes sense," Hal said.

"He was still one of us," Allen said and tried to look like he was rubbing his eyes because he was tired. "Just do me a favor, okay?" Allen looked Hal straight in the eyes. "Ignore my previous advice and do what you need to do to take care of your friends. Don't let this happen to you. Hopefully, Ryan was only smoking weed with them and that was it, but keep an eye on him to be sure. If he gets mad at you for getting into his business, don't give up on it. Let him hate you if it comes to it. His family might thank you someday…" Allen barely got the last word out before he completely broke down, and Hal sat there with him for nearly an hour.

Hal had assumed the other guys had gone back to their accommodations for the night, but when he and Allen finally walked out to the lobby, all five of them were still there, silently waiting. They got back to the motel sometime after midnight. Nobody had said anything since they left the hospital, not even Ryan, who sat looking vacantly out the window on the way back. They found their bags right where they had left them in the parking lot, and collected them up before heading for the motel room door once again. Hal took out his phone and started to dial Jim's number, but before he could finish, his phone started to ring again. Jim's name appeared on the screen, and he hit the answer button. "Hi, Jim, I was actually just about to call you."

*"Oh, damn. I was hoping to give you the good news myself."* He sounded more energetic than he should have been at that time of the night.

"Excuse me!?" Hal said.

*"Whoa, whoa. What was that for?"* Jim asked.

"The *good* news?"

*"Yes! The good news!"* Jim repeated.

"Not the *bad* news?" Hal asked.

*"What bad news?"*

"About Tod?"

*"What about Tod?"*

"That's not why you're calling?"

*"Um, no..."* Jim said. *"So... what about Tod?"*

Hal shut his eyes and shook his head. "Sorry, it's late, and I'm confused. But please, if you have good news, give me that first."

*"Damn right I have good news! I just checked the American Top 40 charts, and I have to say, it's not every day your band has a song hit number one..."*

It wasn't the note on which they had expected to part ways, but Battle Creek and Holy Hell said their goodbyes the next day. The final tragedy of the night before was they only had four shows left before the tour would have been over anyways. So, not only were Tod's friends and family suddenly without him, but a couple thousand fans were left wondering if they had barely missed their last chance ever to see Holy Hell in concert. Allen wasn't sure yet if they were going to try and find another guitarist, or if they were going to retire.

But Gunder told Uli to not hesitate to give them a call if he ever wanted to learn how to play guitar. Even if the answer was no, he promised they would meet again someday. They never had much of a chance to reflect on the tour afterwards when they came home to an onslaught of questions and scheduling changes from Jim. They barely got a few days rest at Hal's house before shipping right back out to appear on a talk show in New York.

"Good evening everyone! I'm Ken Shocker, and this is…" The host held his hands out in the direction of the audience, and all at once they answered: "Shock Therapy!"

"Thank you!" The host replied. "Anyways, our first guests tonight are an up and coming band who have just gotten their first number one single on the national music charts, so if everybody can please help me welcome to the set, Battle Creek!" Ken announced, and a round of applause greeted them as they stepped out onto the set. They took their seats on the couch, waving and smiling humbly, and the host motioned for silence.

"Well, good evening, gentlemen."

"Evening!" Hal said.

"Okay, so I get the pleasure of introducing new bands all the time, and it's one of my favorite things to do. So, we'll just start from the beginning. What are your names, where are you from, what do you do…?"

"Alright, well…" Hal laughed nervously. He'd prepared a whole speech for what he was going to say, but it all completely left him when he sat down and looked out at the audience. He was so used to *playing* to audiences, he oddly forgot how to talk to them. "I'm Hal, I'm the lead singer, and I also play bass guitar a little, and… yeah."

"Okay, now I have to ask you about your hair," the host said. "I've had bands with all colors and shades on the set here, but this may be the first time I've seen grey. In a young band, that is. Why dye it grey? I mean, is that your method for not getting carded at bars?" The audience laughed.

"Uh, well, no. It just grows that way," Hal answered.

"Wait, that's not dyed?"

"Nope. That's how it is."

"Oh my God," Ken said sympathetically.

"I'm kinda hoping it will turn brown when I get old," Hal said, and Ken laughed. "Yeah, well, hope springs eternal, but..." He looked up at his own grey hair, and the audience laughed again. "Anyways, how about you?" He looked at Uli.

"I am Uli Von Wolff, and I am from Dresden, Germany. I play piano, violin, saxophone, and trumpet."

"Uli is our one-man symphony orchestra," Hal added.

"Wow, that's an impressive skill set, to say the least. So, how did you end up in the band?"

"Hal and I met when we went to the same music academy together in New York. We started the band together while we were there."

"So, you're from New York?" the host asked Hal.

"No, no. I just went to school there. I'm from Battle Creek, Michigan, and that's actually where we're based."

"Ah, I see," the host said. "Germany. New York. Battle Creek. We're slowly working our way west here." The audience laughed a little.

"I'm Ryan, I'm from Seattle, I play the drums, and I am single," he said as he looked out at some girls in the audience. He got a small response of giggles.

"Oh, yeah, yeah. I've seen your type before." Ken stopped him from going any further. "And finally, we have… you," he said as his gaze stopped on Ricky. "No! Wait! Let me guess." He cut Ricky off before he said anything. "We've got Germany, Battle Creek, Seattle, and New York worked in there somehow too, so you must be from… Texas? Am I right?" he asked, and Ricky shook his head no. "Well, damn. How close was I?"

"Arkansas."

"Arkansas! Of course!" He laughed again. "And your name is?"

"Ricky."

"And you play?"

"Guitar."

"Ah. There's the guitarist."

"Ricky's from Battle Creek, Arkansas," Hal spoke up.

"Wait… he's from Battle Creek, Arkansas and you're from Battle Creek, Michigan?" Ken asked.

"Yes," Hal said. "But before you ask, no, that's not why we named ourselves that. The name came solely from Michigan. Ricky joined us after we had taken the name, and it ended up being a huge coincidence," Hal said.

"That *is* a big coincidence," Ken agreed. "Now, I've heard of Battle Creek, Michigan, but not Arkansas. I'm assuming that's not a large town? You know what the population is?" Ken asked Ricky. Ricky looked down on his hands and started silently counting on his fingers. The host watched silently and counted along in his head as Ricky made it somewhere in the mid fifties, then stopped and looked like he was lost in thought. "Okay, I think I get the idea," Ken said, and the audience laughed again. "Moving on, I heard there's something of a story behind the night you found out your first song made it to that number one slot a few nights back."

"Yes, unfortunately it's sort of a sad story. We found out on the last night we were touring as the openers for Holy Hell. Though, we didn't know it was the last night at the time because that was the night that Tod Williams, one of the two guitarists, died of a heroin overdose," Hal said quietly. "We had just left the hospital to go back to the motel, and we were all really depressed about what happened, so when we got the news, it was… I dunno, it didn't really affect us. We should have been celebrating, but we were all still in shock. So, I think I told our manager 'okay, that's nice', and then we went to bed."

"Must have been quite an emotional rollercoaster over the last few days," Ken said in a more serious tone.

"It was. I mean, in a period of a few hours we lost someone who had become a close friend, our first real road tour ended abruptly, and we had our first single hit number one."

"Wow. It's like they say, when it rains, it pours. And after it pours, sometimes the floodgates break too," Ken said.

"Yeah, hopefully we won't get hit like that again," Hal said.

"That's the hope, but tell me now, after all this has happened, I'm sure you're probably trying to re-organize and figure out what's happening next, but… what's happening next?" he asked, and they laughed. "What's next for Battle Creek after having their first number one hit?"

"Well, we're getting dates put together for our first tour. Our first tour where we're not opening for someone else, that is. And… we're going to take it from there, I guess."

"Good enough. So, I just have one more question before we end the show and we let you go back home to… everywhere, and that's where did you get that thing on your head? Because I haven't seen one of those in decades," Ken said as he looked at Ricky.

"Ricky's brothers accidentally hit it on State Route 21," Ricky said.

"Oh, no. No, no, no, no," the host groaned. "You're kidding, right?"

"No," Ricky answered.

"No, he's really not," Hal confirmed.

"They cleaned it and tanned it and everything," Ricky assured him, and the host shuddered. "I'm sorry I asked, ANYWAYS, ladies and gentlemen let's give Battle Creek a big round of applause for taking some time out of their explosive schedule, to come on the show and talk to us tonight," he announced as he stood up and started clapping, and the audience joined in and gave them a final round of applause.

When they got back from New York, they were expecting Jim to have a whole new list of places he was going to send them, but they did get a little break at home. Three weeks, to be exact. Excluding local press events and interviews, shooting two music videos, and recording demos for a couple new songs. Demos are like 'first draft' recordings. After the demo is done, they figure out what can be done to improve the song. Then, once all the adjustments are made, they work on recording the master, or 'final draft' recording, which is what will ultimately end up on the album. The master isn't necessarily a whole new recording, but often a digitally sewn together mash-up of pieces of the demo, and new bits of recording they'll do. They might record the instrumental bit completely separate from the vocals, and sometimes even the separate instruments will be recorded apart from each other. Then, the lead singer will sing along to the pre-recorded music to try and get the most polished piece possible. That way, if the chorus comes out perfect the first time, but not parts of the verses, the verses will be re-sung, but the first chorus can still be used in the final piece. The process of inserting bits of new recordings between bits of old recordings is called a 'punch-in,' which got its name from back when music was literally on tape. Trying to piece together a song by 'punching in' between broken tape could run the risk of ruining the whole recording if it wasn't done in exactly the right spot. On a computer, it became only a matter of a few clicks of a button and no danger to the original material. They knew they might not get the masters for the new songs finished in a few weeks. But if they ran out of time, Jim said he could either set them up at a different recording studio on the road, or they could wait until they got back from their tour; though he warned that could be a while. He had gotten them a short-notice booking at a small concert hall in Chicago, so that would be the first stop. After that, they'd basically keep going as long as record sales were still good, or until they couldn't take it anymore and had to stop for a while. Where they went on tour depended on how well the album was selling in certain areas, something Jim called a 'sound scan.' If they were selling a ton of albums in New York but only a moderate amount in Seattle, they might do two shows in The Big Apple, and only one in The Emerald City. They also got to see the first merchandise set that had been done up for the tour. A few buttons, a couple of T-shirts, and a poster of the full image that was their album cover. They all agreed the shirt with their four-piece guitar logo on it was the best. Ricky, however, did not like one of the other shirts with a photo print of them on the front. He said seeing himself on a shirt was 'weird.' Ryan told him that if they sold it in ladies' sizes, it might be the closest he'd ever get to a woman's chest.

When it really started to sink in that they were no longer going to be an opening act for someone else, Hal realized that meant *they* were going to have their own openers. When he asked Jim about it, he said that it was unlikely they'd have the same group with them for the entire trip, especially since they didn't have a set end date like Holy Hell did. He didn't even have anybody set up at all yet, but for most of the tour it would probably be three or four shows with a local band from whatever area they were in. Most openers don't have the endurance for continuous travel for the small pay like they did, Jim explained. "You guys are sort of a rarity, which is why you're charting on the radio, and why you're getting to be the headliners now," he added. The change had come nearly overnight, which was a big shock from the slow progress they had labored over for the last few years. But the final details were falling into place, and a simple few weeks is what they had before the tour started. A few weeks to prepare themselves to be introduced to the world.

# CHAPTER 8

## (On the Road Again)

100. "Don't Trust Me" by 3OH!3

**Hal put his lips to** the microphone and sang the first few lines. Uli played a couple notes on his keyboard, and the first lights came on. Hal sang the next few lines, and Ryan started a beat on his drums. He sang the final line before the chorus, and as Ricky hit the six strings on his guitar, the rest of the lights came on, and they launched full force into the opening song of their own tour. They'd felt a little nervous beforehand, something that hadn't really gotten to them for a long time. The concert hall wasn't even close to being sold out, but it seemed worse than the packed shows they opened for, since these people were all there to see them. If they made a mistake, they couldn't run and hide behind the main act anymore. They *were* the main act, and they needed to be perfect. Hal picked someone out of the crowd near the front, and sang to him for a few moments to keep his focus. The man sang back at the top of his lungs. He felt a grin forming at the corners of his mouth. He picked someone else out and sang to her, she sang back and raised her hand out to him. She was too far back to reasonably touch him, but Hal raised his hand out to her to let her know he would if he could. It confirmed what he had hoped all along, that he too could have the ability to touch people without touching them, just as his favorite bands had done for him through his headphones.

> **End Song 100**

101. "Honky Tonk Badonkadonk" by Trace Adkins
102. "Rise Above" by Black Flag
103. "Monster" by Skillet
104. "Power of Love" by Huey Lewis & the News
105. "Wake Me Up" by Avicci
106. "Johnny, I Hardly Knew Ya" by Dropkick Murphys
107. "Murmaider" by Dethklok
108. "Demons" by Imagine Dragons
109. "Dirt Road Anthem" by Jason Aldean
110. "I Predict a Riot" by Kaiser Chiefs
111. "One Shot at Glory" by Judas Priest
112. "Summer in the City" by The Lovin' Spoonful
113. "You Look Good in My Shirt" by Keith Urban
114. "American Idiot" by Green Day
115. "Sacrifice" by Danzig
116. "One Headlight" by The Wallflowers
117. "I Walk the Line" by Johnny Cash
118. "Why Don't You Get a Job?" by The Offspring
119. "Wrong Side of Heaven" by Five Finger Death Punch
120. "Up Around the Bend" by Creedence Clearwater Revival

After the first song was over, Hal made sure to announce that it was their very first concert on their very first tour where they were the headliners. He had meant it to be an early apology, but the audience cheering loudly like that made it a special privilege to be in the crowd that night. He smiled as he reminded himself these people were just here for a good time, which is the exact same reason why they had started a band in the first place. What was even more ironic was when he had sung alone in his room, he would look in the mirror and imagine a huge crowd of people in front of him. But now that there actually was an audience, whenever he found himself getting distracted by his own nerves, he'd shut his eyes for a few seconds and pretend he was only singing to his mirror again, and it would calm him down enough to keep the show going. He needed to remind himself what he had longed for all those years looking into the mirror, and then open his eyes to see he had finally got it, and let the feeling of victory help move him forward. This, after all, was just the beginning.

> End Songs 101 – 120

121. "Gonna Make You Sweat (Everybody Dance Now)" by C+C Music Factory *to play over this scene*
122. "Sexy and I Know It" by LMFAO
123. "Dirrty" by Christina Aguilera
124. "I Like to Move It" by Reel 2 Real
125. "Livin' La Vida Loca" by Ricky Martin
126. "Whine Up" by Kat Deluna ft. Elephant Man
127. "Sandstorm" by Darude
128. "The Power" by SNAP!

129. "Jumpin' Jumpin'" by Destiny's Child

130. "Angel" by Shaggy ft. Rayvon

131. "Better Off Alone" by Alice Deejay

They ran laughing into a packed nightclub afterwards to celebrate. They brought their opening band with them, a three-man alternative rock group from Springfield. No matter that they were only doing four shows with them. They wanted to share the success and carry on the tradition Holy Hell had shared with them. Hal was feeling incredibly good about how their first show had gone. They were all happy with it, really. They stayed in the club until sometime after 2 a.m., and then Hal, Uli, and Ryan went back to the hotel each with a girl for the night. Ricky had disappeared about an hour earlier. He seemed like he was having a good time up to that point, but then they turned around and he was gone. It was something they had gotten used to, since he had done the same thing most every night they were out on the road with Holy Hell.

End Songs 121 – 131

The next morning, Hal turned the key to the door to Ricky's room, and pushed it open a crack. He moved it slowly to keep it from squeaking. Ricky was lying on his back on the bed, his head turned towards the window on the other side of the room, strumming bits of songs on the old guitar he had when they first met him. Hal closed the door as quietly as he had opened it.

"Just like clockwork," Ryan whispered. "We party, he disappears, we go to bed, we wake up, and he's back and acting depressed."

"How could he be depressed after last night? I mean, that was the most awesome night ever," Hal said.

"I don't know," Ryan replied.

"I mean, for a while I thought he was just miffed at the whole club partying thing, and you harassing him about getting laid, but… that can't be it."

"Yeah, and he left last night before I'd even tried to hook him up with anyone," Ryan added.

"It's got to be something else," Hal mused.

"I bet it's something that's been bugging him since before he joined up with us. Think about it, he said he left a family of what, fifteen or twenty or something back home to aimlessly wander around the country? He's never given us a better explanation than that," Ryan said.

"He may have felt trapped in that small town," Uli replied.

"But would that make you leave home and never talk to your family again?" Ryan asked.

"Well, he's occasionally called home. He's just really sneaky about it," Hal said. "This weird number started showing up on our phone bill, and when me and Mom looked up the area code it was an Arkansas number. So, he has called them a few times, but somehow he always made sure no one was around when he did. So… I don't know."

"Well, I don't either," Ryan agreed. "I suppose, we could be over thinking this. I mean, maybe he's just off raiding people's garbage cans at night."

Hal slowly turned to stare at Ryan.

"Oh, come on! You're just mad that I beat you to that one!" Ryan said.

"I just wish he'd talk to us," Hal said.

"Yeah, well, good luck with that," Ryan replied.

"I can take a few guesses on why he might not want to talk to you…" Hal snapped at him. "But maybe I can see if he'll talk to me."

"Maybe," Ryan mumbled.

"Have you considered the possibility that he might be bi-polar or depressed or something similar, and there's nothing really wrong? Other than possibly being depressed, that is?" Uli asked.

Hal sighed. "I dunno, Uli, but I can't stand to see him like this."

"Well, let's snap him out of it, then," Ryan said.

"How?" Hal asked.

Ryan grabbed the door key from Hal and slipped it into the lock. "Bandpile on Ricky on 3…"

"Ryan…" Hal said, unsure.

"*Just trust me*," Ryan said through his teeth, then started to turn the lock. "One… two… THREE!" he yelled as he threw the door open, and Ricky barely had time to look up before Hal, Ryan, and Uli landed on top of him.

"GAAA!" Ricky yelled.

"Good morning, sunshine!" Ryan said as Hal pulled the guitar out from under them and set it to the side while they pinned him down. "You looked depressed, so we decided to come cheer you up! Are you cheered up now!?" Ryan asked. He was never the master of subtlety.

"He looks scared," Uli noted.

"There's nothing to be afraid of Ricky. It's just us," Ryan assured him, but Ricky only stared at them, speechless.

"Hmmm. Not cheered up yet. Gentlemen, this leaves us with only one option," Ryan declared, and they all grinned.

Ricky's eyes widened. "Nooo…"

"TICKLE RICKY!" Ryan yelled.

"AAAAAAAGGGHHH!" Ricky struggled to throw them off as he got up off the bed. He caught Hal and Uli in a headlock under each arm and tried to keep Ryan back with one foot. "NOT FAIR… NOT FAIR!" he yelled, hopping backwards on one foot while pushing at Ryan with the other. Ryan grabbed the foot and tickled it, and Ricky tripped and fell backwards over a chair. They landed in a tangled heap, and Ricky's head smashed through the wall.

"Oh… shit," Ryan said as he stood there looking at the mess. Uli and Hal slowly sat up, and Ricky pulled his head back out of the wall and blew the plaster out of his nose, one nostril at a time.

"You okay?" Ryan asked.

"Yeah!" Ricky laughed as he rubbed the white chunks out of his hair.

"Attaboy!" Ryan said.

Hal looked at the wall and started to laugh. "Our first stop on our first real tour, and we've already damaged a hotel room," he said, and they all laughed with him. "I guess we're official now," he added.

"Sorry we christened it with your head," Ryan said.

"Is good." Ricky laughed it off.

"Sooo, what should we do to celebrate?" Ryan asked. Hal glanced from the wall to Ricky, and then had an idea. "Why don't we go roller skating?" he said, and Ricky looked up at him. "Thought you guys didn't like skatin'?"

"Whoever said that?" Hal asked. "Just because a few of us suck at it doesn't mean it isn't still fun. Plus, you still have that mission to skate at every rink once. I know you got to a few of them while we were touring with Allen and crew, but it couldn't have been that many. I bet we could find one around here."

"Well, if you's sure…" Ricky said, and Ryan reached a hand down to help him up off the floor. "We're sure. Let's go."

MARCH, *6 MONTHS LATER*

Their first official tour was over half a year after it had started. Not for lack of ticket sales, but rather, they were being sold out too quickly, and the crowds were getting too wild for the small-ish to medium venues they were having them in. Their second album came out in December, and it had been going nowhere but up on the charts since the day it was released. Jim pulled the plug to 'regroup' and get a whole new tour put together immediately. One with far more road staff, and with stops at much larger concert halls and stadiums. While he worked on the new tour, they got some time off again to go back to Hal's house and catch up with his parents.

"I was starting to worry I'd never see you all again," Cecilia said as she took the lid off a steaming pot on the stove and stirred its contents. "I think dinner's ready."

"You know, you don't have to cook us dinner every time we come home. We're not kids, we can cook our own food," Hal said.

"Yes, that's exactly what I'm afraid of. Because if I could take a wild guess, I bet you've been living off nothing other than pizza, beer, and those little instant cup-of-noodles. Am I right?" She glanced back at the guys, who looked less than innocent. "Exactly. And so, tonight we're having grilled salmon, penne pasta, and steamed broccoli to try and balance some of that garbage out. Capiche?"

"Yes, Mom." Hal knew when his mom started speaking Italian in the same tone her dad had used on her, it meant the conversation was over.

"Good. Grab a plate," she said.

"So, anything new and exciting happen here since we've been gone?" Hal asked as he got up.

"Not a lot, really. Though your dad decided his trucking days are over and got a job at the steel supply yard. Oh, and Linda is considering retiring, so that might land me as the head manager at the bookstore sometime in the near future."

"Oh, well, that'll be good. A little more money, right?" Hal asked.

"Yeah, it'll be a raise," she agreed.

"Speaking of money…" Hal started to say. "We're actually starting to make some." He said it like he thought they wouldn't believe him, or maybe like he didn't believe it himself.

"Well, good! That was the idea, right?" Cecilia asked.

"Yeah, it's just… weird," Hal replied.

"Suddenly you have money, and you don't know what to do with it?" Cecilia said.

"Yeah," he agreed.

She walked over and put her hand on his shoulder. "My condolences."

"I'm not complaining!" Hal said. "I'm just not sure what to do with it."

"You buy things, kid," his dad chimed in from across the dinner table.

"No, no, well, yes, but…" He paused. "Let me start over."

"Okay," Harvey said.

"I really don't have anything on my 'small things' wish list at the moment. So that leaves the bigger things like a house and maybe a newer car, though I have no plans of getting rid of the Twinkie. But it looks like we're still going to be on the road a lot so stuff like that doesn't make sense since it'd just be sitting around. So, what do we do with it until then? Invest it?"

"You could, though investing can be sort of a pain in the ass with how the market fluctuates. So, unless you find a few good stable investments, you run the risk of actually losing money. Of course, you could also gain a lot by investing, but it's a gamble. If you want something more guaranteed, you could put it in a high interest CD or a money market account. You might not make as much as investing, but you're guaranteed to turn profit without losing anything on it," Harvey explained.

"Okay," Hal said. "Maybe you and Mom can help explain all that to me in more detail, and set some of that stuff up?"

"Of course, we can do that with everybody if you guys want," Cecilia said, and Uli, Ryan, and Ricky all nodded.

"Great. Thank you," Hal said.

"Sure," Cecilia answered back.

"But, um, before we do that. What do you have left on the mortgage for the house?"

"Nothing," she said.

"What? I thought…"

"Your dad beat you to it. He paid it off with a chunk of the money he's *acquired* over the years," she said, and raised an eyebrow at Harvey, who smiled smugly with one corner of his mouth.

"Okay. Then, are you behind on any bills?"

"Nope."

"Do the cars need any repairs?"

"Not at the moment," Harvey said.

"Well, is there anything else you want?"

"Hal, I'm fine. It's your money," Cecilia insisted.

"But you've spent so much on feeding us, and housing us, and…"

"And that's what parents do for their children, and that's exactly what you're going to do for all the wonderful little grandkids you're going to make for me someday," Cecilia said.

"Come on, Mom, give me something here. Do you want to sell this house, and move into a bigger one in a nicer part of town?"

"Hal, no force in heaven or earth will make me want to pack up all our crap and move it all into a different place. I like our house. Invest your money and buy some things *you* want."

Hal sighed, and looked at her for a few moments while he tried to think. "So, there's no little art thingies in any of the local stores you had your eye on, or any landscaping you want done in the yard, or…"

"Okay, Hal, I don't think you're listening. My desires of the physical world are completely satisfied at the moment. I think you have the right idea by wanting to invest a lot of that money for later, but if it's absolutely burning a hole in your pocket, I can make a suggestion."

"Okay," Hal said.

"Go on vacation. Do some travelling. Go somewhere you've always wanted to go and have a bit of fun before your next tour starts. If it were me, my guess is it's about 85 in Hawaii right now, and I bet the ocean breeze would feel wonderful standing on the beach with your toes in the sand," she said. Hal looked like he was considering the idea, and looked back at the other three to get their impression on it.

"I've always wanted to go to Hawaii," Ryan said, and Uli and Ricky nodded.

"*Now*, if you wanted to take your dorky parents with you, I'm sure we could get a separate room on the other side of the hotel and find ways to keep ourselves busy and stay out of your hair…" Cecilia continued as she scooped a heaping spoonful of pasta onto her plate.

---

132. "Surfin' U.S.A." by The Beach Boys *to play over this scene*

133. "California Sun" by The Rivieras

134. "Surf City" by Jan & Dean

135. "Pipeline" by The Chantays

136. "Wipeout" by The Surfaris

137. "Miserlou" by Dick Dale and The Del-Tones

138. "Walk, Don't Run" by The Ventures

139. "Kokomo" by The Beach Boys

---

They got to the beach and ran towards the water with the rented surfboards. "So, do any of you guys know how to do this?" Hal asked.

"I do not," Uli answered.

"Nope," Ryan agreed.

"Never been to the ocean before," Ricky said.

"Good. We're all on the same page then," Hal said as he dove into the water on the board. By sunset, he and Uli were able to ride most of the smaller waves without falling, but Ricky was by far the best at it, even though he'd never done it before. He was riding down the more medium sized to even larger waves without wiping out. Ryan had given up hours ago, and had been laying back on the shore, working on his tan.

---

End Songs 132 – 139

---

After it got dark, they started a small bonfire on the beach and sat around it, talking. "I've been thinking…" Hal said.

"Uh, oh," Ryan mumbled.

"We advertise ourselves as the ultimate variety band, and we do play all sorts of songs. But, I dunno, I feel like we're not taking advantage of the whole four-genre thing as much as we could be."

"What do you mean?" Uli asked.

"Well, I guess, because we're not… living the lifestyle? That probably didn't make any sense. Um… shit, how do I explain this…" Hal said as he looked down at the sand. "We're not… playing it up on stage? We're a band that plays pop and punk and metal and county songs, but we don't have any elements in the show to indicate that we actually *are* partially a metal, punk, or country band," he said. "If our premise is we're the band that does everything, I feel like we really need to sell that or we're going to look like a bunch of posers. Plus, we would be missing out on all the fun we could have with it."

"Okay…" Uli nodded. The look on his face made it seem like he was sort of following what Hal was saying.

"I mean, like, Uli, when we were opening for Holy Hell, you were much more… I don't know, energetic? Passionate? You got your stage clothes out, and you really looked and played like you were in a metal band," he said, and Uli tried to remain stoic, but was clearly feeling a little self-conscious by having that brought up. "And we're hitting the big time here. So, we need to spice up our concerts anyways. Just playing around with the lights isn't going to be good enough anymore. We need to come up with something to really make a name for ourselves. We've always scattered the different styles of songs throughout our shows. But what I was thinking was maybe we could instead divide the show into four parts, and do the Pop, Country, Metal, and Punk songs in their own segments? And I was also thinking for each segment we could all do four different outfit changes and dress to each style." Uli, Ryan, and Ricky all looked at each other, then burst out laughing.

"No, I'm serious," Hal insisted. "I'd have no problem wearing a cowboy hat and western shirt, or a long black trench coat, or a torn T-shirt and some chucks. Yes, it'll look a little strange at first, but I'm sure we could find something to suit everybody."

"Hal, how the fuck are you going to make Ricky look metal?" Ryan asked, and Ricky looked at him as well and raised a questioning eyebrow.

"Well, um… we'll figure something out when we get there," Hal laughed. "But really, I think this could make the whole show a lot more epic. If it goes down in flames, it goes down in flames, and we go back to what we've been doing. But if it works, I don't think any other major band has ever done anything like this. We could really make it our thing."

"Here is my concern about doing this now that we are going big," Uli said. "It goes back to what we worried about from the start. What if we do all this, and we get certain fans for the certain styles, and they come to the concert, and then are bored during the other three parts? What if the punk people boo us during the country songs?"

"Well, I'm not saying it won't be a risk, and it might not ultimately work. But, my thought is I have all kinds of music in my own personal collection, and a lot of my friends growing up had all sorts of different types of songs they listened to as well. So, I'm betting there has to be a certain potential to gather a following of eclectic music lovers who go for at least three out of four. Ryan, I know you have a few metal songs you like, and Uli, I know you have a couple recent Top 40 songs next to all your head banger stuff. As far as the people who only go for the certain types, I know I might be putting a little too much faith in humanity to hope they'll always behave themselves if we mix them together, but that's what the security staff is there for; to break up any fights that start. I already put some thought to the problems that could happen with this a little bit myself. What I came up with was, if we could try and, like, set things up so we make a sort of mock fight out of it on stage during the show? In order to try and channel some of that tension and make it part of the experience? We could script some lines for in between songs like: 'Oh, hey, Ryan, that was pretty wild, but can you handle *this*?' and then maybe get the fans to join in by which group is cheering the loudest and stuff… like… that…" The flat line stare Ryan was giving him made it difficult to keep talking.

"My GOD, you are such a dork," Ryan said.

"Yes, yes, I know, it's a little weird…" Hal said again, "But can any of you guys see this? Because I can really see this working, and it sort of excites me," he said, his voice dropping off a little at the end.

Uli and Ricky contemplated this quietly, until Ryan said: "We can try it," in his usual doubting, dismissive tone. But it was the same tone he had used when they had just met Ricky, and when they were spending long hours recording early on with Jim. Hal wasn't quite certain of what Uli was thinking, and Ricky hadn't said a thing the whole time, though he got the sense that maybe they were at least half on board with the idea. He could see it very clearly in his head, he'd never seen anything so clearly as this. He needed to figure out how to make it clear to them. Maybe it was a little dorky, but when he thought about it, many famous shows were at their core. He couldn't think of anything else to say at the moment to convince them of it, so he decided he'd show them what he meant when they got back. They sat around the fire talking until midnight, then gathered up the boards and started their hike back to the hotel, the waves washing over their feet as they left a trail of short-lived footprints along the tide line.

# CHAPTER 9

## (It's Still Rock and Roll to Me)

### LOS ANGELES, CALIFORNIA

**The sound of the audience** on the other side of the curtain had a vastness to it that couldn't be produced in the small concert halls. It was a deep rumbling, like standing at the ocean's edge. At one time or another, they had each been in the audience at large concerts themselves, (except Ricky). But being on the other side of the stage seemed to amplify it beyond anything they could remember.

"Shit almighty, are we sure we're here on the right night? These people aren't expecting someone else to walk out onto stage in twenty minutes, are they?" Ryan asked, staring at one of the security monitors. The screens showed bits and pieces of the stadium, though they knew they weren't getting the whole picture at once.

"Unbelievable," Uli agreed.

"So... everything's going to work, right?" Ryan asked.

"Have a little faith, man. We're going to do fine," Hal answered.

"No, not us..." Ryan snipped. "I meant the equipment. They did the sound check and everything, right?"

"Sound check?" Hal asked. "Sound check!?" He repeated it again, suddenly feeling very rash. "Sound check THIS!" he said loudly and ran towards the stage. He pushed through the curtain and bolted across the stage. As they saw his feet come back into view under the curtain on the other side, a tidal wave of screaming and cheering rose up and continued even after he had disappeared again behind the curtain. As he walked back up to them, he put his hand to his ear. "Yep, it's turned all the way up," he said.

Ryan shook his head slowly. "You are one crazy fuck."

The new opening band whom they didn't even really get to meet had finished their set thirty minutes earlier, and while the stage crew was taking down their equipment, they went over the plan one more time amongst themselves. "Alright, so, hopefully, we will be able to clump the four styles together on their own later. But to test out the crowd tonight, we start off with the fourth and fifth highest charters. Then do three of Ryan's songs, followed by two more of the big ones. Then three of Uli's songs, followed by the two that tied for second place on the charts, followed by three of Ricky's country songs, and then do the grand finale with the two that hit number one," Hal said, and they all agreed to that being the plan they had worked out. "I'm hoping, judging on how the audience reacts, that the order we can sink into would be doing the country songs first, then the pop songs, then the punk, and finish with the metal seeing as that is sort of the order of intensity. And I'm not saying anything like country is the worst and metal is the best or anything like that, I'm just..."

"Yeah, yeah, we know what you're saying," Ryan cut him off.

"And we'll see how it goes," Hal finished, and the first dim lights came on over the main stage, which was their sign to start getting ready. "Greatest show on earth?" he asked, and they all put one hand in the center between them and rallied on it. Taking the show transformation in steps, they had settled on not *all* dressing for each musical style at first. Instead, they would just do themselves up for their own genres.

Hal was in black slacks and a violet button up shirt with a black tie, as well as his favorite dark grey fedora hat with a black band around the middle. Uli had worked his outfit up a little bit more than what he had been wearing on their small tour, but still not to the full extent Hal figured he secretly wanted it to go. He'd bought a new pair of black leather pants, and a new studded black leather jacket that only came to his waist, as opposed to the full-length gothic trench coat he kept locked up in his suitcase. One spiked cuff on each wrist, the huge platform boots with the spikes on the toes, and a new metal chain necklace with a pendant in the shape of a dagger hanging in the middle. Still no black eye shadow. Ryan had on a pair of extremely torn up blue jeans as well as a torn white T-shirt that had the remains of a faded skull printed on it. Lime green converse sneakers on his feet with no socks, and a few studded leather cuffs similar to Uli's. He had also spent over an hour spiking up his hair into as tall of a Mohawk as he could make. Ricky had on his Raccoon hat, the old red plaid shirt, but also a pair of new blue jeans, as well as a new leather belt with a big western buckle that was molded into the shape of a curled up raccoon. The buckle was too perfect. It was in the very first shop they had dragged him into, and he didn't even resist getting it. The pants, however, took a lot of pleading from Hal and Ryan. And they were totally unsuccessful in convincing him to get a pair of cowboy boots because he said they were uncomfortable. The man helping them at the shoe store said his feet were the length of a size 9, but they were unusually wide. He said he could custom order in an extra-wide pair of boots, but Ricky refused, and left wearing his same black sandals that were about to wear through on the soles. It wouldn't matter to Ricky even if he went barefoot, Hal figured, since the bottom of his feet were so thick and callused he could probably step straight on a rusty nail and it would bend the nail before it ever broke the skin. But, he was simply trying to get him to work up the western effect for the show. Now that he thought about it though, maybe having him go barefoot on stage would be vaguely funny. He might suggest it to him later. The pants and belt were progress, at least.

They took their places on the stage. It was dark, though they could see okay since they had been waiting in the dimly lit backstage area. While the crew was setting up their instruments, they had the screens overhead lit as bright as they would go. That way, when they went dark, the people in the audience wouldn't have time for their eyes to adjust to the darkness in time to see them sneak onto stage. It was an old tried-and-true concert stadium trick. The screaming started as soon as the lights went down anyways, but they could at least get into place to make their grand entrance.

140. "Tubthumping" by Chumbawamba

141. "Sharp Dressed Man" by ZZ Top

142. "Punk Rock 101" by Bowling for Soup

143. "I Don't Want to Grow Up" by The Ramones

144. "Rock the Casbah" by The Clash

145. "The Wanderer" by Dion & The Del-Satins

146. "Desert Rose" by Sting

When the show lights came on and they were finally face to face with the crowd, it was such a wall of sound Hal nearly forgot to start singing. There were so many people in front of them, it went right past the point of making them nervous to just quietly having to accept that if they screwed up, they were going to die. Ironically, that somehow made it easier to concentrate. Hal stole glances back at Ryan and Uli during the show, hoping he'd see them getting into it. Ryan wasn't having much trouble. Despite all his negativity, he wanted the attention and success as much as Hal did. Now that he was up on stage and out of time to be pessimistic, he looked like he was having fun pounding like hell on his drums.

End Songs 140 – 146

147. "Dragula" by Rob Zombie

148. "(s)AINT" by Marilyn Manson

149. "Through the Fire and Flames" by DragonForce

Uli was always harder to read. He put everything he had into their concerts, but it was like he would do at a hard day of work. Satisfied at his effort,
but unknown to them if he was enjoying the labor itself. They were about to
do the first metal song, and Hal traded places with him at the keyboard since
he didn't have the right voice for metal vocals. Hal started the pre-recorded
sound effects as the lights started flashing in a strobe light pattern, and Ryan
started the beat on his drums. Shortly thereafter, Ricky started shredding
metal like a god on his guitar. They had practiced and rehearsed the song
plenty, but when Uli started to sing, it wasn't how he had done before. He had
a naturally deeper voice than Hal, but what rose up out of him sounded like it
was right out of a horror movie. Where had he gone to practice *this* voice that
they hadn't heard it before? Hal would have been curious to be a person down
in the audience to see exactly what Uli looked like right then. The voice by
itself was creepy enough that it made the hair on the back of his neck stand on
end. As he looked closer, he thought he saw Uli's hands shaking slightly, but
it became less obvious as he took the microphone tight in both hands. There
was a little shudder in his voice, but it was well masked as a characteristic of
the growling tone. A couple girls towards the front who had been watching,
mesmerized, slowly raised their hands up into metal horns. Hal's heart was
pounding like he had been running, even though he was only an observer.
The audience was buying it. While Uli was center stage, Ryan was at his drums
looking like he had just dropped in from another decade, and Ricky was next
to him in a western shirt and a raccoon hat, shredding metal on his guitar,
and the audience was buying it. It was a frustrating moment. They were so
close to seeing their plan work, so close to laying claim to victory that it was
like they had already made it. But they had one more segment to get through,
one more hurdle between them and success, and it was that last hurdle that
made Hal the most nervous. He knew the musical shift from metal to country
was something of a speed bump. He also knew from growing up in a big city
that country music had acquired a sort of bad reputation for being lame, or
something. But he wanted to do the other three first so if the audience did

have that sort of feeling about it, they at least saw those parts of the show beforehand. They also had their second highest hit to put between the two, so hopefully that would ease the transition as well and keep their attention. Hal crossed his fingers and hoped as the third metal song came to an end.

> End Songs 147 – 149

"God, I broke a sweat just watching that!" he said after taking the microphone back from Uli. "I think we need to take it down a notch or two before I have a heart attack!" he said as they immediately started the next song.

> 150. "Misery" by Maroon 5
>
> 151. "I Fought the Law" by Bobby Fuller Four

So far, so good. Giving the people something they recognized seemed to keep the positive energy going. It was a moment to take a break, in a way. For the hits, at least, they didn't have to worry about getting a bad reaction. But it brought its own sense of foreboding. It was during the hits Hal realized just how stressed out he was during the other parts of the show, worrying if they'd be received okay. It wasn't going to be like this for every show, however. By the end of the night, they'd have their answer to whether his grand plan for their shows was going to work or not. There was just one more segment to get through.

> End Songs 150 – 151

"Alright," Hal huffed into the microphone while catching his breath. "We've already done a few songs to suit me, Uli, and Ryan, so I think it's time we do something more along the style of our axe man, Ricky," he announced, doing his best to hide his anxiety. They weren't going into this segment completely unprepared, however. They had a plan put together to mitigate any damage should the country music try to turn the feeling sour. Hal hoped with all his might that it would work as they got into place.

152. "Ticks" by Brad Paisley

153. "She Thinks My Tractor's Sexy" by Kenny Chesney

Ricky started strumming, and the audience sat quietly, watching and waiting. A few people started getting up and walking up the aisles. Important phone calls, snack run, bathroom breaks, perhaps? Hal glanced back at Ricky, who was happily engrossed in playing, and didn't seem concerned about the audience at all. Stupid little carefree jerk. Hal would have been lying to himself had he tried to believe he wasn't the slightest bit jealous. Hal started singing, and when they got to the chorus, several heads in the crowd suddenly turned back to them, and then they started laughing. *Yes!* Hal thought. Some of the people who had been walking up the aisles were now standing where they had stopped, and a few even went and sat back down. They had them now. Because, even if the sound of the country guitar didn't mean anything to them, there is one language that everyone speaks the same: the language of humor. And the first two country songs they had were anything but serious.

End Songs 152 – 153

154. "Follow Me" by Uncle Kracker

After getting through the first two, it went well enough that they decided to take a little risk with the third. Now that the crowd had warmed up to the idea, the real test would be to do something more serious. Ricky pulled a small metal stool up near the microphone and sat down with his guitar. He still didn't look nervous. It always amazed Hal how some mundane parts of daily life scared the crap out of Ricky, and yet, he could play in front of an audience of thousands without even flinching. It might have been a skill he picked up in the little taverns he went through while travelling on his own, but it was like he was more comfortable with strangers than he was with the people he actually knew. He really was a good singer, too. He had the potential to put Hal out of a job, though most of the time he seemed to prefer playing in the background. But when Ricky started strumming that guitar, the stadium fell silent, and nobody seemed to be bailing out on them. They looked engrossed, even. It reminded Hal of the night they met him. Despite Uli's and Ryan's misgivings, there was something captivating about Ricky that made it impossible to dislike him. A few lighters and phones even appeared in the rows of seats and started rocking back and forth. It wasn't as intense of a moment as few they'd had earlier, but that was when the uncertainty really began to lift. They had saved the two biggest hits to end the show, and that's all there was left to go. This was it. They'd made it.

> End Song 154

> 155. "Summer of '69" by Bryan Adams
>
> 156. "Come with Me Now" by The Kongos

> End Songs 155 – 156

After the show was over and Hal had taken a few minutes to sit down in back and breathe into a paper bag with his head between his knees, all four of them snuck up into the rafters over one of the main exits from the arena where they couldn't be seen. There, they spent some time listening to the people below as they left. A couple in their mid-thirties went by below.

*"Well, that wasn't quite what I was expecting."*

*"Me either, but I thought it was an interesting concept."*

*"Oh, I agree. I enjoyed it. That was probably the most unique concert I've ever been to…"*

Three men about their own age followed next.

*"Holy shit, the guy in the spikes could really belt it out."*

*"Seriously, right? I've only heard a few other bands with singers that could do that. It's really hard on the vocal chords."*

*"Why is he with this group, and not a death metal band? Because I would buy that album."*

*"I don't know…"*

A group of older teenagers were behind them.

*"I think I just became a country fan."*

*"That's something I never thought I'd hear you say."*

*"Don't do it, Mike!"*

*"Were all those songs they did on the CD?"*

*"No. Some of them were new."*

*"Well, I hope they put the rest out on their next one!"*

Two young, well-dressed business looking women went by.

*"Ugh. What the hell did they do all that weird music for?"*

*"I don't know. I wish they would have done the good songs first instead of last. Then, we wouldn't have had to sit through all that."*

Three girls and a guy in their twenties walked out the doors.

*"See? I knew you'd enjoy it!"* one of the girls said to the guy.

*"I didn't know they were going to do some real music! I thought it was all going to be the boy band stuff on the radio,"* he replied.

*"It's not boy band music,"* one of the other girls said.

*"Not all of it was, that's what I'm saying."*

*"I wouldn't even call the ones we heard on the radio 'boy band.'"*

*"Whatever. That was some real punk music."*

*"You want to borrow the CD when we get home?"*

*"If the punk songs are on there, then yes, yes I do…"*

A girl dressed in all black with black eye shadow and black fishnet gloves walked by with her parents.

*"That whole concert was so wicked awesome! Except for the country music."*

*"That figures, that's the only part of it I liked…"* her dad said as he pulled a pair of earplugs out of his ears.

They didn't get to go out and do any partying that night because they had to be up at five the next morning for a phone interview for a newspaper in Portland, Oregon where they were doing their next show in two days. Then, immediately after the newspaper, they were off to a local radio station for the same thing. The day after that, they'd repeat the process again in Seattle. They got good at their story and their answers, since it was usually the same questions over and over wherever they went. They made it into a mini behind-the-scenes travelling show. Ricky would start to say something, Ryan knew exactly where to interrupt him, and they all knew their lines from there. Sometimes they'd try to guess if the reporters could tell it was staged. Most appeared clueless throughout the entire meeting. Any that raised an eyebrow at them while they were doing their skit were few and far between. It was how they kept themselves entertained doing the same thing day after day. Eventually, that would be how their shows went, timed and polished, though they still had work to do to get there. The more albums they sold, the busier their schedule became, and it started becoming the norm that they wanted to go back to the hotel and sleep after their shows more than they wanted to go out and party. They knew they'd have some down time before the show in Seattle, so Ryan said he'd take them to a good club he knew. But first, he said they were going to a restaurant in a neighboring city. They walked in under a big sign that read:

## JOHN HOWIE STEAK

"We went here for my high school graduation. This place is the *shit*," Ryan said.

"That good?" Hal asked.

"Oh, yeah, and that was even from ordering the cheapest stuff on the menu. You know how you go to some fancy-ass restaurants, and they bring a big plate out with an itty bitty bit of abstract art made out of god knows what in the middle of it? And you're like, 'What the fuck is this?' Then you bite into it, and then you have to go to the bathroom to spit it out so your relatives don't see, and then you sneak down to McDonalds afterwards? Yeah, that's not this place. My parents hauled my little brother along when we went here, and that little fuck wouldn't eat anything other than junk food. Whenever we tried to take him to fancy places in the past, he'd usually spend the whole evening making a big scene. But when we went here, he ate everything on his plate in five minutes, and when Mom asked him if he liked it, he looked down at the table and mumbled 'yeah, it was fine.' THAT'S how good the food is here," Ryan insisted. "And I decided if I ever got any real money, I'd come back here and go for it," he said while the hostess took them to a table.

"So… do you want to visit your family while you're here?" Hal asked after they sat down.

"Nope," Ryan answered, then opened his menu. They waited about an hour to get their food, but it was worth it. "Oh, God, you weren't kidding. This is good," Hal said with a mouthful of steak. "I've got bad news for Dave when we get home…"

"Yes, this is the best lobster I have ever had," Uli agreed.

"I told you!" Ryan said, carving up his salmon.

"You get salmon at every restaurant we go to, doesn't it ever get old?" Hal asked.

"Okay, first, this is John Howie salmon, second, no, and third, that's what us Seattleites do. Eat salmon and drink lattes."

"Well, going by the whole 'You are what you eat' thing, it makes me wonder how long it will be until you try swimming up a stream to spawn," Hal said.

"The ladies do tell me I have an awe-inspiring breaststroke," Ryan answered.

"How's your potato?" Hal asked Ricky, who kept his eyes on his plate and didn't give any indication that he had even heard him. He looked like he was deep in a trance, or maybe having an intriguing religious experience with the heavenly creation on his plate that was called the "5 Cheese Twice Baked Stuffed Potato". "RICKY!" Hal said louder, and Ricky looked up with a jolt. "How's the tater?" Hal asked again. Ricky looked at him and for a few seconds like he was going to say something, then his eyes sort of wandered back to his plate and he kept eating. Hal laughed.

"See? Indulging can be *fun*," he said. Ricky didn't respond. "You really ought to go and spend some money on stuff you want now and then," Hal continued, thinking he was just talking to himself at that point, then to his surprise, Ricky answered quite clearly.

"*Don't got no money...*" right before taking another bite.

"Ricky, you're a great guy and all, but there are days when you're even more full of shit than Ryan," Hal said.

"Ain't got no money," Ricky repeated before taking the last gulp of his cranberry juice.

"Well, you did the last time we got paid, so... WHAT HAPPENED TO IT?" Hal glared at him.

"Sent it home..."

"ALL of it!?" Hal asked.

"Uh, yeah," Ricky said quietly.

"Why!?"

"Well, family had been needin' a new harvester-combine since the old one had been on its last legs for years now, so Dad finally got to put a big down payment on a nice new one," Ricky explained as Hal put his head in his hands and shook it back and forth slowly.

"Ricky… you selfless little ass," he mumbled.

"Hey! What you gettin' mad at Ricky for!? Y'all went and tried to pay off your mom's house!" Ricky said. "

"YEAH… but… I figured she only had about fifteen thousand to go. I wasn't going to spend it *all* on her…" Hal said sheepishly. "I mean, God almighty, how much are those harvesting things anyways!? We've each made enough to buy a small house!"

"Uh, well, for a new one, they range from three hundred an' fifty, to five hundred thousand," Ricky said.

Hal's eyes widened. "Really…?"

"Yeah…. most people don't know it, but farmers got two mortgages. Their house, an' their machinery."

"Well…" Hal paused. "You're going to get that thing paid off really quick then, huh?" he said, and Ricky nodded proudly and said: "Prob'ly by the end of next year!"

"You know what that means?"

"That it will be paid off by the end of next year?" Ricky asked.

"Yes, that, but we get our cuts again tonight, so I'm thinking you'll be able to afford to take a few Benjamins and BUY YOURSELF SOMETHING," Hal said sternly.

"Why?" Ricky asked.

"Because it'll be good for you," Hal said. "Plus, this is an expensive meal. We can pay for you tonight, but you're going to have to pay your own way going forward." He couldn't even believe he was having this argument. Ricky, of course, resisted all the way back to the hotel.

The next morning, Hal shoved him out the door without giving him a key, and told him he wouldn't let him back in until he had bought something. He was gone for a few hours before they heard a knock on the door. *"Okay, you can let Ricky back in now."* His voice was muffled on the other side. Hal went up to the door and put his ear to it.

"Did you get yourself something?" he asked.

"*Yes,*" Ricky replied.

"What?"

"*A new set of wheels*" Ricky answered, and the door was suddenly flung wide open, and Hal, Uli, and Ryan almost tripped over each other trying to get out to see. Hal looked around the parking lot at all the cars.

"Where!? Which one is it!?" he asked excitedly, and Ricky held up his old roller skates with eight new, clean, red wheels.

"Here," he said with a smile. They looked at the skates, and the excitement quickly disappeared from their faces.

"What?" Ricky asked confused.

Hal looked at the skates for a few moments, then back up at him. "Cute," he said.

"Huh?" Ricky asked again.

"Alright Ricky, I'll admit it, you had us going there for a second. But the war is far from over," he said, and they turned to go back into the room.

"What're y'all goin' on about?" Ricky asked. "These are the wheels with the metal hubs! They cost a hundred an' fifty bucks!" He huffed as he walked inside after them. *"Coulda bought two new tires for that…"*

## Las Vegas, September

If they hadn't already reached the conclusion by then, the day they got the request from the concert board in Vegas to add them to the lineup, was the day they really felt official. It was a multi-band concert that happened at the end of the summer every year, and all the performers were always A-list bands. On top of getting a bid to perform at the concert, a local radio station ran a contest the month before for four people to win front row seats and a chance to meet any group of their choosing before the show. They were surprised to hear the winners chose them. They had heard a lot of their songs on the radio lately, but they still thought they were certainly the least of the performers there that night. They were informed the day before it was four kids who were eleven or twelve years old, and they had no idea what they were going to say to them. While they had started imagining having to babysit for half an hour before they went on, they were pleasantly surprised when they met them face to face. Jay, Brayden, Liam, and Aoife (pronounced Eee-fah, the one girl while the other three were boys), wanted to start a band themselves. They were very excited to get to talk to a real group about what it was like, and to hear any tips they would be willing to share.

"So, just out of curiosity, why did you guys pick us out of everyone else here?" Hal asked.

"Because you're the closest to what we want to be. Making music with meaning, not just the shallow mainstream stuff that most of these other singers do that all sounds the same," Jay replied.

"Yeah, that other stuff is fine if you're at a party. But when I'm having trouble thinking, I like to listen to your first album, and it helps clear my mind so I can figure things out again, if that makes any sense," Aoife said, and Hal had a huge smack of déjà vu as he remembered that was the exact line he had in his head to say to Holy Hell if he ever got to meet them in person. The ironic thing is he never did tell them, because he didn't want to come off as just another 'fan.'

"You know, it does. I've thought that same thing about some other bands myself," Hal said. "You guys are probably too young to have ever listened to any Holy Hell…"

"Are you kidding!? Holy Hell is awesome!" Brayden said, and Hal imagined he probably looked really stupid with his mouth hanging open.

"Has anyone ever told you guys that you're awesome?" Ryan asked, to which they replied no. "Well, I have a newsflash for you, then," Ryan said with a smile. "You are."

Talking to the four of them made that concert a little different. Instead of just thinking about the people in the audience, it made Hal think about all the people who weren't there. The ones who couldn't afford a ticket, or who lived too far away. He did give *some* thought to the people in the audience, of course, but he tried to focus on the people in the back. The people who weren't dancing crazy or screaming. The people at the end with the cheap seats, sitting, watching, listening. When he looked into the eyes of the girls close to the stage, they would start screaming and then make sure all their friends were witnessing it. But now that he tried looking into the eyes of people further back (as far back as he could go and still functionally look someone in the eyes), they would sort of sit up straighter, or look at the other people around themselves, then back up at him. A few of them would even look him straight in the eyes and start lip-synching along with the lines. It was captivating, and he spent most of the show doing it; going from person to person. Later as they were heading backstage, he became a little concerned that he let himself get distracted, so that he might not have sung very well. It was like when he let himself get lost in a daydream while driving a familiar road, and he'd be shocked when he finally snapped back to reality at a traffic light without memory of getting there. Then he'd be left wondering if he'd done anything stupid while driving up to that point. But their road manager, Kevin Larson (or Kevlar, as they called him), said it was one of the best show's he had seen them do, and that they might consider trying to sell the live recordings.

"I sort of want to stick around for a bit before we go get dinner," Ryan said.

"I was thinking the same thing," Hal agreed.

"It has been very educational talking to the other groups and with those kids," Uli added.

"Yeah, and that was a damn good show we just did," Ryan said. "Hate to say this, but you did good, Hal."

"Uh, thanks," Hal replied.

"Sure. Anyways, I don't know exactly what we're going to do here, but it's been an interesting day and I sort of don't want to cut it short," Ryan explained.

"Oh yeah, I agree…" Hal said, right as another one of the singers walked quickly by them. She had been running around frantically, talking to the venue staff and her road management crew all evening, ever since they arrived hours earlier. She had dark blueish purple (or purplish blue?) hair, and it was cut in a short pixie bob except around back. At the base of her neck, a small patch had been allowed to grow out much longer and was tied into a narrow ponytail that stopped at the top of her jeans. She stood quite tall over most everyone else in the room in her enormous platform heels, which were black in color and adorned with purple star buckles on the straps. Matching purple stars sparkled on the belt and necklace she was wearing. The rest of her outfit consisted of white flare pants, and a shirt that had black collar flaps and cuffs, but was otherwise white, and had been cropped extremely short right below her breasts to show off her toned stomach and back. The shirt was a perfect choice, Hal thought to himself, as he watched her. He already knew her name, like most everyone else on the planet. Lyrica Wordsworth. He ran his fingers through the length of his hair once, then started walking in her direction. "Speaking of which, I'm gonna go talk to her," he said quickly, and barely even heard Ryan ask '*What…?*' as he left. She was going over her set list at the entrance to one of the back hallways and didn't even notice him standing there for the first few moments. "Hey…" he finally said, and her eyes appeared over the top of the paper, glancing at him impatiently. "You're going to stress yourself out if you keep running around in circles like this, why don't you come over and hang out for a while with me and my band?"

"No, thank you," she said and grabbed up another few papers off the top of a stool before starting to walk away.

"W… wait, I wasn't trying to be a jerk, it's just that everybody is relaxing out back except for you, and I wanted to invite you to join the party since you still have time before you…"

"I'm busy," she interrupted and started walking faster.

"Too busy to come chat with everybody for a few minutes?" he asked, and she stopped and started to turn around, then Hal felt someone else grab him by the back of his shirt.

"Hey, I'm really sorry about this…" Ryan said. "…he got off his leash." And then Hal felt himself being drug back in the other direction while she took the opportunity to disappear around the corner.

"Hey! What gives!?"

"Out of your league," Ryan said.

"What do you mean, out of my league? We're both on the same stage tonight!"

"Hal, she had a career going when we were sitting in the back yard wishing we did. Beyond all that, you were annoying her, dumbass," Ryan said.

"Well, listen to you, Mr. Admirable Intentions…" he snapped as he tugged his shirt free. "Or is this because I beat you to her? Is that it?"

"Hal, when have you *ever* seen me force myself on a woman?" Ryan asked.

"You mean, like, every day?"

"Nope. Try again. If I invite a lady to entwine and she declines, I'm not going to get slapped, or worse, have the police called on me. If she wants to spend her night alone and bored, it's her loss. I move on," Ryan said, and Hal was speechless. Now that he thought about it, Ryan was right. He couldn't ever remember seeing him chase after a girl who was resisting. "You can thank me later for saving you from getting yourself kicked in the nuts." Hal looked around to find Lyrica far off down the hallway, surrounded by her crew again. He went back with Ryan and sat in the giant common area with Uli and Ricky, and over the next few minutes, a couple more groups joined them. Mostly those who were done performing for the day, or who wouldn't be on for at least another few hours. Some of the other people there had been famous for so long that idle chat with random people was a rare treat, as they were hounded in public wherever they went. Because of this, many of them only conversed with their inner circles most of the year. Gathering like this constituted the only time they got to mingle with other people who weren't screaming in their faces. Hal sat with them, sharing stories and gathering industry tips until it was Lyrica's turn to go on. He then excused himself, saying he was going to go to the bus and change clothes because he'd gotten too sweaty. He went out the back door and walked swiftly all the way around the concert stage and came back in on the other side where nobody would see him. He found a small, dark nook down a maintenance corridor, and peered through a grate in the wall so he could watch Lyrica's performance in peace.

157. "Bad Reputation" by Joan Jett & The Blackhearts

158. "...Baby One More Time" by Britney Spears

159. "Before He Cheats" by Carrie Underwood

160. "Roar" by Katy Perry

161. "It's My Party" by Leslie Gore

162. "Hella Good" by No Doubt

163. "Mama's Broken Heart" by Miranda Lambert

164. "Crazy on You" by Heart

165. "U + UR Hand" by P!nk

166. "Girlfriend" by Avril Lavigne

167. "That Don't Impress Me Much" by Shania Twain

168. "Girls Just Want to Have Fun" by Cyndi Lauper

169. "Poker Face" by Lady Gaga

170. "Lovefool" by The Cardigans

171. "Sweet Dreams (Are Made of This)" by The Eurythmics

172. "Bad Guy" by Billie Eilish

173. "All About That Bass" by Meghan Trainor

174. "Building a Mystery" by Sarah McLachlan

175. "We Belong" by Pat Benatar

He'd always had a silent admiration for her, and when he tried to envision what he wanted to become, in an odd way, she was what came to mind. An artist, a star, a force to be reckoned with. She had a powerful voice, one he could feel when listening to her recordings. When she sang, every word had emotion behind it; nothing was there only to fill space. Seeing her live now, her wild outfits dancing with her across the stage while she released her spirit out in front of the crowds, she never flinched or shied away from anything, no matter how strange and edgy the show became. The movements, the rhythm, the words, it was different from the usual Hollywood façades. It was the type of perfection that stemmed from a single creative mind. And she wasn't afraid to mix up the genres either. She had a few songs that could be considered punk, as well as numerous country-inspired pieces. He hadn't necessarily set out to model his band after that premise of hers, it just sort of happened that way. But, he certainly couldn't say he was the first one with the idea. She really was everything that he wanted to be as a performer. But, like many other people, he had those little voices in the back of his head whispering: 'What if they laugh at you?', 'Lyrica rocks it, but you'll look stupid.', or 'Uli and Ryan will never let you live it down...' all the time, holding him back. How did she let go of it all? Did it come naturally for her, or did she have those little voices to silence as well? "My GOD, you are such a dork..." He could hear Ryan's voice over the campfire in Hawaii. Is this why she sang alone instead of being in a band of peers? Is that what it took to let it all out? To tell everyone else to piss off, and go it alone? Alone on stage, yet attracting thousands of people every night to marvel at what she did. He'd fantasized about the two of them together, and what they could accomplish. He'd never make fun of her ideas, and when he put his own forward, she'd be the only one on earth who'd understand them. It was a daydream he'd played with for years, never thinking there was any chance of it becoming real. "*Out of your league*," he could hear Ryan say again. But, there was another voice that had started travelling around with him recently. One that was gradually getting louder with time, and would flare up when he saw her perform. He could hear it clear as day now, saying: "*Don't let her walk away, Ryan can go piss off…*"

> End Songs 157 – 175

After they got back to the hotel, Hal left again on his own, saying he needed to go get more tea for his throat, and he'd be back in a bit. Once he was on the street, he pulled out a little piece of paper with the club name on it, along with the address he had looked up. A hundred-dollar bill was all it took to get the name of the place she liked to go after shows in Vegas out of one of her roadies. Once he had found it, he looked around inside for a while and didn't see her. Right as he was about to leave, he glanced over and saw a woman in baggy blue jeans and a plain pink T-shirt sitting alone at the bar. She was discreetly stuffing a few loose strands of purple hair back underneath her white sun hat. He went over and sat down next to her, ordered a beer, then spent a minute or two trying to figure out his next move. She didn't look at him. "I've heard this is the best place in the whole city…" He broke the silence.

"Yeah, it's alright," she said, quickly, almost mechanically, without looking up.

"Man, if there's a better one, I'd love to hear about it. I need all the tips I can get. I'm from out of town."

"Sorry, this is the only one I go to when I'm around. I don't live here either," she said.

"Oh. Well, this is Vegas, I guess. Most people here at any time are probably tourists, huh?" Hal said.

"Probably," she answered in a completely flat voice.

"You here on vacation?"

"No, business. Insurance, property-casualty. Our company is going through a merger with a firm based here."

*Damn. She's good,* he thought to himself. Now he needed a story. "I actually just moved here... tentatively. If I can find a job, that is. Not much going on in Michigan, and I can't say I'm going to miss the winters there, either."

"What are you looking to do?" she asked.

"Stage production. Mostly working with sound equipment. Since there's no limit on shows down here, I figure this would be a good place to start."

"That's a tough job, I hear. Lots of work for very low pay."

"Yeah, but at least it won't follow me home every night, you know? I don't want one of those jobs you have to think about all day. Thinking gives me a headache," he said, and he thought he saw the smallest curve of a smile forming at the corner of her mouth. "I admire people like you who can do those jobs though, I wouldn't be able to handle it," he added.

"Yeah, it's boring, but it's a salary. I don't want to live in an apartment the rest of my life. I want a house with a yard," she said.

"Quite a price to pay for someplace you don't get to spend much time at," he answered, and she paused briefly before drooping her head a little lower, the brim of her hat further obscuring her face. "*Yeah.*"

"Sorry for bothering you, but thanks for the conversation. I don't know anybody down here yet, and it's getting kind of depressing not having anybody to talk to," Hal said, and she nodded a little.

"No problem."

"I hope your merger goes well."

"Thanks."

"So, from one traveler to another, can I buy you a drink? Or maybe pay for one of the glasses you've already had?" he asked, and she shook her head.

"That's very nice of you, but it sounds like you need all the cash you can hold onto until you get settled in. Save it for groceries, and rent, and…" she turned her head and looked up at him, and as her eyes appeared from under the brim of the hat, the quick glimpse of kindness he saw suddenly vanished. "Oh, *god*…" she said.

"Oh, uh… hi! It's you!" Hal choked, and it came out sounding far from convincing.

"Can I get my bill?" she called out to the bartender, who nodded and went over to the order screen.

"Hey, wait… that's all I wanted, was to just talk to you for a while…" Hal said.

"Yeah, I bet," she mumbled, tapping her fingers on the bar waiting for the receipt to print out.

"I didn't mean to ruin your night. I'll leave."

"No, that's really okay. I need to get back to the hotel to work out my scheduling, anyways," she replied.

"Uh… can I at least still buy you that drink before you go?" he asked, and as the bartender brought the bill over, she took it and slapped it down on the counter in front of him.

"Be my guest," she grunted, then got up and walked straight out the bar door. Hal slowly swung around on his stool and picked the receipt up and looked at it.

"*Ice Queen*…" he whispered to himself.

# CHAPTER 10

## (Bad Moon Rising)

### HOUSTON, TEXAS. LATE SEPTEMBER.

**"And no peeking!" Ryan said** while pushing Ricky around the corner. "The blindfold's still tight, right?"

"Yes," Ricky answered, annoyed.

"Good, because this will be the best damn present you'll ever get."

"Don't need any more stuff," Ricky mumbled.

"It's not about needing, it's about wanting, and you're the only person I know who's stupid enough to not want anything for his own birthday. But fear not, you'll love this," Ryan said.

"Ricky never said it was his birthday," Ricky insisted.

"No, but your driver's license did. And if you really didn't want us to know, you should have hidden the key to the lock on your bag better," Ryan said. "Ready?" He stopped pushing, and Ricky sighed. "I'll take that as a yes," Ryan pulled out the knot to the blindfold, and when it came off, Ricky found in front of him the most beautiful guitar he had ever seen in his life. The body of the guitar was shaped into a double-sided axe; the medieval execution-style kind. The edges of the two blades were lined with reflective chrome plating that was so polished it could be used for a mirror. The main part of the body was black, with flames rising from the base that were painted with metal flaked hot rod paint. The base of the flames were red, but faded into orange in the middle and to yellow at their tips. The flames undulated and appeared to be burning like real fire as the guitar was viewed from different angles. Ricky bit his lower lip. "Do you like it?" Ryan asked.

"Uh…"

Ryan squinted at him, and leaned in close to his face and whispered: "*Do you love it?*"

"Ye… ees…"

Ryan had never seen Ricky in that much mental pain. It made him smile. "Happy birthday, stupid."

"God knows you already look like a lumberjack in that plaid shirt of yours and the hat. We figured maybe you'd like an axe to complete the look," Hal said. "We saw a guy with one of these in one of the studios we visited out on the first tour. We got a hold of him and asked him where he got it. It was a custom job, but he gave us the name of the artist who made his, and he agreed to make one for you. The other guy's one had green flames though, so yours is unique. I got it all tuned up, so it's ready for tonight, if you want." They weren't sure if Ricky was listening or not as he slowly moved one hand in the guitar's direction.

"*Touch it…*" Ryan whispered next to him. Ricky took the guitar gently off the stand and picked a couple strings. The sound was like liquid velvet drifting into the ears. He hardly blinked as it faded out.

"Should we leave you two alone?" Ryan asked, and Ricky turned around and glared at him, but then quickly looked down at the floor.

"Thank you, guys."

"Aww, you're welcome," Ryan said, and Hal looked at his watch.

"About time to do the sound check." He had made a habit of the run he took across the stage at the first show of the tour. He did it at every show from then on out when they thought they had about fifteen minutes to go. Ricky had started going with him, and he set the guitar back down on the stand. "Ready?" Hal asked. Ricky nodded, and they took off. As they disappeared out of sight at the first turn, the screaming started, and a few seconds later they reappeared from the opposite direction.

"Not bad," Ryan said as they listened. "Not the loudest I've heard, but not bad."

"Is everything else ready?" Uli asked.

"I think so," Hal said. They had gradually modified the show to be closer to what Hal had initially envisioned, but made a few changes along the way. They did do the country songs earlier in the show, followed by the punk rock and then the metal. But, instead of doing all the mainstream pop all at once, they scattered it between the other parts in 2-3 song installments, since that was still what sold the best on single downloads. The fans, however, had developed a saying that you weren't a 'true fan' unless you 'wanted it all.' This became an unofficial motto, and it got so popular with the audiences that their merchandise department started making five special shirts to be sold at the shows that read: 'Don't stop till you get the pop,' 'I come 'round for that country sound,' 'This shirt is so METAL,' 'My punk shirt is smarter than your metal shirt,' and finally, 'I WANT IT ALL!' Amongst the other merchandise was a 6th shirt that read: 'Dance like no one is watching,' in honor of Hal's 'shuffle' he'd do during their shows. The one he promised Ryan he would continue to do no matter how much he pleaded with him not to. That, too, had become a staple of their performances.

The other adjustment they made was to the outfits. While they did all start dressing to the four different music styles, instead of trying to stick to the more 'accurate' portrayals of each genre, they let everyone put their own influence into the costumes. For example, Uli found a black leather cowboy hat that he attached metal spikes to for his 'country' outfit, as well as a black western shirt with an artistic skull and paisley design on it. Ricky got similar pieces for his metal outfit. For Ryan's pop outfit, he found a neon green button up business shirt which he wore with a very loose black tie dangling from his neck, black slacks, and equally green leather lace-up dress shoes. Finding a 'pop' outfit for Uli, Ryan, and Ricky was the hardest to do as pop music changes over time like current fashion trends, and doesn't have much of a set stereotype. But they mostly decided to go with what they called the 'rich businessman at a night club' look. For Ricky's punk outfit, they took a pair of scissors to a white and grey western shirt and a pair of blue jeans for the 'distressed' look. They also got a cheap pair of fake leather cowboy boots which they painted up to look like red converse sneakers. For Hal's outfits, he mostly took a subtle, clean, and as Ryan called it, 'preppy poser' approach to the metal, punk, and country looks.

"How are you doing tonight, Houston!?" Hal shouted into the microphone, and the stadium shook with the sound of the crowd's response. Ricky lifted his new, shimmering axe into the air, and threw the strap over his shoulders. As he did, the overhead lights lit the flames ablaze, making them dance back and forth between his hands as he started to play.

176. "Money for Nothing" by Dire Straits

177. "Joy to the World" by 3 Dog Night

178. "I Like It, I Love It" by Tim McGraw

179. "Wagon Wheel" by Darius Rucker

180. "The Gambler" by Kenny Rogers

181. "One Week" by Barenaked Ladies

182. "What Makes You Beautiful" by One Direction

183. "Blitzkrieg Bop" by The Ramones

184. "Holiday" by Green Day

185. "Ring of Fire" by Social Distortion

186. "Pop" by NSYNC

187. "I'm a Believer" by The Monkees

188. "Crazy Train" by Ozzy Osbourne

189. "Land of Confusion" by Disturbed

190. "Chop Suey!" by System of a Down

191. "My Sharona" by The Knack

192. "Peace of Mind" by Boston

No matter how many times they had done it, the start of the show was always the most nerve-wracking time. As the night went on, they were able to relax more. But Hal reveled in those intense beginnings, and the feeling of the blood in his veins tingling while it turned to adrenaline. Thousands of colored lights danced across the expanse in front of them; glow sticks, phones, and light wands. Rocking, spinning, and jumping in time to the sound, like clusters of rainbow fireflies moving on a dark hill. It was like revisiting a beautiful, surreal dream a few nights every week. A dream he had no trouble getting lost in. It was a show night like any other as he sank deeper into the feeling, then a loud crack and screams suddenly shook him out of the moment. He looked behind him to see Ricky's new guitar lying on the floor. One of the tips of the chrome blades was smashed and splintered, and broken wood jutted out from underneath the bent metal strip. Then he saw Ricky, falling down onto all fours, and running to the front of the stage. Where he was heading, a young boy was up on the edge of the platform, peeking into the dark cylinder of a metal pyrotechnic tube. A frantic woman was rushing up directly behind the boy, and two security guards were on their way from the side as well, but Ricky beat them there. With a flying leap, he caught the back of the boy's shirt in his mouth, and did a complete flip off the stage with him. He landed on his back with the boy on his chest. Seconds later, a five-foot eruption of fire shot out of the pipe, right on time with the show. Once the flames retreated, the two security guards and the crying woman were standing in a ring looking down at Ricky. The boy was crying, not out of pain but bewilderment. Hal could only see Ricky's legs from the angle of the stage, he could pick out a familiar voice with a slight southern accent saying: '*Uh... hi...*'

End Songs 176 – 192

Uli and Ryan stopped playing, and Hal broke into a cold sweat while he stood there feeling stupid, having no clue what had just happened. "What?" he said, forgetting he was still holding the microphone, and the single word echoed throughout the stadium, perfectly summing up what everyone else in the building was thinking. The woman picked up her son, still too stunned to say or do anything other than hold him. Then Ricky stood up and pulled his shirt straight, and turned and glanced back at them on the stage with a look that could almost be described as shame.

One of the two security guards suddenly yelled: "MAN! THAT WAS THE BEST SAVE I'VE EVER SEEN!" And it had become so quiet in the stadium that Hal imagined even the people in the back heard him. A low rumble of chatter rose up from the crowd, then a minute later, the big screens behind them briefly went dark, then lit back up with a replay of the scene, as caught by one of the overhead cameras. They watched as the small body of a boy appeared to the side of the stage, climbed up, hobbled over to one of the metal cylinders, and peeked inside. Then, there was Ricky looking in his direction, throwing the strap of his guitar over his head and letting it hit the floor, and running on his hands and feet over to the boy. The scene played a few times over, though it was on the second replay that a few people in the audience stood up and started clapping and cheering loudly. Shortly thereafter, everyone was on their feet applauding. Ricky stumbled back onto the stage, his back against the wall while he looked bewildered out into the crowd. He tripped over a cord as he walked past Hal but caught himself on a post and stood against it, the sweat starting to pour down his face. Hal thought he heard him whisper 'help,' though he might have just read it on his lips.

Hal tried to snap out of the confusion as he raised the microphone to his mouth. "Ricky, you weirdo..." he said, and immediately regretted it. It was the first thing that came to his mind. The audience started to laugh and cheer louder. There was no denying the strange events that were playing over and over on the screen above them. Ricky looked desperate now, and Hal looked back up at the screen and watched it again a few times, trying to compose his thoughts better. "You know… that is the best save I've ever seen," he said, and the cheering got louder still. He looked back at Ricky. "Alright, well, if you're done being a hero I suppose we can go back to playing?" he asked, and Ricky nodded his head eagerly, and walked over to his guitar and picked it up by the neck. Part of the broken tip detached, but he caught it mid fall, and looked at it painfully before putting it in his pocket. Up to that point, Hal wasn't sure what to make of the situation, but seeing that look is when he started to feel really, really bad for him.

He glanced back at Uli and Ryan to make sure they were ready, but both of them were still watching the screen. "READY?" he asked again loudly into the microphone. Uli looked back down to his keyboard and started flipping switches slowly, methodically, trying to sort out what he had just seen. When Hal turned to Ryan, he didn't pick up his drumsticks, but held a stare of serious suspicion under a furrowed brow. He looked quickly back up at the screen, then back to Hal, motioning with his eyes like he thought he hadn't seen it himself. "So, I think we should start that one over, what do you say?" Hal said into the microphone as he turned away from Ryan, and the crowd cheered loudly. He did a quick countdown, and was relieved to hear a guitar, keyboard, and drumbeat all start on cue. Ricky seemed mostly normal for the rest of the evening onstage, and after the show, spent a little time talking with the parents of the boy.

That stare Ryan had given him made Hal nervous, but they got packed up and made it all the way back to the hotel without him saying anything. Hal was hopeful Ryan was going to drop it, but about an hour later, he suddenly threw open the door to Hal's room. "Get your coat on, he just left."

"What!?" Hal said. "Like, he took all his stuff and left!?"

"No, he left all his things in his room, so I think he's gone out for one of his walks, and we're going to follow him this time," Ryan said.

"Ryan, he probably just wants to go clear his mind. It was a weird night, and I don't think he's going to disappear for good if he left all his stuff here. You know how he is with his things."

"Hal…" Ryan came in and leaned on the couch next to him. Uli appeared as well, pulling the door shut behind him. "Ricky fucking ran like some sort of animal on all fours and grabbed that kid's shirt with his teeth to get him out of the way. What the hell sort of reaction is that when he could have just run over and grabbed him with his hands!?"

"I… don't know," Hal said. "I mean, he's sort of weird, I guess."

"No, no, Hal… this is getting beyond weird. Aside from what happened tonight and disregarding these long 'walks' he takes at night alone in places he's never been before; his eyes fucking glow in the dark. I've never seen or met any other person on earth who has eyes that do that, and I think it's time to figure out what his deal is. Now, let's go before he gets out of sight." Ryan grabbed Hal's coat and threw it at him, then marched out the door. The three of them got in the elevator and started putting on their disguises on the ride down. Something they had never really put much thought to when they got their own tour was that they would start getting mobbed in public if they weren't careful to hide themselves. So, they all came up with a quick outfit they could put on that would make them easy to ignore. Uli had a tourist T-Shirt from their Hawaii trip that Hal lent him, as well as a plain pair of blue jeans, large dark sunglasses, and a grey knit beanie to cover his hair. Ryan would wash all the gel out of his hair to take his mohawk down, then stuff it all into a black hoodie, which made him nearly unrecognizable. Hal got a cheap blue windbreaker jacket and a Detroit Lions baseball hat he would throw on.

"What are you trying to say his deal is?" Hal asked Ryan.

"Look, I don't know. And to be honest, I'm not even sure I believe in the sort of shit it's looking like. I'm sure there is a logical explanation for it, but regardless, even if he is just 'weird,' I still want to know where he goes at night," Ryan replied.

"What do you mean you don't believe in what it's looking like? What the hell does that mean?" Hal asked.

"*Never mind,*" Ryan grunted. The elevator opened into the hotel lobby, and they quickly shuffled out the main door. Ricky was still in view down the street. The three of them made sure to walk casually, and not make any eye contact. The darkness made it a lot easier than if they were trying to sneak around during the day. Ricky had his street outfit on as well. A brown cowboy hat, a white button up shirt, and blue jeans. In certain cities it got him momentary looks, but in Houston, nobody paid him any mind. They followed him down a few city blocks until he walked into a public park. They waited behind a grove of trees until he had made it across an open area of grass before they went any further.

"Wait…" Hal said before they started again. "You aren't thinking he's a werewolf, are you?" Hal could barely stop himself from smiling at the ludicrous thought, and Ryan slowly turned and looked at him.

"GOD… DAMN… are you slow," Ryan replied, and he sounded so genuinely offended Uli had to stifle a laugh. "And that's not what I said. I said I didn't believe in what it was looking like, just that it was vaguely looking like that," Ryan clarified before they walked out to follow Ricky into another cluster of trees across the grass. They lost sight of him for a few moments, but upon getting to the edge of the grove, they ducked down as they saw him about twenty feet in front of them. He was sitting on a park bench in a small clearing with his arms crossed over his knees, looking off into the trees in front of him.

"*Well, there you go!*" Hal whispered, motioning at Ricky. "*Taking some time to clear his mind. Are you happy now?*" he said.

Ryan seemed to quietly concede, but added: "*Even if he is only going on walks, there's still something up.*"

"*I have to agree with Ryan,*" Uli said.

"*And I'm not denying that,*" Hal agreed. "*But look, it's even a full moon out, and he's still just a human being.*" Hal pointed upwards. A small amount of moonlight was coming through the branches over the clearing and hitting Ricky straight on his face and bare arms. "*Not to mention he sneaks out way more than once a month.*"

"*Like I said, it was vaguely looking like that! I never said that's what I honestly thought was going on!*" Ryan was clearly getting irritated.

"*Not to mention, if Ricky is a were-something, I somehow doubt it's a wolf….*" Hal said, and there was a moment of silence as the same ridiculous image ran through all of their minds at the same time. They heard a rustling sound nearby and crouched down lower, then watched as a large raccoon appeared out of a bush and waddled up to the park bench. Ricky looked to the side as it jumped up on the seat next to him, and he had a sort of sad, yet amused smile as he raised his hand for it to sniff.

"*And I completely forgot about that!*" Ryan said. "*Attracting wild animals isn't normal either!*" And no sooner had he said it, then a small screech owl glided by and landed on a low branch right next to the bench. Over the next few minutes, they watched as two more raccoons, a possum, and a few mice made their way over to the bench to crawl up on it or run between Ricky's feet. "*And it's not like he's occasionally able to get a squirrel to come up to him and take food from his hand with a lot of coaxing. Look at this! He's like a damn magnet!*" Ryan added.

"*I don't know, okay, Ryan!? But he's not growing fur, or getting abducted by aliens, or playing poker with Bigfoot, so we should probably leave him alone and get back to the hotel before he sees us!*" Hal whispered, and they started to turn around to sneak away, but as Hal turned, he put his face straight into a large spider web and choked loud enough they knew Ricky must have heard it. They looked back, and the animals around Ricky scattered back into the woods as he flung around and looked at them. His eyes stopped right in a thin band of moonlight that lit them up in a brilliant green. They started screaming, and scrambled to get to their feet as they started running back to the entrance to the park. They ran all the way back to the hotel, even though they never saw any hint of Ricky following them. No one dared to slow down or say anything until they were back in one of the rooms.

"WELL, THAT WAS FUCKING BRILLIANT!" Hal yelled at Ryan. "I BET GETTING SCREAMED AT MADE HIM FEEL LIKE A MILLION BUCKS!"

"YOU SCREAMED TOO!" Ryan yelled.

"ONLY BECAUSE YOU GUYS DID! YOU TWO ARE THE ONES THAT SCARED ME WHEN YOU SCREAMED LIKE LITTLE KIDS! NOT HIM!"

"BULLSHIT!" Ryan said back.

"IT DOESN'T MATTER!" Uli said and pushed them apart. "But what is he going to think! We need him!" Uli said, and Hal and Ryan quieted down. They glared at each other for a moment more as what Uli said sank in, then Hal sighed. "I'll stay up and watch for him to come back. I really don't think he'd leave his stuff behind. I'll talk to him."

"That sounds like a good plan, unless you want to try and go back to the park and find him," Uli said.

"I could try," Hal agreed.

"Yes, try to go find him. I will watch for him here until you get back," Uli offered, and Hal went back to the park alone. When he got there, he didn't find Ricky on the bench, or anywhere else he looked. Eventually, he gave up and came back to the hotel around 1:00 a.m.. Ricky still hadn't shown up. Uli went to bed, while Hal decided he'd spend the night on the couch in Ricky's room and wait for him. He didn't fall asleep until about three in the morning, and only got a couple broken hours of sleep until around five thirty when he heard the door creak. He opened one eye to see a figure in a cowboy hat come into the room. Ricky gently shut the door behind him, flipped on the light, and didn't notice Hal under the blanket on the couch. He walked back into the little kitchen and turned on the second light, and Hal took the opportunity to get up and go lean against the door to block it. There was a bit of shuffling in the kitchen, and then Ricky walked back out the other side of it, carrying some of the food he had brought in and started heading towards his duffle bag on the floor.

"Ricky?" Hal said gently, and Ricky dropped half of the items he was holding. "I… I'm sorry…" Ricky stuttered, starting to back away.

"Wait, what? No! What do you need to apologize for? I'm the one who needs to apologize! I'm here to apologize for all three of us. We were acting like a bunch of little kids following you to see where you were going at night. Then, when we were going to sneak away I put my face straight into a god-damn spider web. When we knew you saw us, from there it sort of became an immature scream fest and Ryan's an asshole, but me and Uli feel really bad about it, and we're sorry," Hal said, but Ricky had his back against the wall by that point, still looking like he thought Hal was going to kill him. They stood at a deadlock for a moment or two before Hal pulled a chair out from the little table in the room. "So, can we talk, or something?" he asked, and Ricky slowly came over and sat down in the chair opposite from him. "So, I guess…" Hal started, then paused. "This has been a weird night," he said, and Ricky nodded a little. "God, I'm really sorry. You didn't do anything wrong at all. I mean, you saved a little kid tonight, and like I said, we were being stupid following you into the park and we only screamed because we knew you saw us."

"And Ricky's eyes were prob'ly glowin'," Ricky mumbled.

Hal looked up. "Well, we… knew you saw us," he repeated, he didn't know what else to say. "So, I'll be honest, we were a little weirded out by how you got that kid off the stage." Ricky didn't even flinch.

"It… just sort of happened," Ricky answered, and then was silent again.

"So… stuff like that happens sometimes?" Hal asked.

Ricky nodded again. "Yeah."

Hal waited for a bit. There was more to it than that, way more. He could read it on Ricky's face. But if Ricky wanted to say anything, he wanted to let him do it in his own time. Hal already knew if he didn't feel like talking, asking questions wouldn't get them anywhere. They sat for a while. There were a few moments where Ricky looked like he was maybe going to speak, then ultimately didn't. Hal could see him getting more and more uncomfortable, and after a couple more minutes, he asked: "So, you weren't planning on packing up and leaving us, were you?"

Ricky replied "no" rather quickly, which made him think it might have been a lie, but hopefully one he was willing to follow through with.

"Because… god, we're screwed without you, and I really enjoy having you around. You're the best damn guitarist I've ever met, and it'd make me really sad if you left." Ricky was looking him in the eyes now, and Hal felt that look cut right into him. "Whatever is going on, we'll figure it out, just… talk to me sometime, okay?" Hal added, and Ricky nodded again, slowly. "Alright," Hal said, then started to stand up. "I'm gonna go to bed. See you in the morning." He opened the door to the room, then paused in the doorway and looked back to where Ricky was still sitting at the table. "'Night, amigo," he said gently.

Ricky answered "'Night" back, then Hal shut the door slowly behind him. He made his way back to his room for the night, one whole door to the left, a trip that took way longer than it should have due to the exhaustion and worry weighing him down. He had a feeling it was going to be one of those nights where he was going to be too tired and drained to get much sleep.

"Hi, Jim Zim…" Hal answered the phone the next day around noon when it woke him up. "Is it really?"

*"Yep. Just about any station you turn to has done at least one little blurb about it. But hey, I don't blame them. That was one hell of a save Ricky made."*

"Yeah, he surprised all of us," Hal agreed.

*"Hey, well, this will be great press for you guys. They say any press can be good advertising, but when you actually get a story like this with a happy ending, people eat that stuff up."*

"Yeah, I think Ricky is a little embarrassed by all the praise he's getting from it."

"*Well, he'll need to get used to it for a bit, because you already have six different offers from various shows to do interviews.*"

"Good, god. He won't like that at all."

"*Too bad for him! Tell him to relax and bask in the glory.*"

"Easier said than done for Ricky, Jim."

"*Regardless, your road team is going to go ahead and drive everything to Santa Fe and get set up for the day after tomorrow, but you'll be on the plane to New York this evening. Then you'll fly straight from there to Santa Fe late tomorrow night.*"

"Great," Hal mumbled.

"*Please don't tell me you just woke up.*"

"Define 'woke up,'" Hal said, and he heard a frustrated sigh on the other end of the line.

"*Just be ready to be at the airport at five for an eight o'clock departure, and pack light, you'll only be there for a little over twenty-four hours.*"

"Can do, Jim. I'll tell the guys."

"*Good, and since I'll be out that way and I haven't seen you guys for a while, I'll meet you at the airport and we can spend some quality time catching up and discussing what happens for the rest of the tour.*"

"Alright Jim, we'll see you there."

"*Yep, see you tomorrow.*"

"Bye." Hal hung up the phone and pounded on the wall behind his bed a couple times. "RICKY? I'VE GOT BAD NEWS…"

When they sat down on the plane that evening, Hal and Uli quickly hustled Ricky into the window seat, then Uli sat down, then Hal, and Hal shoved Ryan down into the aisle seat. There was exactly seven seconds of peace before Ryan looked over to Ricky and asked: "So, when are you and I going to chase some tail again?"

Hal glared at him.

"What?" Ricky asked.

"You know, get some tail?" Ryan asked again, and Ricky looked at Hal.

"Is that a code word for sumthin' dirty?" he asked, and Hal nodded. "Thought so," Ricky said, then started to put his headphones on. Ryan reached over and pulled them off.

"So, you really have fourteen siblings?" Ryan asked.

"Well, prob'ly more by now. Been gone a few years, after all," Ricky said.

"So, did your mom have all of you one at a time, or did she have you guys in a couple litters? I mean, are any of your siblings twins? Triplets?"

"Uh… well… Randy and Ray are identical twins, they's the only two who are identical. Ruby and Rex are fraternal twins…" Ricky paused and looked like he was thinking. "Other than that, everybody else was separate."

"Hmm. Interesting," Ryan said. "So, you have any plans to visit your family anytime soon?"

"Uh… well, no…" Ricky said.

"Oh. You not get along with them? Because if that's the case, I totally understand. I don't get along with my dirtbag family either," Ryan said.

"Ricky's family ain't no dirtbags!" Ricky said firmly, and Ryan smiled.

"Well, if that's the case, you should go visit them! I mean, you haven't even dropped by to say hi in what, four years?" Ryan said.

Ricky looked downwards, obviously ashamed. "Uh… five," he answered.

"And you know what, you guys haven't met me and Uli's family since we're sort of on bad terms with our parents. But if you're still doing good with your family, maybe you could take us *all* down to meet them," Ryan said.

"Hey, that sounds like it'd be a fun trip," Hal added. He knew somehow Ryan was up to no good, but the thought of meeting Ricky's family was intriguing.

"Uh… if you really want to…" Ricky replied.

"If it's okay with you," Hal said.

"S'okay with Ricky. Do y'all know what you're getting yourselves into?"

"Oh, I'm sure we can handle your family for a week," Hal added.

"Seventeen or more people not 'cluding you three, four bedrooms, one bathroom with plumbin'..."

"I know it won't be Hawaii, but we can sort of think of it as camping. We can sleep on the porch if we need to. I mean, we're done for the year in two weeks. We could go there before we head back to my house. It'll still be warm enough, right?"

"Should be," Ricky answered.

"Well, let's do it. If it turns out to be a disaster, you have full permission to say you told us so," Hal said.

"Uh, okay. Will do," Ricky answered uneasily, and Ryan left him alone for the rest of the flight. Once they were backstage on the talk show set the next day, Hal pulled Ricky to the side.

"So, we need to figure out a plan here," he said.

"You always do most of the talkin'. Can't you talk to 'em?" Ricky pleaded.

"Unfortunately, I don't think that's going to work for tonight. You're the one they want to talk to. If I do the talking, it won't seem right."

"But… what should Ricky say?"

"I can't tell you that. Just… say what you told me. If that doesn't sound like a good idea, make things up as you go."

"*Lie?*" Ricky asked.

"No, *act*," Hal replied. "It isn't going to hurt anybody; especially not you. Think of it as preventing trouble." Ricky still looked unsure, but they were running out of time, and Ryan would be back from the snack machine any second. "Look, I'll try and help whenever I can. Just think of this as *Improv Theater*." One of the stage crew leaned into the hall right then to tell them to get into place, and they made their way to the side of the stage, barely out of sight of the audience. About a minute later, they heard Ken Shocker announce: "Now let's welcome our special guests for tonight's show, the four young men who are *Battle Creek!*" They walked out onto the stage to the usual cheers and screams and smiled and waved for a few moments before taking their seats. Ricky sat the furthest away from Ken's desk. "Good evening, gentlemen!"

"'Sup!" Hal said.

"Okay, when was the last time you were on my set here? A year and a half ago?"

"That sounds about right," Hal said.

"Okay, first, I want to thank you for coming up to New York tonight. I know you're still out on tour right now and are going to be playing in Santa Fe the day after tomorrow, so you're on a tight schedule, and thank you for allowing me to make it tighter," Ken said, and the audience laughed. "Anyways, you know I'm always happy to have you all here simply to chat, but we have something of a special mission tonight, so we're going to start with a quick game of musical chairs. First, you are going to trade with him..." he pointed to Hal, who was sitting in the seat closest to the desk, and then to Ricky. Ricky stood up and reluctantly switched with Hal. "And then, I'm going to do this." Ken came out from behind his big desk, grabbed a stool in the corner of the stage, and pulled it up right next to Ricky. He took out a small notepad and a pencil, then put on his glasses and looked him right in the eyes. "So, myself and most of the people in the audience have already seen this infamous footage from your concert the other night, over and over, so we already know *what* happened. But inquiring minds want to know *why* things happened the way they did," Ken said, and Ricky was wearing a pitifully fake smile. "So, the other night, you're in the middle of a song, and you look over and see this little boy climbing up on the stage and sticking his head in one of those, ah, pyrotechnic tubes that shoot flames during the show. What was going through your head at that moment?"

"Uh… that it was pro'bly really gonna hurt," Ricky said, and the audience started laughing.

Ken nodded his head slowly in agreement. "Fair. And I imagine the next thing that went through your head was you were going to prevent that from happening?"

Ricky nodded and answered, "Yup."

"Okay, so, going step-by-step here, you had to get that big, beautiful guitar out of the way. You threw it over your shoulder, and let it hit the ground, and that broke a little chunk off the tip of one of the blades. This guitar is shaped like a double-sided axe for anybody who hasn't seen it," the host said to the audience. "Here, let's get a picture of the guitar up on the screen." The host gestured to the screen behind them, and a picture of Ricky on stage holding the guitar appeared a moment later. The audience oohed and whistled at it. "A young man who was at the concert that night sent this in to me. This was obviously before you had to drop it. Now, if we may deviate from the story for a few seconds, I'm told this is the first time anyone had seen this guitar in your possession, and what a beautiful guitar it is! Was it new for that concert?"

"Brand new," Hal interrupted. "The first time he saw it was about fifteen minutes before the show started."

"It was his birthday present from us," Ryan said proudly.

"Birthday present!?" the host said. "All that craziness happened on your birthday!?"

"Uh, yeah," Ricky said quietly.

"Well, *HAPPY BIRTHDAY TO YOU!*" Ken sang the one line, and the people in the audience clapped. "Oh, boy. That is a gorgeous instrument. I am willing to bet you at least have the means to get it fixed?"

"Yeah," Ricky nodded again.

"Good. I'm sure your fans are eager to see more of it in the future. Anyways, getting back on topic now, you drop this gorgeous guitar to go save this kid, and then what happens next is the most talked-about part of the entire night. Now, I think *most people*, if placed in that situation, would probably have tried to run over, you know, on their feet, and grab the kid with their hands to get him out of harm's way. But as we already know, sometimes musicians are not normal people…" The audience started to laugh. "…and you dropped down to all fours, ran over to him like a dog, grabbed him by the back of his shirt with your mouth, and leapt off the stage. Thus sparing him from becoming an overtoasted marshmallow when that fire tube went off moments later. So, the initial reaction a lot of people had that night was that it was all a strange stunt for the show, but we've already established that's not the case. So, that leaves some questions to be answered. It leaves lots of questions. The main one being: Why? Why the four-legged thing?" Ken asked, and silence fell over the room.

Ricky looked down at the ground, then shrugged his shoulders. "Just sorta happened."

Ken stared at him for a few moments, and spotted laughter started breaking out of the crowd. "Just... sort of happened?" Ken repeated.

"Just sort of happened," Ricky confirmed.

"And?"

"And...what?" Ricky asked.

Ken examined him for a long moment. "You aren't actually going to answer the question, are you?" he asked, and Ricky thought about it for a few seconds, then shook his head 'no.' The audience laughed again. Ken sighed, then stood up and picked up his stool and moved it over about six feet so he was in front of Hal. He sat down again and got his pen and notepad back at the ready. "I remember you. I know you'll talk. So, what's with him and the four-legged thing?" he asked Hal.

"Oh, that just sort of happens sometimes," Hal answered casually, and the audience started laughing harder. Ken nodded in disbelief.

"So, then, does he do this all the time when you're on the road?"

"Oh, yeah," Hal said.

"Like, how, specifically?"

"You mean... how does he act like an animal?" Hal asked.

"Yeah," Ken confirmed.

"Well, um... he's usually more active after dark, he loves to hang out in attics, his favorite hobby is to go dumpster-diving for unique treasures people throw away, and during the off season when we're all living at my mom's house, we will occasionally get phone calls late at night from angry neighbors asking us to please come get Ricky out of the cat food in their kitchens…"

# CHAPTER 11

## (I Was Born in a Small Town)

**"Faster!" Ricky yelled as they** sprinted for the train.

"This is insanity!" Hal yelled back while they tried to catch up. Ricky ran alongside one of the cars and jumped onto a service ladder. He climbed to the roof, put his bags down, and then hung upside-down by his feet from the top rung of the ladder and reached for Hal and Ryan. "Come on!"

They got within range, and he pulled them up to the ladder. Uli jumped on the small platform on the back of the train, then climbed up the second service ladder on the back and crawled over to them across the top of the car. Ricky remained hanging by his feet as two little boys appeared from a patch of woods alongside the tracks and ran up to the train. He pulled them both up, and they ran fearlessly down the roof to the front of the train where another small group of boys sat. He then pulled himself upright and joined the other three.

"I don't care how long of a drive it would have been, getting a rental car would have been a lot safer," Hal panted.

"Told you, Battle Creek is up a long, dead-end road. Only one way in an' out, and that way is opposite from the direction we're comin' in. The train saves hours, and the conductors are fine with it," Ricky said.

"That's because they are *in* the train," Hal said. "When you said, 'We'll ride down *on* the train,' I didn't know you meant that literally!"

There were about ten other hitchhikers scattered about the roof with them. As they looked around, more and more eyes were beginning to turn towards them, and concealed whispers were starting to go from person to person.

"Good Lord, you do still exist!" a man who was sitting a few feet from them said abruptly.

"Uh… think so," Ricky answered.

"Huh. And here we were startin' ta think you had gotten too famous to ever show your face back here again," he said in a hardy tone.

"Na. Just busy," Ricky said.

"Jesus, what's it been, like, seven years?" he asked, and Ricky started counting on his fingers. "No, maybe… five," he answered, and the man shook his head.

"That's it?"

"Yeah," Ricky said, and Hal leaned over to him.

"*Is he one of your brothers?*"

"*Nah, he's a neighbor,*" Ricky answered.

"And what the hell is all this you've drug along with you?" The man pointed to Hal, Uli, and Ryan.

Ricky looked casually behind him, and then back. "A few friends," he said, and the man shook his head at them again.

"You have my condolences if you've been having to deal with… *this,*" he said jokingly as he looked at Ricky, then reached a friendly hand out to Hal, and the other passengers around them started to move in closer to talk to them.

---

193. "I've Got a Name" by Jim Croce

194. "Let Your Love Flow" by The Bellamy Brothers

195. "Me and You and a Dog Named Boo" by Lobo

196. "End of the Line" by The Travelling Wilburys (Bob Dylan, George Harrison, Tom Petty, Roy Orbison, Jeff Lynne)

197. "Everybody's Talkin' at Me" by Harry Nillson

198. "Babylon" by David Grey

---

The early October sun lit up the yellow grain fields from its evening position on the horizon, and the Southern heat began to taper off for the evening. Not only had they all jumped onto the train with a backpack of supplies for the week, but Ricky had his old acoustic guitar in tow as well. He took it out of its case and sat it on his knee. He started playing a few songs that went well with the moment; warm and soothing, much like the setting sun itself. The melodies flowed smoothly alongside the train and darted in and out of the empty windows of the abandoned homestead houses that dotted the route. At least, that's how Hal imagined it as he lay on his back, watching the scenery go by. He had the greatest appreciation for somebody who could use the right music to make a moment in time reach its full potential. It's something he had strived to do himself at parties back when he was a DJ for hire. But DJ-ing couldn't even begin to compare to the satisfaction of making the music personally, and creating their own moments from scratch.

> End Songs 193 – 198

"We're here." Hal heard Ricky's voice, and he sat up suddenly as he realized he had nodded off for the last part of the trip. The train started to slow as they entered a wooded area along a river.

"So, you'll bring 'em over to the diner on Sunday to meet everyone?" The neighbor who Ricky had been chatting with asked, and Ricky nodded.

"Yep. We'll see y'all then," Ricky answered, and started gathering up his luggage. He climbed halfway down the service ladder and looked back up at the other three. "Hit the ground runnin', makes it a lot easier!" he yelled, then jumped off. He landed sprinting, then gradually slowed down and started becoming smaller in the distance as Hal looked back.

"*This is bullshit,*" Hal heard Ryan mutter behind him as he looked down at the fast-moving land.

They heard Ricky yell: "Gotta jump before you get over the bridge!" Hal cringed and let go of the ladder. He landed on his feet running, but tripped over a sunken rock and smashed into the dusty ground. Uli and Ryan did roughly the same. Ricky walked up and leaned over Hal. "Well, not bad for the first attempt… sorta," he said, and then reached down to help him up.

Once Hal was standing, he rolled up his sleeve to find his elbow bleeding. "Damn…"

"You are one crazy shit, Ricky," Ryan mumbled as he brushed the dead grass off his knees.

"Sorry," Ricky shrugged. Uli looked at the train turning out of sight around the trees down the line. "Nobody else got off?"

"Our house is at the North end of town. Everybody else rides it a couple miles further," Ricky said, then started walking towards the head of a narrow foot path beaten in the grass leading into the trees. Uli and Ryan started following him. They got to the edge of the grove before noticing Hal wasn't with them. They looked back and found him standing in front of a tree closer to the tracks, his back turned to them and the two ends of his belt hanging loosely against his sides.

"Hold on, somebody needs a minute," Ryan announced.

"Hey! That was a long train ride!" Hal yelled over his shoulder.

"I didn't say it wasn't!" Ryan yelled back. "Just wanted to make sure we didn't leave without you!"

"Thanks. Appreciate it," Hal answered.

"Anytime!" Ryan said.

"Should probably get used to it," Ricky said. "Gonna spend the next week in a house with sixteen other people, one bathroom, and a medium-capacity septic tank. Plus, the girls get priority. There's two outhouses by the barn, but that's only a total of three at once, so if you don't wanna wait, you get to 'get creative' as dad used to say."

Ryan replied: "Jeez. That's living the rugged life."

"That's one word for it, 'suppose…" Ricky said.

The wispy clouds overhead began turning pink as they made their way along the trail. The route twisted and turned under the cover of intertwined branches, and the dusk was alive with birds calling above them. Hal caught glimpses of them as they darted out from behind the dry leaves, and he could swear it was the same flock of ten or fifteen following them through the woods as they walked. The trail eventually emptied out into an unkempt field of wild grass. Sitting in the middle of it was another abandoned homestead house, but this one was by far the most magnificent they had seen. Adorned with ornately carved posts and flourishes on the trim, it was eerily beautiful, even in its state of neglect and decay.

"Oh, we gotta go say hi to Charlie real quick," Ricky said as he shifted his course for the house.

"Dear god, someone still *lives* in that thing?" Hal said.

"Are you sure he's home? There's no lights on," Ryan added.

"Oh. Charlie's dead. He's a ghost," Ricky answered.

"Say… what?" Ryan said as they started into the knee-high grass.

"There's no such thing," Hal said firmly, but Ricky ignored him as he kept talking.

"Charlie and his family came out here in a covered wagon to start a farm, and his dad an' him built this house together. Couple of years after they finished, Charlie died from a bad flu going 'round, but he stayed to watch over his family and the house. His family died a long time ago, 'course, but he still wants to take care of the house him and his dad built."

"How do you know all this?" Uli asked.

"Charlie said so. Used to go hang out with him all the time and play his old banjo," Ricky answered. The old stairs creaked loudly as they walked up onto the porch.

"Is this place… stable?" Ryan asked as he dodged a hole in the floor.

"Enough. Ricky helped Charlie replace a few of the beams and posts over the years so it wouldn't collapse," Ricky answered. They walked through the front door and into the main room. One healthy tan post stood out brilliant against the weathered grey-brown wood of the rest of the house. The furniture inside was chipped and spotted, though not too covered in dust thanks to the wind that let itself in. "Charlie, it's Ricky. 'Know it's been a while, but promised t'come back and say hi so… here I is!" They waited for a moment or two with no reply. "Oh, uh, these guys'r with Ricky. They won't hurt anything." Hal smiled politely as the silence continued. "Hmmm." Ricky went over to the most stable wall and beat his fist against it twice, sending two loud bangs throughout the house. A few moments later, another two bangs sounded out, but it sounded like they came from upstairs. Ricky knocked three times, and his inquiry was answered with another three knocks.

"Nice trick, how are you doing that?" Hal asked.

"Not Ricky, Charlie's doin' it." He knocked four times, and four knocks were returned.

"You're causing something upstairs to shake," Hal said.

"Am not. Here…" Ricky pounded out the first five beats of an old tune, and the final two notes were added from the upper level.

"Okay… how are you…" Hal started to say.

"Not Ricky, Charlie," Ricky answered patiently. A small ball of light suddenly appeared at the top of the stairs, and zipped down and wove itself between them at super speed before zooming back up the stairs to the second level.

"Holy shit!" Ryan yelled and jumped back towards the door.

"What was that!?" Uli yelled.

"That was the biggest firefly I've ever seen!" Hal said.

"No, no, that was Charlie. Sometimes he's a little ball of light," Ricky said, and bounded up the stairs. Ryan, Uli, and Hal followed cautiously. The upper level was one single, large room that had several bed frames that were all different sizes, and completely devoid of any pillows, sheets, or mattresses. One large window on the far wall framed the dwindling sunset perfectly, and illuminated the whole room with a deep, pink-gold light. Under the window, an old wood stool and a banjo case rested against the wall. Ricky went over and pulled out the banjo and sat down with it on the stool. He tugged the strings gently to make sure they wouldn't snap, then started tuning them. The other three sat down on the edge of the bedframes. He strummed a quick melody on the banjo and glanced up at the back corner of the room. Hal was tired and really wanted to get to Ricky's house for the night, but sitting down for a while was a nice break after jumping on and off of a train. He figured they had also walked what he guessed might have been a mile and a half. He figured he'd give it at least another ten or fifteen minutes before he tried to get him to move, but out of curiosity asked: "So, how close are we to your house?"

"Mmm. 'Bout half way from the tracks," Ricky answered. Hal looked around. It really had been a well-built house. He couldn't even get the tip of his fingernail between the floorboards, they were so closely fit. The peeling wallpaper was adorned with flowers done in simple black ink outlines, and the window was framed with the same nice curls-and-crests wood molding as was on the outside of the house. The view was nothing to complain about, either. He saw the last strand of the sun dip below the horizon, and as it did, the air suddenly went icy cold. Cold enough that Hal saw a wisp of his breath rise in front of his face.

"What the hell? How did it get cold so fast?" Ryan asked, and Ricky stopped strumming the banjo mid-song, and looked back up towards the far corner.

"Hi, Charlie!" he said.

Hal, Uli, and Ryan turned to see a set of legs in straight pants, the lower half of a torso, and the outline of a shoulder appearing out of the wall. The form was white-grey like their breath in the air, and they could barely make out what looked like suspenders over the shoulder. The legs took a step towards them, and Hal jumped to his feet. "Holeeey SHIIIIIIIT!!!" he yelled, and he, Ryan, and Uli took off running down the stairs.

"HEY! You scared him…" Ricky's words faded into the distance as they ran down the stairs, through the front door, leapt off the porch, and sprinted across the field. They didn't stop until they had gotten back to the trail.

A few minutes later, Ricky appeared in the doorway, and walked casually down the stairs, carrying Hal's backpack in one hand, and Uli and Ryan's in the other. When he caught up to them, he handed them their bags, then shook his head in disappointment before starting back down the trail. Hal's heart was still pounding like a drum in his ears, and he forced himself to swallow to keep his throat from drying up.

"So, how about now?" Ricky asked.

"How about now… what?" Ryan answered.

"Oh, sorry. Was talkin' to Hal. You a believer now?" Ricky asked, though Hal's face was frozen in shock as they kept walking, and he didn't even so much as look back at Ricky to acknowledge he had heard the question.

"404. Answer not found," Uli quipped after a few more moments. "Yeah, so, what happened to Charlie's head?" Ryan asked.

"It's there. Y'all just didn't give him enough time to form all the way. Charlie's got short hair, a mustache, an' he always wears a bowler hat," Ricky replied, and they walked in silence through the woods for most of the rest of the way.

Once the failing twilight had reached its end, Uli finally asked: "Ricky? Are we very close? I brought a flashlight I could get out of my bag."

"Nah, we're almost there. 'Nother couple minutes and…" The sound of a large branch snapping sounded out in the woods near them, followed by a sort of muffled grunting noise.

"What the…" Hal started to say, and they all stopped dead in their tracks. Nobody dared breathe as Ricky looked off into the woods around them. They could barely make out a look of uneasiness on his face.

"*What is it?*" Ryan asked quietly.

"Nothing…'guess," Ricky concluded after a short inspection, then started walking again.

"You GUESS!? What did you think it was!?" Ryan asked alarmed.

"Dunno," Ricky answered.

"Maybe an animal? We are following the critter magnet," Hal reminded Ryan. They heard loud rustling again, and looked behind them in time to see one of the bushes along the trail stop shaking, and heard the dull thumps of something running away. "Okay, THAT wasn't a small animal!" Ryan said.

Ricky looked behind them again, and then up into the tree branches overhead. "*Uh oh*," he whispered.

"WHAT!? Are we about to be attacked by bears!?" Ryan asked, and Ricky shook his head.

"Worse... SIBLINGS!" he said, and a swarm of small bodies immediately appeared from behind every tree trunk, out of every cluster of thick brush, and a few even jumped down out of the tree branches above and descended upon them in a screaming mob. They tried to run away, but were quickly overtaken and tackled to the ground amidst crazed chanting and laughter. Ricky struggled to get up with two children on each arm, one on each leg, and one on his back, but only made it a couple steps before collapsing again.

"RICKY!... RICKY!... RICKY!..." the kids chanted as they all jumped up and down. They gradually fell silent one by one and stared at the terrified men on the ground in the way that children will stare at something interesting and dead.

"*Hi, guys...*" Ricky mumbled with his face in the dirt, one small boy sitting on the back of his head.

An old white farm house came into view as they were pushed along by the mass of kids. The wooded, brushy landscape ended abruptly at the edge of the house, and a vast expanse of crop fields could be seen past it. Three cars were parked out front; a 70's era orange pickup truck with rust at all of the edges of its bed, a turquoise 1950's car with huge tailfins, and a short school bus that was much more recent. The tempting smell of fresh cooked dinner emanated from the house, and the door suddenly opened and a Golden

Labrador the size of a large sheep came shooting out and tackled Ricky to the ground. "SPUD!" Ricky yelled, trying to hold him back as his face was being licked. Ricky pushed the dog off him and rolled him on his back, then started rubbing his tummy. "Spud! Spud... spud… spud… spud… spud … spud… spudspud spudspudspudspud!" The dog's tail was beating against the ground forcefully enough that it sounded like someone hitting the crusty dirt with a hammer. And the way it was frantically barking and whimpering made them wonder if it was about to have a heart attack and die from joy. A forty-something looking man appeared in the doorway moments later, and stood there with his arms crossed, smiling at the sight. The semblance between him and Ricky was undeniable. He had the same wide-shouldered stocky stance, square jaw, and bushy eyebrows. But his hair appeared jet black, while Ricky's was much more of a true brown. He nearly looked like an older, shorter Elvis Presley, had The King been relinquished to a life of hard farm work rather than decadent stage performance. He started to come down the stairs, but a woman with short brown curly hair rushed past him in a flurry. She had on a pair of very vintage looking black framed glasses that came to a point at their corners, and a bright pink-with-black polka-dots dress that bounced down the stairs with as much enthusiasm as she did. She threw her arms around Ricky from behind and pulled him up off the dog. "I thought I heard my baby's voice out here!"

"*Hi, Mom…*" Ricky gasped as she squeezed him.

"It's been too long! Why don't you come and visit your poor mother more often? I've wanted to see you again for a long time now, oh, you must be starving! Dinner's ready! Come in and eat!" she said as she started half-leading, half-dragging him inside the house. The dog followed close behind.

"I guess a guy has to take a number 'round here to say hi to his own son," the man on the stairs said out loud, then motioned at the other three. "Welcome to the madhouse. C'mon in!" They followed him inside while crowded on all sides by children shoving past each other, and were greeted by a massive dinner table with huge vats of food in its center. The table itself was uneven with a few sections that were lower than other spots, and Hal suspected the enormous tablecloth over it was a mask for four or five different tables pushed together. Right as Ricky was getting out of his mom's grasp, he turned around right into the arms of another man who was at least a half-foot taller than him, and had the chiseled facial features of a movie star.

"Rob!?" Ricky looked up at him shocked, and Rob hugged him tightly, then gave him a slap on the back.

"Little brother! It has been way too long!"

"Didn't know you'd be here!" Ricky said.

"Hey, when I heard you were finally comin' down for a visit, I rescheduled a few patients and decided to take a few days off to come see everyone. Plus, me an' Emily have a little announcement to make," he said, and the woman standing next to Rob reached out to give Ricky a quick, polite hug.

"Ricky, how are you?"

"Ricky is doin' good, Emily. How are you?"

"I am doing wonderful, thanks for askin'. And I see you're still referring to yourself in the third person." She laughed. "Good. Don't you ever change, hon."

"Alright, alright, I get a turn here don't I?" Ricky's father finally took him up tight in his arms, and Ricky hugged him as tight back. "How ya doin' kid?" he asked.

"Doin' good," Ricky answered.

"You sure?" his dad asked as he looked him straight in the eyes, holding him back at arm's length. Ricky hesitated for a moment, then nodded solemnly. "Good," his dad said and looked at him for a few moments more. "Look at you, you done well for yourself. Proud of you." He hugged him again.

Hal found it strangely refreshing to see Ricky getting showered with attention for once while the rest of them were left in the background. "You and Rob, couple of heavy-hitters," Ricky's father said as they started to walk towards the table. "Don't know where you got that from, sure wasn't me or your mother." He smiled.

"Dad! The farm still's harder than what we do. Just with a lot less cameras," Ricky answered back.

"If you say so. I can tell you this, though, your siblings sure appreciate the bar you two set for them," His dad laughed as he took a seat at the table. Hal, Uli, and Ryan followed Ricky to four empty seats in a row on one side of the table. All the other kids filtered into their seats, which they noticed seemed to wrap around in order of age. The boys were on the left side with them, and girls on the other side, ending with the youngest children on either side of their parents at one end. The dog ran underneath the table as well, then laid down to wait for scraps. Sitting directly across from them were the oldest of Ricky's sisters, some of whom were whispering and laughing amongst themselves as they stole glances at Hal, Uli, and Ryan. Hal tried to politely ignore them so as not to embarrass Ricky, but Ryan raised one eyebrow as he smiled at them, and they went into a fit of giggles. The older sisters were admittedly rather pretty. Ricky's father was observing this from the other end of the table and taking detailed mental notes. "WELL!" He stood up and set his hand down hard against the tabletop so loud it startled nearly everyone in the room, and all the talking fell silent. "Everyone's here…" he said in a much calmer voice, gazing down the table at Ricky and Robert. "And then some!" He added, looking at Hal, Uli, and Ryan. "So, I do believe introductions are in order. Ricky? You wanna start?"

"Sure." Ricky stood up. "Uh, everyone, this is Hal, Uli, and Ryan," he said, and they waved and said hello.

"HELLO!" all of Ricky's siblings said in unison, then began to laugh at their own perfect timing. They all had the same rambling laugh.

"Good to meet y'all, finally," Ricky's father said. "I'll introduce the family here, and take notes, because there will be a test at the end." Some of the younger kids giggled. "My name is Ronald Ransom, or Ron, and this is my lovely wife, Ruth Ransom." Ricky's mother nodded her hello. "And then we'll start with the girls, oldest to youngest, well, plus Emily." He motioned to the girl sitting next to Rob. "First of all, this is Robert's lovely wife, Emily, who is joining us tonight as well. Then we have Rose, Ramona, Renee, Roxanne, Rachel, Ruby, Rebecca, and Rhonda." He ended with a little girl in a high chair next to her mom. "For the boys, we have Robert, Rusty, Randy, Ray, Russell, Rex, Riley, Ross, and Robin." He ended with a little boy barely able to look over the top of the table. "Oh, I should also prob'ly mention number nineteen…" He put his hand over Ruth's slightly rounded stomach. "We think this is Rodney, but it could end up bein' Regina."

"*Mother of God…*" Hal heard Uli whisper.

"And on that note…" Ron began. "Dig in!"

"Oh, wait, before we do that…" Robert suddenly stood up. "Emily and I have an announcement to make," he said, and Emily stood up next to him and he put his arm around her.

"I'm pregnant! We're expecting our first baby in seven months!" Emily said, blushing with excitement. A short silence followed. A few of the kids looked around at each other confused, wondering why this was even news, but then Ron suddenly stood up and threw his hands in the air.

"WHOOO! SWEET LORD, THAT'S THE BEST NEWS I'VE HEARD IN YEARS!" he said, and Emily was beaming with delight until Ron suddenly turned to face his wife. "You said we could stop becoming new parents once we became grandparents! You promised!" he said, pointing at her.

"Ron!" she snapped. "I said that because I didn't think any of the kids would move so terribly far away, and we'd be able to help raise the grandkids! Robert and Emily have done moved all the way to Little Rock! They won't be 'round except for rare visits!"

"You never made that part of the deal!" Ron retorted, smiling almost maniacally. "You promised!" Robert was desperately trying to maintain a smile as he watched his parents argue, however, he was putting so much effort into it, his right eye began to twitch. Emily's smile was also slowly morphing into a look of vague disappointment. Vague, because she had spent enough time around Rob's parents before, and in the end, wasn't terribly surprised.

"Ron, we will discuss this all later after dinner," Ruth said firmly, pointing her finger downwards dramatically to motion for him to sit back down in his chair. Ron took his seat, still smiling, hopeful of his eventual victory over her.

"Anyways, congratulations, you two," he said to Rob and Emily.

"Yes, that's wonderful news, I'm so happy for you," Ruth said cheerily, then added: "Ooh! Do you have potential names picked out yet?"

"Well, we were thinkin' if it's a boy maybe Lucas, or Harper if it's a girl," Rob answered. Ruth stared at him blankly for a few moments. "Robert, darlin', those don't start with an 'R,'" she said.

"Right, well, thanks for the congratulations and well wishes Mom and Dad. We'll have to talk more about the names later," Rob said dramatically. "Right now, let's get to dinner, shall we?" he added as he and Emily sat back down, and Emily leaned over to her husband.

"*You don't want to have twenty children, do you*?" she whispered through clenched teeth, still holding a fake smile.

"*I'm good with two*," he whispered back.

Seconds later, chaos erupted as all the kids were suddenly grabbing for food off the various platters and out of the many dishes, like piranhas on a cow leg. Hal, Uli, and Ryan found themselves scrambling to secure even a little food for themselves. "Oh, sorry, forgot to mention ya have to be quick at meals," Ricky said, his plate already miraculously piled with food. "And don't take your eyes off it for even a second once you have it," he added, and Hal looked down to find the bread roll he had grabbed already missing.

"Yeah, listen to Ricky..." the oldest girl, Rose, said as she stood up to go retrieve more rolls from the kitchen. "He always was the expert on not lettin' his food git away from him," she said as she reached down and teasingly pinched his side.

"Heyheyheyheyhey!" Ricky swatted her hand away.

"Wait a second!" Rose said as she stopped and pinched at his side again. "Where's my little brother gone!?" she asked loudly, and Ricky quickly twisted in his chair to get out of her reach and batted her hand away a second time.

"Always runnin' around all day every day now, makes it hard to keep it on," he answered embarrassed as he grabbed the bottom of his shirt and pulled it down tighter over himself.

"I don't believe it!" she said, grabbing the second dish of rolls off the counter. "If you aren't careful now, you're gonna lose your title of being the only one of us that isn't a total string bean!" she announced from the kitchen, and Hal looked around the room. She was right. Everyone else at the table was quite slender, minus Ricky's father who was stocky and muscular like he was. A couple of the older boys were getting there, but they still had slim waistlines even if they were developing some muscle in their upper arms and chests. Another thing Hal noticed looking around during dinner, Ricky was indeed the only one with green eyes. The rest of his family had unremarkable brown eyes.

"Well, Ricky, come now an' tell us all about what you've been up to! We've only heard bits and pieces of it. You must have so many excitin' stories by now from your travellin'!" his mother Ruth insisted.

"Uh, well…" Ricky began. "We go all over the country playing shows in different cities."

"Yes! Tell us all about it, hon!" Ruth said excitedly.

"Uh… don't know what to say, really. It's tiring, but fun. Seen a bunch of different places… and… um…."

While Ricky struggled to find something more to say, his father quickly came to his aid. "Ruthie, you know Ricky isn't much of a talker," he said casually. "Prob'ly why he plays the guitar."

"And does he ever!" Hal agreed. "Ricky's the most amazing guitar player I've ever met. I mean, you know we do a bunch of different music styles and such, and Ricky's the master of all of them."

"Huh, and to think this all started with that worn out guitar that had been sittin' in the living room that whole time. And here you took it and went on to discover somethin' you're really good at," Ron said.

"Yeah, Ricky certainly has some unique abilities," Ryan added, and Hal kicked him hard in the shin under the table without looking up from his food. Ryan flinched, but kept going. "We've seen him do things I've never seen any other human being do. He's a force of nature, to be sure," Ryan said, and as he looked around the table, nearly everyone seemed to be ignoring what he was saying, except for Ricky's mother, who was beaming with pride. But when he glanced over at Ricky's father, the look Ron was giving him made the hair on the back of his neck stand on end. Ron's fist was clenched tight around his fork, his brow furrowed in deep folds as he glared at him. It wasn't a quick glare either, he kept staring at him. It made Ryan so uncomfortable he tried to look away a few times, hoping when he looked back Ron would have quit, but no luck. Hal and Uli were both thoroughly creeped out by it, and they weren't even the ones on the receiving end. Ron kept it up as long as he could without any other family members noticing, then eventually went back to eating his food. Ryan was silent the rest of the dinner, as was Ricky, who kept his head down, carefully examining every spoonful of mashed potatoes before he ate them.

After dinner, Ryan mentioned he was going to go out to smoke. Ruth scolded him thoroughly for having the habit, and then made him walk all the way to the back of the main barn so he was well away from any of the windows of the house. As he was walking out there, Hal and Uli noticed Ron had vanished, but then caught sight of him disappearing down the opposite side of the barn. They both excused themselves casually, like they were going to go hang out with Ryan while he had his cigarette. They quickly ran into the barn and headed for the far wall. It was an old, red barn with crevices between the boards barely large enough to see and hear through. They were almost to the back when something hit the barn hard enough to cause the whole structure to shudder. "What'n the *hell* is wrong with you!?" they heard

Ron say. He was talking quietly so as not to alert anyone in the house, but they could hear the anger in his voice. As they crouched down and peered through the slats, they saw Ron had Ryan pinned against the wall, holding him by the collar of his shirt. "I thought you were his friend, but friends don't stab each other in the back!" Ron said, and they could barely see the look of fear on Ryan's face. "Maybe he didn't tell you this detail, so let me enlighten you: no one else in the house knows about it except for him and me! And do you know how hard it is to keep a secret like that in a house with this many people, especially when most of 'em are children!? The walls have ears!" Ron growled, but Ryan remained silent. "Answer me! What are you trying to do, expose him!?"

"So, there is something…" they heard Ryan say meekly, and as Hal tried to lean in for a closer look, he brushed against a shovel, causing it to fall over onto an old metal bucket with a loud crash. Hal barely had time to look back up before the back door of the barn was flung open. Ron was holding the handle in one hand while he kept Ryan's shirt collar in a tight grip with the other. Hal and Uli looked at him terrified, while Ron quickly developed his own look of alarm. He looked at Ryan again, then back at the other two. "He… hasn't told you?" Ron asked in a whisper, and Hal could barely bring himself to shake his head no.

"We have come to understand there is something… unusual … about him, but he has not told us anything specific," Uli answered in a shaky voice. Ron's face was turning an angry red, though Hal got the feeling it wasn't them he was angry at in that moment.

"Shit," Ron whispered, looking around at the three of them. "Well, apparently he thinks you can't be trusted, then. You ain't gettin' anything out of me, that's for damn sure! It's for him to do if he changes his mind. But so help me if I find out any of y'all say anything about this to anyone else…" Ron said, and Ryan shook his head back and forth vigorously. "We won't, we won't, I swear…"

"We won't say anything," Hal agreed.

"You'd better not. For your sake, and his," Ron said menacingly as he let go of Ryan's shirt, then pulled the door shut again on the barn as he turned to go back to the house.

Later that evening, Hal, Uli, and Ryan stared at the ceiling restlessly while six of Ricky's brothers were snoring and mumbling in their sleep.

"*Ricky, how the hell did you deal with this for so long? Ricky?*" Hal looked over to find him sound asleep.

"*Well, that answers that,*" Uli whispered back.

Hal sighed. "*Yeah, we're off to a miserable start.*"

"*Yes, but only with his father,*" Uli said, and he and Hal both looked over at Ryan.

"*Yeah, I got it. Sorry,*" Ryan whispered as he rolled over to have his back towards them. For the first time in a long time, his apology sounded genuine.

"*Tomorrow there are some things that need to be dealt with,*" Uli said.

"*I know...*" Ryan mumbled.

"*It's something we can all work on together,*" Hal added. "*Step one should probably be to quit pestering Ricky when he's never done anything to deserve it…*" Hal was interrupted by a fit of even louder snoring coming from the brother they think was named Rusty, and Hal grabbed his pillow and held it down on top of the back of his head. "*And step two might be to concede to Ricky that 'he told us so.'*"

# CHAPTER 12

## (Strange Magic)

**They were all groggy at** breakfast the next morning, having only gotten a few hours of sleep through the constant noise. They couldn't complain about the food, though. Somehow around caring for eighteen children, Ruth was able to make the most amazing feasts twice a day.

"Ricky, when we mentioned you were comin' for a visit, your grandma Myrtle requested that we send you over to see her for a few hours at least," Ruth said as she started working on a mountain of dishes.

"OK," Ricky answered. "There a certain time ta go over?"

"Oh, no. She's home all the time now, so anytime," Ruth answered.

"Could go now, 'spose," Ricky said.

"That would be fine. Though it should probably just be you goin'. She hasn't been gettin' any younger, and too much activity or talkin' wears her out very quickly," Ruth added. Ricky looked over to the other three.

"Yeah, no problem," Hal said, yawning. "You go see your grandmother, and we'll hang out here for a bit."

Ricky finished his breakfast, then headed out. Things finally got a little quieter shortly thereafter, once most of the kids left for school. Only a few of the oldest and a few of the youngest stayed. Hal, Uli, and Ryan decided they'd take the opportunity to go back to bed, but before they reached the stairs, Ron caught them outside the living room.

"Good morning, boys," he said, leaning against a wall.

"Uh, morning," Hal answered nervously.

"Sleep well?" Ron asked.

Hal shook his head. "Nope."

"Yeah, story of my life," Ron answered. "Don't worry, you'll start sleeping better once you get too exhausted from not sleeping. Hey, why don't we go for a walk 'round the property? I'll show you the place, and it'll help you wake up." Hal, Uli, and Ryan sort of looked at each other, then back at him.

"Uh, we were going to go back to bed for a while, uh, unless you really want us to?" Hal asked.

"Yeah! It'll get you out of this cramped house for a while, get some fresh air, and give us time to talk." He sounded oddly cheerful, probably because Ruth was still listening in the next room.

"OK…" Hal answered reluctantly. They followed him to the back door of the house, though what exactly Ron was thinking made all three of them uneasy. They walked in tense silence until they were out of sight down the outer border of an almost ready-to-harvest wheat crop field. "Harvest this year is going to be much easier with that new combine," Ron said, grabbing one lone stalk to chew on as they walked. "Tryin' to make ends meet was gettin' harder for the longest time. But beyond what Rob contributed, I suppose I should be thanking you three as well. You invited Ricky to join you, and y'all did what you did together," Ron said without looking back at them.

"Uh, yeah, well, we certainly couldn't have done it without him," Hal answered.

"Yes, but he couldn't have made all that money without you either, so I still have to thank you."

"Uh… sure…" Hal said.

"So, I talked to Ricky for a while last night, while you three were gettin' acquainted with the outhouse," Ron started to say. "Mostly I went to apologize to him and give him a heads up that I hadn't done him any favors by talkin' to y'all. But we ended up having a nice little chat."

"OK…" Hal said.

"Y'all know somethin's up. He knows you know somethin's up. So, I asked him why he hadn't filled you in. He said he really wanted to, 'cept there's one of you that makes him nervous." Ron glared at Ryan. It was one of those moments where Ryan wished he could have made himself invisible.

"I've... done and said some things to Ricky he didn't deserve..." Ryan stammered out. "And I'm sorry."

Ron observed him for a moment, before looking back ahead. "That's good of you to say and all, but tell it to him, not me," Ron said.

Ryan looked down at his feet. "I will."

"Good," Ron answered, then sighed. "I also had told him a long time ago to never tell anyone else about it for his own safety, but he was still a kid back when I said that to him. I figured when he got older, he'd know when he'd found another soul or two to confide in, but that boy never did know when to break a promise. Regardless, we both agreed last night that there's no point in keepin' you in the dark anymore. And normally, I'd encourage any of my children to talk to their own friends 'bout their own issues, but Ricky has never been much of a talker as you probably know. And the truth of the matter is, what happened is my fault, though God knows it was an accident and it never should have led to what it led to," Ron said, and he certainly had their attention now. "Not to mention, it all act'lly started before Ricky was even born, so I'm the one with the complete story, though I certainly have told that part of it to him. But, since he doesn't like talkin' and I was the one who saw the whole thing through, I agreed to be the one to fill you in."

"Only if Ricky's okay with it," Hal said.

Ron looked back at him. "You're Hal, right?" he asked, and Hal nodded. "Thought so. Ricky told me he came closest to telling you, and I can see why. So, first of all, I don't know what y'all believe in and what y'all don't..."

"I think we're in a believing mood," Hal said, and Uli and Ryan both agreed. "I mean, we've seen Ricky attract animals, we've seen his eyes glow at night, and he did sort of save that kid by running over to him on all fours and grabbing his shirt in his teeth."

Ron sighed wearily. "Yeah, I saw that on the news. The whole damn town has seen it," he lamented. "I couldn't think of anything to tell th' neighbors other than yeah, my son may be a little strange. Farm kid raised in a small town in a house with too many people would drive anyone nuts, right? But, that was a new one. Never seen him do anything like that before," Ron said, and hearing that came as a bit of a surprise.

"So… you mentioned what we do and don't believe in…" Hal said. "And, I mean, I guess we didn't really believe in this, but we were sort of wondering if he was a… werewolf?" Hal asked, looking over at Ryan.

Ron stopped in his tracks. "A werewolf!?" Ron said in a louder voice than he had been using, but they were a safe distance from the house now. "Do you know how much easier that'd be to explain to folks!?" he asked, and none of them knew what to say in response. No, no they didn't know. They had no idea. Ron sighed again. "I will warn you, it's a long story."

"I believe we have time today," Uli said, and Ron nodded.

"Alright. But my offer from last night stands. If you ever tell anyone else about this, it's gonna be your funeral," Ron said, making sure to look in Ryan's direction.

"*Got it…*" Ryan said quietly. Ron spit the remnants of the wheat stalk out of his mouth and crossed his arms. "So, back when Ruth was 'bout six months pregnant with Ricky, we had a stretch where we noticed some of our chickens were goin' missin' during the night. Our neighbors were havin' the same problems, so we reckoned we had us a brazen coyote gettin' in and taken' 'em. So, four of us guys decided to get together and stake out someone's farm each night until we got the thing. We didn't have much luck for the first few days, but finally one night we were sittin' up at our neighbor Hank's farm when I saw somethin' moving through the grass towards his chicken coop. Now, I should mention the other guys had taken the stake outs as an opportunity to do a little drinkin' without their wives knowin', but I was there to kill a coyote. I thought I had a big family at the time you know, three kids with a fourth on the way, and we needed the eggs for breakfasts. I might have been one to let Hank do the honor since it was his farm, but by that hour he was in no state to shoot straight. So, I grabbed the rifle and waited for it to get a li'l closer to the coop, then took aim and fired. It fell over, but when it did, it made the most horrible shrieking noise I'd ever heard. It scared the hell out of me. It was a noise I didn't think no coyote could make, so I ran down to take a look. When I got down there, I turned the flashlight onto a lady named Daisy Beauregard. I'd shot her in the stomach." The sound of shame in Ron's voice was palpable. "I think she had to have been crawlin' on her hands an' knees through the grass, because if she'd been walkin' like a person, I would have seen that. I'll have to tell you a bit more 'bout her in a minute, but I yelled for the other guys to come down and help me carry her to the truck so we could take her to Doc Leroy. I rolled her onto her back, and she looked up at me and said my name, 'Ronald Ransom... how dare you!' And I said 'My God, I'm sorry, ma'am! I thought you were a coyote comin' to steal chickens! I wouldn't have ev'r shot you if I'd have know it was you down here! But we're goin' to get you to the doctor, so just hold on...' But before the guys could get down the hill to help me, she grabbed me by the neck with one hand an' dug her nails into my throat and said: 'A curse upon your next born. May he have troubles he can never escape from, a spirit that will haunt him wherever he goes.' And then she said a few words in another language I couldn't reckon what it was, before letting go of my neck, and her head slumped back against the ground."

"RICKY GOT CURSED BY A WITCH!?" Ryan asked.

Ron cringed at the question, then answered: "Yes, that is what happened as far as I can tell. All the kids in town called Daisy a witch, but none of us adults ever fully believed it. We just thought she was a deranged, angry woman who lived by herself in the woods."

"You knew her name, so, I mean, where did she come from?" Hal asked.

"OK, so, Daisy's story is... well, first of all, she was related to a number of folks in town. Her nieces an' nephews and their kids still live here. So, everyone knew who she was, the weird part was how she got the way she did. She was born in town about a hundred years ago, back when Battle Creek was an even smaller farming community than it is now. The Beauregard family at the time was mom and dad, Mary and Andrew, and their four daughters, Rose, Iris, Daisy, and Lily. By all accounts, they were a normal, hard-working family. But I think it was 'round the time Daisy was twelve they had an unusually bad winter, and a nasty flu went through town. The whole family caught it, but it was Daisy who got the sickest. Accordin' to the story, she had a fever of 106. Not sure if that was exaggeration or not, but by the end of it all, it wasn't Daisy who died, but their youngest, Lily. The family was devastated, but losing a child like that wasn't uncommon back then, so they did their mournin', then tried to move on. All except for Daisy. Ever since she'd got sick, her personality changed. She got depressed, angry, and violent. One day she even ended up stabbin' the schoolteacher in the arm with a pair of scissors for no apparent reason. Literally grabbed 'em off a desk, walked to the front of the room and did it. Everyone in town assumed the death of her younger sister was too much for her, an' it drove her insane. But lookin' at the story, I always wondered if she did have a fever of 106, if maybe it caused some brain damage."

Uli agreed. "At that temperature, that is a possibility."

"Yeah, that's what I've heard. Anyways, one night her parents found her out in their field, throwin' stones hard at the dry ground and yellin' nasty words at the dust clouds the impacts were causin'. After that, they finally decided they'd have to commit her to an asylum to protect her and everyone else in town. They planned to make the trip into the city over the next few days. Whether Daisy was listenin' in on that conversation or not, nobody knows, but the next morning, the window to her second story bedroom was broken, and she was gone. Everyone in town joined in the search for her, but after a few days, they reached the conclusion she hadn't stuck around. Nobody saw her for a good few years, until one day she just came back. One of the neighbors spotted her at the edge of town. She said her clothes were all tore up, and her hair was really long and dirty. She also said she was carrying somethin', though she couldn't see what from the distance. Battle Creek of course was too small to have its own sheriff, so the residents decided to watch her for a few days to see what she was up to before they tried to approach her or go to any larger towns for help. She was elusive, but a few days later her mother saw her walkin' into the woods, and she tried to go up to her, but Daisy ran away into the trees. Over time, people would see her every few days, or every few weeks, or every few months. But eventually, a group of boys playing in the woods found a crude shack someone had put up, an' they waited around and saw Daisy go into it. In the end, people decided they didn't want to deal with the hassle of tryin' to catch her to take her to the asylum as long as she stayed away out in the woods. And that's how it went for another sixty years or so."

"Oh my God," Hal said.

"Yeah. What went on with her in the woods or where she'd disappear to nobody knows, but I guess she got into some dark, nasty stuff somewhere along the way. After she died, me and the other guys drove her body up to the chapel and told the reverend what happened. He said he'd find a place for her in the cemetery. I said I'd call the county sheriff in the morning and tell him the story, but the reverend and the guys told me not to. The reverend said I was right with God for admittin' what I did, and he didn't want to see me get any trouble for somethin' that was an accident. He said for us to say we'd found her dead in the woods while we were out looking for the coyote. I never felt quite right 'bout that, but I did have a family to take care of, and I didn't know how it would go for me if I went to the sheriff and said I shot an old woman. So, it became a secret that stayed with us guys. Anyways, after we took her up to the chapel, we didn't tell anyone else she was dead for a few days and met up again the next evening sayin' we were still lookin' for the coyote. We decided to go find her shack out in the woods and see what was in there. I'd be lyin' if I said we weren't the slightest bit curious. Her sister Iris was still alive at the time, livin' in town with her son and his wife, so we decided to see if there was anything of value in there to pass along to her. When we finally found it, there was this horrible smell comin' from it, and we were still a good couple hundred feet away. We figured on account that she was insane, that maybe she never set up a proper outhouse or anything. But, when we opened the door, we realized it wasn't shit we were smelling, but rotten meat. It turns out I *had* killed our coyote, because we found our chickens inside. Their heads were arranged on an altar in the middle of the room, there was a bucket of feet and feathers on a table, and, of course, none of this was properly cleaned or prepared or anything. There was flies everywhere, and we barely set a foot inside before we'd had enough and decided we'd come back the next day and clear some brush to do a controlled burn on the thing. We all agreed we didn't want none of our kids pokin' around in there after word got out she was dead. From the brief look we got, we didn't see anything valuable inside, anyways. So, the next day after we got done clearing the brush, I volunteered to go inside and plant a bit of dry kindling to help the inside burn. While I was holdin' my breath and layin' the kindling around, I noticed back behind a log stool there were a few large books against the wall. I'd been thinkin' 'bout what she'd said before she died, an' I decided to take them in case there was something useful in 'em. I never was superstitious, but I figured I'd see what they were. I snuck 'em out back to the truck without the other guys seein', and then we lit the shack on fire and stayed until the flames went out and it was nothin' but ash. I took the books home that night and didn't 'mediately go through 'em, and stuck 'em in the barn in an old metal bin and sort of covered them up with old tools and rope so no one would know they were there."

"As far as what happened to Ricky, the rest of Ruth's pregnancy went fine, and she was only in labor an hour or two before he was born. I had been a bit concerned in the back of my mind, but everything seemed fine until we got our first look at those green eyes of his. It gave me a start, but Ruth was all excited and said: 'Look, Ron! He has my grandmother's eyes!' I hoped that's what it was, though I know green eyes are rare, and I hadn't known of anyone on my side with any green. Usually ya' have to have green somewhere on both sides to get more green. Other than that, years passed, and Ricky grew up to be a healthy, normal kid. Well, maybe not normal, but, you know, not a screamin' demon or any such thing. So, I'd long written off what Daisy had said until one day when Ricky was around twelve years old or so, he came up to me after dinner lookin' upset, and asked if we could talk alone out by the barn. I said sure and didn't think anything of it because that was the look I'd gotten many times from my kids usually when they had diarrhea or somethin' and needed to be taken to the doctor and didn't want their siblin's to know about it. So, I walked back there with him and asked him what's wrong, and he immediately started cryin' and said '*Daddy, I think I'm possessed!*' Now, he was the one who was cryin', but I just about shit myself when he said that. I didn't want to jump to conclusions though, and I tried to calm him down. 'Whoa, whoa, Ricky, son, what in the world makes you say somethin' crazy like that!?' He didn't answer me right away, but then went into a rant: '*I... I... I haven't been messin' with witchcraft or Ouija boards or sayin' any curses or anythin' like that and I don't know how this happened an' I swear I ain't been doin' nothing wrong and...*' Honestly, that's when I started really gettin' scared because that was the longest string of words I'd ever heard come out of that boy's mouth. I asked him again what made him think he was possessed, and he got sort of quiet all of a sudden. I asked him a third time, an' he said he wasn't sure how to explain it. I told him just to tell me whatever he could, and after a while, he finally said he'd been mad 'bout somethin' the day before, and he'd went for a walk out in the woods to be alone. While he was out there, he kept thinkin' about it and gettin' madder and madder, and then he kicked a rock with his foot down the trail in front of him, and suddenly a ring of plants and grass around him shriveled up and turned brown."

"What!?" Hal said.

Ron looked at him. "Yeah, that's pretty much what I said. I tried to tell him it was just his imagination, and he had walked into an area of dead grass without noticin', but he insisted he watched it happen. He said it scared him so bad, he turned to run out of the woods, but brushed against another bush as he turned 'round, and that one shriveled up too. He also said later that same evenin' he was questionin' himself if he had imagined the whole thing and decided to see if he could make it happen on purpose. So, he said he went out and found a dandelion in the far back of the yard and tried to think about what he had been thinkin' about earlier while he looked at it, and it dried up and shriveled on sight. I didn't know what to say to him at that point, but I was hopin' to all heck he just wasn't right about what he was sayin'. Next I did somethin' stupid and asked if he could show me, and he said yes, and looked over at a vine crawlin' up the backside of the barn where we were talkin'. Lord help me I watched as that vine turned from green to brown, fell off the sideboards, and withered to the ground." Hal, Uli, and Ryan's mouths were hanging open with shock, and Ron continued. "That was 'bout the scariest thing I've ever seen in my life. After seeing that, I told him everything that had happened with Daisy like I told y'all, and that seemed to calm him down a bit. Knowin' that he wasn't goin' crazy, and that it wasn't anything he brought upon himself."

"After that, neither of us was quite sure what to do, but I did mention those books, and I told him maybe it was time we went through them to try and see if there was any way to 'cure' him of it. So, we went out again the next night. I told Ruth we were goin' for a 'walk,' which is a code word of sorts in our house when somethin' needs to be dealt with that maybe doesn't need to be talked about in front of the whole family. We went down into the barn where I had them books stashed. I hadn't looked at 'em since I first hid 'em twelve years before, and when we opened the metal bin, they were covered in a layer of dead mice. Some were skeletons and others looked to only be a few days old. There were other bins and buckets throughout the barn, and maybe we'd occasionally find one dead mouse that got stuck in em', but never a layer like that. I slammed the lid back on, and we decided maybe we'd try somethin' else first. We went up to the chapel to go talk to the reverend, and we were downright nervous about it, but I ended up tellin' him what Daisy had said and how now Ricky was havin' problems. God bless our poor reverend, he took us seriously and promised never to tell another soul and he never did. He said that he'd try to do a blessin' or exorcism or somethin', though he'd never really done one before. Well, he did his little blessin' ceremony on Ricky, and Ricky told me he didn't feel anything different way after he was done, but we thanked him and said we'd tell him tomorrow if it worked or not. Needless to say, it didn't work, but we both agreed we didn't want him to have to try again, so we put on a couple of big smiles and went up the next night and told him it worked and thanked him. After that, we realized we might have to get into those nasty books, so I got a pair of gloves and dug 'em out from under the mice and wiped 'em down with a rag covered in rubbin' alcohol. Then we got in the truck and decided to drive somewhere and park and read them in there. Now, the two of us weren't exactly experts on wardin' off evil, but we brought an old cross necklace Ruth's grandmother had given her, and we also brought a can of salt to make a ring 'round the truck. We both had a good laugh about it as we hung the necklace from the rearview mirror and circled the truck with salt, and then we got down to readin'. Those books were big though, and we realized real quick it was gonna take us a couple of nights to go through 'em all, but we got to it. Now, a lot of what was in them was Olde English, so we were only able to make out some of what was written, and other parts were in French, and then another language we didn't recognize at all. But after readin' what we could out of 'em, we figured out a couple things. First, I had always wondered why Daisy decided to curse Ricky and not me since I was the one who shot her. But one of the things we read was that adults are much harder to put spells on than children since they are more mentally... hardened, I guess, than kids are. So, I guess Daisy wasn't feelin' too good about her chances of cursin' me, so she decided on someone more vulnerable, and you don't get more vulnerable than an unborn baby. Second, we discovered you couldn't exorcise anything that wasn't truly evil, that bein' anything other than a demon. So, we figured between the failed blessin' and reading that, that Ricky had somethin' other than a demon put in him. It also mentioned demons couldn't be controlled whatsoever after they were summoned, and seein' as Ricky seemed to have some control over it, we reckoned it wasn't an evil spirit. That answered another thing I'd been wonderin' 'bout, that bein' if Daisy really wanted him to suffer, why hadn't she possessed him with somethin' more awful. But it makes sense now because a demon can be exorcised and driven out while a non-evil spirit can't, so she knew we wouldn't be able to get rid of it."

Ron took a moment to catch his breath, then with a quick sideways nod of his head, continued. "That's my main theory, anyways. I might be givin' her too much credit, because when she did her curse she was sort of dyin' from a gunshot wound and she was crazy anyways. So, maybe she did mean to possess him with a demon but wasn't exactly thinkin' real clear at the time and messed it up. Regardless, we think we found out what exactly she did put in him, and that was somethin' called an 'elemental.' An earth elemental, to be exact. So, as you loudly pointed out at dinner…" Ron shot Ryan another nasty glare. "Ricky is sort of a force of nature."

"So, what all can Ricky do? If you're willing to tell us, that is," Hal asked.

"Well, earth elemental spirits supposedly have control over a few things, 'cluding dirt, rocks, plants, and that kind of stuff. Also over animals," Ron said. "As far as what all he can do with these things we don't know 'cause it's mostly not somethin' Ricky ever wanted to mess with for fear he'd do somethin' bad. So, he's tried to keep it under control and not play around with it."

"And you've kept this hidden from your whole family for all this time?" Uli commented.

"Yeah, and that wasn't easy," Ron said. "It took us about a week to get through those books, and Ruth certainly noticed me and Ricky had been going on a lot of 'walks' as of late. After we got back one night as I was gettin' into bed she turned over and asked me what we'd been up to and *'please tell me nothin's wrong with our sweet Ricky.'* I knew that was a rhetorical question 'cause Ruth knew full well somethin' was up. She may be a little nutty, but she's not stupid. I'd never lied to my wife before in our entire time bein' together, but I couldn't exactly tell her our son had been cursed on account that Ruthie came from a much more religious family than me, so it might have really freaked her out. Plus, I didn't think she'd believe me anyways. So, I sort of leaned over to her and whispered '*puberty*' and held my finger to my lips to let her know to keep it a secret. She looked all kinds of relieved and nodded back, then rolled over and went to sleep," Ron said right as they stopped at the southern boundary of the field. He panned his gaze out across the land for a moment, then added "And that's, kind of it."

"Damn…" Hal said quietly, and that seemed to speak for all of them as they stood looking at the distant woods.

"So, over the years we figured a number of things out, though there are still some things that are a mystery," Ron added. "On top of everything else, lookin' back on what happened, one of the things that still scares me to this day is I have no idea how Daisy Beauregard knew my name. Or how she knew I was havin' another son soon. Like everyone else in town, I'd occasionally caught a glimpse of her walkin' on the edge of the woods, but that was all the closer I got. I'd never spoken to her, and I don't believe anyone in town had for nearly sixty years. So, barring she had learned what she did through some 'mystical' means, the thought that she may have been creepin' around closer to our houses at night doin' more than stealin' chickens was not a cozy thing to think about." The other three nodded in agreement as they turned around to walk back towards the old white farmhouse.

When they got back, Hal, Uli, and Ryan went back to bed for a few hours before Ricky returned. When he came in, they were just finishing the sandwiches they had made for lunch. "Hey," Hal said casually as he came through the door. "How's your grandma doing?"

"Uh… s'okay. Just slowing down a little," Ricky answered.

"So, what are we doing the rest of today?" Hal asked.

"Dunno," Ricky said.

"Well, what did you do around here when you had free time?"

"Uh, mostly hung out in the woods…" Ricky said as he shot a quick glance at his dad, who was working on a small stack of financial paperwork on the table. Ron looked up and nodded at him briefly. "…and explored all the abandoned houses. We could do that, there's more cool ones up in the hills and…"

"NO! No, no…" Hal said, motioning with his hands. "I think we'll leave the abandoned house exploration to you," he said, and Uli and Ryan nodded in agreement.

Ricky's dad slowly looked up again from his paperwork. "You didn't take 'em to that house up halfway between here and the tracks, did you?" he asked.

"Uh, yeah," Ricky answered, looking guilty.

"*Ricky, Ricky, Ricky…*" Ron said, shaking his head sarcastically as he went back to his paperwork.

"Well, if y'all don't wanna explore, then 'dunno what else we could do," Ricky said. "Could hang out here, or… wait, we could go see John!"

"Who's John?" Ryan asked.

"John's the one who taught Ricky to play guitar," Ricky said. Hal and Uli perked up.

"Hey, now THAT sounds like an awesome idea," Hal said. "I'd love to meet him."

"Okay,. Wanna go now?" Ricky asked.

"Yeah, let's do it," Ryan replied.

"Should someone call him to let him know we're coming?" Uli asked.

"John don't have a phone. He's always home, though."

"He doesn't have a phone!? Like, not just no cell phone, but no phone at all?" Ryan asked as they went out the door.

"That's right," Ricky answered.

"What in the hell," Ryan quipped.

"John leads a simple life," Ricky said as they started down the road in the other direction from which they had come the night before.

Half an hour later, Hal noticed they'd only passed two or three other houses. "This place really is desolate," he said. "And it's so quiet during the day. This is the only place I've ever been that was louder at night than during the daytime."

"Yeah, sorry 'bout all the snoring," Ricky answered.

"Well, not just that…" Hal laughed. "All the frogs and crickets and that owl in your yard last night. I know lots of people like to think cities have an 'active night life,' but they've got nothing on this place. And now, during the daytime, everything is asleep apparently. It's weird, I guess, having grown up in a city, to suddenly realize what it's like to be someplace truly quiet. I mean, when I thought I was someplace quiet back home there was still the sound of traffic in the distance, or the neighbors making noise, or the furnace running, or *something*. But, there's just *nothing* here."

Ricky shrugged his shoulders. "Never really noticed."

"Never really noticed there was nothing to notice?" Hal asked with a smile. "No distractions, nothing running around you, no ads vying for your attention. I'm a little jealous, actually." He laughed.

"Yeah, well, it's a nice break here an' there, but after a while it gets really borin'." Ricky said as he suddenly turned onto another beaten footpath at the edge of the woods.

"I suppose it would be," Hal said. "Ah! Here's another thing I never got growing up: woods to play in. Real woods. Not small, litter-covered city parks. I woulda killed for something like this." Uli and Ryan seemed to agree.

"Yeah…" Ryan said, "…somewhere to get away from other people." And Hal could hear a small trace of longing in his voice that sounded all too familiar.

"Alright, explorin' the woods is kinda fun," Ricky relented. They followed him down a sloping hill, and at the bottom, the trail turned to loop around a marshy lowland. Within a few moments, Uli and Ryan began swatting mosquitoes landing on their arms. Ricky took notice. "But maybe not everything about the woods is as great as ya might think."

"Thank God for long sleeves," Hal said smugly, then suddenly swatted at the back of his neck.

"Trick or treating in this town must have been a nightmare," Ryan grunted. "Are we almost there?" he asked, and Ricky gestured ahead of them.

They saw off in the distance a classic-looking log cabin nestled way back in the woods among a patch of evergreens.

"Holy shit…" Ryan muttered. "You weren't kidding about the simple life."

"Nope," Ricky agreed. They made their way up to the cabin, and Ricky knocked on the door. "Hello? John?"

The door swung open, and a tall woman wearing a long, tan dress appeared in the doorway. "Who the hell are you!? What do you want!?"

Ricky took a step back, startled. "You… must be Grace?" he asked, and the woman appeared taken aback. "Yes…"

"Your dad was always talkin' about how much he missed you. He must be happy that you came to visit."

"He is…" she answered as she studied Ricky suspiciously.

"Grace, who the hell is at the door?" a raspy voice yelled from inside.

"Four white boys," the woman yelled back, and Ricky cringed.

"Well, get rid of 'em!" the man's voice yelled back.

"IT'S RICKY RACCOON!" Ricky bellowed into the house.

"RICKY!?" The raspy voice was suddenly more welcoming, and moments later, footsteps were heard coming towards the door.

"Daddy, you need to lie down," Grace said as she walked quickly back inside.

"I'm gonna die anyways, might as well do it standing on my own two feet and not laying in bed like a worthless old man!" They heard him argue back. An elderly man appeared around the corner with his arm around his daughter's shoulder.

"Ricky! Where the hell have you been?" he asked excitedly.

"John! Been everywhere! Got so much to tell you!"

"And what is all this that you brought back here with ya?" he asked lightheartedly, shaking a wood cane in the direction of the other three.

"Oh, this is Hal, Uli, and Ryan," Ricky said, pointing to each as he named them. "We's all in a band," Ricky said excitedly.

"You're in a band!? Attaboy Ricky!" John said as he made it to the door with the help of his daughter. He held out a hand. "John Benjamin Goode," he introduced himself.

"Sir, it's a pleasure. We've heard a lot about you," Hal said as he shook his hand. After all the introductions were done, John lowered himself down into a wooden rocking chair on the front porch with some assistance from Grace. Everyone else found a seat either on the railing, or on a few wood crates that were stacked to the side.

"Alright, Ricky, I'm listenin'. Start from the beginning and tell me all about it," John said.

"Well, we met in Memphis in a tavern. Ricky was on stage playin' for a little money and they was in the audience," Ricky said.

"And we were in the market for a guitarist, and Ricky was one of the best we'd seen in a long time," Hal cut in. "And I'm told we have you to thank for that."

"Yeah, well, I taught him to pick a few strings," John said humbly.

"Never be as good as you, though," Ricky said.

"Oh, cram it all," John said. "So, y'all met up in Memphis, and what happened from there?"

"Well, we all went to Hal's house where we mostly live. Though we're out touring an awful lot now, so we're not there much anymore."

"You're doin' that well, huh?" John asked.

"Yeah. Sellin' out stadiums, gotten a couple songs to hit #1 on the charts..."

"What!?" John said. "You pullin' my leg, or are you serious?"

"Ricky wouldn't lie to you," Ricky said. "Things are goin' real good. Even bought the family a whole new combine. Paid for an' everything!"

"Ricky! That's incredible! You actually hit the bigtime!"

"Yeah, who woulda' thought, huh?" Ricky answered.

"What you guys call yourselves? I do listen to the radio on occasion."

"Battle Creek," Ricky answered.

"You're Battle Creek!?" John said loudly. "Well, goddamn, I guess I should get the dumbolt of the year award for not figurin' that one out."

"Well, in all fairness, we didn't actually name the group after this place, though it did work out very nicely for Ricky. See, I'm from Battle Creek, Michigan," Hal explained.

"Alright, that makes me feel a little better, I guess," John laughed. "See, when I'd first heard of this 'Battle Creek,' I assumed it was regardin' another Battle Creek since there are a few places in the country named that. I figured there was no way the group was named for this place."

"John, you enjoy your solitude an' privacy and all that, but maybe you should get out into town and talk to people a little more. They coulda' told ya," Ricky said.

"I'm too old and weak for that now," John muttered.

"Yeah, you... don't look as strong as you used to," Ricky said quietly. "Are you doin' okay?"

"I'm getting' old, that's all." John brushed him off, but Ricky didn't look convinced.

"So, sir, Ricky has said some amazing things about you over the years, and seeing as he is the best guitar player I've ever met and you're the one who taught him, I don't suppose we'd be able to have the honor of listening to you play a few songs?" Hal asked.

"Oh, Lord. Well, I can guarantee you most of what Ricky has told you is likely exaggeration at best and fabrication at worst, so I wouldn't get your hopes up too high. But I certainly never turn down a chance to pick up the guitar and play a bit," John said as he struggled to lift himself back up out of the chair.

"Dad! Sit back down right now! You've done enough for today already," Grace insisted.

"I already done told you Grace, I'mma die up on my own two feet! I'm only goin' a couple steps inside to get the guitars, goddamn," he grumbled.

He came back a few moments later, one acoustic guitar in each hand, and sat back down.

"So, did anyone teach you to play?" Ryan asked.

"Nope. Taught myself a long time ago. Got a hold of an old guitar and a few worn instruction books and learned in my free time between plowin' the fields," he answered. John gave the guitars a quick tuning while the men sat around chatting, but at the same time, Hal noticed Ricky talking quietly to Grace, who looked concerned. "Now you see, I got raised on Blues and Motown, so that's where I started," John explained. "And that's what I always go back to. Probably a little different from what you boys play."

"That is totally alright," Hal said. "It will be nice to try something new."

"See now, that's a good attitude to have. Probably why you've been so successful. Ricky, you wanna help out here?" John asked, handing him one of the guitars.

"Always," Ricky replied.

199. "Maybellene" by Chuck Berry

200. "(Sittin' On) The Dock of the Bay" by Otis Redding

201. "Build Me Up, Buttercup" by The Foundations

202. "Stand by Me" by Ben E. King

203. "My Girl" by The Temptations

204. "Silhouettes on the Shade" by The Rays

205. "Hit the Road, Jack" by Ray Charles

John began strumming a few chords, and out of him came a gritty, raspy, yet wonderfully melodic voice that sang of decades past by its tone alone. Hal and Uli snapped their fingers and tapped their feet while Ryan kept rhythm on an old metal tub sitting nearby. Grace even sang a little bit of backup for one of the songs. Minutes turned to hours as one song followed another. They sat there playing on the porch of the log cabin while the sun made its way down the sky to the cradle of the hills in the distance, and then even long after it had gone down below. The fireplace emitted a comforting glow as they got ready to leave for the night.

End Songs 199 – 205

"You know Mr. Goode, with the way you play, we know people who could sign you onto a label in no time," Hal said.

"Nah, I'm too old for that now. If you'd a' come to me with that offer fifty, forty, heck even twenty years ago I might a' taken you up on it, but it's too late now."

"It's never too late," Hal insisted.

"Boy, I'm too weak to travel, and even if I don't go out on a full tour like you do, I'd still have to do a little travellin' to record, and I don't have it in me anymore. But it's a nice offer anyways, so thank you kindly."

"Well, if you ever change your mind, just let us know," Hal said as he shook his hand again.

"I'll remember that," John said. "Ricky, it was wonderful to see you again, I was startin' to worry I'd never get another chance to talk to you. You done well and got yourself some wonderful friends. Thanks for bringin' 'em down today. This was the most fun I've had in years. But why don't you come back by yourself tomorrow so we can catch up and talk a bit, just you and me."

"Sounds good, John. Will do," Ricky said. "We can also talk about movin' you into a better house."

"What in God's name are you talkin' about?" John asked him.

"You taught Ricky everything he knows, and Ricky has money now, so as a thank you, Ricky would like to move you into a place that has plumbing and all its roof shingles," Ricky responded.

"Ricky, it'll be over my dead, cold body that I'll leave this cabin."

"We'll talk about this tomorrow, John," Ricky replied, rolling his eyes.

"Oh, we'll talk tomorrow alright, but it won't be about me leavin' this cabin."

"'Nite John," Ricky said with a smile as they ventured back out onto the marshy trail.

The glow of the cabin quickly faded behind them, delivering them into nearly total darkness. "Shit, I can barely see my hand in front of my face. How are we going to get back?" Hal asked as he stopped at the edge of the tree line.

"Follow Ricky. Ricky knows the way back," Ricky answered. "I get that you know the trail really well, Ricky, but how can you even see the damn thing?" Hal asked, then looked in the direction he thought Ryan and Uli were. "Neither of you have a flashlight, do you? I didn't think to bring one. I didn't know we were going to stay that long."

"Ricky can get us back," Ricky insisted.

"What, do you have night vision?" Hal asked sarcastically.

There was a small pause before he heard Ricky answer: "Well... yeah."

It caught Hal off guard for a moment. He hadn't thought much of what he had asked, he was just teasing him. "Oh, uh... well then, lead on," Hal answered. He knew at some point they were going to end up having a strange conversation or two with Ricky, but his plan was to leave the subject alone for a while. He struggled to follow Ricky's dark silhouette ahead of him as he held his hand out to avoid running into a tree, or even into Ricky if he stopped suddenly. He wished he had his phone on him for a little light, but there was no reception at all anywhere in the area, so he'd left it at the farmhouse since no one would have been able to call him. He tried to keep a conversation going so he could at least hear where Ricky was, so he didn't wander off the trail away from everyone. "John is a super cool guy. He has one of the most powerful voices I've heard in a long time. He looked a little frail, though, I wonder if maybe he should see a doctor."

"Yeah, somethin's not right. Ricky was gonna ask Rob to pay him a visit before he goes back to Little Rock. John's gonna resist, but Ricky was gonna ask him to agree to a meeting with Rob as a personal favor tomorrow," Ricky said.

"Yeah, that'd probably be a good idea," Hal answered. "So, do you want to postpone going skating then until the day after tomorrow?"

"Nah, ther'll be time for both. Saturday is skate night. Gotta go on Saturday. Ricky'll go see John earlier in the day. Plus, Sunday we're gonna go meet everybody from town at the diner. We might be there all day."

"Oh, that's right," Hal said. He made it a few more steps before catching his shoe on something and fell forward into Ricky's back. Luckily, he didn't knock him over. "Uh, sorry!" Hal laughed as he straightened back up. "Tree root, I think."

"Y'all really can't see anything at all?" Ricky asked.

"No!" All three of them answered at once.

Ricky was silent again after that. They couldn't see his face of course, but Hal guessed from the tone of his voice that it was a genuine surprise to Ricky that their sense of vision wasn't as good as his. Hal tried to follow him by the sound of his footsteps on the dried twigs and leaves that littered the forest floor, but it was hard to pick out which were his, and which were Uli and Ryan's. "Ricky? You still right in front of me?" Hal asked.

"Yeah…" Ricky answered.

"We need to, like, talk about something here so I can know I'm still following you," Hal said.

"Uh, okay. What should we talk 'bout?" Ricky asked, and Hal thought about it for a second.

"Come on, Ricky. It's late. Don't ask me tough questions like this when it's late."

"Um…" Ricky started to say, then Ryan interrupted: "Hey! I know! Why don't we play a few rounds of I-Spy?"

"I hate you," Hal replied.

"No, no, really, I'm serious! Okay, okay, I'll choose first. I spy with my little eye something black," Ryan said.

Hal thought about it for a second, then answered: "Uli's soul?"

Another couple moments of stunned silence followed, then they heard Uli say: "*Excuse me?*"

"HOW THE FUCK DID YOU DO THAT IN ONE GUESS!?" Ryan yelled.

"I've lived with you long enough. I know how you think," Hal said, then added: "Sorry Uli, nothing personal. I just knew that was what he was thinking."

"Um… apology accepted… I think…" Uli replied.

"Okay, my turn," Hal said. "I spy with my little eye something black."

"The empty, dark space between Ryan's ears?" Uli asked.

"Oooohh. Good job. See? I'm not the only one good at this," Hal said.

"Ha… haa… *ha*…" Ryan answered.

They walked a few more yards ahead in the stillness while Hal pondered what to say next, when they started to catch sight of a few very small, dim lights in the distance. He watched in wonder as they slowly got closer and strained his eyes in the darkness to focus on them and try to figure out what they were. Once a few of them were within 50 feet or so, he finally realized what he was looking at: fireflies. A whole cluster of them. Over the course of about ten minutes, about 25 to 30 flew in and gathered around them, letting them see each other again out of the dense shadows.

"Is that better?" Ricky suddenly asked. Hal turned to look at him, stunned, but was met only with the sight of the back of Ricky's head. Ricky was walking with his hands in his pockets, hunched over slightly like he was trying to hide himself from the dim light.

"Uh… yeah. That's much better," Hal replied. "I… should be able to see what I'm stepping on now."

"Okey dokey," Ricky simply replied, and they continued in a silent march. The little bit of light made it so they could see Ricky to follow him, but it was only enough to let them see about three feet in any direction.

As they walked, it was like the earth appeared below Ricky's feet as he took each step, and then disappeared again behind Ryan's. Being in the complete dark was one thing, but now that they were travelling in what looked like a little moving bubble of existence through a dark abyss, it was oddly claustrophobic. Hal knew it was ridiculous because they were surrounded by open woods, but the darkness around them was so complete, it nearly looked like it had mass and substance to it as it enveloped them. It was like they were moving through a long tunnel of black fabric that was lifting barely enough to allow them to pass. It was one of the stranger things he had ever seen in his entire life. He felt his hands start to tingle, and he realized he was hyperventilating. He looked down and tried to focus on the visible tree debris passing under foot while he attempted to calm his breathing. *We're surrounded by open woods... we're surrounded by open woods.... we're surrounded by open woods....* he thought to himself. He looked forward to make sure he was still right behind Ricky, and was startled to see Ricky looking back at him. His eyes had the night animal glow on them, thanks to the light from the little bugs, and he looked concerned. *Was I breathing that loudly?* The thought went through his head.

"*You okay?*" Ricky formed the words with his lips without actually saying them. Hal looked at him for a moment, while he made himself start breathing more slowly. He nodded very slightly. Ricky obviously wasn't convinced, but he looked forward again, so he didn't run into anything as they kept walking.

"So, Ricky…" Ryan suddenly said, piercing the silence. It made Hal jump. "I gotta ask, do you talk about yourself in the third person because there's two of you in there?"

*Yeah, so much for leaving it be for a while,* Hal thought to himself. He felt bad for Ricky for having Ryan prying at him again, but as they walked, hearing normal conversation again helped to calm him down a bit.

"Uh… maybe…" Ricky answered quietly.

"So, like, what do you two talk about inside of your head?" Ryan asked.

"It's… not like that," Ricky said.

"Oh?" Ryan asked.

"It's not like it talks to Ricky, it's just… there."

"It is not sentient?" Uli asked.

"Uh, Ricky don't know what that word means." There was a hint of shame to his voice as he said it.

"Sentient. Having a human-like intelligence. Being greatly aware of one's own existence. Capable of developing elaborate plans to achieve one's goals. Having goals and reasons behind them…" Uli explained.

"No, no, it's not like that," Ricky said. "It's hard to explain. It's… it's sort of like havin' a pet that won't leave you alone. Like a dog that keeps jumpin' up on ya' and ya' have to keep shoving it off and tryin' to get it to sit down and behave so you can get your work done."

"So… it, like, wants you to do stuff sometimes, but it doesn't ever talk to you or try to take over?" Ryan asked.

"Yeah, kinda like that." Ricky answered.

"Hmm," Ryan replied. "Your dad mentioned that you seem to be able to call it up on command if you want."

"Yeah…" Ricky mumbled.

"But sometimes it will just show up on its own?"

"Yeah. Sometimes. It really is like a dog," Ricky said.

"An interesting way to think about it," Uli commented.

"Okay, so, what exactly does it want you to do when it shows up?" Ryan asked.

"Various things," Ricky said. "Mostly it's happy if Ricky goes and hangs out in the woods or a park for a while. That'll calm it down for a bit."

"Kind of like taking the dog for a walk," Ryan said.

"Yep," Ricky replied.

"So, all these times you've gone and snuck out at night, you were always finding a park or a patch of woods to just go hang out in?"

"Yeah," Ricky answered again.

Hal was listening to all this, amazed. Ricky was being unusually forth-coming with his answers. He wondered if it was a huge weight off his chest now that they finally knew. Then they heard Ryan sigh. "Ricky, I've sort of been an ass to you over the years when you didn't deserve it. I'm sorry, man," Ryan said, and Hal nearly felt his jaw hit the ground.

"It's… okay," Ricky said very quietly.

"No, it's really not," Ryan mumbled.

"Don't worry about it," Ricky replied.

After that, they walked without saying another word until they were the rest of the way out of the forest. When they stepped out of the tree line back onto the main dirt road, Ricky started heading back in the direction of his family's house. It took him a few moments to notice the other three weren't following anymore. He looked back to see them all standing still, gazing up. Sometime during their walk back, the clouds had broken, and the sky had opened to reveal more stars than any of the three of them had ever seen in their entire lives. Every inch of the sky had thousands of tightly clustered lights, with very little dark space between them. Shooting stars streaked across the sky every few minutes, and a few satellites, which, from where they were standing, looked like slow-moving shooting stars, made their way leisurely along their orbit paths. The Milky Way arced overhead and down to the horizon, revealing the circular curve of the earth, and removing the usual illusion of a flat sky. Ricky smiled to himself and walked back to join them. Another thing the country had that the city didn't that they hadn't experi-enced before. The little cluster of fireflies that had been with them began to disperse and flutter out into the field in front of them; gradually becoming little earth-bound stars themselves as they made their way into the distance. They ended up staying there for well over an hour, and by the time they got back, they were all tired enough that they ended up getting some decent sleep that night despite all the noise; both inside the room and out.

# CHAPTER 13

## (Welcome to the Jungle)

### BATTLE CREEK, MI

**The trip to see Ricky's** family apparently had quite an effect on Ryan and Uli, as Hal found (and secretly read), a hand-written letter from Ryan to his mom that he had hidden in his duffel bag. The letter was unsent, but at least written. Hal had been digging through Ryan's bags in search of his electric razor. The occurrence of finding each other's things in each other's luggage was an ongoing problem with them. Hal still couldn't figure out how it happened as much as it did since nobody seemed to be doing it on purpose. At first he thought the paper was going to be notes for a new song, and he decided to be nosy on what Ryan was working on. Ryan really didn't get enough credit for being a decent co-writer, and it was oddly something he didn't brag about. Though song notes, this little piece of paper was not.

> "Mom,
>
> I know it's been a while and that you and Dad probably still hate me, but please read this all the way before you decide to burn it. I know I've been a pain in the ass, but I do miss you guys sometimes. Yes, I just said that, and for what it's worth, I'm sorry. Anyways, as you can see I've enclosed 4 checks, one for you, one for Dad, one for Becky and one for Jeff. They won't bounce, but if you don't believe me, you can wait for them to clear the bank. Do whatever you want with them. Pay off the house, get a new car, buy stuff, whatever. If you want to talk to me, my email is —"

Hal dropped the letter back into the bag as he heard a door open, and he quickly darted out of the room and into the kitchen. Ryan was, thankfully, still sitting at the table, messing with his phone. Uli appeared a few seconds later and took a seat across from them.

"Well… how'd it go?" Hal asked.

"They said they love me and are proud of my success, but still want me to consider giving up music and come home to learn how to run the family business someday."

"Well, they said they're proud of your success. That's a start… right?"

"Yes, it is a start," Uli agreed.

Jim hung up his cell phone and looked up at Hal. "Okay… you guys have your first international tour set up starting in London on New Year's Eve. Your next album goes on sale in two weeks, you currently have five songs on the Billboard Top 40 and…"

"JIM! Good god, we just got home. Give it a rest, man. Don't you ever relax?" Hal said.

"No," Jim replied.

"Well… welcome to the Hulsing house! This is a good place to practice," Hal said, gesturing to the room around him. "Your first time here you're not supposed to be working."

"Just let me finish, there's only one more point of business," Jim insisted.

"Fine," Hal said.

"Okay, in two weeks I've got you booked to do an interview on the Marla Mathers show and…"

Hal, Uli, and Ryan all suddenly looked at him, appalled. "Please tell me that was a joke," Hal said.

"What?" Jim asked.

"That woman is a stupid airhead with a tacky show," Ryan said.

"Yeah, and that's coming from Ryan!" Hal pointed out.

"A stupid airhead with millions of viewers!" Jim replied.

"We already have millions of listeners, why subject ourselves to her mind-numbing drama?" Hal asked.

"Because it's good for your careers."

"But not for our mental health," Hal replied.

"Just… do it," Jim grunted. "You go on, you talk to her for half an hour, you have millions of women watch you, and you leave. It won't kill you."

"Jim, seriously, I want to keep the 'classy' rating at a certain level for us. I really don't want to be seen on her show," Hal pleaded.

"Okay, first of all, she's interviewed plenty of A-listers over the years and they've all survived to tell the tale. Second, just because you think she's 'tacky' doesn't mean you have to be. You're only the guests. Heck, give her a lesson in being classy while you're there. I don't care what you do. Whenever you make appearances on talk shows, the ratings always go up for the show, and your albums always see at least a little bump in sales following the episode airing. It's a win-win. You'll live," Jim said, then looked back down and began writing in his date book again.

Hal, Uli, and Ryan all tried for the next few days to talk him out of it, but nothing they did worked, and all too soon they found themselves in New York preparing for the show. They at least got to stay in a very upscale hotel. As their income increased over time, so did the quality of the accommodations. The elevator door opened on the sixteenth floor, and in their most boring street outfits, they made a quick dash for the room. They passed a few people in the halls, none of which gave them a second look. They found the room and slid in the key card, and as the door clicked open one last person went by. They held their breaths, then let out a sigh of relief as she passed. One thing none of them had pondered when they set out to make it big was the most terrifying thing in the world would turn out to be average people on the streets. They had good management and security, but a few times they were caught off guard, and once one person recognized them and yelled it out loud, it would become a mob scene very quickly. As they pulled their luggage in through the door, Hal gave one final glance down the hall, and saw the woman who had just passed them getting into the elevator. A few strands of purple hair hung out from underneath her hat. It gave him brief pause, but he reminded himself there were plenty of other people on the planet with purple hair. They threw their bags down and pulled out various laptops and phones.

"And now, for another episode of '*The Glamorous Secret Lives of Rock Stars,*'" Ryan announced as he popped open a bag of cheese doodles and sat down on the couch with his smart phone in the other hand.

"Day 153, we have successfully infiltrated the next facility without being noticed," Uli said.

"We are secure for the night, but what may be our toughest challenge yet awaits us in the morning," Hal added.

"Will our heroes survive to see another day? Stay tuned," Ricky finished.

Hal set up his laptop on the table, and he, Uli, and Ryan spent the next hour checking sports scores, posting updates on their Facebook Page, and reading the news. Ryan had given Ricky his old laptop to use, though he made sure to say he was just 'lending' it to him. And while Ricky had been skeptical at first, after much insisting, Ryan was able to convince him the internet was an amazing source of funny cat videos. Ricky was not disappointed. From there on out, while the other three of them would browse the internet quietly, they would do so to the sound of Ricky giggling to himself in the background. Hal finished posting his daily musings to their site blog, then had a quick flashback to the woman in the hall. On a whim, he went to Lyrica's website and clicked on the 'upcoming tour dates' tab. He scanned the screen for a few moments before he found she was playing a show at Madison Square Garden, only a couple blocks away from the hotel, the day after next. He had to stop himself from getting carried away. There were still tons of people in New York with purple hair. But… how many of them could afford to stay at a hotel like this? Hal looked at the other three briefly over his shoulder. "I'm hungry. I'm going to go down and get something in the bar."

"Why? We brought food," Ryan said.

"I know, but those cup of noodles get boring after a while. Plus, I'm just feeling restless. I want to go walk around for a while instead of being holed up in here," he said.

"Bad idea," Ryan warned.

"Yeah, I know," Hal said.

"What if someone recognizes you?" Uli asked sternly.

"I'm sure you'll hear the screaming. We're only on the sixteenth floor after all," Hal answered as he put his hat and glasses back on and got up.

"Good luck. Be careful. Make good choices," Ryan told him, and Hal replied he would as he left.

Ryan sighed disapprovingly. "Just as our heroes thought they were safe and sound for the night, Agent H decided, once again, to go do something stupid..."

Hal moved quickly across the lobby into the restaurant bar. The restaurant had more security than the main lobby of the hotel, so Hal took off his glasses, but left the hat on. He figured the whole time that she'd already be long gone, but to his surprise, there she was, sitting right in the middle of the bar in front of him. He sat down right next to her. She looked up, and he smiled warmly and waved. "*Are you stalking me!?*" she hissed at him.

"Well, no, actually. Our manager is forcing us to do the Marla Mathers show tomorrow around the corner, and you walked right by us as we were getting into our room," Hal said, and her eyes went into a squint as she glared at him. "True story," he added. She rolled her eyes as she took another sip of her drink. "So, did we start off on the wrong foot? I never meant to irritate you. I just thought it'd be interesting to talk to you since you've been in the industry longer than us."

"So, what do you want? A beginner's guide? A list of tips?" she asked.

"No, no. Just to talk. I mean, there's only so many people I get to talk to anymore. We talk to reporters and magazine people all the time, but we don't really *talk* to them, you know? Just answer their same questions over and over. The only people I get to talk to now are my parents and band mates,"

Hal explained, and as she was looking at him again now, stone-faced, he got the definite, unnerving feeling that she was scanning his soul for lies.

"I guess I… also have to admit I sort of would like to spend some time in the company of a beautiful, talented female singer as a last request, since I'm not entirely sure we're going to survive whatever Marla Mathers is going to do to us tomorrow," Hal said. She gave him a mildly disgusted look. "So… have you ever been on her show?" he asked.

"Unfortunately," Lyrica mumbled as she took another sip of her drink.

"Okay, um… so… do you have a list of tips, or a beginner's guide on surviving her drama?" Hal asked, and he thought he almost saw her smile, but she was quick to put a stop to it.

"Use very small words and don't mention puppies, whatever you do," she said, and Hal laughed.

"Good to know." The bartender came over and Hal ordered a drink, and while he did he watched Lyrica chug down the remaining half of hers, then order another.

"So… how's your night going?" he asked.

"Oh, y'know, same old, same old," Lyrica answered.

"You on a tour right now?"

"Yeah, I play Madison Square Garden the day after tomorrow."

"How long have you been on tour?" Hal asked.

"Sixteen months."

"Oh my God! That's too much! How much longer do you have?"

"One more month."

"Well, good luck! I know touring is tiring," Hal said.

"Thanks," Lyrica mumbled.

"So… you always drink alone when you're not working?"

"Yes."

"Just seems kinda lonely."

"Yeah, well, lonely is nice and quiet," she replied.

"Right..." Hal answered sheepishly. "But, uh, would it be too awful if I joined you for a bit tonight, and then take care of your whole bar tab again?"

Lyrica slowly turned to look at him. "You're one of those guys that likes to be abused, aren't you?"

"Well, uh, maybe," Hal replied. "I was a waiter in a steak house for many years, so I sort of got used to being abused, I guess."

Lyrica sighed. "Fine. Tomorrow is a rest day anyways. You can buy me all the damn drinks you want," she said as she took another long gulp.

You've had a bad day, huh?" Hal asked.

"What the hell does it matter to you?"

"I guess I hate to see someone who makes people so happy be so miserable themselves," he answered.

"What do you want?" she asked, exasperated.

"What do I want?" Hal said. "I... don't want anything. I have everything. What do *you* want?" he asked her back.

"What do I want?" she repeated, surprised. She realized she didn't know what to say. Nobody had asked her that for years. "What do I want?" She repeated it again.

"Yeah," Hal said. "What does Lyrica Wordsworth want?"

She squeezed the glass in her hands tightly, out of bewilderment and anger. *It's been another day from hell. I want some damn peace*, she thought to herself, but before she said it out loud, she was suddenly struck with another idea. The expression on her face softened as she looked back at him again. "Do you... *actually* like being abused?"

"Umm... uh... maybe?" Hal answered nervously.

"And you were a waiter, so I imagine you're pretty good at taking orders?"

Hal's eyes widened, and he looked at her for a moment or two before answering: "Yeah..." She leaned in closer to him, and in a hushed voice asked: "*How good?*"

He felt himself starting to sweat as he answered: "*You'll... have to tell me...*"

She pushed the door to her room open forcefully with her foot, holding the hotel keycard in one hand, and pulling Hal along by his tie with the other. The door slammed shut behind them, and she put her hand on his back and shoved him onto the bed. "Wait there," she said as she walked into the bathroom. Hal pushed himself up so he was sitting, wiping the sweat from his brow as he looked around the room. He couldn't believe this was actually happening. He took his hat and coat off and tossed them onto the floor, then waited. He waited for what felt like a long time. She was taking forever in there. Perhaps this was her first method of torture. He got up to walk around the room a bit and made his way to the window to look at the city lights below.

> **206.** "Mirrors" by Natalia Kills *to play over this scene*

Suddenly, everything went dark as he felt a piece of fabric pulled over his eyes. "Ready to take some orders, waiter?" he heard her say in his ear.

"*Yes, ma'am,*" he answered eagerly.

She tied whatever it was she had over his eyes into a knot, and he was once again shoved down onto the bed. He rolled over onto his back, then felt her weight on his chest as she sat down on him, straddling his stomach. She began to unbutton his shirt. "Generally, I'm a chicken sort of girl, but I suppose I could go for a steak tonight."

"Excellent choice. How would you like it? Rare, medium, well done?"

"Oh, let's go medium-well. I don't like my meat too pink," she said as she pulled his tie off and used it to tie one of his wrists to the bed post.

"Alright. And can I interest you in a red wine to pair with it?"

"A simple pinot noir please." She finished the knot, then pulled off his shirt, which she used to secure his other wrist to the headboard.

"Coming right up," he said in a shaky voice.

"*I bet…*" she whispered under her breath as she started to undo his pants, and he exhaled heavily as she pulled them down his legs, his boxer shorts going along with them. "You know what, hold on a second. I want to see what else there is on the menu." Hal started hearing scraping and dragging sounds in the room.

"Okay…" he answered. The dragging sounds stopped, then there was the light clicking of what sounded like writing. He waited with great anticipation, until suddenly he heard a door open and close, and then there was silence.

> **End Song 206**

"Uh… Lyrica?" he asked. There was no response. "Lyrica?" He leaned his head over and nudged the blindfold up off one eye with his shoulder. He was alone. The side table next to the bed had been moved to the foot of the bed, and the room phone sat on top of it. The picture on the wall directly in front of the bed had been taken down, and in its place a scribbled note had been forced over the nail:

*Front desk is *1*

*And to answer your question,*
*you are very good at taking orders.*

*Love, Lyrica*

Hal tried to pull his wrists free, but found the knots she had tied him up in to be quite strong. He got the feeling she had tied a few other men up in her time. He brought his foot up over his head, and tried to work his toes into the fabric with no luck. He struggled and strained for a few minutes to try and loosen the fabric, but eventually gave up and kicked the phone off the receiver and dialed the *1 keys and then hit the speakerphone button with his big toe. There had been some doubt in his mind before, but this removed all uncertainty. He was in love.

"Good morning, everyone! And welcome to Marla's Matters! I'm really excited for today because we have not only one, but two totally hot bands to talk to!"

"Huh? Who else is here?" Hal whispered to Ricky, Uli, and Ryan. None of them had any idea.

"Battle Creek and Sugar Swamp!"

The audience shrieked and cheered in a crazed frenzy.

"You've got to be kidding me..." Hal said.

"Shit, we have to deal with those jackasses as well as her!?" Ryan asked.

"This is going to be a *great* day," Hal mumbled.

"It is my extreme pleasure to welcome both of you onto the show today. Come on out, guys!"

Hal, Uli, Ricky, and Ryan walked across the stage waving and attempting to smile while the audience made up entirely of teenage girls went crazy. Sugar Swamp appeared from the opposite side of the set, waving enthusiastically and flashing confident smiles. Battle Creek sat down on the couch on the left side of Marla and Sugar Swamp took a seat on the right.

"Oh my gosh! Hi guys! I'm sooo excited to meet you. I'm like, both of your biggest fan!"

"It's a pleasure to meet you as well," Hal said politely.

She turned her attention to the other side of the desk. "And a very sweet *hello* to you guys too!"

"Hi, sweetheart," the lead singer of Sugar Swamp, Brad, replied.

"So, guys, the reason I invited you both here today is because I heard that you were having an argument over who was the better, hotter band. And me being the caring person that I am, decided myself and my viewers would help settle this for you once and for all!"

"*What? When did that happen?*" Ryan whispered to Hal, who rolled his eyes as the crowd started screaming again.

"Why do you even need to invite them here? You already know the answer," Brad said.

"I dunno, they're both pretty hot, right girls?" she asked her audience, and they screamed wildly at her queue.

"Honestly guys, I have to say that I think it's a tie in the sexy category. What I want to try and settle is which one of you is the better band."

"And how do you plan on doing that?" Hal asked, pretending he cared.

"Okay, so you both have an album coming out in a week or so. The winner will be decided by who sells more albums on the first day. Isn't that a great idea!?" Marla giggled.

"Oh, okay. That's not so bad. That'll be an easy win," Ryan said confidently, and Hal and Uli nodded.

"Not so fast, punk boy. This next album is going to be our big one. Yours doesn't stand a chance," Brad replied.

"Punk boy? Really?" Ryan mocked him.

"You know what, you skinny little…" Brad stood up, but was held back by his drummer.

"Whoa, whoa, whoa. No fighting on set. My producers said we don't have that type of insurance. However, I do have a little twist to this competition, if you're up for it," she said, slyly.

"What's that?" Brad asked, intrigued.

"My challenge to you, if you can handle it, is the losing band gets to do a concert here in New York… BUTT… NAKED…" The audience gasped at the suggestion. Brad immediately developed an intrigued smile, while the four members of Battle Creek looked at each other confused, and Hal shrugged his shoulders.

"Well, do you guys accept my challenge?" Marla asked.

"Of course," Brad said.

"Uh, sure?" Hal answered. "If they really want to get naked that bad."

"Oh no, you guys will be the ones flashing your pale asses in New York," Brad said.

"Um, I'm really not interested in arguing here, but I do think we sell more albums than you, by, like, a lot," Hal said calmly. "I don't have the numbers in front of me, but I think it's a pretty big gap."

"And I'm not saying you're wrong about the numbers right now, what I am saying is you're going to get a big surprise in a week when the tables turn on who sells more with their new album."

"If you say so..." Hal didn't really want to keep the conversation going anymore.

"Oh, we do say so," Brad growled, then added: "Have fun in New York." And the audience stood up and burst into screams and applause.

Once they got home later the following day, Hal relayed the strange events to his mother. "It was bizarre. This other band Sugar Swamp was there, and they agreed to a bet with us they have no way of winning."

"I think I've heard of that group, unfortunately," Cecilia said. "They're always on the tabloid covers for all the immature things they do."

"Yeah, well, they can add this one to the list," Hal said.

"What did they bet you?"

"Well, they didn't bet us, Marla came up with the idea, but they agreed to a bet that that their album will sell more copies on its release date than ours will. And, the group that sells less than the other on the first day would have to do a concert naked in New York."

"What?" Cecilia said, disgusted.

"Yeah, really. I dug up the numbers for our last release and their last release. They sold 35,000 total copies in the first week it was out. I couldn't find data for the first day alone, but our last album sold about 100,000 on the first week. So, 100,000 compared to 35,000 in the same amount of time isn't exactly a close margin."

"Not exactly," Cecilia agreed.

"So, I'm not quite sure what they were thinking by agreeing to this, but I've developed three theories," Hal explained.

"Okay…" Cecilia answered.

"Theory number one, they thought it would be a good publicity stunt, and they have no intent on following through with it. Theory number two, they actually wanted to do a concert naked, and were conveniently handed an excuse to do so. Theory number three, they're complete idiots. And then I guess I have a fourth theory, and that being it's some combination of the other three."

"Fame makes some people crazy. It seems to me like it's this big, nasty game of who can get more attention, and the thing behind all of it is money," Cecilia said.

"Sounds about right," Hal agreed.

"Well, have fun with that," Cecilia said.

"Yeah, we will. Have a good time at dinner," Hal told his mom as she pulled her coat out of the closet.

"We will. See you later," she said as she and Harvey went out the front door, leaving Hal alone in the kitchen. Uli was in his room listening to Holy Hell's fourth album loud enough that Hal could hear every word, even though he was listening to it with his headphones on. Ryan had left earlier to go hang out with a few of his former co-workers from the hardware store that he had sort of been friends with. They had planned to meet up at one of the guy's houses for a long night of drinking and video games. Ricky had been in his room for hours, strumming slow songs on his guitar, and even singing quietly by himself.

207. "Song Sung Blue" by Neil Diamond

Hal pushed the door open a crack and found him sitting on the edge of the bed, looking out the window as he played. Since they'd gotten home from the trip to see his family a few weeks ago, he'd been acting more depressed than ever before. Hal couldn't figure it out. His family appeared happy to see him and was supportive of him. They'd gotten successful enough that he was able to help them pay off their house and farm equipment. He got to see his friend John, and they'd all finally found out about his bizarre secret, which Hal thought would have been a huge load off his mind. But something was still bothering him. Hal thought for a while maybe he had been worried about John's health, which would have been completely understandable. But he had to remind himself he'd been acting like this since before he saw John looking sick. Had one cause to worry led straight into another when the first ended? Something didn't seem right about that. Hal could understand why he would have been occasionally nervous and scared about them finding out, but it didn't make sense that it would have made him depressed as much as he was. Hal began to wonder if Ricky was a classic case of someone unwilling to take their own advice and see a doctor. From what he had observed of Ricky for the last few years, that seemed quite possible. He was concerned enough about a friend to force them to get help even if it upset them, but was then unwilling to admit to himself that maybe he needed help. Hal figured it was long overdue that he go ask him what the hell was bothering him so much, though he was hoping for a better opportunity than just barging into his room.

> End Song 207

He pulled the door shut gently and walked into his own room and sat down at the desk. They were leaving on an international tour in a few months, and that was going to be a lot of stress, so it'd be good to figure out what's going on and deal with it soon. He knew all four of them were going to have to be in the best state they could be if they were going to survive travelling all over the world for a whole year. They wouldn't just have the tour to survive, they'd have to survive dealing with each other with no breaks for that long as well.

After a long day of recording footage for a music video, Ryan collapsed down on the couch next to Hal in the fancy L.A. hotel suite. "This is going to be good," he said as he opened a can of beer. "Maybe we can take a picture of all our butts and send it to them as a consolation gift."

"Wouln'mf wont to brefk ur kamra…" Ricky said from the kitchenette with half of a ham sandwich in his mouth.

"Ricky, if only you knew what that camera phone has seen," Ryan responded. Uli sat alone at the table behind them writing lyrics. "Oh, come on Uli, you know you want to watch this."

"Not really. There is no plot, and the ending is predictable," Uli replied.

"Whatever," Ryan mumbled and turned up the volume on the TV.

"As you all know, today the highlight of our show is the opening day's sales results for Battle Creek's and Sugar Swamp's albums that came out this last Tuesday. This will decide who wins the bet, and who loses and will be obliged to put on a super-awkward concert in New York. We're going to cut right to the chase here since I'm eager to find out for myself…" Marla said. Hal and Ryan leaned closer to the TV. "Battle Creek opened with 25,000 in sales…" Hal and Ryan froze.

"Why… so… low…?" Hal whispered.

"And Sugar Swamp opened with a surprising 40,000 sales, which means that Battle Creek will be doing a women-only concert completely naked at the…" Uli's pen fell silent and Ricky started choking on a piece of his sandwich in the kitchen. Hal looked over to see Ryan staring at him in shock. Marla continued: "But, I think it should also be noted that on day two of the two albums' releases that Battle Creek caught up with a whopping 150,000 in sales while Sugar Swamp only had an additional 20,000…"

"Our fans boycotted us!" Ryan said in disbelief. He stood up. "OUR FANS... FUCKING BOYCOTTED US... TO... TO SEE US NAKED," he said loudly. Then added, in an admiring tone: "That's... amazing..."

Hal stared at the TV in silent terror until he felt the back of his neck burning, then slowly turned around to see Uli giving him a homicidal stare. "HAL..."

"Hey, hey... wait a second..." Hal said, standing up, slowly backing away across the room. "You heard the numbers, we really *should* have won that bet... plus, none of you were screaming 'No!' because we were all thinking the same thing. Don't blame me..."

Uli stood up and walked quickly across the room, grabbing a cowering Hal by his shirt collar once his back was against the wall. "You are going to explain to the TV reporters and all the fans that we will not be participating in this idiocy as the bet was not fair. They can see from the day two sales that we should have won that bet, but agreeing to it out loud ultimately skewed the results. You will explain this to them when you let them know we will decline to do this show."

"Yep, will do!" Hal agreed with a nervous smile.

"Good," Uli said, then let go of him, and went back to the table where he began furiously writing more lyrics. Ricky leaned into the room from the kitchen, catching his breath after coughing out the piece of sandwich. "Yeah... what... he said..." he agreed, pointing in Uli's direction.

"I don't know, it might not be that bad. I mean, we clearly should have won. It's obvious what happened looking at the numbers, so there's really no argument *'we're the better band'*..." Ryan said in a high-pitched girly voice, mocking Marla. "But lots of our lovely lady fans obviously think it's a popular idea, and it might be kind of fun... to..." Ryan quit talking as he turned to look at Uli, who was also giving him a homicidal stare. "Um, yeah. Never mind. Have fun with that, Hal."

Hal sat back down on the couch, looking miserable as he watched the rest of the announcement. "I don't know about you ladies, but I can't wait for the tickets to go on sale!" the TV blared loudly, and the show's audience was screaming so loud it looked like Marla was trying to say something else, but even with her microphone on, it all got drowned out by the sound.

"I'll call Jim first thing in the morning and get it all straightened out," Hal muttered.

"Yes, yes you will," Uli agreed.

The next morning, Hal woke up to the sound of the phone ringing. He picked it up blindly. "Hello?"

"Morning, Hal."

"Hi, Mom," Hal said.

"Um, have you been watching the news as of late?" Cecilia asked. Hal had to think for a second before he realized what she was talking about. "Oh, you saw the announcement on the Marla's Matters show last night, huh? Yeah, I didn't see that one coming, but I was going to call Jim today to get it all straightened out since the results were obviously skewed."

"Um, you might want to get on that... soon," Cecilia said, concerned.

"What?" Hal asked.

"You obviously just woke up and haven't turned on the TV yet today, have you?"

"Um, no... why?"

"You... might want to turn on the TV and call your manager ASAP," his mother warned. The concern in her voice was suddenly making him feel more awake.

"Um, okay. I'll do that right now." Hal jumped up out of bed and went looking for the TV remote.

"Okay... let me know how it goes," his mom said.

"I, uh, will, thanks."

"Okay. Love you, Hal, good luck."

"Love you too, Mom, bye." He hung up the phone, found the remote, and turned the TV on in a panic.

"Ohmygod, I'll live on the sidewalk in a tent for a month if I have to in order to get a ticket!" A wild-eyed young woman said into the microphone in the reporter's hand. The huge crowd of women behind her yelling and waving at the camera. Hal threw open the door from his room to find the TV in the common room of the suite turned onto another news channel that Uli, Ricky, and Ryan were all watching in terror. "Well, we haven't heard anything yet, but we'd certainly be willing to re-schedule a few shows if they'd like to contact us and make this the venue of choice since this is obviously going to be such a huge event," a slightly confused looking man in a suit said to another reporter.

"These people are all sick!" Hal said loudly, startling the other three.

"Ah! The sleeping prince is finally awake!" Uli said angrily as he started to stand up.

"Okay, okay! You don't have to say anything! I got it! I'm going to put a stop to this insanity right now!" Hal said as he pulled out his cell phone, dialing a number as he marched back into his room, quickly changed out of his lounge pants into a better outfit, and marched out the suite door. "Hello, Jim? We need to talk!" He pulled the door shut hard behind him, leaving the other three speechless, though in a rather impressed sort of way.

A few hours later, however, he returned looking a lot less confident. "Uh, we've got problems…" Hal said uncomfortably as he stepped back into the room.

"What do you mean we've got problems!?" Uli said sternly. "They had better not be naked concert problems!"

"Look! I tried to talk sense to Jim for two whole hours! He's being as stubborn about this as he was about us going on that stupid show in the first place!"

"Are you saying Jim thinks this is a good idea!?" Uli asked.

"He thinks it's going to be amazing for publicity and that the show itself is going to be a cash cow," Hal said.

"Too bad! It is a simple matter of explaining to him we are not going to do it, period!"

"Okay, YOU tell him that!" Hal said, shoving his phone into Uli's hands. "I tried!" Hal went into his room, slamming the door behind him.

"I will!" Uli yelled after him and began dialing Jim's number. The phone rang, and Jim picked up.

"*Hello, Hal…*" Jim said calmly.

"This is not Hal, this is Uli," Uli replied. "Hal may be weak-minded enough for you to manipulate him and send him on a guilt trip or whatever it is you did, but those tricks will not work on me!"

"*Uli, let me explain to you what I explained to Hal. This is already all over the news, and if you back out now, not only will you be losing out on all the money there is to be made on this, but you will also be branded as cowards.*"

"Cowards!? What about the branding of classless, disgusting slimeballs we are going to get if we do go through with this!?"

"*I'm not denying either way you're going to get labeled as something unappealing because of this. But if you go through with it, you at least end up as slimeballs who got another fat paycheck as opposed to cowards who didn't make a single dollar on the deal.*"

"That is insignificant! That is only short-term thinking! We are making good money and will continue to do so regardless, but doing this could cost us some fans who think it is a disgusting act and will make them think less of us! Plus, we do have fans who are children!"

"*Uli, this is really simpler than you're trying to make it. You lost a bet. Explain to your fans that this isn't something you'd normally do, and that you really didn't think you were going to lose that bet, but that you wish to be men of your word. They'll understand.*"

"Perhaps you have forgotten, Jim, you technically work for us. We can fire you and get a new manager," Uli growled.

*"Yeah, you certainly could. You're right. But I am only doing my job. You hired me to make you famous and to make you money. That's exactly what I did, and what I'm continuing to do. And you don't have to take my word for this, but there's plenty of nastier managers out there than me. I only wish the best for all of us financially."*

"That is all there is to you in this world? Money?"

*"Yeah, pretty much."*

"Well, at the end of the day it is not worth our self-respect. We will not do it. Please start explaining this to the press."

*"Okay, I'll do it. But after you see the reaction from your followers, you may change your mind."*

"We will deal with our fans," Uli reassured him.

*"Okay… suit yourself…"* Jim replied with disturbing confidence, and then hung up.

# CHAPTER 14

## (Hot Stuff)

*NEW YORK*

"I can't believe we're doing this," Uli mumbled as he peered between the curtains.

"After that onslaught of media questions and fan bitching, I can," Hal grumbled, then added: "I'm just glad this whole mess will be over in a few hours."

"I will never live this down with my parents," Uli lamented.

"Uli, you'll probably make more tonight than your parents will in the next six months, remind them of that," Ryan said as he pushed Uli aside to look at the audience between the tiny gap in the curtains. "I didn't know that there were this many pretty girls on earth," he said, excited.

"Guys, I'm really sorry about this," Hal said.

"It is not your fault Hal, you were right when you said that. None of us tried to stop you because we didn't realize what would happen," Uli answered.

"Yeah, we'll all survive," Ryan said, unflustered.

"I sure hope so," Hal said as he looked back at Ricky, pacing nervously back and forth while pretending to be tuning his guitar. "I really hope he doesn't pass out or get sick or something."

"What he needs is some liquid courage," Ryan said, pulling a gold colored glass bottle out of one of his bags.

"You know he's not going to drink any of it," Hal said.

"Well, maybe tonight he'll make an exception," Ryan replied as he went over to him. "Hey, man," Ryan said, and Ricky looked up at him nervously. "Here, take a few gulps of this." Ryan tossed the bottle to him, and Ricky reacted in just enough time to catch it. "A bit will make you less nervous, a little more and you won't be nervous at all. Or, if you really want to go for it, a few glasses and you might actually want to take your clothes off."

"An' then forget how to play the guitar," Ricky said as he handed the bottle back.

"Uh, well, there is that…" Ryan admitted. "But you don't hit that point until at least a few glasses." Ryan held the bottle at arm's length. "Couple sips?"

"No thanks," Ricky mumbled.

"Ricky, you're going to be miserable. This will help lessen it. Do yourself a favor and be less miserable," Ryan insisted.

"Never had any before. Don't know what it will do to Ricky. Don't want to get sick or look stupid on stage," Ricky said.

"Ricky, first of all, we're all going to look stupid on stage, so don't worry about that. Second, a little glass won't make you drunk, even if you've never had any. I promise."

"Really shouldn't…"

"I've never seen anything else upset your stomach, I think this would help you relax a bit. It's going to be much worse if you go out on stage and have a panic attack."

Ricky stared quietly at his feet. "Just… don't want to risk doin' anything… weird," he finally said.

"Like I said, a little bit won't bring you to that point, but should anything happen, we're all here with you. Remember, Hal is the master of elaborate excuses," Ryan said. "We've got your back, I promise."

Ricky examined the bottle carefully for a little while, but ultimately answered 'no thanks.'

"Alright…" Ryan relented. "If you change your mind when we're between songs, just let me know."

"'Kay," Ricky answered.

Ryan headed back over towards the other three with the bottle, and Hal spoke up: "He might not want any, but I think me and Uli might take you up on it."

"I figured you would," Ryan said, pulling a couple paper cups out of his bag. "A couple shots for good luck." He poured three small cups and passed them out. "To the best concert we'll ever do."

"May it be over quick," Hal added.

"And may we never speak of this night again," Uli finished.

"God, you'd think we were leading you two to the gallows," Ryan said with disdain.

"Hey, you and Ricky at least have your drums and guitar to sort of hide behind. Me and Uli are screwed," Hal said.

"Hopefully, we'll all be screwed after the show is over," Ryan replied, taking down the glass in one long gulp. "And don't worry, I will do my best to not hide behind the drums all night," he promised.

"Well, are we ready to do this?" Hal asked.

"No," Uli answered.

"Cool. Let's go." Hal got up and reached for his bass. Ryan was right behind him while Uli and Ricky followed reluctantly. The set had just gone completely dark from the lights that were on during set up, and in the dark they were hit with the first round of wild screaming. They got into place, then waited for the queue to start right before the beginning lights came on.

208. "Sexy Back" by Justin Timberlake

Uli started a beat on his electric keyboard, and Hal swallowed hard, then began to sing right as the lights came on. There was screaming, immediately followed by a little booing, which Hal expected. They all agreed walking out onto stage naked would be too artless, so they would lose their clothes throughout the first song. Once Hal started taking his shirt off, the booing stopped immediately, which he also expected. The instrumentals for the entire first song had been pre-recorded, since it's a little hard to undress while trying to play an instrument, but they were going to play over and along with it as much as they could. Hal worked one finger into his tie and began to slowly loosen it. It hit the floor, and the screaming got louder. He started on the shirt next. He hoped to hell that nothing was going to go wrong throughout the night, and that Uli, Ricky, and Ryan would just do their part so he wouldn't have to look back at them much. He wasn't too concerned about Ryan, but the thought that Uli and/or Ricky might get too freaked out to keep playing at some point lingered in his mind. He threw the shirt out into the crowd, and there was a mad dash for it. He'd seen Ricky get quite red a few times when his mom would compliment him or something, and Hal imagined he was about that shade of red by this point, if not worse. Hal was going to find the nicest restaurant in town the next night and buy them all dinner, since they were about to spend a few hours having to look at his pale backside. None of them really deserved that. He started on his pants, the screaming got louder. There had been a few other points of screaming while he was in the middle of working on an article of clothing, which made him think the other three had lost at least a few things. He slowly worked his pants down his legs. He'd worn his dorkiest pair of boxers for laughs, and laughs he heard as he stood there in his yellow smiley face shorts. This was the part he was looking forward to the least. He had resolved to try and enjoy the performance as much as possible, but even with thousands of screaming women in front of him, he still had a bit of trouble losing the shorts.

End Song 208

When the song came to an end, he wiped the sweat from his brow, trying not to tremble as he raised the microphone. "Uh… hello ladies," he said casually. The screaming nearly drowned his voice out entirely. "We thought it would be a little weird to just walk out here naked, so I hope you can forgive us for that." The screaming that followed certainly sounded like forgiveness. "So, I guess we thought the moral of this story for Sugar Swamp was going to be 'don't make bets with people who are smarter than you.' But I guess we've found out the hard way you shouldn't make bets with people who are dumber than you, either. Because, who knows. Maybe that one time, they were smarter than you," Hal said, and the audience laughed as they started the next song.

> 209. "Light My Fire" (Radio Edit) by The Doors
>
> 210. "Burning Love" by Elvis Presley
>
> 211. "Pour Some Sugar on Me" by Def Leppard
>
> 212. "Do Ya Think I'm Sexy?" by Rod Stewart

The shock value gradually wore off throughout the rest of the show, and by the end they were mostly playing like they would any other night. Though Ricky kept his guitar quite close the whole night. Fear is tiring, and it wasn't something they could keep up while trying to focus on playing. Despite this being the case, the lights falling after the last song ended sent them scrambling for the safety of backstage.

> End Songs 209 – 212

Hal woke up the next morning on the hotel room couch with a nasty hangover. He lay still for a few moments trying to figure out what day it was, then remembered what they had done the night before. He sat up quickly, which was a mistake as it sent his head pounding. Ryan noticed from the kitchen nook, where he and Uli and Ricky were eating breakfast. "Look, he lives…" Ryan said.

"Sort… of…" Hal said, clutching his forehead.

"Yeah, I think you took a few too many shots between songs," Ryan said.

"Did I?" Hal replied.

"Oh, shit, do you not remember last night?"

"I remember most of it… just, not the end, I guess. Did we survive?"

Ryan looked briefly around the room before answering: "Yeah, I think we survived."

"That's good," Hal mumbled.

"So, what's the last thing you remember?"

Hal had to sit and think for a moment, then said: "Burning Love?"

"So, you don't remember anything after that?" Ryan asked.

"I might later, but not at the moment," Hal admitted, then noticed Ryan, Uli, and Ricky were looking at him a little oddly. He cringed. "Oh, God, what did I do? Did I start singing off key and ruin the end?"

"No, that was all fine. We made it to the end."

Hal put his head in his hands and asked again: "What did I do?"

"Well, you… sort of… did some pole dancing with the microphone stand," Ryan informed him.

Hal spread his fingers over his face so one wide-open eye was visible. "So… basically I was being a stupid drunk ass all over the stage?" he whimpered.

"Well, I wouldn't quite say that," Ryan said.

"What do you mean?" Hal asked. Ryan sat silently for a moment, thinking. "What?" Hal insisted.

"I'm trying to figure out how to put this without it sounding really weird coming from me," Ryan answered, then sort of squinted at him suspiciously. "That wasn't the first time you've done some pole dancing, was it?"

Hal took a moment to come up with one of his elaborate excuses, but was too hung over to think straight, so he gave Ryan the honest answer instead. "Uh, it was the first time I had a full audience watching."

"Fair enough. MOVING ON," Ryan replied.

"Okay, wait, it's not what you think…" Hal said.

"Dude, I don't want to know," Ryan tried to stop him.

"No, look, when I was in college in New York I dated a stripper for a while. And sometimes when she was drunk, she'd start teaching me her moves. And, I don't know, she was sort of cute when she was drunk and trying to teach me to pole dance. And chances were if she was drunk, I was probably drunk too, so I just sort of went with it, and we usually had a good laugh about it the next day."

Ryan looked at him blankly for a few seconds. "Okay, you're right. That was way less disturbing than I thought it'd be."

"Yeah," Hal said.

"Yeah," Ryan agreed.

"That was Annaliese, right?" Uli asked with an amused smile.

"Yep," Hal confirmed.

"Anyways, while we're still sort of on the subject, I should probably mention Jim called earlier."

"Oh, what now?" Hal asked.

"Apparently last night was professionally recorded, and since it all went well-ish he was thinking about having it put on DVD for sale since the show sold out so quick," Ryan said. Hal developed an even more glazed over expression, and slowly lay back down on the couch.

"Tell him to take that idea and shove it up his…"

Right then, Hal's phone began to ring. Ryan went over and grabbed it off the counter. "Here, you can tell him yourself." Ryan looked at the screen. "Oh. Never mind. It's your mom."

Hal's open hand appeared over the back of the couch, facing Ryan. Ryan tossed the phone, and Hal caught it, and it disappeared out of sight as it made its way down to his ear. "Hello?"

"*Morning, Hal. Just calling to make sure you're all okay.*"

"We survived," he mumbled.

"*OK, you don't sound too good, though.*"

"Oh, I'm fine. Just took in a little too much, um, 'liquid courage' throughout the show."

"*Oh, OK. I don't need any other details, just wanted to make sure you were all alive and accounted for.*"

"Yep. Ricky, Ryan, and Uli are all mostly OK too."

"*Good. Well, that was mostly why I was calling. There was one other thing, but it's not urgent. Maybe I should call back later.*"

"No, I'm awake. Go ahead," Hal answered.

"*Well, I mean, it's not urgent, but it is sort of 'news' for us. Why don't you go back to bed and call me when you're not hung over.*"

"Well, now you have my attention," he said. "What's the news?"

"*Well, I called to tell you… just how close you came to being an only child.*"

"Wh… what?" Hal asked quietly, and as quiet in some ways can be louder than it seems, Ricky, Uli, and Ryan were all suddenly leaning over the couch in wonder.

"*Um… Hal, you're going to be a big brother in eight months or so.*"

"No… way!" he said, sitting up.

"*Way,*" Cecilia answered.

"I thought you… uh…"

"*Yeah, that's what me and your dad and my doctor thought too. But, uh, surprise!*"

"Wow, Mom, that's… awesome. I guess. I mean, are you going to be okay?"

"*Well, I think so. The doctor's going to keep a close eye on my progress, of course. So, yeah. Huge surprise, but might be fun.*"

"Well, congratulations."

"*Thank you, Hal.*"

"So, Ricky and Uli and Ryan are all hovering here wondering what the hell we're talking about. You want me to tell them, or should I put you on speakerphone and you can do it?"

"*Oh, put me on speakerphone.*"

"Alright." Hal pushed a button, and the fuzzy backdrop sound of the speakerphone function could be heard.

"What's up Mrs. H?" Ryan asked loudly.

"*Hi, guys. I was just telling Hal how close he came to being an only child.*"

"WHAT!?" Ryan, Ricky, and Uli shouted together.

"Wait, are you adopting a kid?" Ryan asked.

"*Nope. I'm pregnant.*"

"Holy shit! Do you know who the father is?" Ryan asked.

"*Oh, Ryan. If only I could reach through this phone and slap you,*" Cecilia said. There was a brief pause before she heard a loud smacking sound on the other end of the line, and the muffled sound of Ryan swearing right afterwards. "There, took care of it for ya mom," Hal said.

"*Thanks, sweetie. I appreciate it,*" She replied.

"Just making sure! Jeez," Ryan complained as he rubbed his face.

"How far along are ya?" Ricky asked.

"*About a month, so the baby will probably be born while you're still on tour, assuming I don't miscarry.*"

"Now, don't say that!" Ricky said.

"*I'm forty-six, guys. It could happen, though I'm going to do my best to prevent that.*"

"It's too bad we will not be around when you're due," Uli said.

"*That's okay. We'll be waiting for you when you get back. Speaking of which, when are you coming home next? I do get to see you before you ship off to Europe in a month, right?*"

"Oh, yeah. I forgot to give you the update. We'll be home for a couple weeks from the 14th to the 28th. We leave on the 29th to do the New Year's show in London," Hal said.

"*Oh, good. So, you'll be home for Christmas.*"

"Yes, we will."

"*Good, we'll have to spend as much quality time as possible before you go.*"

"Yes, Mom. We'll have a lot of prepping to do, but I think quality time is certainly going to be part of that."

"*Good. Alright, well, glad you're all OK, and let me know what time to expect you on the 14th when you get your agenda.*"

"I will. Hopefully you'll be feeling OK in the weeks, and I guess, months to come."

"*I'll be fine. See you all in a bit.*"

"Good luck, Mrs. H," Ryan said.

"*Thanks guys.*"

"Love you, Mom."

"*Love you too, Hal. Get some sleep. Bye.*"

"Bye." Hal hung up, but couldn't go back to sleep after that, not with a new worry to add to the list as they prepared for their upcoming tour. And on top of it all, there had been something else on his mind that now resurfaced and added itself to the mix. They wouldn't be home for most of the upcoming year, and he had unfinished business with a certain fellow singer. Away from prying eyes in his room, he pulled out his laptop and brought up Lyrica Wordsworth's website. He clicked on the 'tour' tab and found the list of upcoming shows. Her tour snaked all across the country, but was set to stop in Chicago on December 16. That'd be about a 2 ½ to 3-hour drive from his house, but that was about as good of a chance as he was going to get. He just needed to come up with some sort of excuse to be gone for a day, but seeing as how close to Christmas it was, perhaps a little 'Christmas shopping' was in order...

He left the house around six at night, to avoid at least part of the rush hour mess on the way there. He knew that'd put him there well before the concert ended, so he brought his best incognito clothes and decided maybe he would do a little Christmas shopping in the area. The show was supposed to end around eleven p.m.. Add a little time for her to get out of her stage outfits for the night, and he figured she'd probably be leaving the venue around midnight. And from the concerts they had done in Chicago, he had a pretty good idea of what hotel she'd be staying at. He started waiting outside the front of the hotel around eleven thirty, and talked on his phone for a while. His mom had called to ask where he was shopping so late, and he told her he had gotten hungry and stopped for some dinner on the way back. He stood there for over an hour, doing his best to look casual and bored so no one gave him a second look. Finally, around twelve thirty, a heavily tinted black car pulled into the parking garage entrance suddenly. He followed it down. Once it had parked, he walked quickly up to the car, and as the door opened, a middle-aged business man stepped out. He caught sight of Hal and stared him down suspiciously. Hal stopped in his tracks. "Oh, you're not Sarah. I'm sorry, sir, her car looks just like yours," Hal said, then turned around and walked back up to street level. A few minutes later, another tinted vehicle pulled into the garage. This time, an elderly woman and her husband stepped out. Hal went back up. Ultimately, he waited until one thirty in the morning before he gave up. Either this was the wrong hotel, she had somehow snuck in the back, or she was still out partying. He started down the road back to the garage he had parked in. A block away from the hotel, a purple sports car suddenly zoomed past, and he stopped. He knew he might be fooling himself, but he had a feeling about it this time. He turned and looked to see it go into the hotel parking garage. He ran back. He turned the corner in the garage in enough time to see a tall woman walking quickly for the elevator. She had on a hat and sunglasses, despite it being one thirty in the morning. Hal ran up behind her. "You know, next time maybe you could at least whip me a little bit before…" He only got a very brief glance at her face as she pulled something out of her purse and held it up in her hand, and then there was a loud hissing noise. "AAAAAGGGH!" he yelled as he clutched his face with his hands, and his eyes began burning as he went into an uncontrollable coughing fit.

"HAL!?" He heard her say his name loudly. "Goddammit, you fucking idiot! What if I had had a gun instead of pepper spray!?"

"You're… *cough cough*… too… *cough*… smart… *cough hoark cough*… to… *cough*… shoot… *cough cough hack*… someone… *cough cough*… without… *cough cough wheeze cough hack*… seeing……" He was unable to keep going from the coughing. She began to cough too.

"Shit… *cough cough*… I breathed in… *cough*… some of it… *cough*… too…" Hal felt himself grabbed by the back of his shirt. "I COULD FUCKING… *cough cough*… KILL YOU…" she said. He couldn't see where they were going, but from the sound around him, he realized she had drug him into the elevator. They began to go up. He felt like a french fry in boiling oil, the spray bubbling and popping on his eyes and nose intensely enough that he could see his skin sizzling in his imagination. The coughing was making it hard to breathe now, and he listened to himself gasping for air for what seemed like an hour-long ride. Finally, the elevator stopped, and a small ding sounded out before the rattling of the doors opening. She started leading him again by his shirt, and he tried to walk the best he could to keep up with her. She was still coughing intermittently. They stopped briefly while a door opened, then she shoved him roughly inside the room and quickly pulled it shut behind them. "I don't think… *cough*… anyone saw us," she said, angrily. He lay on the floor unable to do anything besides cough and listen to her moving around the room. "If they did… *cough*… this will be all over the fucking tabloid news… *cough cough*… first thing in the morning." What sounded like a fridge opening and then bottles clinking was noticeable while she talked, and then he heard a sink turn on. The thought of cold water was the most amazing thing, but he could barely breathe, let alone try and get up.

After a few minutes, she grabbed him by the shoulders again and pulled him onto his feet, and then he was shoved against a counter, where he felt in front of him a faucet with handles. He turned the cold water on full and shoved his head underneath the spout, but was frustrated to find the burning was completely immune to water. His face was getting cold, yet, was also still burning at the same time. The sound of glass clinking caught his attention again.

"Here, try some milk. *Cough.* I thought I heard once that milk *cough cough* helps." Hal grabbed the glass and tried to open his eyes as he poured it over his face. He couldn't keep them open though, and the milk didn't seem to help much, either. The only thing that finally made the burning stop was time. About an hour's worth of it. Once Hal could keep his eyes open long enough to find a chair, he went and sat down. Then when it really started feeling like it was wearing off, he looked at his watch and saw it was 2:45 a.m.. He'd been expecting Lyrica to leave the room at some point and call the police to come get him, and he'd been working on what he was going to say in his defense to try and take his mind off the burning. But while there were periods of quiet, he'd eventually hear her moving around the room again, and at three in the morning, he was surprised to find her still there, sitting across from him, glaring at him.

"So, how was that for a little pain?" she asked.

"You win," he mumbled.

"If you think I didn't know how to deal with stalkers, hopefully tonight removed all doubt."

"I wasn't trying to stalk you," he said.

"Oh, yeah, right. You somehow found out where I was, I'm assuming travelled a fair distance to get here, showed up unannounced, snuck up behind me… no, you're not stalking me. What was I thinking? That's how all guys ask a lady for a date."

"Well, the first two attempts didn't work out so well," Hal said quietly.

"Right, and stalkers also totally know how to take 'no' for an answer," she said sternly. "You're not fooling anyone. I've had many overzealous fans hauled off by the police. I could write a book on the subject," she snapped.

He'd never meant to harm her in any way, but now that she had repeated back to him what he had been doing, it started to sink in. He hadn't thought it through very well. "I'm sorry," he said.

"OK…?" she said sarcastically, like she was expecting more of an answer, and an awkward silence followed.

Hal looked down at his feet and asked: "Not that I'm complaining, because I'm really, really not, but why haven't you had me hauled off yet? Or is that still on the agenda for tonight? Because I think I can see well enough to leave…"

"Oh, I don't know. Boredom, I guess. I'm still trying to figure you out. I mean, you actually look vaguely sorry. But if you're smart enough to be sorry, why aren't you smart enough to think that maybe sneaking up behind a woman in a parking garage in Chicago at one thirty in the morning and whispering something about being whipped wasn't a good idea!?" She stopped to catch her breath, then added: "You have to be the dumbest stalker I've ever had!"

Hal was speechless. She was right. What had he been thinking? "You're… you're right!" he said. "I must be an idiot. But… I… really never meant to cause you any distress. I just… wanted to talk to you."

"You keep saying that!" she yelled. "But every time we meet, all it leads to is '*Hi! I'm Hal! Nice weather we're having! Do you have any tips on surviving talk shows?*' So, is that it!? Is your greatest dream in life to make small talk with Lyrica Wordsworth!?"

"No! No, that's not it. I dunno, didn't want to go straight to the questions without building up to it… I guess."

"OK, well, here I am! It's three in the morning, I don't have a show tomorrow, you're here and I'm listening, so do tell! What do you want to know!?" she asked, slouching back in her chair and putting her feet up on the table.

"I… I guess, I don't want to risk sounding like another fan, but I wanted to tell you what an inspiration you are, and that your shows and your voice are mesmerizing and powerful, and they regularly shake my soul watching them. And… I guess I hoped that you'd share the secrets of your universe with me?" Lyrica was looking supremely unimpressed. "SUCH AS, like, how you're so good at coming up with addictive melodies, and with the lyrics, because most of them are unique and wondrous while others are what some people might call cliché. But the way you sing them, it makes them sound new and rare and powerful and fresh. And I just wondered how is it you know exactly when to use unique lyrics and when to use time tested ones. And like, how do you find that balance? And then there are your shows. Your stage performances are so… weird, I guess, but in the most wonderful, whimsical weird sort of way, and I always wondered where you get the imagery. Like, does it just come to you, or I always wondered if any of it was from dreams you had? And with everything I listed, how did you find the courage to go out and accomplish all this!? Did people call you strange? And did that bother you? Did you have to learn to find the courage, or were you always able to just say 'fuck them all, I know what I'm doing?' And… how is it that you're such an incredible, brilliant badass because that's exactly what I wanted to learn to become in my life!?" Hal stopped to catch his breath, and to his surprise, Lyrica no longer looked disgusted, she looked horrified.

"You think I came up with all that!?" she asked, panicked.

Hal answered: "Uh… yeah?"

"Well, I've got news for you!" she said, standing up out of her chair. "I don't write my own songs, OK!? I don't create the melodies, and I don't write the lyrics either. And my shows!? Ha! Professional set designers, professional choreographers, and professional costume makers! I don't do any of it! Everyone does everything for me! I just show up and do a little singing! That's all!" Hal looked at her, stunned. "So, there you go." Lyrica continued. "The secrets of my success. Happy now?" she asked, throwing her hands in the air.

He sat there with his mouth half-open for a few long moments, unsure of what to say at first. "Oh. Well… that… wasn't exactly what I was expecting, no," Hal said, looking down at his feet. "But… that's probably error on my part, I suppose. You've never exactly said you do all those things. You go out and nail it on stage. And there's nothing wrong with that." He stole a quick glance back up at her. You're an amazing singer, and that's not something everyone can be." If he hadn't known better, she was actually starting to look guilty now. "Knowing it's a team effort is sort of cool actually," he continued. "A set designer gets a chance to shine, a costumer gets a chance to see their hard work make the show stunning, a choreographer has a means to show off their talents, a writer and composer get a chance to hear their creations come to life. And, maybe perhaps while they can write, they have no singing talents of their own. I mean, it gives a number of people a chance to create something great together."

"Yeah, and I get all the de-facto credit for it," Lyrica mumbled.

"Well, hey, it's not like you're outright claiming all that for yourself," Hal said. "Plus, I think several industries are sort of that way. I mean, look at the movie industry. The main actors and actresses and *maybe* the director get all the credit for something hundreds, or maybe even a few thousand people worked on. But no one *ever* gives the actors grief if they didn't write the whole damn movie, or even any of it, themselves. What they do is bring it to life, and it takes a certain, rare talent to bring those characters to life just right. And that's what you do; you bring songs to life. Trust me, there's plenty of people out there, hell, probably most of the population, who, if handed one of your songs to sing, would never be able to do it an ounce of justice. And let's be honest, a number of them might turn it into a rather unpleasant sound at that." Lyrica scoffed at the thought. "I'm serious," he insisted. "Even if those writers and composers gave a song to five different professional artists, each one would come out different, and I can guarantee you there'll always be one version that rises above the rest. It's like with famous songs that have been covered by many different bands. For any listener, there will always be one version that speaks to them more strongly than the others, even though it's the same damn song. And I'm sure you don't need me to tell you this, but judging by your popularity and how many albums you sell, I'd dare say a lot of people think you give a lot of power to your music."

"Yeah, well, if you say so." Lyrica brushed him off, and Hal caught a quick glimpse into her eyes as she turned her back to him.

"You don't enjoy what you do anymore, do you?" he asked quietly. She sighed.

"You could have the most fulfilling, exciting job in the world, but if you do it too often for too long, anything can become a chore," she said.

"Well, I certainly love it when you put out new songs, and I'm always eager for the next one, but if this is what it's become for you, it sounds like you should really take a nice, long break to recharge. Or…" Hal could barely believe what he was about to say, "…retire from it and pursue something new in your life."

"I can't," Lyrica replied.

"Why not?" he asked.

"My contract to do continuous performances and recordings for years to come."

"What? That doesn't sound right. That can't be legal?"

"Apparently so," Lyrica said.

"I'd highly question that. I mean, maybe you signed an agreement that you'd give them exclusive producing and recording rights, but if you're exhausted, I don't think they can force you to work."

"Well, it's not like I have anything else to do if I quit."

"What are you talking about? Go home and sleep! Read a book, read a bunch of books! Travel to your favorite vacation spot and stay there a while. Watch your favorite movies, draw a picture. I don't know what your hobbies are, but take some time and indulge in them!"

"I don't have any other hobbies other than singing. It's what I do. It's everything I've ever done since I was eight years old."

"Since you were eight!?" Hal asked. "You knew that young what you wanted to be when you grew up!? Shit, when I was eight, I think I wanted to grow up to be a Tyrannosaurus Rex!"

"Well, I always liked singing enough I guess, but Mom was certain it was what my future was. She said that if that is what I wanted to be, I had to start young if I was ever going to compete, and she was probably right," Lyrica explained.

"It's long overdue you take a break then! Maybe on your down time you'll discover some other side talents you never knew you had."

"You're not listening! I *can't* take a break! I'll never hear the end of it from my manager and my mom."

"Well it sounds like your manager may have questionable motives at best, and if your mom cares about producing new hits so much, maybe she should get her own singing career."

"SHE TRIED AND FAILED!" Lyrica said, nearly shouting as she turned fully back around to face him. He could see the anger in her eyes, a very specific type of anger. Anger on defense, like a wild animal backed into a corner.

"And so… you can't," he replied quietly as the realization crept over him. "You never had a chance to become anything else."

"I could have become anything I wanted!" Lyrica said bitterly. "God knows there's plenty of people our age who were allowed to try and forge their own path, and still haven't figured out a damn thing! But Mom certainly had a plan: '*Let's name her Lyrica Wordsworth and make her become a singer!*'" Lyrica said with her tongue out, gesturing with her hands.

"That's horrible," Hal said.

"What's horrible!? I have a steady job, more money than I know what to do with, and everybody loves me!" Lyrica said as she kicked at a small waste can on the floor, sending it flying across the room. "What's there not to like!?"

Hal gazed at her for a while, silently. He could tell she was on the verge of tears, but was well-versed in hiding it. He reached over and grabbed a small notepad and a pen off a side table.

"What are you doing?" she asked.

"I'm giving you our manager's phone number. He's a little busy, of course, but he knows other potential managers who will work for you, or at least with you, instead of over you or against you. I'm still going to tell you that you should take a break, but if you won't, at least consider dumping your current overlord for a nicer one."

"You don't tell me what to do!" she yelled.

"I'm not telling you what to do, I'm only making suggestions, for your consideration, because I think it could make things easier on you."

"You think I haven't already tried to make things better!? You think you know more about how these things work than I do!? You've been in the industry for what? A few years!? Well guess what, I've been doing this professionally for a decade, and not quite on a professional level for a few years before that. And if you think you're going to show up with some golden tips and become my savior, then you're even dumber than I originally thought! Sure, I could try and get a new manager. But my current one isn't going to take that lightly, and he's got a huge arsenal of lies he'd be ready to seed to the media, so they chase me day and night and never give me a moment's peace! And they already have their own stash of unflattering pictures of me that were taken at bad angles or between expressions that they'll use as 'evidence' I'm on drugs and about to crash and burn in a fiery Hollywood train wreck!"

"Lyrica… my god…" Hal started to say.

"And yeah, I could certainly tell my mother to take a hike, and then she'll turn around and spread a bunch of lies about me to alienate me from everyone else in the family and make them think I've lost my mind and am trying to flush my 'amazing' career down the drain. So, yeah, that's that. Your pitiful advice won't prevent all that from happening."

"I…"

"Anyways, it's late, and I'm quite tired, so now that you've heard my whole life's story, hopefully that satisfies your need for conversation, and you can move on to bothering someone else," Lyrica said as she went over and opened the door for him. Hal stood up, put his hands in his pockets and looked at her. "I'm sorry, I never meant to…"

"GO!" she grunted.

Hal walked up to the open door, saying in a quiet voice: "I hope your life gets better someday…"

"I SAID GET OUT OF HERE!" she screamed as she grabbed a coffee mug off the counter by the door and threw it at him. It shattered against the wall as he ran out into the hallway, and the door slammed shut behind him.

He didn't get home until around five forty-five in the morning. He came through the front door, expecting everyone to be asleep, but jumped as Ryan said loudly: "Holy shit, where have you been!?"

"He's back!?" Uli came running into the entryway. Ricky was right behind him. Ryan switched on the light, and Hal cringed as the light hit his tender eyes. They were still red and swollen, along with most of his face. "Oh shit, what happened!? Did you get beat up!?" Ryan asked.

"No, no. I didn't get beat up," Hal said, trying to keep his head down.

"Did a mob of crazy fans do something to you!? Is the Twinkie wrecked!?" Ryan asked.

"Were you out doing hard drugs?" Uli asked half-heartedly as he examined his face.

"No, no, and no," Hal said.

"Well, what then!?" Ryan insisted.

"Look, guys, it's a long story and I'm really tired. I'll explain it tomorrow," Hal mumbled.

"Dude, at least give us a quick summary. We were afraid you were dead or something!" Ryan said.

"Why didn't you call?" Hal asked.

"We did call! A lot. You didn't answer," Ryan said.

"What? My phone was on me the whole time." Hal pulled his phone out of his pocket and looked at it. A red battery icon flashed dimly on the screen. "Oh."

"Give us a quick rundown, then you can tell us the whole thing in the morning," Ryan insisted.

"Okay, look, I sort of got pepper sprayed," Hal answered unwillingly.

"PEPPER SPRAYED!?" Ryan said loudly.

"Yeah, and I couldn't see for a while, so I had to wait for it to wear off before I drove home."

"Who the fuck pepper sprayed you!?"

"I told you, I'll explain it tomorrow."

Hal went up the stairs and was halfway to his room when his mother's bedroom door opened. "What's going on?" Cecilia said groggily as she turned on the hall light and saw Hal in front of her. "Hal? Oh my God, what happened!?" she said as she pulled him into the bathroom and turned on the bathroom light to get a better look at his face.

"I got pepper sprayed, it's a long story, and I just want to go to bed," Hal said as he tried to get out of her grasp.

"Pepper sprayed!?" Cecilia said horrified.

"That sucks. Been there, done that," Harvey said as he leaned out of the bedroom doorway.

"Yep, it was quite an experience. I highly recommend against it. I'm okay. I'm not dead. I'll hopefully look better in the morning. We'll talk tomorrow. I'm going to bed now. Goodnight," Hal said as he made his escape into his room and pulled the door closed. Everyone else was left standing in the hall. Cecilia stared intently at his door for a few moments, like she might burn a hole through it to drag Hal back out. Her expression gradually turned from fear to distrust, and then to something resembling anger after that.

"I don't like this one bit," she finally said, quietly enough that Hal shouldn't have heard it. "If he had gotten caught in the middle of someone else's fight accidentally or had just been at the wrong place at the wrong time, or was mistaken for someone else, he'd tell us." Her voice was so intense, no one dared say anything in response. A few more moments of silence followed, then she turned to look at Uli, Ryan, and Ricky. "I have a favor to ask of you guys. Can one of you please find out what he did, so I know how hard he needs to be kicked in the butt, and how long of a talk I'll be having with him?" she said, and Ricky looked down at the ground uncomfortably, while Uli and Ryan regarded her solemnly.

"Yeah, we'll find out," Ryan said. "We'll get the truth out of him."

"Thank you," she answered, then sighed and rubbed her eyes. "I'm going back to bed. Goodnight, again."

"'Night, Mrs. H," Ryan replied, and they dispersed to go get ready for bed as well.

Hal didn't wake up until after three in the afternoon, and he stayed in bed until 3:30 p.m. thinking about what he was going to say. He finally went to the kitchen to re-heat some pizza for his breakfast, or lunch, or dinner, or whatever it was at that point. Ryan, Uli, and Ricky were in the living room working on the beginnings of a new song. He sat down at the table with his pizza and waited. He knew they had heard him, and the fact they weren't already pestering him was a little worrying. Part of him wanted to get it over with, and the other part of him had the unrealistic hope they would just drop the whole thing and forget about it. He had pondered coming up with a different story to explain what happened, but he knew they'd be able to tell he was lying, and so he had surrendered to the reality that he was probably going to have to tell them the truth.

"Feeling better?" Ryan asked from the living room.

"Yes, quite a bit," Hal answered. He heard Ryan put down his papers and a moment later he turned the corner to the kitchen. "You look a lot better."

"Yeah, my face is burning a lot less," Hal replied. Uli and Ricky silently appeared, and all three of them sat around him at the table. Ryan and Uli looked like buzzards moving in for the kill while Ricky looked almost shamed to be joining them. "So, how'd the Christmas shopping go?" Ryan asked.

"Oh, that went fine," Hal answered.

Ryan stared at him for a bit, then leaned back in his chair and demanded: "Alright, Hal, what happened?"

"I got pepper sprayed because I did something stupid without thinking it through, and, yes, sometimes I'm an idiot. But I can guarantee you I learned my lesson and it's not going to happen again."

"Good to hear," Ryan said, a little annoyed. "So, any chance are the police looking for you?"

"No, they're not," Hal answered.

"Are you sure?" Ryan asked.

"Yes," Hal assured him.

"Well, you got off lucky then. Now, WHAT HAPPENED?" Ryan asked louder.

It was obvious Hal was getting quite nervous. "So… I drove out to Chicago last night…"

"Chicago!?" Ryan and Uli said together.

"Because… Lyrica was playing a concert there…" Hal said, and he watched as Uli's and Ryan's expressions turned to disgust.

"You drove all the fucking way to fucking Chicago to go stalk Lyrica Wordsworth, and she fucking pepper sprayed you…" Ryan said.

"I never intended to 'stalk' her!" Hal said. "I just… wanted to talk to her."

"Oh… my… God…" Ryan said. "You know, Hal, there's being stupid, and then there's being a fucking creeper. I can deal with you being stupid, but I'm not sure I can deal with you being a stalker."

"Yes, it was stupid, I didn't think it through, I got it," Hal said angrily. "Trust me, I got it. We had a long conversation after she drug me up into her hotel room so no one would see us after she pepper sprayed me."

"You followed her to her hotel!?" Uli said.

"Yes, and I certainly got what I deserved," Hal said. "She's apparently had a rough couple of years, and not only did I startle her accidentally so she pepper sprayed me, but I managed to single-handedly remind her of how shitty her life is. I guess spending an hour on her hotel room floor with my face fucking on fire wasn't enough for me, because I was clueless enough to ask the right questions to get her even more upset and angry about all her other problems. I'm a massive fucking dirt bag, okay!?" He got up and shoved the chair forcefully back under the table, then turned and walked out the front door, slamming it behind him.

He walked swiftly across the yard, then shoved the door to the garage up forcefully and got in the van. He wasn't sure where he was going, but it was somewhere that Ryan and Uli weren't. The tires screeched briefly as he started down the road, and he drove aimlessly for about ten minutes before turning into a park. It was a cloudy December day, and the beginnings of dimming daylight were already starting to show at 3:45 p.m.. He got out of the van, kicked the snow off a park bench, and sat down. The cold didn't bother him, the damp bench didn't bother him, and nothing else could possibly bother him up against what was already weighing on his mind. He felt physically hot and feverish from the anger itself. He sat there for a half hour, watching the approaching darkness coming in, when Ricky suddenly showed up out of nowhere and sat down next to him. "How'd you find me!?" Hal asked. "Do you have a built-in radar system too?"

"No, just a lucky guess, actually. This is a good park to hide in. Lotsa twists an' turns," Ricky said, and a small grey possum climbed down a nearby tree and waddled over to him and jumped into his lap. Ricky started casually petting it like a cat. "Plenty of wildlife too," he added, and Hal gave him a quick sideways glance.

"Are you sure you can stand to be seen in public with me?"

Ricky hesitated a moment or two before answering: "At first Ricky was a little weirded out at what Hal did, but obviously Hal didn't mean any harm. Just sorta did somethin' rash without thinkin' it through."

"Yeah, pretty much," Hal answered morosely.

"Which isn't good, but… everyone's been there at least once or twice, for one thing or 'nother," Ricky assured him.

Hal shut his eyes and shook his head slightly. "You can't possibly have ever done anything this stupid."

"Ev'rybody does stupid stuff, just maybe not the same type of stupid stuff as other people. Life is like a box of stupid chocolates. There's lots ah' different types to choose from," Ricky explained.

Hal pondered this for a bit. "I guess…" he sighed. "Ryan and Uli are probably right about me. I rush into stuff too quickly without giving it any good consideration. I probably need to learn to think things over first."

"Well, not a bad idea, but not everything Hal has ever done on a whim ended up badly."

"It often seems to. What hasn't?" Hal asked.

"Well, there was this one time Hal offered a random homeless drifter in a bar a spot in his band. Ricky thinks that turned out okay. Certainly worked out well for the drifter."

"You were not a homeless drifter! You had a home. You were *travelling*," Hal corrected him.

"Still probably took an incredible lack of thinkin' to do somethin' like that," Ricky said with a smile.

"Well, no. More thought went into it than you know. Ryan tried his best to talk me out of it for a good half hour," Hal said, and Ricky nodded.

"Right. And Ryan suddenly joined y'all after comin' up to tell you how bad he thought Uli was at playin' drums," Ricky said.

"Ye… yeah…" Hal answered. "Alright, those two worked out," he admitted. "But I don't have any good excuse for this time. As crappy of a day as I had, I made someone else's far worse. Ryan and Uli can make me feel awful to their heart's content, but what really bothers me is I don't think I can do anything to make Lyrica feel better. Part of me wants to send her an apology note or something…"

"Ah'd be real careful 'bout doin' that if ah was you," Ricky said.

"Yeah, I know. She doesn't want to talk to me. But at the same time, maybe it would do some good if I promised her I wasn't ever going to bother her again, and… did you just refer to yourself in the first person?" Hal looked up at Ricky, who suddenly looked away.

"No!"

Hal raised one eyebrow at him, then got back on topic. "But that's maybe all I'd put in the note is I'm sorry I made your night shit, and I promise I won't bug you anymore."

"Now, is that to make her feel better, or to make you feel better?"

"What?" Hal asked.

"Do ya'll want to send her a letter to try an' make yourself feel better by apologizin' again, or would that actually make her feel better?" Ricky asked. Hal had to think about that for a moment. "Cuz' you prob'ly got one of those dark little clouds hoverin' over ya and makin' anythin' and everythin' seem miserable because y'all can't make it go away. And when one of those things is followin' somebody, all they want to do is get rid of it. So, would sendin' her a letter be to help get rid of that cloud, or would it actually make her feel better?" Ricky asked. It was times like this Hal wondered how Ricky got so good at his disarming '*Oh, I'm just a simple country boy*' guise, because it was easy enough to believe when he wasn't saying or doing something disturbingly smart. Or even when he was being smart, but happened to be holding a possum in his lap.

"Well…" Hal said. "I suppose you might be right, but I still wonder if maybe telling her I won't come around to bother her anymore might give her a little peace of mind."

"Well, perhaps so. Ricky wasn't there, so it's a call only you can make," Ricky said. "But, this might be one of those things to think about for a while before decidin.'"

"Probably a good strategy," Hal agreed.

"Yeah, right so. Anyways, don't stay out 'til five forty-five in the morning this time. Y'all scared us good," Ricky said as he stood up, and the possum climbed up to his shoulders, then jumped up onto a low-hanging tree branch and climbed up higher through the branches to disappear into a hollow in the trunk.

"Did you walk all the way here?" Hal asked.

"Yeah," Ricky replied.

"Well… I think I'm cold enough to go home now. Come on, we'll drive," he said, nodding in the direction of the parking lot.

Once they got home, they stepped outside the garage, and as Hal turned to reach up and pull the door shut, he was suddenly grabbed by the ear. His mother started leading him across the yard towards the idling Mustang waiting right out of sight around the corner. "Ow… ow… ow… ow… ow! Mom! Stop! I got it! I'm in trouble! But I can walk on my own!" he pleaded, but she said nothing, holding a slightly terrifying, distant smile on her face as she brought him around the side of the car and forced him into the passenger seat. She got into the driver's seat, shut the door, then took off, leaving a stunned Ricky standing in the snow-covered driveway. Ryan and Uli appeared around the corner of the garage a few moments later and stood next to him as they watched the Mustang disappear down the road. "Dead man walking," Ryan commented, then took another drink of the bottle of beer he was holding.

They got back about an hour later, and when Hal came in he looked like he had been thoroughly chewed up and spit out. He gave a passing glance to the other three sitting in the living room before quietly ascending up the stairs to his room. Cecilia came in a few moments later and collapsed onto the couch.

"So, how'd it go?" Ryan asked.

"Oh, I think it went very well, for what it was. He got the message loud and clear that what he did isn't okay, and he will not be doing anything like that ever again," she said confidently, though she looked rather drained.

"That's good," Ryan said.

"Yeah." Cecilia sighed. "Hal's from a long line of charismatic psychopaths, and I told him when he was younger that he could grow up to be as charismatic as he wanted, but if he ever started going down the psychopath route that there would be an intervention."

"I acknowledge what he did was in no way okay, but at the same time I don't think he meant her any harm," Uli said.

"Oh, no. I'm sure he didn't," Cecilia agreed. "I'm sure his intentions were only to take her out to dinner, buy her some nice gifts, and then get frisky. But, he needs to understand he can't just decide someone belongs to him if he wants them. That was something my dad did all the time. If he liked the look of someone else's bodyguard, they immediately became *his* bodyguard. If he heard good things about a local accountant, they became *his* accountant. And, if he saw a beautiful woman he wanted, she basically became his girlfriend on the spot whether she wanted to or not. That's how my mother ended up with him," she lamented. "Hal collects people he wants to do his bidding in the same way, but up until now it has been with their consent."

"What the hell are you talking about?" Ryan asked. "Who has Hal collected?"

Cecilia slowly looked up at Ryan, then gradually glanced over to Uli and Ricky. Ryan followed her gaze, and the color gradually went out of his face. "Oh…shit…"

"Yeah, but he's still a much nicer human being than his grandfather was, and I'm going to see to it he stays that way," Cecilia said. "He can find himself another girlfriend who actually *wants* to be with him, and from what

I understand there is likely a waiting list by now, so he can figure it out," she added, then bid them goodnight and went to bed.

Hal spent the next few days thinking about what Ricky had said. And about Lyrica. And about what he had already said to her. And about what his mom said. He thought about it quite thoroughly, and finally decided he was going to go ahead and send her the written apology. Nothing fancy. No Hallmark card, no flowers, no delivering it in person. Just a piece of lined paper saying what he wanted to say. He reached the conclusion that apologizing to someone wasn't a selfish thing to do, though he understood where Ricky was coming from in suggesting he just leave her alone completely. He was sure she had left Chicago by this time, so he called up Jim under the premise that he was working on a new song. He told Jim that it was to be a duet with male and female vocals, and that he wanted to ask Lyrica if maybe she'd like to do a collaboration with them for it. He also told Jim that he wanted it to be a surprise to Ricky and Uli and Ryan if she said yes, so he hadn't mentioned it to them, and if he could keep it a secret as well. Jim thought it was a neat idea and said sure. Hal explained he was being old-fashioned by writing the request in a letter, and asked Jim if he could figure out how to get the letter directly to her through his contacts. Jim said he'd make it happen, and Hal thanked him, and sent it out in the mail to his office the next day.

Lyrica sat alone in her trailer, staring at the letter on the table. It stared back. Her conscience had been nagging at her since that night. She didn't feel bad for pepper spraying him, because he had snuck up on her in a dark parking lot. She didn't feel bad for telling him off for trying to tell her what to do, because she'd never asked for his damn opinion. And she didn't feel bad for trying to get him to go away in general, because he had functionally been acting like a stalker… but at the same time, she felt a little bad for all of it. Maybe he actually had been trying to be nice to her and help her. Nobody had done anything like that for so long, she might have forgotten that it was even a possibility. She'd thrown a mug at the first person in years who had tried to compliment her. Like, really, honestly, compliment her; even after finding out she didn't do all the things he thought she did. And then, the very next day she went back to putting on her best face for those who forcefully manipulated her life for her without her consent. Everybody seemed to always want to get something from her, and this was the first person in years who had offered to give something in return. She reminded herself it still wasn't that simple, though.

He had been following her even after she told him to go away. That was never a good sign. She fell back on her couch and stared at the ceiling. Her mind was going in circles around the whole thing. She tried to get the two possibilities to hold still for a second so she could examine them properly. Either he was so maliciously brilliant that he was waging a psychological war on her to get her to let her guard down and make her more vulnerable to whatever it was *he* was trying to get from her. Or, maybe he actually was a painfully clueless, though vaguely sweet, moron. She was beginning to lean towards the latter. Having someone to yell at (who didn't yell back louder), had been oddly therapeutic. But now what? Give in and say she was sorry for the whole thing, even though he had crossed a few lines? Or go on as is, and be left wondering if the universe had maybe tried to send her some much needed help, and she turned it away even though she had silently been begging for company in the depths of her soul for years?

Once she had made the decision, then there was the issue of what to *functionally* do about it. Ignore him, or send him a note back through his manager? That seemed anti-climactic. She thought about it for a moment, then sat back up and pulled her laptop across the table over to her. She got on Battle Creek's website and looked around for a bit. *Oh shit, they're leaving for an international tour in a few weeks.* He was right, he wasn't going to be around to bother her. *Hmmm.* She clicked on the 'About Us' tab. They are based out of Battle Creek, MI. *Well, that should have been a no-brainer,* she thought to herself. *Did he drive to Chicago from there? That's a long drive, but not unthinkable. He should be home around this time since it's almost Christmas.*

She was leaving in the morning to go home for about a week as well. Against maybe what was her better judgement, she decided to call up a few of the lesser managers on her staff who weren't such massive assholes and ask them for a personal favor. Namely, could they find out what flight from what airport from what terminal, etc., Battle Creek would be leaving from to go to London on their tour. She made up her mind, at least for now. She was going to give Hal something before he left, and then there would be a good year in between to see what became of it. She was going to bring her pepper spray to the airport with her though, just in case.

# CHAPTER 15

## (Leaving on a Jet Plane)

**At the Detroit Metro Airport,** a jet was getting ready to take off for London. They were waiting in a private lounge until it was time to get on board. Once it was boarding time, they would rush into first class, and then the door would be shut right behind them to minimize any issues with possible lurking paparazzi. While they waited, a woman wearing a long white coat, dark glasses, and a wide-brimmed hat had gone through the security process and was now on her way to the gate. Once everyone else was on the plane, they were called to board.

"This will be quite the adventure. Be safe, call often," Cecilia said as she hugged Hal.

"I will, Mom. I'll be sure to give you regular updates. I'm really sorry I won't be around to help out if you get sick later in the pregnancy."

"It'll be okay, Hal. Remember, I do have help," Cecilia said as she shot a glance in Harvey's direction. He made a weak attempt at looking excited.

"Alright, but remember, if anything major happens, just call. We can always catch the next flight home," Hal insisted. Cecilia and Harvey said their final goodbyes, then strolled out of the lounge while the guys donned their disguises and got ready to do a speed walk to the gate.

"Alright, we're ready for you." A security guard leaned into the lounge and motioned for them to go. They began their walk. They got to about twenty feet from the gate when a woman began quickly approaching them. One of the security men noticed and was getting ready to confront her and hold her back when she suddenly took off her hat and glasses and threw her coat off onto a nearby chair. He paused in shock. Hal noticed something was starting behind them and looked back to see Lyrica walking towards them like she was on a fashion runway. Her hips were swaying gently back and forth in a fancy pair of white, studded designer jeans, and her rhinestone-covered halter top glistened brightly in the light.

"Wha… what…?" Hal started to say. This alerted Ricky, Uli, and Ryan, who also stopped and watched in disbelief as she made her way up to Hal.

"Hey, I thought I'd come down and wish you good luck on your tour. And, I know you're always looking for tips, so remember…" Her voice became quiet as she leaned in close to Hal's ear. "It's called the lavatory or loo, not the bathroom," she said, then gave him a quick kiss on the cheek before turning around and walking away as sleek as she had come.

"Bu… bu…" Hal began to stutter.

Ryan threw his hands in the air. "WHAT THE FUCK!?"

"Bu… but… but…" Hal took a step in her direction, but Uli quickly grabbed him by his shoulders.

"No! We have to board!" he reminded him.

"OH MY GOD, NO WAY!" A younger teenage girl a few feet away yelled, and Lyrica was quickly enveloped in a crowd, obscuring her from their sight. The last Hal saw of her before she disappeared though, he thought he could see her smiling.

"But…" Uli drug Hal down the loading hall to the plane door, and the gate entrance was quickly pulled shut behind them.

"Did you write her that apology note afta' all?" Ricky asked as they stepped into the plane.

"Yeah…" Hal whimpered in reply.

"Uh, good job," Ricky said, then the main plane door was sealed behind them.

"HOW ARE YOU DOING TONIGHT, LONDON!?" Hal yelled to the screaming crowd in front of him. "Are you all ready for the best damn New Year's party ever!?" he asked, and the screams got louder. "Good! I know I am! Before we begin, I want to thank you all for the warm welcome, and I have a feeling this will be a great start to our very first international tour." The crowd cheered and whistled. "Well, we've only got an hour left till the New Year begins, so let's get this party started!

---

213. "Bittersweet Symphony" by The Verve

---

End Song 213

---

"Ricky, you want to start the next one for us?" Hal asked. Ricky smiled as he started to strum the mighty axe. Its tip had been all fixed up back into a chrome point, and the lights over the stage set ablaze the orange and yellow flames so they danced and shimmered when he strummed the opening chords.

---

214. "Cruise" by Florida Georgia Line

215. "Enter Sandman" by Metallica

216. "Anarchy in the UK" by The Sex Pistols

---

End Songs 214 – 216

---

217. "The Final Countdown" by Europe

Once midnight was almost upon them, during a musical interlude near the end of the final song of the year, Hal announced: "Well, I think it's about that time, everyone." A large red clock behind him started counting down from 10.

"...nine, eight, seven, six, five, four, three, two, ONE!" The entire city shouted it at once and then exploded into a frenzy of cheers and noisemakers.

End Song 217

"Alright! And in celebration of the New Year, we've decided to play a new, unreleased song for you all tonight to start this year off right." The announcement caused the cheering to go even louder than the screams for midnight, and Hal smiled. "This one is something we made especially for celebrating the New Year here in London, and to help kick off our first international tour, so here we go with the first song of the New Year!"

218. "One More Time" by Daft Punk

Uli started an enticing beat sequence on his synthboard that went out to the crowd like a call, and when Hal started to sing, everyone in the crowded square started to dance. It was one of those moments in life that played like a picture-perfect scene from the ending of a good movie. They stayed and played for another hour, until one in the morning, and nearly the entire crowd stayed until the very end when they finally said goodnight.

End Song 218

"I think that was a huge success!" their European tour manager, Mason Harding, said triumphantly after the show had ended. Mason was tall and lanky (though not as tall as Uli), and had chin-length brown hair and a chronic case of five o'clock shadow. Never clean shaven, never enough to call it an actual beard.

"I believe the people screamed louder for your new song than they did for the New Year itself!" Mason's niece, Nora, said. Nora would be there to assist her uncle while they toured through Europe, acting as an intern to try out her skills in the professional talent management industry.

"I know, right!?" Hal said excitedly.

"They really did," Nora agreed. "And that guitar is amazing," she said to Ricky. "It actually looks like its burning!"

"Yeah, they got it for Ricky for his birthday," Ricky said, pointing to the guys.

"Well, they did a good job, and you wield it well!" she said.

"Thanks," Ricky said quietly. As much as his guitar looked like it was burning brightly, Nora's short, curly red hair could have given it a run for its money. Red hair over ocean blue eyes, fire and water side by side, separated only by a cute button nose, and all on top of a thin, short, slight frame.

"Only bad part of headlining a New Year's show is you miss the party yourself," Mason said.

"Pfft. We didn't miss the party, we *are* the party," Ryan replied.

"Nice! But what I was getting at was everything is going to be winding down for tonight, but maybe we can all go out and celebrate the start of the tour tomorrow," Mason said.

"That sounds good. I think we figured out a long time ago that trying to party after doing a show is too much for one day."

"Speak for yourself," Ryan interrupted.

"I am," Hal said, yawning.

"Well, if you want to go out, I can't stop you, but I do prefer to go out after a full night's sleep," Mason said.

"Yeah, let's plan for that tomorrow and call it a night," Hal agreed.

"Alright. Excellent job again, everyone. Day two begins tomorrow, sometime around noon, perhaps," Mason said, and they all agreed on that before parting ways to go pack their things up for the night.

"I like Mason. He gets it better than Jim," Hal said.

"Yeah, he's probably going to help us avoid 6:00 a.m. interviews instead of push for them," Ryan agreed.

"God, I hope so," Hal replied. "*I gotta feeling…*" he started to sing. "*This is gonna be a good tour, this is gonna be a good, good tour…*"

They went out to lunch the next day, and then walked around downtown for a bit after doing everything in their power to make themselves as unrecognizable as possible. They took a few pictures, went through a few shops, and then went past a business that really caught Hal's eye. "Ooooohhh shit, look at that thing!" Hal backed up a few steps and was suddenly plastered to the window like a kid outside of a toyshop. The other three joined him in ogling a sapphire blue car reminiscent of the vehicles in a James Bond movie. It was smooth and streamlined like a blue bullet on wheels, and the black and silver dashboard shined like polished ice in the sun.

"Oh yeah, I feel it," Ryan agreed.

"Indeed," Uli added.

"Guys, I know this may seem a little fast, but I think I'm in love. I'm bringing her home with me tonight!" Hal said as he went for the door.

"Geez, don't tell Lyrica," Ryan said under his breath as they followed him.

"Premium Unleaded V-12 6.0 L engine, 8-Speed Automatic Transmission, Titanium and Quartz dash…" the salesman rambled on, and Hal was nearly drooling. "Convertible or hardtop, coupe or sedan…"

"Let's do sedan and hardtop. Gotta have enough room for these guys, and as much as I'd like a convertible, the hardtop keeps the crazy people out more effectively. Oh, and I can't really do much with it here since we'll be travelling non-stop, so is there one of these located in the U.S. I can buy through this dealership? Or can one be shipped there? And the steering wheel will have to be on the left side, of course."

"Yes, that can all be arranged. I'll check stock with the American dealerships first…" the sales rep. said.

Ricky tried to get a better look at the paperwork while they waited for him to bring up more information on the computer. "So, how much is this Austin Martin thing?"

"AS-TON Martin," Hal corrected him, and then the price came up on the computer screen as the salesman loaded a new page.

"THAT'S HOW MUCH ONE OF THESE COSTS!? Y'all could buy a house for that!" Ricky said, appalled.

"How many years, exactly, is it going to take for you to get over the whole you're-not-broke-anymore thing?" Ryan asked.

"It's just a waste is all! Y'all can get a really nice car for a quarter of that!"

"Yeah, but any other car isn't an Aston Martin. You only live once, Ricky," Hal answered.

"I think we have a new challenge," Ryan announced. "We have to find Ricky an expensive car he'll like."

"Good luck with that," Ricky said, doubtfully. They stayed there for three hours until everything was finalized, and Hal had signed a pile of paperwork. They took a spin in one of the cars at the dealer to test it out and did some donuts in the parking lot. But the specific car Hal bought was at an American dealership, and would be shipped to his mom's house. If he had bought a car that was there, he would have had to ship it home eventually anyways. He wouldn't have gotten a lot of chances to drive it while they were travelling in the tour bus and always busy doing shows. His mom got an email later that night that read:

Hi Mom,

I bought a car today! I'd tell you what kind, but it's a surprise. :) I'm having it sent to your house since I won't have much of a chance to use it while we're on tour. You'll find I've transferred some money into your account, if you could use that to have the garage expanded to fit three cars, that would be great. This car sort of needs to be locked up at night. If you need more for the expansion, just let me know. The car won't be showing up for about a month, so hopefully the expansion will be done by then? If not, and it has to stay outside for a few nights, I know Dad would be more than happy to shoot at anyone who tries to steal it. Anyways, since we'll be gone for so long, yes, you and Dad can take it out for a few drives. It shouldn't be left to sit for months on end, since that's not good for cars. Just tell Dad to control himself when he sees it. I know you will.

We had a great first concert last night. The crowd cheered louder when we said we were going to play an unreleased song than they did when midnight hit! It was pretty cool. I'll send another update after the next concert, the day after tomorrow. Oslo, Norway is next. Followed by Sweden, then back to England for a few days in Manchester and Birmingham. Our great European adventure continues!

Love, Hal

And right as he said would happen, about a month later, a large car carrier pulled up in front of their house and parked in front of a freshly remodeled three car garage. Cecilia and Harvey went out to greet the driver and watch it be unloaded. "I bet it's a Ferrari," Harvey said.

"This may sound strange, but I don't think a Ferrari is Hal's style," Cecilia replied.

"What *is* his style, then?" Harvey asked.

"Well, I'm not quite sure how to explain it. He's more, I don't know, an old-world sophisticated sort of type? Not that Ferraris aren't sophisticated, but Hal would maybe be more in the direction of a Bentley or Rolls Royce than a Ferrari," Cecilia said.

"He was in England, so actually, a Bentley or Rolls Royce isn't a bad guess. Unless he just bought an American or Asian car over there," Harvey said.

"Well, that's true. What other car companies are British?"

"Let me think, Bentley, Rolls Royce…" Harvey recapped. "MG, uh, Mini Cooper…"

"I somehow doubt it's a Mini Cooper," Cecilia laughed.

"Jaguar… Triumph…" While Harvey was still thinking, a sapphire blue car was rolled out of the back of the truck, and Harvey's jaw dropped. "And ASTON MARTIN!"

"Oh… my… God…" Cecilia said quietly. Harvey ran down to look at it while the drivers finished removing the shipping harnesses. Cecilia came up beside him. "You realize this is our son's car and not yours, right?" she said with a raised eyebrow.

"He said we could drive it! And the kid's right. It's not good for cars to sit in storage. The fluids start to settle."

"He said we could drive it, not take it street racing," Cecilia said sternly.

"I won't speed in it while the police are around. I'll get it a radar scanner," Harvey said, and Cecilia put her hand over her eyes and shook her head in disgust.

A few weeks into their tour, Hal noticed something at their concerts that was different from their U.S. shows. They were getting much more of an audience reaction to the metal songs they played. He also noticed Uli had been letting his hair grow longer than he usually kept it. Hal started thinking maybe they needed to do a little adjustment to their set to add in a few more metal songs. They'd done adjustments before to better suit certain places. The overall theme was still that they were the band that did everything, but if they were in an area that tended more to a certain style, they might throw in a few more of those songs to please the crowd. The Midwest and Southern states reacted well to the country songs they did, so they'd do a few more of them for those shows. It was a nice break from the norm, and it was sort of neat to occasionally see Ricky, Uli, and Ryan get a little more well-deserved appreciation. Ricky and Ryan had certainly had their days, but Uli was well overdue.

"You gonna let your hair get long enough to put it in a ponytail?" Hal asked him as he walked by on his way to the little kitchen in the hotel suite. It obviously caught him off guard, but Uli answered 'maybe' casually. "I've noticed we've been getting much more of a reaction from the metal songs since we got over here. So, I was thinking we do a little adjustment to add a few more of them in."

"Sure," Uli answered, turning on the stove to make some soup.

"And we should probably figure out a way to play it up a bit more visually. Any suggestions?"

"Just the usual things. Moody visuals on the back screen, lots of pyrotechnics..." Uli answered.

"We gonna get to see that amazing trench coat of yours, finally?" Hal asked.

"Yes… might as well use it," Uli answered hastily.

"Mmm, hmm," Hal answered. Uli heard the doubt in his voice loud and clear. Metal music was what he loved, and he should have been happy to revel in it. But somehow, even after the time that had passed since he left home, there was still the lingering feeling of guilt and shame. What was worse, he was fully aware all that guilt was an unfounded, nasty present from his parents. But despite realizing this, he still couldn't shake it. It wasn't supposed to work that way. He couldn't remember how he originally got into metal, but he did remember the first time his parents found the CDs in his room, and he got a stern yelling at. He could remember that, but not how it originally came into his life. He got more CDs and hid them better, and they stayed in the shadows for many years. It was fitting in a strange way, having to have secret rendezvous with his music in the dark. Perhaps that's what happened. It felt good to have a secret, and so it couldn't see the light of day.

Still, he loved music too much to hide all desire for it. He asked his parents for a guitar, but they gave him a violin. He asked for a drum set, he was given a piano. They sat in his room for a long time, collecting dust, until one day his parents gave him an old Disney movie to watch 'for inspiration' in his musical endeavors. "I loved this one when I was young," his mother said. "A few parts of it are a little girly, but not all of it. Getting visualizations to the classical musical pieces can help develop an appreciation for them." He sat there watching it disdainfully, a fake smile on his face whenever they checked in. It wasn't bad, no, even he had to admit the whole compilation was a masterpiece of music paired with animation; but most of it just wasn't his thing. However, after two hours of fairies painting dew on spider webs, mops dancing with their buckets, dinosaurs setting out on a death march, colorful centaurs and flying horses dancing around rainbows, and finally, hippos and ostriches in tutus, there came the last musical score of the movie. It was that last piece that hypnotized him in a way he'd never experienced before. To the eerie wailing of stringed instruments and a monstrous bellowing of horns, he watched as a demon, or perhaps Satan himself, sitting atop a mountain on a dark and dreary night, sent forth the tremendous shadows of his hands over the city below to raise the wispy souls of the damned out of their graves. They came up through their cemetery plots, backwards through a hangman's noose, and out from the flooded dungeons to join him on his mountain. There, they would dance furiously in his presence until morning light banished them back to their abodes. It was the most terrifyingly beautiful thing he had ever seen. He watched that part, only that part, over and over again for days. 'Night on Bald Mountain,' or 'Chernobog;' that was the name of the musical score. Mussorgsky was the composer. He realized he could play this on his violin, and there was probably a way to learn it on the piano too. He found the sheet music for it. He taught himself to play. He played it repeatedly. And as he began to study classical music more, he discovered this wasn't the only piece of its kind. He found 'Toccata and Fugue in D-Minor' by Sebastian Bach, a song that frequently plays when the hero of the horror movie is approaching an old, haunted castle at night. 'In the Hall of the Mountain King' by Edvard Grieg, 'Danse Macabre' by Camille Saint-Saens, Beethoven's 5th Symphony in C Minor, even the theme song to the Phantom of the Opera play. There was more, as well. And as he learned them, he came to discover the spirits of classical darkness were nearly as good of company as the souls of modern metal. His parents were not amused. That Christmas, he asked them for a pipe organ. They said no.

"Uli! Find something brighter to play for God's sake! I feel like I'm living in Dracula's Castle!" his mother would yell up the stairs at him.

"I'm sorry, Mother, I just find Mussorgsky very inspirational," he'd yell back, to spite her. And so, it went for the rest of his childhood, and into his teenage years. Classical music after school, and heavy metal in his headphones after his parents were in bed. He also discovered that there were certain metal bands that incorporated the use of classical instruments into their songs alongside of the electric guitar. Effectively paying homage to the original dark and mysterious composers of old. He'd listen to the songs at a volume low enough to fall asleep to, but still loud enough to have it fill his dreams with misty forests, shrouded moonlight, dusty bones, raging fire, and all manner of monsters and ghosts. All things that were supposed to be repulsive, but that he found so very friendly and beautiful. He knew there were others out there like him, who appreciated the same kind of beauty; but he didn't get the privilege of finding and meeting any of them as he grew up. They certainly weren't in his neighborhood. He had only the music for company. The thought, now, of bringing those spirits fully out into public with him was unnerving. He sat down later that night and pulled the coat out of his luggage. He smoothed out the wrinkles and hung it up on the back of the door. He liked that coat a lot, and it had been bothering him that he had apparently bought it to carry it around in a bag and never wear. Perhaps, the time had come to let it see the lights of the stage.

Over the next few days, they laid out their plans to adjust the song set and effects. The first place that would get this adjusted show was Berlin, Germany. They saved the metal segment for last as they always did, to be the grand finale; but with a bit of extra flair this time. They finished off the punk rock segment and the few high-charting pop songs that followed, then the stage went dark. The giant screen overhead played some visuals in the meantime while they changed outfits, and the stagehands prepared the next round of scenery. Covered in black leather and spikes head to toe, Uli took one final look in the mirror, then grabbed the long trench coat and put it on. He liked what he saw in the reflection. He liked it a lot. He just needed to get used to knowing it was okay to like it. He took a deep breath and opened the changing room door and nearly ran into Hal, who was standing a few inches outside.

"Well, we gonna go full metal, here?" Hal asked.

"Let's do it," Uli replied confidently, then started to walk towards the stage.

Hal stopped him. "Hold on, there's something missing," he said, then pulled a small tube of black eyeliner out of his pocket. "I'll do it if you will…" Hal said.

A few minutes later, as they approached the stage, Ryan caught sight of them, and announced loudly: "Well, look at this! We have not one, but TWO gods of hellfire!"

"Oh, I'm no god, I'm just the apprentice to hellfire right now," Hal laughed.

Ryan went up and got right in Uli's face to get a better look. "Ooh, honey, you have to tell me who does your makeup for you, it's divine! Though I think you missed a spot right…" Uli grabbed Ryan tightly by his skull T-shirt, and shoved him away, causing him to trip backwards over an unused amp, and land in a pile of light rigging with a loud crash. He smashed his head against one of the metal light hoods, and sat back up slowly, clutching the back of his head. "*Shit…*" Ryan said as he looked at his hand to see if there was any blood.

Uli looked back at Hal, who nodded his approval. "Think about it this way, at least we're not naked," Hal said.

"I thought we agreed we shall never talk about that night ever again," Uli said.

"But it *does* put it in perspective, no?" Hal replied as they started back towards the stage to get into place.

---

219. "Twisted Transistor" by Korn

---

One spotlight came on pointing towards the stage, Ricky's signal to start playing. With his axe slung low over his shoulder, he strummed the opening chords, which cut through the air like a sharp blade. Lights came on from the floor behind him, illuminating his silhouette as he played. A small amount of fog rolled out of the side fog machines. Ryan started the beat on his drums a few moments later, his head pounding in rhythm with the beats as he tried to ignore the pain. Hal began to sing. They'd generally had Uli sing for the metal songs because he was the only one who could get his voice low enough. But Hal had been practicing on his own metal voice. Uli had mentioned if he was at all able to learn to do it, it'd be good if himself and Hal split the work since it was hard on the vocal cords. Hal couldn't get his voice as low as Uli could, but with enough practice, he eventually figured out how to add enough grit and rasp to it to get away with singing a few octaves higher than the average. He was able to get a creepy effect without having to go too low.

When they hit the first chorus, more lights came on. Enough to make them more visible, but still keep the stage in a moody state of shadows. Ricky could shred like he'd always done metal, clad in his black cowboy hat with skull band, black western shirt, black jeans and western-style skull belt buckle. His guitar always shined brightest when they were all in black, looking literally like embers against a pile of ash.

During the chorus, Hal got down on his hands and knees, and began to crawl to the front of the stage. He stopped once he was face to face with a woman he picked out of the crowd and sang the chorus directly to her with an intense stare. The girl watched him intently, though she started to look a little unstable. Hal reached out his hand and gently ran one finger down her cheek, and in a state of visible euphoria, she started to fall backwards. One of her friends caught her and held her up. Such the showman, Uli thought. It made him jealous at first, but now it made him mad. Ricky and Hal, who never had a personal interest in metal, had adapted to it very well, while it still made him uncomfortable. He wasn't mad at Hal and Ricky, of course. They weren't the ones to blame. And once it came down to it, neither were his parents.

---

End Song 219

---

220. "Amerika" by Rammstein

---

The next song was Uli's to sing. Hal traded places with him at the keyboard, and he took his place center stage. Hal started a very slight musical intro on the keys, and Uli joined in as well with a deceptively calm vocal lead in. A couple seconds later, Ryan started increasing the beat on his drums, and then all hell broke forth. The guitar had no intro, suddenly raging to life in an explosion of sound accompanied by a powerful jump in the drums and vocals. Then, just like during the show they did back in L.A., they found out Uli had been holding out on them again. He was calm, calculated and cultured most of the time, but very good at hiding what he was actually capable of. It was his voice they heard, but somehow slightly different again;

stronger, heavily marinated in a coating of thick evil, and carrying like an echo roaring through a deep canyon. He stalked slowly to the far end of the stage and back again, walking along the edge barely out of reach of all the people trying to touch his spiked boots. He was getting really hot from the heavy coat and the pyrotechnic blasts going off next to him. He was hot and mad, but it felt right for the song. A lot of people in front had their hands in the air in metal horns, jumping to the beat, a few of them with their teeth bared as they screamed the lyrics along with him. It confirmed what he had suspected the whole time: that he was really going to enjoy it when he finally did break free. He still had to wonder what it was that felt *necessary* to keep depriving himself of the feeling for as long as he had. And all to maintain an image he didn't want, but was supposed to keep for the sake of someone else. He looked down and noticed a group of either older children or very young teenagers singing along with him with strong enthusiasm, and then an even stranger thought crossed his mind. Maybe now he was one of the voices on hidden songs stashed in a bedroom, keeping somebody else company in the dark. Thinking he should be himself for his own sake hadn't been fully convincing, but pleasing a few thousand fans was clearly superior to pleasing two disgruntled parents. It was simple math. He sang straight to them for a few moments, and as they pumped their fists in time with the beat and looked him straight in the eyes, he started getting a better understanding of why Hal enjoyed singing directly to the people in the audience as much as he did. Getting worshipped did wonders for one's self esteem. He could get used to this.

> End Song 220

> 221. "From Paris to Berlin" by Infernal *to play over this scene*
> 222. "The Way I Are" by Timbaland ft. Keri Hilson

223. "I See Right Through to You" by DJ Encore ft. Engelina

224. "Whoomp! (There It Is)" by Tag Team

225. "On the Floor" by Jennifer Lopez ft. Pitbull

226. "Days Go By" by Dirty Vegas

227. "We Found Love" by Rihanna

228. "It Takes Two" by Robb Base & DJ E-Z Rock

229. "Whenever, Wherever" by Shakira

230. "Summer Jam" by The Underdog Project

231. "Scandalous" by Mis-Teeq

232. "Music Sounds Better with You" by Stardust

They went out partying afterwards. This had been an unusually good concert. Very few of their shows ever went bad, but once in a while they did one that felt far better than the rest. One where the audience was more amped up, they were more awake, and everything seemed to go just right. This had been one of those nights. Since they had a few days before they had to be at their next location, Mason and Nora and a bunch of the other road staff joined them. Hal, Uli, and Ryan spent the night drowning themselves in alcohol and women out on the dance floor, while Ricky watched from the side. He had eaten a meal of chicken strips and orange soda, and was about to sneak out to find a nice park to sit in for a while when he noticed Nora sitting up towards the other side of the bar alone. She had her back turned to the counter, and was watching everyone else below. Out of curiosity, he went up to her. "You okay?" he asked, and she looked up at him, surprised.

"Oh, yeah, I'm fine. Just watching," she said.

"You don't do any partyin'?" he asked.

"Oh, no. I'm not much for it. It's not what I do. And I can't drink either. I tried it a few times a while back, and I really didn't have that much, and then I was so very sick in the morning I never wanted to do it again," she said.

"So, you're really just here to learn the job?" Ricky asked.

"Yeah, mostly. But if you can keep a secret, I'm also sort of keeping an eye on my uncle for my father."

"Why's that?" Ricky asked, sitting down next to her.

"Well… like I said, this is all under wraps, but Dad said Uncle Mason had started acting strangely a few months back. He sounded different on the phone, and some of the things he said apparently didn't make much sense. So, Dad started worrying he was doing a little more than occasionally partying too hard with his clients. I'd sort of had a little interest in what it would be like to be a road manager like him for famous groups anyways, and since Dad is too busy with work to spend any amount of time spying on his brother, we figured out I'd intern with him for a season. I'd keep an eye on him, and I'd also have some impressive experience to put on my resumé when I was done."

"Well… you noticed anything goin' on?"

"I'm not sure yet. Up until now, I never spent much time with Uncle Mason, so I'm not sure yet what's him acting normal and what's not. He might also be trying to behave better since I'm around," she said, and immediately afterwards, they watched as Mason lifted his glass upside down in the air over his head to get the last few drops of whatever was left inside. But he apparently leaned a little too far back, and went down with a loud thud on the dance floor. "Or perhaps not." She and Ricky watched for a moment as Hal, Uli, and Ryan went to help Mason up. "I'm beginning to think my family duped me into babysitting a full-grown adult for a few months," Nora said. Mason was helped back onto his feet for a few moments before he suddenly went down again, taking an unstable Hal and Ryan to the floor with him.

"Ricky knows the feeling," Ricky said, and Nora let go a sympathetic laugh. "You at least enjoy travellin' around?" Ricky asked.

"Oh, this is a trip I'll never forget, that's for certain, but I'm not sure I could do this job the rest of my life," she said. "It's too tiring. I like seeing all the sights, but I miss my own bed in my own room."

"Fair 'nuff," Ricky answered.

"So, why aren't *you* down there partying with your friends?" Nora asked.

"Oh, uh, Ricky doesn't party. Not what Ricky does, either."

"Do you always talk about yourself in the third person?"

"Yeah, mostly."

"Alright, well, whatever suits you best," she said, then added: "So, what does Ricky like to do for fun?"

"Oh, uh, walk around outside. Spend time out in nature. Go bird watching."

"Seriously!?" she asked. "That's so cool. If you'd rather take a walk than drink, then you're certainly a rare breed. Especially in this business."

Ricky shrugged his shoulders. "S'pose. Was going to go out and try to find a park in a few minutes and wander around."

"What, in the middle of the night?" she asked.

"Uh, yeah," Ricky answered.

"Ugh. You men are so lucky. You can do stuff like that without having to worry about being followed by creepy guys."

"Do… you want to come too?" Ricky asked.

"Oh, I didn't mean that. I wouldn't want to impose. You probably use that time to clear your mind and unwind, right?" she asked.

"It'd be fine. It's just walkin'," Ricky answered. "But, you prob'ly gotta stay and watch your uncle, huh?"

"Oh, my goodness, my uncle is a grown man. He can watch himself for a while," she said. "You really wouldn't mind if I joined you? It'd be nice to get out of here. It's too loud."

"No, Ricky wouldn't mind at all," Ricky answered. As they got up to leave, Hal, Ryan, and Mason all got to their feet this time, and started moving as one unit towards the wall, where they'd be able to hold onto something until the world quit spinning so fast. That way, it wouldn't be able to keep knocking them over.

Hal woke up on the hotel room floor the next morning. He hadn't done that in a long time. He knew better than to try and sit up right away, and instead stared at the ceiling until his eyes regained focus. He looked over and found a naked woman on the floor next to him, sound asleep and with her makeup smeared all across her face. He wiped the back of his hand across his mouth, then looked at it. Yep, that was the same shade of lipstick that she had on. Next step was to take stock of his clothes. Shirt? Nope. Pants? Nope. Underwear? Present, but bunched sideways. He put his hand on the floor and stared to push himself up. Slowly, slowly, slowly, and he was sitting. He looked around the room. Empty beer cans and other bottles littered the floor, as well as a few pizza boxes and empty condom wrappers. The fact the wrappers were empty was probably a good thing. He looked around more and was shocked to see Uli asleep on the couch, completely nude, and with a long-legged brunette passed out on top of him. It must have been one hell of an after party they had last night.

Next step was to stand up. He turned over onto his hands and knees and used the arm of the couch to hoist himself up. He found his pants on the floor and drug them behind him into the bathroom. He came out a few minutes later and started the coffee machine warming. Once it began brewing, it was back to taking stock. Lead singer? Check. Pianist /orchestral specialist? Check. Bracing himself against the counter, he turned around again, and scanned the entire room. The other two were still unaccounted for. He was only seeing the main common room of the suite, however. He tried the first bedroom door to the side. Drummer? Check. Also, one, two, three, holy shit, *four*; four naked women as well. He closed the door quietly. He wasn't entirely expecting to find Ricky in this disaster, but there he was in the next bedroom. Alone, and sound asleep in a perfectly clean and straight room. He shut the door. Poor Ricky. He wondered at what point in the night he had come back, and what he must have had to step over to get to his room.

He poured himself the first cup of coffee and took a few minutes to wake up. The next thought that managed to form in his head was if there was a roller rink anywhere nearby. After this, they owed Ricky some skate time. He took another sip and surveyed the scene again. It was rather impressive. He really wasn't one for trashing hotel rooms, but they'd outdone themselves this time. He'd probably end up cleaning it all up himself out of guilt. He still couldn't believe Uli was asleep on the couch. He almost always was sober *enough* to get himself into bed at the end of a party. And Ryan had outdone himself, too. Four might have been a new record.

---

233. "Dancing Queen" by ABBA *to play over this scene*

234. "Relax" by Frankie Goes to Hollywood

235. "Y.M.C.A." by The Village People

236. "Blue (Da Ba Dee)" by Eiffel 65

237. "Celebration" by Kool & The Gang

238. "One Night in Bangkok" by Murray Head

239. "MMMBop" by Hanson

240. "September" by Earth, Wind & Fire

241. "The Loco-Motion" by Little Eva

242. "Cotton Eye Joe" by The Rednex

243. "I Will Survive" by Gloria Gaynor

244. "Walk the Dinosaur" by Was (Not Was)

245. "You Sexy Thing" by Hot Chocolate

---

Hal made the mistake of asking Ryan later that day how he managed to handle four girls at once. He imagined they had to take turns waiting for a few minutes each, but that was not the case. Ryan explained: "Two hands, a mouth and a dick. That's four."

"Damn," Hal replied, lacing up his rental skates. Ryan's eyes were still bloodshot red, too, even though evening was approaching. That *really* must have been one hell of a party they had last night.

End Songs 233 – 245

# CHAPTER 16

## (Around the World)

**Everything was moving so fast,** it was easy to lose track of where they were, and what was going on. All of them had days where they woke up and had to remember what country they were in. Most days were get up, travel, get ready, do a high-energy show, go to bed exhausted, and wake up the next morning to hurry on to the next city or across the next border to do it all over again. It took at least a month before any of them started to realize they were passing by some of the most amazing places in the world without stopping to appreciate them. "We have to carve out time to see some of the sights!" Hal insisted as they rode in their bus on the way to Paris. "It would be nice, but what time do we have to do so?" Uli asked.

"I dunno, anything. Even if it's just a few hours here and there. We're travelling through Europe for God's sake, and not only that, we're being paid to do it! I'm not saying we stop to see everything, but we need to at least see the Eiffel Tower, and Stonehenge, and Neuschwanstein Castle when we get back to Germany! I put together a 1,000-piece puzzle of that castle when I was a kid," Hal said. Even though they had already done shows in England and Germany, they would be back to do more in different cities. It would make more sense if they got all the shows in the same country done in one go, but quite often it didn't work out that way due to scheduling conflicts with the various venues. And so, they found themselves bouncing back and forth between the same countries multiple times.

"While we are in France, we should really see the Louvre Museum as well, and Notre Dame," Uli added. "And when we get back to England we should see the British museum."

"Sure," Hal agreed. "Here, I'll start making a list," he pulled out a piece of scrap paper from his notebook and started writing.

"Dude, we should spend the night in one of those old castles in Ireland when we do Belfast and Dublin," Ryan said. "And Ricky can talk to all the castle ghosties."

"Okay!" Ricky agreed. Hal cringed as he added 'Irish Castles' to the list.

"That made me think of another place, we need to do the tour of the French Catacombs," Uli said.

"That's where the hallways are made up of stacks of skulls and bones right?" Ryan asked.

"Yes. Piles of skeletons," Uli answered.

"Sweet!" Ryan responded.

"Catacomb tour…" Hal repeated, writing that one down somewhat unwillingly as well, then added: "I know another one, the Roman Colosseum in Italy! I mean, yes, we're busy, and there's tons of things to see, but if we can at least hit these main ones that'll be good."

"Hell yeah, get our skuzziest clothes and darkest sunglasses and do the tourist thing a little bit. It'll be a nice break from the action," Ryan replied.

"I'm sure the planning crew already has our accommodations all laid out, so they'll probably be really thrilled about us wanting to change a few things. But if we don't seize the opportunity to go see some of these places, I know I'll regret it the rest of my life," Hal said.

"No, you're right," Ryan agreed.

"We are in Paris tonight, let's eat dinner in the Eiffel Tower," Uli said.

"Wait, there's a restaurant in the Eiffel Tower!?" Hal asked.

"Yes. More than one, I believe."

"Huh, just like the Space Needle," Ryan added.

"There's a restaurant in the Space Needle!?" Hal asked.

"Yeah, duh, everyone knows that," Ryan answered. "Though the one in the Eiffel Tower probably doesn't rotate."

"The Space Needle restaurant rotates!?" Hal asked in disbelief

"Yup. The view you get below changes throughout your dinner, but the part with the windowsill next to the tables doesn't rotate with the tables. So, you can't set your camera or whatever on the windowsill next to you, because if you aren't paying attention, it's gonna be next to a different table by the time you realize what happened."

"That's so cool! I mean, not the losing your camera part, but that the Space Needle rotates!"

"Not the whole thing, just part of the restaurant inside," Ryan corrected him.

"Still!" Hal said. "Godammit, we missed most of the good spots in the U.S. too. I guess we did Vegas and Hawaii, but we need a U.S. list for the next time we tour at home." Hal pulled out a second piece of paper.

"Space Needle," he said out loud as he wrote it.

"Uh… Disneyland?" Ricky spoke up.

Hal smiled. "Disneyland." He wrote it on the list.

"The Grand Canyon," Uli said.

"And Bryce Canyon and Zion National Park," Ryan added. "My parents took us down there in an R.V. once. The rock formations in Bryce Canyon are really, really weird. And Zion National Park has this rock alcove in the face of a cliff that drips water out of it, even in the middle of summer. I think it was called the 'Weeping Rock.' You can get up in the alcove and sit down and watch the water drip in front of you. Sort of like being behind a really, really slow waterfall in a shallow cave. It's up a trail of steep stairs in this cliff, so the view is amazing too."

"Bryce Canyon, Zion National Park - (Weeping Rock)…" Hal tried to keep up.

"Yellowstone National Park!" Ricky said.

"The Golden Gate Bridge," Uli added.

"New Orleans," Ryan said.

"Mount Rushmore?" Ricky suggested.

"Skiing in Utah and Colorado…" Uli said.

"Okay, okay… hold on…" Hal said.

Once he had caught up, Ricky began again. "Florida Everglades."

"Alaska and… you know, all the Alaska stuff that comes along with it," Ryan said.

"The Smithsonian Museum of Natural History, and everything else of note in Washington D.C.," Uli added.

"What is it with you and museums?" Ryan asked.

"They are efficient. Lots to see in one building," Uli explained.

"Well, if we're going to do D.C., we have to do New York too. The Statue of Liberty, Central Park, the Entire State Building…" Ryan said.

"Did you just call it the *Entire* State Building?" Hal asked.

"Oh, yeah. That's a running joke in my family. That's what my little brother thought the Empire State Building was called."

"Nice," Hal said as he wrote it down. "I guess the dumbest thing I thought as a kid was… well, first, for some reason Mom always called ambulances 'Aid Cars.' Because, I dunno, maybe she thought I'd have an easier time remembering that when I was little. But I misheard her and always thought if you got hurt or really sick, something called the 'Egg Car' would come help you."

"Ricky thought there was a State of New Hamster," Ricky said, and they all laughed.

"You would think there was a state called New Hamster," Ryan said.

Hal looked at the list again. "I think we have all the big ones," he said, then thought of something else. "Hey, Ryan, isn't there that place in Seattle called 'Pike Place Market' that's really famous?"

"Yeah, we can do Pike Place, though I don't know how it gets so much attention when there's better stuff around. I mean, I see it often as 2nd or 3rd on the lists of things to do in Seattle when it really deserves to be 6th or 7th. It's alright. It's really old and weird and it's supposed to be haunted. The shops are in layers, and guys throw fish to each other upstairs, which is amazing to people who don't live on the coast, I guess. But there's other things we need to hit as well next time we're there."

"Like?" Hal asked.

"Well, lemme think. There's the shops on the pier, which are way better than the ones in Pike Place if you ask me. Especially the 'Ye Olde Curiosity Shop.' There's the Seattle Underground, the Pacific Science Center, the Seattle Aquarium with the awesome dome room where you can see the fish swim above you. There's all the little independent art cafes around the city…"

"Whoa, whoa, whoa… wait a second…" Hal said, writing furiously.

"What is the appeal of all these things?" Uli asked.

"Okay, so, the Curiosity Shop is this weird Shop/Museum thing on the Pier. The Museum stuff is hanging from the ceiling and on the walls, and the shopping is all in the middle of the store surrounded by the museum on all sides. The store specializes in weird things, so for shopping you can buy gag gifts, small import art pieces, little cool and weird trinkets, and what not. The museum stuff is random items from all over the world, but they really specialize in dead, preserved things. They have several taxidermied animals born with extra limbs and body parts. They have a few stitched-together 'trophies' like a mounted jackalope head, a creepy-ass 'mermaid' mummy made out of a monkey and a fish, and they have at least four dead people in there, maybe more."

"Mummies?" Uli asked.

"Yeah, three of them are. The other one I remember is a bare skeleton. The mummies aren't Egyptian mummies, though. One's an unidentified cowboy who was found dead in the Southwest Desert. One's from South America. I forget where the other one is from. Oh, they also have a collection of shrunken heads. So, yeah, more than four dead people."

"Damn," Hal said.

"Yeah, there's other stuff too. There's some old swords, random antiques, and other crap like that. But yeah, it's a really neat place if dead things don't bother you. Um, now, the Seattle Underground tours underneath the streets in the Pioneer Square area, and you see parts of some of the buildings that got buried when they did the Seattle regrade," Ryan said. Hal, Uli, and Ricky stared at him blankly. "Yeah… okay, so, Seattle used to literally be lower and more hilly. Then, when the city started to get built up they decided to try and flatten parts of it out to make it more buildable and easy to travel, I guess. They were also having massive plumbing problems at high tide, like, toilets would erupt in literal shit-splosions. So, they decided to raise parts of Seattle up higher by taking down some massive area hills and using the dirt to raise the altitude of the lower areas. In the process, sections of existing Seattle buildings were buried and built on top of. Someone figured out much later that the buildings underground are super creepy and would make a great tourist attraction, and so the Seattle Underground tours were set up."

"There's an entire abandoned second city under Seattle!?" Hal asked.

"Well… there's bits and pieces of it. Most of it got completely obliterated, but there's a few specific areas under the streets where you can go and see chunks of historic brick buildings underground. It'd be much cooler if there was more of it, because there's actually not much left. Even during the tour you sometimes have to go back above ground, walk a few blocks, and then go back down into the underground in a separate entrance because it's not all connected. But it's still sort of a cool thing to do at least once. What's even weirder is sometimes you walk under open grates where you can see people walking on the streets above you. And also, part of the tour goes under a building that has an extremely popular nightclub in it. So, if you're down there at the right time, you could be looking through the window or door of an old, buried building while listening to people six feet above you partying."

"Alright…" Hal said, intrigued.

"The Aquarium pretty much speaks for itself, but like I said, there's a cool dome room where you can see the fish 360 degrees and above your head… um, what else did I say?" Ryan asked.

"Pacific Science Center," Hal said, looking at his paper.

"Ah, yes. If you grew up in Seattle as a kid, you ended up at the Science Center at least two or three times on school field trips. And it's not as boring as it sounds. It's made for people who don't have an interest in science to try and get them interested. Like, they have huge animatronic dinosaurs, and a human-sized hamster wheel over the water pools outside that you can run in. There's also a set up of two big funnel thingies that are like, one hundred feet apart, but they face each other, and if someone says something into one of them, the person across the room hears what they said in the other funnel even though they have no wired connection. There's a big IMAX theater that they run science movies in, plus there's the laser dome where you can see laser light shows on the ceiling set to music. There's always presentations you can sit in on where they blow shit up inside, there's the naked mole rat colony… there's just a ton of stuff. It was really cool to go there as a kid. Now, I haven't been there since I was a kid, so maybe some of the exhibits have changed or been replaced, but it'd be worth checking out again."

"You know, to really see a city, I think you have to have a local show you around," Hal commented. "Because I'm sure there's lesser known attractions around Europe that are really cool and deserve to be seen more, but you'd never know about it unless someone who lives nearby shows you."

"Yeah, pretty much. Once we get back to Washington, I'll take you guys on a really good Sea-Town tour."

"Yeah, I think we've already done Battle Creek *and* Battle Creek the best we can," Hal joked.

"Oh, hey, nature boy…" Ryan said to Ricky. "You were mentioning some of the national parks. We should also go to Olympic National Park if we can get at least a week off in Washington. Parts of the forest there look like something out of Middle Earth. Huge trees that would take at least ten people to hug them. Forests with so much moss hanging from the tree branches that they form moss-curtains and make the trees look like fuzzy moss monsters. Lots of wild animals you can see at close range. A few really unique waterfalls…"

"Okay!" Ricky said.

"Olympic National Park…" Hal wrote it down.

"And we can certainly work on this list more as we think of more places, but I say tonight we dine in the Eiffel Tower," Uli said.

"I think that'd be a great start," Hal agreed.

Later that evening, they lined up against the window looking out at Paris, and Hal handed Uli his phone. "You get to do the honors, you have the longest arms," he said, and Uli held the phone up over them. "Eiffel tower selfie!" Hal said, and they all briefly pulled back their hats and glasses as the phone clicked. The days that followed brought a Mona Lisa selfie at the Louvre Museum, a Notre Dame selfie, and a 'creepy' selfie in the catacombs under Paris. They checked off everything else on the list in the months that followed until finally, they spent the night in an old Irish castle. The next morning, they met Mason, Nora and part of the road crew for breakfast.

"So, how are you liking the Emerald Isle?" Nora asked.

"It is beautiful," Uli answered.

"Well, this castle is sure awesome!" Ryan said. "Spending the night in an old, haunted castle isn't exactly something we can do back home."

"So, did you see any of the castle ghosts last night?" Nora teased.

"We didn't see one, but we had a chair move on its own in our room," Ryan said.

"Really!?" Nora asked.

"Yeah! Pulled itself back from the table about a foot. Scared the shit out of us, especially Hal."

"Yeah… let's… talk about something else…" Hal mumbled.

"Hey, Ricky, what did the ghost say his name was again?" Ryan asked.

"Uh… Sheamus…" Ricky said quietly.

"The ghost told you his name?" Nora asked startled. "You heard him talk?"

"Well, Ricky… did…" Ryan said, suddenly realizing what he had done. An apologetic look of '*crap… sorry man*' spread across his face as he glanced over at Ricky.

"You heard the ghost say his name?" Nora asked Ricky.

"Uh… yeah…" Ricky replied, uncomfortably.

"So, Nora, what part of Ireland are you from again?" Hal asked.

"Oh, Dublin. Good ol' Dublin," she said. Hal was obviously trying to change the subject, so she dropped it for the time, but Ricky wasn't going to get out of it that easily. Later, when they had a moment alone, Nora pulled him to the side. "Not only do you attract animals, but you talk to ghosts as well?" she asked quietly.

"Well… sometimes…" Ricky answered. Nora raised one eyebrow at him. That look made him nervous every time.

"What else is there?" she asked.

"Nothin'," Ricky said quickly.

"You're a liar," she said, the Irish accent she tried to hide making a very noticeable appearance. "And you're going to tell me everything."

"Uh, yes, ma'am…" Ricky answered, though he was hoping to put it off until they were back from the leg of their tour through Asia and Australia. Nora and Mason wouldn't be joining them for that part of the tour; different road managers would handle those areas. But after they were done, they had more dates to play in Europe. That'd give him a little time to think through how much he was going to say.

"See you in a month and a half," Mason said, waving them off at the airport as they boarded the first of a series of change-over flights that would eventually take them to Australia.

"Bye!" Hal called back as they started down the corridor, all except for Ricky.

He stood facing Nora, who gave him the warning again: "Enjoy your month and a half, because we're having a talk the next time we take a walk. And don't think you're going to come up with a good story, because you are a terrible liar." He smiled and nodded.

They stood there looking at each other a moment more, Ricky slowly, slowly beginning to blush… but then she started to step away. "See you in a bit," she said.

"'K," he answered quietly. He turned to join the other three on the plane and saw them all standing in the doorway of the gate, staring in disbelief. He held his breath as he went over to them. Wide, prying grins formed on all three of their faces as he walked past. This was going to be a long plane ride.

246. "Land Down Under" by Men at Work *to play over this scene*

"This is torture," Ryan said, laying on a deck chair in the light of the sunset with a bottle of beer next to him.

"Hey, Jim warned us touring would be miserable," Hal reminded him.

"This is so awful, I might have to move here someday," Ryan added.

"Told you this would be fun," Hal said.

"Well, you guys didn't mention there'd be such nice accommodations when you said you wanted to see 'That Giant Rock in Australia'!"

"It is not just a rock, Uluru is one of the world's largest free-standing monoliths, surrounded by bountiful native Australian animals and plants. Not to mention, this is a place of spirits for the Aboriginal people," Uli explained.

"Yeah, see, if you'd have just said that in the first place, it would have made more sense!" Ryan insisted.

"And it's going to make for a great hike tomorrow," Hal said.

"So, what else are we gonna hit in Australia?" Ryan asked.

"Well, obviously the Sydney Opera House, and we have to go see the Crocodile Hunter's zoo," Hal said.

"Yeah, that was such a great show," Ryan said.

"I know. I think when he died that was the only time I was actually, honestly really upset about hearing that a celebrity had passed away," Hal lamented.

"Ricky can't go," Ricky said. "But you guys have fun there."

"Oh, come on. I'm going to feel terrible if we go without you," Hal said.

"It's okay. Don't feel bad," Ricky insisted.

"But you like animals more than any of us," Hal retorted.

"Yeah, but if Ricky goes into a zoo, things will get weird real quick," Ricky replied.

"Well, we'll just have to deal with it as we go. We can't be in Australia and not see the animals," Hal said.

"Oh, Ricky plans on meeting all the critters," he said, tipping his sunglasses up and looking off in the direction of the sunset.

"Wait… you can't be serious," Hal said.

"Why not?" Ricky asked.

"Because it's hot and there's a ton of poisonous shit out there!" Hal said.

"It'll cool after the sun goes down, and poisonous things don't bite Ricky," Ricky reminded him.

"Yeah, Hal, the worst he has to fear from all the snakes is that they'll all want to cuddle at once," Ryan said.

"Yep," Ricky agreed. "Well, see y'all in the morning," he said as he suddenly stood up and jumped over the railing of the deck and took off running towards the open outback.

"Uh… be safe, make good choices!" Hal yelled after him. Ricky raised his hand in the air and called back "Yes, Mom!" It was still hard to accept

Ricky could do things that would get the average person killed, but it was nice to see him smiling for once as he ran off into the night.

End Song 246

247. "Under the Milky Way" by The Church

He could feel the last wisps of heat leaving the desert floor for the night; rising between his fingers and up his sides as he lay on his back, scanning the arc of the Milky Way above. The silhouettes of kangaroos and dingoes blocked the starlight close to the horizon as they moved around him. Some came up to inspect him. It was interesting, they came close like all other animals did, but they seemed a little confused and wary, like they could sense he was from a place far away. It made it more of a treat to see them, because they didn't jump straight into his lap. He'd made it far enough from the resort that he couldn't see the building lights anymore, but he could tell from the little movements of shadow that there were still more animals off in the distance ahead of him. He got up. A few young dingoes had been hanging around him. Rushing him and then running away, trying to get him to react. The predators are always the least afraid, and the most playful.

He took his sandals off and set them on a nearby rock. He'd make sure to retrieve them on his way back, but the warm sand felt good on his feet. He looked at the dingoes, then took off running. They pursued playfully as he made his way further into the dark of the desert. He caught glimpses of glowing eyes in the bushes watching him go by, and snakes and lizards scattered ahead of his feet while jumping mice bounced to and fro in the shrub. Parks were perfectly nice to spend time in, but it felt really good to be out in a true, healthy wilderness once in a while. The desert landscape was so different from what he was used to, he might as well have been running over the surface of an alien planet, even though he was simply on the exact opposite side of his own. When he looked up at the stars, it also oddly felt like he might have been running through outer space itself. He aligned himself with the path of the Milky Way, and ran towards where it touched down on the horizon in front of him. It didn't look too far ahead, so surely he could reach it before sunrise. He felt a rare and welcome fire in his chest. His spirit was most pleased by this. The Australian Outback beat the crap out of little city parks any day, though not *all* of the heat was from the desert. Part of it was from the thought of glowing red curls.

End Song 247

The baby kicked, and it woke Cecilia up. "Uh oh, what's he done now?" she mumbled. She had decided, just to amuse herself, that whenever the baby kicked, it meant Hal was in trouble. There was another kick. "Uh, huh?" she said quietly. A third kick. "Really?" A fourth kick, the hardest so far. "Wow, he's really in a mess this time, isn't he?" Things settled for a bit after that, and she was about to fall back asleep when her stomach muscles suddenly seized tight, and sharp pain shot through her. She sat up instantly, breathing hard. She waited a few moments, then her stomach seized tightly again, pulling her into a sitting fetal position. Her midsection felt like it was being sucked into a black hole forming in her own belly. She started a cold sweat, then as a third shot of pain hit, she yelled "HARVEY!!!" at the top of her lungs. He jumped up and fell out of the bed. It was still the middle of the night.

"ZZZ… ZZ… ZOMBIES!!!"

Ryan hit Hal hard on the back of the head. "SHUT UP, HAL, YOU'RE NOT FUNNY!" They backed into a tight huddle as the mob got closer. Five hundred, maybe six hundred fan girls had them surrounded on top of one of the tour busses behind a stadium in Tokyo. A few of them caught sight of them sneaking around outside, and their giddy screams quickly alerted many more. Now they were starting to climb up the sides of the bus. "THERE'S TOO MANY OF THEM!" Ryan sounded more frustrated than scared.

"WHAT DO WE DO!?" Hal yelled.

"WE'LL HAVE TO KICK THEM IF THEY GET TOO CLOSE!" Uli said.

"I CAN'T KICK PRETTY GIRLS! ESPECIALLY NOT FANS!" Hal replied.

"I DON'T WANT TO EITHER, BUT WHAT ELSE CAN WE DO!? IF THEY GET A HOLD OF US, THEY MIGHT TEAR US APART!" Uli insisted.

Just then, they caught sight of a familiar figure way in the back of the crowd. Ken Daisuke, their road manager for the Asian portion of the tour, was waving at them while talking loudly into his cell phone. "KEN!!! HELP!!!" Hal yelled.

"POLICE ARE ON THE WAY! POLICE ARE COMING!" Ken yelled back. The stadium security crew was doing their best to get to them, but they were vastly outnumbered. Ken was about ready to pull his hair out. "*Not good! Not good!*" he said to himself. The police seemed to be taking their time, or at least, it felt like they were. A few girls were nearing the bus roof.

"WE HAVE TO DEFEND OURSELVES!" Uli said, sticking the heel of his shoe out, ready to push at the hands about to come over the top.

"NO! NO! KEEP YOUR ARMS AND LEGS IN! IF THEY GET A HOLD OF YOU, THEY'LL PULL YOU DOWN!" Ken yelled from the back. Uli quickly brought his foot back in close to himself. They watched as a few sets of fingers grasped onto the top.

"It's been a pleasure working with you guys," Hal said.

"Hey, if we have to die, death by hot Asian chicks will be a pretty glorious way to go," Ryan said.

"RICKY WOULD RATHER DIE OLD IN HIS SLEEP THANKYOUVERYMUCH!!!" Ricky bellowed at Ryan.

"HEY! I DIDN'T SAY THIS IS MY PREFERRED METHOD, BUT IF WE HAVE TO DIE YOUNG, THIS IS THE WAY TO DO IT! IT'LL BE A HELL OF A HEADLINE!" Ryan yelled back.

*Oh shit, we are going to die,* Hal thought to himself. If Ricky was screaming at Ryan at the top of his lungs, then the end truly was near.

The first girl's head peaked up from the edge. The look of desperate, unconditional love on her face sent a chill down Hal's spine. It was a look he'd never forget. The wave of despair had just begun to wash over him when the first sounds of sirens barely began to make themselves heard over the crowd.

About an hour later, they slammed the door shut behind them, safely inside the backstage of the stadium. The police had just cleared the crowd out of the loading area, and they were about to finally start getting ready when Hal's cell phone started to ring. "Hello?" Hal answered, frazzled.

*"Hey, kid. Your mom's gone into labor."*

"What!?" Hal said. "She's not due for another month and a half!"

*"I know, trust me. But apparently the baby has other plans."*

"Is she okay!?"

*"Just a sec…"* Harvey's voice became quieter. *"'Celia, Hal wants to know if you're okay?"*

Hal heard her strained voice answer: *"Yeah… great…"*

"Shit, and we have a show tonight, so…"

*"Hal, don't you dare think about cancelling your show to come back here,"* his mom grunted. *"I'll be alright. We just wanted to let you know what's going on."*

"Mom, you're way more important than a concert, so I'm going to head out now."

"*Hal, I'll be okay. We're almost to the hospital, it's not like we're stuck in the middle of nowhere. If you must come home, wait until you have a few days break between shows.*"

"How the hell am I supposed to concentrate on a show knowing this is happening? It's going to be ruined anyways, and I'm NOT blaming you, I'm just saying there's no point in staying here, we'll re-schedule it."

"*Hal! Absolutely not! I'm not going anywhere! We'll see you in a few days, okay?*" Cecilia said loudly, followed by a small shriek of pain that made Hal's stomach tie itself in a knot.

"*I got her, Hal. You're not the only one who loves your mom. We'll take care of her,*" Harvey assured him.

"But…"

"*Hal, if you cancel your show that's going to upset me more, okay? Please come home in a few days when you have a break.*"

"Mom…" Hal said.

"*It's not up for debate,*" he heard her say.

"Alright," Hal said. "Promise you'll call me if anything happens. I'll keep my phone in my pocket during the show."

"*I'll call if we need to,*" Harvey said. "*And feel free to call as soon as you're done for the night, and we'll give you the full update.*"

"Okay…" Hal said quietly.

"*Have a good show sweetheart, we'll call you later,*" Cecilia said.

"Love you, Mom. Be okay," he answered.

"*I will. Bye.*"

"Bye," he said, then leaned back against the door to keep himself from falling down completely.

"Sorry, man," Ryan said quietly. Him, Uli, and Ricky were standing to the side, Uli and Ricky looking down at their feet.

"Your mom is a strong lady. She'll be alright," Ricky said. Hal nodded silently. "I have a feeling this might be another one of those liquid courage concerts," Ryan said.

Hal sighed. "Yeah. Pretty much."

"I'll get something strong out…" Ryan said as he went over and started rifling through his bag.

Never had three days felt like such an eternity, but they finally made it home. Cecilia and Harvey met them at the hospital. Cecilia had spent the first night there, then was discharged the next day. Baby Charlotte was in for a longer stay. "Hi, Mom," he said as they met in the lobby, and he hugged her gently.

"Hi, sweetheart," she said. "Hi, guys."

"How are you doing?" Ryan asked.

"Oh, still weak and tired, but I've been feeling a little better each day," Cecilia answered.

"That is good," Uli said.

"Yes, I'll be fine. Squeezing out a tiny human is a bit of a chore, but I'm on the mend."

"I'm glad. We were worried about you," Hal said.

"I know you were, but the worst of it is over now."

"So, how's my sister doing?" he asked.

"Charlotte's still stable and responding to treatment. She's premature, but it's looking good that she'll survive. They haven't found any abnormalities, so hopefully she'll be able to grow up healthy."

"Medicine has come very far, she has a good chance," Uli agreed.

"Yes, it's exciting. But I bet you want to see her for yourself."

"Well, I am slightly curious," Hal laughed, though he had no idea what he was in for.

The little baby in the neonatal intensive care unit barely looked real; a squirming, pink creature lying in the incubator attached to every possible wire and tube there was. "Hello my sweet, Charlotte. We're back, and your whole family is here now. This is your big brother, Hal, and his three best friends," Cecilia said quietly to the little girl.

Hal thought he'd want to spend a while taking in the sight of this miraculous sibling, but now he wanted to get out of the room as quickly as possible. Seeing his mom doing okay had removed the sense of panic, but now it was replaced by a slow, sinking feeling. Hal could only imagine how horrible it had to feel having that many tubes rammed into her little body, and it made him sick. Apparently he was a total wimp. It wasn't even his kid, after all. He didn't have to deal with her except on the rare occasion he was visiting home. But he had to wonder if that was what was so distressing about the whole thing. There was nothing he could do to help her. He was doing his best to retain a poker face, but as he looked over to Ryan and Uli, they didn't look particularly comfortable either. Ricky, however, seemed perfectly at ease. He'd probably seen enough newborn babies in his life.

"My God…" was all Hal could manage to say.

"She's so little," Ryan added quietly.

"Yes, but she's going to grow up nice and strong," Cecilia said, reaching her hand into the attached glove for the incubator box and stroking the side of Charlotte's head.

They stayed for about an hour, then decided to go back to the house with Cecilia and Harvey for a bit. As they were walking through the parking lot, Ricky leaned in and said quietly to Hal: "Don't worry, she's gonna be okay."

"I hope so," Hal replied somberly.

"No, she will be okay. She's real uncomfortable from all the wires, and from bein' born and all, but bein' born ain't comfortable for anybody. She ain't strugglin' to stay alive, so unless somethin' serious happens, she'll be fine," Ricky said, and Hal slowly turned to look at him, but Ricky made sure to keep his eyes straight ahead as they followed Hal's parents back to the van.

# CHAPTER 17

## (Hot N' Cold)

It was a steamy hot night in Madrid, Spain, so Hal blamed the sweat running down his face on the heat. They were preparing for their second concert back in Europe. The first one in Portugal had gone well, but Hal had a bad feeling about tonight's show. The last thing he ever wanted to do was disappoint their fans with a poor performance, but with how Ryan had been acting the last few days, he was certain Ryan had started using some sort of drugs again. He'd been doing so well since they parted ways with Holy Hell. To everyone's surprise, he hadn't kept up the Marijuana habit once they set out on their own tour. Everything was fine during the domestic segment of the tour, but once they started the European segment, Ryan started acting strangely again. He went back to acting normal on the Asia and Australia leg of their tour, but now that they were back in Europe the odd behavior was back. Hal had a theory why that was, and his theory was named Mason Harding. Mason seemed to be the common link lately for when Ryan was and wasn't acting like he was on drugs. And he had watched Mason and Ryan party really hard after the show in Portugal. Hal wasn't mad yet. And he didn't want to be, but they'd all worked hard to get where they were, and he didn't want it to come undone over something this stupid. He held onto the hope that if Ryan could possibly do anything well while intoxicated, that it would be drumming. "*Please, God, say he can drum high…*" Hal whispered, right before the first lights came on.

The night wasn't a huge disaster, like Hal had feared, but Ryan was a little off the whole time. No one would have ever guessed it, though, from the energetic performance he put on. He obviously thought he was doing a great job. Luckily, Uli and Ricky were so good they didn't really need him to keep themselves on track, and Ryan wasn't off enough that the audience seemed to notice. They spent so much time screaming it made a great cover for mistakes, but they wouldn't get away with it forever. Hal felt like he really should have been mad, but the anger wasn't forming. It just made him depressed, and anxious for future shows. He confronted Ryan after the show, even though he knew he was likely still high. He decided to start with the friendly approach. "Hey, Ryan…"

Ryan looked up from his bag on the ground with an oddly alert smile. "Yeah?"

"Did you take some good shit before the show and not share it with the rest of us?"

"What?" Ryan answered quickly, still smiling. His pupils were disturbingly huge looking.

"I'm asking if you have a secret stash of something you're not sharing," Hal said.

"I dunno. I dunno what you're talking about," Ryan replied.

"Mmm, hmm," Hal responded. Mason came around the corner. "Hey! Great show everybody! So, we ready to go party!?"

"Fuck yeah!" Ryan said loudly.

"And you guys?" Mason asked Hal.

"I don't know, I'm sort of beat," Hal said.

"Not tonight, Mason," Uli agreed.

"Suit yourselves," Mason said. "You ready? I think the road crew can get the rest of this," Mason said to Ryan.

"Oh, yeah!" Ryan replied, pulling a regular cigarette out of his pocket and walking out the back to Mason's waiting car. The other three watched them go.

"Try again when he is sober," Uli said. "Not that he will be any more cooperative, but he might at least understand what you are saying to him."

"Yeah, I know," Hal said. "I guess I was hoping maybe I'd catch him off guard, and he'd be a little more forthcoming since he was high."

"I did not think about it that way," Uli said. "But what are you hoping to accomplish? We already know he's doing drugs. What is the benefit of getting him to admit it?"

"I don't know. I guess I just wanted to see what he'd say. See if he said anything useful we could use against him," Hal explained. Uli seemed to be considering that. "I'll try him again when he's not high," Hal repeated.

"I would offer to help, but he is far more likely to talk to you than me," Uli said.

"Oh, I know. Don't worry about it."

"If there is anything we can do to assist that does not involve trying to get him to talk, let us know," Uli said, and Ricky nodded in agreement.

"Thanks, I will."

They went back to the hotel to rest, and Ricky did his usual disappearing act, but tonight, he wasn't alone. "Pretty sure your Uncle Mason and Ryan are usin' drugs together," Ricky said.

"Great…" Nora mumbled. "Well, I'll tell my father about Uncle Mason. But there's probably not much he can do until we go back home."

"Yeah. Sorry," Ricky said.

"It's okay. Thank you for the information," she said.

"Sure," Ricky replied.

"But now it's *your turn*," she said, getting in front of him and walking backwards as she poked him playfully in the chest. "Start talking."

"Uh, 'bout what?" Ricky asked.

"Oh, mercy," Nora sighed. "You know exactly what. You. Animals. Ghosts. Start talking," she insisted.

"Uh, well…" Ricky said.

"Yes?"

"It's a really long story, and a little hard to believe…"

Nora looked at her watch. "Well, if that's the case, you had better start soon."

Ricky sighed. "'Kay, so… it all started before Ricky was born…" They walked slowly through the park as he told her the story. He could tell at times that she was having trouble buying some of what he said, but she listened patiently all the way through until he had finished. "So… yeah. That's sort of it," he said nervously.

"That was… quite the tale you just told," she said with noticeable uncertainty. "Though, it sounds like you could prove it, somehow."

"Well, yeah…" Ricky mumbled. "You promise not to scream or pass out or anythin'?"

"I will do my best," Nora replied.

Ricky stopped walking and looked around the park to see what he could use, and noticed a tree to the side of the path that had a crop of small brown nuts hanging from its branch tips. He walked over and picked one, then held it in his palm in front of her. "Ready?" he asked.

"Yes," she answered quietly.

"Alright…" he said, looking down at his hand. She watched as the outer shell of the nut split, and a small, green shoot began to emerge. It made a few spirals as it grew, and then a bright green leaf opened at its tip. She looked up at him, her mouth agape. It was the look of she had tried to believe what he was saying, but she hadn't actually, *actually* thought she'd see it with her own eyes.

"Um, yeah..." Ricky mumbled, looking away from her.

"You're… really an amazing man."

"Well, it's not like Ricky earned it or practiced it or... somethin'. Just got born with it."

"Yeah, but it's still unique. And it's not the only thing that makes you amazing," she said, and he looked back up at her. "Your friends are out partying and drinking, and one of them is doing drugs, but here you are instead, walking around a park with a clear mind, sprouting seeds. Even minus the sprouting seeds, the fact that you're here instead of doing what they're doing makes you unique."

He started to blush. "Yeah, well, you're doing the same. You're here instead of doing drugs with your uncle," he replied.

"Yeah," she agreed. "And so… here we both are." She crossed her arms and gazed at him silently for a while, and he felt his face getting warmer the longer the awkward silence ensued.

"Uh… so, after we're done walkin', do you want to go back to the hotel and play Yahtzee again?" he asked, and a gentle smile formed at the corners of her lips.

"That sounds lovely," she answered. As they started walking back along the trail, he felt her hand slip into his, and he closed his fingers gently around hers as they made their way deeper into the shadows down the path.

Ryan's reliability came and went in the weeks that followed. Some nights, everything was fine. Other nights, he was barely able to keep a beat. Hal wished he'd chosen one path or the other. Of course he would have preferred Ryan choose the sober path, but if he would at least be consistent with not being able to do his part, they could quit playing the guessing game of '*maybe he'll be okay tonight*' and take drastic action. They all knew deep down this was only going to get worse, but when he wasn't high, the hope that maybe the worst of it was past kept showing up to cloud their judgement. '*Guys, I'm fine, don't worry about it,*' he would say when they would approach him when he was sober, and for some stupid reason, they kept believing it, even though no lie had ever been more obvious. It was easier to see the problem when they looked at it from a distance, rather than when they were in the heat of the moment

"I am not trying to make excuses for him, but this isn't uncommon for our line of work," Uli would say to Hal, to try and offer some comfort.

"Unfortunately, I know many bands have a long history of drug use within their ranks, but many of them keep performing for years and sometimes decades to come," Uli added, and Hal sighed.

"Yeah, but too many of them don't make it work, and join that growing club of artists who die young from their addictions."

"Yes, that happens too," Uli agreed somberly.

"Dammit…" Hal groaned, putting his head into his hands. "We need to do *something* about him."

"What?" Uli asked.

"I don't know. I mean, I've already tried talking to him. I literally don't know what else we can do."

"Legally, probably nothing. But you have been talking to him nicely. Have you tried really confronting him?" Uli asked.

"God, that's just going to make him mad."

"Yes, but that is the last thing we have to try. You have been very patient with him. And yes, it probably will make him mad, but it might be the last way we have to get a message across to him. He has been brushing off your patient concern and not expecting anything more to come of it."

"I guess that's all that's left," Hal agreed. "I'm not going to do it before the show though, that'll cause him to be more distracted than he already is."

"I agree," Uli said. "Catch him right after, that way he has the night to cool off before we go to Budapest."

"Alright," Hal agreed, then added: "Why does crap like this always happen right at the end of our tours? Can't we ever make it through the end of one without a ton of drama coming up?"

"It is actually very logical that things start falling apart towards the end. We have been travelling for months, and the longer we are away from home without a break, the more emotions are going to flare."

"Alright, Spock," Hal said.

"I am merely trying to make sense of our situation. You asked a question, and that was my answer."

"And I wish I could do more to keep us going smoothly, but dammit, I'm a singer, not a therapist," Hal replied.

"No, but you are persuasive, and a good leader, so you might be the next best thing," Uli said, and it caught Hal off guard.

"Uh, thank you. I… do my best."

"And I wish I could do more to help…"

"Oh, no. I get it. Ryan would shut out anything and everything you say. I'm quite aware," Hal said. "I know you two have never gotten along. Thanks for at least trying to work with him."

"He is a good drummer and a valuable team member as long as he is behaving himself," Uli said.

"Ha! I'll have to tell him you said that."

"He won't believe it," Uli replied.

"Or worse, he won't even remember it in the morning," Hal sighed. "I'll try getting through to him again after the show."

"Okay," Uli agreed.

Hal did check in with Ryan right before they started that night's show, so he could prepare himself for what they were in for. "Hey, how are you feeling?" Hal asked him.

"You act like I'm sick," Ryan snapped.

"We're worried you are," Hal answered.

"I'm fine." Ryan insisted.

"Ryan, I am worried about you. You didn't do too well the other night in Prague. And I'm not saying that to be a dick. I'm saying it because I've seen you do so much better. Don't do this to yourself."

"Hal! I'm fucking fine! Look! I can walk in a straight line!" Ryan yelled as he put one foot in front of the other. "I can touch my nose!" he added as he held his arm all the way out and then brought one finger to the tip of his nose. "You want to hear the alphabet backwards, too?"

"No, I want to hear you stay on beat tonight."

"I *am* fucking on beat! You're the one who's singing too slow. And Uli and Ricky need to learn to fucking keep up too! You're the ones who are slacking off, and you're trying to blame me to try and make yourselves feel better about it!"

"*Ryan…*" Hal said wearily.

"No, I'm not taking this bullshit anymore. You can do your part or not, but don't blame me for every little thing that goes wrong when it's your fault!" he said as he turned and stormed off.

*Well, crap,* Hal thought to himself. He really hadn't meant for it to escalate that far before the show. Ryan was in an exceptionally foul mood tonight, and he may have just kicked the hornet's nest out onto the stage. He hoped not, but his fears were only yet to be confirmed.

Ryan's mistakes were like an irritating itch that wouldn't go away. It made it hard to concentrate. It made it impossible to have a good time. And as much as he tried to ignore it, it just wouldn't stop. Every time Ryan hit the beat wrong, every time he quit playing completely for a few seconds, it gnawed at him. He hoped since he knew the songs inside out he was the only one really noticing, but it was getting bad enough that he got the feeling the audience was catching it this time too. He could swear he saw people pointing behind him and talking to their friends, and not in the usual, excited way. He did his best to keep going and not let it show on his face, but it killed him inside. This was what he had worked his whole life to achieve, and he wanted every show to be the best it could. Sure, they had been on the road for a long time, but these people paid a lot of money to be here. And for some of them, this was perhaps the only chance they'd ever get to go to a show like this. And Hal felt like if he, Ricky, Uli, or Ryan couldn't appreciate that, it was nearly as bad as if they had just robbed every person in the audience of their money.

"WHAT THE HELL WAS THAT!?" Hal's mood flipped instantly after they had finished and gone backstage for the night.

"Huh?" Ryan barely turned around before Hal was in his face.

"Ryan! This has to stop! You're doing so goddam much drugs that you can't keep a beat anymore! What are you doing, by the way? Does it happen to be cocaine? Judging by your symptoms, that was Google's diagnosis."

"I'm not doing anything…" Ryan answered, somewhat sluggishly.

"Right, well, you're not drumming properly, that's for damn sure," Hal said.

"Hal, come on, you know it doesn't matter. Those people are just here to see our pretty faces in person. Live music never sounds very good," Ryan defended. He wasn't nearly as loud or nasty as earlier. Now he looked tired.

"What the HELL are you talking about!? Our concerts have always sounded good! Well, until *recently*, that is!"

"We sounded fine," Ryan replied.

"No, we did not! You were off all night, and it was so bad the audience noticed too. I saw a bunch of them pointing at you and talking to each other throughout the night."

"Hal, it's all… in your head." Ryan paused in the middle of his sentence like he had forgotten the rest of what he was going to say. "They were pointing at us because… we're us."

"They were pointing at YOU!" Hal insisted. "Ryan, we can't keep going on like this. You're getting worse, and don't try to tell me you're not because you ARE! When is this going to end? Huh? What are we going to do about this!?" Hal stopped for a moment, and it took Ryan a little bit to realize Hal was actually waiting for an answer from him.

"Wh… what are we going to do about what?"

"YOUR DRUG PROBLEM!"

"I don't have a…"

"You are full of shit!" Hal snapped. "You go out at night and do cocaine or whatever it is with Mason! Speaking of which, WHERE IS MASON!?" Hal yelled, looking around them backstage. Mason, who had been listening in from around a corner, took off running before Hal caught sight of him.

Nora, who had been standing right next to him and giving him a firm, angry stare, took off after him to try and have their own talk.

"Hal... calm down." Ryan put his hands out in front of him.

"Ryan, that's the problem! I've tried talking to you calmly, and it doesn't work!"

"Alright, alright. I get it. Let's... all sleep on this tonight and we'll talk in the morning."

"No, Ryan, we're going to figure this out now! I don't know what else to do, so you tell me, how are we, no, how are YOU going to fix this!?"

"I... I'll..."

"No, wait, let me guess. You'll promise to do better and promise that you'll be okay in order to get us to leave you alone, then you'll keep snorting cocaine and messing up concerts. That's your plan, right!?" Hal yelled. "Here's the problem, we're not going to keep playing that game. As far as I'm concerned, there's three options here: Either you quit doing drugs, which I know isn't happening, OR we end our tour early and check you into rehab, which I'm willing to do if that's what needs to happen, or...WE FIND A NEW DRUMMER!" Hal bellowed at him, and Ryan's face went pale as they stared at each other for a moment. Ryan took a step back, then turned around and walked slowly away in shock. Hal started to walk after him.

"Wait," Uli stopped him. "Give him a bit to think about it."

"No, I shouldn't have said that, I..."

"No, Hal, that got his attention. Being nice to him was not getting his attention. It had to be done. Give him at least a little while to think about it," Uli insisted. "Let's go pack up." Uli turned Hal around so they were heading back to their equipment, and they started putting their things away and helped break down for the night, all in an uneasy silence.

It took about two hours for them to get everything packed back up, and Hal decided it had been long enough for Ryan to have done his initial 'thinking about it.' "I'm going to go check on him," he told Uli and Ricky before he went out back.

He figured he'd start with the tour bus since it was the most likely place. He went up the stairs and turned the lights to the main part of the bus on. "Ryan?" he called. There was no answer. He walked up into the bus and checked each room, finding all to be empty. He was about to leave when he noticed the bathroom door was shut. Hal went and tried the handle, and it was locked. "Ryan? I know you're in there," Hal said. There was no response. "Look, I'm sorry. Things got out of hand back there. I don't want a different drummer, and I shouldn't have said that. I want to keep you in the group, but it's been frustrating since you started not playing as well, okay? We want the old asshole Ryan back, not the new one you've turned into." Hal tried to lighten up the mood a little. There was still no response. "Ryan…" Hal said quietly. "Let's get through the last few shows of this tour, then please check yourself into a nice rehab place somewhere. We'll take a break for a few months and then go from there, okay?" There was nothing besides silence from the other side of the door. "Ryan, please just say something so I know you're not dead in there." More silence. "Ryan? Ryan!?" Hal started pushing and pulling at the door trying to shake the lock loose. When he pushed, he felt like there was a weight against it. He took a few steps back and kicked at the lock as hard as he could. The metal bolt held good, but after a second kick, the plastic notch that it locked into cracked and gave way. The door flew open as Ryan's limp body fell sideways onto the floor at Hal's feet. His eyes were half open in another eerie, dilated stare, and his arms and legs were shaking in series of little tremors. "RYAN…!!??"

Sitting in the hallway of the hospital E.R., nobody said anything, but they all knew it was a depressingly familiar scene. "I shouldn't have yelled at him like that," Hal said.

"Hal, don't even start trying to blame this on yourself," Uli cut in. "You yelled at him for messing up not only our performances, but also his own life by doing cocaine, and what does he do? More of it!"

"Yeah, but he's not in his right mind anymore. He's addicted, and I knew that, and I should have known getting mad at him would do nothing besides make him stressed out. And now, I might not even get a chance to apologize," he said quietly. On the ride over, the EMTs said his heart rate was dangerously fast and irregular, his temperature was extremely high, and that he was having trouble breathing. But, judging from all the shouting coming from the room and the fact that more doctors kept rushing inside, there was still a battle going on, and it wasn't clear yet which side was going to win. Uli leaned his head back against the wall and said something in German, while Ricky kept his arms crossed and his eyes down on the ground. "*If he gets mad at you for getting into his business, don't give up on it. Let him hate you if it comes to it.*" Allen's words echoed through Hal's head. He had tried to follow his advice, yet, here they were, all the same. Maybe he'd gone about it the wrong way, or maybe the problem was there simply was no right way to go about it. Hal pulled out his phone to try and call Mason again, to give him the update since they couldn't find him before they left for the hospital. He dialed the number and put the phone on speaker. It rang. And rang. And rang. And rang. Still no reply.

Time crawled by. Gradually, the voices on the other side of the door were becoming quieter, and after about an hour, the door finally opened, and the doctor stepped out. "Your friend is stabilizing."

"What!?" Hal jumped up. He was overjoyed to hear the news, but it caught him so off guard, he realized the tone of his voice might have made anyone else think he was mad about it. "I mean… we thought…"

"He would die? He was not in good shape when he got here. But you think I would let him die?" the doctor asked.

"Oh, no, no. I didn't mean to…"

"No, no, *you* don't understand. He dies? I die. My daughter kills me!" the doctor said in a thick Eastern-European accent. "Her bedroom is covered in pictures of you! She has bought every song! I cannot let him die!" he said dramatically. "He will live. But you also must sign, something, I don't know what, something for my daughter. Because she finds out I met you without bringing her a present? She also kills me!"

"Sign something!?" Hal yelled. "Hell, we'll give her backstage passes and take her out to dinner!" he said excitedly as they got up and went through the door of the room.

Ryan was unconscious, attached to multiple machines, and looking very pale. But the heart rate monitor was beeping in a regular pattern, and they could see his chest rise and fall normally with each breath. "You are a miracle worker," Hal said gratefully to the doctor.

"Eh? I do my job. Excuse me, I must check on another patient. I call my daughter and tell her you offered to meet her. If you hear screaming? That is her a few miles away. I will be back in a few minutes," he said as he left them in the room. The other doctors and nurses also began to file out one at a time. They gathered around and sat down in the chairs next to the bed.

"Are we certain he is not going to die?" Uli asked.

"ULI!" Hal snapped at him.

"It was a joke!" Uli defended. They heard a slight groan and looked back down at Ryan and were stunned to see one eye half open, staring at them. It looked like he was having a little trouble focusing, however. He started to move one of his hands, which was a difficult task for him judging by how bad it shook. He managed to turn it over and curl four of his fingers in so only one remained upright in Uli's direction.

"You know, Uli, I'm a singer, not a doctor, but I think I can say with fair certainty that's a good sign he's not dying," Hal said quietly.

By the time Ryan was well enough to be released, he had been in the hospital long enough that he started going through withdrawals. Hal begged him to stay and ride it out with some help, but he refused and demanded to be checked out. Once they got back to the hotel, he immediately locked himself in his room to get another fix. They had a show the next day, and once they had packed up and were back on the tour bus, Hal spent a few hours trying to come up with a plan. He waited until Ryan was in a downswing before he approached him. "Ryan?" He asked it very calmly. Ryan slowly turned to look at him. He had just come out of the bathroom and was about to dart to his room. He had been actively trying to avoid Hal since he got released. "We only have a few weeks to go. Can we come up with a plan to make it through until then?" Hal asked.

"Like what?" Ryan asked back.

"I don't know…" Hal said, sitting down on one of the bench seats. "I don't know if this is possible, but, are you able to, like, coordinate and time things so when we're on stage you're not at the peak of a high, or crashing…?"

Ryan thought about it for a moment. "Yeah… I can do that," he replied.

"Okay, and…" Hal started to say, but with a slam of the door, Ryan disappeared back into his room. Hal sat there staring at the door for a few moments before turning around on the bench, so he was facing Uli and Ricky. Hal sighed. "That was a productive conversation. I think we got a lot done," he said, wearily.

"It is like you said, the three of us will give the remaining shows all we have got to cover for the bad drumming, and we will make it through," Uli replied, and Ricky nodded in agreement.

"Thanks, guys. I really appreciate that," Hal said. He at least had them to count on. "We just need to get through the next few weeks, and then once we get home, we can work on a more permanent solution, whatever that is."

"Send him to rehab, and if he refuses, get a new drummer?" Uli asked, though he did it without the usual contempt or sarcasm in his voice.

"Yeah, I think that's what we're down to," Hal said quietly, hoping Ryan wasn't listening in. "Though, as much of a pain in the ass he is…" He wrung his hands together thoughtfully a few times, then looked up. "I'm going to see him personally to the front door of the rehab facility."

"No, *we* will be seeing him personally to the front door of the rehab facility," Uli corrected him. "I will not allow Ryan to attempt to kill himself with drugs again. If anything is to kill Ryan, that pleasure will be mine alone," Uli said firmly.

Hal smiled weakly. "Alright. That's a plan I can live with."

"Yes, we are in this together. The three of us against Ryan, and Ryan against himself," Uli said. The statement was so true it hurt, but step one is to admit there is a problem. And now that they had accepted Ryan was going to screw up and the rest of them were going to do the best they could to put on a good show, it removed the stress of trying to stave off disaster when it was simply unavoidable. It also gave Hal a new sense of drive. It was a fresh challenge, to be so good he could overshadow what was going wrong right behind him. A welcome sense of relief was present the next night as they were setting up before the show. When they started to get in to place, Ryan seemed calm as he joined them, though to the point of being distant. He didn't exactly look like he was crashing, but it was hard to describe exactly what he did seem like. The lights were on, but no one was home. Hal glanced back at him as he took his place at his drums. Ryan intentionally avoided making eye contact. *Well, at least he isn't in a manic fit,* Hal thought as he took the microphone.

"Good evening, Zagreb!" he shouted to the screaming crowd. They were in Croatia that night.

248. "It's My Life" by Bon Jovi

Ricky, Uli, and Ryan all started the song off at the same time. Ricky with the guitar, Uli with some sound effects on his keyboard, and Ryan with the beat. Hal looked out to the crowd. He was in a rather intense mood, and so they didn't start out slow. He sang at the top of his lungs, with the most perfect pitch he could muster, though he was surprised to hear behind him what sounded like an even drum rhythm. He kept waiting for it to go bad, though as the minutes passed, it kept beating like a healthy heart. He took a moment and glanced back at Ryan again. He had his eyes shut, and was lip synching the lyrics to himself as he played. The sweat was running down his face at an incredible rate. As it dropped off his chin onto the drum skins, the spotlights illuminated it like falling diamonds, and then it was split and sent flying off in all directions by the next strike of the drumstick. Hal had never seen Ryan look that focused on anything in his whole life, not even when boobs were involved. He was actually *trying*. Hal looked back out to the audience, on their feet with their hands in the air, and started feeling that little rush he'd get when a song was going perfectly. He'd been taking that little feeling for granted up until recently. He loved it so much, but he was afraid to let it flare tonight only to have his buzz killed if Ryan did start screwing up. He looked over at Ricky, who had his full attention on playing fast and hard with all his might. Then he looked to Uli, who caught his gaze and shrugged his shoulders optimistically as he looked over at Ryan. Hal turned back to the crowd. What the hell. Might as well enjoy it while it lasts. He shouted the lyrics out to the crowd as hard as he could without messing up the melody, and the people screamed it back to him, pumping their fists in time with the drum beat. Hal started tapping one foot in time with the drum and fists, hoping by some non-sensical wanting and wishing that the fists and his foot would somehow help Ryan keep the rhythm on time. As the night spun around them and the beat went on, he couldn't be one to say that it wasn't working.

End Song 248

# CHAPTER 18

## (Take Care)

"So, what do y'all like to do when you're home?" Ricky asked. They had already established that it wasn't drinking and partying, unlike some people. Ricky had Mason by the wrists, and Nora had his ankles as they carried him through the hotel lobby door. He, Hal, Uli, and Ryan may have partied a little too hard after the show and may have gotten a little too drunk to be able to stand. Or walk. Or remain conscious.

"Well, whenever I can, I like to go out to the moors or to the ocean and take photos for my portfolio. Especially if it's a foggy day, or if a storm is coming in along the coast."

"Neat!" Ricky said. "You sell your pictures?"

"I'd love to, but it costs so much to get big enough prints made and have them framed, and then if they don't sell, I'll have spent all the money for nothing."

"Have ya even tried it?"

"Well, no," Nora answered.

"Cuz, they're definitely not gonna sell if ya never make prints and put 'em up for sale."

"Yes. I know," Nora sighed.

"So, try it with a couple of 'em. Once the first few sell, then you'll have money to print more."

"That would be the smart thing to do," Nora agreed.

They were about halfway across the lobby when they suddenly noticed the woman at the front desk staring at them, as well as the few other people in the lobby at that hour of the morning. "Oh, goodness, this probably looks a wee bit odd, doesn't it? This is my uncle. He's passed out drunk. We're taking him to his room to sleep it off," Nora spoke up. "We have a few more drunk friends we'll also be bringing in." The various people in the lobby gradually went back to what they were doing. The woman at the front desk shook her head in disgust as she went back to reading her book. She was likely not looking forward to the mess they might find in those rooms in the morning.

Uli was the only one of the four who had been drinking who was stable enough to walk himself to his room, though he was in no shape to help Ricky and Nora carry the others. He had already gone in ahead of them, and he got in the elevator and leaned against the wall to keep himself standing as he pushed the button for the tenth floor. Ricky and Nora made their way to the second elevator bay and maneuvered Mason inside, then set him down on the floor as they took the ride up. "You at least have any small prints of your photos to show people?"

"I don't have any physical prints, no, but I do have them all on my computer. Do you want to see a few once we get everyone to their rooms?"

"Yeah! Love to!" Ricky answered. Once the elevator stopped on the tenth floor, they picked Mason back up, and carried him down the hall to room 1040. They set him down on the floor again in front of the door while they looked for the key card to his room. Nora checked the right pocket on his pants while Ricky checked the left. Ricky pulled out his wallet, and the keycard fell out from one of the folds. "Got it." Then his face lit up as he looked at the wallet again. "Hey! Look! Money for you to get prints with!"

Nora burst out laughing. "I really hope no one turns the corner right now, this wouldn't look good."

"Just tell him he spent it drinkin'. He'll never suspect a thing."

"You are too much!" she said as she slipped the card into the lock slot, the indicator light flashed green, and she opened the door. They lifted Mason up and started walking him through the door, and there was a loud thud as his head hit the door frame. They both stopped and cringed. Mason let out one brief groan, then went still again. They looked at each other in mutual guilt. "We'll... tell him he fell on the dance floor. He'll never suspect a thing," Nora said.

"Okay." Ricky nodded in agreement, and they turned him carefully to get him in the room, then heaved him up onto the bed. Nora set the key card down on the side table next to him. "That's one. On to two?" Ricky asked as he headed back to the door.

"Actually, wait a second," Nora said. "Maybe we should roll him over onto his stomach."

"Why?" Ricky asked.

"Well, uncle Mason himself actually told me once the most unglamorous death in the music industry is when someone chokes to death on their own vomit. It happens when they drink too much, pass out lying face up, and throw up in a daze without waking up fully. If they're face down, however, it won't run back down their throat into their windpipe," she explained. Ricky took one, uncomfortable moment to ponder that image, then they both went over to opposite sides of the bed. Ricky pulled as Nora pushed, and they rolled Mason over onto his stomach. Nora moved his head so it was facing sideways, so he wouldn't suffocate in the sheets, either. They examined him for a moment more, called it good, then went back to the elevator to go back down to the lobby. The limousine driver was still waiting outside. Hal was next. As they set him down in the elevator, he woke up briefly. He looked around with blurry eyes. "Huh? Where... are we?"

"In the hotel elevator takin' you up to your room so you can sleep. Y'all got really drunk," Ricky said.

"Oh... that's... nice of you guys... you don't... have to do that..." Hal slurred.

"Well, we can't exactly leave you in the limo all night, the fare in the morning would be terrible. They charge more for wait time than they do for actual driving," Nora replied.

"Man… you two are so nice… I'm lucky… to… have friends like you…" he said, then slipped back into unconsciousness. Ricky and Nora tried to stifle their laughter as the elevator opened, and they carried him to room 1042. They found his keycard in his back pocket, opened the door, and were extra careful to not slam his head against the door frame. Once he was inside, lying on his stomach, with his head turned to the side, they went back out for Ryan.

"Alright, so, what do *you* do for fun when you're not playing sold out concerts?" Nora asked.

"Hang out in the woods," Ricky replied.

"I meant other than that!" she said. "What do you do when you're home?"

"Mostly helped with tillin' and plantin' and harvestin' in the fields," Ricky said. They opened the limo door and hauled Ryan out of the back seat. Ricky held him by his armpits as Nora grabbed his ankles, then they started walking him through the main lobby door.

"That can't be all," Nora said. "Eating, sleeping, working on the farm and spending time out in the woods? There must have been *something* else!" she insisted.

"There wasn't much else to do back home. That's how it is in a place that small," Ricky said. "Other than workin' the farm, a kid in Battle Creek pretty much had three other options: Spendin' all day readin' the Bible and workin' on your relationship with Jesus, becomin' an alcoholic, or makin' mischief."

"What do you mean by 'making mischief?'" Nora asked, intrigued.

"All kinds of stuff. Ricky's brothers an' some of the other boys in town came up with all sorts of crazy plans."

"Like?" Nora prodded. They stepped inside the elevator and set Ryan down on the floor. He was out cold, though they did make sure to check that he was still breathing. "Well, uh, once Rusty an' two other guys from town decided to see how many rolls of duct tape it would take to keep someone on the roof of a car goin' at freeway speeds."

"What!?" Nora spit out the word.

"Yeah. They rolled down the windows an' Rusty got up on the roof and laid down, and Brad and Hunter started rollin' the tape 'cross him. They pulled it down through the open windows, across the ceilin' inside the car, then back out the other side and across him again."

"Oh my God! And they drove on the highway with him up there!?"

"Yup."

"Did he fall off? Or get hurt?"

"Nope," Ricky answered.

"Well, that's good. So, how many rolls of duct tape did they use to keep him up there?"

"Four."

"And they got away with it all?"

"Nope," Ricky said. "Sheriff Frye was waitin' in a grove of trees for anyone speedin', and they was speedin', so he pulled them over. He found Rusty duct taped to the roof, called everyone's parents, and they was all grounded for weeks."

"My goodness," Nora said. The elevator door opened, and they picked Ryan up and walked him to the door of 1046. Nora took the right pocket and Ricky took the left to find his key card. Ricky pulled out his wallet, a few unopened condoms, then a small bag of white powder.

"Found it." Nora pulled the key card out of his other pocket, then saw Ricky holding the bag, looking disgusted. "Lovely," Nora commented as Ricky put it back in Ryan's pocket.

He sighed. "Yeah. Hal and Uli are comin' up with a plan to make Ryan go to rehab when we get back."

"I don't think they can legally force him to go." Nora slipped the card in the slot and opened the door.

"They're makin' a plan, somehow," Ricky said. "Ricky heard 'em use the word 'blackmail.'" Ricky grabbed Ryan's shoulders and Nora got his feet.

"Ryan has no shame about anything. How in the world are they going to blackmail him?" Nora asked.

"Not sure," Ricky answered. "Only heard part of what they were talkin' about." They set Ryan down on the bed, rolled him on his stomach, and turned his head to the side.

"You know, I just had a thought," Nora said.

"Yeah?" Ricky asked.

"What if we hid his cocaine somewhere in the room and made him look for it in the morning?" she said. It was an idea. An awful idea. It was a wonderful, awful idea. They thought about it for a second, then started looking for hiding spots. Ricky, however, realized shortly thereafter that Ryan might literally tear the room apart looking for it the next morning, and the hotel staff really didn't deserve to clean that up. They abandoned the idea and left the room. They had to make one more run to the limo to make sure no other stuff was left in there.

"So, you had a chance to talk to your uncle yet 'bout his issues?" Ricky asked as they got back in the elevator.

"No," Nora sighed. "He knows I'm going to, so he's doing everything he can to avoid me. But he can't stay away forever. We're on the same tour, after all, so I'll keep trying."

"Good luck," Ricky added.

"Thanks," she replied. They got down to the limo, pulled a few articles of clothing and Ryan's phone out of the back, then Nora tipped the driver and sent him on his way. They got back into the elevator. "You said your brothers and their friends came up with all manner of crazy things to do to amuse themselves…?" Nora asked.

"Yeah?" Ricky answered.

"Indulge me, I want to hear more."

Ricky thought about it for a second. "Uh, well… a bunch of guys in town spent a whole summer a couple years back buildin' a giant wood ramp down by the lake for kids to ride their skateboards and bikes down. It's 'bout twenty feet high an' curves up at the bottom, so it'll launch ya into the air before ya fall into the water."

"That sounds like fun!" Nora said.

"Yeah! Bunch of people worked on it, and even a few of the dads from town helped too. They built a wood ladder on the back, and a lil' flat ledge at the top to get ready on. They even made a rope pulley to pull the bikes up with."

"Wouldn't the bikes sink to the bottom of the lake once they fall in?" Nora asked.

"Well, the spot most people landed in was only 'bout ten feet deep, so if they lost the bike after goin' in, it wasn't too deep to not dive down an' get it back."

"Okay," she said. "Did you ever try it?"

"Yeah, went down it a few times sittin' on a skateboard. Some of the kids could go down it standin' up on 'em, but Ricky never made it to the water tryin' to stand up on one. So, Ricky just sat on it."

"That still sounds like a lot of fun," Nora said. The elevator opened, and they stepped out onto the tenth floor for the fourth time that night.

"Yeah, it was, but that's not even the best part of the story."

"There's more?"

"Yeah, so, when they first got the ramp finished, everyone was tryin' to decide how to christen it, and what some of the guys came up with was they were going to ride a couch down it."

"A couch?"

"Yep. A couch."

"Don't couches not roll very well?"

"Not usua'ly, but they put some of those little furniture-movin' roller thingies under it."

"Where did they get a couch to throw into a lake?"

"Lady named Mrs. Boundsguard. She had a couch she was goin' to take to the dump 'cause her cats had scratched it up so bad over the years that the stuffin' was starting to get all over her livin' room."

"Okay. Third question: Was this a full-size couch? And how did they get it to the top of the ramp? Was the bike pulley rope strong enough to bring a couch up?"

"No, they didn't take it up with the pulley. Mr. Adkinson had rented an excavator to dig better drainage ditches on his property, so he drove it over to the lake, an' they chained the couch up to the digger arm and lifted it to the top platform that way."

"It sounds like your entire town got together to help send a couch down a ramp."

"They did. After a long day out in the fields, most people wouldn't be able to resist qual'ty entertainment like that."

"So... did it work? Did they get the couch to go down the ramp?" Nora asked.

"Yep," Ricky said. "Rusty, Russell, Jackson, Tucker, and Mike rode it all the way down to the end of the ramp, and got 'bout six feet of air over the lake before fallin' in."

"Did any of them get hurt when it hit the water?"

"Nope, they all landed on top of it, and then it slowly sank," he said as they made a quick stop at Ryan's room, and Nora slipped Ryan's phone in underneath the door.

"You didn't volunteer to be one of the couch riders?" she asked teasingly.

"There was lots of volunteers," Ricky said. "Not ta mention, had it not gone so good, Ricky didn't want his head stone to read: 'Ricky Raccoon. Beloved Son & Brother. Killed in unfortunate accident with high-speed couch.'" Nora started laughing again.

"Oh, come now! That would have been the best headstone in the whole cemetery!"

"Well, Ricky can still get that on his head stone someday, just didn't want it to be true."

"Oh, you couldn't tell a lie like that even if you were dead!"

"Ah'd hope not! 'Cause then you'd have to start talkin' with Hal about how to deal with zombies," he said as they stopped outside of Nora's room, a few doors down from Ryan's.

"Yeah, I learned my lesson already about mentioning zombies around Hal. I think he ranted about his plans for surviving a zombie apocalypse for forty-five minutes at dinner on the third night of the tour," she said.

"Yeah, Ricky's already sat through that rant a few times," Ricky said.

"Well, I'm not sure he's ever going to get his wish, but *we've* survived another night, and the boys are all safe in bed. So, go team!" she said as she raised her hand, and Ricky gave her a high-five.

"It sure is nice havin' help. Thank you," Ricky said.

"Have you carried them in by yourself before?"

"Yeah, the only way to do it alone was to carry 'em slung over a shoulder, and once all the blood had rushed to their heads, that sometimes made 'em even more nauseous," Ricky said.

"Oh, Lord. Did any of them ever throw up on you?"

"Hal did, once."

"Ewww. I hope he paid you back for that one."

"Eh, never told him 'bout it, and he prob'ly don't remember doin' it."

"You didn't even send him on a little guilt trip for it?" she asked.

"Well, it ain't like he did it on purpose. And it's not the first time Ricky's been puked on. Grew up with fourteen siblings, ya know. Though that number's grown to eighteen now."

"I hope they appreciate how good of a friend you are to them," Nora said, and Ricky shrugged. "Just glad Ricky never had to carry Uli in like that, he's always awake enough to get himself to bed. Heck, his feet prob'ly would have drug in front while his hands drug on the floor behind!"

"Okay, he's not *that* tall," Nora said.

"With his arms hangin' down over his head he is! There's so dang much of 'im! If you and Ricky had to carry him, don't think we could hold him high enough to keep his stomach from draggin' on the ground!" Ricky said, and Nora giggled a little.

"Yeah, he's tall enough I bet he can get things off high shelves by himself without a step stool," she said.

"And see what's on top of refrigerators," Ricky added.

"My goodness, it's nice to talk to someone who understands the struggle," Nora said. She was perhaps a half inch shorter than Ricky, if that. It was close. "You and I are almost the same height." She stepped closer to him and tried to hold her hand flat from the top of her head towards his. The scientific method.

"Yeah, it's close. Ricky's 5'3", how tall are..." Nora leaned in quickly and kissed him on the cheek, startling him into silence.

"Gotcha," she said, and he stood there with his mouth half open, slowly turning red. "I told you that you wouldn't be able to get away forever. Have a good night," she said with a wink, then slipped her card into the door lock and opened her own hotel room door.

"W... wait..." Ricky said, and she stopped and looked at him. An awkward moment of silence followed. He took half a step in her direction, then stopped and gazed at her silently. She took a curious step back towards him, and he looked down at his feet for a moment, then reached out and took her hands in his. He lifted his eyes back up from the floor to look into hers, searching within them for a brief measure before he started to lean in towards her. Her eyelids fell shut instinctively as she leaned in and met him halfway. It was the early hours of the morning in a long, empty, well-lit hotel hallway. One of the countless random places over the centuries where the best high to be had has been stumbled upon by unsuspecting participants. The type that can't be bought on dirty city streets, or down dark alleys.

"Uuugghh…" Hal had the worst hangover he'd had in years next morning at breakfast. He had his head down on the table, pondering a small plate of food with disdain. Uli and Ryan were in roughly the same shape. Mason was still passed out in his room. Ricky and Nora sat next to each other, eagerly eating through a few short stacks of pancakes.

"You know, if you didn't drink so much and party so late you wouldn't find yourselves like this in the morning," Nora said, between bites.

"Did you hear something, Hal?" Ryan mumbled. "Because I sort of thought I heard talking, but it sounded meaningless and distant."

"Yeah, I heard it," Hal mumbled back. "But, you're right. It was so unhelpful that I couldn't quite make it out," he said without raising his head off the table, then added: "We're on a world tour, goddammit. The entire point of this is to get so hammered every night that you can't remember the day before," he said, though there was a tiny twinge of regret in his voice.

"We're certainly all here to have a good time, I'm not trying to say otherwise. But have you considered ever having fun *without* alcohol?" Nora asked.

"There it is again. That pointless, unhelpful voice," Ryan said.

"How, exactly, is someone supposed to have fun without alcohol?" Hal asked.

"There's plenty of ways," Nora said. "Get a bunch of people together and play a board game…"

"Go skatin'," Ricky said.

"See a movie…" Nora continued.

"Go for a walk…" Ricky added.

"Go out to dinner and enjoy pleasant conversation with friends…" Nora suggested, and Ryan started breathing in the quick, short breaths that usually prelude a sneeze.

"Aah… ah… ah… AHCHNERDS," he sneezed.

"Bless you," Nora said.

"Go bowlin'…" Ricky kept going.

"Read a good book…" Nora said.

Hal suddenly drew in one hard breath. "AHCHDORKS."

"Bless you," Nora said again.

"AHCHNOTPUKIN'," Ricky suddenly sneezed.

"Oh, no, you're not coming down with it, are you?" Nora asked him.

"Might be," Ricky replied.

Nora suddenly drew in a few quick breaths. "AHCHNOTHUNGOVER." She rubbed her nose. "Oh dear, now it looks like I'm getting it too!"

"Do you hear this bullshit, Hal?" Ryan asked.

"Yeah. It sounds like they're spending too much time around us," he answered.

"You may be right. We may be spending too much time around you. Maybe you should try spending some time with us, instead," Nora suggested.

"I think they're trying to seduce us to the dork side," Ryan said.

"I don't know, could you even handle a whole day of sober fun?" Nora asked, skeptically. "Or would you be lost without your drinks?"

"Oh, we could make it a whole day," Hal said confidently, rolling his eyes. "Done it plenty of times in the past."

"Okay, prove it," Nora challenged him.

"Fine," Hal answered quickly. "We'll go a day without drinking."

"So, what are we going to do? Spend the day knitting and playing role playing games?" Ryan asked.

"Oh… my… goodness!" Nora said sarcastically. "You know what might be fun? If we all went to that carnival going on a few blocks down the road."

"That would be fun, but we'd just get mobbed," Hal said.

"Well then, what if we played a little dress up?" she asked.

"Even with our alter ego clothes on, I think we'd get found out. That only really works if we're sneaking around briefly after dark."

"Okay, but what if you did more than clothes? What if we did a little hair and makeup?" Nora asked.

"What are you talking about?" Hal asked, and Nora smiled. Her family had a long history in the entertainment industry, though not all of it specifically in talent management. Her mother had spent a long time working in the costuming department of a city theater and had given Nora more than a few lessons in professional stage makeup.

After a few hours in the trailers, the four of them emerged, transformed. Hal was sporting a very convincing brown wig that was parted down the middle, and was a little longer than how he usually wore his hair. His sideburns and goatee had also acquired a brown shade, though it was a temporary dye that would wash out in the next shower. Brown contacts completed the transformation. He put on blue jeans and a Star Wars T-shirt, and for the rest of the day, would be known as 'Luke.' "Now in Technicolor!" Hal joked as he looked into the mirror, and then took a selfie to send to his parents. Ricky had been given a blond wig with bangs that were swept to one side, blue contacts, and full-length blue jeans. He was given a heather-grey T-shirt with the image of a young Simba, Timon, and Pumbaa walking in a line together. Underneath them it read: 'Squad Goals.' Ricky would be 'Walt' for the day. Uli was much more of a challenge as he had too much hair to hide under a wig, so Nora pulled in up into a tight bun, and then hid it under a brimmed straw hat with a red hat band. "Don't take the hat off at any point..." she warned him and gave him a pair of dark sunglasses to wear. Uli never wore shorts, so shorts it was; knee-length khaki shorts with a black tank top that read on it in bright white ink: 'THE BEATLES.' He would be 'Paul.' Finally, Ryan's line of black dyed hair that was usually in a mohawk was hidden under a short-haired brown wig, shorter than what Hal was given, and blue tinted sunglasses. He got black cargo shorts, and a white sleeveless muscle shirt with the Superman logo on the chest. He would be 'Kent'.

Hal looked at the other three. He had to hand it to Nora, they really didn't look like themselves. "We ready to go trick-or-treating?" Hal asked.

"Ready!" Ryan answered. They cautiously stepped out of the trailers in the back parking lot, and looked around. No one in sight. They quickly made their way to the front sidewalk, then started casually walking down the street. Hal held his breath as they passed by the first group of people. They walked by without giving them a second look. He exhaled. As they passed more and more people on the street, nobody was really paying any attention to them. He was starting to feel a little excited. Maybe they were actually going to get to spend a day at the fair without getting attacked by mobs of fans. They made it the few blocks to the fair entrance and got in line at the ticket booth. Once they got to the front, Hal handed them his credit card.

"Five adults," he said, then had a sudden shock of fear as he realized whose name was on the card. The lady in the ticket booth swiped it without looking, then handed them five tickets.

"Enjoy." He took his card back and slipped it back into his wallet. He was going to have to watch it if he bought anything inside the fair. They went in, and a wave of nostalgia went over him. The smell of hot dogs being barbequed, and sweet, sugary things wafted through the air. The sound of rollercoaster cars running along their tracks, and kids screaming when the cart took a downwards plummet. "Well, where do we start?" Ryan asked.

"I always like to begin with the animals." Hal answered as he set his sights on one of the livestock barns.

"Ric… err… Walt can't join y'all in there, so we'll see ya later," Ricky said.

"Alright, you got your phone on you?" Hal asked.

"I've got mine," Nora said.

"You don't want to see the animals, either?" Hal asked Nora.

"I've seen plenty of farm animals in my life. Haven't seen nearly enough roller coasters, though," she answered.

"Alright," Hal laughed. "We'll catch you later, then."

"Yes!" Nora agreed, then grabbed Ricky by the arm. "Come on, Walt!" she said excitedly, then started leading him towards the rides. He looked back briefly to see Hal and Uli smiling at him smugly. Ryan had his back turned to them, his arms crossed over his chest while he rubbed his hands up and down the sides of his back like he was making out with someone. Ricky rolled his eyes then started running faster to keep pace with Nora. The other three started for the first livestock hall.

"So, why are we doing this instead of going straight to the rides?" Ryan asked.

"Because the chickens are awesome, trust me," Hal answered. As they went inside the first door, they entered a hall full of rabbits and chickens. Towards the front were a line of rabbits in cages that were white except for rings of black fur around their eyes, like they were all wearing eyeliner. "Well, those are adorable." Hal said.

"Yeah," Ryan agreed. "I know you're not supposed to test makeup on bunnies, but I didn't know there were some that came with their own." They moved down the aisle to a row of small, grey, fluffy bunnies that looked like little ash piles in a fireplace, then to a cage of white bunnies with such long fur that they looked like mini sheep. As they went down the lines of cages, there were fluffy rabbits, tiny rabbits, long eared rabbits, short eared rabbits, grey rabbits, brown rabbits, white rabbits, black rabbits, spotted rabbits, and at the very end… giant rabbits. Giant. Grey. Rabbits. Over the cage of the biggest one, a small blue first place ribbon hung, and the tag next to it read: 'Flemish Giant. Thumbelina.'

"Yeah, that figures," Hal said. Thumbelina was bigger than half the dogs he had ever seen. Nearly unreal to look at.

Next, they moved onto the chickens. Standard looking chickens, colorful chickens, extremely fluffy chickens, chickens with afro hairdos, and chickens with feathers down to their feet that made them look like they were wearing thick socks. There were roosters with extremely long tail feathers, black and white chickens that had white feathers with black around the edges, and then, a massive rooster, much like Thumbelina. "God, that thing could probably do some damage if it attacked you," Hal noted, and then a few cages down from the giant rooster, was another cage containing the tiniest, neatest, most perfect looking mini-rooster they had ever seen. Every feather was meticulously groomed, his red head crest held high, and his colors were a mix of everything else they had seen to that point. Some red, some brown, some white rimmed with black, and some iridescent green. "Well, aren't you dapper?" Hal said to the rooster.

"That is the smallest cock I have ever seen in my life," Ryan said. As soon as he said it, the rooster suddenly perked up, fluffed its feathers, and lunged at him with a loud screech; hitting the side of the cage with enough force to move it slightly forward on the table. "Jeez!" Ryan said as he took a sudden step back.

"He seems to have taken offense to that," Uli noted.

"Remember Kent... it's not size, it's attitude," Hal said with a smile. As they started to move further down the aisle. They walked out to go to the next barn, but lining the outer wall of the first barn were cages of turkeys and ducks. "Hoogaboogaloogle!" Hal said to the turkeys, who all frantically answered back with a round of synchronized gobbling. "That never gets old." Hal said proudly. The turkeys were all a little bedraggled looking, possibly in the middle of a molt, but the ducks were all looking their finest. Most were standard breeds, but they came upon one breed that stopped them all in amazement. A cage of four tall, black ducks stood very upright, as if stretching to see over a high wall. And as they walked, they did not waddle, they very neatly walked in a straight line. They were taller than any duck had the right to be.

"Are those alien ducks?" Ryan asked.

"I was thinking demon ducks. If I woke up to find one of those standing at the foot of my bed in the middle of the night, I'd probably shit myself..." Hal answered.

"I like it. This could be the next great bad horror movie," Ryan said.

Hal walked up to the cage tag. "Indian Runner Duck," he read.

"Oh god, they run fast too?" Ryan asked.

"I dunno, I would assume so from the name...?" Hal answered.

"This is totally the next bad B movie. Attack of the Indian Runner Ducks," Ryan insisted. The only thing preventing the black ducks from being any more unnerving, is they still had the same vacant, brainless look in their eyes that all the other regular ducks possessed. "Hey, Ul… err… Paul. If you ever start a farm, you could get some of these. They're creepy and all dressed in black," Ryan said.

"I shall keep that in mind, Uli said, incredulously. They moved onto the next barn, which had the goats.

Inside, the first pen had tall goats with white fur and black faces. "Ooh! These are the ones that scream!" Ryan said excitedly, then began to draw in a breath.

"YOU KNOW…" Hal said as he suddenly grabbed Ryan by the back of his shirt and pulled him back, "…we're trying to *not* attract too much attention to ourselves," he said through clenched teeth.

"Well, maybe you shouldn't gobble at turkeys then!" Ryan said.

"There is a big difference between gobbling at turkeys *outside* and screaming at goats *inside*," Hal replied.

"Have you ever considered the possibility that whispering to one another might actually be more suspicious than screaming since that is what most people do at fairs?" Ryan asked.

Hal glanced around. A few people were casually observing them. He looked back at Ryan. "Hey, I have an idea!" he said brightly. "Let's go check out the cattle!" He started pulling Ryan towards the door. Ryan pulled himself free from Hal's grasp, and walked after him grudgingly.

As they reached the door, Ryan suddenly pivoted on one foot and yelled at the top of his lungs into the barn. "AAAAGGGHHH!!!" Nearly everyone inside jumped. One of the goats put its hooves part way up the rail and hoisted itself up, then looked right in his direction. "AAAAAAAAAAGGGGGHHH!" it replied, and then most everyone inside started to laugh. Ryan turned triumphantly around and walked out the door with Hal, who did his best to suppress the urge to laugh along with them.

In the cattle barn, they passed by the giant bovines; black, white, brown, spotted, all groomed to their finest… except for the ones with dung running down the lengths of their backsides and legs. "That is why it is important to never drink unpasteurized milk." Uli said.

"Yeah, and these are *show cows*," Hal agreed.

"Oh, cows are revolting," Ryan said. "There is a reason you can smell them for miles if you're out in farmland. And it is also why I try to eat as many of them as I can to reduce the population."

Uli shot him a sideways glance. "You have never heard of the economic rule of supply and demand, have you?"

"Hey! It's not my fault if they keep breeding more! I just do my part by eating them!" Ryan said.

"I'm not sure if I want to eat another steak again after this…" Hal said as they moved on. They didn't spend a lot of time with the cows due to the smell and went straight through to the horse stables and arena. A few of the horses trotting in the arena were quite stunning. Far from the standard frumpy brown ponies seen at the usual festival pony rides, there were vivid black and white appaloosas with spots from head to foot like Dalmatian dogs. Next to them in the ring were shining white horses with accents of pink skin showing through their coats, giving them a nearly angelic appearance. Horses with grey-blue fur and black faces and manes, dun horses with primitive, tiger-like stripes on their legs, and black and white pinto horses so flashy that it appeared their patches were painted on individually also mingled in the arena.

After the horses, they left the animals and moved on to the fair booths. Row after row of white tents filled with troves of tacky trinkets and treasures. One table had long metal finger pieces on it. Not quite rings. Rather, the finger of a medieval knight's armor, hinged in the middle so the finger could bend. The tip came to a point, like a removable claw. Ryan put one on all five fingers on one hand, then flexed the claws open and closed. "These are cool…" he said as he admired them, then his eyes lit up. "I could poke Paul with these!"

Uli gave him a stone-faced stare. "*Great*," he said under his breath. Ryan ultimately bought five of them. What he didn't see was Uli quietly returned to the tent later and bought ten.

They moved down the rows of tents one at a time, finding much of the same items in each, until they reached an end tent that was blasting deep bass techno music. Inside, lights across the wall pulsed in time with the music. The lights were on the fronts of shirts, hats, and half-face masks that covered just the mouth, similar to what skiers use. Clothing with small electronic setups that had digital displays on them that reacted to nearby sound. Some of the shirts had simple sound bars that would rise and fall like on a stereo display, while others had pictures or objects that would pulse in layers of color. One of the half masks had a pattern that made it look like a gas mask, and the lights within the circular shapes throbbed in and out with the music.

"Oooh… yeah… here we go…" Hal said quietly, and each of them ended up buying multiple shirts and hats. It was dark in the tent to show off the lights, so luckily, "Luke" doubted the cashier working the stand was able to read his actual name on his card. They had the stand hold onto their items in labeled bags so they could come back for them later, and then moved onto the food stands.

Lunch was giant hamburgers and fries, followed by elephant ears and deep-fried chocolate covered Twinkies for desert; compliments of a stand entitled 'Deep Fried Everything.'

"Well, now what?" Uli asked as they threw the napkins away in a nearly overflowing trash can.

"What do you mean *now what*?" Hal said. "There's only one thing left to do!" As they walked out of the food court, all the rides came into sight in front of them. Ferris wheels, roller coasters, carousels, and numerous other attractions that spun, rolled, and swung. "Place your bets. The one who makes it the longest without puking wins," he announced.

"How high of a bet are you thinking?" Uli asked.

"I don't know… uh… $250 each?" Hal answered.

"Alright," Uli said.

"Kent, are you good with that?" Hal asked. There was no reply. "Kent?" Hal turned around. He was suddenly nowhere to be seen.

"Apparently this is going to be a two-person bet," Uli said casually.

"He was just there a second ago!" Hal complained.

"I noticed he was starting to look a little anxious when we were eating," Uli said.

"So… he went back to the hotel to get a fix…" Hal sighed as he turned back around.

"Most likely," Uli said.

"Either that, or someone abducted him," Hal mused.

"Well, if that is the case, they will return him shortly with a letter of apology," Uli said.

"God dammit, this was going to be the fun part. I guess we should have done the rides first," Hal admitted.

"Perhaps, but he is gone now, and there is nothing we can do about it," Uli replied. "But, this is still a viable two-person bet."

"Alright. We'll make it work," Hal agreed. "You ready? Winner will be $250 richer."

"I am ready," Uli replied, and they headed on towards the rides. They passed by Ricky and Nora a few times in the crowd, during which they exchanged awkward nods and waves. Later in the afternoon, Hal managed to snap a quick picture of the two of them smooching on the ferris wheel right as the roller coaster cart himself and Uli were in reached the peak of its climb.

A few hours later, they all met up again, and Hal and Uli picked up their (and Ryan's) light shirts, then all went out the front gates together. Uli was $250 richer, and Hal was slowly sipping on a Sprite.

"Where's Kent?" Ricky asked.

"He disappeared. Probably went back to the hotel to get a fix," Hal said, sounding queasy.

"Oh," Ricky said quietly.

"Yeah. Didn't get to join us on the rides. But, hey, did you have a good time?" Hal asked.

"Of course!" Nora answered, and Ricky nodded. "The question is, did *you* have a good time?" she asked.

"Oh, this was awesome! I haven't been to the fair since I was a little kid. It brought back good memories. And I guess we made some new ones, too," Hal said.

"See? Wasn't this better than getting drunk and passing out?" she asked.

"I wouldn't quite say *that*, but it was a different sort of fun," Hal replied, and Nora sighed.

"So, what treasures did you find?" she asked as she pointed to the bags.

"Oh, THIS is awesome…" Hal said excitedly as he set the bags down and they stopped along the sidewalk. He pulled out one of the shirts and flipped the switch on the small control box. "Check this out." He started beatboxing with his mouth. "Ooomm cha, oom cha, oom cha, oom cha…" As he did, the sound bars on the shirt rose and fell in time to the beat.

Ricky's mouth dropped open a little bit. "That's so cool!" he said.

"Yeah!" Nora agreed.

"You know, we could go back in for a few minutes and you could get a few for yourselves," Hal suggested.

"Well, they's neat, but it's not something Ric… err, Walt would probably wear…" Ricky said as he looked quickly around.

"Oh, come on! These would be badass to wear on stage for the pop out-fits! Oh, and you could wear it when you go skating! Think about it, you'd be the envy of the entire rink…" Hal insisted.

Ricky looked hesitant, then looked at Nora. "I actually… would rather like to get one," she admitted.

"Okay! Back through the gate!" Hal suddenly turned them all around and marched them back the direction from where they'd just come. Ricky ended up getting a shirt with a tree on it that pulsed light from its center in the upper trunk. If the noise got loud enough, it would light up the very upper leaves and branches at the top, and the jagged roots down low at the bottom. Nora got a shirt with a lightning bolt on it that would also pulse from its center. Afterwards, they left through the main gates again with more bags in tow.

"So, now that we took your challenge and had a day of sober fun, you two are going to get shitfaced with us tomorrow night, right?" Hal asked.

Ricky and Nora looked at him and turned a few shades paler. "I believe it would only be fair to try spending a night as we like to, now that we've spent a day doing what you want to do," Uli said with a sly smile.

"Uh…" Ricky said uneasily as he looked at Nora.

"Great! Glad you agree!" Hal said. "Don't worry, we'll start you off easy. No keg stands until at least a few hours into the evening," he reassured them, and he and Uli shared a terrifying laugh.

Ricky and Nora were uncomfortably quiet the rest of the way back to the hotel. When they got there, they headed towards their rooms to plot how they were going to get out of a night of hard drinking while Hal and Uli went to Ryan's room to check on him. They found him on the computer flipping through pages of porn at an unnecessarily quick pace.

"Hey, you missed all the rides," Hal said.

"Sorry… got a headache… didn't want to make it worse…" he said in broken sentences.

"Right," Hal said quietly. "Know what else you missed?" He pulled out his phone and put the most recent picture he'd taken on the screen. Ryan looked at it in disbelief.

"REALLY!?" he said. "ARE YOU FUCKING KIDDING ME!? AND I WASN'T THERE!?"

"Why no, no you weren't," Hal replied.

"I… got a bad headache…" Ryan said again, quietly.

"Yes, we need to talk about your headaches," Hal said.

"I know…" Ryan said through clenched teeth. "When we get home, okay?"

"Alright…" Hal said. "But we ARE going to deal with this once we get home. Not the day after we get home, not two days after we get home, not…"

"Okay, okay, I get it…" Ryan said.

Meanwhile, on the way back to their rooms, Ricky and Nora had ruled out faking illness as Hal was going to know they were lying. Now they were debating between arguing that they made them do something wholesome as opposed to them wanting them to engage in something unhealthy. Or perhaps, they would just take off out the back door and disappear for a few hours and ditch them entirely. Nora knocked on her uncle's hotel room door to check on him. "Uncle Mason?" she asked. No answer. She took a key card out of her pocket. She'd swiped one of his when he wasn't looking. She unlocked the door, and began to open it slowly, "Uncle Ma…"

"Shit! The hell!?" Mason suddenly jumped up from his chair, holding his nose. A small trickle of blood began to run out of it. The door opening startled him, and he had taken a small core sample of the inside of his nostril with the white straw he had been using. A few lines of white powder were on the surface of the small hotel table.

"UNCLE MASON!" Nora said sternly, putting her clenched fists on her sides. "WE NEED TO TALK!" Mason suddenly ran at the door and shoved past them, then took off down the hall. It stunned Nora for a moment, before she yelled and took off after him. "HEY!"

"Good luck!" Ricky called down the hall after her.

"Thanks!" she yelled back as she waved quickly at him before turning a corner.

Mason went out the back door of the hotel and bolted towards the road. He already knew exactly what Nora was going to say to him, and he didn't want to hear it. What was worse, he had tried to go a little longer between highs because he already knew this was a habit that was going to start pulling him down into a dark hole. But, he needed his next fix *now*, and if he tried to sneak back to his room, one of the others would see him and probably call her to rat him out. He knew from his contacts in various places that there was a dealer somewhere nearby, but his other problem was he was out of cash until his next paycheck came through in a few days. He turned the corner onto the sidewalk and pulled the small piece of paper out of his pocket to figure out where to go. A few seconds later, he heard Nora yell behind him: "Uncle Mason! Please just stop for a second!" He looked over his shoulder to see her catching up to him, and he began to run faster, looking around for any escape he could find. A small alleyway came into view up ahead, and he ducked sideways into it. By the time Nora made the turn, he was out of sight. She ran to the end and took the next corner only to be faced with a maze of alleys and exits behind an old apartment complex. He could have gone down any one of them. "Nnngh!" she grunted to herself, then picked a direction and began her search.

Back on the main road, Mason slowed his pace as he got further from the back exit of the apartments and pulled the piece of paper out of his pocket again. He made his way a few blocks to a very old brick building that was currently in use as a motel. He went up two flights of stairs and knocked on door 30. Within a few seconds, two very well-dressed men answered the door. One had curly brown hair and a short beard and was wearing a tight-fitting white T-shirt while the other was clean-shaven with a buzz cut and a brown leather jacket. Both had fancy designer jeans and pointed brown leather shoes. They invited Mason inside. Nora was watching from across the road. She had caught sight of him again and had been following him for a while. Knowing if he saw her he'd start running again, she decided to change her strategy and wait for an opportunity to sneak up on him. She worked her way as close as she felt comfortable, and waited barely out of sight behind a parked truck. She wasn't going to interrupt whatever meeting was going on inside, but once Mason came back out, he was in for a stern yelling at.

About five minutes later, the door opened, and he was forcibly shoved out onto the stairs. "You don't have money, you don't get anything," one of the men said.

"Oh, come on! I told you, I'm getting paid the day after tomorrow, then I just need to go to the ATM!"

"Yes, yes. You have all the good excuses we have heard many times before."

"But I do get paid the day after tomorrow!"

"No money, no goods," the second man insisted as he shut the door between them. Mason slowly began to make his way down the rusted metal stairs and back onto the sidewalk. Nora was about to make her appearance when she saw him pull a bag of white powder out of his pocket.

*I'll come back and pay them double for it tomorrow. That should make them happy,* he thought to himself. The door to the apartment suddenly swung open.

"HEY!" one of the men yelled at Mason. He took off running. "*Well, shit. They noticed that fast!*" The two men ran down the stairs and chased after him. Nora watched for a few moments, and once they were far enough down the road that she knew they wouldn't see her, she began to follow. Mason turned another street corner, then saw an abandoned warehouse down the block up ahead. He located a break in the chain link fence around the outside, and slipped through it as fast as he could. He thought he was far enough ahead that they wouldn't see where he went, but they made the corner just in time to catch him disappearing through a side door into the building. They slowed to a walk and casually followed him inside. Mason was working on catching his breath inside when they suddenly appeared next to him. Nora ducked down against the side of a car parked across the street and caught glimpses of them beating her uncle to the ground through the broken windows of the warehouse. Some of the hits were hard enough that she could hear them across the road, accompanied by unspecified snapping and crashing noises.

She waited fearfully for them to finish, and a few minutes later, finally saw them come out of a second door on the other side of the building. They sauntered slowly into the shadows down the back, and she heard one of them say: "Stupid shit thought he was clever."

The other one answered: "Eh, he must be given a small amount of credit. His plan worked for a whole minute."

"Yes, we must be losing our touch," the first one answered, and then they both shared a slimy chuckle amongst themselves.

She waited until they were out of sight before she ran inside. Mason was lying face down on the ground, a small pool of blood forming around his face; draining from his mouth and nose. He wasn't completely unconscious as she reached down and began to help him up. "I'm here, Uncle Mason." He could only groan in response as she put one of his arms around her shoulder and struggled to stand him up on his own feet. "Let's get you back to the hotel." She began to walk him towards the door. One of his teeth had been cracked in half, and his nose was bruising noticeably before her eyes. The tell-tale iron smell of blood was in the air, masking the smell of gas seeping into the room from behind them. A freshly broken pipe by the back door was slowly losing its contents, while the two men outside had stopped and were standing at the rear of the building. The one with curly brown hair had flicked a lighter on, and was working on cramming a small splinter of wood down the side of the button to keep it lit. "He will not try this again!" he said with a smile, and they both laughed as he threw the lighter through the window. They turned and ran down the back of the next building, where they were just out of reach of the crashing wave of flames from the explosion.

# CHAPTER 19

## (Rehab)

**When they got the news,** Ricky locked himself in his room. He stayed in there for days, hardly coming out. A few times to use the bathroom, never to eat. He wouldn't talk to anybody, not even Hal, not even through the closed door. After many hours of wondering where Nora and Mason had gone, and why they wouldn't pick up their phones, they called the police. Everything came together rather quickly the next morning once the police realized their descriptions matched those of the two victims found in the warehouse.

Once again, their tour was cut short, and a few days later, they got on the plane to head home. It was the longest plane ride of any of their lives. Nobody dared to talk about anything, because Ryan was a powder keg ready to explode, and Ricky had clammed up so tight they could barely get a mumble out of him. He wouldn't even look at any of them. If he was walking, he kept his eyes on the ground, and seemed to have to will his own feet to keep moving. Hal and Uli sat between the two of them. Hal wanted Ricky next to the window so he could see the clouds and sunshine, for any good it may do for him. And he wanted Ryan on the aisle so he could get to the bathroom quicker if another bout of nausea struck. Ryan had gone about twelve hours now without a fix, since they knew they couldn't bring him to the airport high, nor was there any way his stash would make it through baggage check or customs. He was going through withdrawals, and to say he was in a foul mood would have been the understatement of the year. He sat in his chair, staring forward the whole trip. Seven hours of angry staring from London to New York, and another three hours from New York to Detroit, plus a five-hour layover in between flights. He had tried, a few times, to listen to music through his headphones or browse the internet, or even to sleep. But his head was throbbing so hard that he couldn't handle trying to focus on anything other than the ugly pattern on the seat in front of him. Both the laptop and music player were stuffed aggressively back into his bag out of frustration, and the staring continued. The staring, the twitching, and the occasional nose blowing. Hal and Uli tried to read or do something on their laptops while taking the utmost care not to make any sudden movements. God forbid if one of them accidentally bumped him with their shoulder. The whole plane would probably go down.

Ricky leaned his head against the wall of the plane and stared out the window the whole ride. Seven hours of blank staring to New York from London, and another three hours to Detroit from New York after the five-hour layover in between. Hal had the horrible darkness and depression of having lost Mason and Nora as friends hanging over him bad enough. He couldn't even imagine how much darker and heavier that cloud was for Ricky. He wanted so much for there to be something he could say or do to lessen the pain for him, but he knew it was only wishful thinking. There was literally nothing he could do, and it was going to drive him crazy.

Once they landed back in Detroit, Cecilia and Harvey met them with the Twinkie van at a private exit around back. Hal had already briefed them on the situation over the phone from London the night before, and they drove home in fragile silence. Two and a half hours of fragile silence. Once they got home, Hal and Uli carried all the luggage up to the house, and Ricky and Ryan trudged slowly behind them. When Hal opened the front door, a grey ball of fur came flying out, but suddenly skidded to a stop in the grass a few feet away from Ricky. Slinky looked up at Ricky, her eyes got wide, then she puffed a little bit and started slowly backing up. Ricky watched her expressionless as she turned around, then slunk back into the house with her body close to the ground. She ducked under the bottom shelf of a side table next to the staircase and observed quietly from a distance. Ricky's eyes went back to the ground as he came inside and started plodding up the stairs. Each step gave a prolonged, melancholy creak as his feet touched down on them, then a quick squeak of relief as he moved to the next. Once he was at the top, he went straight to his room, and pulled the door shut behind him.

Slinky came out from under the table and crept up the stairs after him. She approached Ricky's door cautiously, sniffed it for a few moments, then laid down and pulled her limbs under her body so she formed into a little fur loaf right outside the door. Cecilia slowly turned her head to look at Hal, her mouth half open in disbelief. Hal caught her gaze for a moment, and she could see the same concern in his eyes as well. They both shifted their attention back up the stairs to Ricky's door. They had never let Cecilia in on Ricky's backstory. They figured the less people knew, the better. And as much as his mother was concerned by the cat's behavior, it sent a truly deep chill down his spine. Hal started to take a few steps towards the stairs, then Ryan spoke up quietly behind them: "I'm going to go get something to eat, I'll be back in a bit," he said, but as he started to leave, Hal caught him by the back of his shirt.

"Like HELL you are!"

"We've been travelling for fifteen hours! I'm fucking hungry!" Ryan protested.

"Well, tonight is your lucky night, because you're getting room service," Hal said. "Tell me what you want, and I'll go get it *and* pay for it." Ryan glared at him furiously. "So, what'll it be?" Hal asked.

Ryan was clearly shaking as he answered: "Big Mac meal… with a Sprite."

"Comin' right up!" Hal said, and took the keys from his dad as he went out the door. "Oh, hey…" He leaned back inside. "Why don't you and Uli spend some quality time together playing video games or something? It'll be a nice break from all the boredom we just endured," he said, then pulled the door shut behind him.

Ryan turned to look at Uli, who had a disturbingly bright smile on his face. "You name the game! It's your choice since you haven't been feeling well lately," Uli said. Ryan gritted his teeth again. Uli was obviously the prison guard until Hal got back.

"I'm, uh, going to go get Charlotte," Cecilia said awkwardly as she left out the front door. A neighbor had been babysitting her for the last few hours. Harvey also suddenly made himself scarce. Ryan sat down, and tried to play a few rounds with Uli, but he had trouble keeping his hands from trembling. On top of that, he was still experiencing a complete absence of concentration, so it became a lost cause. Uli shut the game off, and they both just sat on the couch and ended up watching a little bit of The Late Show. Uli watched it, anyways. Ryan may have listened to parts of it. Ryan was starting to tremor harder than he had been earlier, and he laid down on his half of the couch with his head on the armrest, facing the wall. The light from the TV was giving him a headache. He had no hope of falling asleep, but he kept his eyes shut and tried to lay still. He didn't have enough energy left to stay angry, and now he was starting to look sick and drained. Uli kept an eye on him until Hal came back through the front door.

"One Big Mac… meal…" Hal's voice dropped off as he saw Ryan curled up on the couch. Ryan slowly raised his head to look at him. Hal went over and handed him the bag as he sat up and set the Sprite down on the side table. Ryan took a small bite of the burger, and slowly started chewing. "So, you know how I said we were going to rehab right when we got back?" Hal asked.

"*Yeah?*" Ryan mumbled between chewing.

"You're getting a reprieve. I'm too goddam tired tonight. We're going tomorrow," he said, and that seemed to make Ryan perk up a bit.

"Alright," he replied, sounding a little too pleased. Hal didn't like that tone in his voice. It made him nervous, but he was too exhausted to drive back another two hours to Detroit tonight. "You've got to be exhausted, too," Hal said.

"Yeah," Ryan answered again. "Great. I'm going to bed. See you in the morning."

Uli got up off the couch and followed Hal upstairs to go brush his teeth. Hal had locked the deadbolt on the front door. While Ryan was certainly capable of unlocking a deadbolt, the old lock was quite rusty, and they would hear the screeching and grinding of the lock from upstairs if he tried to escape. Still, Uli and Hal took turns peeking over the railing down to the living room to make sure he was still eating, until both of them were completely ready for bed. At that point, Hal came halfway down the stairs and announced in a less than subtle tone: "Whelp, time for bed. YOU should go to bed too." Ryan stared at him out of the corner of his eyes, then slowly got up and turned off the TV.

Hal listened from his bedroom as Ryan brushed his teeth, then went into his room and shut the door. A few moments later, Hal came back out of his room. "God dammit," he said out loud, to no one in particular, then walked down the stairs. Their luggage was still in the living room. He wanted Ryan to think he was looking for something. He came back up the stairs with one of his bags, but also with three kitchen pots and pans. He tossed the bag in his room, then very carefully and very quietly stacked the three pots and pans on top of each other right outside of Ryan's door. He repeated this twice more, bringing two more bags up to his room, as well as six more cooking pots.

Once the tower of kitchenware was nine items high outside Ryan's door, he went back into his room and announced out loud: "Ah!" Clearly, he had found what he was looking for. He examined the precarious tower one last time, then pulled his door shut. *'Please, God, please say Ryan will just fall asleep and stay in his room tonight.'* Hal turned off the lights, then laid down in his bed. That bed had never felt so good in his entire life. He felt himself sink into it. He breathed in the smell of the sheets he knew well, but hadn't laid on for over a year. He held the breath in for a few moments, then let it out. He shut his eyes and began to nod off immediately. He spent ten seconds in pure bliss drifting off to dreamland, before there was a tremendous, thundering crash in the hallway. He opened his eyes wide. Ten seconds. Ten. Fucking. Seconds. He couldn't have at least gotten an hour's nap first? That made him mad. Really, really, mad. He slammed his hands on the bed and pushed himself up. He pulled on a pair of shorts, then threw open his door and flipped on the hall light. Ryan had the deer-in-the-headlights look as their eyes met, standing amongst the scattered pots and pans. "I SEE WE ARE GOING TO REHAB TONIGHT AFTER ALL!" Hal nearly yelled it.

---

249. "Rehab" by Amy Winehouse *to play over this scene*

---

Ryan said nothing, but suddenly took off running down the stairs. "HEY!" Hal jumped over the pots after him, and with a flying leap, tackled him halfway down the stairs. A split second later, Uli was there too, helping to hold him down.

Upstairs, Cecilia and Harvey were lying in bed, wide awake. No crying yet. Cecilia looked over to a sleeping Charlotte in her bassinette. Somehow, all this noise hadn't woken her up. "It's nice to have the boys home," she said, pleasantly.

"Yeah," Harvey agreed. Unintelligible screaming started coming from the stairwell. "Do you hear something?" Harvey asked.

"Nope. Not a thing," Cecilia answered.

Harvey nodded. "Okay. Goodnight then." He rolled over and pulled the covers over his head. Cecilia checked Charlotte to make sure she was still breathing and everything, and after confirming she was fine, laid back down herself and settled into the sheets.

"Let go, you don't understand, *please* let go!" Ryan begged. He was starting to cry, and it didn't appear to be manufactured drama, either. "I can't do this, I can't! It's like having a big, sweaty, dark monster scratching at the inside of my skull! I have to make it stop!"

"Ryan, you've already made it this far, it's going to get better on its own if you can make it a little bit longer!" Hal said.

"A little bit longer!? It might be another week! I can't do this for another week!" he pleaded. "I've made it over a day. I need to get a fix to stop this. Then, I'll make myself go another day before another one, and I'll slowly work myself off it, I swear!"

"Ryan!" Hal said. "I know in the heat of the moment you think you mean that, I know you really, really want that to be true, but it's *not* what's actually going to happen, and you know it! You're this far in, don't lose all this time and have to start over from the beginning! Please, let us take you to rehab!" Hal pleaded.

"I can't do it, Hal, I'm not strong enough, alright!? You two have ten times more willpower than I'll ever have! There, I said it! Now LET GO OF ME!" Ryan bellowed.

Hal and Uli kept their grip on him firm. Hal looked slowly to Uli. "Time for plan B?" Uli asked.

"Yeah, I think we've hit that point. Can you hold him by yourself for a second while I get things ready?" Hal asked.

"Yes, I can keep him here," Uli assured him.

"Okay," Hal said, and loosened his grip as Uli grabbed both of Ryan's arms and held him down on the stairs. Ryan began to kick and flail as hard as he could, but Uli had enough strength over him to keep him from breaking his hold. Hal went upstairs into his room for a few minutes, then came back out and went back down the stairs and grabbed Ryan by the ankles. "Ready?" he asked Uli.

"Ready," Uli answered, and they picked him up and carried him into Hal's room.

Inside, a wood chair was waiting in the middle of the room, facing Hal's computer. They forced Ryan into the chair, and Hal pulled a roll of duct tape out of his desk drawer.

"Are you FUCKING KIDDING ME!?" Ryan screamed.

"Will you SHUT UP!?" Hal yelled back, pulling a length of tape loose from the roll. "My parents and Ricky are trying to sleep!" he said as he wrapped the first loop of duct tape around Ryan's chest. They knew Ryan wasn't going to hold still, and if he had been at full health, both of them combined might not have been enough to restrain him. They were only able to overpower him this time since he was weak and uncoordinated from the withdrawal symptoms. They got both legs taped to the chair legs, his wrists duct taped together, and plenty of duct tape around his torso and the back of the chair.

"So, now what? Are you going to make me an offer I can't refuse?" Ryan snapped.

"Yes, exactly." Hal nodded as he sat down at his computer.

"You think you're a fucking gangster, huh?" Ryan said.

"Well, maybe 'mobster' is a slightly more accurate term in today's world, but yes. I am 100 percent mobster by birth," Hal answered.

"I see *you've* been demoted to goon," Ryan said to Uli.

Uli shrugged. "The pay has been excellent."

"Anyways, let's begin," Hal said as he brought up a blank email template on his screen. "So, first of all…" Hal rotated the chair, so he was facing Ryan, and put his fingertips together. "I had an excellent phone call with your mother about a week back."

"You did WHAT!!??" Ryan yelled. Hal held up one finger to signal for Ryan to wait before he said anything else.

"I told her you had expressed to us that you really did want to patch up things with her and the family, but you were concerned she was going to think you weren't serious and continue to be resistant to talking to you. So, I told her I was calling her without you knowing to assure her you were serious. And to let her know ahead of time that you were considering writing a long apology to her and everyone else in your family for your behavior in the past, and ask if they could forgive you and let you start anew," Hal said, and Ryan rolled his eyes. "She was so happy to hear this, she told me she wanted to share it with everyone in her church congregation. So, if you were willing, she was wondering if maybe you could send them all a copy of the apology as well? I said I could mention it to you. She said you knew quite a few of these people growing up, and that they'd love to hear that you're doing better. She sent me the current congregation email list," Hal explained, then pulled a piece of paper off the desk. "Do these names look familiar to you?" Hal held the paper up in front of Ryan. On it, Ryan did recognize most of the names of the people from his parents' church congregation, which also included his own grandparents.

"Yes," Ryan answered dryly.

"Good!" Hal said, then turned halfway back to the computer, changed the 'From' address to Ryan's email address, and then typed in the subject line: 'I just want to say sorry, for everything'. After that, Hal opened a note where he had all the email addresses typed out and copy and pasted them in the 'To' line. "Next, the body of the email, so to speak." Hal clicked on the main text box and typed: "I recorded what I wanted to say to everyone, I thought it might be a bit better than me trying to write it all out. See attached," Hal typed into the email body, then minimized the email itself, and brought up a video player. He went to his video list, clicked one, and brought it up full screen. "I'm sure you'll remember this. It was a pretty wild night, as far as you've told us," Hal said as the video started to play. On the screen, shaky cell phone video showed a drunken Ryan in a hotel room, pulling two girls down onto the bed with him. A third girl appears from off screen and joins them, quickly pulling her shirt off. About half of what was being said wasn't discernable due to the video quality, but the images were clear. One of the girls began pulling Ryan's pants off him while he was otherwise occupied with his head up another girl's skirt, pulling her pink thong off with his teeth. "See, I liked this one due to the sheer number of players that ultimately end up on the field, as well as the complexity, dexterity, and variety of plays that are used throughout the game," Hal explained. "And so, we have attachment number one… tada!" Hal said as he attached a copy of the video to the email, and then saw some of the color go out of Ryan's face. "Next, a somewhat different piece." Hal pulled up a second video and hit play. Ryan immediately recognized it. It took him a while to wipe the lens on his camera phone clean the morning after he recorded it. "This one is only two players, a one-on-one game, but I liked the extreme attention to detail that went into it. The crisp close-ups, the sounds, the textures that were showcased. You can nearly taste the flavors and smell the smells that were present," Hal said as he turned to face Ryan, while behind him, the phone made its way deeper and deeper in between the girl's thighs. "I figured this would be a good supplement to the first video as it provides a very different perspective." Hal turned back around and added the second video as an attachment to the email. "Ka-chow!" he said dramatically as he clicked the button to upload it, and Ryan's face just ghostly, turned a whiter shade of pale. "Now, *this* is the part where I make you an offer you can't refuse," Hal said. "And I'm just going to get right to the point, here. Agree to go to rehab, or I click the send button," he said menacingly. Ryan hadn't really quit crying, but he looked like he was on the verge of a new wave of tears.

"You… you know I'm trying to patch things up with my family. It'll never happen if you send them that!" Ryan said.

"I know," Hal replied calmly.

"They didn't do anything to you! You want to torture me? FINE! But leave them out of it! If you send that, Mom and Dad are going to be the laughingstock of the entire church!"

"So?" Hal replied.

"SO!?" Ryan yelled. "This is MY problem, not theirs. This would just screw everything up for everyone!" Ryan said. Hal suddenly looked like he had an idea.

"You know, I just thought of the PERFECT solution to keep me from sending this email!" he said.

"Okay, look, I've got a drug problem! Okay!? I've fucked myself up! I've always fucked everything up! Don't do that to my family and make them hate me more!" Ryan said.

Hal rolled the chair over next to Ryan and looked him closely in the eye. "You know, they're not going to like you very much as a coke addict either," Hal said. "So, are you going to let us take you to rehab, or am I going to push the button?"

Ryan started to cry a bit harder. "I can't do it, okay!? My head hurts too much, I'm not going to make it! I'm not strong enough, ALRIGHT!?" Ryan begged, and Hal looked at him for a moment, then sighed as he swiveled back around in his chair. He pulled the email back up and moved the mouse straight to the send button. "WAIT!!" Ryan suddenly yelled.

Hal swiveled back around again, slowly. "Why?" he asked, irritated.

"Because what good is it going to do!?" Ryan asked. "If I don't go to rehab and you send the email and screw everything up for my parents, what good will it do at that point!? It will only make everything worse for everyone!" Ryan said.

"Ryan, apparently I have to explain this to you," Hal said. "This is a little litmus test, if you will. If you care enough to still have an ounce of shame for yourself and an ounce of respect left for your family, then you might have an ounce of willpower left to still be our drummer." Ryan fell silent. "All I'm trying to do is see if you've gone over the edge of the cliff yet or not. If you're past the point of no return where you love the drugs more than your own family, then I'll know that you're also at the point where you'll never be as dedicated to drumming again as you are to worshipping the magic white powder. And then I'll know we need to start having tryouts to replace you." Hal saw a few, large tears run down Ryan's face. "And if you're more dedicated to the drugs than your family or drumming, then it really shouldn't matter if I send this email or not. You haven't seen these people for years, and you may never see them again. So, what would it fucking matter?" Hal asked. "I mean, hell, it'll be better for you this way. After this, you can be alone with your drugs, and your family won't try to bother you anymore about anything ever again."

Ryan's voice quivered as he answered: "I need help, okay? I need help. You sending that email isn't going to help anything. I don't know if I'd make it through rehab, but, please, don't send it. Just… don't send it!" Ryan pleaded.

Hal examined him for a second. "Look at you," he said. "Look what this has done to you. You're begging and pleading and crying like a little kid. You should only ever be on your knees begging for one thing in this world, and this sure as hell isn't it." Ryan looked at him, broken. Hal continued, "You know, Grandpa told me once that sometimes, to get the results you need, you have to hurt innocent people. Or threaten them, at least. So far, all the attempts we've made to help you by being nice haven't accomplished anything at all. Now we're at least getting a reaction, so it seems he was right."

"What the hell is wrong with you?" Ryan whimpered.

"Ryan, I'm from a long line of nasty people," Hal said. "It all comes down to business. Like I said, I'm just trying to figure out if I need a new drummer or not. So… do I, or don't I?" Ryan hung his head as another wave of pain hit him, and he started to cry harder. Hal sighed. He turned slowly in his chair and grabbed the mouse. He moved the cursor to the 'send' button, and Ryan watched as his pointer finger positioned over the left side of the mouse.

"OKAY! OKAY! I'LL GO TO REHAB!" Ryan suddenly yelled with every ounce of energy he had left. Hal remained still for a moment, staring silently at the screen as a wave of relief hit him. He exhaled slowly. Ryan watched in tense anticipation as Hal's finger slowly backed off the mouse.

Hal shut his eyes for a moment, said a quick 'Thank you' in his head to any possible deity that may have intervened on their behalf, then swung back around in his chair, a renewed smile on his face. "See! I knew we could reach an agreement!" he said. "And guess what? Your bags are already packed for a long trip!" Hal stood up and headed for the stairs. "I'll load them up into the van now! Uli? Can you make sure he doesn't go anywhere until I get back?" he asked, and Uli nodded. "Thanks."

"I… fucking… hate… you…" Ryan mumbled, then turned his head so he was facing out the door and yelled louder: "I FUCKING HATE YOU!"

"I can live with that!" Hal yelled back. Uli held down the chair as Ryan struggled to break free of the layers of duct tape, until Hal came back upstairs about ten minutes later. He opened a can of Red Bull, chugged half of it on the spot, then looked at Uli. "Ready?" he asked.

"Ready," Uli replied, and Hal leaned the chair back and grabbed the back rest as Uli lifted the legs, and they started carrying Ryan towards the stairs. "Are you FUCKING KIDDING ME!?" Ryan yelled. "I said I'd go! Cut me out of this!"

"Nah. It's going to be much easier this way," Hal said, and he and Uli carefully carried Ryan and the chair down the stairs, then out across the yard to the garage. They loaded Ryan onto the back seat, laying him down on his side, and looped a seatbelt through the back slats of the chair, as well as lacing it tightly around the legs.

> End Song 249

"I'M GOING TO FUCKING KILL YOU TWO!" Ryan yelled.

"Not while you're stuck in that chair, you're not," Hal answered, and then he and Uli burst out laughing. Hal jumped in the driver's seat, Uli in the front passenger seat, and Hal pulled the door shut. They laughed for at least another two minutes straight. It was only that funny because it was way too late and they were way too tired to be dealing with something like this. Ryan swore and screamed the whole drive there. Two hours of screaming and whining. It was oddly refreshing compared to the hours of silence they had endured earlier in the day.

"Would you like me to add one more piece of duct tape?" Uli asked as they went up the first ramp onto the interstate.

"Nah, this will help me stay awake," Hal answered. He felt like he hadn't slept for days at this point. He finished the first can of Red Bull and started on the second. By the time they got to the rehab center, he had finished the fourth. They unbuckled the chair, and Hal took the chair legs and held them over his shoulders while Uli grabbed the back rest. They carried Ryan in through the front door, like a pig on a stick on its way to a giant outdoor barbeque. Ryan protested loudly the whole way across the parking lot.

The receptionist did a double take as she watched them walk in. "Goooood evening!" Hal said in a loud voice. He was completely strung out on nerves and Redbull. "We'd like to check my buddy into rehab!" he announced. The receptionist examined them for a moment. Hal could tell she knew who they were. He could see it in her eyes. Pretty much everyone had heard of them, though there were still many people who didn't know what they looked like. Heard of the band, liked the music, seen the logo, but never took a moment to pull up any pictures of them on the internet. Hal had seen enough of both groups to tell which was which by the way they looked at them. The young receptionist with long brown hair knew who they were, though kept a professional demeanor. She'd likely dealt with celebrities before. This was the nicest rehab center they could find in the area.

"Sir, you actually can't check someone in against their will. It's against the law. They have to be willing to be here and check themselves in," she said.

"Oh, did I say we were here to check him in? I'm sorry, I meant we're here as moral support for our friend as he makes this life-changing decision to check himself in," Hal explained.

The receptionist took another good, long look at them, then her eyes moved to a miserable and exhausted looking Ryan, hanging face down from the chair. His face was red, his eyes were red, and his mohawk had not been properly done in over a day. The line of black hair hung down over the side of his head, except for a few pieces that clung to the duct tape on the chair.

Hal looked over his shoulder at Ryan. "Oh, right. That," Hal said. "I imagine that does make it look a bit like he's here against his will, huh? Long story, but Ryan here was in the middle of something sort of… *kinky*…" Hal whispered it with emphasis, "…when he suddenly had the realization that his life was spiraling out of control due to his drug problem. He decided right then and there that he couldn't wait another moment to get back on the right track, so he called us in and begged us to take him to rehab where he could make those important first steps to recovery. We agreed we would deal with getting him out of the chair once we got here."

Ryan slowly turned his head to glare at Hal. Uli gave him a bit of a look, too. The receptionist was clearly trying to keep a straight face.

"Well, um, would you like to deal with the chair *now*?" she asked politely.

"Yes, lets!" Hal answered, and he and Uli carefully set Ryan down, then she handed Hal a pair of scissors. It took a few minutes to cut Ryan free. As they tore the last piece of duct tape off from his shirt, Ryan got up and went and leaned against the counter. His back had started cramping a bit. The receptionist was skeptical as she put a pile of papers on the counter in front of him.

"As I mentioned, per law you have to check yourself in only if it is of your own will to do so, and then you'll have to sign a few things to consent to us providing care for you," she said. Ryan looked dismally at the papers, then to Hal and Uli. Hal had a nearly homicidal smile on his face; worse than it had been earlier when he was taunting him with the email. Ryan examined the papers again, then reached for the pen and started filling out the first form. Once he had finished and signed his name, the receptionist turned the dial on a walkie-talkie on the desk and said: "New patient for check-in, already experiencing intense withdrawal symptoms."

A few moments later, a male nurse in blue scrubs came out the door behind the check-in desk and walked out to them. "Good evening… or… morning?" He looked at his watch. "Good morning," he corrected himself.

"Mm… orning," Ryan said weakly. The nurse grabbed the papers off the desk and flipped through them quickly, then looked at Ryan. "I imagine you probably have the worst headache of your life right now. You want to come back and we can get you something to help with that? And then you can lay down for a bit?" The nurse asked as he gestured towards the door behind him. Ryan pondered it for a second, then shook his head 'yes' slightly. That sounded really nice. He started walking back with the nurse, turning to look back at Hal & Uli one more time as he went through the doorway.

"You can do this," Hal said, and Ryan stopped for a moment. "You're strong enough," Hal added. They shared a hard stare for a little bit, then Ryan turned away without a word. The door closed with a quiet click behind him.

"I'm assuming he has clothes and a toothbrush and everything? Or do you need some supplies to be purchased for him?" the receptionist asked.

"Oh, no. We've got all his stuff packed up in the van. We'll bring it in," Hal said, and he and Uli picked up the chair and went out to the van to bring Ryan's bags in. Once they were back in the lobby, another employee came out to bring the bags back to Ryan's room, and then Hal went up to the reception desk. "Thank you for everything. Here, let me give you my number. Please call us if he checks himself out before you think he's ready," Hal said as he grabbed a post-it note from the corner of the desk and started to write his number on it.

"Sir, I can't do that. I know you're trying to help him, but it's a violation of patient's privacy rights for us to contact anyone to let them know they've checked out without their explicit permission," the woman said.

Hal looked slowly up at her. *Are you frickin' kidding me?*' he thought to himself. It was way too late for a charm offensive. Way too late. Did he really have to try one now? He shut his eyes for a second to compose himself, then opened them again slowly, looking the young receptionist strait in the eyes. "Look…" He glanced at her name tag. "Melissa… we're trying to make sure he gets better. For his own sake. Ryan doesn't have the greatest sense of self-control. He needs help. And we want to help him," Hal said quietly.

"I know, and trust me, we've had many other people who want to help see to it that their loved ones stay here until they're better. But unfortunately, we cannot keep someone here against their will, nor can we disclose confidential information to outside parties without their consent. That includes alerting anyone that they have checked out," she replied solemnly, adding: "I'm sorry."

Hal tried to keep his gaze with her soft, though it was teetering on the edge of irritation. The girl was only doing her job, he knew that. But he was trying to do his, as well. "You know we're just trying to help him," Hal repeated.

"I know, trust me, I know. And he's lucky to have friends like you who are willing to offer support, but this is a rule we can't break. He needs to find his own strength to get through this, that's part of beating an addiction. If he doesn't, he's going to fall right back into it as soon as he checks out," she answered.

*Employee of the frickin' year,* Hal thought to himself. This was going to require a different approach. He pulled his check book out of his pocket, put it on the counter, and started writing.

"What are you doing?" the girl asked.

"Look, Melissa, we're at odds here. And it's difficult odds, because you're doing your job by following the law, but my job is to get Ryan clean at all costs. I am going to do whatever it takes to make sure that happens, so we need to figure out how to end this standoff." Hal began writing out one of the checks.

"I can't take any bribes," she said, annoyed.

"Well, you say that now, but give me a few more seconds here, and we'll see if we can change your mind," he insisted, and to her disbelief, she watched as he started with a 1, and then added one zero, two zeros, three zeros, four zeroes. $10,000. Her heart stopped for a second. "You're doing very important work here helping people get their lives back, but, sadly, I imagine that being the receptionist at a rehab center probably doesn't pay very well." He ripped the check out of the book along the perforated lines. "I would know. A few years ago, when I was a server at a steak house, my mom and I were doing our best to break even on the bills and not go into any debt." He held the check facing her on the counter. "Now, I don't know if you're married, have any kids, need a new car, have medical bills to pay, need a little help with rent, all of the above or none of the above. But I bet you'd be able to put this to good use somehow," he said.

"I can't take that!" she said, terrified.

"Well, actually, you can," Hal said. "You've been told you can't, but physically, yes, you can take this check, cash it, and call us if Ryan leaves," Hal explained. "And the reason for all this is to keep our drummer from destroying himself, not to hurt him in any way." Hal held the check closer to her. "This is pocket change for us. I make more than this every day. And, my offer is that you go straight ahead and cash it. I'm not asking you to wait for Ryan to check himself out. This is a payment just to keep an eye on him. Even if he doesn't end up checking out early at any point, don't worry about a thing. It's yours. This is simply peace of mind for us." Melissa was clearly starting to ponder it. "And no one's going to sue you if you make the call. If Ryan somehow finds out and gives you any trouble, we'll beat the crap out of him for you and deny any allegations he makes, don't worry. So... how 'bout it? Help us help a friend?" He gave her his best rock-star seductive eyes, and a charming little smile. Melissa slowly reached out and took the check, looking pained to do so. She glanced around, and then quickly put it in her pocket, and Hal took the post it note back up and finished writing his number on it. "Here. This is my personal cell phone number. I would appreciate it if you don't give this out to anyone," he said as he handed her the note. "And in case you're wondering, no, that check will not be bouncing. All I ask is you call or text if he checks himself out, and if you could let us know the general direction he heads in after going out the front door. That's all. I'm not asking you to follow him down the street or anything." Melissa nodded slightly. "Do you need anything else for him before we go?" he asked.

"No... I think everything is taken care of," she said.

"OK, we're going to head out, then. You can also call us if you need us to bring anything else for him, but he should have everything he needs in his bags. We literally just got back from a tour. You have a good evening, okay? And Melissa…" He waited until she was looking him in the eyes again. "Thank you," he said quietly.

"You're welcome," she said in a near whisper, and Hal gave her one last smile and a quick wink, and then he and Uli left out the front door. They trekked back across the parking lot and got back in the van.

Once the door was shut, Hal and Uli slowly turned to look at each other. "I cannot BELIEVE that worked," Hal said.

"Which part of it?" Uli asked.

"All of it," Hal answered. "The pot and pan alarm, the duct tape, the email, the bribe…"

"It was… a well-executed series of plans," Uli admitted.

"Yes, it was. But god, let's go home." Hal turned the key in the ignition. The van chugged a few times before starting, and the shocks squeaked as they always did when he turned out from the parking lot onto the road. At least they wouldn't have to deal with any traffic at this hour of the night… or morning. As soon as they got onto the onramp, Hal put the pedal to the floor to start bringing the old van slowly up to freeway speeds. Zero to sixty in two minutes flat.

"I am glad your mother raised you and encouraged you to pursue music," Uli suddenly said. Hal glanced over at him, one eyebrow raised. That was random. "You would have been a terrifying mob boss," he added. A giant, gratified smile began to form across Hal's face, and as he turned his attention back to the road, Uli heard him chuckling to himself under his breath. Perhaps, though he would have had trouble killing people. He could certainly toy with anyone he needed to until he got what he wanted, but he had impressed even himself tonight. He wasn't completely sure the email scheme was going to work, but Ryan's mother was right. Hal ran the actual phone call he had with Lana Summerfield through his brain again…

He'd found her number in Ryan's phone while Ryan was otherwise occupied. They were still in Eastern Europe at the time. It was evening, and they'd just gotten back from a dinner date with a very starstruck doctor's daughter. The phone rang a few times, then a woman picked up. "*Hello?*"

"Hello, is this Lana Summerfield?" Hal asked.

"*Speaking,*" the woman on the other end answered impatiently.

"Hi, Lana, my name's Hal Hulsing. I'm, uh, one of Ryan's friends." That caused a momentary pause on the other end.

"*Oh. Uh, yes. I've… heard of you,*" Lana said slowly. "*What can I do for you, Hal?*"

"Well, I'm actually calling to ask you for help with something," Hal said. "Ryan's unfortunately taken up to doing some hard drugs. Cocaine, to be specific, and we're trying to figure out how to make him go to rehab when we get back from our tour."

"*Oh, Lord,*" Lana said, nearly a whisper. "*I wish I could say I'm shocked to hear that, but unfortunately, I'm not. I am sorry to hear he's taken it that far, though I'm not surprised. He never respected any limits set for him, nor did he know how to set any of his own. I wish I could help you somehow, but, I spent so many years trying to help Ryan, and he's not going to listen to anything I have to say.*"

"Oh, I know," Hal said. "I know Ryan can be a tremendous pain in the rear, trust me, I know. And I know he's had a bad history with you, but Ryan's been our problem for many years now, and it may sound crazy, but we want to keep him our problem. And I actually wasn't calling to ask you to talk to him, but to see if you maybe had anything we could use against him."

"*What do you mean?*" Lana asked.

"Well, to be perfectly honest, we were thinking of trying to blackmail him into going to rehab. But, since Ryan has a much less developed sense of shame than the average person, we're having a little trouble trying to come up with something to blackmail him with," Hal explained.

"*And you're wondering if I know anything that might work?*" Lana asked.

"Yes, exactly."

Hal heard her sigh. "*Oh, boy. I mean, I could tell you all sorts of stories that the standard person would find horribly embarrassing, except I'm sure Ryan would wear each one like a badge of honor.*"

"Yeah, that's kind of the problem we're having," Hal agreed. "But what I was thinking is, since Ryan has a certain *type* of reputation he likes to keep, if you have any old, dorky pictures or video of him? I think everyone goes through a super-awkward stage between ten and fourteen, so do you have anything that might be embarrassing to him in a G-Rated nerdy kind of way from that era?" Hal asked.

"*Well, that's an idea, I suppose,*" Lana said. "*Nothing is immediately coming to mind, but I could take some time over the next few days to go through the photo albums and our old videos.*"

"That would be fantastic if you could. Sorry to ask this of you."

"*No, no. It's no problem. I appreciate that you're trying to help him. But, as you already know, you have your work cut out for you.*"

"Yes, we know," Hal answered.

"*Alright, well, can you give me a few days to go through everything, and I can call you back if I find anything useable?*" Lana asked.

"Yes, of course. Take your time," Hal said.

"*Okay. Is this number you're calling on the best number to call you back at?*"

"Yes, this one would be perfect."

"*Okay Hal, I'll see what I can find.*"

"Lana, thank you so much. I really appreciate it."

"*You're welcome. And thank you for trying to take care of him, at least.*"

"No problem, it's part of our job."

"*Okay, well, I'll call in a few days.*"

"Okay, thanks again. Have good day."

"*You too. Bye.*"

"Bye." Hal hung up, and he and Uli spent the next few days trying to figure out the details of how they were going to blackmail Ryan with dorky pictures. That was all the further they had gotten with their plan. They didn't have a solid idea of how precisely they were going to execute it, other than maybe releasing them to the media, or posting them online someplace where they would be seen by a ton of people. They still didn't have a solid plan when Lana called back three days later.

"Hello, Lana, how's it going?" Hal asked.

"*Well, to be honest Hal, I went through all our old photos and videos, and I just don't know if I have anything blackmail-worthy,*" she replied. "*I mean, I have a short video of Ryan playing in a mud puddle when he was three, and a picture of him in the fifth grade behind his first drum set, smiling with his braces on. But I don't think either of those are going to scare him into doing much of anything.*"

"No, those don't sound terribly juicy," Hal agreed.

"*Yeah, but I've spent the last few days thinking about how one might go about blackmailing my son. Unfortunately, it was a far more entertaining thing for me to think about than it really should have been, which probably makes me as bad of a mother as Ryan says I am. But I think maybe I've come up with a different plan for you to try.*"

"I'm listening," Hal said, intrigued.

"*Okay. It's a little more complicated than what you had and needs a bit of explanation. Do you have a few minutes?*"

"I do," Hal said as he sat down at the table in his hotel room. "Shoot."

"*Alright, so, first of all, do you have any pictures or video of Ryan engaging in his usual debauchery?*" Lana asked.

"Oh, yes, we certainly do," Hal said.

"*Okay. Because you and I both know that if you sent stuff like that out to the media or posted it online, it wouldn't bother Ryan. But I may know a few people, who, if you threatened to send something like that specifically to them, it might scare him a little bit.*"

Hal sat up straighter in his chair. "Go on..."

"*So, believe it or not, there were a few members of our church congregation that Ryan did have some respect for when he was younger. And, threatening to send those videos or pictures to them might sway him a bit.*"

"Okay, that is a little hard to believe. But you know him better than me, so if you think it'll work, then I'm game," Hal said.

"*Yeah, I know it's hard to believe. But it's true,*" Lana replied. "*It's actually quite the story. Though I imagine you don't have THAT much time to hear the whole thing.*"

"Well, actually, we're in between show nights right now, so I have a few hours, to be honest. The more specifics I know, the better I might be able to understand things so I can really give Ryan a scare."

"*Okay, well, there was a number of very sweet, elderly church patrons that we had the pleasure of knowing, including many that had far more patience with Ryan than I did. But, there was one gentleman in particular who made quite an impression on him. His name is Daniel Wilkinson, though Ryan took to calling him 'Crazy Dan.' Dan and his wife Cindy moved to Seattle from Minneapolis when Ryan was about eight. They joined our church and attended for a few weeks before we ended up sitting next to them one Sunday morning. Ryan was being his usual, charming self. We let him play his Gameboy in church because it was absolutely, positively, the only way our poor pastor was going to get through his sermon without getting interrupted. It was horribly rude, and Ryan's brother and sister, Jeff and Becky, would always pout at us for letting Ryan do it but not them, but it was the only way to keep him quiet. We explained to them over and over that it was because Ryan was much less mature than them, and we were so proud of them for being able to sit through church without having to resort to that. Then they would always give us their best stone-faced stares. Anyways, even though we caved and let Ryan play his Gameboy, he still found ways to make a pest of himself. He liked to put his feet up on the back of the chair in front of him and push on it, and he was doing this the morning we sat next to Dan. I grabbed his ankles and pulled them down to*" the floor and told him to stop, because someone was sitting in the chair he was kicking, and it was making them uncomfortable. Now, everyone there knew we had our hands full and we were doing the best we could with Ryan, except this was the first time Dan and Cindy had really seen him in action. Anyways, I told him to keep his feet on the floor and not kick the chair, and he just looked at me and asked 'Why?' in his usual bratty tone, even though he knew exactly why. That's when Dan first looked over in our direction. He told Ryan: 'Young man, you are being very rude to your neighbor in front of you, and to your mother.' He said it in a very civil tone, and Ryan sort of slowly looked up at him and said, 'What does it matter to you?' Dan looked at him silently for a moment, then asked: 'I guess I'm just curious. Do you think it's okay to be rude to people and make them uncomfortable?' Ryan told him yeah, then Dan said: 'Well, you know there has to be equality in this world, right? If you're rude to people, does that make it okay for them to be rude to you?' Ryan told him: 'Yeah, fine, whatever.' Then went back to playing his Gameboy and put one foot back on the chair in front of him. Dan said: 'Oh, okay'. Then looked over at me and Steve. I guess he was trying to read us for what we might do after what he was about to do to Ryan. I'm sure it was perfectly clear to everyone in the room that we were both at the end of our ropes trying to deal with him, so Dan stood up, moved one seat over, and sat on him. This completely caught Ryan off guard, and he yelled: 'What the hell!?' really loud. Normally I would have had to haul him out of the sanctuary for saying that word during the sermon, but me and Steve were so flabbergasted we didn't know what to do. I remember Dan's wife Cindy got this horrified look on her face and slapped Dan on the arm and told him: "Dan! We've already talked about you sitting on other people's children without their permission! Get off him!" And then she looked at me and Steve and said 'I am so sorry about this! Dan, stand up!' But Steve told her that it was okay, and don't worry about it, and if Dan wanted to sit there, then he could sit there. And I remember Ryan shot Steve the nastiest look I've ever seen in my life and yelled at him: 'Are you serious!?' And Steve told him that hey, Ryan, you're the one who's always complaining that no one listens to you or takes you *seriously, but it appears this man listened to what you had to say and acted upon it. Steve, I'm sure, was enjoying watching Ryan squirm, and Jeff and Becky were laughing their heads off. Ryan kept yelling and called Dan a freak and threatened to call CPS on him, but Dan didn't move, and told Ryan: 'No thanks, I like this seat better.' To that, Ryan told him: 'Well, I'll move! Get off me!' And Dan said: 'Nah. I've never been a tall person, and I can see a little better if I'm sitting up on something. I know you might not like being sat on, but you said it was okay if other people make you uncomfortable. So, like your father said, I'm going to go ahead and take you at your word.' Now, the whole sermon had stopped at this point, and everyone was staring and laughing. I think even our poor minister was trying to resist laughing himself and get back on track. Dan ultimately sat on Ryan for another fifteen minutes until we all rose for a hymn, at which point Ryan ran to the back of the building and sat in the back quietly for the rest of the service."*

"I would have paid money to see that," Hal said.

"*Oh, me and Steve were in awe. And that was just the tip of the iceberg with Ryan and Dan. The next Sunday, when Dan and Cindy came in, as soon as Dan spotted us, he made a beeline for the seat next to Ryan. Dan sat down, and Ryan looked up and suddenly took his feet off the chair in front of him. And Dan asked him: 'Why'd you do that?' And Ryan said: 'Because.' And Dan asked: 'Because why?' And Ryan just said 'Because.' again. And Dan said: 'There has to be more of a reason than just because. Is it because you didn't like being sat on?' Ryan didn't answer him, and looked down at his Gameboy and was kind of trying to scoot closer to me. Then Dan said: 'So... you don't want to be sat on, so you quit making the lady in front of you uncomfortable?' Ryan kept ignoring him, and Dan finally said 'Interesting...' And then we started the sermon as usual. I had never seen Ryan that quiet during church in my entire life. It was amazing. Anyways, later in the service, our pastor did something he'd do once a month, and passed out a bunch of scrap paper and pens. He'd have everyone write down an anonymous prayer request for something they needed help with. Then, every Sunday for the rest of the month at the end of the service, he'd always go through a bunch of them, and we'd all pray on the request together. Ryan usually wrote something lovely like he wished his family would drop off a cliff, or that his teacher would quit giving out homework. Our pastor usually skipped over them. Or sometimes, he'd modify them to be a bit more palatable, like he'd have us pray for the Lord to help all the children to understand their schoolwork and grow in their knowledge through their lessons. But today, as the paper and the cup of pens was being passed down the aisle, Dan handed the paper and a pen to his wife, himself, and Ryan individually before handing the pile to me to keep it moving. Ryan put his paper on the back of the hymn book and clicked the pen, then suddenly screamed and threw the pen down. I wasn't sure what had happened, but I figured that maybe he'd pinched his finger with the pen somehow. I picked the pen up and asked him if he'd pinched his finger, and I remember he sort of looked at the pen, then looked at me, then said he didn't know. I thought that was a sort of odd answer, but I picked the pen up and was going to click it on for him and then hand it back. I think Dan had just started reaching over to try and stop me, but I clicked it and got the shock of my life, literally."*

"Oh! It was one of those zappy pens?" Hal asked.

*"Boy, was it ever. I think most gag pens might give you a tiny jolt, or really, most of them nowadays don't even shock you anymore and only vibrate to startle a person because you're not expecting it. But that pen Dan had was, I don't even know how to describe it, a professional stage quality magician's gag pen? That thing dished out quite the shock. My hand was tingling for about ten minutes afterwards from only a split second of touching it."*

"So, Dan struck again," Hal said.

*"Yes, indeed,"* Lana said. *"Poor Cindy smacked Dan on the arm again and scolded him for electrocuting other people's children without their permission. But once Ryan realized what had happened, and that Dan had subtly handed him a special pen from his own collection, Ryan spent the entire rest of the sermon clicking it and zapping himself with it over and over."*

Hal laughed. "Yeah, that sounds like something Ryan would do."

"Yes. And I was at the point with him that I didn't really care if he gave himself a bit of nerve damage from repeated use. I figured maybe it would make it harder for him to pinch Becky and Jeff. Anyways, for the second weekend in a row, Dan kept Ryan amused, for better or worse, through the entire service. After the service, I saw Ryan give Dan his pen back, but six days later on Saturday, I found it in his room while I was picking up some of the laundry. Somehow, he had taken it back out of Dan's pocket without me or Dan noticing right after he gave it back to him. I decided I was going to talk to him about that after church the next day, so he didn't have reason to make an exceptionally big scene during the service. But I did give Dan his pen back, and I remember Dan said: 'Oh, that's where that went!' And I told him yes, and that I was very sorry, I had no idea Ryan had it this whole time, and I would be having a long talk with him later that night regarding stealing from people. Dan didn't seem too concerned that Ryan stole his pen, and he asked me if Ryan knew he had it back yet. I told him no, but assured him that I was absolutely going to have a sit down with him about it after church. Then Dan just asked again: 'But... he doesn't know I have it back right now, correct?' And I told him no, Ryan did not know he had it back yet. And then I remember Dan got this really excited smile on his face, and then he sort of twirled the pen through his fingers a few times before asking: 'Lana, I don't suppose it would be okay with you if I addressed him first about the pen after the sermon, would it?' I told him that was perfectly fine with me since he was the person who had been wronged, and then he said thank you and walked away, smiling."

"Uh, oh," Hal said.

"Oh, yes. Dan definitely let Ryan know after the service that he had his pen back. He went and got one of those yellow rubber dish gloves from the church kitchen and held the pen cap down and got Ryan on the back of his neck when he wasn't looking. That was the loudest I'd heard Ryan scream in quite a while. Then Dan apparently told Ryan he had been an American Spy in Russia during the cold war, and that every item he owns has a microscopic tracking device on it. He said that he had tracked it to Ryan's room and took it back while he *was at school. Then, he pointed out to Ryan that he had technically stolen his pen, and asked Ryan if it was okay for him to steal things. At that point, I think Ryan knew Dan was leading him into another trap, but he was too proud and snotty to not walk right into it, so he said 'Yes.' Then Dan asked him if he was allowed to steal stuff, if that made it okay for other people to steal stuff. Ryan said 'sure', so Dan grabbed Ryan's Gameboy right out of his pocket, then held it above Ryan's head while Ryan tried to jump up and grab it. Boy, Ryan was mad about that. But Dan reminded him that he had just said it was okay, and then I recall he looked at the screen and said: 'Oh! This must be that peek-achoo thing everyone is talking about.' And told Ryan not to worry, because he'd figure out how to feed it over the next few days for him, then walked out of the church and said 'Thanks, Ryan!'"*

"Brutal," Hal laughed.

*"Yes, indeed. Dan dropped by the next day while the kids were at school and tried to give me the Gameboy back, but I told him to keep it until next Sunday. Which I sort of ended up regretting, because it meant Ryan didn't have his Gameboy to distract himself, so he spent the rest of the week attacking his siblings relentlessly. But, it was a good lesson for him to learn."*

"Yeah, I mean, it sounds like Dan was trying to give Ryan some moral coaching in his own way," Hal commented.

*"Oh, he absolutely was. And as entertaining as it was, at first I was a little suspicious as to why Dan had taken such an interest in my son. But, what I ultimately found out was Dan and Cindy had raised three difficult, rambunctious boys of their own. And over time, in trying to deal with them, Dan had developed what he called the 'Don't-Get-Mad-Get-Even' style of parenting that he was now re-using on Ryan. Dan apparently started having such a good time figuring out new ways to torment his boys, that when they had all grown up, calmed down, and moved out, he found himself bored and lonely. He apparently tried a few of his pranks on Cindy, which won him more than a few nights of sleeping on the couch. So, he was more than ready to take on a new challenge with Ryan, to, as Cindy put it, 'relive his glory days.'"*

"God, that's incredible," Hal said.

*"It really was. And this went on for years. The sheer number of different pranks and gags that man had up his sleeves was beyond belief. Dan and Ryan ended up developing this interesting dynamic, in that Dan was both Ryan's best friend and arch nemesis at the same time. Ryan started looking forward to going to church to see what 'Crazy Dan' had planned for him each week. It was a challenge for him to see if he could outwit Dan, which he never did, of course. Or to at least be able to figure out what Dan's latest trick was without Dan having to explain it to him. Poor Cindy kept apologizing to us for the things he was doing to Ryan, but the fact that Dan got results from his antics was such a blessing to me and Steve. And not only the behavioral results, even just the simple fact that he was keeping Ryan distracted every Sunday so me and Steve could at least enjoy the sermon with Jeffrey and Rebecca. Dan could do some basic slight-of-hand magic tricks with playing cards and little toys, too, and he would sometimes do them silently for Ryan while we were all sitting. He would listen to the sermon and do the tricks in his hands without even looking at them, while Ryan would watch and try to figure them out."*

"You know, that is so cool. That would have been such a neat thing to any kid, I think," Hal said.

*"Oh, yes. Dan became quite the enigma to Ryan. I remember another time he came through the church doors on a summer Sunday with his hands cupped together and told Ryan he had found a giant beetle in the parking lot. Ryan wanted to see it, of course, but Dan suddenly squeezed his hands together, and there was a loud crunching noise, and then green juice started running out from between his fingers. Dan then opened his hands while keeping his palms pointed towards him, so Ryan couldn't see what was in them, and started licking the green juice off his fingers. He told Ryan bugs were an excellent source of vitamins. The look on Ryan's face when he thought Dan had actually crushed a bug in his hands and was eating the guts was priceless."*

"What did he actually do?" Hal asked.

*"If I remember right, he had a little open packet of sweet relish in his hands, as well as an empty wrapper from a candy bar or something. The wrapper was to make more of a crunch noise since relish packets don't crunch very well."*

"That's awesome. I can't believe Ryan's never mentioned Dan to us."

*"What? And admit there was once an adult in his life he looked up to and respected?"* Lana asked.

"Well, okay, I suppose there's that, but still, I don't know how you could go that long without talking about someone that awesome."

*"Which leads straight into my theory. Most of Dan's antics had a lesson to them, and if Ryan told the stories, he might have some things to answer for. I want to believe Ryan has a teeny, tiny bit of shame regarding what he's become hiding somewhere in that messy, uncontrollable brain of his. And as much as he'll never admit it, by the time Ryan left home, I think he knew what Dan had tried to do for him. So, if Dan found out now that Ryan didn't ultimately turn out like his boys did, I bet it would hurt Ryan to know that he let Dan down."*

"Interesting idea…" Hal agreed,

*"Yeah, and like I mentioned earlier, there were some other church elders that Ryan didn't hate either because they had way more patience with him than I did. Me being a horrible failure of a mother and all, so I think threatening to send Dan and them some videos or pictures of what Ryan has been up to lately might make him think twice."*

"Lana, you're not a horrible mother. Remember, the people from church were only seeing Ryan for a few hours one day a week. There is a big difference between that and having to live with someone 24/7. Trust me. We've been touring with Ryan, and he's our friend. I'll never say he's not. But, there have certainly been a few times me and Uli wanted to strangle him until he passed out."

*"Well, I appreciate that. Ryan would tell you a different story, of course, but yeah, that's my plan. Threaten to show the people he actually liked some incriminating pictures or videos."*

"Well, judging from the story you just told, that sounds like a plan that could work. I just need to figure out how to spin it to Ryan."

"*How to spin it to Ryan?*"

"Yeah, I need to come up with a story for how I got a hold of some of your church member's contact info."

"*Uh, well, you could tell him you called me, and I gave it to you.*"

"That would make him mad at you."

"*He's already permanently mad at me, why not?*" Lana asked.

"Because he's told us he's wanted to try and patch things up with you guys, but he wasn't sure how."

"*Wait… he said that!?*" Lana asked.

"Yeah, he wrote you guys a little apology note around this time last year. Did he never send it to you?"

"*Uh, no, we never received anything.*"

Hal sighed. "Oh well, Ryan did… wait, I think I've got it!"

"*Got what?*" Lana asked.

"How to tell Ryan I got ahold of the church email list. I'll tell him I called you to tell you he was thinking of sending you an apology note, but was afraid you wouldn't take him seriously. So, I decided to give you forewarning of it and to let you know he was serious, in order to help him out. Then I'll tell him that you were so excited to hear this that you gave me the congregation email list and asked me if I could ask him if he could send the note to everyone at the church as well. "

"*Well, that works!*" Lana agreed.

"Yeah, hopefully it will. I do have one concern I'd like to run by you, though. If the threat of emailing the church members doesn't scare Ryan, and he calls my bluff, I would think the next step would be to actually send out an email with something not quite as bad. Then, once he sees we're serious, threaten to send some worse things next time. But, I wouldn't actually want to email any of that stuff to your church group."

"*You know what, Hal, I'll let everyone in on the plan. I'll tell them Ryan's started doing drugs, and that you as his friends are trying to make him go to rehab, and that you asked for my help. I'll tell them the whole plan. Normally, I don't think you'd find too many church congregations that would be willing to be complicit to blackmailing someone, but a lot of the people there remember Ryan, so they'll understand why blackmail is the plan of choice. Plus, the fact that this is purely to help someone, and no one else is at risk of being hurt by it. I will explain to them that you might have to make good on your word to show him we're serious. So, I'll warn them if they receive an email from Ryan or yourself, that for the sweet love of the Lord Jesus to not open it or any attachments.*"

"Lana… that's perfect," Hal said.

"*Oh, well, you know, I've only been waiting to get some payback against Ryan for years now. You give him your best pitch for the email, and I'll make sure everyone on this end knows the plan to avoid any mental trauma.*"

"I love it! I'll do my best to make it believable, and I'll let you know what happens."

"*Okay. Just text me the email to send the list to.*"

"Thanks, I'll do that as soon as we hang up."

"*Okay. And Hal… thanks again for trying to help him,*" Lana said.

"Of course. He's our friend," Hal said, then thanked Lana a final time before hanging up.

Hal was more excited now to get back to the house and send Lana an email than he was to go to bed. When they did get home, it was around four thirty in the morning. Hal and Uli went in as quietly as they could, and Hal woke his computer back up and wrote a quick message:

Dear Lana,

This is Hal. Operation Email Blackmail was a success! The eagle is in the nest. Repeat: the eagle is in the nest! I'll send you updates on his progress as we get them. Thank you again and have a good night!

-Hal

He sent the email, then took off pieces of clothing one at a time and left them in a short trail on the floor directly from the desk to the bed. He collapsed onto the mattress. Oh, bed. You feel so good. Oh, god, yes. More, MORE. He pulled the blankets over himself, and shut his eyes. What a day. And that was only one down, with one more to go. He got the easy one out of the way first. Tomorrow would be the real challenge: What to do about Ricky.

# CHAPTER 20

## (Numb)

Hal woke up around three in the afternoon. He could have easily gone back to sleep for longer, but after looking at the clock and seeing what time it was, he figured he'd better get up so he could start readjusting back to Michigan time. He came down the stairs, and, in a groggy haze, pulled some cereal out of the pantry and headed for the fridge to get some milk. Cecilia was sitting in the kitchen, bottle feeding Charlotte.

"Good… morning?" she asked, turning to look at the clock on the oven. Hal stopped dead in his tracks.

"HOLY SHIT! I FORGOT! I HAVE A SISTER!" he blurted out. Harvey slowly lowered the classic car magazine he was reading and gave Hal a judgemental stare.

"It has been a long week for you, hasn't it?" Cecilia asked.

Hal ignored both of them as his eyes lit up at the sight of Charlotte, who was looking much healthier and less red. She was a cute little girl dressed in a lilac onesie covered in fluffy pastel owls. "Now, *that* looks like a baby!" he said as he sat down and pulled the chair up right next to his mom.

"Oh, yeah, she's been doing fine since she came home from the hospital," Cecilia said. Charlotte had been starting to fall asleep as she neared the end of the bottle, then the sounds of their voices caused her to stir a bit. She opened her eyes and looked in Hal's direction.

"Hi, sis!" Hal said as their eyes met for the first time. As Charlotte looked at him, she developed one of those truly offended looks that only babies can properly pull off.

"Charlotte, this is your big brother, Hal. Your brother Hal is home," Cecilia said gently to her as she bounced her gently in her arms. "You want to hold her?" she asked.

"Of course," Hal answered, and Cecilia handed the little baby to him. Hal cradled her against his chest. "*Hi*," he said.

Charlotte looked at him for about three seconds before starting to cry. "Ah… aga… ahh… aaaaaaaaahhh!!!"

"Uh oh, stranger danger!" Hal laughed as he handed her back to his mom.

"Oh, dear. She'll get used to you once she's spent a little more time around you," Cecilia reassured him. Charlotte quit crying after a few moments back in her mom's arms, and Hal reached back behind him and grabbed the cereal and milk off the counter and started pouring them into a bowl.

"Is Uli up?" he asked.

"Haven't seen him," Harvey replied.

"I think for once he may be sleeping in later than you," Cecilia agreed.

"You three had a late night last night," Harvey said.

"Yes… is Ryan at the rehab center?" Cecilia asked.

"Yep," Hal replied. "He put up quite the fight, though. I'll have to tell you the whole story."

"Well, I think we overheard a good portion of it last night," Harvey grumbled.

"Oh, right, sorry about that," Hal said.

"Did you really drive all the way back to Detroit last night?" Cecilia asked,

"Yes, yes we did."

"When did you get home?" she asked.

"I honestly don't know," Hal mumbled. "Somewhere between three and six in the morning?"

"Good God," Cecilia said.

"Yeah, I don't even remember getting into bed last night. But it was all worth it. We gave Ryan the scare of his life, and now he's in rehab," Hal said triumphantly, then ate the first few spoonfulls of cereal. "You guys haven't seen Ricky since he went into his room last night, have you?"

"No, I haven't," Cecilia said. "The way he was acting last night has me worried, though. And then there was the way slinky was acting."

"Yeah, I know. I'm really worried about him too," Hal agreed. "He hasn't eaten much of anything for the last few days."

"That's really not good," Cecilia said.

"No, it's not. I've tried a few times to talk to him, but he's built a wall around himself and gone into silent mode."

"And all this over a girl he only knew for a few months," Cecilia said. "Not to trivialize it, because it was a terrible tragedy. But to go as far as to quit eating…"

"Well, I'm pretty sure there's more to it than that," Hal said. "Ricky's had something that's been bothering him since the first day we met him that we could never get him to talk about. He would go into these little depressed fits occasionally. Then, once he met Nora, that sort of quit happening, and it was like he finally started letting go of whatever had been haunting him all that time. But now, he's right back to where he started. Except, you know, way worse."

"Do you think whatever was bothering him that whole time also had something to do with a girl?" Cecilia asked.

"Oh, I'd put money on it," Hal replied. "He's always so dodgy with the subject. And whenever Ryan tried to set him up with a date it would make him really nervous."

"If that's the case, that's just horrible," Cecilia said.

"I know. I feel awful, and I don't know what to do," Hal agreed.

"I guess there might not be much you can do other than let him know you're there if he wants to talk."

AUGUST WANDERLUST

"He's not going to talk. He won't. I've been trying to get him to for years. But I really wish he'd eat something. I was going to try and see if I could get him to eat a bit today."

"That's probably the best place to start at this point. If he keeps not eating, he's going to make himself sick," Cecilia agreed.

"Yeah… I know," Hal agreed somberly. After he finished his cereal, he went upstairs to make the first attempt. He knocked gently, then asked: "Hey, Ricky, you want to go to the steak house for a late lunch? I'll buy."

"*Not hungry…*" Ricky mumbled from inside.

"Ricky, you haven't eaten for days. You must be starving. You're going to make yourself sick," Hal said. Ricky didn't answer. "Alright, what if we went there for dinner in a couple hours?" Ricky remained silent. Hal sighed, but decided to leave him alone for a bit so he could think about it. He hoped if he had a few hours' notice, that maybe he would be willing to get up and go out for a while.

He came back around five thirty to try again. "Alright, Ricky, get ready, we're leaving for dinner in five minutes," Hal said.

"*Not hungry…*" Ricky replied.

"Ricky! I guarantee you that you are. You have to be. You've probably hit that weird stage where you've gotten so hungry it doesn't feel like you are anymore. And that's not good. You've got to get up and eat something," Hal insisted. Ricky didn't say anything. Hal leaned his head against the door. "Ricky, come on. Let's go to the steak house, get you a plate of chicken strips, and you tell me about all your problems," he said. "Please."

"*Ricky can't eat when he ain't hungry,*" Ricky answered. Hal stood there for a moment, then wrapped his fingers around the doorknob and started to turn it, then got a different idea and stopped. He went into his room and pulled out his incognito street clothes instead.

"Any luck?" Uli asked as Hal walked past the kitchen. "No, he won't come out. But I'm going to try something else," Hal said as he pulled his shoes on and went out the front door. He came back about half an hour later

415

with some raw chicken breast strips, a few packets of seasoning, a large jug of ketchup and a bottle of orange soda and went to work in the kitchen. Forty-five minutes later, he knocked gently on the door to Ricky's room with one hand, while holding a steaming plate of chicken strips in the other.

"Ricky? I'm coming in," Hal announced, then opened the door. When he did, Slinky, who had been crouched right outside the door, ran in, then suddenly stopped in the middle of the floor and turned around and crept back out to the hall and huddled back down against the door frame. Ricky remained motionless on the bed, not even acknowledging Hal as he set the chicken strips and a glass of orange soda down on the side table next to him. "I brought you something, man. Please eat it," Hal said, then walked back out and pulled the door shut gently behind him. Ricky looked over at the plate. Five juicy chicken strips sizzled in its center, surrounded by writing in ketchup that read: *'Please eat. We're worried about you.'* The strips looked obscenely good. They smelled obscenely good. And yet, he just wasn't hungry. He wasn't hungry to the point that he had a feeling of aversion to the thought of even trying to eat. If he reached over and took a bite out of one, he didn't think he'd be able to force himself to swallow. He knew Hal was right, that he really needed to eat something, but the desire wasn't there, and so he just laid there for a while, staring at them.

Hal went in to check on him later in the evening. He knocked on the door, then let himself in. Ricky was asleep, and Slinky went all the way into the room this time and jumped up on the bed and laid down next to him. Interesting, Hal thought. He looked at the plate of chicken strips. Four remained untouched, one seemed to have one or two bites out of it. *'Please eat'* was intact, but *'we're worried about you'* had been rubbed into a smear. About a quarter of the orange soda had been drunk. Hal sighed. It was a start, at least. He grabbed the plate and carried it out into the hall, and set it on the floor, then looked back in the room at slinky. Part of him wanted to leave her in there because Ricky could really use a cat to cuddle right now. But whatever it was about him that had been freaking her out might start again once he woke up. So, he went in and picked her up, and she mewed delicately in protest as he carried her out and set her down at her waiting spot right outside the door.

In the days that followed, Ricky started eating a bit more of what Hal brought him, but they still couldn't get him up out of bed. "Ricky, come on. Let's go for a walk in the park down the road. That'll make you feel better," Hal said through the closed door. No reply. That was the third time that day he had tried to get him to get up and do something. He still wasn't budging. Hal wearily went back down the stairs and sat down on the couch next to Uli.

"We have to get him up at some point. He is starting to look sick. I saw him briefly when he came out of the bathroom last night," Uli said.

"I know," Hal replied. "You think I haven't been trying?"

"It is time to take more drastic measures," Uli said.

"What do you mean by 'drastic measures'?" Hal asked.

"Force him to get up. One of us can take the arms and one can take the legs if we have to, like we did with Ryan."

"I don't know, Uli. This is different. Ryan's problem was entirely self-inflicted, and he was being an ass about it, so he deserved to get duct taped to a chair and hauled to rehab. Ricky didn't do anything to deserve any of this. And he certainly didn't do anything to cause any of it. He's just… depressed."

"Lying in bed, not eating is going to make him even more depressed. Getting him up will be for his own good. It won't fix the overall problem, but it will keep him from getting worse," Uli said.

"You're probably right," Hal said. "But, I wonder if it's going to seem a little harsh. He needs support, not someone forcing him to do something he doesn't want to do. I'm worried that making him get up will cause him to get irritated and maybe even make things worse. I dunno, maybe he just needs a little bit more time," Hal pondered out loud.

"How much more time?" Uli asked.

"I don't know."

"Hal, I don't think Ricky has taken a bath in over a week."

"Probably not. He hasn't shaved at all, that's for sure," Hal replied.

"As angry or annoyed as we make him, it will be by us trying to help him. Ricky is smarter than Ryan, he should understand that," Uli said.

"Okay, say we do make him get up…" Hal mused. "What are we going to do with him? I'd like to take him on a walk, but I don't think he's going to cooperate."

"Maybe make him watch a movie with us?" Uli asked.

"He's not much of a TV watcher, but we could try. I guess that would be the next easiest thing to lying in bed," Hal said, and reached over for the TV guide. "Let's see if there's anything good on."

"Perhaps for Ricky we should put on the discovery channel?" Uli asked.

"Yeah, that might be a good one," Hal agreed, flipping through the programs. "I just want to see if there are any other options… oh, hey, one of the X-Men movies is on. Let's try that. I mean, Ricky is a damn X-Man himself. I don't know if he's ever seen any of the movies, but I always wanted to watch some of those with him to see what he thought."

"Worth a try," Uli agreed, and Hal got up and went to Ricky's door. He knocked on it three times. "Ricky? Why don't you come and watch some TV with us? One of the X-Men movies is on," Hal said. No reply. He opened the door. He went in and sat down at the foot of the bed. "Ricky… you can't spend the rest of your life in bed, man. You're making yourself sick just lying there. I can't imagine the hell you've been through, but you need to get up at some point."

"*Maybe later,*" Ricky mumbled.

"No, Ricky, you can't keep going like this. This isn't good for you. You have to get up," Hal insisted. Uli listened in from the living room. "*That wasn't a suggestion…*" he heard Hal say. "*I know you don't feel good, and I don't blame you, but it's going to get worse if you spend any more time just lying there… no, no more laters… we're not going to let you waste away… I know, but X-Men is on, and it's TIME TO GET UP!*" Hal said loudly, and he appeared a moment later, leading Ricky unwillingly down the stairs.

"Sit!" He forced him down on the couch next to Uli, then sat down on the other side of him. Ricky was barely recognizable to either of them. He'd noticeably lost weight in a short period of time from eating basically nothing for days, he had a short beard, and he was pale with dark bags under his eyes. "Hey Uli, want to make us some popcorn?" Hal asked. Uli got up and went straight to the kitchen. He returned a few minutes later with a giant bowl of it, and they spent a few hours watching X-Men. Hal figured Ricky would be in a bad mood at least at first, but as he stole glances at him throughout the movie, he never seemed to show any emotion of any kind at all. His eyes were pointed at the screen, but despite Hal's best efforts, his mind was obviously elsewhere the entire time. When the movie ended, Ricky simply stood up and walked back to his room without a word. "This is worse than we thought…" Uli said, somberly. It took Hal a long time to fall asleep that night, his brain was so racked with worry, trying to figure out what to do next. He woke up earlier than usual, too, at the first sign of dawn, and couldn't go back to sleep. He got up, put on some clothes, and went to Ricky's door. They were going on a walk. He needed Ricky to talk to him. He wanted to talk to him. He knocked on the door. "Ricky?" He opened the door. Ricky wasn't inside. The bed was made, his green duffel bag was gone, though his guitars were still leaning against the wall. There was a note on the bed. Hal ran over and grabbed it:

Going home.

Sorry you had to deal with me the last few days.

Maybe we'll meet again someday.

– Ricky

"Uli!" Hal yelled as he ran into his room. Uli sat up in bed with a start. "What! What!?"

"Ricky's gone. He took his duffel bag with him but left his guitars."

"What!?" Uli said again.

"Take a look at this," Hal said, and handed him the note. Uli read it a few times over before saying: "Perhaps he just needs to spend some time at home with his family?"

"That wouldn't bother me, but there's something about that note I don't like. And that's the 'maybe' part."

"It is a little… questionable," Uli admitted. Normally Uli had an unbreakable poker face, but Hal could see a little bit of worry making itself known in his expression.

"I don't like what that might mean. I don't like it at all. As a matter of fact, I'm genuinely a little scared right now, so I'm catching the next plane to Arkansas. You coming?" Hal asked.

Uli took a few more moments to read the note again before answering. "Hal, this is concerning, and it is not that I do not want to help, but you are a much better therapist than I. You know he doesn't like talking about his problems or being scrutinized, so maybe it would be better if only you went."

"Alright," Hal said. "I'm going to go get packed."

"And I will be here if Ryan gets out of rehab and does something stupid. Call me if that lady calls you."

"I like it. It's a plan," Hal said. He quickly packed up a few essential things into a back pack, put on his incognito outfit, then headed for the door. "Can you tell Mom and Dad what's going on when they wake up?" Hal asked Uli.

"Yes, of course. I cannot believe they slept through you yelling, but I will certainly tell them."

"Alright, thank you. They're probably worn out from being up late with Charlotte."

"I cannot believe *she* slept through you yelling," Uli added. A few seconds later, Charlotte started crying.

Hal hesitated as he heard someone getting up in his parent's room, but then went out the door. "Aaagh! I need to go!"

"Yes, go! Go! I will tell them what is going on," Uli promised.

"Thanks!" Hal called back. He jumped into the van and started it up, then took off down the road. He pulled into the Park N' Fly lot at the Detroit airport a few hours later and locked the van up. *"Please have all your windows intact when I get back,"* he whispered to the van and kissed it on the driver's side mirror before running for the departures terminal.

250. "Hey Brother" by Avicii *to play over this scene*

He dashed up to the ticket counter and pulled his hat low as he got the attention of the woman behind the counter. "I need to get on the next flight to Arkansas. We're having a family emergency." He had to wait for six hours before the next flight left, and it was late afternoon before the plane touched down in Little Rock. He hailed a taxi outside the airport. "Okay, this is going to be a little weird, but this is where I need to go…" he told the taxi driver. An hour later, the driver dropped him off at the bend in the railroad tracks in the middle of nowhere that Ricky had taken them to last time when they jumped on the train. He sat down and waited, and waited… and waited.

The sun was low in the sky and turning an evening shade of gold by the time he heard the train coming in the distance. He threw his bag behind his back and got ready. The train wasn't going all that fast, but it was still a force to be reckoned with as it started going by him. He began running as fast as he could, and as the next service ladder came along side of him, he jumped and grabbed it. He hit the side of the train hard, but secured his feet on the bottom rung, then climbed carefully up to the roof. By the time the grove of trees on the outskirts of Battle Creek came into view, the sun had already dipped below the horizon. He climbed down the ladder and readied himself to jump. *"Hit the ground running, 'makes it a lot easier!"* he could hear Ricky say in his head, and he leaned out from the train, holding on with one hand as he crouched, then jumped. He already had his feet moving when he landed. He faltered for a second, then regained his footing and kept running straight to the head of the footpath at the edge of the trees. He pulled out a flashlight and held it in front of him, pointed down at the ground to make sure he didn't lose the thinly-carved trail. He ran without stopping for what felt like miles, and eventually made it to an area where there was a field to the side of the trees. Breathless, he stopped.

An old, abandoned homestead house sat in the center of the field. He wanted nothing more than to keep running for Ricky's family's house. But that was still a ways down the path, and if Ricky wasn't at the house when he got there, he didn't want to have to backtrack this far up the trail to go looking for him… at night… in the dark…. *in there.* Hal may have whimpered a little bit out loud by accident as he started across the field. He stepped carefully on the stairs to avoid the scattered holes in the boards and pushed the creaky door open. "Ricky!?" he called into the house. "You in here!?" He got no reply, but he knew that didn't necessarily mean Ricky wasn't in. *"So… your name is Charlie, right?"* Hal said much more quietly as he took his first cautious step inside the house. *"I'm Hal… one of Ricky's friends. You might remember me from last time Ricky visited. Sorry about the screaming thing… and all…"* Hal scanned the room nervously with the flashlight as he crept forward. *"I'm just here looking for Ricky. It's a long story, but I'm a little worried about him and I can't find him."* Hal jumped as something dark shot past him out the window; either a startled bird or a bat. No oversized fireflies yet. Still, it got his heart racing. *"B… bu… but anyways, if he's not here, sorry to bother you. I'm going to look upstairs really quick, then I'll leave. Don't let me interrupt you if you're in the middle of… something… whatever it is… you do around here. Don't feel you need to come help, or anything… I've got it handled…"*

Hal started up the stairs. Each one creaked and groaned in a different key as he stepped from one to the next. This was probably the most scared he'd ever been in his life. He was more okay with the possibility of facing down a transparent apparition than with the thought that Ricky was upstairs, and wasn't answering for reasons other than he was just ignoring him. Hal reached the top stair and quickly whipped the flashlight into the room. It was empty. Empty, except for a vacant chair, and a banjo case leaning against the wall. There was one closet in the room, and the door was wide open, revealing it to be empty as well. Hal took a deep breath and shut his eyes for a second to try and calm his nerves, then started back down the stairs. *"Okay... Ricky's not here, so I'm going to head out now. Enjoy your evening..."* he said, and his pace quickened as he reached the ground floor and ran back out and down the porch stairs. The creaky door screeching one more time as it swung shut behind him.

He made it through the last length of tall grass and stepped back onto the trail when a man's voice suddenly called out behind him: "PLEASE FIND HIM!"

Hal swung around with the flashlight, but saw no one on the trail, or anywhere else in sight. That voice was clear as day. He knew he hadn't imagined it. "HELLO?" Hal called out. Only the sound of crickets answered him. He looked shakily back at the old house but saw no one in its windows. He hesitated for a moment, then yelled out: "I WILL!" and began running again down the path.

End Song 250

The lights of the Ransom family's house finally came into view, and he bolted up the stairs and knocked loudly five times before throwing the door open without waiting for an answer. It hit the inside wall with a loud bang, and Spud suddenly jumped up and growled at him, but then quickly fell silent and stepped back when he realized it was Hal. Ricky's parents and all his siblings were seated at the table inside, eating dinner, and Hal had heard them all talking and shouting from outside, but now silence had fallen as all eyes were staring at him. Some of the kids still had their forks half-raised to their mouths. A quick scan of the room revealed Ricky was not with them.

"Uh... hi, Hal," Ron finally said.

"Uh… yeah… hi. Is Ricky here?" Hal asked.

"Well, he was. He got back a little earlier today, but he went on a walk a few hours ago. Hasn't come back yet," Ron answered.

Hal's heart sank. "Uh, okay. Sorry to have barged in like this. I'm just going to go see if I can find him," Hal said casually. "Is it okay if I leave my bag right here?" he asked, setting the bag down to the side of the front door.

"Yeah, that's fine," Ron answered.

"Okay, thanks. I'll… we'll be back later," he said, then shut the door gently behind him.

He went down the stairs and looked around to try and decide which direction to go first when Ron suddenly came out the door, letting it slam closed. "Hal, what's going on?" he demanded.

Hal turned around. "Well, it's… a bit of a long story. He left my house this morning suddenly without telling us, except he left a note for us to find saying he was going home, and I'm a little worried about him. Was he, like, acting weird when he got here?"

"No, not really. I noticed he looked a little thin and tired, but you guys have been runnin' around all over the world, so I figured he was exhausted from the tour y'all were on."

"Did he have a beard and smell like he hasn't bathed in a week?"

"No, no, nothing like that at all. What happened!?"

"Okay… so… on our international tour we got a new road manager to take us through Europe, and his niece Nora was there to help him and sort of job shadow him and learn what he did for a living. Anyways, over the course of the tour, her and Ricky sort of… got a little thing going. I mean, I guess he fell in love with her. Then, right at the end of our tour about a week ago, she and her uncle were found dead in a burnt down warehouse."

"WHAT!??" Ron yelled.

"Yeah, it was horrible. We don't totally know what happened, but we think it probably had something to do with a bad drug deal. We're pretty sure Mason, our manager, her uncle, was doing cocaine. We know she wasn't though, so she might have gotten caught in the middle of something. Ricky has been extremely depressed ever since. He's eaten basically nothing for the last week, he was barely leaving his room, but then he just up and left last night. The note he left saying he was going home also said that 'maybe' he'd see us again someday, so… I'm really worried about him."

"Shit…" Ron grunted, looking around panicked. "Shit, shit, shit."

"Yeah, so… I was going to go check and see if he's at his friend John's cabin," Hal said.

"That's a good idea," Ron agreed. "I know a few other places he could be, so you go that way and I'll go the other direction."

"Oh, I already checked the abandoned house halfway back to the train tracks on the foot path," Hal said.

"Okay. Good to know. That was brave of you. I still know a few other places he could be. There are a lot of old houses out here he'd hang out in. Here, hold on a sec." Ron said as he ran back up the short porch steps, leaned in the back door of the kitchen, and pulled something off the shelving unit inside. He came back out and tossed Hal a yellow walkie-talkie. "Those are long range, they'll work a few miles apart. That way, who ever finds him first can let the other know."

"Awesome, thank you, Ron. And, thanks for helping me look for him," Hal said.

"No, my God, thank you for comin'. I had no idea. Ricky's very good at hidin' things when he wants, and really bad at askin' for help when he needs it," Ron said as he pulled his keys out of his pocket and got into their old pickup truck. Hal started running down the road in the other direction.

Ron was already halfway out of sight before Hal realized he should have asked him to refresh his memory on how to get to the cabin. It was too late now, so he got the flashlight back out and decided to try his best to find it. He knew roughly what direction it was in. A few minutes later, he found the little trail off the side of the road and started through the woods. This trail wasn't used nearly as much as the one that led in from the train tracks, so the path was harder to see and follow. Luckily, he ultimately came out from the trees along the swampy area he remembered from their last trip and saw a dim light in the evergreens off in the distance. He was heaving breaths from running and could only manage to walk the rest of the way up to the cabin. He went up the stairs and knocked on the old cabin door. "John!? It's Hal, one of Ricky's friends. Is Ricky here?" he called out. Footsteps could be heard, and then the door opened. It was Grace.

"Oh, hello, Hal."

"Hi, Grace. Sorry to bother you at this hour, but is Ricky here?"

"Well, he was here for a while earlier, but he left about two hours ago, hon."

Hal sighed. "Okay, at least he was here. It's a long story, but something happened on the tour we were on that sent him into a depressed fit. He came back here suddenly without saying goodbye to us and just left a note. I'm really worried about him. I figured he'd come here to talk to your dad for a bit. I mean, did he seem okay? Was he in a better mood after talking to your father?" Hal asked. Grace looked away from him, suddenly looking like she was on the verge of tears. "Hal, my father passed away three days ago."

"*No…*" Hal said in disbelief.

"Ricky's brother who's the doctor had come down an' taken a look at him and put him on two medications, and he was doin' much better for a few months after that. But three nights ago he went to bed, and never… woke up…" she said as she started to cry gently. She wiped away a tear from under one eye and added: "I don't know if it was a stroke or a heart attack or what happened. But I buried him out back 'cause this cabin has been his home for most his life, an' I know he don't ever want to be anywhere else. I've been here cleaning up and figurin' out what to do next…"

"Grace, I'm so sorry…" Hal said gently.

She nodded slightly. "It was bound to happen. He was old. I just feel bad I wasn't back sooner to take care of him."

"You did come back though, and you were here, that's what mattered," Hal said. "And if you need anything, or any help, just let us know. I don't know if your father left any bills unpaid, or if you might need help moving any of his belongings out of the house or anything, but please let us know what we can do for you."

"Thank you, that's very kind of you. He didn't leave no bills, but I'll let you know if anything comes up."

"OK. Sorry to change the subject back, but this makes me a lot more worried about Ricky. He probably came here for some comfort, and finding John gone can't have helped. He's really depressed, and I need to find him," Hal said again.

"Of course, of course. You got your friend to take care of. He was here an' sat by the grave out back for a few hours. I gave him Dad's guitar, because Dad mentioned a while back Ricky was to get it when he died. But he left a few hours ago, an' I don't know where he is now."

"He didn't say anything at all about where he was going or what he was going to do?" Hal asked.

"No, he didn't. He just said thank you an' left. He went back up the path, but that's the only way in an' out of here, so he could be anywhere now."

"OK, thank you so much, Grace. I'm sorry about your father. We'll be sure to drop by in the next few days to see if you need anything."

"Thank you, Hal. I do sure hope Ricky's okay."

"I hope so too. Thank you," Hal said as he left and started back up the trail. Once he made it back to the dirt road, he continued further on down it to see if he could find any other abandoned houses to look in. It was so dark he couldn't see much further than twenty feet in front of him, even with the flashlight.

After another hour of searching, he didn't find any other vacant houses, and eventually, the road came to a dead end. He was out of places to look. "RICKY!!!" Hal yelled out into the darkness. "RICKY!!! WHERE ARE YOU!!?? PLEASE, ANSWER ME!!!" Hal begged. Only crickets and frogs could be heard calling back. "RICKY!!?? PLEASE!!" Hal stopped and put his hands on his knees. He was getting really tired. He heard a rustling noise next to him, and he swung the flashlight over to find himself face to face with a raccoon. He sighed, then asked: "You haven't seen Ricky have you? He's about 5'3, brown hair, maybe he's a friend of yours?" The raccoon looked at him terrified for a few moments, then turned and ran off into the woods. *Worth a try,* Hal thought to himself.

He stood back up and looked around. He had nothing left to try, so he decided to head back to the house and wait to see if Ron came back with Ricky, or maybe if Ricky would come back on his own. He didn't get very far before something to the side of the road caught his eye. He moved the flashlight over to find two of the trees that lined the side were wearing their fall color early for the season. All the other trees all around them were still completely green. He made his way slowly over to them, and as he pointed the light upwards, saw that the trees directly behind them were going into shades of orange and red as well. Same with the ones in the third row directly behind them. He found this pattern kept going deep into the woods, and he started to follow it. There was no treaded foot path between these trees, and he pushed aside thick brush and stepped over fallen logs until he found a clearing that was something of a small meadow. At the far end of the meadow sat another old, abandoned homestead house. As he pointed his flashlight at it, saw it was grander and more ornate than any of the others he had seen. Even fancier than Charlie's house. He began to run towards it, but stopped as two green orbs came into view in the light of his flashlight up ahead in the grass. He examined them for a moment, then went into a full sprint. "RICKY!!!"

"STOP!" Ricky stood up, and Hal froze. That's when he noticed Ricky was standing in the middle of a circle of dead grass, about twenty feet in front of him. "DON'T COME ANY CLOSER!" Ricky yelled. Hal realized he was about a foot from the circle's outer edge. He took a step or two back.

"Ricky, me and your dad have been looking all over for you! We were worried you weren't okay!"

"Well, that's 'cause ah'm not!" Ricky said.

"Understandable," Hal said, more quietly. "We just… wanted to find you."

"Well, here ah' am. Out here, killin' grass," Ricky answered.

Hal sighed. "I see that." He reached down and turned the dial on the walkie-talkie up, and briefly ducked down into the grass and whispered into it: "I found him. I'm going to try and talk to him."

A short pause followed before Ron's grainy voice answered with a hushed 'okay,' and then Hal stood back up and turned the dial off. "I went to John's cabin looking for you. Ricky, I'm so sorry." Ricky turned around and ran both hands through his hair to the back of his head, where he gripped his hair tightly, looking like he might pull it out from frustration.

"AH' CAN'T TAKE IT ANYMORE, HAL! AH' TRIED FOR YEARS TO KEEP GOIN', BUT AH' JUST CAN'T!!!" Ricky kicked his foot into the grass, and suddenly some of the green grass in front of Hal began to brown as the circle spread. He took a few panicked steps back until it stopped. "WHY DO THEY ALL GOTTA DISSAPPEAR OR DIE!?" Ricky stood with his back turned to Hal, his fist clenched at his sides.

"Yeah, I know, and it's total bullshit, because you bring that happiness of yours wherever you go, and it puts everyone in a better mood; people and animals alike. But it seems you don't get to have any in return! And this may sound like the stupidest thing you've ever heard, because you're the one who's lost two people in as many weeks, but this is the most miserable I've ever been in my life because I don't know what I can do to help you! And that kills me… because… you don't deserve this." Ricky turned slightly to look at Hal over his shoulder. "You do realize…" Hal continued, "…that I owe our success to you. It was my dream to be in a rock band. But as hard as I tried, as hard as me and Uli tried, as hard as me and Uli and Ryan tried, we just didn't have any success until you joined us."

"Could have been anyone…" Ricky mumbled.

"NO, IT COULDN'T HAVE!" Hal said sternly. "You're the most amazing guitarist I've ever met. Heck, you're awesome regardless. But apparently you don't see that in yourself, which is really sad." He and Ricky stared at each other in silence for a few moments, until Hal asked: "Ricky, what happened, man? I know this is about Nora, and about John, but I also know this isn't *only* about Nora and John. What made you leave town?" Ricky's gaze sank away from his, down to the ground in front of him, leaving Hal once again waiting for the answer he could never seem to find. "Tell you what, you don't have to tell me if you don't want, you don't ever have to tell me. But I'm not going back to your house without you. You scared us good, and if you're going to stay out here until five thirty in the morning, then so am I. I'll just lay down in the grass here and do some stargazing until you want to go home," Hal said as he sat down on the ground and put his hands behind his head as he lowered himself down. "And seriously, no rush at all. As you know, we don't get views like this back home in the other Battle Creek."

Ricky stood there for a few more moments, letting the silence creep back in all around him before sinking down into the grass himself. It was dark, but despite having night vision, all he could see were shades of grey, black, and brown. Grey rocks, black shadows, a prison cell of brown dead grass. Then, a faint glimmer caught his eye, and he looked over to the old blues guitar lying in the grass to his side. The body was polished enough to catch and reflect a tiny bit of starlight, giving its outline a hushed, blue glow. An angelic apparition in the darkness. He grabbed the instrument and pulled it into his lap as if he were going to play, though he knew he had no music in him tonight. It made a solid brace to lean against; something to hold him up as he began to speak, barely loud enough that Hal could hear. *"It was back in the summertime. When ah' was sixteen…"*

Hal spent two more days in Battle Creek before he was satisfied that Ricky would be alright. He left alone, but with the promise from Ricky that he'd come back to join them after he'd taken some time to rest. Hal got back in the late evening and collapsed onto the couch next to Uli. "Welcome back," Uli said.

"Thanks," Hal replied.

"So, how did it go?" Uli asked.

"He should be okay now," Hal answered.

"Good. Did you get him to talk to you?"

"Yes, he did talk."

"And?"

"Sorry, I'm sworn to secrecy," Hal said.

"Wait, you got him to tell you about old stuff?"

"Yep," Hal said.

Uli raised one eyebrow at him. "Impressive."

"Oh, you know, I got my skills," Hal replied.

"Hmmph," Uli grunted.

"Yeah… poor guy," Hal said quietly, then glanced over at Uli and changed the subject. "So, you aren't going to have a massive personal crisis anytime soon… are you?"

"I do not plan on it," Uli replied.

"Good, because I'm tired," Hal said as he slouched down deeper into the couch.

He slept in the next few mornings. He felt a little better after that. A few days later, Uli decided to go home to Germany to see his parents. Hal recommended he fan himself with a handful of 100 dollar bills in front of them at the dinner table.

"I will think about it," Uli said, rolling his eyes.

Hal and his family went out to dinner the next few nights. He spent some time holding his sister, to the point where she quit screaming whenever he picked her up. He and his dad played catch in the alley behind the house. He drove his Aston Martin around on some local county highways. A week later, he was thoroughly bored. He tried working on bits and pieces of some new songs, but without the other three to bounce ideas off of, he could only get so far.

He now found himself having spent two hours lying in bed, staring at the ceiling. It wasn't even dark out. "*Uugh…*" He rolled over, pulling his pillow down on the back of his head. It was strange. He wasn't running from one appointment to another, one interview to the next, or preparing for the next show after the current one. No one in the house was fighting. He had no idea what to do with himself anymore. How the hell did he deal with the boredom before they went on the road? Oh, right. He worked long hours as a waiter. Almost forgot about that. He lay there for a few minutes more, then suddenly had a welcome moment of inspiration. He jumped out of bed and pulled up an internet window. He checked a few pages, bought a plane ticket, and packed one small bag. "Going to Texas! Be back at some point!" he yelled as he ran out the door.

"Uh… have fun, be safe, make good choices!" his mom said, mostly to herself, as the door swung shut and Hal was already halfway across the yard.

251. "Material Girl" by Madonna

252. "Teenage Dream" by Katy Perry

253. "Bitch" by Meredith Brooks

254. "Jolene" by Dolly Parton

255. "Black Horse & the Cherry Tree" by KT Tunstall

256. "We R Who We R" –by Ke$ha

257. "Ironic" by Alanis Morissette

258. "My Boyfriend's Back" by The Angels

259. "Walk Like an Egyptian" by The Bangles

260. "Girl Next Door" by Brandy Clark

261. "Spice Up Your Life" by Spice Girls

> 262. "Get the Party Started" by P!nk
>
> 263. "That's the Way It Is" by Celine Dion
>
> 264. "Believe" by Cher
>
> 265. "Goodbye Earl" by Dixie Chicks
>
> 266. "Love Me Like You Do" by Ellie Goulding
>
> 267. "C'est La Vie" by B*Witched
>
> 268. "A Thousand Miles" by Vanessa Carlton
>
> 269. "Into You" by Ariana Grande

A strobe light flashed madly as a row of pyrotechnics went off, and Lyrica yelled into the microphone: "Goodnight, Houston, and never stop dreaming!" Her voice faded in time with the lights.

> End Songs 251 – 269

She made her escape to backstage, grabbing her schedule off a stool to remind her how quickly she'd have to pack up for the next show. She nearly ran straight into him. "*Et tu*, Lyrica?" Hal asked, suddenly face to face with her.

"JESUS CHRIST!" she yelled, dropping her schedule and all the other papers she was holding all over the floor.

"You can call me Hal," he answered, leaning against the wall with his elbow, then shut his eyes and puckered his lips.

"*Ugghhh…*" she grunted in disgust. Hal raised his eyebrows while keeping his eyes closed and puckered his lips harder. Lyrica hesitated, then put her open hand flat across his face. "I suppose you can make me dinner, waiter," she said.

"*Ife Queef.*" Hal's voice was muffled from behind the palm of her hand.

# CHAPTER 21

## (Light 'Em Up)

**Months went by. Ryan checked** out of rehab after the minimum recommended ninety days and went back to Hal's house. Another month after that, Ricky called to say he was coming back. He would have been back sooner, but his family wanted him to stay through Christmas. Hal picked him up from the airport on December 27th. "You have no idea how happy I am to see you," he said. "Ryan got back from rehab, and he and Uli have been fighting nonstop. I've had no one to give me any backup while they're at it."

"So, Ryan's feelin' better?" Ricky asked.

"Oh, yes," Hal lamented. "Ryan's all back to normal. And Uli only had to track him down and tackle him four times to take him back to the rehab center. But, how about you? Are *you* feeling better?"

"S'pose," Ricky answered quietly, looking out the window.

"You know… I'm no John, but you're always welcome to play out anything on your mind with us," Hal said. "That's what we're here for. That's part of why we do what we do. We could all sit down and make a night of it or two, or three, or eighty. If that's okay with you."

Ricky thought about it for a moment, then said: "You ain't no John, no. But, then… John wasn't no Hal either." And Hal glanced over at him. "I missed talkin' to you guys," Ricky added rather quickly, still staring out the window.

"And we've missed you, too," Hal said. "And, hey, when we start writing and working on demos again, you can use your new Christmas present that's waiting for you at home," Hal said, a grin creeping across his face as he looked back ahead at the road.

"Christmas present!?" Ricky said. "No, it's too late. Christmas was two days ago!"

"Yeah, nice try, Ricky. 'A' for effort, though," Hal added.

When they got home and went inside, Ryan greeted them at the door and eagerly hustled Ricky to the living room, and to the last unopened present under the tree. "You'll never guess what it is!" he said excitedly as they brought him in front of it. Multiple layers of wrapping paper covered something clearly shaped like a guitar. "Guys, Ricky already has two, no, three guitars! Ricky doesn't need another one!" Ricky insisted.

"Ricky, haven't you ever heard the saying *'He with the most guitars wins?'*" Ryan asked.

"No," Ricky answered.

Ryan glared at him. "Well, you have now, so open it!" Ryan shoved Ricky forwards, and he reluctantly started pulling off the layers of paper. Hal nodded at his father, who walked out the back door. As Ricky pulled the pieces off, what came into view was a most unique electric guitar. The head and neck were a generic electric guitar assembly, but the top left quarter of the body was in the shape of a wood grain acoustic guitar. The top right quarter was part of a standard Fender Stratocaster. The Stratocaster piece flowed seamlessly downwards into a midnight black and sharply pointed warlock guitar. Then, on the other side of the lower half underneath the acoustic shape, was the rounded bottom of another standard electric guitar body that could easily have come from the same Stratocaster donor, except for the Union Jack flag sketched across its face. Their logo. "Had to be done, and you know it!" Ryan said. Ricky admired it, speechless. Ryan leaned in closer to him. "*Do you like it?*" he asked teasingly.

Ricky sighed. "Ricky loves it," Ricky answered.

"AHA!" Ryan jumped up. "HE CAN BE TAUGHT!"

"Thank you," Ricky said quietly.

"You're welcome. And like Ryan said, it had to be done. That logo had to come to life at some point. It's just too amazing to remain an image," Hal said proudly. "I do have a confession to make, however. This wasn't originally your Christmas present, it was your birthday present."

"Uh… what?" Ricky asked.

"Well, you weren't here for your birthday when we were going to give it to you, so it sort of became your Christmas present. Then we realized it wasn't right to just skip your birthday, so we went and got you something else to replace your birthday present that became your Christmas present. Dad should have brought it around to the front of the house," Hal said.

"WHAT!?" Ricky said.

"Birthday present time!" Ryan shouted, and all three of them started pushing Ricky back in the direction of the front door. "You remember back when Hal was buying his Aston Martin, and I said our new challenge was to find you an expensive car you'd like?" Ryan asked.

"*Oh, no…*" Ricky said.

"OH, YES!" Ryan responded.

"Ricky doesn't need a car! Ricky doesn't drive anywhere! We all get driven and flown places by other people!" Ricky complained as they forced him through the entryway.

"We've already been through this, Ricky. It's not about needing, it's about wanting. And you'll want this car. You just don't know it yet," Ryan insisted.

"Now, before we show it to you, I do want to apologize for giving this to you in the dead of winter, because this is really more of a summer car. But hey, maybe we can catch some air over a few snow drifts in it?" Hal said.

"What do you mean 'summer car?'" Ricky asked.

"It sort of has no roof," Hal answered.

"It's a convertible!?" Ricky asked.

"No, it's not a convertible. It doesn't have a convertible top. It… has no roof," Hal said.

"It's missin' part of the body?"

"Well, sort of," Hal replied.

"Ricky thought y'all said it was an expensive car?"

"It is!" Ryan said excitedly. Before Ricky could say anything else, Hal pushed open the front door, and they all yelled at once: "HAPPY LATE BIRTHDAY!"

In the driveway sat a heavily customized 1932 Ford rat rod. The whole body was hopelessly rusted, but the chrome engine and inner workings shone brilliantly through the sides of the hood, and whitewall tires with a thin red stripe glowing around new disc brakes. The hood was also adorned with pinstriped flames, and the otherwise stark interior was brightened with a black and red blanket that was being used as the upholstery for the bench seat. The long stick shift in the center was crowned with a polished 8-ball ornament, and a little raccoon tail hung from the top of the radio antenna, ready to blow in the wind. The redneck portion of Ricky's country soul did a spit take with his root beer.

"Well? Can't you see yourself bombing down the highway towards the skating rink in that beauty on a hot August night with a couple siblings in the back?" Hal prodded him. Ricky's jaw dropped.

"Aww, he likes it," Ryan said.

"No, he loves it," Uli corrected him.

"And the tail on the antenna is artificial, so it is certified animal lover friendly," Hal assured him. "Oh, I also had the garage expanded again while you were gone, so you can park it inside and it won't get full of snow," he said, pulling the keys out of his pocket and dangling them in the air next to Ricky's face. Ricky slowly turned his head to look at them, then snatched them out of Hal's hand.

"Alright! Let's give it a run!" Ryan yelled and ran over and jumped into the front passenger seat of the car. Uli and Hal jumped into the back. The car started with a deep, thundering roar as Ricky turned the key in the ignition. They got more looks than usual driving through town. Not only were they them and not only was the car impossible to ignore; but once they had been driving for a bit and the engine got nice and hot, it began creating a cloud of steam in the frigid December air that left a trail behind them like an antique locomotive. It bounced nicely through the snow on the side streets thanks to the updated suspension, and took corners on the plowed, icy roads well thanks to the new tires. They drove around for two hours before they went back to the house to have dinner.

Hal started a fire in the basement fireplace later that evening, and pulled the door shut so they could practice and write without waking his sister up. "So, I do have a few ideas and pieces of new songs I've been working on to bounce off of you guys. And if anyone has any ideas of their own, please do share them with the class," Hal said as he sat down with a small stack of paper. "Anyone want to start?" Nobody seemed eager to volunteer. Ricky tugged at the strings of his guitar nervously, but without making any sound. He had his original, acoustic guitar out for practice to keep from making too much noise and disturbing Charlotte. Hal watched him for a few moments before continuing: "Alright. So, I came up with…"

> 270. "Dream On" by Aerosmith

Hal stopped as Ricky began picking a gentle, melancholy tune on his old guitar, and played it over and through a few times while they listened. Ryan joined in after a few cycles with a gentle beat on his drums. He only tapped them with his fingers. He wasn't using his drumsticks to keep from waking the baby up. Uli began shadowing Ricky's melody on his keyboard, with the volume turned way down so Hal's little sister could sleep. Hal listened intently, his brain working to shape words to it. He had some lyrics written already, and he had a little melody to go along with them, but this was much better. He could make what he had work to this. He listened a few times over to get a general idea. Then, a few times more while he sang it in his head to make sure it would sound good. Then as it started over again, he began to sing to it out loud. He sang quietly, so as not to cause his infant sibling to stir, but he could hear it already in full glory in his head; loud and electrified. Though playing it quietly like this gave it a unique, haunting appeal, too. The light from the flames in the fireplace danced across the floor, up the walls, and over their faces as they passed the song back and forth. They molded and morphed it until the fire burned out in the early hours of the morning, and then decided it was time to go to bed.

> End Song 270

The song spent the entire next day turning over and over in Hal's head. He was more than ready to polish it with the new changes he came up with once they began their work again after dark. But before he could even finish getting the fire going for the night, Ricky was playing something else sad and beautiful.

> 271. "Just Dropped in (To See What Condition My Condition Was In)" by The First Edition w/Kenny Rogers

The fire flared up, and to their surprise, Ricky started doing his own singing to the melody. His face wasn't showing a lot of emotion, but some-how, the side profile of his shadow on the wall was full of expression. His head hung down and his hair dangled over his eyes while each word formed a unique shape on his lips. Ryan joined in with a little beat on his drums, and Hal and Uli listened while watching the shadow put on a performance all its own. Partway through, Ricky re-adjusted and pulled the guitar's body back in closer to himself, causing the guitar's head and neck to move fur-ther outwards. The shadow of the guitar head moving appeared as if it was Ricky's heart bursting out of his chest, and then floating mid-air as if to mock him while he sang to it. His reasoning seemed to be in vain as it appeared unmoved all the way to the end of the song, until Ricky loosened his grip on the guitar, causing the shadow to slide lifelessly down the wall onto the floor.

End Song 271

272. "Clint Eastwood" by The Gorillaz

Ryan was the next to offer up some new material. He'd composed nearly an entire song on his own, including the base melody and lyrics. Once he had given the lyrics to Hal and worked with Ricky and Uli on bringing the tune to life on a guitar and piano, they did their first full play through. As Ryan played the slow beat on the drums, the shadow of his mohawk bouncing to the rhythm on the wall appeared as a giant clawed hand over his head. It grabbed at his skull and released it over and over, and the fingers at times seemed to go in his nose and ears, reaching and straining to get at his brain. Where Uli was sitting, he was casting two shadows, a darker one and a lighter one. The lighter one was higher up on the wall, and was mostly overlapped by the darker one, so it was only his head and shoulders. The ponytail of the lighter shadow was covered by the shoulders of the darker shadow, giving the illusion that his hair was still short. The darker shadow showed him in full profile, ponytail and all.

Hal hadn't gone through anything as severe as the other three, and he knew it, but from the way they played, he could almost feel the pain as intense as they did. Misery, fear, anger; it was a universal language, and they filled the room with the dark sentiments until he was completely covered in it. Being the mouthpiece for the group, it was his job to sing the emotions out as if he was experiencing them firsthand, and so he let it all absorb into him like a demonic possession.

End Song 272

A number of strange shadows appeared on the wall for all of them in the weeks and months that followed. The shapes and forms changed depending on what harsh memory was thrown in the flames as kindling on any given night. Then, by early spring, once everything had been reduced to ash, they had a new album put together. Jim arranged for it's production, and for them to get out on the road again by mid-summer. The album was released in early summer, and on the day it came out, a review of it in an online news site caught Cecilia's attention. She printed it out and took it to the living room to read to them. She cleared her throat dramatically to get their attention:

"Battle Creek's new *Bonfire* album is an expressive masterpiece, taking on a more serious, mature tone than their previous work to date. Straying from the usual upbeat content, *Bonfire* delivers a compelling dose of darkness and angst, but with hints of hope and perseverance mixed in seamlessly throughout, like a gentle seasoning on a gourmet dish. The tracks on *Bonfire* are pure emotion that should be allowed to flow through you, commiserate with, and inspire better days to come. The vocals have an intoxicating allure to them, the guitar is a raging river to be caught up in, hints of violin, piano, and horn add sophisticated edges, and the drums add a unique heartbeat to each song. Fans who have become accustomed to the brighter side of Battle Creek may find *Bonfire* a bit of a shock, but it is a lovely sojourn to the darker side of life, and contains what may become some of the finest, enduring melancholy songs of this generation. Five out of five stars." Cecilia finished, and looked up at Hal.

"Mature?" Hal said, raising one eyebrow. "Shit."

"Hal!" Cecilia scolded him, even though she knew he was kidding. "This is an amazing review! You should be proud of yourselves. I'm proud of you!"

"Thanks, Mom," he said.

Ryan came running up the stairs from the basement. "You'll never believe what I just found!" he shouted and threw something at Hal. Hal flinched as a small, brown, fuzzy thing hit him in the face. *Wahoooo!!! Oooof!*

Hal looked down where it landed in his lap. "HOLY SHIT, IT'S THE LAUNDRY WEASEL!" He grabbed it and stood up.

"Right!!??" Ryan answered. "He was wedged between the wall and the water heater. We would have had to have stepped just right to move the clothes against that part of the wall. That's why we had so much trouble finding him."

"He is *so* coming on this tour with us!" Hal laughed.

"Damn right!" Ryan agreed. "Hey, let's tie him to the horn of Ricky's new guitar, so he's hugging it."

"I like it!" Hal said, and they both ran up the stairs and down the hall to Ricky's room.

"Right…" Cecilia said to herself, "…mature."

Before they left for their next tour, Ricky decided to have his car sent home to his family. He wouldn't be around to drive it for months anyways, and he figured they might get a kick out of it. A large, flatbed delivery truck showed up unexpectedly one night around dinnertime at the Ransom house. Thinking the driver was lost, Ron went out to give him directions. A flock of children went to the doorway to watch. This counted as entertainment in a town this small. As Ron stepped outside, he suddenly saw before him the most beautiful vehicle he had ever seen being unloaded in their dirt and gravel driveway. "Whoa… whoa!" he yelled. "I think you guys have the wrong house! As much as I'd like to take that gorgeous machine off your hands, and all."

"Oh. Is this not 2301 Upper Battle Creek Road?" The driver picked up a piece of paper off the passenger seat.

"Uh, yes, it is," Ron said, confused.

"This is the address I got on the delivery order," the driver replied.

"Really?" Ron said, and walked over to take a look at the paper for himself.

"I know there's a note on the windshield I was supposed to give y'all at delivery. Maybe that'll explain things?" the driver said. Ron went over and pulled the small, folded piece of paper out from under one windshield wiper.

Dear Mom and Dad,

The guys gave it to Ricky as a Birthday/Christmas present. Neat, huh? We're going on another long tour, and Ricky won't be around to enjoy it, so decided to send it to you guys so you can drive it around and it won't be sitting for months. Please put it in the barn when it's raining or snowing. Have fun, keep it nice. Inform the siblings that if there is any damage on it when Ricky next visits, Ricky will find the guilty party and kill them.

Love, Ricky

P.S. It's mine whenever I'm home.

"It's Ricky's car!" Ron said out loud, and was immediately mobbed by screaming children begging to be the first to get a ride.

"HOLD IT!" Ricky's mother Ruth appeared, and all screaming stopped. "Your father and I will take the first ride alone to make sure this thing is even safe before anyone else gets in it," she said firmly. "Now, everyone back into the house to finish your dinner!" she commanded, and the mob of children began shuffling back through the narrow back door into the kitchen. Once they were all back inside, Ruth turned to Ron and announced: "No way any of them get to ride in it before I do."

Ron laughed heartily, putting his arm around her. "Yes, dear," he said, and they left Rose, the oldest girl, in charge until they got back from their first joyride.

They started their newest tour relatively close to home, in Columbus, Ohio. Hal was nervous. They were going to mix in all their big hits amongst the new songs. That's what they did on any tour anyways, but despite the good critical reviews, he still wondered how the moodier songs would go over with a live crowd. People generally went to concerts to party, not cry themselves to sleep. The opening band had finished thirty minutes ago, and now they were in position, ready for the curtain to be pulled. Hal looked around to the other three, who all looked uneasy too. He smiled and nodded at them. He really had the least to lay on the line publicly, but as the singer, he had the odd responsibility of expressing their fears for them. He'd tried to convince the other three to sing at least a few of their own songs, and they'd settled on one song each to do as the lead vocals. But much more than that was really their work, and he hoped he'd be able to do them justice.

> 273. "In the End" by Linkin Park

Uli began playing a few notes on the piano, and they echoed out through the stadium. The screaming began, and the curtain pulled to the side as cool blue lights came on behind them, casting them as black silhouettes on the stage. Hal started to sing right as the drumbeat and guitar hit. He kept his eyes closed at first as he walked across the stage. He wanted to make sure he had his focus before he took in the crowd's reaction. He was right about in the center as they hit the chorus. He looked out onto the audience, and they were on their feet, singing and chanting along with them in a moody trance.

> End Song 273

274. "Bullet with Butterfly Wings (Rat in a Cage)" by The Smashing Pumpkins

They went straight into playing a few of their older hits to bring the mood back up before going back to another one of the new, intense songs. It was Ryan's turn to sing, and he and Hal traded places. Hal had practiced long hours to learn to drum properly for this one song. As many times as Ryan tried to talk him out of doing the switch (due to Hal's bad drumming at first), Hal insisted he'd get it right. They practiced the song over and over and over until it got Ryan's approval. Hal barely had to give Ryan any pointers on singing. This song was mostly Ryan's work, and he'd had his own vision for it. Ryan, Uli, and Ricky were all good singers in their own right, even though they preferred to just play their instruments. But occasionally, Hal liked to see each of them take the microphone for a bit. The audience loved it, it gave the show more variety, and Hal wanted to see them sing their own songs to see how they thought they should sound. That way, he could pick up any tips he could for singing each genre. Ryan had a great punk voice on stage. Rough around the edges, energetic and raucous, but always in the right key. He poured his heart out into it on stage, and Hal tried to match that wild energy whenever he sang their punk songs. It was nice, though, to occasionally watch Ryan as a refresher for how it should be done.

End Song 274

275. "Working Class Hero" by Green Day
276. "Greenfields" by The Brothers Four
277. "Precious" by Depeche Mode

Hal took the microphone back for a few songs, then it was Uli's turn to sing his.

End Song 275 – 277

278. "Snap Your Fingers, Snap Your Neck" by Prong

This one wasn't as much of a challenge since Uli had sung it before, and all Hal had to do was cue in a few custom sound effects on Uli's mix board. Uli had gotten a lot more confident over time with being up front, even stomping his foot to the beat as he belted out the words, but he had another new move for tonight's show. His hair was down past his shoulders now, and in one quick, glorious movement, he reached up and ripped the hair band out to free all that hair. He began swinging it in a circle while head banging during the chorus, and it crested high into the air before going down low almost to the floor of the stage. "Yeah!" Hal said aloud. Luckily, the closest microphone was off so no one else heard it, or he would have felt a little silly.

End Song 278

279. "Dust in the Wind" by Kansas

280. "Beds are Burning" by Midnight Oil

281. "Lonely People" by America

282. "Sound of Silence" by Simon & Garfunkel

Four more new songs and two older ones after that, then it was Ricky's turn to sing his.

> End Song 279 – 282

> 283. "Lonesome Town" by Ricky Nelson

The crowd whooped and cheered like crazy when Ricky took the microphone. It was adorable. The fans knew it was a rare treat when Ricky sang. Wondering what the fans knew about each of them from their performances/interviews/music videos etc. was kind of weird compared to what they knew about each other from basically living together. But Hal was always happy to see Ricky get the recognition he deserved, even if he would have preferred to stay in the background. He got a lot of love from the crowd as he sang his song, and thousands of lighters and phones rocked back and forth like waltzing fireflies over the audience.

> End Song 283

> 284. "Paint It Black" by The Rolling Stones
>
> 285. "Rhythm of the Rain" by The Cascades
>
> 286. "The One I Love" by R.E.M.
>
> 287. "Iris" by The Goo Goo Dolls

Hal took over for the rest of the night, and they finished out the show with four of the most emotional songs. As he sang, it sounded like the entire stadium was echoing each word back. He looked into the eyes of the people closer to the stage, and they would look back with haunted faces. They spent so much time worrying about whether their new songs would be accepted or not, that they sometimes forgot that for many people, it went well beyond simple acceptance. He knew every person singing back at them had a story behind what the songs meant to them, and he could only guess how many thousands of stories those were. The people right at the foot of the stage were reaching their hands up towards Hal, and he walked along them and let his hand brush through theirs. Some people would grab it and squeeze it, some would let it slide over, and some would let their fingers lace between his as he passed. They gazed upon him like a sort of god, which he found humbling, because he was only the one singing the songs, while the people below him and behind him were the ones living them.

End Songs 284 – 287

After the concert, Ryan and Uli were ready to go out partying. Hal was very happy with how the concert had gone, but he wasn't in a drinking and partying sort of mood. He told them he might meet up with them later. Ricky had taken off to find a park to spend time in, and Hal made a note of the direction he was headed and went after him. He found a park a couple blocks down the road, and quickly located Ricky lying on the grass in a clearing. He had attracted a small family of skunks that were huddled to one side of him. "Hey," Hal said, sitting down on the grass next to him.

"Hey. Y'ain't goin' partyin' with Uli and Ryan?" Ricky asked.

"No, I'm not really in a partying mood tonight. Relaxing out in a park sounded kind of nice, actually. If that's okay with you," Hal said.

"Fine with Ricky," Ricky replied.

"And if it's okay with your friends."

"Oh, yeah, they won't spray you," Ricky assured him. "Wanna hold one?" Ricky asked, picking up one of the babies.

"Uh, no, that's okay," Hal said.

"Okay…" Ricky put the baby back down at his side.

"That was a hell of a show tonight," Hal said, lying back in the grass.

"Yeah," Ricky agreed.

Hal caught something moving off to the side of them and looked over to see a doe step out from the shrubs. She made her way up to Ricky and leaned down and touched her nose to his.

"Ricky, why don't you ever mess around with your nature powers? So, you can see what all you're capable of doing with them?" Hal asked.

"Uh… so Ricky doesn't get harassed by the news and kidnapped by scientists to be experimented on?" he replied.

"I didn't mean *publicly*," Hal said. "And I doubt you'd be kidnapped by scientists. Maybe a landscaping company, or National Geographic at worst." Ricky raised a doubting eyebrow at him. "Okay, yeah, maybe you'd get abducted by scientists… but I didn't mean publicly!" he repeated. "I know you come out here and hang out with animals, but I know you can do more than attract animals. I mean, how do you resist not messing around with it and seeing what else you can do?"

Ricky thought about it for a while before answering: "Because nature can take care of itself, it doesn't need Ricky messing with it."

"And I understand that, but you've been given this amazing ability, and why not try and understand it better, in case you ever can find a good, solid use for it?" Hal asked.

"*Cursed*…" Ricky corrected him. "*Cursed* with the ability."

"You know, it's only a curse if you let it be," Hal said. "For better or for worse, you have it and it's part of you. I think that gives you the right to use it and understand it."

"Maybe," Ricky sighed. "Just… don't want to mess anything up if things get out of control."

"Can you undo it if that happens?" Hal asked.

"Depends," Ricky said.

"Ah, so you have messed around with it before!"

"Yeah, and that's why ah' don't wanna mess around with it more. So far, all ah've killed is plants. Like to keep it that way."

"Yeah, but, you only accidentally kill stuff when you're in a bad mood, right?" Hal asked.

"Yeah…" Ricky answered.

"So, don't mess with it when you're mad. Only when you're in better spirits," Hal said. Ricky looked away nervously, pretending to be occupied petting one of the skunks. "So, I know you said nature can take care of itself and doesn't need you messing with it, but people have done a lot of damage to the planet. Now, I'm not trying to talk you into a career change here…" Hal said with a laugh, "…but when we are on break between tours and recording, have you ever thought about going out and trying to reverse some of the pollution and deforestation humanity has done?" Hal asked.

"Ah've thought 'bout it a little…" Ricky admitted. "But it's a matter of what can Ricky do without bein' caught. Cuz' if a loggin' company chops down a forest, and Ricky grows it back overnight, somebody's gonna notice," Ricky said. "And then somebody figures out it was Ricky, an' then the scientists show up, and we're back to where we started."

"Well, just do little things then. Save one tree. Help one injured animal. It may not be much, but it's better than nothing," Hal said.

"You're right," Ricky admitted, nodding slowly.

"You *do* like helping nature out, right?" Hal asked.

"Yes!" Ricky said. "Of course."

"Alright, then do a few things here and there. What you've got is too amazing to not use it. Use it to do a bit of good and make yourself happy," Hal said. Ricky turned to look at him. "Sorry, I know it's really not my business, but you and Uli and Ryan are all like brothers to me. The brothers I never had growing up."

"Hal, we ain't no brothers to you," Ricky said. "If we was your brothers, we'd break all your stuff, tell your mom you did it to get ya in trouble, and kick ya in the head while you're sleepin' just cuz we could." Hal stared at him blankly. "We ain't brothers, Hal. We're friends. Much better than brothers," Ricky clarified.

"Alright, if you insist," Hal laughed. They sat and talked for a while longer before Hal left to go join Uli and Ryan at the club. Ricky stayed in the park until it was very late. He walked along a little creek that ran through the center, picking up a few pieces of trash as he went to put in the garbage can on his way out. Further down, he came along a tree with a big section of bark missing off its lower trunk. The bark had obviously been ripped away by bored kids. Squirrels and birds sometimes take bark for their nests, but not in a patch that large. What was worse, the bare wood exposed on the trunk had all kinds of graffiti carvings in it, including many swear words. Ricky looked around to make sure nobody was nearby, then set the garbage down and went up to the tree. He took a deep breath, put his hand on it, then shut his eyes and tried to concentrate. The carvings disappeared as new wood grew to fill them in, and then a new layer of bark began to form in patches under his hand. He held it there for a few seconds, then took his hand away to have a look. Almost as good as new. The bark was still a little thin in places, but as he was about to work on it more, he heard voices, and looked up to see a couple coming along the path up the hill. He picked up the trash again and ran to the outer edge of the park as fast as he could. He dumped everything in the garbage can at the entrance, then put his hands in his pockets, and walked casually down the sidewalk back to the hotel for the night.

At the next show they did two days later, Hal was determined for Ricky to experience a little bit of what he had experienced while singing to the crowd during the first show. "Look into their eyes and run your hand along theirs when they reach up to you," Hal said quietly to Ricky as he handed him the mic.

"That's not Ricky's thing," Ricky replied.

"Just try it once, okay? Please?" Hal stared at him intently, and Ricky gave in and said he would.

---

288. "Always on My Mind" by Willie Nelson

---

Hal plucked the first few notes on the guitar, and Ricky started singing in the gritty, quiet voice he saved for occasions like this. The crowd started singing back. He really preferred to do his singing sitting on a stool. That is what he got used to when he was first singing and playing his guitar at the same time in the little bars. But he got up, and started walking along the stage and forced himself to look into some of the people's eyes. Normally he stared off into the far reaches of the crowd or kept his eyes on his feet. Looking strangers in the eyes was a daunting thought. The first person he made eye contact with smiled wide and started waving, and he smiled and nodded, then quickly looked away. He didn't like that kind of attention. He didn't want to be anyone's idol. That one look was more than enough for him, but he promised Hal he'd give it an honest try, so he picked out someone else and made eye contact. The woman didn't smile or start freaking out, and instead started singing louder, holding a concentrated gaze on him, like she wanted him to know she knew every word. He moved his eyes onto someone else, a man about his age, who gave him a quick nod as their eyes met, and sang along as well; his eyebrows furrowed in a solemn, knowing expression. A lady a few rows over held her hand out as their eyes met, palm out and fingers spread, like she wanted to grab him by the hand, even though she knew she was too far back. She kept her hand out as she nodded her head to the beat, whispering the words over her lips. He wandered a little closer to the edge and looked down at all the people who were close enough to touch. They held their hands up towards him in the hopes it would happen, and he drew in a deep breath as he let one hand drop down to them as he walked past.

---

End Song 288

---

"So, how was it?" Hal asked after the show.

"It was… interestin'," Ricky mumbled.

"Did you, I don't know, get the eerie feeling that some of them knew exactly what you were talking about?"

"Yeah, kind of," Ricky agreed.

"Yeah. It gave me the chills that first show. Just knowing how many people were feeling what we were singing to them. Sort of blows away that whole myth that nobody else on earth could understand what you're going through, huh?"

"Yeah," Ricky answered casually, picking up his guitar case as they started taking their things out the back door. Hal sighed. Maybe it was only him, but he'd really felt something strong that first night. They crossed a patch of dry grass between curbs that separated the back parking lot into separate sections for large trucks and small vehicles on their way to the tour bus. They put the first load of important equipment inside, then went back for more. On the way back, Hal noticed a few patches of green amidst the dead grass. They were randomly spotted in the middle, not in the shade or along the edges where any water might have lingered. Odd. Those weren't there a moment ago, were they? As he looked closer, he noticed they were all in a line. A few feet apart. About the size of a foot. He looked ahead at Ricky, who was a ways ahead of him as he made his way back to the stadium. He was looking up at the night sky, his hands in his pockets as he walked, oblivious that he was leaving a trail behind him.

# CHAPTER 22

## (Magical Mystery Tour)

### LATE SUMMER

Towards the end of August, they found themselves in Nevada to play an unusual show in an unusual venue. Hal had personally arranged for them to participate. Every year in the Black Rock Desert in Nevada, the mother of all hippie festivals takes place, and Hal had heard stories for years and always wanted to give it a try. The festival runs for a week, and they'd play a concert one night, but then be there for the entire event as a mid-tour vacation. Hal had mentioned to the other three he had requested to play a festival, and they thought it would be a neat idea since they hadn't done something like that in forever. But they didn't realize what they were in for.

"Shit, are we playing a show on the surface of Venus?" Ryan complained as they waited in the intake line in the RV. They had traveled in a bunch of unmarked vehicles since it's an open area, and they'd have no stadium or buildings to hide behind.

"It's 103 degrees out," Uli noted, looking at the thermometer.

"Yeah, they turn this big open desert into a temporary city every year for this. It's really amazing," Hal said.

"We're playing in the evening, right?" Uli asked.

"Yeah, it should be around sunset, so it won't be this hot when we're on stage," Hal answered. When they finally got to the front of the line of cars and RVs, the driver checked them in so they could remain hidden, and then they were shown to their spot. The RV was parked in one location while the trucks carrying their equipment went towards one of the stage areas.

"Are we just in with everyone else?" Ryan asked.

"Yeah, that's how it is here," Hal answered.

"So, we're not going to be able to sneak around," Ryan noted.

"No, not really," Hal said. "But we're in a remote location with a set number of people. A large number, yes, but not an inexhaustible supply. We'll probably get mobbed a bit, but we're here for seven days so we should still be able to find time to enjoy ourselves."

"Well, at least we don't have to worry about sneaking around in a hot disguise," Uli said, taking the last sip of his third bottle of water. The RV pulled into place and parked, and the driver got out to go meet up with the rest of the road crew.

"So, do we wait in here for a bit, or what?" Ryan asked.

"No reason to. We're not playing until tomorrow night. We might as well venture out," Hal said.

"I would prefer to wait a bit for the heat to die down," Uli said.

"It's 5:00 p.m., it should get cooler from here on out," Hal answered.

"Yeah, what the heck." Ryan pulled out his fourth bottle of water and twisted the top off. He took a few gulps, then wiped his mouth with his arm. "Let's go."

Hal, Uli, and Ryan decided to go shirtless, tossing their shirts onto their designated beds. The RV had air conditioning, but it was struggling to keep up with the desert heat. It was about eighty-five inside, and they knew they'd be in for a blast of heat as soon as they opened the door.

They jumped out, momentarily hidden from main view in the maze of other RVs, and Ryan kicked the ground. "Dude, this isn't even sand, it's dust," he said, sending a small cloud into the air around his legs.

"Yes, that would be why they gave us information on what to do in the event of a dust storm," Hal said. "And I've heard this crap will pretty much be on everything by the time we're done. We can't leave the instruments out of their cases. They need to be protected unless we're using them. And if we see a dust storm coming while we're onstage, we'll have to stop and throw the covers over the amps and everything as quick as we can, and then finish out the show later," Hal explained as they started past rows of RV's, all of which were ultimately situated in a giant half-circle formation around the core center of the festival. The whole setup was known as Black Rock City.

When they passed the last row, Uli, Ryan, and Ricky stopped in their tracks. A group of people dressed as flowers ran by, slowly being chased by a vehicle made to look like an enormous bumblebee. Two women dressed in elaborate pink jellyfish costumes went the other direction, both bobbing gently up and down and side to side as they moved. A large piece of art being brought in on a trailer went by next. A sculpture of Darth Vader made entirely of asthma inhalers.

"Dude… this is like a Seattle festival on steroids…" Ryan said.

"Hal…" Uli said, slowly turning to look at him. "What the *hell* is this?"

"Burning Man!" Hal said proudly. "Come on, you know all festivals have a little weirdness to them, that's what makes them festivals."

Right then, a man wearing makeup to make him look like The Joker from Batman rode by on a bicycle that was covered in fluffy yellow feathers and had a yellow duck head mounted to the handlebars. He had no clothes on.

"Was that like something you'd see at a Seattle festival on steroids?" Uli asked Ryan.

"No, that was more like something at a normal Seattle festival," Ryan said calmly, pulling a cigarette out of his pocket and lighting it. "Especially during Pride Week," he added.

"Excuse me, sirs…" A man walked up to them holding what looked like a giant potato. He had long brown hair, a short beard, and was wearing a pair of brown pants with fringe around the ankles. "I'm trying to get one hundred people to bless my yam before I cook it for dinner tonight. Would you all be kind enough to bless my yam?"

"Uh… sure," Hal said. The man held out the yam, and Hal put one hand on it. "Uh, may this yam be blessed to he who eats it?"

"Thank you, thank you very much. And you?" He held the yam up to Ryan.

"Um, may this yam be blessed?" Ryan said.

"Bless this yam…" Ricky said uneasily as the man brought it to him. The man then went to Uli, but Hal put out his hand to stop him. "He… he's not good at blessing vegetables. It's a long story," Hal said.

"Oh, okay," the man said calmly. "Well, thank you kindly for your blessings. That brings it to eighty-three. Seventeen people to go!" he said cheerily, then took a step to go, but stopped again and turned back around.

"You know, you guys look sort of familiar. Did you bless my yam last year?" he asked.

"Nope, this is our first time here," Hal answered.

"Huh. I swear I recognize you from somewhere."

"Yeah, we get that a lot," Hal laughed.

"Righteous. Alright, thank you again!" he said, then went on his way.

"Hal, this is not a festival, this is madness! This is like a book that has so much going on, that it has completely lost its focus! This is Alice in Wonderland shit!" Uli said.

"You do realize Alice in Wonderland is one of the bestselling books of all time for exactly that reason, right?" Hal asked.

"I will wait in the RV," Uli said, turning around.

"Uli…" Hal said, stepping in front of him and holding his hands up to stop him. "Yes, this may be a slightly weirder festival than most, but we've barely seen the tip of it. And it's not all going to be creepy weird, there's something here for everyone. We just have to get out and look," he explained. "Now come on, let's go explore." They set off out into the open space of the festival. A couple people recognized them as they walked around and came up to chat and get autographs, but they didn't get mobbed like they feared they might.

"Dude, this is weird. Not that many people know who we are," Ryan commented.

"Yeah, this is sort of an alternative festival, if you hadn't already noticed. I wasn't sure how many people *were* actually going to recognize us," Hal said.

"Kind of a nice break," Ryan said.

"I know, right?" Hal laughed. "Though the night is still young. We may still get mobbed." As they walked towards the center of the festival, they came to find Hal was right in saying they'd barely seen the beginnings of what Burning Man had to offer.

The landscape was alive and brilliant with tons of amazing art sculptures, and bizarre modified vehicles driving around. A giant metal coyote sat on the desert landscape howling skywards, the sun sitting perfectly within his open mouth, ready to go down it's throat as night approached. As they were admiring the coyote, a man in an elaborate costume strolled past. They struggled to decide what he was supposed to be. He had translucent fairy wings on his back, but the delicate wings were countered by his creepy split snake eyes, vampire-like fangs, green leather chest harness and spiked headdress. A demon? A warrior from a mythical race? An ancient god? They didn't stop him to find out. They made their way further and came upon an igloo made of old CDs. The discs were bottom side out, so they shone brilliantly in the setting sunlight and scattered little rainbows all across the white desert dust. Near it, a short tree stood covered in bells that sounded like the heavens opening as Hal shook one of its branches. A lady rolled past the bell tree in a human-sized hamster ball, followed by a large car done up as a cat ready to pounce. They heard shouts and cheers and turned around in time to see a man engulfed in flames run past.

"Holy shit!" Ryan said as they jumped back. Ricky sprung into action to chase after him and help, but Hal grabbed him by the arms and held him back.

"Wait, wait. I think that was intentional," he said.

"I assume that is the burning man?" Uli asked.

"Um, no, actually. That was *a* burning man, but not *the* burning man," Hal said. He turned around and pointed towards the horizon. "*That's* The

Burning Man." A giant effigy stood in the distance, towering over all other sculptures. The figure was in the rough shape of a man, though his head was shaped more like a policeman's badge, and his face was devoid of any features. An exoskeleton of neon lights lined his entire body, most noticeably on his chest, where the horizontal tubes took the form of a ribcage. "The climax of the festival is when they light him on fire, and people dance and party beneath him as he burns."

"Is that the idea of all this, to '*stick it to the man*?'" Ryan asked, making little quotation marks with his fingers.

"Yes, I believe that is the idea," Hal said. "Though I'm sure there's also stuff like how artists are 'burning with creativity' and whatnot. It's just that… I've been hearing about this for years, and after seeing pictures of the art and costumes online, I really wanted to check it out. This is supposed to be a place where everyone lets it all out, you know? Nothing is taboo. People are allowed to express whatever they want, however they want, and I think that's a beautiful thing, and that this would be really inspiring for coming up with new ideas for the tour and for songs," Hal said.

"I… suppose," Uli said as a small herd of single-seater cupcakes drove past them.

"You'll be a believer by the end of it, I promise," Hal insisted.

"Well, let's go take a look at that thing," Ryan commented as he nodded in The Man's direction, then spit the butt of his cigarette onto the ground.

"AH! No! Pick that up! This is a 'leave no trace' event. No littering," Hal scolded him. Ryan stared at him for a few moments, then rolled his eyes and picked it up and dropped it in the first trash can they came across on their way to The Man.

289. "Hey Mama" by David Guetta, Nicki Minaj, Bebe Rexha & Afrojack *to play over this scene*

They walked by a twenty-foot-tall boom box with a small crowd of people sitting up on top of it. At its base, a group of women with amazingly detailed butterfly wings danced in a giant circle. These were no cheap Halloween costume wings. They looked like real butterfly wings that had been put under a growth beam and enlarged. Music came from all directions. So many people were playing instruments throughout the festival, it was hard to tell what was live and what was being broadcast from the many radios and portable stereos. Though they could feel the giant stereo was certainly making sound as the low bass sound waves hit them in the chest.

End Song 289

About halfway to The Man, a giant copper penis drove by. Ryan looked to the side. "What the fuck is that!?"

"That was a dick, Ryan," Hal said.

"No, not the car, dumbass! That!" Ryan said, pointing to the right of them. Hanging from a metal frame was a man submerged in water contained in a roughly human-shaped clear plastic membrane sac. He had a snorkel tube in his mouth so he could breathe. He wasn't doing anything. He was just hanging there. In his water sac.

"That…" Hal said, "…is more dedication to getting attention for oneself than even I am willing to commit to."

"That's, like, the third freakiest thing I've ever seen in my life. And, you know, I've seen some shit," Ryan said.

"Yes, and I'm pretty sure none of us want to know what number one and two are," Hal said. Ryan obliged and didn't tell them. But on the way to The Man, they did end up passing something else that made it into the top five of Ryan's list. A life-size reproduction of an old prairie homestead church building propped up off the ground by a giant stick that had a rope attached to the end of it. 'The Church Trap' as it was called, made in the style of the trap made of a wood box on a stick with a carrot under it that was supposed to catch Bugs Bunny. They all agreed they had no interest in going anywhere near that thing for a better look. But it did inspire both Hal and Uli to start their own top ten lists of the freakiest things they'd ever seen. They never quite made it to the base of The Man. They could have gotten closer, but a couple dressed in Steampunk wedding outfits were getting married at the bottom, and they didn't want to disturb them. They made it plenty close enough to get their fill of his imposing presence, however, as he stared vacantly out across the desert at a height of eighty feet overhead.

"Alright, where to next?" Ryan asked.

"I've been trying to figure out what that is this whole time…" Hal said as he pointed to a tall object off to the east of them. "And I still have no idea, so why don't we head that way?"

"Let's," Ryan answered. Whatever the thing was, it was huge. Not quite as tall as The Man himself, but as far as they could see, it was likely the second tallest thing at the festival. They made their way through a disembodied exit door set up in the middle of the open desert, then paused briefly to let a giant silver shark drive in front of them before they got close enough to start making out what the enormous sculpture was. Two big-rig semi trucks fused together vertically, twisting and curving skywards like a snake rising out of a basket to a flute player's tune. Even Uli had to admit it was rather impressive.

"I'd never even heard of this event, but it would appear there are artists here who are willing to go to extreme lengths to put on a show," Uli said.

"Exactly," Hal agreed.

"Where is the stage we are playing on tomorrow?" Ryan asked.

"I believe it's this way," Hal said as he turned back in the direction of the center of the festival. They were about halfway across the big open space they had already walked across once when a group of four young women walked by. They were completely naked except for some body paint and curled ribbons in their hair.

"Woah, woah, woah. Hello. Well, see you guys later," Ryan said as he did a 180 degree turn to chase after them.

"Hold it!" Hal grabbed him by the shoulder.

"Dude! I'm trying to see the sights here!" Ryan said.

"I know, and that's fine. I figured we might end up splitting up at some point anyways, but there's one thing I want to say first."

"*What?*" Ryan whined.

"So, I realize I'm not your mom, and you are technically free to do as you wish, but as the leader of this band I have an investment I'd like to protect, if you will, and…"

"Yeah, yeah, yeah. I'll use a condom."

"That's not where I was going with that, actually."

"Then what!?" Ryan yelled.

"NO DOING DRUGS!!!" Hal yelled in his face loud enough to make the people immediately around them stop and stare.

"Drugs! No! No way. Never touch the stuff. Don't know what you're talking about!" Ryan said sheepishly.

"Good," Hal said with an equally fake smile, then let go of Ryan's shoulder as he took off running after the women. Hal, Uli, and Ricky started walking again, and came upon a very impressive temple-like building shaped like a giant leaf. Someone sitting directly outside of it on a bench got up as they walked by. "Excuse me. Sorry to bother you, but if I may take a moment of your time…" the man said, then introduced himself. "I'm Kale, and I'm with the Holy Temple of Mother Gaia. We're trying to make sure everyone follows the core principle of 'Leave No Trace' by reminding everyone to pick up any garbage you produce, and not leave it to tarnish the beauty of Mother Gaia's desert."

"Totally, thanks for the reminder," Hal said with a wave.

"Oh, one more thing. There is native wildlife in the area, even here in the driest, most barren core of the desert. Even though the festivities and people usually scare off the animals into the outlying areas, if you do happen to find a butterfly in the way of being trampled, or have a desert hare run into your tent, we are willing to come help catch and escort any animals to safety if you don't wish to do it yourself. Our services are available any time of the day or night, feel free to come and find us." The man handed them a piece of paper that read: 'Members of the Holy Temple of Mother Gaia' at the top, and had a picture guide to area wildlife on it. "And, of course, if any of you want to meditate on the beauty and perfection of nature, or help volunteer to preserve the wildlife, our doors are open, and all are welcome." Hal and Uli both immediately looked at Ricky. Inside the temple, people were occupied in various activities including weaving crowns out of dry grass, painting nature-inspired art on the wall, and engaging in friendly chatter. Ricky looked over at Hal uncertainly. "*Go!*" Hal said quietly, gesturing towards the temple.

Ricky hesitated for a moment, then nodded and ran over to Kale. "Uh, can Ricky join y'all for a bit?"

"Of course! Who's Ricky?" Kale asked, looking back at the other two.

"Uh, me," Ricky answered.

"Oh. Okay. Yes, welcome, Ricky! Are you an animal lover too?" Kale asked as Ricky followed him inside.

"There, we haven't even been here an hour yet, and Ryan and Ricky have already found something of interest. Now we need to find something you'll like," Hal said to Uli.

"We'll see," Uli said doubtfully. They found the stage in the center of the festival, and an electronic DJ was setting up for the night.

"Seems pretty standard," Hal commented, looking up the black metal rigging on either side of the stage platform.

"A comforting thought compared to the rest of this madness," Uli said.

"Hey, let's go look at the schedule over there and see who else is playing this year. Maybe there'll be a few shows we can go to as spectators. Wouldn't that be something?" Hal laughed.

"You go and get a copy of the schedule, or take a picture of it, or some-thing. I think I need to go back to the RV for a while. It is too hot," Uli said, and Hal noticed Uli was quite red in the face and drenched in sweat as well.

"Oh, shit. You don't look good. I'm sorry, I didn't realize the heat was getting to you that much." Hal handed Uli the last unopened water bottle he had been carrying around. Uli drank down half the bottle in a matter of seconds. "Alright, let's go back. I'll come with," Hal said.

"No, you're enjoying this. I'll be okay. I just need to go sit down where it is cooler. I'll find you later," he said as he started back towards their RV.

"Alright. If you need anything call me. I've got my phone in my pocket," Hal said.

"I will," Uli muttered. The massive collection of RVs on the other side of the festival stretched on for what seemed like miles, though he was fairly sure he knew where theirs was. Right in front of them was a giant black RV with lime green accent striping on the side. It was hard to miss, so while they had travelled incognito in a standard white RV, he knew he'd eventually find the black and green one. It was also right on the end of one of the rows, along a pathway.

His boots were already covered in the desert dust, and the layer only got thicker as he drug his feet across the dry ground. He was getting dizzy from the heat and the bright sunlight. He wanted to sit down and rest for a bit, but he knew if he tried to take a break, he probably wouldn't get back up again, so he kept forcing one foot in front of the other. He made it to the first ring of RVs and tents. He thought they were probably in the third row back, but as he was about to cross the path from the first row to the second, he stopped as he came across a small garden under a tent. Next to it was a large white shipping container that seemed to have been converted into a portable house of sorts. Maybe he really was losing his mind due to the heat, because all the flowers in this mini garden looked black. They must be silk. He crouched down and felt the leaves of one on the edge and found it to be real. He took the flower head in between two fingers and gently pulled it a few inches forward into the direct sunlight. The petals really were black. He'd been hearing flute music, amidst all the other noise around him, and as he held the flower, he realized it was coming from the garden. He stood back up, and found a woman sitting on a chair in the center of all the flowers, her back turned to him, playing the flute.

"Ma'am?" he called out. She stopped playing and looked at him over her shoulder. As she turned her body, a long, auburn brown braid came into view laying down her chest over the ridge of her other shoulder. A few strands were escaping from it, and blowing across the silver skull design on her black tank top. She had light brown eyes, an aristocratic cleft chin, and was wearing studded black shorts that matched the tank top. "I'm sorry to bother you, but are these real black flowers?" Uli asked.

"They are indeed!" the woman answered with a smile, and she stood up and put her flute down on the chair.

"How did you get them like this? Was it an absorbed dye?" Uli asked.

"No! These are all natural! They grow this way," she said.

"I've never heard of such a thing," Uli said in amazement.

"Well, I guess maybe they're not *all* natural seeing as a botanist probably bred them like this. Some of them, at least. But they are natural in the sense that they produce their own black. It's not dye."

"Incredible."

"Yeah…" she said proudly, cupping one of the black flower faces in her hand. "This one is a pansy. The *Viola* family, to be specific. This variety is known as *'Molly Sanderson.'* And the smaller ones over there are also pansies. The *'Bowles Black'* variety." She moved to another ceramic pot. "This flower here on the stalk is *Alcea Rosea 'Nigra,'* also known as black Hollyhock, and this one with the cute black bells is *Salvia Discolor.*" She then lifted up a bowl planter with a burst of little black flowers that had shocking white edges, like a black ball gown adorned with white lace. "*Nemophila Menziesii 'Penny Black,'*" she said, then nodded towards the most elaborate flowers of all on long, tall stems. "And this impressive flower is a black Iris."

"I do not suppose you could write this down for me? If I ever buy a house I'd want to put some of these in the yard," Uli asked.

"Of course I can," she said. "I keep a notepad handy because I get asked about them a lot," she said as she took a notepad off a small table nearby and started writing.

"What is the black grass over there?" Uli asked.

"*Ophiopogon Planiscapus Nigrescens*," she answered without hesitation. He was sure glad she was writing this down. He had no idea what she just said. "It's a mouthful!" she added with a laugh. "The more common name for it is Black Mondo Grass. And the thing next to it with the black leaves is a Black Pearl ornamental pepper."

"Thank you, that answered my next question," Uli said.

"Not a problem! So, are you a first-time Burner?" she asked.

"A what?" Uli asked back.

"I'll take that as a yes," she said with a smile. "Is this your first time at Burning Man?"

"Oh, yes. It is."

"Feeling overwhelmed yet?" she asked.

"You could say that," Uli replied.

"Well, don't worry. It's a lot to take in at first, but it's going to be amazing. By the end of the week you'll wish you could live here and never leave," she assured him.

"I take it you are a veteran here," Uli said.

"I suppose.. This is my fourth year."

"Did you come with your family?"

"Oh, no. They'd probably think this is a load of insanity. I'm here by myself this year. The last three years I came with my best friend. She was the one who convinced me to try this in the first place. She didn't come this year because she's seven months pregnant with her first child, and she didn't think she'd be able to take the heat. I started looking forward to this so much every year I didn't want to miss it, so I'm here without her this year."

"I'm sorry to hear that," Uli offered.

"Oh, no. It's fine. I mean, I wish she was here, but you're never alone at Burning Man.

"And you brought an entire garden with you," Uli added.

"Yes, well, after two years of going here as an observer to other people's creations, I decided I needed to bring something myself to show. And I realized there was no better thing to bring along than a slice of my little garden of darkness. My whole yard is done like this, but I keep most of them in pots all year now for this purpose, so I don't have to keep transplanting them."

"It is certainly unique."

"Thank you. It's a little refuge in the desert heat, and it makes a great conversation piece," she said, winking at Uli.

"Yes, yes it does," Uli admitted. She finished writing the names down and handed the list to Uli. "Thank you," Uli said.

"Of course," she answered. Uli turned around to go the rest of the way back to the RV, but, suddenly feeling lightheaded, tripped over his own feet and fell down onto his knees.

"Oh my god!" the lady said, running out of the tent to help him up.

"I'm fine, I'm fine! Just a little overheated," Uli said, embarrassed, as he struggled to get up.

"You need to go to the medical tent and get checked for heat stroke!" she said.

"No, no. I'll be fine. I just need to get back to the RV and sit for a while."

"Here, why don't you at least sit in my crystal cave for a few minutes?"

"… what?" Uli asked.

"My crystal cave," she said, pointing at the white shipping container. "I keep it cold with an air conditioner running on a generator. It's insulated really well, so once it's cool in there, it stays cool. Here…" She opened a cooler and handed Uli an icy bottle of water. "Go chill out in there for a few minutes. The crystals will help you find your center and give you a sense of calm, as well." She led him over to the container, and sent him in as she opened the door, then shut it quickly behind him.

Inside, the walls were painted black, and rows of shelves housed many large crystals of various shapes, sizes and colors. Many of them were illuminated by lighted bases. It was marvelously cool inside. He twisted the cap off the water bottle and began to chug it as he sat down and leaned against the wall. He felt really awkward sitting in there, but he really needed to cool off. The crystals cast competing shades all across the wall, and it looked like something out of a fantasy movie. Aside from the welcome chill, it was indeed very calming. Within a few minutes, he could hear quiet flute music playing again from outside the walls.

He shut his eyes and spent about twenty minutes in there before he was feeling better and worked up the strength to get up. He opened the door and darted out, closing it quickly behind him to keep the cold in. She heard the door open and set the flute down again. "Feeling better?"

"Much, thank you," Uli answered.

"You gotta be careful with this heat. Plenty of people here aren't used to this kind of environment, and if you don't keep enough water on you to drink, the heat'll drop you before you know what happened."

"Yes, I will be more careful. Thank you. I assume you are from somewhere hot, then?"

"South Dakota. It's not hot all year, but when it's hot, it's hot as hell," she answered. "Don't ask me why I'm still living there. Laziness, I guess. It's where I was born.

"I see," Uli said, then added: "You play the flute beautifully. Do you belong to an orchestra where you are from?"

"No, nothing like that. It's something I learned in school, and I do it as a hobby when I have time to spare. It helps the plants grow," she said. Uli gave her an amused look, and she raised one eyebrow at him. "You don't believe it? Turns out its true. Talking to plants and playing them music actually helps them grow. Not because they enjoy rousing conversation or appreciate fine music, it's the sound waves. Noise stimulates growth."

"Really?" Uli said.

"True story," she replied. "So, you play anything?" she asked.

"Yes, I play a few instruments."

"A few?" she asked.

"Yes. The piano, the violin, the saxophone, and trumpet. I also do keyboard and mixing work …"

"That's more than a few!" she said, surprised. "Do *you* belong to an orchestra?"

"No, but I do play in a band."

"Oh, cool! You playing at all here?"

"Yes, tomorrow night, at seven."

"Well, I might have to go watch, then. You on the main stage?"

"Yes."

"Alright. I'll go check it out," she said. "So, what's your name?"

"It's Uli."

"Ooli?"

"It's German."

"It's… unique."

"Thanks," Uli said.

"I didn't mean that as a bad thing!" she laughed. "I'm Claudia," she said as she extended a hand to him.

"Claudia," he repeated, taking her hand in his.

"Alright, what did everyone do yesterday?" Hal asked at breakfast. They had all gotten back to the RV at different hours of the night.

"It's not so much a question of what, as it is a question of *who* I did," Ryan answered.

"You don't say…" Hal responded.

"Uh, we saved a lizard from being run over by a giant pink rabbit," Ricky said. Hal reached an open hand out to him and gave him a high five.

"What is it with pink bunnies and rubber ducks in this place? They're fuckin' everywhere," Ryan said.

"I'm sure it's a giant inside joke we're not in on yet," Hal replied. "So, I spent a lot of the night listening to that DJ that was setting up yesterday when me and Uli went and checked out the stage. He was pretty good. Danced with a few cute girls, talked to a bunch of different people. After the DJ finished, some acrobats came on and did a show. I tell ya what, I thought I was in pretty good shape until seeing them do their thing. I hadn't felt that inadequate in a long time," Hal laughed. "It was a guy and girl, and he was flipping her up in the air and catching her like she was a rag doll. And at one point, she was holding herself on the trapeze by nothing but the back of her neck. It was crazy."

"I have seen shows like that before, they are incredible. Too bad I missed it," Uli said.

"You never told me you liked circus acts. I would have called you!" Hal said, adding: "They said they were going to do a show every other day though, so we'll have to find out when they're performing again tomorrow, and all go watch. See? I knew we'd find something you'd be interested in!"

"You were right," Uli admitted.

Later that evening when they were setting up, it finally became clear to them why Hal insisted they practice some old, obscure songs by other bands. *"Because I really like this one, and I always wondered how it would sound if we did it…"* he had insisted as he introduced the next one, and the next. And none of that had been lies, but rather, incomplete reasons. As one of the most popular mainstream groups at the time, bursting onto stage at the biggest counter-culture event in the country might not have gotten them the best reception. There were fans everywhere they went, but the percentage was certainly lower in the Nevada desert at the end of summer. Hal had it all worked out. He was going to introduce them as a garage band from Michigan. They'd only cover old songs for at least the first hour. He had come up with a nice, weird outfit to wear; something that had nothing to do with the whole 4-genre thing they usually did. It would be glorious.

He came out from the back wearing an antler headdress. It wasn't huge or fancy or anything, a simple brown leather headband that held small 3-point buck antlers on each side. He also had a couple leather arm bands with a few brown and black feathers on them, and he was barefoot and shirtless in his jeans. Ryan took one look at him and said: "Nice rack."

"Thank you," Hal said. "We're in the desert with a bunch of artists, and I'm going to make the most of it."

"Man, I wish I'd have known this was such a big deal, I'd have figured out something better to wear," Ryan said, then suddenly developed a terrifying look of excitement. "WAIT! I KNOW!" he said, and started tearing his clothes off as fast as he could. Hal, Uli, and Ricky turned to look away, disgusted. "At least he'll be behind us," Hal mumbled. Uli was dressed a little strangely himself, though more out of necessity than intention. He had a black leather lace up vest over his bare chest, black leather jeans, and that was all. The vest would normally have been over a black shirt and under a black coat, but that combination would have cooked him alive. He was also barefoot. All four of them were, actually. Ricky had been mostly barefoot as of late, even before they were in the desert, as he had finally gone through the soles of his black sandals. He refused to get new ones.

"Hey, Ricky!" they heard someone shout and looked to see a few members of the Temple of Mother Gaia run up to them. "We came to wish you luck, and may the Raccoon Spirit bless you and guide you throughout the night," Kale said as he reached up with two paint-covered hands and spread a crude, tribal-looking black raccoon mask across Ricky's eyes.

"Uh, thanks!" Ricky laughed.

They took the stage casually, no smoke or explosions or sudden light after darkness. Hal walked up to the microphone. The crowd was oddly silent, then they heard a murmuring rise, followed by a mixed reaction of cheers and boos. Boos. A few people were booing them. They hadn't had a real challenge like this in a long time; Hal was nearly beside himself with how eager that made him.

"Uh, hello. We're Battle Creek. We're a garage band from Michigan. Thanks for being willing to give us a chance to play for you tonight, and… yeah. I hope you enjoy," he said, as awkwardly as he could manage, then they began.

---

290. "The Riddle" by Gigi D'Augostino

---

Ryan started an antique sounding beat on his drums, something like a Civil War march, followed shortly by some flute-like sound effects from Uli's keyboard. Another thing they were doing differently besides covering songs from other groups was for the first song, Hal was going to sing with a voice filter. They had routed the microphone output through Uli's synthboard to add a mystical sort of sound to his voice. It wasn't Autotune, but rather, a warping filter that gave him a slightly robotic echo. He pulled the microphone off the stand to carry it, and at the first chorus, started doing something of a tribal-like dance in a circle. Ryan rolled his eyes. Hal was doing one of his stupid dances again. Must he do crap like that on stage in front of everyone? Hal kept his eyes on the floor. He just wanted to enjoy the moment. He had the familiar sinking feeling that Ryan was probably judging him. It didn't get to him that much anymore, but he didn't want to let it in to distract him. Once he had spun around back to the front again, he let himself get a look at the audience. The booing had stopped, and plenty of people were dancing themselves, some even in the same fashion he was. Shit, that was a fast turnaround. That was faster than even he could have hoped for. Sometimes he impressed even himself. Ryan must be pissed. Another uplifting thought.

> End Song 290

> 291.  "Pet Sematary" by The Ramones

The first song played straight into the second. They didn't let a moment of silence in between when the last note of the first song stopped, and the first note of the second song started. It wasn't the smoothest transition, the songs weren't that close musically, but Hal saw a similar quality in both. Despite their differences, both gave him the inexplicable but irresistible urge to dance wildly around a campfire in the dark. He had planned on avoiding eye contact with his band mates for the most part, but as he sung the line: "…*and at night when the wolves cry out…*" he heard a loud howl behind him, and looked back to see it was Ricky who had done it. On a whim, Hal pointed straight at him right as the next chorus was coming on, and Ricky, apparently having read his mind, joined in and they danced in a circle opposite of each other; like two predators sizing each other up for a fight. Ricky had the biggest smile on his face, and looked like he was genuinely having a good time. Hal could at least count on Ricky to be weird with him when nobody else seemed interested. Thank God there was at least a few other weird people on the planet who thought like he did. Weird people are more fun.

> End Song 291

Towards the end of their two-hour show, they played some of their own songs, and it went fine since the audience had warmed up to them by then. The people in the crowd who were fans had started screaming for them to play some of their own stuff at that point, and they ended it with a straight run of their seven biggest hits. When they finished, they left their instruments to be packed up by the few road crew members that had come with them, and they jumped down from the stage straight into the audience to mingle. Hal, Uli, and Ryan were instantly mobbed by women. Ricky hit the ground running and made his escape towards the group from the Temple of Mother Gaia waiting for him off to the side.

"You didn't say you were in Battle Creek!" Uli heard behind him, and turned around to see Claudia standing there. "It… didn't come up?" Uli answered. Claudia squinted at him, disbelieving. She stared at him for a while until she could see he was getting uncomfortable, then casually said: "Your third album was the best."

"You think so?" Uli answered. He managed to divert all the people trying to talk to him to Hal & Ryan, and despite how many people were around them, he knew Hal and Ryan were observing them closely. They talked for a while. They'd had minimal set up and break down with their show since there weren't any special effects, and within a few minutes, another artist was up and ready to play.

292. "The Greatest" by Sia

293. "The Mummer's Dance (Faster Radio Edit)" by Loreena McKennitt

294. "Under a Violet Moon" by Blackmore's Night

295. "Only Teardrops" by Emmilie De Forest

296. "Only Time (Faster Radio Edit)" by Enya

Inspired by their show, a group of people had gotten a large fire going out in front of the stage and took to dancing around it. Ryan had a girl under each arm grinding against his body, and Hal was joined by a woman who was willing to dance in circles with him around the flames. Ricky found himself jumping up and down in unison with everyone else from the Holy Temple of Mother Gaia.

"Come on!" Claudia grabbed Uli and pulled him into the center with her. They went into something like a fast ballroom waltz, stirring the smoke from the fire into a large halo around their heads, and causing all the lights of the festival to form into one giant spinning ring. The sun went down, the moon rose, more artists came and went across the stage as the hours went by, and they ended up dancing all night, until daybreak began to creep over the desert horizon. It barely felt like it had been that long as the time had rushed past them, but they were suddenly quite tired as they called it quits to go back to the RV.

End Songs 292 – 296

They slept all the next day. It was a pattern they fell into for the rest of the week; hiding from the heat in the RV during the day, and setting out at night to explore. Things got more interesting after dark. When the sun went down, the dry ground sprouted a neon jungle of art as far as the eye could see. They made their way through a light portal shifting all colors of the rainbow, and on the other side, found themselves in a garden of neon flowers tall enough to make them feel like ants. A ring of pillows encircled each stem, making an inviting place to sit and talk for a while in the company of friends and strangers alike. A giant wire sculpture of a nude woman dancing kept watch nearby. They walked under a dome of white umbrellas with strings of white lights falling from them like luminescent raindrops that caressed their shoulders as they walked through. A whole room of lit beaded curtains, friendly jellyfish, or perhaps white weeping willows. After exiting out the other side, they hitched a ride in the largest Volkswagen Beetle any of them had ever seen to the stage, where the acrobats would be performing again tonight.

As they watched them flipping and throwing each other through the air, it instilled a sense of wonder that these people had spent long hours learning to fly by briefly touching the earth, and each other, to the greatest effect. Not lingering on a bar or another person for more than a second, then sending themselves airborne again. They did it effortlessly, too, unlocking the power of their own bodies and concentration, putting full and complete trust of their lives in the hands of their friends. Art by nothing except movement; much like singing. One of the acrobats made his entrance by falling down to the stage from the full height of the rigging while unraveling from a long, loose sheet. It had been wrapped around him in an alternating pattern that allowed him to fall, pause, fall, pause, and then lightly touch down on the ground. The lady who had suspended herself from the trapeze bar by the back of her neck performed the stunt again, and then later, spent time hanging from a vertical rope by wrapping her legs and feet around it. No hands, no horizontal bar to hook legs on, just like a spider with its silk. A body full of fully utilized and perfected muscle, doing stunts with ease that could have killed the average person.

Another man took an extremely tall, non-folding, two footed wood rung ladder, stood it up on stage, and then climbed up, over the top, and down the back side, in the middle of the stage. Nothing for it to lean against, nothing holding it up besides two unstable feet. He didn't climb slowly, either. Had he not used his hands, one would have said he ran up and down it. With his hands, he skittered up and down it like a fleeing mouse. After him came the grand finale, aptly named the 'Spinning Wheel of Death.' It was two wheels, actually. Human sized hamster wheels, affixed to the opposite ends of a giant metal pole, the center of the metal pole attached to a stand that held it up and allowed it to spin around with the rings on either end. Visualize an airplane propeller spinning around its center point, and the rings being on the tip of each end of the propeller blades. The rings themselves did not spin on their own center points, they only rotated around the main center of the "propeller blade" as the bar holding them spun. It was a towering apparatus, stretching almost to the ceiling of the stage. It started in a vertical position, with one ring nearly on the stage, and the second straight up in the air barely below the ceiling rigging. Two men in costumes that made them look like ancient warriors from a jungle tribe walked out to it, and one gave it a little push to get it going. It started to swing back and forth, like a pendulum, then one of the men jumped inside the lower ring. As he grabbed its edges and forced his weight against it, he got it going faster, faster, like a kid pumping their legs in a playground swing. He gradually worked it until the ring he was in crested at the peak, straight up in the air, and with one more well-timed shove, it slowly, slowly started to move again. Not back the way it came, but forward this time, making the first full rotation. It made a few turns, then the second man on the ground reached up with one arm and grabbed onto the edge of the other empty ring and was instantly snatched skyward. He swung himself into the ring, and both of them ran inside like hamsters as they spun over and under. This was impressive enough in itself, but they were only warming up. Each of them had a jump rope in their pockets, and they pulled them out and began to jump rope in the rings. That was part two of the warm up. As high as the rings got in the air at their peak, a fall inside would most likely mean the men would be tumbled around like loose change in a dryer. Unpleasant, but not deadly; and this was the Spinning Wheel of Death. One of the men grabbed the rigging holding the ring to the bar and swung himself out of it, and, in a split second, he was suddenly running around the outside of the ring. Now faced with a possible 50-foot fall should he trip at the top, he pulled his jump rope out again. He and the other man managed to remain upright as this giant apparatus spun, creating a strange illusion, like watching parts move contrary to logic in a well-oiled machine. The man jump roping wasn't satisfied to just jump rope on the outside of a giant spinning wheel. He began to jump higher, higher, higher, until he threw the jump rope to the side, let it fall to the stage, and did lone high jumps over the ring. He jumped at the top as it was about to descend again, and free-fell over it until his feet touched down again at the bottom right before his ring was about to go under the center. The second acrobat was now on the outside of his ring, both jumping and running as it turned over faster and faster. Hal, Ricky, Uli, and Ryan were all thinking the exact same thing: They were about to watch two men die on stage. It was terrifying, yet impossible not to watch. How the two of them were running fast enough to keep up with the rings and avoid being slammed to the ground was one miracle after another as the seconds ticked by. Finally, one of the men did a back flip in the air as his ring reached the highest peak, landed partially down its side as it was already well into its descent, but, in a blink, caught up, and was back on top. Hal's heart was pounding watching it. What these two were doing was so dangerous and difficult that they were giving people who were just standing still and watching them a heavy cardio workout. *That* was how you do an impressive show. When they finally decided they had tempted death for long enough, they climbed back inside, quit running, and let the spinning wheel of death slow to a stop. They both jumped out, and with prideful, borderline egotistic smiles of victory, they threw their hands up in the air to demand applause, and the desert roared in response. They had earned the right to wear smiles that demanding. Not a single person in the audience would have disagreed.

"RICKY! You're not going to believe this!" Hal came running up to the rest of them. He'd gone out earlier the next afternoon when it was still hot out. He couldn't wait for evening to do more exploring. It was their last day. The Man would burn that night. Now that evening was approaching, it was starting to cool off, and the rest of them came out of the RV.

"Uh, what?" Ricky asked.

"There's a roller rink here!"

"What!?" Ricky answered.

"Yeah, somebody's totally set up a temporary roller rink over that way. They laid out a bunch of plywood planks to make a floor," Hal said. Ricky looked around uncertainly.

"Ricky's not sure he wants to take his skates out here. They'll get full of dust and get ruined," he said.

"That's the best part, they have a whole fleet of sacrificial rental skates for people to use! They're the designated dust skates," Hal said.

"Really!?" Ricky said.

"Yeah! Let's go!" Hal said, leading them off into the desert.

---

297. "Funkytown" by Lipps, Inc. *to play over this scene*

298. "Mr. Sandman" by The Cordettes

299. "Walk This Way" by Run DMC & Aerosmith

300. "I'm Too Sexy" by Right Said Fred

301. "Hot Stuff" by Donna Summer

302. "Who Put the Bomp" by Barry Mann

303. "Love Shack" by The B-52's

304. "Zuit Suit Riot" by Cherry Poppin' Daddies

305. "Disco Inferno" by The Trammps

306. "Eye of the Tiger" by Survivor

307. "The Rockafeller Skank (Funk Soul Brother)" by Fatboy Slim

308. "Car Wash" by Rose Royce

---

Underneath a large plywood sign that read 'Black Rock Roller Disco,' they sat down and put on their rental skates, then headed out to the skate floor. It was cooling off, but the air was still heavy with heat, and the floor was full of people. Some were skating naked, or mostly naked, something Ricky very objectively noted wasn't a very good idea, on account more skin was exposed to potential floor burn if they fell. It was Ryan who added the comment that certain body parts that are usually protected would also be in danger of getting run over.

"Hey, Ricky! I'll whip ya!" Hal yelled back at him, holding his hand out. By whip, he meant 'crack the whip,' a move where a whole line of skaters is holding hands, and then as the group takes a corner, the person on the end gets launched forward away from everyone else due to the extra momentum. Ricky skated up, grabbed Hal's hand, and Hal pivoted and swung him fast around the corner, then let go, sending him off ahead of them. Shortly after Hal let go, however, Ricky hit the edge of one of the plywood sections, and normally it would have been fine, except he was going too fast and it caught him off guard and he went down hard. "Oh, shit!" Hal said loudly as he skated over to him. "Sorry, man. You alright?"

Ricky sat up. "Yeah, Ricky is fine," Ricky said, examining his knee. He had skinned it a little, though not enough to make it bleed. "That's why ya don't go skatin' naked. That could have been Ricky's entire right side." He laughed.

"Sorry about that." Hal helped him up.

"S'alright," Ricky said.

"*NO PLAYING CRACK THE WHIP.*" A loud, monotone voice suddenly came through the speakers, followed by muffled laughing the microphone picked up. The DJ wasn't being serious, and his friends mingling behind him knew it.

> End Songs 297 – 308

They skated for a few hours, watching the sun slowly make its way closer to the horizon. It started to get a little hazy though, and it wasn't quite time for it to set. "Is that fog rolling in?" Hal asked. "Isn't it too hot for that?"

One of the people around them heard him and looked, then screeched to a stop. "DUST STORM! INCOMING!" the man yelled out. "COVER YOUR EYES!" Everyone on the floor slowed to a stop as they noticed the haze approaching rapidly, and then people began pulling their skates off and running to find shelter. Once the four of them got their skates off, they pulled bandanas out of their pockets and put goggles on. They had started carrying these things with them at the suggestion of more veteran Burners they'd talked to, since dust storms could descend upon them without much warning. Once their faces were covered, they started running back in the direction of the RV. They were surprised to see only about half of the people they passed seemed to be looking for shelter. The calls of 'DUST STORM!' were bouncing across the desert now, moving from person to person, camp to camp, like a game of pinball. Some people simply covered their eyes and noses, then went right back to what they were doing. These were people who had been through a few of these in years past, Hal reasoned. They ran past a large metal sculpture of a circle flanked on either side by large silver wings right as a man jumped up into it. He had on a headdress of black feathers, a vintage looking gas mask, and steam punk goggles. He reached up and grabbed the top part of the ring, and waited, facing the approaching storm. Hal's pace slowed as he watched him, the thin front of the storm just starting to pelt him in the chest. He was welcoming it. Taunting the storm to come closer and face him head-on.

They made it back to the RV, and Ryan pulled his goggles off and jumped up to close the ceiling vent. Uli pulled the door shut behind them right as the outside world began to disappear into the haze. They sat inside for about an hour and a half; watching the storm hit its peak and create white-out conditions. Once it began to thin again, the world came back into view, revealing a deep red sunset. It wasn't a very long storm, but it was a potent one, covering everything in sight with a layer of white dust. When they dared to venture back outside, they saw a few stray dust devils in the distance, chasing the storm's tail. Making their way through the camp, anyone who had braved the storm outside had been turned into a dust ghost. Skin was rendered paper white by the blowing ground cover, a stark contrast to the rings of tanned skin around eyes that were revealed when the goggles came off. People had little time or resources to wash themselves off at this point. The Man would burn in an hour. Several people spit on their fingers, then pulled them across their faces in stripes and patterns. This had become their final war paint for the evening as they began to make their way to the grand finale.

"You all realize what that storm was, right!?" the announcer yelled into the microphone while standing at the base of the imposing Man. He held the microphone in one hand and a lit torch in the other. "The Man knew we were coming for him tonight! But he has lost. There is no escape now, for we are victorious!" he yelled, and people whooped and cheered loudly. "We will not be repressed, we will not be held back, and we will not be silenced, for we are the lifeblood of the earth! Our voices will be heard, and our art will be seen!" Everyone began to scream louder. "Nobody can stop us. Not society, not the government, not the weather, not even the barriers that exist in our own minds. And certainly, not *The Man*!" Amidst more thunderous cheers, he held the torch to The Man's leg. The fire caught, and quickly spread, turning The Man into an 80 ft pillar of fire. Even standing far back in the crowd, they could feel the heat radiating off him, licking their faces and making them squint and look away to keep their eyes from burning. A few moments later, fireworks began filling the sky with rainbow flower blooms. This was the beginning of the wildest, and last, celebration of Burning Man. Music began coming out of speakers and from live instruments all across the desert. Most everyone was dancing, and if they weren't dancing, it was only to throw back a few drinks or psychoactive drugs first.

They lost track of Ryan immediately, likely to the nearest orgy. Uli had disappeared, too, though Hal thought he saw him out of the corner of his eye a few minutes earlier, talking to that woman with the long braid he had been dancing with on the second night. Hal walked out from the thick of the crowd, out to where there was open space and only a few people milling around, and leaned against a giant flower stem as he looked out into the desert. In the distance, a neon-lined pirate ship rolled across the dry ground, tossing up dust around it that appeared like sea mist breaking in its wake.

"Watcha' doin'?" Ricky was suddenly next to him.

"Oh… thinking," Hal answered.

"'Bout what?"

Hal paused for a moment, before answering: "Anything. Everything. Art. Neon lights. About how I want to come back and do this again next year. About how I wish this wasn't coming to an end to begin with." He hesitated again before adding: "Our upcoming shows." A particular sculpture he had seen earlier that week was capturing his attention again. It was the see-through wire exoskeleton of two adults sitting back to back, one with its head in hands, the other with the base of its chin resting on the top of the knees, both in obvious frustration. Inside their wire frames, however, were two additional solid sculptures of small children. The children were standing and facing each other, reaching out and touching hands through the backs of the adults. The children radiated a bright, white light. "Song writing, connecting with people…" Hal said. Ricky remained silent as he examined the sculpture too; a quiet concentration seemingly coming over him. "All the wild things the human mind can create," Hal added, while the fire popped and cracked like far off thunder behind them.

# CHAPTER 23

## (On Top of the World)

**Packing up and leaving to** continue with their tour was like waking up from a seven-day dream. The type a person could spend eternity in, and is devastated to wake up from.

"We're going back next year, right?" Ryan asked.

"You know it," Hal replied. As they pulled onto the highway, Uli made sure to keep his right wrist facing down on the seat, so nobody would see the phone number written on it. A South Dakota area code, followed by 867-5309.

*They really liked the violin, I think. They all seemed stronger the next day. Next time you're around Minnesota or Iowa or Nebraska, you know, the party states, you'll have to drop by and play for them again,* he could hear Claudia say in his head.

Hal was unusually quiet the next few days. The storm of new images in his mind kept him busy for hours at a time. Their shows would be bigger, better, more stunning. But how? The ideas were fighting for attention. Could they add some low-scale acrobatics? Could the outfits be improved? Could they just put more energy and oomph into everything? And all the while entertaining these thoughts, new songs were taking shape as well. It took a few weeks, but Hal finally brought before the other three his battle plan. *"Guys, we're going to make a few changes..."*

Truth be told, the changes Hal proposed weren't all that drastic; mostly embellishing what they were already doing. But the embellishments made a world of difference in his mind. He was going to personally add some acrobatics to the show. Once the adjustments had been made, they were ready to test it on their first audience. On this night, they were in Raleigh, North Carolina. They still sometimes shuffled the song order in their concerts depending on where they were. And, being down in the South tonight, they would do the country songs sooner rather than later. The pre-show images flashing across the screen went dark with the rest of the room, and the crowd started to scream. They'd still start with something popular, they always did. It was the only way to greet all that pent-up energy the people had from waiting.

309. "Larger Than Life" by The Backstreet Boys

Flashing blue and white lights scattered across the stadium, and Hal walked out from the side, making his grand entrance with a maniacal laugh. He never went a show without running his hand along the outstretched hands reaching up over the front of the stage, and he was especially in the mood for it tonight. He went straight to it, much to the delight of the audience. He knew they'd be a little more zealous at first, and he was prepared to be grabbed and possibly held onto. But, as he finished his first pass and turned around at the end of the stage to walk back, he felt a quick jerk as someone grabbed his foot. He barely looked back in time to see a quick glimpse of his shoe disappearing into the audience. The screen overhead had captured it rather well, and half of the screaming turned into laughter. He stood still on the stage for a second staring at the crowd, though he didn't stop singing. He looked back, and the other three were laughing too. He laughed as he stepped on the heel of the other shoe, using the foot with only a sock on to loosen it. He took a few steps back, and then kicked his other foot hard, sending the second shoe flying out into the audience. It disappeared into a flurry of outstretched hands. Too bad, he liked that pair.

End Song 309

310. "Centerfold" by J. Geils Band

As the first song came to an end, they launched straight into the intro of the second song, and the screaming came back anew. This was one of the hottest songs they had at the moment, and once the audience recognized the beginning of it, they went wild. Hal started pumping his fists in time to the beat as he sang, and a group of five girls at the front all wearing the 'Dance Like No One is Watching' shirts sold at their shows all started cheering in his direction. There were nights he really loved his job. Even if he lost one of his favorite pairs of shoes. "LEMME HEAR IT!" Hal yelled out into the audience, and they all started clapping along.

End Song 310

311. "Devil with a Blue Dress" by Mitch Ryder & The Detroit Wheels
312. "Roll to Me" by Del Amitri
313. "Gimme Some Lovin" by Spencer Davis Group
314. "What I like About You" by The Romantics

Hal did more of his signature improvised dancing than usual. He was really getting into it tonight. And even Ryan had to admit, the crowd was eating it up. He picked out a few girls near the front throughout the song and sang right to them to watch them giggle, but he also sang to the crowd as a whole. It was impossible to make eye contact with every single person in a 20,000 seat stadium, but he'd see how many he could connect with at each show. He'd also be sure to at least look in the general direction of every part of the stadium throughout the night, even the farthest corners in the back, to see if he could pick anyone interesting looking out of the crowd and sing to them for a bit, even if they didn't notice.

> End Songs 311 – 314

Once they had done the first set of pop songs, the lights went dim, and the overhead screens came on with some old footage of them while they ran backstage to change outfits. Splitting up the top-charting songs throughout the show made the outfit changes a little weird since they didn't really want to change every other song. So, occasionally they did some songs dressed for a different genre. But since they started out the show that night with a few pop songs, they started in their 'pop' clothes, and now were scrambling to get into their country outfits for part two. Hal came out in his blue plaid shirt, cowboy hat, western boots, and tight blue jeans. Ricky was in the original red plaid shirt he had on when they first met him, his famous raccoon cap, blue jeans, and the curled-up raccoon belt buckle capping a black leather belt. Uli had a black button up western shirt with white embroidered skulls and flourishes on the shoulders, as well as black leather cowboy boots and a black cowboy hat with metal spikes. Ryan had shredded blue jeans, a faded T-shirt that had the NASCAR logo on it, and an American flag bandana tied around his head. Each of them putting their own flare on the country look.

> 315. "I've Been Everywhere" by Johnny Cash
>
> 316. "Small Town Saturday Night" by Hal Ketchum
>
> 317. "Chicken Fried" by Zac Brown Band

318. "Danny's Song" by Loggins & Messina

319. "Country Girl (Shake It for Me)" by Luke Bryan

320. "The Cowboy in Me" by Tim McGraw

Starting up the country songs was sometimes as fun as starting the pop songs if they were in the right area. A couple of the slower, more moody country songs they had done as of late were doing really well on the charts, so they'd perform them tonight. But Hal wasn't going to start the segment like that. When they got a good, energetic country song going, they could get the crowd nice and wound up with them and turn it into a party real quick. Something that had surprised Hal over the years was that girls in the audience would flash them more often during the country songs than during the other three genres. Playing the country set in the South was the gift that kept on giving some nights. The girls who were in front with the 'Dance Like No One is Watching' shirts had apparently come in layers. They all stripped off their first shirts, and underneath they had the matching 'I Come 'Round for That Country Sound' shirts, and were bumping and grinding together to the country beat. Hal was liking this group more and more. This was the other part of country Hal liked; people would dance to it. And it wasn't only the girls dancing side by side, even the guys would sway and rock in time. Country music was the closest thing in sound form to actually singing a sunset to people, and Hal had fun faking a subtle southern accent for it. When he first asked Ricky to teach him how to sing in an accent, Ricky gave him the most intense vacant stare, like what he was asking was total madness. But he explained to Ricky that he wanted it to sound genuine, and added he always thought the accent gave country vocals a unique and beautiful appeal. Ricky eventually relented and gave him a few vocal lessons. Hal had already picked up some of what he needed simply from listening to Ricky talk, but hearing him do the singing helped a lot in developing the right cadence. Ricky had said as of late he was getting 'scary good' at it, too, something Hal took as the highest form of compliment.

End Songs 315 – 320

321. "I Took a Pill in Ibiza" by Mike Posner

322. "Smooth" by Santana Ft. Rob Thomas

323. "Baba O'Riley" by The Who

324. "Jump" by Van Halen

325. "Little Lion Man" by Mumford & Sons

326. "Love Potion #9" by The Searchers

After the country portion ended, they did another set of pop songs while still wearing their country clothes. Once the pop songs were done, the stage went dark, and the overhead screens played a few more minutes of footage of them as they went back to get into their punk clothes. Hal would put on an old Ramones T-shirt, shredded jeans, and a few spiked leather cuffs to create the classic look. Uli's punk clothes were all black. And shredded. Shredded black clothes with skulls and chains and safety pins. Making Ricky look punk wasn't easy, but they finally got him another red plaid shirt that they sewed a handful of punk band patches on, and put a few tears in it. They also had jeans with the knees worn out, and cheap cowboy boots they had bought and painted to make them look like red hi-top sneakers. Ryan wore what he usually wore. Jeans; shredded. T-shirt; faded. Converse sneakers; neon green.

End Songs 321 – 326

327. "Self Esteem" by The Offspring

328. "Wild One" by Iggy Pop

329. "Ruby Soho" by Rancid

330. "Action" by Sweet

331. "Addicted" by Simple Plan

332. "Still Waiting" by Sum 41

"*Laah laa lalala lah lah lalalaaaa...*" The lights came back on after a playfully off-key intro to the first punk song of the night. It never ceased to impress Hal how fast and hard Ricky could play. The sweet wailing of the guitar rising above the voices of the crowd, and also combining with them to create an even more blood-pumping sound. After a rousing country set, the energy in the room felt like it was ready for riot music. The girls in front stripped off another layer to 'My punk shirt is smarter than your metal shirt', and there was something about that greased-lightning guitar that got heads banging. Hal had never lied when he said he was an eclectic music lover, but the only lifestyle he had ever known before he met Uli was the mainstream usual. While he had never set out to start such a varied band, it was incredible what fate had thrown at him. He got to live four different lives every other night now, and each one of them had its own appeal. And as much as the other three wouldn't admit it, he would sometimes catch them taking a liking to it in their own way as well. In an attempt to train Ricky in the ways of punk, Ryan had once told him during the punk songs to occasionally get up onto an amplifier and jump off right as he was going into a guitar solo. In response, Ricky slowly cocked his head to the side, like a confused cat, as he stared at Ryan.

"*Just do it, alright?*" Ryan had insisted.

"*Uh... okay...*" Ricky replied, obviously still lost as to the reason why. But, now as they were approaching a solo, Ricky scrambled up onto an amp, and jumped right as the solo hit. He landed and slid forward onto his knees as he shredded it out, and the audience right in front of him screamed and reached for him on the stage. Hal saw it in his eyes. If later Ricky had told him he didn't feel anything different about doing a guitar solo that way, Hal would have told him he was full of shit. Hal shifted his weight quickly back and forth between his two feet as he sang now, like he was warming up to run a race, and it felt good to scream it out. He always wanted to do a stage dive so bad during the punk segment, but unlike in their earlier days, if he did it now, the crowd probably wouldn't give him back. It was tempting anyways, though their manager had thoroughly warned them against it, so he had to keep the jumping on stage. Hal kicked his foot up high in the air over his head to the finale of the punk set, and fire shot up from the edges of the stage. It had taken him a while to perfect that high kick. The first time he tried it backstage, he knocked himself over into a pile of wires. Ryan couldn't stop laughing, and Hal told him rather angrily, "Why don't you try it then!" Ryan did try it, pulled a groin muscle, yanked a spotlight down on top of himself as he fell, and walked funny for a week after that. Hal made sure he did it at least once a show now, and each time he got his foot a little higher over his head *without* falling over.

End Songs 327 – 332

333. "This Ain't a Scene, It's an Arm's Race" by Fall Out Boy

334. "Ob-La-Di, Ob-La-Da (Life Goes On)" by The Beatles

335. "China Grove" by The Doobie Brothers

336. "Your Woman" by White Town

337. "You Shook Me All Night Long" by AC/DC

338. "Great Balls of Fire" by Jerry Lee Lewis

They did the next pop set in their punk clothes, the girls in front stripped off another layer to 'Don't stop till you get the pop!', and then the stage went dark again as they ran back to get in their metal clothes.

End Songs 333 – 338

They had permanently started doing the metal songs last every show, due to a big PR firestorm that had happened earlier that year. A group of parents had brought their children to one of the shows and complained loudly to the news afterwards about the obscenity in the metal segment when they thought the whole show would be reasonably family friendly. The whole thing turned into a big media mess, until they publicly announced from there on out they would always do the metal segment last. That way, anyone who wanted to bring kids to the show could enjoy at least 75 percent of it with them there, and then could leave early. Or, at least take them to the bathroom or merchandise stand for five or six songs before coming back for the final round of pop songs. It sort of worked out for them as well. Now, they could paint their faces up more elaborately without having to worry about hurriedly washing it off in the quick break between sets. As of late, they'd even got Ryan to agree to wear a little face paint and 'guyliner' with them.

339. "Hall of the Mountain King" by Apocalyptica

340. "Night on Bald Mountain" by Dead Rose Symphony

341. "Ace of Spades" by Motorhead

342. "Bodies (Let the Bodies Hit the Floor)" by Drowning Pool

343. "Resist & Bite" by Sabaton

344. "Last Resort" by Papa Roach

The metal segment is where things always got the most intense. It was where Uli did his transformation, and where all of them got a chance to let out some aggression under the guise that it was only for show. Uli had ultimately embraced his classical orchestra instrumental training in the metal segment, electrifying some of the old, dark, classical songs. When he was really warmed up, he could shred on his violin like Ricky could shred on the guitar. The hand with the bow would get moving so fast it would nearly turn into a blur. Tonight, the fast-paced shadow cast what looked like a frantically beating heart on the chest of one of the five girls, across the words: 'This shirt is so METAL.' Uli and Ricky had been working on a song together, a metal version of 'Night on Bald Mountain.' Since the song had no words, it would be a two-guitar duet, but Uli wanted to be part of it, so Ricky had been teaching him how to play the guitar a bit. Uli played the slower, deeper guitar part while Ricky took the fast moving, high-pitched half. Uli looked right at home playing that guitar with his long coat flowing at his sides, and Ricky had on the black studded cowboy hat and the black western shirt with the skulls and flourishes on the shoulders. He and Uli traded those two things throughout the show. Uli's country outfit was Ricky's metal outfit. The audience did often notice this and would post about it on Facebook and Twitter after every show, but Uli and Ricky didn't really care. Uli's hair was long enough now to really head bang with and swing in a circle. He got it going good tonight, while the girls raised their hands in metal horns and swung their hair along with him. Hal had been working on his metal performance, too. He'd go for the full-on possession performance, crawling around the stage like a spider and twisting and contorting on the floor during the songs he sang. Uli would still sing most of the metal songs since he did it best; but Hal got at least one per show, and he liked to ham it up. Then he'd get accused of promoting demonic worship in their songs by the media, when honestly, he just sort of had fun writhing around on the floor.

End Songs 339 – 344

Finally, drenched in sweat with their face paint running, they'd do the final pop songs of the night with the energy in the room at its peak. It became a personal motto for them that if at the end of the night they weren't sweaty

and filthy with their face paint running, and the audience didn't leave coma-
tose and exhausted, they hadn't done their job right.

The biggest change Hal had made was what he did for the grand finale
song. Inspired by the acrobats at Burning Man, he wanted to add some
acrobatics into their show. Not satisfied to have it done by back up dancers
or hired acrobats, he'd worked something out with the effects crew to create
a harness he could swing from. He wasn't afraid of heights, but he wasn't a
trained acrobat either, so he decided as long as he was firmly strapped into
a good rigging harness, he could go as far and as high above the stage as he
wanted. He'd sing the final song swinging back and forth high overhead, like
a pendulum, upside down. He wouldn't do the whole song like that because
three plus minutes upside down gave him quite the headache when he practiced it, so he decided to do it only at the final chorus. He had the vision
he'd start the swing by standing upright on a platform, then simply falling
backward as if he were going backwards off a cliff. Behind them on stage, the
screen would project a starry sky while he sang this grand finale. It wasn't
really all that fancy, but for people who came expecting a concert and not a
circus, it was a stunning addition.

345. "Never Let You Go" by Third Eye Blind

346. "Daydream Believer" by The Monkees

347. "Bad to the Bone" by George Thorogood & The Destroyers

348. "Shelter from the Storm" by Bob Dylan

349. "Got My Mind Set on You" by George Harrison

350. "Counting Stars" by OneRepublic

The first, gentle strings on the guitar started the final song, and Hal sang
the intro slowly until the beat dropped, and a burst of dancing stars exploded
on the screen behind them. He took his victory lap along the front to touch

hands before climbing up the side ladder to strap into the harness. Then, as the last chorus hit, he put his hands up and leaned backwards into a freefall. He'd sing the final moments of the song swinging overhead, his hair blowing back and forth across his face, watching Uli and Ricky and Ryan swing in and out of his view below. He put the last amount of energy he had for the night into those few seconds, projecting his voice as loudly as he could for an explosive ending. Then, with the blood fully rushed to his head, he'd be lowered down and take the final bow and wave goodbye to the crowd for the night.

> End Songs 345 – 350

It also became the ritual to have to take a long shower to wash one show away before moving on to the next. They wore themselves out so extensively with their performances now that they hardly ever went out partying anymore right after a concert. Show nights were for sleep, in-between nights were for partying, and the daytime was for welcome moments of boredom, rest, and plotting.

"So, I have an idea," Hal said the next day on the bus, doodling on his note pad.

"Oh God, not again," Ryan answered.

"We need a house," Hal said. Uli and Ricky looked up from what they were doing. "But not just any house. *The* house. A lair. The Batcave."

"We?" Ryan asked.

"Yes, we. I'm not saying we all live there all the time for the rest of our lives. I'm sure you three will all end up with your own places closer to home. But, for when we are prepping for a tour, or finishing an album, or when there are a few weeks break between shows, we need a place to stay in that's not a hotel. I know that's what my mom's house had always been for, but now that Dad is back and they have Charlotte, I think we make it a little too crowded in there."

"It was rather full at Christmas," Uli agreed.

"So, where are you thinking? New York? L.A.?" Ryan asked.

"What? No. Battle Creek," Hal said.

"You're expecting to find an amazing mansion for sale down the street from your mom?" Ryan asked doubtfully.

"No. I'm not looking to buy one. We'll have a custom one built!"

"Oh. Now we're talking," Ryan said, intrigued.

"Yes. There's plenty of vacant land for sale in the area. We'll start with a clean slate. Now, I'm taking suggestions. What should we put in it? No rules."

"A recording studio!" Ryan said excitedly.

"Well, duh!" Hal said. "That was the obvious one. Now, I mean, GET CREATIVE. Private roller coaster? Indoor waterfall?"

"The rollercoaster would be too much work," Uli said.

"A waterfall into a pool!" Ryan said.

"There we go!" Hal said, writing.

"And a large screen theater room to play video games on!" Ryan said.

"*That* was already on the list," Hal assured him.

"How about a spiral staircase leading up to a tower with a glass ceiling for stargazing?" Uli was being sarcastic, but Hal's eyes widened as he thought about it for a second, then began writing frantically. Uli looked taken aback.

"How about a slide from the second floor to the first! Because, you know, slides," Ryan said.

"I like it!" Hal laughed.

"Oh, and please have a stripper pole installed in my room," Ryan added.

"Stripper pole for Ryan to practice his stripping," Hal said aloud as he wrote.

"Oh, that reminds me… YOU BETTER STAY OFF IT," Ryan said.

"I have no idea what you're talking about," Hal answered as he continued writing.

"Oh, and a hot tub. In my room," Ryan continued.

"Hot tub. Chlorine bleach. Cans of Lysol," Hal repeated. "Ricky, you're being too quiet over there. Don't tell me you haven't thought of anything?"

"Uh, well..." Ricky started to say.

"Yes?" Hal said.

"Eh, dunno," Ricky answered.

"What?" Hal asked.

"Nothing," Ricky answered. Hal stared at him. "Never mind," Ricky insisted.

Hal stood up, walked over, and sat down on the bench seat right next to him. "YOU GOTTA SPEAK UP, RICKY, I DIDN'T HEAR YOU. WHAT DID YOU SAY!?" Hal shouted.

"Uh... what about... a... tree house?" Ricky stuttered.

"A... TREE HOUSE!?" Hal raised both eyebrows.

"Dude... I always wanted a tree house," Ryan said.

"Me too! Ricky, you're brilliant. You've done it again," Hal said, adding tree house to the list.

"Uh..." Ricky started to say.

"Shhh," Hal stopped him.

"Hell, we can make the tree house just as cool as the regular house!" Ryan said. "We could put in a bar, and a flatscreen TV, and..." Ryan suddenly caught a look at Ricky, doing his best to maintain a fake smile. "Or, uh, actually, scratch that. We need someplace quiet to unwind after a tour and, uh, get inspired. Um. It's gotta have a ladder though, no stairs. That's cheating."

"Agreed," Hal said, getting up and going back to his side of the bus. "What else does it need, Ricky?"

"Uh... dunno... just... high up."

"Why, of course," Hal said. "No pansy safe tree houses in my yard. I'll make sure when I look at property there's at least one nice, big tree."

"I knew it. Ricky enjoys being high as much as the next guy," Ryan said.

"Shhh!" Hal said in Ryan's direction. "Alright, what else?" Hal asked.

"For the tree house, or the regular house?" Ryan asked.

"Yes," Hal answered.

"That's all I have at the moment, but I'll let you know if I think of anything else," Ryan said.

"Same," Uli agreed.

"Alright, well, think fast, because I've already been looking at land listings online, and I was thinking I'd fly back home for a few days in the gap we have next week and take a look at some of them."

"Are only you going?" Ryan asked.

"Well, I wasn't going to make you guys go, but if you really want to, I'm not opposed to it."

"Oh, I'm coming with. Someone needs to make sure you don't screw this up," Ryan said.

"It would be nice to see your family again, even if it is only a day or two," Uli added. Ricky nodded in agreement as well.

And so, they all flew back to Michigan in the middle of the next week. Hal didn't tell his mom they were coming. He hadn't pulled a good prank on her in a long time, and he felt it was overdue. He was planning to have them all stay in a hotel, anyways. He had arranged with an agent to take them on an all-day land safari in the morning, but first things first. They got in a little after 3:00 p.m. and got to the house around seven o'clock. Ricky, Uli, and Ryan waited out of sight around the garage while Hal crept into the back yard, climbed the trellis up to his bedroom window, and gently jiggled the window open. He crawled inside, and barely got both feet on the ground before his bedroom door flung open. "Holy shit!" Hal said as he saw his dad in the doorway with his gun drawn. *Damn, you are a good guard dog!* Hal said quietly.

"Hal?" Harvey said, lowering his gun.

"*I was gonna surprise Mom…*" Hal whispered.

"Oh," Harvey said.

"Harv? What is it?" Cecilia called from down the hall.

"Oh, uh, it was a squirrel chewing on the window frame. I scared it off," Harvey answered as he pulled the door shut and went back downstairs.

Hal opened his closet and pulled out his old UPS uniform and put it on. He grabbed a small cardboard box, dumped its contents out of it onto his bed, and jumped back out the window. He ran around front and pulled his brown baseball cap down low over his eyes as he rang the doorbell. He heard his mom's light footsteps coming down the stairs, and then the door opened. "Good evening. Just need a signature for this," he said.

"Oh, I wasn't expecting anything…" Cecilia said.

Hal pushed the bill of his hat up. "Ma'am, no one expects the Battle Creek Inquisition."

"AAAHH! HAL!" She hugged him, and Ricky, Uli, and Ryan jumped up onto the stairs. "Oh my gosh! What's the occasion!? Not that I'm not happy to see you all."

"We came back to look at vacant land to have a house built," Hal said.

"A house!?" Cecilia said.

"Yeah! I figured it was time. It was a sort of last-minute decision, so I figured we'd surprise you."

"Well, consider me surprised," she said.

"Yeah. Dad almost shot me though, so that might be the last one for a while."

"I knew I heard that window opening!" Harvey said.

Cecilia paused, took a deep breath, let it go, then continued. "If I'd have known you were coming I would have made you something."

"Mom! It's okay. We ate at the airport," Hal said.

"Oh god, Ricky's and Uli's rooms are full of stuff now and…"

"MOM! I planned out this whole surprise thing. We're staying in a hotel. We didn't want to crowd you."

"Oh, Hal, I feel bad."

"Well, stop it. I just wanted to surprise you, that's all."

"Alright, alright," she relented.

"Okay, where's sis?" Hal asked.

"In her crib…" Cecilia headed that way, and Hal and the guys followed her. She opened the door, and Charlotte was sitting up, clutching a stuffed toy cat. Within a few moments, Ricky had a real cat on his shoulders. Charlotte looked up curious as the group moved towards her. "Hi, honey! Look! Your big brother is here again!" Cecilia said to her as she lifted her out.

"My god, what is that!?" Hal joked. "It's huge, it has hair… IT'S BROWN!" Hal exclaimed.

"Yes, it was quite the surprise! She gets that from your dad."

"Dad has grey hair," Hal said.

"It wasn't always that way." Cecilia rolled her eyes. "Charlotte! You want to let your brother hold you again?" Cecilia asked her, bouncing her gently up and down. "Let's try." She handed Charlotte to Hal.

"Hi, sis," Hal said. Charlotte's big round eyes stared at him blankly, then she began to cry. Hal sighed. "Really, sis? We've already been through this."

"Oh, once she starts talking and we can explain to her that you're her brother, then she'll think you're the coolest thing and won't leave you alone."

"We'll see," Hal said. He turned around and handed Charlotte to Ricky. "Here, take this." Hal hastily stuffed her into Ricky's arms. Charlotte immediately stopped crying, looked up at Ricky, reached one small hand up and touched his face, then let out a tiny giggle.

"Jerk," Hal mumbled.

"Now, that's not fair…" Ricky said.

"Hey, sorry, Hal, the girl's a good judge of character," Ryan said.

"Alright, we should probably head out to the hotel for the night. But tomorrow we're all going out to dinner after we're done with the real estate agent, okay?" Hal said.

"Okay," Cecilia said.

"And then we'll come back here for a bit and play with rug rat," he added.

"Alright, sounds like a plan," Cecilia said, and Hal hugged her again before they left.

"Charlotte, round two tomorrow." Hal pointed in her direction as Ricky handed her back to her mom, and then they left for the night.

"I liked that one better than the first," Hal said as they got back in the car.

"Yeah, that one was just... easier to see?" Ryan said.

"Yeah, I know what you mean. I suppose the first could be fine, but it was so overgrown it was hard to visualize it. Anything could be cleared, but it's nice to be able to already see it that way so there's no surprises," Hal said.

"Yes," Ryan agreed.

"On to number three?" Hal asked the agent.

"Yep, just let me get the directions ready," she said as she put the address into her phone. They drove about a mile and a half north before pulling into a rough gravel driveway ending in a grassy patch that went back about a hundred feet to a thick greenbelt.

"Ooh. They're getting better and better," Hal said as they got out.

"Okay, so, this one is a little shy of five acres. It doesn't look that big, but you get a lot of the woods back there," the agent said.

"We could set up a paintballing course in there!" Ryan said excitedly. "Yeah! You know what else that looks good for?" Hal asked.

"A tree house, perhaps?" Uli interjected.

"A tree house," Hal confirmed.

"Shit, you could do a whole tree house village in that," Ryan said.

"That'd be cool," Hal agreed. "And there's already a clearing for the house up front," he said as he wandered a few feet into the grass. "This might be it."

"It's a good one," the agent agreed. "Though there is one more I want to show you."

"Sure. This one is going to be hard to beat, though," Hal said.

"Hey, let's at least go explore back there for a few minutes before we move on," Ryan said, and they all followed him back to the tree line. Looking into the wooded patch they couldn't see out the other side, the trees seemed to go on forever. "Shit, this is big. This would be our own private forest," Ryan said. "Hey Ricky, how'd you like to have your own private park?" Ryan asked. Ricky smiled wide as he put his hand against one of the trees and gazed up to its highest branches. A small flock of chickadees began to gather over them. "This would be paintball city," Ryan said to Hal.

"I know, I'm in love already," Hal agreed. "But let's go see the last one, then we can decide for sure."

As they got back into the car, the agent said: "I'll be honest, I saved the best for last. I know you liked that last one a lot, but wait and see our last stop of the day," she said. "And to be clear, I didn't do this on purpose. This just happens to be the furthest one from the office." They went south again across the city, about three miles this time, then pulled into a thickly wooded lot. When they came to a stop at the end of the dirt road, the water came into view.

"Hold on a second, you didn't say there was one on the lake!" Hal said as they jumped out again. A plateau on top of a gentle slope looked out on where the land rolled down to the waterfront. On the plateau, a crumbling brick chimney covered in ivy stood precariously at the end of the remnants of a concrete foundation where an old house once had been. In front of it, a path flanked by tall trees created a shadowy tunnel leading to the shining water at the end. Lily pads grew in little clusters on the edges of the lake, and dragonflies flitted in and out of view among the cattails. Ample woods surrounded the property all around. As Hal looked around, he suddenly noticed Ricky had wandered off. He caught sight of him again down closer to the water off the main path, looking awestruck up into the towering branches of one of the biggest cedar trees Hal had ever seen. It was wide and gnarled with age, but still sporting a full, healthy canopy of green at its top. Ricky took a step closer and put his hand on it.

"You know how I said the last property would be the one?" Hal said.

"You lied?" Ryan suggested.

"I lied," Hal agreed, then turned to the agent. "Sold."

They sat down with the architectural designer, and Hal laid out their requirements. The designer listened quietly, though he had a smile that was getting wider and wider at the mention of slides, hot tubs, and glass ceiling towers.

"I think we can make this all work," the designer said after Hal handed him the list and doodles he had made. "But you should be aware, between doing the plans, waiting for all the permits to go through, and the actual construction, you're looking at at least two years, if not longer."

"Yeah, I figured," Hal said. "But it will be worth it."

"Oh, yeah. This is going to be a masterpiece once it's done. But I'm glad you already had a good idea of the wait you're in for. It makes my job easier when clients aren't chewing on my ankles waiting for the project to get finished. I'm going to make this happen as fast as I can, but that comes with the caveat of we can't control how long permitting will take, and we don't want to rush construction and risk lower quality work."

"Of course," Hal agreed.

"Well, it's a deal then," the designer said as he stood up and shook his hand. "I'll be in touch once the preliminary blueprints are drawn up, then we can make any necessary adjustments."

"Sounds good, thank you, sir," Hal said. He knew the wait was going to suck, but he also knew exactly how to take his mind off it. Boston was next, then New York, Atlanta, and then Miami. Down the East Coast before they started making their way west again, in their newest march across the country. And when they were done with the US, Canada would be next, followed by Mexico and South America. Then finally, back to Europe and the other side of the world, in their second grand march around the globe.

# CHAPTER 24

## (Working My Way Back to You)

*LOUISVILLE, KENTUCKY*

---

351. "Thunder" by Imagine Dragons

---

**Lightning flashed across the giant** screen behind them as Hal walked out onto the stage. This was one of their most popular songs at the moment. It was all over commercials, in movies and TV shows, and being played in sports stadiums as an inspirational anthem. It was completely clean, so it was a huge hit with kids as well as adults. In this particular song, a high-pitched voice sang in part of the chorus, and Hal let the kids sing that part along with him. He would hold down the microphone to any kids close enough to the stage to do the back-up vocals. He had his wireless mic that wrapped around his ear, and then he carried a traditional hand-held microphone for the kids to sing into. As the first chorus neared, he laid down on his stomach, and the seven-year-old boy directly in front of him was clearly nervous, but also thrilled to have been chosen. Hal held the microphone to him, and he began to sing: "*Thunder, thunder, thunder, thu-thu-thunder…*" As Hal sang with him, he slammed his hand down on the stage to the beat of Ryan's drums to simulate a thunderclap, and the sound echoed around them through the stadium.

Once the first chorus was done, the boy looked up at his parents, overjoyed, and they smiled wide and his father gave him a high five. Moments like that warmed Hal's heart. That boy was never going to forget that. Had he gotten to do something similar as a kid at a Holy Hell concert, he could only imagine how excited he would have been. It probably would have been the best day of his young life. Now that he was able to do something like that for the kids at their concerts, it was the best feeling in the world.

He looked around for his next young assistant, and saw a little girl in a wheelchair towards one side of the stage. Oh, yeah. This was going to be a Kodak moment. Once her parents saw he was coming their way, the mom reached down and patted her daughter's shoulders and said something to her excitedly. Her father leaned over the back of her wheelchair and said something to her as well, a huge smile on his face. The girl didn't respond to her parents, but her eyes got wider and wider as Hal approached. He crouched down and quickly realized he wasn't going to be able to hold the microphone low enough to her if he stayed up on the stage. But with the chorus upon them, he wasn't going to let this moment be ruined. He rolled on his back and slid halfway off the stage, catching his feet on an amplifier and a vertical rigging bar so he was hanging upside down.

His eyes were right on the level with hers, and he held the microphone to her, and she shut her eyes as she started to sing: "*Thunder, thunder, thunder, thu-thu-thunder…*" Her voice was stunningly perfect. It caught him off guard. She sounded so professional he almost forgot to start singing his part. The stage film crew quickly got a camera down to their level to project it on the big stage screen, and as they sang together, the audience got noticeably quieter. Once the chorus was done and she opened her eyes again, there was a wave of cheers, and at least half the stadium stood up as they applauded. Hal started singing the next verse, but before he tried to get back up on the stage, he reached an open hand out, and the girl hit it with a strong hi-five. Hal then did a sit-up and pulled himself back onto the stage. He was going to have to get her another round of applause after the song ended. But for now, he had one more kid to pick. He looked back out to the crowd, and any and all kids against the stage were going crazy at that moment; reaching and screaming, hoping to be picked. All except for two. Brother and sister, he assumed, since they were standing right next to each other. Amidst all the chaos, they were both standing there silently with their hands raised. They were at a wild concert, patiently raising their hands. It was adorable. Third helpers located. He started walking over to them, and the girl put her hands over her mouth excitedly, and the boy did a quick, little excited dance. Hal laid down on the stage and put the microphone between them, and they brought the song to a perfect ending in perfect harmony with him.

End song 351

The entire stadium rose to its feet and gave them an extended round of applause. Once it started to die down, Hal said: "I agree. That's the finest help we've had so far on the tour." The crowd clapped and screamed again. Hal walked back over to the girl in the wheelchair. He got down on his stomach again, and the camera man followed as Hal asked: "Hey, what's your name?" He held the microphone as close as he could to the girl.

"Isabella," the girl said, shyly.

"Isabella, has anyone told you that you have an amazing singing voice?" he asked, and she only giggled, seeming too nervous to answer him. "Because you're going to be a star someday." The crowd cheered and applauded.

"I can't be," the girl said quietly, and Hal looked at her confused.

"Why not?" he asked, then held the microphone back to her.

She looked away, then said quietly: "I can't stand up."

"WHAT!?" Hal said. "You don't need to stand to sing! You just sang with me a few minutes ago, and you did great! Wasn't she amazing?!" he asked the crowd and was greeted by loud applause. "You're going to be a star, you do not have to stand up to sing…" Hal repeated again as he got up, walked center stage, and then sat down. He looked behind him at the other three, and sort of waved at them to indicate they should start the next song.

---

352. "Fly" by Sugar Ray

---

He did the entire next song sitting. It was a little weird to not be able to dance around, but he put as much spirit as he could into it, gesturing with his hands and holding his arms out to the side as if he were flying. A lot of people in the audience followed suit with mimicking his movements, though while still remaining standing, which went to prove his point perfectly.

---

End Song 352

---

When the song ended, he walked over once more to Isabella. "You're going to be a star someday with that voice of yours. You do NOT have to stand up to sing! Got it?" he asked, and the crowd cheered and screamed once more as the camera caught Isabella nodding her head in response. "Good," Hal said, and then went back to continue the show. A few days later, he got word that the whole event had made the local news in Louisville, and from there, had started to go viral on the internet. A few recording studios came forward to offer Isabella a chance to record with them. He knew the studios were probably doing it for the publicity associated with the story, but he hoped they would be pleasantly surprised with her talent. Maybe the world would be hearing about her debut album in the years to come.

---

353. "Shut Up and Dance" by Walk the Moon

---

They started another popular, family-friendly song. With the upbeat energy they had going now, everyone was ready to dance. As they went into the first verse, a woman holding her small daughter felt her pants sliding down, so she put the girl down briefly to pull them back up. When she looked down again, three seconds later, her daughter was gone. She started looking around frantically, but in the tight packed crowd, she could have gone anywhere. She crouched down to look around people's feet but didn't see her from that view, either. Panicked, she looked to the side of the stage to find the nearest security guard to help her, and that's when she saw her little girl running behind the guards and up the stairs towards the stage.

Her first reaction was to run over there and grab her, but with how packed in she was with the other concert-goers, there would be no way she'd make it in time. This was obviously about to be an incident. The joys of parenthood. The question now was whether the guards would see her in time and remove her from the stage before she interrupted the song. Or would the girl be too quick for them, and was she herself going to have to climb up onto the stage to get her while apologizing like crazy to the members of her favorite band? As the girl reached the platform, her mom frantically started waving and calling to her to try and get her to come over so she could grab her. But, no, her daughter started going straight for Hal. As the little girl in her yellow sundress made it within a few feet of him, Hal caught sight of her out of the corner of his eye and looked down as she stopped right next to him. She stood there for a few moments, smiling. She saw him talking to the other kids, so she knew he wasn't scary. This was her absolute favorite song, so she'd decided she wanted to get closer. By now, security had seen her and were coming up the stairs. Hal held out his hand to signal for them to stop. Ricky, Ryan, and Uli now saw her as well, and Hal held out his pointer finger and moved it in a circle behind him to let them know to 'keep going.' This was apparently going to be kid's night. The little girl started rocking back and forth on her feet, and sort of raised her hands and started shaking like a little excited chihuahua. Hal felt a dance-off coming on. He'd never done a dance off with a toddler before. This was going to be a challenge. He started doing a quick jog in place as the verse was nearing its end, and when the chorus hit, both of them immediately started dancing and flailing wildly. The crowd went wild. It was terribly cute. The girl's mother was thoroughly embarrassed by now, but she knew this was going to be a once in a lifetime event, so she pulled out her phone and started recording. Hal and the girl did two more rounds of the dance-off at the next two choruses, then, when the song ended, Hal gave her a high-five as well. The girl's mother got her attention and waved her back over. She ran giggling into her mother's arms, and her mom grabbed her off the stage and then lipped 'sorry' to Hal. "Sorry? For what? That was awesome!" Hal said to her, then announced to the entire crowd that he believed he had been defeated.

**End Song 353**

354. "You Give Love a Bad Name" by Bon Jovi

355. "Kodachrome" by Paul Simon

356. "Runaround Sue" by Dion & The Belmonts

They did a few more pop songs without any additional interruptions before moving on to the country portion of the night.

**End Songs 354 – 356**

The big screens put on footage of them doing a particularly funny interview with a local news channel while they went backstage to change. While the interview was playing, a woman who was down in the very back of the standing-room-only section on the main floor took the opportunity to try and inch a little closer to the stage. She was about 5'2, with sandy blond hair pulled back in a short ponytail, and every inch of her skin from her face to her legs was absolutely, positively, completely covered with freckles. She'd never been to a concert like this before. She knew a lot of people would be there, but she honestly had no idea HOW MANY people there would be, and she had come ill-prepared. She wished she had a sign to hold to get his attention, but she hadn't even thought about it beforehand. She managed to get about twenty feet closer in the break before they came back out in their country clothes, and the concert continued.

"So, this has been one of the most fun nights we've had the whole tour," Hal said, and the audience cheered. "I'd say we're having too much fun, but I don't think that's possible, am I right?" Hal asked the crowd, and they screamed and whistled back. They knew exactly what was coming next.

357. "Too Much Fun" by Daryle Singletary

358. "Honey, I'm Good" by Andy Grammer

359. "Bubba Shot the Jukebox" by Mark Chestnutt

360. "The Snakes Crawl at Night" by Charley Pride

361. "Theme from Rawhide" by Blues Brother's Movie Version: John Belushi & Dan Aykroyd

Hal started singing with his convincing Southern accent, and instantly, the energy in the room changed. It moved through the arena like a wave, bringing the feeling of late summer at the state fair with it. It really was sort of magic, exactly like the people who had been to their shows before had told her. She had been enjoying a pop concert, but now, she was in the midst of an amazing country show, and everyone was clapping and singing along. She imagined people would have been square and line dancing if everyone wasn't as tightly packed, though a few were trying, regardless. And even though they were inside, she could see in her mind the golden light of sunset emanating from the stage behind them and flowing from the instruments as they played.

> End Songs 357 – 361

After the fifth country song ended, Hal took the microphone, and talked to the audience for a bit. He thanked them for being there and told a few funny stories they had acquired from touring. It flowed perfectly in the show, as everyone assumed they were taking a quick break. What was easy to miss was Uli had subtly crept off the stage. When he returned, he had acquired a few extra garnishes to his outfit, and then they began their final country song.

> 362. "The Devil Went Down to Georgia" by Charlie Daniels Band

The surprise of the night was both Uli and Ricky picked up violins for the next song. Ricky had spent time teaching Uli guitar for one song, and in return, Uli had taught Ricky violin for one song as well. Though in this case, it might have been more accurate to say Uli taught Ricky the fiddle for one song. Both of them started playing the intro together, and Hal threw the strap to a bass guitar over his shoulder and began narrating. It was a folk-style story song.

Uli had acquired a pair of brown horns jutting from his forehead, red contacts, and a pointed, blond goatee. He made a very handsome devil as he stalked across the stage towards Ricky. Ricky initially had his back to Uli, but now he turned around and looked at him, startled. Uli lip synched the words as Hal sang, and then Ricky acquired a look of fire in his eyes as he lip-synced his part back. Hal sang the whole song, but with Uli as The Devil, and Ricky as the young man with the fiddle, they duked it out with their violins on stage.

Smoke rose from the tips of Uli's fingertips as he played, and somewhere during the song, the whole show had changed again. They were still playing country music, but now a short theatrical play was happening as well. It was so enthralling, the girl in the crowd forgot to try and make any more progress forward for a few minutes. She stood there mesmerized until the song was over. Once it ended and the spell wore off, she snapped back to reality, and tried to push onward. But the people in front of her were totally unwilling to budge, and she made no progress at all during the pop songs that followed.

End Song 362

363. "Beautiful Day" by U2

364. "Rebel Yell" by Billy Idol

365. "Where Do You Go" by No Mercy

366. "Time of the Season" by The Zombies

367. "I'm Gonna Be (500 Miles)" by The Proclaimers

368. "She Drives Me Crazy" by Fine Young Cannibals

As people started jumping up and down for the second and third pop songs, she felt oddly like a kernel of popcorn in one of the big popcorn machines at the theater. One tiny person in a storm of chaos. The mass of bodies in front of her was becoming an insurmountable obstacle as she took in the sheer number of people she had to get through to get to the front. The notion that she might be able to get his attention when so many other people were trying to do the same thing started seeming stupid and naive of her. But, this was likely the only chance she was going to get, so she tried to just focus on the people right in front of her, and on making progress one person at a time.

End Songs 363 – 368

Once the pop songs ended and they took another break to change out-fits, she managed to gain a little more ground by slipping in between people as they settled down to catch their breath. She made it about fifteen feet this time before they came back out on stage to do the punk set.

"Hey, Hal…" Ryan said into his microphone.

"Yeah?" Hal answered.

"There was this girl I had a crush on when I was about thirteen. Her name was Stacy," Ryan said, and the crowd started to whistle and '*Oooooh*'.

"Oh, yeah?" Hal said.

"Yeah," Ryan answered. "But there was a problem…"

"What's that?" Hal asked.

"Her mom was hotter."

"Uh, oh," Hal said.

"Yeah," Ryan answered. "Stacy was pretty, but…"

369. "Stacy's Mom" by Fountains of Wayne

370. "Pretty Fly for a White Guy" by The Offspring

371. "All the Small Things" by Blink 182

372. "London Dungeon" by The Misfits

373. "I Fought the Law" by The Clash

374. "Dirty Little Secret" by All-American Rejects

Ryan's voice trailed off as Ricky started to play a few short riffs, and then Hal started to sing the introductory lyrics that would finish Ryan's sentence. The feeling in the room changed again. It turned from ease to eagerness. Usually those go in the other direction. A sense of building energy began to take hold. The anticipation right before a party breaks out. It built all throughout the first song, then broke free at the first guitar riff of the second song. People started moshing and shoving each other, and she found herself caught in the middle of a riot. She got shouldered by someone into the person next to her, and he shoved her forward into the back of the woman directly in front of them. She didn't sign up for *this*. She tried to hold still and steel herself to keep from being knocked to the ground, but she had never been a big person, and she was vastly outpowered by everyone around her. She changed her plan to best anticipate the next hits, and let herself be moved by them instead of trying to resist, like a small fish being pulled through a strong current in the vast, open ocean. That seemed to work a little better, and then she noticed that a few gaps would open in front of her as people were shoved side to side. She rode the tumultuous current forward a few feet per song until the punk songs had ended, and they arrived at their next pop set.

End Songs 369 – 374

375. "Handclap" by Fitz and the Tantrums

376. "California Dreamin'" by The Mamas and the Papas

377. "Drops of Jupiter (Tell Me)" by Train

378. "Pretty Little Angel Eyes" by Curtis Lee

379. "How Bizarre" by OMC

380. "(I Just) Died in Your Arms" by Cutting Crew

As she took a moment to catch her breath, she started getting the odd feeling that she might have actually been travelling through time. Perhaps attending a few moments of every concert that had occurred for the last seventy years. Now that the punk movement was suddenly over, everyone was singing together again to the newest Top 40 songs, and she was about sixty feet away from the stage now. Her destination was not so far away. She made another ten feet of progress through this less turbulent time, singing along with the people beside her, and rocking her phone back and forth in time during the slower song. She hoped with all her might she wouldn't end up messing this up. She just wanted to say hello and talk to him for a bit, but at the same time, she didn't want to distract him or interrupt the concert. That gave her a very small window during which to get his attention before he disappeared backstage, and off into the night again. The greatest challenge remained, however. The proverbial haunted woods at the end of the journey. The metal songs were next.

End Songs 375 – 380

When they went back to change into their final outfits, something she hadn't thought about was that several people who had kids with them would leave at this time. Not a huge amount, but it was enough for her to make it another ten feet. Every little bit helped. She was very close now, but due to her short stature, she was easily hidden from view by the crowd. She would really need to get right up to the stage for him to see her. The lights went dim as the mood in the room took a very dark turn. This ought to be interesting. She had never seen him like this before, and never thought she would. This wasn't his style. It was going to be intriguing to see a part of him that likely would have never manifested had it not been for joining up with a band that did everything under the sun, and then everything in the dark as well.

381. "Feel So Numb" by Rob Zombie

382. "mOBSCENE" by Marilyn Manson

383. "I Stand Alone" by Godsmack

384. "Poison" by Alice Cooper

385. "Symphony of Destruction" by Megadeth

386. "Demons Are a Girl's Best Friend" by Powerwolf

The guitar and vocals came on hard and fast, along with the fog and flashing lights. When the lights became barely bright enough to see them all, they appeared as four dark spirits hiding in the mist. This kind of music had never been her thing, but surrounded by a bunch of people who were excited by it, she started seeing little glimpses of its draw. It may have been as simple as this was the first time she was giving it a chance, but it was the other side of what she was familiar with. In a weird way, part of it was also fun and freedom, like exploring an abandoned house and finding treasure hiding in the decay. And to think, they had gotten here after starting with a motivational speech and a dance off with a toddler. This wasn't only a journey through time, this had also been an entire lifecycle. The four seasons might have been in there somewhere, too. What a wild concert. She'd liked their songs on the radio, but now she saw why people kept telling her to see them live. And he'd been one of them the entire time without her even realizing it. Apparently she had been living under a rock. A dark, heavy rock. A rock called working on her master's degree and never having a social life.

End Songs 381 – 386

387. "Californication" by Red Hot Chili Peppers

388. "Take Me Home Tonight" by Eddie Money

389. "Pop Muzik" by M

390. "Walkin' on the Sun" by Smash Mouth

391. "The Night Has a Thousand Eyes" by Bobby Vee

392. "Hanging by a Moment" by Lifehouse

As the band went into their final set of pop songs, she readied herself to make it the last forty feet. As much as it didn't sound like a difficult task, she was now faced with the final, most devoted group of fans who were likely in no mood to give up their spots. She found it to be about as tough as she feared. Trying to progress that final stretch was like trying to swim through syrup. She had the will to get to the stage, but everyone in front of her happened to be taller and stronger. The story of her life.

She tried a few different methods to get through the crowd. Attempting to gently and politely sneak between bodies wasn't working. Trying to force her way a little more powerfully between people didn't work either. Waiting for a small opening to appear between people as they danced turned out to be like waiting for the Great Pumpkin. It wasn't happening. She finally tried loudly asking a few people if they'd let her ahead of them because she had been trying to get to the front of the stage all night, and it was a dream of hers to spend a few moments right in front. A few people relented and let her ahead, though most did not. She gained about ten feet by this method. Thirty more feet to go. The minutes ticked by, and eventually, they made it to the final song. As she saw Hal climbing the ladder to get in position for the grand finale, she knew she was out of time. As much as she felt like a jerk doing this, she started shoving her way to the front of the crowd as fast and hard as she could.

The final chorus hit, and Hal fell backwards and swung across the stage, the audience cheering and singing along as a multitude of stars swirled behind him. She was probably the only one not watching him swing at that moment. She was about twenty feet from the stage. This was obviously as close as she was going to get. She shouted his name, but her voice was completely lost in the crowd. She shouted it a few more times. He wasn't looking. Of course he wasn't looking. He had more important things to focus on. She didn't want to distract him and ruin the end of the final song, but unfortunately, it was now or never.

*Come on… look up!* she thought. She filled her lungs with air and shouted his name as loud as she could. "RICKY!" She saw him suddenly jerk his head up, and he looked around, startled. RICKY!" She shouted it again, and he started frantically scanning the crowd. She jumped up and down, raising her hands in the air and shaking them around as hard as she could. *Yes! Just a little more to the right… a little further…* He was about to look right to where she was when the song ended, and suddenly the arena burst into applause and cheers. Everyone in the crowd threw their hands in the air, completely obscuring her from sight.

> End Songs 387 – 392

"LOUISVILLE, YOU GUYS ROCK! 'TIL WE MEET AGAIN, PARTY HARD AND DANCE LIKE NO ONE IS WATCHING!" Hal called out to the crowd, and a few moments later, the regular overhead lights came on. She could barely see Hal between people's heads as he started to walk backstage, and then she saw Uli give his final wave to the crowd before following him.

*No! No, no, no, no…!* she thought to herself and called out his name again as loud as she could. "RICKY!!!" She was expecting people to begin leaving so she'd be able to get a better view of the stage, but no one was moving. *Come on! The concert's over! Start leaving!* she thought, but then things suddenly got worse as a wall of people behind her started trying to crush in on the stage. *What the hell!?* The chatter exploded. From what she was hearing, she could only guess maybe they had come back out onto the stage to talk to people and do autographs? She got excited. Maybe she still had a chance! Even if Ricky had gone backstage, maybe she could convince one of the other three to go get him.

She started trying to shove her way through the crowd again more frantically than before, then, after a couple moments of chaos, something else strange started to happen. Nobody was leaving, but the crowd started getting noticeably quieter. She quit struggling and looked up, and finally got a clear view of the stage. Hal, Uli, and Ryan were standing right next to the exit to the backstage area, looking confused. Then she looked over to see Ricky still standing right at the front of the stage, staring directly at her. Their eyes met. A lot of people were looking around, trying to figure out what he was staring at, but once they realized it was her, they backed off a few feet and gave her a small space bubble. He stood there with his guitar hanging from his shoulders by the strap, and his arms hanging loose at his sides. Her hands were still half raised in the air, where they had stopped when she was still trying to keep herself from getting crushed. No one would have said the arena fell silent, but in the moments that followed, that was probably the quietest a building full of 23,000 people could have gotten. It was mostly down to whispers; 22,995 curious whispers, four people who had achieved perfect, stunned silence, and then there was Ricky, who forgot his microphone was on, so his soft-spoken voice echoed all throughout the arena: "Mm… Melody?"

# CHAPTER 25

## (Dancing in the Dark)

**Ricky had researched the area** earlier, and had already chosen the park he was going to disappear to after the show. Tonight, he didn't go alone. He grabbed Melody's hand and pulled her up on stage, then they disappeared out the back door together without another word. Him, and the neighbor girl from back home that he hadn't seen in years. After a silent dash through the night to the edge of the park, they sat back in a wooded area, out of sight.

"Jeez, Ricky, look at you. Playing in a successful band. You've done really well for yourself," she said, nervously. "And, apparently I'm totally oblivious because I've been hearing about Battle Creek for years, and I've downloaded at least twenty songs, but never took any time to look up any pictures of you guys on Google."

"Not that weird, really. Now that ah' think 'bout it, ah've no idea what a lot of the bands that've done some of mah favorite songs look like," he replied.

"But, you've prob'ly been all over TV and in the magazines, and I just haven't been payin' attention. Until I saw you on that magazine cover at the grocery store while I was waitin' to checkout a few weeks back, that is.

"Well, ah' haven't been watchin' TV or readin' magazines either. Been too busy for any of that," he said, and she sort of smiled.

"You have to tell me all about it," she said. Ricky shrugged his shoulders. "Just been travellin' everywhere and playin' the guitar."

"Oh, come on! There has to be much more to it than that," she insisted.

"Well, yeah, but, you first! What've you been up to the last few years? Ah'm assumin' you moved out from your dad's house…?" he asked.

"*Oh, yeah,*" she mumbled. "Me and Mom made a break for it one night after Dad fell asleep. That was 'bout two years after we moved. We got an apartment and I worked as a waitress while she got another job at a salon. We just sort of worked all the time for a few years until I graduated, then I managed to get a full ride scholarship for veterinary school since we were completely broke. I just completed my degree two months ago at the University of Kentucky."

"Th… that's great, Melody! That's what you always did want to do!" he said excitedly.

"Yeah, it is. Thank you," she said, shyly.

"So, where are you workin' now?" he asked.

"At the moment, I'm still in Lexington working as a waitress, but that's only temporary until I figure out where I want to move to, and apply for a permanent job at a veterinary hospital."

"Oh, okay. So… what finally made you and your mom leave?" he asked.

"Nothing in particular, you know, as far as something unusually bad happenin' or anything. She'd just finally had enough, and so did I."

"He still the manager of the dump?" Ricky asked.

"You know, he was only manager for three months before the head of the waste management division realized what an idiot he was and fired him. Dad begged and pleaded to get his job back, and eventually they hired him back on, but only as a garbage truck driver again. So, he ended up right back where he started. I didn't ask about movin' back, because I already knew what the answer would be," she said quietly.

They sat there for a while in silence after that, until he mustered up the courage to ask: "So, why didn't you ever write?"

Letters were old fashioned, but it was what they had hinged their hopes on. She couldn't have called his house since her dad would have seen the number on the phone bill. They wouldn't have gotten a moment's peace anyways since he had thirteen siblings at that time, and they knew someone would have tried to listen in on their conversations. Both of their families were too destitute to afford to buy them phones to text with, and it would have been great to talk to him over the internet, except none of the kids in the Ransom house were allowed to use the computer. Their parents needed it for records keeping and taxes, and they knew if one of the kids was allowed to use it, then the others would have screamed and cried until they were allowed to use it too. Then, one of them would have undoubtedly broken it, and Ron and Ruth wouldn't have been able to afford to replace it. And so, letters are what they decided on, but apparently, snail mail had failed them too.

"I did," she replied. "I wrote you a long letter late the first night we got there, and I put it in the mailbox that night so it'd get picked up early. But, Dad had been up late that night, too, workin' on address change paperwork, and he got up and went straight for the mailbox in the morning and found my letter in there. He saw who it was addressed to, and opened it and read it, and… I woke up to a beatin'." She said it without much emotion in her voice, but Ricky felt an old knife in his chest that hadn't moved for a long time turn again at the thought. "Left me cold on the floor for a few hours, at least," she added. "When I did wake up, he called me a whore, and garbage, and a few other things I won't repeat, and promised me a few broken bones if he ever caught me tryin' to talk to you again. And it's not like him sayin' that made me not want to talk to you, but, every time I went to write you another letter… I mean, even if I took 'em across town to the post office or a public mailbox or someplace else safe, he still might have found the ones you sent back, and I was… scared," she said quietly. "I was really depressed for those first few years. I really missed you," she added, with an embarrassed smile. "Which is why I was excited when I saw you on that magazine, because I'd thought about you here and there, and I had wanted to talk to you again, someday."

"Why didn't you write or come visit after you an' your mom moved out?" he asked.

She sighed. "I don't know. It had been two years at that point, and that doesn't sound like much, but it seemed like an eternity. And, I guess, I didn't know if you were mad at me for never writin' like I said I would, and I didn't know if you had, I dunno, moved on," she said.

"Ah' was…'fraid your dad had killed you," he said in a shaky voice. "Ah' was worried 'bout you, Mel'dy," he said, and she looked away and started to fight back a few tears. "Ricky, I really owe you an apology…"

"No, Melody, there wasn't nothin' you could have done 'bout it. You did what you had to do to stay safe," he said. She didn't look terribly convinced, and he wasn't completely convinced of what he was saying, either. But, he had promised God that if he ever got to see her again, he wouldn't get mad at her, no matter what. And here she was, so that was that.

"I'm sorry," she said.

"No, Melody…" He took her by the shoulders and turned her, so they were face to face. "You went and became a vet. You woulda had to leave home to do that anyways, and ah' woulda just held you back. And ah' wouldn't of met Hal and Uli and Ryan and started playin' in the band with 'em," he said. She stared at him stunned for a few seconds, and eventually he took his hands off her shoulders and they sat quietly again, side by side.

"Ricky…" she said quietly.

"I'm really glad you're okay," he interrupted, then asked: "So… where you thinkin' 'bout movin' to?"

"I honestly don't know yet. I wasn't sure if I wanted to find work around here or move… somewhere else," she answered. "There's so many options, because a vet can get hired literally anywhere. It's sort of overwhelming trying to decide."

Ricky glanced at her out of the corner of his eye, and wrung his hands together nervously a few times before saying: "Mrs. Lovett is still workin."

"That poor woman still hasn't retired!?" Melody asked, and Ricky shook his head. "What is she now, like, seventy-five?"

"Seventy-seven," Ricky answered. "She's wanted to retire for years now, but they couldn't ever find anyone who wanted to move into town or anywhere nearby to take her place."

"Good Lord, she was trying to retire when we were in the fifth grade!" Melody added.

"Yeah…" Ricky said, "…and she's real tired, but she feels bad because if she does retire, no one will be 'round to take care of any of the cows or horses or Mrs. Boundsguard's cats. But, if you moved back home, you could take over and everyone already knows you."

"Well, I suppose that's a thought," she said. "You still live with your parents when you're not travellin'? Or have you moved out, or…?"

"Ah' guess ah' sorta don't live anywhere right now. We're always on the road, but when we're not, 'suppose we all sorta live at Hal's house. But ah' was thinkin' since ah' got some money now, ah'd hire somebody to finish renovating the old house."

"Oh my God!" she said. "It's still standin' and everything?"

"Yep." Ricky nodded. "Oh… uh… that reminds me…" he said. "Ah', uh, have something of yours…"

"You do?" she asked, and Ricky took his raccoon hat off, flipped it over, and pulled a wadded piece of fabric out of a tear in the inside lining. He kept his eyes down on the hat as he held it ashamedly at arm's length, and it unrolled into a small pair of purple underwear with little flowers all over.

"Sorry. Ah', uh, know when, when you woke up and asked where they went, that ah' said ah' didn't know, but, ah', uh… lied…" he said, and even though it was dark, she could see his face was bright red.

"You… carried those around with you this entire time?" she asked. "Uh… yeah…" he answered slowly, then ventured a glance in her direction. She had her hand over her mouth, staring intently past the underwear at him. She reached up and took them, and held them in her lap with both hands, running her fingers across the edges. He took the opportunity to take a better look at her. She wasn't as skinny as he had remembered, but then, she was a young, semi-starving teenager the last time he saw her. She had gained a bit of weight and filled out quite nicely. She had curves now, lovely, lady-like curves, and the front of her shirt seemed a little fuller as well. If he'd had a tail right then, it would have been wagging.

"You know, Ricky, when me and Mom packed up and ran 'way from Dad in the middle of the night, I left most of my clothes and things behind. So, I'm sort of glad you held onto these for me. But, 'til I get settled again…" She reached over and took his hat out of his hands. "You've done such a good job takin' care of them, maybe you should hold onto them for me a little longer…" She stuffed them back into the lining tear, then loosely set the hat back on his head. "If that's okay with you," she said, and he nodded, reflexively. She began to notice he had lost a bit of weight since she last saw him. His shoulders had gotten wider and his arms were bigger, and she didn't see his stomach hanging over the brim of his jeans anymore. And even in the dark, she could easily make out the light green of his eyes she missed so much; glowing from the faint light of the street lamps as he looked at her. If she'd have had whiskers right then, she would have been purring. Something moving down by his hand caught her eye, and she looked down and saw a few blades of grass were growing up out of the dirt around his fingers, getting visibly taller as she watched. "You're, um, leaking forest spirit… again," she said softly.

393. "Sparks Fly" by Taylor Swift *to play over this scene* and

394. "All I Want is You" by Barry Louis Polisar *to play over this scene*

She'd spent a large amount of her childhood playing in a dump. Literally. It was where most of her toys had come from, and about half the furniture and fixtures in her parent's house. Her dad drove the garbage truck for the whole rural area, and back when she was very young, before he started drinking heavily, he would often bring her home little treasures he had found in the trash on his daily runs. Stuffed animals that just needed a good run through the washing machine, toys that their owners had simply grown out of, even her first bicycle. It was a treat she looked forward to all the time. But, once he started drinking, he quit caring as much, and the little treasures stopped showing up. Eventually, she started going to the dump on her own on the weekends to do her own treasure hunting. She also taught herself to sew by reading her grandmother's old sewing books, and any scraps of fabric she could get a hold of she would sew together in unique patchwork dresses and shirts. One of a kind pieces, as they would say. A few of the mean kids at school called her various names having to do with trash, though some of the other kids actually thought it was a really unique, cool thing she did and kind of admired her for it. They also admired her for simply being brave enough to do it, though they never told her any of this because they were kids, and they had no idea how much it would have meant to her and how much it would have helped to take the dge off of the things the bullies called her.

A while later, Ricky started joining her on the treasure hunts. They had always played together from the time they were very young, but as time passed, they became the inseparable duo known as Ricky Raccoon and the Garbage Can Girl. Dirty jokes flew behind their backs like crazy. It was something they learned to ignore. On days when the dump was proving fruitless, or when they wanted to do something else, they would go exploring in the sprawling woods together. Both of them had a love of animals, and the fact that Ricky could attract them to himself was pure magic to her. They would find a nice secluded spot, and he would get rabbits, deer, foxes, and all manner of critters to come up to them so she could see them up close. It was what ultimately made her want to become a veterinarian. Animals were so perfect and wonderful, unlike most people, and to be able to help any of them that were sick or in pain seemed like the best way she could possibly spend her life.

Ironically, it was on one of their forest expedition days that they found the greatest discarded treasure of all: a house. There were tons of abandoned homestead houses around; tons of them. Little ones, big ones, ones in bad shape, ones in better shape, and even a haunted one halfway to the train tracks. But, there was something exceptional about this one. The most ornate and fancy one around, to be sure, and left out in the woods to rot by the previous owners. The light blue paint was badly chipped, and tree debris and dirt coated the roof and the higher parts of the outside walls. A couple stray saplings made their homes in the gutters, and birds flitted in and out of a broken window over the attic. Inside, the ceiling and support beams were dull and faded but lacked any holes, and there was very little dirt or debris on the floors that had found its way in. All except one of the glass windows to the main part of the house were free of cracks. There was no graffiti, needles or beer bottles around, either, which meant they were the first ones to find it since it had last been lived in. A grand spiral staircase flowed down from the upper level and landed directly under a tarnished chandelier in the main room, like something out of a fairytale book. The entrance of this staircase had a most unique feature neither of them had ever seen in any other house. At the tip of the railing, a flower arrangement sprouted from the wood. The stems were metal, but the flowerheads were made of glass, and unscrewed to reveal small lightbulbs that once must have filled the room with color as they illuminated the bouquet. A piece of art added years after the house was built when it was first retrofitted for electricity. Because of this, they started calling it the 'Glass Flower House.'

In their younger years, the house served as the ultimate woodland fort and two-member clubhouse. But, over time, it turned into something more. Actual plans, long hours of work, and an honest attempt at a restoration to turn it back into a livable home occupied most of their weekend days. They cleaned the whole thing. Swept it out, dusted the furniture that had been left, wiped the dirty wallpaper clean, and even replaced most of the floorboards and railings on the porch to make it safe to walk on again. Their supplies came from the dump, or from spare material inside neighbor's barns that they got permission to take and use. The house had one damaged interior window upstairs in what had been the master bedroom. The radiating pattern in its center told the story of where the end of a large, broken tree branch had made impact years ago during a storm. That very branch was still leaning against the side of the house on the ground below. The web of cracks it left made for the most unique sunsets to be viewed through it. It threw the light in multiple angles and directions across the room and appeared like a glowing petroglyph on an ancient temple. Because of this, they decided to leave the window as it was.

They did their work during the day on the weekends, and then at night, they'd go up to the roof and gaze at the never-ending spread of stars overhead and talk. Just talk. They'd talk about anything and everything, happy or sad. It was where their deepest, darkest secrets were exchanged, and where Ricky first showed her a seed sprouting in his hand when he was twelve years old. They labored on the house for many years. But, in between projects, whether they were taking a short break, or for longer periods when needed materials were scarce, they worked on something different inside those walls. She had seen it on TV in the old movies and shows, and it gave her such a sense of longing and sadness. There were no more sock hops, or late nights at the drive-in. There were no malt shops, hot-rod cruising, or saddle shoes to be seen. Their generation didn't know how to dance. She would listen to her grandmother's old records, and she could feel it as she closed her eyes. She wanted to know what it was like to swing dance. She asked for the old albums on CD, and for a portable CD player to play them on, and her mother granted her wish on her next birthday. She brought the little battery-operated boom box out to the house one day and showed it proudly to Ricky.

End Songs 393 – 394

"Cool!" he said. "What CDs ya got?"

"Oh, lots! Bill Haley and the Comets, Little Richard, Jerry Lee Lewis, Elvis Presley, Buddy Holly and the Crickets, Chuck Berry, Bobby Day, Bobby Lewis *and* Bobby Darin…"

"What?" Ricky asked.

"It's all 50's and early 60's music."

"Oh," Ricky said, confused.

"It's swing music," she said excitedly. "Ricky, we should learn to dance."

He stared at her for a moment. "*Dance…?*" He said it like he had just won an all-expenses paid trip to the dentist.

"Yeah, dance! Like, real dancing," she said. "Not like our school dances where everyone stands around and don't do nothin'. We should learn to swing dance!" she said. She could tell from the look on his face it hadn't been something on his to-do list, but the old songs were so goofy and upbeat and fun, she knew she could make him fall in love with them just like she had.

---

395. "Shake, Rattle & Roll" by Bill Haley & His Comets *to play over this scene*

396. "Splish Splash" by Bobby Darin

397. "Do You Love Me?" by The Contours

398. "Tossin' & Turnin" by Bobby Lewis

399. "Jailhouse Rock" by Elvis Presley

400. "Land of 1,000 Dances" by Wilson Pickett

401. "New Orleans" by Gary U.S. Bonds

402. "Oh, Boy!" by Buddy Holly and the Crickets

403. "Rockin' Robin" by Bobby Day

404. "The Twist" by Chubby Checker

---

It was awkward at first, her holding his hands while she tried to show him how to move his feet. But luckily, the music did a lot of the teaching on its own. It was hard not to dance to it. At first, they moved carefully back and forth. After a few days of practice, they were coordinated enough to do a bit of spinning around. Then, in the months that came, they got faster, more polished, until he was able to dip her fast, and even flip her completely over his shoulder. Sometimes, they'd start on the upper floor, dance from one side of the house to the other and back again, then make their way down the big stairwell while doing their fancy footwork. They'd do wide swings through the main entryway, then move to the porch and out into the yard.

End Songs 395 – 404

405. "Earth Angel" by The Penguins *to play over this scene*

406. "Perfect (Dancing in the Dark)" by Ed Sheeran

407. "Will You Love Me Tomorrow" by The Shirelles

408. "I'd Love to Lay You Down" by Conway Twitty

She asked for more albums for Christmas and her birthdays, and a couple slow songs made their way into her collection over time. They would dance to those out under the moonlight on clear nights, parting clusters of fireflies as they moved through the field. They'd leave thin trails of trampled grass that would trace their path in zig-zags and spirals that they would admire from up on the porch after they were done. Their own down-to-earth crop circles, carved with the greatest of care.

End Songs 405 – 408

It was all coming to an end though, unbeknownst to them, the year he was sixteen and she was fourteen. She came running to him one evening. He was waiting for her in the house, and she burst through the door in tears. He opened his arms wide and caught her, thinking it was something awful her father had done, again. He was ready to hold her for a while, let her cry it out, wipe the tears away, and maybe do some slow dancing later to put a smile on her face again. He wasn't prepared for what she was going to say this time. Her father hadn't told her he applied for a position as dump manager at a different site in a different state. He only told her when he was accepted. The three words brought his entire world crashing down. *"Ricky, we're moving…"*

They did their hardest thinking over the next few weeks, trying to explore every angle, any solution, but nothing seemed to be the right answer. Every plan he came up with had gaping holes, every idea was flawed. As hard as they tried, they couldn't figure out how to stop it from happening.

409. "Forever Young" by Alphaville *to play over this scene*

On the final night before she would have to leave, they sat on the porch of the house, shattered and vacant, and watched the rising moon cast a pale blue light across the countryside. A summer breeze moved through the tall grass in waves, and the fireflies rode up and down on the light wind, looking much like the glistening sun on the ripples they made with their toes at the lake. He didn't know what he was going to do with himself once she was gone. They spent so much of their time together, they were hardly around their own families anymore. She sat with her chin resting on her knees. Tears slowly welled in her eyes, then broke and rolled down her cheeks. He reached out and put his hand on her shoulder, and she looked up at him forlorn. He couldn't stand that face. He had seen it a million times before, but this time, he couldn't make it go away. "Ricky?" she asked quietly.

"Yes?"

"You'll come and rescue me in a couple years, right?"

"Of course," he answered, and she nodded blankly. "Ah' just wish there was a way you could stay here, and just your parents could move."

"Even if there was somebody who'd let me stay with them, Dad would never allow it. I mean, you'd think he'd be happy to leave me here, because then he could go spend more of his money on whiskey and beer without havin' to pay for any of my expenses. But I think he likes having someone around to blame his being poor on. He'd still have Mom, but the more, the merrier, I suppose," she said, and his heart sank. Normally she was the one with never-ending optimism. Seeing some of the bitterness she had been fighting back all that time show itself was painful. He stared at her silently, and the anger on her face slowly faded and turned to regret. "I'm sorry Ricky... I shouldn't be talkin' like this to you."

"What? You're not talkin' like that *to* me. And ah'm here to listen..."

"It's still not nice of me."

"Hey, you've always listened to all mah stupid complainin's 'bout my family, even when they prob'ly sounded like heaven compared to yours."

"Ricky! Nothing you've ever said was stupid! You're the only person 'round here who isn't stupid! And now, I won't be able to... see you..." She started to sob quietly, and he took her gently by the shoulders and pulled her into a firm embrace.

"Ah' might not be there with you, but you know right where ah' will be," he said softly. "You write me whenever you can. Whenever somethin' bad happens, just put it all down on paper an' send it mah way. Ah'll be here waiting for it, okay?" She nodded against his shoulder, and he sighed. "Good. Because ah' don't think ah' could go two years without at least bein' able to talk to you either. And that way, ah'll know right where you are so ah' can come get you on mah' eighteenth birthday."

"Ricky, you'll be eighteen, but I'll only be sixteen. Dad could still take me back then."

"Yes, if he can find ya," he answered. "Cuz, see, ah'll come steal you while he's not lookin', and we'll get us a little apartment somewhere to live in until you turn eighteen too. Ah'll get a job to support us, and your dad won't know where you are to come ruin it." She almost smiled, and he continued. "We'll prob'ly have to hide in a bigger city to disappear for a while. But then, after two years, we'll come back here when your dad won't be able to do nothin' about it, and we'll get the house finished and not have to worry 'bout anythin' anymore."

She smiled a sad, disbelieving smile, and asked: "Promise?"

"Promise," he said, and she threw her arms around his neck and hugged him, and they sunk back against the front wall of the house and slid down until they were nearly lying flat together. He kicked his sandals off and stretched his bare feet out against the railing posts at the edge of the short deck, and she watched as a firefly came up and landed on his foot. It crawled up to the tip of his big toe, flashing brightly, and she laughed a little to herself. His animal magnetism was endlessly amusing. It was a strange talent, but whenever she saw the little birds and creatures come up to him and take crumbs from his hand, she thought she knew exactly why they did it. There was something incredibly comforting about being near him, and whatever it was she needed at the time, he always had extra to share. But that was exactly it. As much as she wanted to believe in all their planning and plotting, if she wasn't going to be able to occasionally reach out and touch him, it felt like it wasn't going to work. She buried her face into his shirt and tried not to cry again. There was so much more she wanted to say to him that she wouldn't be able to put into writing, but she didn't know if she could make it all make sense in a few hours. Two years would be a long time to hold in the words she didn't know how to speak, and the thought of it made her want to scream. As she was thinking about it more, she suddenly caught a flicker out of the corner of her eye, and looked over and saw another firefly had come up to the porch and was hovering above the railing near them. The two insects flashed in perfect time with each other, and the little bug on his foot signaled its pattern once more, and then was airborne. They did a quick spiral together, and then flew away out into the field. As she watched them go, they gradually joined into a single pulsing light, and then disappeared entirely in the distance.

"Ricky…" she said in a low whisper.

"Hmm?"

She pushed herself up a little, so she was looking at him, and her head blocked out the moonlight from his face. He could barely make out her features backlit against the night sky, but her messy blond hair caught the light, and glowed in a brilliant halo around her head. "You're pretty…" he said quietly, and she raised one eyebrow at him and shook her head.

"Uh, huh!" he answered.

"Ricky…"

"Yeah?"

"I love you."

He stared at her for a moment, then felt his heart hit an extra beat when he realized what she said. He shouldn't have been surprised. It was something he could have figured out from all the time they spent together, or at least from the first time they had kissed almost six months ago. But, she'd never said it straight like that before. Even worse, he realized he'd never told it to her either. She watched him in tense anticipation, and his mind went blank. She was beautiful, and she made him happy, and he never wanted to be apart from her for a whole day, let alone two years, but he wasn't sure how to tell it all to her, so he inhaled a quick breath and said the only thing that came to him: "Mm… Melody, I LOVE YOU TOO!" He sat up quickly and slammed his forehead into the windowsill above them, then fell back down to the deck with his head in his hands.

"Ricky! Are you okay!?"

"Ricky… is… fine…" he managed to stammer out as he slowly sat back up. He saw her put her hand over her mouth to try and stifle a laugh, and he felt his face go red. "Uh… sorry, ah' got excited…" he said, and she leaned in closer to him until their noses were almost touching. Her amber-brown eyes were barely in focus in front of him, and he stared at her cross-eyed and grinned sheepishly. "Um… made you smile…"

"Yeah, you're good at that," she answered, and he shut his eyes as her lips pressed up against his. She'd always had a subtle taste to her he couldn't liken to any food he had ever eaten. It was sweet, but not like sugar. More like cold water on a summer's day, or warm milk on a winter's night. Kissing her left traces of it at the corners of his mouth, but he'd always wondered what it would be like to get more of it on his tongue. He felt himself blush again at the thought, but he had little time left to find out, and he knew if he didn't, wondering about it was going to torment him for the next two years. He opened his mouth slightly and held his breath while he ran the tip of his tongue gently across her bottom lip. She pulled away suddenly and stared at him, and his chest tightened.

"Ah'… AH'M SORRY…"

"No, no… it's okay…"

"Ah'm sorry."

"Don't be…" she said firmly and glanced down at her knees.

"But you…"

"It's okay. You just… I wasn't expecting that," she said as she brushed a little bit of hair out of her face, then looked back up at him. She had a new expression in her eyes he had never seen before. He couldn't quite place it, but whatever it was, it made him believe that she really wasn't mad at him. She leaned in and kissed him again, and then the tip of her tongue brushed lightly over his bottom lip. He felt a rush of excitement, and he pulled one knee up to his chest in between them. She'd always given him a little thrill when they were together, but that one was much stronger than usual. The tips of their tongues accidentally met on the next pass, causing both of them to jump at the same time, but then giggle it off together a few moments later. They took it easy for a little bit after that, kissing more carefully with their mouths closed, but ultimately those kisses became longer and more daring on their own as the minutes passed, until she finally put an end to their game by slipping her tongue slowly into his mouth.

"*Mmmm.*" he sighed as he wrapped his arms around her and pulled her in closer, their tongues beginning to wrap over and around together in slow circles. They sat there making out for what felt like only a few minutes, but it had apparently been a few hours as a little beep sounded out, and Ricky stopped and glanced down at his watch. The misery in his voice was undeniable when he spoke. "Mel'dy, it's midnight…"

"That's nice," she said.

"Your parents are gonna be mad."

"Ricky, Dad's been stressed from packing. When he's stressed, he drinks even more. He'll probably be passed out 'til noon, and I'm sure Mom is higher 'an a kite right now on her pills."

"What if he isn't? What if he's out lookin' for you, getting madder by the second?"

"I don't care," she said. "He can beat me as hard as he wants, I wanna spend as long as I can out here with you."

"Mel'dy! Ah' ain't worth no beatin'!" he said, sternly, then added in a gentler tone, "We should get you home." She knew he might have been right, but it didn't matter right now. She wasn't going to get another chance to commiserate with him, and she wasn't going back to her house until she absolutely had to. "You're prob'ly right…" she mumbled, looking out across the meadow. "But you're gonna have to catch me first."

"Wha…"

With that, she jumped up and leapt off the porch, and took off racing into the tall grass. "HEY!" He sat up with a jolt, and then rushed towards the stairs. His tracks hit the dusty ground a foot further than hers, and he tore across the field after her. His feet had such brief contact with the earth it was like he was nearly flying, and the grass slashed his legs as he ran, but the little cuts went unnoticed as he gained on her. He reached out and caught the back of her dress, and she lost her footing as he pulled her backwards. He ran into

her and tripped over her, and they hit the ground in a tangled heap. "Ah'…
AH'M SORRY…" he tried to say, but she sat up laughing, and draped her
arms around his neck and hugged him.

---

End Song 409

---

Any or all:

410. "Night Moves" by Bob Seger

411. "Because the Night" by 10,000 Maniacs

412. "Let Her Go" by Passenger

413. "Twilight Time" by The Platters

414. "Hold Me, Thrill Me, Kiss Me" by Mel Carter

415. "Kiss Me" by Sixpence None the Richer

416. "Can't Help Falling in Love" by Elvis Presley

417. "I'm on Fire" by Bruce Springsteen

418. "Unchained Melody" by The Righteous Brothers

419. "I'm Not the Only One" by Sam Smith

420. "Blueberry Hill" by Fats Domino

421. "Save Tonight" by Eagle-Eye Cherry

422. "Airplanes" by B.O.B. ft. Hayley Williams

423. "Can't Fight the Moonlight" by LeAnn Rimes

424. "I Just Called to Say I Love You" by Stevie Wonder

425. "Cupid" by Sam Cooke

426. "If You Leave Me Now" by Chicago

427. "Nights in White Satin" by The Moody Blues
    (*To play over this scene*)

She pulled him down so they were lying side by side in the tall grass, and they kissed completely still for what felt like a long, long time. The golden stalks danced and swayed around them, and they didn't look so tall when they were standing, but at the roots, became a towering cover of shadows overhead. Hidden beneath it, a realization began to creep over him. There was no way he'd be able to let her go in the morning. No matter how hard he messed things up, she was never mad, and they'd laugh it off together. It wouldn't be the same trying to laugh at himself alone. He had nothing else he looked forward to in his life besides seeing her, and he wasn't going to lose his one source of happiness. He made the decision right then, maybe the first decision ever on his own, the first of his adulthood, or the first of his own solid will, but he wasn't going to allow her dad to take her away the next day. He didn't know how he was going to make it work, but he'd come up with a plan by morning, and he wasn't going to take no for an answer. He just wouldn't allow it to happen. Once he decided that, he felt amazingly better, like he actually had some control over his own fate. It gave him a huge sense of relief, but the longer she held her lips to his, the more restless he became. He broke the kiss for a second as their noses brushed together, then they went straight into another one. That next kiss lasted a little less time, as did the next, and the next. He didn't notice until she was already finished that she had apparently been unbuttoning his shirt. It was when he first felt her hands on his bare skin that his hands reflexively snapped up and grabbed her by her wrists. It made her jump a little, but then everything went still. He wasn't even looking at her. Rather, staring past her, over her head, off into the night. Her heart was racing, but she shut her eyes to compose herself, then slowly pulled her hands free, and he let them go without a fight. She reached out and ran them down his chest, and the muscles in his torso and stomach tightened and contracted as she went, like they were trying to escape her touch. He suddenly grabbed her hands again. "*MELODY!?*" He was staring straight into her eyes this time; searching them for answers to a question that he didn't have the guts to ask. She looked just about as frightened and confused as he was, and in that moment he'd never felt closer to anyone in his whole life. They could even be scared together, and it was okay. He saw a flash of conviction in her eyes as she pulled her hands free again, and started sliding his shirt down from his shoulders. He sat up long enough for her to pull it down his arms and off onto the ground behind him. He crossed his arms in front of him, apparently feeling a passing chill in the thick evening heat, and then glanced at her nervously like he was waiting for her disapproval. She didn't mean to stare, but she couldn't help it. He had those nice broad shoulders that gave him a firm stance, and that irresistible collection of uneven tan lines where many days of work faded to pale under his sleeves. She knew he'd probably never believe her if she told him how much she loved those little lines.

They laid back down, and she snuggled up close to him and started rubbing her hands down his sides and over his back. The feeling of her fingers on his body did all kinds of conflicting things to him. It made him horribly nervous, but at the same time, it felt good. It felt really good. Really, really good. He put one hand on her cheek, holding her face tenderly for a long moment before trailing the backs of his fingers thoughtfully across her shoulder, then running his palm down her side to her hip. Even though she didn't say a thing, he could tell from the way her body responded under his hands that she didn't want him to stop, either. He started to slide his hand back up again to hold her at her ribs; higher than he normally would have touched her for a prolonged period of time. The uncertainty in his brain was nagging him to move it back down to her waist where it belonged, but instead he let it creep a little higher, one tiny movement at a time, until it was nearly at the point where he truly wasn't going to dare go any further. But, right as he was about to stop, she drew in a jagged breath and let her head rest back against the ground, and her eyes closed in tense anticipation. It caught him off guard, and instead of stopping, he let his hand brush lightly up onto the front of her dress. "Ah…", she made the tiniest, most satisfied noise, and it sent a bolt of electricity through him. On a normal day he would have died from embarrassment, but because of that little sigh, he decided he might let himself live through it. She put her hands on the back of his head and pulled him into another kiss, and lips began to seal and unseal faster and faster between quick, needed breaths. Being able to breathe at all soon became a coordinated effort. Inhale, kiss, exhale. Inhale, kiss, exhale. Coming closer together on the inhale, and then pulling back on the exhale. Closer on the kiss, then back again. But, unlike dancing, the more they kissed, the more the both of them seemed to be losing their coordination. Mouths ended up partially on cheeks and tongues on chins, despite their best efforts, and after a few moments, she broke from his mouth entirely to start working her way down his neck. She could taste the salty residue forming on his skin. He was sweating hard, and she drew in a deep breath and sighed it back out. Working on the house all day was always quite the exercise, and when he got hot, he would start to smell like barbeque smoke and spice. It was one of the stranger attractions she had to him. That, and the little trail of hair that ran from his stomach down into his shorts. She reached down and started playing with it; massaging her fingertips into his stomach and feeling his heart beat faster and faster as she gradually made her way toward the top of his pants. Just as her fingers were about to go under the brim, he grabbed her by her shoulders and rolled her onto her back; rolling himself up on top of her in the process. As his weight came to rest on her, it lit up an intense warmth in her that seethed out below her waist and above her knees, and she curled her toes in delight as they started to kiss even more frantically.

He immediately regretted his decisions. He shut his eyes tight as he tried to maintain control of himself. He really, really shouldn't have done that. Straddling her body was a rush harder than any he had ever experienced, and all he wanted to do was press himself to her even more firmly. He could feel every one of her little movements underneath him, and it was driving him insane. He caught himself reacting to her without even thinking about it, like he was becoming only an observer in his own body, and it was genuinely starting to freak him out. He stopped kissing her, and looked gently in her eyes as he whispered: *"Ss… sorry…"* He started to get up, but suddenly felt himself trapped with her arms around his back.

*"Hey, where you goin'?"* she asked quietly.

*"Melody… I… we can't do this…"* he stuttered.

*"Why not?"* she asked quietly, a little tremble in her voice.

*"Because… we… we ain't married…"* he said in a forced breath. A thinly veiled excuse for nervousness.

*"But we will be someday, right?"* she asked it so frankly, he was stunned. Just like that, with no hesitation at all, she had said those words. He had to run the sentence a few times through his head to try and accept it even happened, then gave her the only answer he could fathom: *"Well… yeah."*

*"I think that means it'll be okay,"* she said.

*"Mm… Melody…"* he whispered, and she reached up and took his hat off and set it on the ground next to them, and the night air that followed behind her fingers felt good in his hair and down his back. A little twinge of euphoria bit at him as what she said started to sink in. Lord knows he'd run this scenario through his head many times before. Nightly, to be honest. But apparently all of that counted for nothing because he was nearly paralyzed at the thought that it was really happening. She pulled him gently back down into another kiss, and he felt her fingers heading down his stomach again. He had already been dangerously close to the verge of losing all of his dignity, and she didn't even get her hands all the way in his pants before it pushed him over the edge. He broke away from her mouth with a gasp and then pressed his face into her neck, and she felt the little nervous lines form in his brow as every muscle in his body tensed up at once. The hot draws of his breath were rolling in and out of the neck of her dress, and the blood was pumping so strongly through her veins that it made the stars above pulse in time to her own heartbeat. She watched them for a few moments as he trembled in her arms, until he finally relaxed again with a long sigh.

He kept his face buried in her neck after it was over. His face felt red hot. He had no idea what he was going to say to her. He couldn't even generate a single coherent thought at all in that moment. He shamefully raised his head to look at her, and he found her staring back at him intently, biting her lip. She looked at him. He looked at her. Neither one of them blinked. "*I... I, uh...*" Ricky started to say, and he saw her lips part a little in preparation for her response, but then her thighs suddenly squeezed together tight, driven by some involuntary reflex judging by the little shudder that ran through her. She shut her eyes as a few more shudders followed in it's wake, and he watched her in frozen, terrified engrossment until she was left gently panting. She looked so vulnerable and fragile and embarassed. He felt bad for thinking it, but that look on her face really did something to him. "*Oh Lord...*" He said it in such a tone that he sounded like he had just witnessed something to be truly ashamed of, but as he kissed her again, he was so overtaken with a feeling of contentment that there couldn't possibly been any thing objectionable going on between them. "*Mmmm... mm...*" She whimpered gently between breaths, and pulled her legs out from underneath him so he was resting between them, then she intertwined them with his and wrapped her arms around his back tightly so her whole body was basically clinging to his. It apparently counted for nothing that she had just gotten him off, because that put him right back on the edge of the cliff. There was no way he'd be able to keep fighting to suppress it, and he tried to discreetly undo his belt buckle and unzip his fly with one hand, but he apparently wasn't being as subtle as he thought, as he felt one of her hands immediately seize the opportunity to slide all the way in. "*Aaahh...* " A sigh escaped him before he even knew what was happening, and his eyes rolled back into his head as he felt a warm surge shoot through him. Her hands touching him was such an incredible relief, and he could barely get his hand between her legs fast enough to return the favor.

The moon rose higher from the horizon as it followed its path across the sky over them, causing the shadows of the trees to rotate around their trunks like a nocturnal sundial. It was only about an hour or two before the sun would be coming up that the final, stubborn remains of apprehension vanished between them, and he hooked his fingers around the edge of her underwear, and tugged them somewhat hastily down her legs, over her knees, and off the ends of her feet. She drew her knees up to her chest and held them there with her fingers interlaced, and the way she was resting, he could almost see up her dress. Almost, but not quite. He kneeled in front of her for a few moments and watched in the terrified hope that she might slip up and give him the pleasure, then she started to giggle, and he realized he was holding her underwear in the air like a prize fish he had caught. He blushed a little as he set them down inside his hat, then felt a hot chill go down his spine as he lay gently back down on her. She gave him the most sincere, longing stare as he tugged down the front of his shorts, and he whispered a quick prayer in the hopes she'd give him some clues before he made and idiot of himself. But, before he could even finish the thought, he felt her body rise up to meet his, and he nearly choked as he grabbed a fistful of her dress and started to push back against her.

They struggled for a few moments, or rather, he struggled. Trying to fig-ure out what position to get into, how to hold her just right, working himself into a panic until he felt her grip tighten on his shoulder, and then the fear melted under the feeling of her smooth body slowly coming over him. He instantly felt lightheaded. He had caught glimpses of the sensation before, alone with only the image of her as his company, but it was different now that she was real in his grasp and not made of air. Her curves fit perfectly to his, like they had both been formed to be in this way with each other from the beginning, and he let one hand wander over them. Taking in her shape without his eyes, and holding her head and neck carefully in his other hand as he dared to start giving her a few gentle thrusts. He did it without thinking, moving in whatever way he thought was right, but despite never having had any practice, whatever he was doing was working. She trembled and sighed with every motion, and as he listened to her, the world around them started to fade off. It's not that it was disappearing, he just couldn't see it anymore. And it's not that they had moved from the spot they were lying on, but they were someplace different now. Someplace where they could be alone, and no one else could follow to bother them. He dug his toes into the ground as he braced himself against her, and then let back before doing it again; her legs relaxing down to the side as they fell into a gentle rhythm. A gentle rhythm the two of them improvised together on that last night they went down to the outskirts of town to go dancing in the dark.

End Songs 410 – 427

He didn't remember falling asleep, only waking up the next morning with the sick feeling of knowing what the coming day would bring. They laid there together for a while. A couple hours passed. They hoped that maybe if they stayed there long enough, her family would just leave without her. But eventually, they started hearing a car horn off in the distance, breaking the silence of the vast woods. Ricky held her tighter and she started to cry. It mocked them more, and they finally got up and began a long, solemn trudge back towards her house.

428. "Goodbye Stranger" by Supertramp *to play over this scene*

When the truck came into view, he held her again behind a tree and kissed her. He was ready to fight with her father to keep her, but the confidence he had felt last night in winning was fading fast.

"Ah'll come find you. Ah'll bring you back," he whispered.

"You can't…" she whimpered.

"When ah'm eighteen I'll be able to."

"That's two years."

"Better than waiting for you to be able to come home in four."

"Ricky… you promise? You promise you won't forget…?" she asked.

He reached down to the ground and drew a little red wildflower up out of the dry dirt. He picked it and handed it to her, saying: "Never. Ah'll be there at your doorstep on mah eighteenth birthday."

"GODAMMIT, WHERE IS SHE…" Mr. Gibson's gravelly voice was full of rage.

"Dad's going to beat me…" she said, fearfully.

"Ah'll make sure he doesn't," he said and kissed her again. They emerged from behind the tree to her father's fiery glare.

"WHERE IN THE HELL HAVE YOU…" he shouted as he stalked towards them.

"It was mah fault. Ah' kept her from gettin' down here," Ricky interrupted him.

"Nobody asked you, boy," the man said as he grabbed Melody by the arm and yanked her towards him.

"I THOUGHT I TOLD YOU…"

"AH' SAID IT WAS MAH FAULT!" Ricky bellowed as he punched Mr. Gibson in the chest.

"YOU LITTLE SHIT!" Stanley Gibson yelled, grabbing Ricky by the shirt and slamming his fist into his stomach. Ricky bent in reflexively over the blow, but managed to kick him in the knee in response. Mr. Gibson let go of him for a few moments as he staggered backwards, and Ricky steadied himself, then lunged at him. In a split second, Ricky was stopped again by Mr. Gibson's fist in his left eye socket. Ricky hit the ground hard from the force of it. He rolled onto his stomach and started to push himself back up, but then felt the smashing force of Mr. Gibson's boot heel hit the center of his back. The whiplash effect of the hit sent Ricky's face slamming into the dry dirt, and then Stanley kicked him hard in his side. Ricky struggled to find the footing to propel himself away from the next kick, but each impact made his attempts at escape more and more difficult.

"DAD! NO! STOP!" Melody yelled. Her father dealt Ricky one final, crushing kick, then turned back towards her.

"GET IN THE TRUCK RIGHT NOW!" he yelled as he pulled his keys out of his pocket.

"RICKY!" She started to run towards him, but her father caught her with one arm and literally threw her into the back seat of the cab and slammed the door. The old engine chugged as it started, and Ricky felt every hair on his head standing on end with rage, but the pain kept him on the ground as the truck backed up, then started down the long dirt driveway.

As he turned to watch it go, the ground below him began to shake, and a crack in the earth began to open in front of him. It widened as it shot forwards in the direction of the vehicle, like a bolt of lightning ripping through the ground. Ricky had to force himself to stop it before it reached the back wheels of the truck. What was he planning to do? Take the whole truck down with Melody and her terrified mother inside? As the truck gained more distance down the road, Melody leaned out the back window and yelled at him: "I'M SORRY, RICKY!"

He struggled to sit up, but the pain in his side shot through him like a bullet, and he could only lay on his stomach and watch her get smaller in the distance. "TWO YEARS! AH'LL SEE YOU IN TWO YEARS!" he yelled back, and the truck disappeared around a grove of trees at the edge of the main road, and the engine faded into the distance.

> End Song 428

He let his head fall back down in the dusty gravel, and he shut his eyes. There went his plan to rescue her. All that willpower he felt the night before, and it was all a delusion. There went all his future plans. There went the rest of his life. And to top it all off, he might have a cracked rib. He laid there on the ground for at least a few hours, finding no will to get up. The tears running down his face eventually formed tiny mud puddles on the ground to either side of his head, and he decided maybe he wouldn't get up for the next two years. That was the plan he decided on at the moment, and he knew he'd follow through with it the same way he followed through with his plan to keep her with him.

In the days that followed, he was the first to the mailbox right after school, only to find every day was a disappointment. Disappointing days turned into frustrating weeks, and frustrating weeks into terrified months. Where were her letters? He'd go up to the house on the weekends just to get away from everyone else, and stew in his fear and misery alone. The pain in his side slowly faded, but the alarm in his head only got worse. It had been too long. They had to have been in their new place now, and she should have been able to get her hands on some paper and envelopes. He worked every possibility he could to explain it away, but the only answer that worked at this point was that something horrible had happened. He didn't want to believe it, because she was smart and resilient But then, where were the letters? All roads kept leading in circles back to the worst possible answer.

He spent many weekends in the house trying to come to terms with it. Something bad happened to her, and he failed to stop it like he promised himself he would. Over time, all the fear and panic slowly melted into a long, sluggish depression. His father noticed it, even through all the daily chaos in their house, and did his best to try and comfort him, but had no means of lessening it. Ricky began spending all his time outside of school helping his dad out in the fields. Anything to pass the time that was his life. Then, at night, he'd struggle to fall asleep, haunted by her fate, which he didn't even get to know. She would visit him most nights in his dreams, only for him to wake up again and find her gone. Sometimes he would go out into the woods at night just to walk aimlessly. If he wasn't going to sleep, he might as well do something. His dad suggested he try to find a hobby to take up; something to try to take his mind off it all. He tried to make himself go back out to the house and work on it alone, so he could show her how much work he'd gotten done once she came back, but most days it was too painful to think about.

He got back from the house late one Saturday night, after having just sat there for a few hours, and found his dad in the corner of the living room, strumming his guitar. That guitar had been in the house since he could remember, but it'd never been anything other than an abused plaything for his siblings. He'd never actually seen or heard it played before. He stood back by the door and listened for a while, until Ruth called down to Ron from upstairs to help her with one of the babies, and he set it down and headed up to meet her. Ricky went over and picked it up, then went back out the door. He sat in the woods for a few hours that night, messing around with it. His dad had tuned it, probably for the first time since he had begun having children, and it sounded nice. He picked at the various strings with his fingers, while holding them down with his other hand in random places along the neck. It was all the more he knew about how guitars worked. He moved his fingers to another position along the neck, but this time when he strummed the six strings, the sound it made was like nothing else he had ever heard. It didn't make sense because it was only noise, yet somehow, that combination he found sounded like how he had been feeling. It sounded sad. He kept his fingers where they were, memorized their position so he could recreate this sound again, and strummed it a few more times. It was mesmerizing. No one knew how lifeless he felt, except for this inanimate object. The inanimate object he gave life to. He found a few more combinations as he played with it, a few other different varieties of sad. He tried putting them together. He made a little song out of it. He heard it in his head as he fell asleep that night.

The next day after school, he went straight for the guitar and took off into the woods with it again. He sat on the stairwell of the house as he played it. It kept him entertained for a few weeks, though ultimately, he could only take it so far himself. He wanted to learn to play it properly. He knew his dad would be more than happy to teach him, if only he could find the time. His mom just had another baby, and they were in that difficult stretch again where the baby was waking up every two hours needing to be fed. He thought about it for a little bit, and then it struck him. The mysterious man who lived in the woods that he and Melody had observed from a distance, playing his guitar. They'd never spoken to him, but he seemed to be alone. He probably had a lot more free time than his dad did. He could ask him for lessons.

Ricky carried the guitar over his shoulder by its neck like a fishing rod as he made his way into the deeper part of the woods, and finally found the little log cabin. Nobody was out on the porch, but a thin trail of smoke rose up from the chimney. Ricky made his way down the hill, to the front steps. He stepped onto the porch, and nervously reached up and knocked four times on the wood plank door. A few moments later, the door swung wide open, and the owner stood on the inside, looking down at Ricky, confused. "Who the hell are you!?"

"Uh, hi, sir. Mah name is Ricky, and, uh, you know how to play the guitar and Ricky was wonderin' if you'd teach him?"

The man squinted at him for a second, trying to figure out if he was serious, then said 'NO!' and slammed the door in his face. Ricky stood there for a second, then knocked on the door again.

"*Go away!*" he heard from inside.

Ricky turned around and left, but came back to try again the next day. He knocked four times on the door. The door swung open.

"Uh, hi sir. Mah name's Ricky, and, Ricky was wondering if you could teach him how to play the guitar?"

The man leaned down to him. "Go. Away," he said sternly, then slammed the door.

Ricky left, then came back the next day. He knocked four times on the door. "*Guitar lessons are cancelled today! So... go away!*" Ricky heard from inside the house.

He walked away, disappointed, then came back again the next day, and knocked four times on the door. The door opened. "No, wait, let me guess…" the man said. "Yo' name's Ricky, and you want guitar lessons?" Ricky smiled and nodded eagerly. "Fine!" The man threw his hands in the air in defeat. "Siddown!" He pointed to a crate being used as a bench on the front porch.

Ricky sat. The man disappeared into the house, and angrily grabbed his guitar. He grabbed a pencil off a desk and started going through the drawers looking for scrap paper, then heard a slow, sad melody coming from out on the deck. He walked over to the door and peered around the frame enough to take a look without being noticed. Ricky was watching his own hands intently as he strummed the tune, enamored by it. It gave him pause. The way the boy was looking at that instrument reminded him of something he once felt, a long time ago. Ricky was so focused, he didn't notice as he came back out with his own guitar and was standing next to him.

"Oh, hi…!" Ricky said, startled, when he finally noticed him.

"What you strummin' that melody for?" the man asked him coldly.

"Uh… it makes Ricky feel better," Ricky said, quietly.

"Makes you feel better!? You're what, thirteen? What the hell you have to be so sad about? Someone call you a bad name at school!?"

"Ricky is sixteen…" Ricky said quietly. "And…"

"And?"

"The girl Ricky had always hung out with had to move away," he said.

The man resisted rolling his eyes as he sat down and started tuning his guitar. "Love of your life, huh? How long you known her for?" he asked.

"Well, since Ricky can remember. Since we were babies. Act'ally, no, wait. She was two years younger than Ricky, and Ricky wouldn't have remembered anything from when he was a little baby, so, uh, guess since she was two and Ricky was four? So, twelve years, 'spose?" Ricky answered. He looked over, and the man was looking at him, taking a quick break from tuning his guitar. "Twelve years?" he repeated back to him, a little more gently.

"Yeah, she was Ricky's only friend," Ricky mumbled. The man went back to tuning his guitar. "What's your name?" Ricky asked. He quit tuning his guitar again and looked up. "It's… John. John Benjamin Goode," he said.

"Ricky." Ricky held his hand out. "Ricky Raccoon." John shook it.

"Your last name is Raccoon?"

"No. It's Ransom."

"So… that's your nickname?" John asked.

"Yeah," Ricky said.

"I see," John said, examining his hat, then he sighed. "Well, Ricky, let's start at the beginning. You know what letter note each string is?"

"No," Ricky said.

"Alright, from the fattest string to the thinnest, you got E A D G B E," he said. "The easiest way to memorize that is make it into a sentence. The one my daddy taught me was Every Amateur Does Get Better Eventually."

"Every amateur does get better eventually," Ricky repeated.

"Yes, now let's start with a basic blues progression…" John said.

Ricky stayed at the cabin and practiced until after the sun went down that evening, until he realized he really should head home for dinner. "Thank you, John. Ricky really appreciates it. Can Ricky come back tomorrow for more lessons?"

"Sure…" John said reluctantly as he waved goodbye from his porch, and watched Ricky disappear back into the woods. "*Fool boy talks about himself in the third person…*" John mumbled to himself as he turned to go back inside.

Ricky came back regularly for lessons after that, and, as John had said, every amateur does get better eventually. Ricky made fast progress, and after a few months, they were past the basics, and John was teaching him full songs.

When John sang, the pain in his voice was vivid. He never shed a tear that Ricky saw, but he could sing himself raw. The pain of his wife leaving him, and his daughter telling him she never wanted to see him again as she too went out the door years later. Things he told Ricky about as the months went by. Ricky ultimately told John his full story as well, and it came to pass many times over that two guitars and two voices would carry out over the swamp instead of one. Casting out the blues again and again, in hopes they wouldn't come back. They always did, but singing it out, even if it was only temporary, kept the sadness moving, so it didn't sit in one place chewing a hole in them. They'd tap their feet slowly to the rhythm, in lieu of drums, and to remind themselves their hearts were still beating despite everything that had happened in the past.

End Songs 429 – 433

434. "I'm So Lonesome I Could Cry" by Hank Williams

435. "Dream Walkin'" by Toby Keith

After a while, Ricky started writing a few of his own songs, with a little help from John, though he wasn't very confident in his singing at first. "I can barely hear you boy, you gotta speak up." John didn't often interrupt him when he was playing, so it was doubly jarring when he did.

"Guess Ricky would maybe rather just play," Ricky answered.

"No, no, you can't be that way. Singin' and playin' go hand in hand. They can hold their own alone, but they're better with each other," John said.

"Ricky doesn't have much of a voice," Ricky mumbled.

"Oh, bullshit. You got a voice, I can tell. You just gotta use it. It won't get stronger unless you're willing to exercise it. Now there ain't nobody out here to make fun of you besides the deer and bullfrogs, and I can guarantee you, they don't give a damn. They ain't made fun of me the entire time I've been out here. Now, let's hear it," he insisted. Ricky started strumming again, and he tried to be louder. At first that was all he sounded like to himself: the same, except louder.

"Alright, that was better. You were louder. Now, quit thinkin' 'bout your voice and start thinkin' 'bout singin'," John said. "It's like playin' the guitar. After a while you gotta stop focusing as much on where and when you're moving your fingers and just let it happen," he said. Ricky looked down at his feet and thought about that for a second. "Alright, now give it a go."

> End Songs 434 – 435

> 436. "Neon Moon" by Brooks & Dunn

He started strumming again and shut his eyes to try and focus on his singing. This time, instead of talking loudly with drawn out words, he could hear his own accent coming out now, garnishing the words, and turning them into lyrics instead of just words. That's how it sounded in his head, at least. For all he knew, maybe he still didn't sound any better. But when he finished that song and looked up again, John was smiling as wide as could be. "You see that? Or, I suppose, I should say did you *hear* that? Did you *feel* it?" he asked. Ricky nodded a little. "You keep that up, you might hear yourself on the radio someday," he said.

"Nah, that's not gonna happen," Ricky said.

"Now, you gotta quit cuttin' yo'self down like that. After all, you never know," John said.

> End Song 436

> 437. "Juke Box Hero" by Foreigner *to play over this scene*

Though he wasn't quite sold on singing yet, playing the guitar certainly wasn't what Ricky was hoping it would be. It was far better. Sometimes he felt bad about feeling moments of happiness again when he was playing, which made for even more songs. The guitar was the answer to everything. It understood him. And he noticed after many months that when he was playing the guitar, he didn't have as much need to go spend time in the woods to satisfy his spirit. Something about playing the guitar was just as nice as running barefoot through the leaves, or watching the sun set from the top of the hill. As content as he felt singing out the blues, though, sometimes he felt that guitar nudging him to keep taking it further and further. He occasionally caught segments of rock and roll solos on the radio, and it made his heart beat faster. He wanted to try some of that, too. Sometimes, if he managed to have time alone in the room he shared with five other brothers, he would turn up the radio and dance around in his pajamas. Holding the family guitar and either pretending to strum the fast chords on the radio, or trying to figure out what they were and play along a little. He'd never had any urge for fame, but sometimes, he could see a crowd in front of him, cheering as he looked down on them from where he was standing up on the bed. The whole vision went in slow motion, his arm coming down from above, strumming a power chord on that guitar at the bottom of its descent, and the crowd goes wild.

> End Song 437

He finally asked John if they could do something… faster? John smiled and picked up his guitar. "You ready?" he asked. Ricky threw the guitar strap over his shoulder.

"Ready!" he said.

---

438. "Shout" by The Isley Brothers

---

They didn't remain sitting long, foot tapping wasn't enough for how fast John was playing. He stood up and put one foot on the crate to hold the big guitar still while he went to town on it. Ricky tried to accompany on his guitar, but this was a little over his head. He lost his place and spent the rest of the song watching John play. This was obviously going to be their next set of lessons.

End Song 438

Even after dedicating time to playing more upbeat songs, the pain that had led him to the guitar never left, though playing really helped pass the time. Two years didn't drag by nearly as long as he had feared, and on his eighteenth birthday, he got ready to say goodbye to his family. As he was packing to leave, his dad leaned against the doorway of his room. "Ricky, what're you gonna do if you don't find her?"

"Ah' don't know," Ricky admitted. "Maybe come home, maybe not. Not like there's anything here for me."

"Your family is here," his dad reminded him.

"Ah' know," Ricky said quietly. "Ah'll come back and visit on occasion."

"Okay," Ron said. "Be careful out there, alright? I do want to see you again someday."

Ricky looked back. "Ah'll be fine," he promised.

As he headed downstairs, his mother and several siblings were waiting at the bottom. Everyone knew he was leaving, but the reason why had been lost on most of the family. The chaos of life in that house and Ricky and Melody's tendency to sneak off into the woods to hang out had somewhat obscured how close they were to the casual observer. He told everyone except John and his dad that he was leaving to find work and a new life.

"Ricky, are you sure about this, hon?" Ruth asked, trying to dissuade him.

"Yep," Ricky answered, heading towards the door with the guitar in its case, and one duffel bag of clothes and supplies.

"Well… when are you coming back?" she asked.

"Dunno, Mom," he said. Stricken with worry, his mother followed him all the way to the train tracks. A bunch of siblings followed as well, because it was something to do. His father brought up the rear of the group, walking quietly with his hands in his pockets.

"Now, Ricky, remember to brush your teeth every night, and don't forget to eat a big breakfast every day. If you're lookin' for work, you'll need your strength," Ruth reminded him.

"Ricky will eat breakfast, promise," he said.

The train came into view on the horizon, and he threw his bag straps around his back and readied himself. He looked back at them once more. "Don't worry, Ricky will be fine. Be back at some point," he said with a smile, then took off running to gain speed as the train got closer. He jumped and grabbed a maintenance ladder with one hand and pulled himself up against the freight car. "BYE!" he yelled back as the group quickly grew smaller in the distance. He settled down on the roof, sitting on the straps of his bag to keep it from blowing away, and tried to sort the racing thoughts in his head. He had a rough idea where he was going, but no idea where he was going to sleep that night, where his next meal was coming from, or how he was going to get money while he was travelling. Melody had said they were going to Tennessee, so that was his destination. It was going to take a few days to get there. He would try to see if anyone affiliated with the solid waste transfer station would give him any information on where her father was, (while making sure to not be directly seen by him). Though he knew they might not want to disclose addresses or telephone numbers. If that didn't work, plan two was to find a library with a public computer to do some searching. Plan three was to ask around in the immediate area, or even check phone books if he had to. Plan three was all the further he had at the moment.

Over all the time he had to think about every angle of the situation in his head, he'd reached the conclusion that there were two possibilities: The first was that she had simply forgotten about him and moved on, and that their time together didn't mean as much to her as it did to him. If that was the case, he would fully understand the meaning of every sad country song he had ever heard on the radio. The second possibility that he reached was that her father had actually killed her, which was something he could barely bring himself to think about. On one hand, he'd felt so sure that they were in love, that he was convinced that there was no way she could have simply forgotten, and therefore, she had to be dead. On the other hand, he was certain she was too smart and resourceful to have not escaped if her father was trying to kill her, and therefore, he was just a fool. Something inside him kept insisting it was the first possibility because he just couldn't fully believe she didn't love him. Yet, he spent all his time praying that it was the second. He didn't want to think that his failing to save her from her family had led to her death. He would be the happiest man in the world as long as he found her alive. It didn't matter if it was years later, in the arms of another man, surrounded by their laughing children. He just wanted to see her again. Even if all he could do was smile, wave, and say he was passing through town, and funny finding her here and it was nice to see her again. If he could just see her again, he could move on. He could spend a little more time on the road trying to make a living as a travelling musician, ultimately fail, and then go home and become a poor wheat farmer like his parents.

*"Now, you keep playing that guitar, you hear me? It'll never do you wrong. And you better come back someday and show me the new songs you wrote out on the road,"* he heard John say again in his head, and he reached back and took the guitar out of its case and checked the strings to make sure they were still well tuned. He strummed a few chords, and it calmed his nerves a little bit. He strummed a few more and laid down with his head on his bag as he settled in for the long trip. He strummed them again, and it turned into the beginning of a new song, one he wrote on top of a train heading off into the unknown, into the darkening landscape, opposite the direction of the sunset.

In the days that came, he would find no site manager who worked for the solid waste division anywhere in the State of Tennessee named Stanley Gibson. In the weeks that came, he found no sign of a Melody Gibson living anywhere in the state. In the years that followed, he would find himself wondering why he hadn't gone back home yet. But, every time he had admitted to himself that was the only option he had left, he would find himself on another bus or train heading in a direction other than what pointed back towards Arkansas. Another day labor job putting up fences or patching roof shingles, another amateur's night at a new bar. He had a feeling he was still looking for something, though he had no idea what anymore. He just knew whatever it was, it wasn't waiting for him at home.

# CHAPTER 26

## (Crazy Little Thing Called Love)

**"Sorry in advance for anythin'** they say," Ricky said as they stood outside the hotel room door. "They're a lil' nosy."

"I'll be fine," Melody laughed. "They can't be any worse than your siblings."

"*We'll see...*" Ricky mumbled as he opened the door. As it swung to the side, it revealed Hal, Uli, and Ryan all sitting in a row on the couch, facing the entry like they had been waiting for them the whole time. It sent a chill down Ricky's spine. "Uh, morning," he said.

"Ricky!" Ryan held his hands up overdramatically. "You must introduce us to your friend, here."

"Um, everyone, this is Melody. We grew up together back home," Ricky said. He knew he must already have been turning red.

"Melody, good to meet you!" Hal said warmly as he got up and shook her hand. He had a rolled-up magazine under his other arm, which Ricky found a little odd since he was going through the trouble of holding it there instead of leaving it on the couch. He could see part of the cover, it was the latest edition of PEOPLE, so it wasn't something he should have been trying to hide. Unbeknownst to Ricky, Hal was keeping it ready to beat Ryan over the head with if he said anything too inappropriate. Ryan had already been warned of this.

"Good to meet you too!" Melody said. She also shook Uli and Ryan's hands. Ryan had the most unnerving look on his face. He looked like he was either plotting evil, or about to burst out laughing. Possibly both.

"Hey, so, I have a question, Melody. I know Ricky loves roller skating. Do you skate?" Hal asked.

"Oh yeah, we used to go skatin' together all the time," she said.

"Well, hey, why don't we all go out to dinner tonight, and then go skating? Spend some time getting to know each other. That alright, Ricky?" Hal asked.

"Yeah!" Ricky answered.

"Alright, we'll make an evening of it. I figure we'll meet up at four thirty. Until then, we do the packing for tomorrow?" Hal said, and they all agreed on that.

Uli, Ryan, and Melody stepped back out into the hall, and Uli asked: "Melody, I don't suppose you play any instruments?"

"Oh, no, I don't play anythin'. I just earned my Veterinary Degree. That's been takin' up all my time the last few years."

"Oh, well, congratulations!" Uli said.

Hal pulled Ricky to the side before he went out the door. "Hey, man, so, what's the plan?" Hal asked quietly.

"The plan?" Ricky asked.

"I know you've been wanting to see her again for a long time. I mean, were you going to stay here for a while, or…?"

"What? No, we got shows to do," Ricky said.

"I know, but, shows can be rescheduled," Hal replied.

"No, Ricky wasn't gonna stay here," Ricky said.

"Are you sure?" Hal said.

"Yeah. But…" Ricky started to say.

"Yeah?" Hal asked.

"Ah… was wondrin', if, maybe she could… travel with us for a while?" Ricky asked.

"What? Really?" Hal said.

"If that's okay?" Ricky asked.

"Okay!? That'd be awesome!" Hal said. "But, didn't she just become a vet? She isn't going to lose her job, is she?"

"She just graduated, but hasn't been hired yet. She was actually packin' up to figure out where to move to. But, we was thinkin' it might be fun to get to travel around together for a while."

"Sure! She can totally come! If that's what you two want to do," Hal said.

"Okay! Ah'll tell her!" Ricky said, and went out into the hall to join the group. Hal breathed a sigh of relief. Ricky had been miserable for so long, he wasn't going to do anything to prevent him from being happy again. But Hal had also been a little worried their latest tour was about to come to a sudden end. Again. But, not this time, fate. Not this time...

439. "Hooked on a Feeling" by Blue Swede *to play over this scene*

440. "Come and Get Your Love" by Redbone

441. "Ice Ice Baby" by Vanilla Ice

442. "Stop in the Name of Love" by The Supremes

443. "Footloose" by Kenny Loggins

444. "Get Down Tonight" by KC and the Sunshine Band

445. "Do Wah Diddy Diddy" by Manfred Mann

446. "Le Freak" by Chic

447. "Mambo #5" by Lou Bega

448. "You're the One That I Want" by GREASE, John Travolta & Olivia Newton-John

449. "The Book of Love" by The Monotones

450. "You Make Me Feel Like Dancing" by Leo Sayer

451. "We Like to Party! (The Vengabus)" by The Vengaboys

Melody tied the top lace into a bow on an old pair of white leather roller skates, and she and Ricky bolted out to the floor. The disco ball spun slowly overhead, and with the lights down low and the black lights on, the laces on, Melody's skates glowed brightly in their zig zag pattern. Other colored lights bumped and flashed to the beat of the music, and Ricky flipped around backwards and took her hands in his as they made their way around the floor; weaving slowly, effortlessly, between all the other people around them. Hal, Uli, and Ryan all sat down in the snack bar with a few cups of soda. None of them wanted to be the third wheel to this date, though it was sort of depressing just sitting there.

"It's… I don't know, weird to watch," Ryan said as Ricky and Melody made another lap.

"Right?" Hal agreed.

"All that work I did to try and get him a date. All of it for nothing," Ryan lamented.

"My deepest sympathies," Hal replied.

Ricky and Melody skated for at least forty-five minutes before they got off the floor to get a drink of water. Melody smiled and waved as she skated by to the snack bar, and Ricky skated up to their table, and, in one motion, spun around and sat down into the chair. "When are you guys gonna come out? You're not gonna sit here all night, are ya?" he asked, and Uli, Hal, and Ryan all sort of looked at each other.

"Uh, no, we were going to come out for the next song," Hal said.

"Good," Ricky said. "Ya don't come to a skatin' rink to sit in the snack bar all night!" Melody came back with her water and took a few big gulps of it before setting it down on the table, and she and Ricky went back out to the floor.

"Maybe he doesn't know he's on a date?" Ryan asked as they got up.

"Or maybe he doesn't need to alienate everyone when someone new comes into his life? I think maybe we're kind of used to people who do that.

But maybe Ricky's too cool to be that sort of person?" Hal replied, and Ryan raised both eyebrows, and then shrugged in agreement.

---

End Songs 439 – 451

---

They skated for about half an hour before the music paused, the lights came back on, and the DJ came on the microphone: "Alright, everyone, right now we're going to do a little activity called the Whoopee Skate..."

"The Whoopee skate!?" Ryan asked.

"Don't get too excited," Hal said.

"Now, this is how the Whoopee Skate works: Step one is you need to get into a group of two or three people, skating side by side, holding hands. Then, once everyone has their group, I'm going to start the music, and you'll all start skating in the regular skating direction. But then, every time I say the word "WHOOPEE!" you're all going to spin around and start skating the other direction around the floor."

There was a low murmuring on the floor amongst the crowd as the challenge was announced.

"And that's all there is to this. The Whoopee Skate isn't a game. There's no winners or losers. It's just an activity, because, you know, you all haven't gone in enough circles yet tonight, I'm sure," the DJ said. "So again, get into a group of two or three holding hands, I'll start the music, and here we go..."

---

452. "You Spin Me Round (Like a Record)" by Dead or Alive *to play over this scene*

or

453. "Turn the Beat Around" by Gloria Estefan *to play over this scene*

---

Ricky and Melody locked their hands together and took off fast. Hal looked at Uli and Ryan, who both looked a little skeptical, but he held one hand out to each of them and gave them the look that meant the topic wasn't up for discussion. They both grabbed a hand, and all three of them started skating.

"Alright, everybody ready?" the DJ asked. "Whooopee!" Hal watched as Ricky and Melody spun in a tight arc together, and were suddenly going the other way. Hal spun Uli and Ryan around as the center person, but he did it a little too fast, and struggled to keep both of them from falling as they tried to keep their feet from going out from underneath them. They all regained their balance and had just started going the other direction when they heard: "Whoooopee!"

"Oh, come on!" Ryan complained as they tried to turn back around as fast as they could. They made it a little further this time before the announcement came again: "Whooooopee!" They got a little faster each time they did it.

"Whooooopee!" They spun around again in time to see Ricky and Melody make another flawless, synchronized turn. Ricky's wheels screeched a little against the floor from the speed at which he took the angle.

"You guys gonna keep letting them show us up like that!?" Hal asked. Uli and Ryan had no time to answer while they struggled to keep pace with how fast he was trying to get them going.

"Whoooooopee!" They stumbled and faltered as they turned around faster, and Ricky and Melody flew by them.

"You two are too slow!" Hal announced as he let go of their hands and grabbed them both by their upper arms where he had a little more ability to stabilize them. He took off as fast as he could, towing both of them with him. "Whooooooopee!" He spun them around fast, and Uli and Ryan were both screaming on the inside as they made the spin. Ricky and Melody passed them.

"Getting the hang of it?" Ricky asked as they went by.

"We're working on it!" Hal laughed. "Whoooooooooopee!" Hal spun them again, and his wheels even screeched a little this time. The way he had Uli and Ryan by the arms gave him pretty good control in swinging them around, though Ryan suspected Hal was starting to cut off his circulation to the rest of his arm. Ricky and Melody came up alongside of them again.

"Ready?" Ricky asked.

"Bring it!" Hal said.

"Whoooooooooopee!" The DJ said again, and while Ricky and Hal's intent had certainly been to do a synchronized spin next to each other, Hal spun left while Ricky went right, and amidst sudden screaming and a loud crash and thud, they ended up in a five-body pileup on the floor.

> End Songs 452 – 453

The song came to an end, and many of the other people on the floor made their way over and stood looking down on them. "Any survivors down there?" The DJ asked through the speakers, and Hal raised a single hand up from the pile and gave a thumbs up, then collapsed back down into the heap.

They had a good laugh over the whole thing as they held bags of ice to various body parts while eating ice cream at the Baskin-Robbins across the parking lot before going back to the hotel for the night. "You should be glad your hat didn't get torn off in that fall, we would have been sitting ducks if anyone figured out who we were," Uli said to Hal as they got out of the elevator on the fifth floor.

"Yeah, that wouldn't have ended well. That pile would have gotten bigger really quick," he agreed. "Sorry about that, Melody."

"What, are you kiddin'? That was great!" She laughed. "If you don't fall, then you weren't skatin' hard enough."

"If you say so," Hal laughed.

"I will see everyone in the morning. Have a good night," Uli said as he pulled out the key card for his door.

"Goodnight," Hal said. Ricky's door was next. Hal wasn't going to stare to see if Melody was going into his room with him or not.

He made a point to look down at his pocket as he pulled his own key out to get it ready, but then heard: "Goodnight you two!", and turned in time to see both Ricky and Melody disappear as fast as they could into the room.

"*Ryan!*" Hal hissed at him.

Ryan turned around. "What!?" he said.

"Would you leave him alone? PLEASE?" Hal said.

"What? All I said was goodnight!" Ryan insisted. Hal glared at him, then took his pointer finger and middle finger, formed them into a 'V' as he pointed them at his own eyes, then quickly turned the hand around and pointed sharply at Ryan.

"*I'm... watching... you,*" he mouthed, silently, and Ryan rolled his eyes as he went into his own room for the night.

Hal sighed. *This must be what it's like to be the parent of a teenager,* he thought to himself, then had a sudden, strange urge to call his own mother and apologize.

Melody travelled with them for the rest of the tour, over the course of a year and a half; and even through the international segment. She helped where she could, since she felt weird about the idea of just following them around without doing anything. She was from a working family. Setup, breakdown, and any coordinating assistance she could provide. During that time, Ricky was paying her rent for her apartment so her belongings had a place to be while she was gone. He was also covering all her grocery bills and other expenses. Melody was super cool. She was fine with Hal, Uli, and Ryan's quirks, and she and Ricky were happy to include them in almost all activities.

They occasionally snuck out to dinner together, but going to see movies, roller skating, anything else they could think of, they always invited the other three. The only difference was when they were all at the movies together, Ricky was paying attention to her, instead of making quiet, sarcastic comments along with the rest of them. And when they'd go out to eat, he was so distracted he was *actually* ignoring their awkward questions instead of *pretending* to. The way Ricky looked at her was like the way he looked at his guitar, only more intense. It stabbed Hal in the heart. It was so nice to see him happy.

After this tour ended, they'd be due for a break. They had been going nonstop for years, so it was likely this would be a longer break than before. Everyone was exhausted, including Hal. Yet, the thought of rest wasn't all that appealing to him. If there were no shows to get up for, what was the point of getting rest? After a few full nights of sleep, he'd be back to 100 percent, and have nothing to spend that energy on. Travelling constantly had been a shock when they first got started, but after a few months, Hal adjusted to it well, and now going back home would be just as big of a shock. He could certainly understand why tour life was an acquired taste for many people, and something others could never quite stomach. But, he had gained quite a liking for it, and now it was what he lived for. Not having new stadiums of people to please every few nights was a depressing thought. He tried to not let his mind run wild with worry about how long of a break it might be, but still, he had a heavy sense of sadness as they went into their final show.

---

454. "Stereo Hearts" by Gym class Heroes ft. Adam Levine of Maroon 5

---

He gave that last performance everything he had. No lazy singing or half-assed dancing tonight. He generally never got lazy on stage, but tonight needed to be exceptionally flawless. He tried to make his voice perfect, he moved with meaning, he took in the faces of the audience, bobbing their heads in time with the rhythm, and the sounds of the screams when they started playing one of their biggest hits. He reached out into the front row and saw the fire in people's eyes as they grabbed his hand and sang along with him. They all knew every word, as usual. He could do this every other night for the rest of his life. He tried to stay in the moment, but knowing this would be the last show for a long time painted the entire night bittersweet from start to finish.

End Song 454

455. "Hotel California" by The Eagles

The lights moved slowly across them on the stage as they started the last song, one they had only played for the last couple shows of the tour. A new one. One that came at an inconvenient time. It had no new album to make a grand entry with. But, instead of putting it on ice for later, they decided to release it as a stand-alone single, and throw it on stage for what it was worth. One for the road. Ricky started strumming the haunting melody, and, covered in face paint and sweat, Hal began to sing. Lighters and phones started to rock back and forth. Even slow songs went by faster than usual on that night. The guitar faded out slowly at the end of this new song. Slowly, but still far too quick, and the last line echoed in Hal's head even after the show ended, and followed him into his dreams later that evening.

End Song 455

"Promise to call now and then, okay?" Hal called down the airplane loading hall.

"Of course!" Ricky yelled back, and he sounded sincere. The way he said it made Hal feel like he was just being paranoid. He'd never felt more relieved about possibly being too paranoid. As Ricky and Melody turned their backs to them, their fingers interlaced, and Hal caught one quick glimpse of a real, genuine smile on Ricky's face as they disappeared around the corner.

Ryan left for Seattle the next morning, and Uli caught a later flight back to Munich… or so he told Hal. The plane touched down in Sioux Falls, South Dakota, a few hours later, and Uli arrived at a little hotel in the rural town late that night after a two-hour drive north. He slept thirteen hours into the early afternoon the next day.

When he finally woke up, he had breakfast, or lunch as it may have been, took a shower, then spent a few hours catching up on all the emails he had been ignoring the last few days. He had called Claudia a few days prior, to see if she was still interested in seeing him, and by the end of the call, it was a date. He was going to pick her up at 5:00 p.m.. He pulled up into the driveway of the little old rental house and turned the car off. He glanced out the side window in disbelief. He had pulled in next to a hearse. A black hearse. It couldn't be hers, could it? He knew she had roommates, so maybe not, but he got out and did a quick walk around it before going up to the front door. Some very familiar black flowers and grass adorned flowerpots to either side of the steps. He was definitely at the right house. He rang the doorbell, and the door opened a few moments later. A woman with short, spiked brown hair stood there looking at his chest, then slowly tilted her head up until she was looking at his face. "Um, hi. Is Claudia here?" he asked.

"Uli!"

He looked up as Claudia appeared around a corner. A black velvet dress that came to her knees was laced tightly around her stomach, the crisscross pattern of the black ribbon created a faux corset look. Her auburn hair was done up in a tight whip of a braid, dark black liner circled her eyes like an Egyptian goddess, and her lips shone a shiny slick of purple lipstick.

"Uh, hi. Hello... Claudia," Uli stuttered out.

"Hey, it's good to see you again!" she said.

"Uh, yes, good to see you... too." He could have killed himself for losing his composure this badly.

The girl with spiked hair suddenly turned and looked at Claudia, and with her thumb pointed back in Uli's direction, asked: "Do you want to share?"

Claudia sighed and put her hand on spikey-hair-girl's face and shoved her back into the kitchen as she walked up to Uli. "Shall we?" She gestured outside.

"Let's," Uli replied as they left. Claudia went down the driveway and opened the passenger door of the rental car.

"So, whose hearse is that?" Uli asked.

"Oh, it's mine," she said.

"Do you... want to take it to dinner? This is just a rental car."

"I wish! It's not running yet. I'm working on it a little bit each paycheck. Hopefully, I'll get to drive it soon."

*Scheisse,* Uli thought to himself. And it was probably a bit too early in the relationship to offer to pay to have it all fixed for her.

They ate out at a local restaurant. People knew Claudia since it was a small community, though some would still put extra space between themselves and her on the sidewalk because of how she dressed. Most people in the area could be found in Church every Sunday, and she was one of the few who wouldn't be seen there. Because of that, rumors were passed through the grapevine regarding her and her roommates engaging in witchcraft. "Oh, for heaven's sake, we just like rock and roll and Halloween," they'd say to people, and then move on. That, combined with their overall friendliness and willingness to engage in other community events had removed a lot of the tension over the years. Though, some of the more conservative members of the community would still harass her parents regarding 'having an intervention' with their daughter. Showing up to the town café with a 6'5 guy in a black Holy Hell T-shirt and black jeans caused the usual breadth of space people would give her to grow a little wider this evening. Her and Uli talked casually, though quietly, to try and avoid too much attention.

"So, the basic idea with Wicca is there is energy in everything, and finding ways to manipulate that energy can help bring about positive changes in a person's life," she explained. "There is likely some actual science behind it, though we're in the very early stages of understanding it. But, there is a college in California called the Institute of Noetic Science that is starting to explore some of the concepts of the mind and natural energy that might be behind some of the main tenants of Wicca. One of their hypotheses is that brainwaves might have some sort of measurable mass. That mass is certainly very small, but if brainwaves do have a measurable mass, it means they could theoretically be used to manipulate certain things and be manipulated themselves." Uli was listening with rapt attention. "I'm not sure I believe in magic per se, but I do believe there are things we still don't understand, and I like playing with those things. After all, a lot of what we know as proven science today used to be called magic or the ravings of mad men in the middle ages."

"Like the earth being round, and the fact that it revolves around the sun as opposed to the other way around," Uli said.

"Exactly!" Claudia agreed. "The standard person in the middle ages thought the earth was flat because no matter where they walked, they never ended up sideways or upside down. And, they thought the sun revolved around the earth because their house never moved, yet, they observed the sun moving around it during the day. These were reasonable observations in the realm of the reality a person knew back then. They had no idea that themselves and their home were actually moving through space upon the earth as it spun. And, that due to gravity, perception, and the question of whether there is actually an 'up' or 'down' in the universe and the fabric of space time, a person who is on the 'bottom' on the earth doesn't feel upside down, and may consider someone on the other side on the 'top' to be upside down," Claudia said, then added, "Sorry if I'm being boring. My dad is an aerospace engineer, and I find this stuff fascinating."

"You are not being boring at all. My parents both have master's degrees, and the community I grew up in was considered to be very well educated," Uli said. "So, I have had many similar conversations before. Though, there is this, arrogance, I suppose, in the scientific community regarding how certain things are impossible, while at the same time, they themselves state there is much we don't know and are working to understand."

"Oh my god, exactly!" Claudia agreed. "When I would look up ghost videos and cryptid sightings on YouTube, Dad would scoff at me and say I was watching a series of hoax videos. But, at the same time, he is the one who believes there are likely thousands of species of fish in the oceans that haven't been discovered yet, and that teleportation and time travel are theoretically possible. And, I'm just like, Dad… how can you be so certain there aren't large, highly endangered species of animals on land we haven't discovered yet, and how, if you state teleportation could be possible, can you immediately dismiss the possibility of human souls existing as a disembodied energy in the afterlife!?"

"Yes, that is exactly it!" Uli agreed. "These scientists think they have open minds and are unbiased researchers. And yet, they still possess some of the same close-minded arrogance the people in the middle ages had that they themselves disavow as dark-ages illiteracy."

"Oh my god… you understand!" Claudia said, her eyes wide.

"YOU understand!" Uli countered back. They stared at each other for a few moments in silence, until they both started smiling.

"You know, going back to the science of brainwaves, I saw a video once on the Ghost Hunters show where they did something unusual and sat down with a self-proclaimed psychic and videotaped the reading with him as he tried to read one of their minds," Claudia said. "The regular camera didn't pick up anything strange, but they had their FLIR heat camera trained on him as well, and during the reading, a plume of heat rose off of the ghost hunter guy, travelled over, and settled down on the psychic guy who was doing the mind reading."

"Really!?" Uli said.

"Yeah, you can look it up on YouTube. It was in season two, episode thirteen of Ghost Hunters. But, they literally caught scientific evidence on camera that the psychic guy physically altered the environment around him and was able to pull energy from the ghost hunter to himself."

"That is incredible. So, was the mind reading successful?" Uli asked.

"Apparently so. The ghost hunter guy said the psychic guy told him things about himself and about experiences he had that he had never, ever told to anyone else."

"Amazing," Uli commented.

"Yeah. But, anyways, I shot off on a huge tangent. But, I guess that is sort of some of the back story to how I think Wicca works. The idea that everything has energy that can be manipulated, and what a lot of people know as 'witchcraft' likely has some science behind it that hasn't been explored yet. Though, there is certainly the allure of playing with something that you don't fully understand."

"The unknown," Uli said.

"Yes, the unknown. My favorite place. The 'Beyond' section of Bed, Bath and Beyond," Claudia replied, and this made Uli laugh. She continued: "But, there is a long list of ways to manipulate various things to get a certain outcome. This knowledge being the cumulative medicinal and 'magical' folk knowledge of ancient peoples who found these correlations, even if they didn't understand how or why they worked. There's spices and herbs that can be used to manipulate both physical and spiritual outcomes. Same with crystals, minerals, and other elements from the earth like salt, fire, and water. Colors, especially colored candles, also have correspondences to certain things, as do seasons, light, dark, time of the day, words, repetitions of certain phrases, as well as the phases of the moon. Like, for example, with the moon, if you're casting a spell to bring something to yourself, like a new job, the best time to do that is during a waxing moon as the moon is coming into its full form and increasing its presence and light. Likewise, if you're trying to get rid of something, like, trying to get someone to stop harassing you and 'banish' their bad influence, you would cast a spell during the waning moon as it is 'lessening' and it's light is going away for another cycle."

"Interesting," Uli said.

"Yeah. As far as all the herbs, crystals, colors, etc. there's all kinds of books you can read on the subject. But, a few examples are, basil seems to attract money, and aids in fertility for couples who are trying to conceive. Amethyst crystal seems to help heal and soothe people, brown candles are good for casting spells for healing animals and nature since brown corresponds with mother earth. You could literally spend years reading on what all the herbs and crystals do."

"So, for casting a spell, how exactly do you do it? Do you always use crystals, herbs, and candles while speaking a certain phrase? Or do some spells only require some of those elements?"

"Some only require some of those elements, while others require all of those things and then some. I've also seen incense, bells, coins, feathers, figurines, and personal items with sentimental meaning to the practitioner used. There are complicated spells and simple spells. And, there's different means to cast them. There's saying a spell over a burning candle, there's putting a written spell and some herbs into a wish box, there's making up a special tea or tonic to drink, there's even spells that involve taking a bath in bath salts blended with special essential oils. And, you can also create your own spells once you know what goes into it. You don't always have to use an existing one out of a book. I worked as a Barista at Starbucks for a while, and it's oddly like learning to make the drinks. You can make your own combinations, or just do one of the recommended drinks off of the menu. But, you start by picking the drink size and what type of drink to work with; like hot, cold, iced, blended, etc. And then there's different types of milk, different flavors, different types of coffee, and a never-ending combination of possibilities for how much flavor, shots, and milk to put into each drink. It's kind of like its own form of math, but in the end, it's really just a matter of knowing what the ingredients are, how much you have to work with, and what your desired goal is."

"Okay. That makes sense," Uli said.

"Yes. And knowing what ingredients complement each other and what ones don't go so well together also helps. Like, a mocha green tea latte might be kinda gross, but a green tea latte with some melon flavor added has worked well for a lot of people. Likewise, trying to attract love during a waning moon while burning a black candle is probably a bad combination that's not going to work too well. But, getting some lavender, rose petals, and amethyst together would be great for attracting romance, or another good combination is basil, citrine crystal, and the color green go well for attracting money…"

"And if you're trying to attract love or money, you should do both during a waxing moon," Uli observed.

"Yes! Now you're getting it!" Claudia said.

"So, I suppose this may be a stupid question, but does this all work?" Uli asked.

"Well, not always. But, I've seen enough of it work that I think it goes beyond coincidence and statistics," Claudia replied. "Some reasons why it may not work is you're not supposed to cast spells out of greed or selfishness, and also, if you're not thinking positive enough when you do the spell. Positive brainwaves supposedly get much better results than negative or disbelieving ones. But, a few years back I had a thirteen-year-old cat that got very sick with a kidney infection. The vets didn't think she was going to make it, but I cast a healing spell for her, and she made a somewhat miraculous recovery. She was on her antibiotics, but the vets still didn't think she was going to make it even with the meds, but she did, and I got another four years with her before I had to say goodbye," Claudia said. "Now, I don't think spellcasting is a replacement for modern medicine, but in this case, it may have been enough to tip the fates in favor of my sweet little Snuggles."

"I see. So, I do have to ask: you have talked about healing and attracting money, but to what extent can you actually hurt someone with spells? I am sure turning someone into a frog is a myth, but can you actually cause harm to befall a person?"

"Okay, so, first rule of white witchcraft, that being, good-intentioned witchcraft, is you never cast spells to cause harm, no matter how much that person may truly deserve it. Now, you can cast a spell to try and stop someone from causing more harm, but not to punish them for what they have already done. As I mentioned earlier, you can cast a spell to get a co-worker to quit harassing you, but not by means of wishing for them to get hit by a bus after work. I'm not saying it's not possible to cast a spell to cause harm, but it is highly recommended against. Dark witchcraft and black magic is a whole separate world in its own; and one I don't plan on visiting. That's dangerous shit. In Wicca it is believed there is a rule of threes. Whatever you send out into the universe, you get back threefold. You send good wishes, you will be blessed three times over. You send out curses, you better be ready for a karmic ass-kicking," she said.

"Okay," Uli said, amused.

"Wicca and witchcraft are like a hammer. That being, they're simply a tool. You can use it to build a house for a homeless family, or you can use it to bash someone's skull in. What it does all depends on the intent of the person wielding it. Now, there is one other rule of white witchcraft I know, and that is you shouldn't cast a spell to change someone's fate or freewill. The most common example that comes up in the Wicca books is casting a spell to make a specific person fall in love with you. Doing that is highly advised against because maybe they're not the right person for you, and maybe they're intended to end up with someone else. What you are allowed to do is cast a spell to attract a romantic interest, but you are supposed to leave it up to fate and the universe who that person is that shows up because of the spell. Be it the person you've had your eye on, or someone entirely new that you haven't crossed paths with yet," she said.

"Hmm. So, did you cast a spell to attract someone at Burning Man?" Uli asked teasingly, taking another sip of his coffee.

"Well… yeah," she replied. Uli paused mid-sip and looked at her. "There's not a lot of selection around here, and I sort of wanted to meet someone. So, yeah, I did cast an attract romance spell the night before I left for Burning Man. I figured there'd be a wide selection there for the universe to pick from, and, hey, maybe there would be someone as weird as me there. And then… you hobbled up to my garden on your way to a heat stroke," she said, sort of shyly.

Uli slowly set his cup of coffee back down. "Oh," he said, looking somewhat stunned.

"So, um, yeah. That's another spell that might have worked. I guess we'll see," she said with a nervous laugh.

"Yes, I… guess we will," Uli said with a soft smile. They sort of looked at each other quietly for a few moments after that, before Uli asked: "So, would you be willing to teach me… more? More about Wicca and spells, that is? I would be interested to learn."

"Yeah, I can totally do that. I can also recommend some good books to read on the subject," she said. "There's a lot of herbs and crystals to learn. Hundreds of them. But there is certainly what might be considered a 'core set' of each that have wide and common applications."

"Yes, that would be great if you could write down those titles," Uli said.

"Okay, I'll do that," she said. "And, I mean, I don't know if you need to head out early tonight to do anything else, but if you want to come over tonight I can give you some lessons. In spells. All my roommates will be there, and they can help teach too."

"Yes, that would be nice, if it's not too much of a bother. I don't have any place else I need to be tonight."

"Okay, we can do that, then," she answered, nervously. "God, it's so nice to meet someone new who I can talk to about this who doesn't immediately want to haul me into the nearest church and make me repent," she said. "I've got Caitlyn and Sarah and Ashley at home, but it's always nice to meet someone... new," she repeated.

"Likewise," Uli said. "No one I knew growing up was into Metal music or horror movies or paranormal studies or anything of the like. And my bandmates are perfectly accepting of me, but they are not personally into it like you are. So, yes, this is wonderful to be able to talk to someone who is," he agreed.

"Your bandmates aren't into spooky stuff? They sure looked like they were on stage when they did those metal songs later in the evening," she said.

"Well, as you know, we are the band that does everything, and we all fully perform to each other's preferences for those parts of the show. But, in reality, we are all quite different, and Hal, Ryan, and Ricky are not specifically into the metal scene on their own."

"Boy, they're good actors then. They sure looked like they were."

"They are good actors. That is part of what the show is all about," he explained.

"Well, that's really cool. That you guys respect each other enough to really partake in each other's interests," she said. "It's nice to be around people who accept you for who you are," she said quietly. "Anyways, if you come over you'll be meeting my roommates tonight. Are your bandmates around? I mean, do we get to meet them too?"

"Not at the moment," Uli said. "I travelled here without them. But, next time they are around, I would be happy to introduce you."

"Sweet. Because, well, you guys are really cool, and we all like your songs. Especially the metal ones, as you could have probably guessed."

"Thank you. We do our best," Uli said, taking another sip of coffee. "Um, just as a heads up for when you do meet them, our guitarist Ricky had a traumatic experience with a woman back in his hometown who was considered a witch, but she was definitely a practitioner of black magic, not white witchcraft. So, Ricky may be a little nervous to meet another witch," Uli said. "I want to be clear though, I am in no way asking you to hide that aspect of yourself. I just wanted to let you know there could be some nervousness on his part when meeting you. I will, of course, try and explain to him beforehand what you just told me, and let him know that he would have no reason to fear you."

"Well, I'd appreciate that," she said. "Wouldn't be the first time, though. Lots of people still have the opinion that witchcraft is always evil and anyone who practices it is evil to the core."

"Yes, and that is unfortunate," Uli agreed.

"If I may ask, what did the woman in his hometown do that traumatized him so bad?"

"Well, um…" Uli scrambled to think up a more believable story than what had actually happened to Ricky, plus he had also sworn to keep his secret safe. "…when Ricky was a young child… he was playing in the woods by himself one day when he happened to accidentally cross paths with her. She invited him to go back to her cabin with her for unknown reasons. When he refused and started to run, she chased after him for a great distance. And, as he told us, in his young mind he actually thought he was going to die," Uli said.

"Ugh. That's awful. What a bitch," Claudia said.

"Yes, well, the woman's name was Daisy, and she was likely very mentally ill. She was also quite old, and after she died and some people from the town found her and buried her, they went through her cabin to see what was in there, and did find what seemed to be paraphernalia for dark witchcraft."

"That's too bad. There certainly are people out there who use black magic witchcraft, but they are rare, and most who practice witchcraft nowadays practice the positive, natural version. That's horrible your friend had to have that happen."

"Yes, Daisy caused a lot of trouble for the town. I do not believe she ever killed or injured anyone, but she kept people in a constant state of nervousness. She scared Ricky so bad that he was afraid to play in the woods for a while after that. When he did dare venture out again, he stayed away from the part of the woods she was known to live in until after she died years later."

"Alright, well, I'll give Ricky a bit of a handicap when we meet," she said.

"And I apologize for that. Like I said, I will talk to him ahead of time, I just wanted to make you aware that he could be uneasy when you meet."

"Sure. Thanks for explaining all that. It's good to know. So, when..."

"Excuse me folks..." The waiter came up to the table. "Sorry to interrupt, I just wanted to drop this off..." He set the bill in the thin black folder down on the table. "And let you know we close in ten minutes." Uli and Claudia looked around, stunned. They were the last ones there. They could have sworn they were surrounded by other diners only five minutes ago.

"Um... right..." Claudia said as she reached for the bill. Uli quickly snatched it away.

"Yes, yes. Here..." He shoved a card into the folder and handed it to the waiter.

"I could have gotten it," Claudia insisted.

"No, no. You need to prioritize. You have a hearse to fix," Uli answered.

Claudia laughed a bit. "Thanks. So, when's the next time you think you'll be in the area after this?"

"I'll be around for a while, actually."

"Really? Are you doing a few shows in Minnesota soon?"

"No, actually. Our tour is over. We're on break."

"So... what do you have to do around here?"

"Um, well, this is a good place to disappear for a while and relax since it is not densely populated. We were touring for two years. I am exhausted. Spending time in the middle of nowhere doing nothing sounds nice right now."

"You're going to hang out around here for a while, doing *nothing*?" she tried to confirm.

"Well, yes, that is the plan," Uli admitted. "If… that is okay with you."

Claudia gave him a quizzical look, then developed a very slight smile. "I think it'll be alright." The waiter came back with the receipt, and they got up and went back to the car. "Seriously though, what are you going to do around here?"

"I have a laptop with plenty of games loaded onto it. Sleeping in also sounds lovely."

"That's it?" she asked as she sat down in the passenger seat.

"Mostly. Boredom will be a nice change for a bit."

"Well, if you get too bored the only other thing I can recommend around here is there are a few ranches that do horseback riding if you're into that type of thing. That's about it."

"I have not ridden a horse since I was a child."

"Think you might give it a try now?" she asked.

"We shall see," Uli said as he pulled the door shut and started the car. "Is there at least a theater around here? I am way behind in the movies."

"Well, the closest one is about an hour's drive down the highway."

"There. I have something to do, then."

"I, uh, know that new slasher film is out this Friday. I read it was a real bloodbath," Claudia said.

"Really?" Uli said, intrigued.

"You wanna go see it…, together?"

"I would not complain," Uli said.

"Well, why don't we make a night of it?" Claudia said.

"Alright. What time works for you?" he asked.

"As long as it's after 6:00 p.m. I'm available. What about you?"

"You know, my schedule is clear…" he replied as they pulled back out onto the road, and started heading back in the direction of her house.

# CHAPTER 27

## (Who Says You Can't Go Home)

**The tires kicked up little** rocks and left a trail of dust in their wake as the rusted hot rod pulled up the long, gravel driveway. They came to a stop, and Melody kept her eyes covered like she promised while she got out. She watched her own feet move through the grass as they walked around front, and when they were at the right spot, Ricky asked: "You ready?" She replied she was. "Okay!" he said, and she looked up at the house. A fresh coat of light turquoise paint adorned the walls, the rotting boards had been replaced, a new roof sat on top like a crown, and all the windows had new glass in them, save for one. It was fully restored to its original glory. She looked slowly from one side to the other. It was hard to believe, even though it was right in front of her. He admired it silently, too. He'd seen it at a few different stages in progress, but it was still going to take a while to get used to the sight.

"C'mon, you should see th' inside," he said excitedly, and they ran up to the front door. He pushed it open, and she was about to step inside when he threw his arm out and stopped her. "Wait a sec…" he said, then suddenly swept her off her feet to hold her in both arms.

"What, you gonna carry me 'cross the threshold!? We ain't married!" she laughed.

He paused and looked at her. "No, but we will be someday, right?" he asked.

"Well, yeah," she answered quietly.

"Ah' think that means it'll be okay," he said, then stepped inside. He set her back on her feet in the grand entry, and she looked around at the room she had spent so much time in, but had never seen like this before. The stairwell was looking very well-dressed in a new layer of bright white paint, and the splinters that once lined its lengths had been completely sanded away. The chandelier was showing its shine again; the shine they knew had been hiding under the layer of tarnish for all those years. It looked like the ballrooms from the old fairytales she read as a kid. Ricky walked past her towards the wall right of the stairwell, and flipped a switch. The flower arrangement at the base of the banister lit up and bloomed for the first time in decades, sending beams of color all across the room. The lights from the petals settled on the walls, making it look like the whole inside was covered with springtime blossoms. She walked up to it and ran her fingers gently over one of the glass flowers. After a few moments, she looked over and noticed Ricky leaning against the wall, watching her with a shy smile. She felt herself smiling, too, in response. She didn't know what to say. It truly left her speechless. He walked over to her and took her hand in his, and, without a word, they started making their way up the stairs. At the top, the memories she had of what the upper floor looked like were slowly coated with fresh paint and new hardwood as they went; like the house was being remodeled before her eyes with each step. They made it to the end of the hall, to the master bedroom, and she walked up to the window to take a look at the golden sunset through clean, though still mystically cracked, glass. She put her hands on the sill, then picked them up again. It didn't feel like she remembered. She looked at her palms. They were completely clean. No layer of dirt and paint chips this time.

"Ah'd figure we'd leave this window alone. Since, you know, we had fun pretendin' it was an ancient symbol," Ricky said.

"Ricky… did we really pull this off? Is this really happening? We really made it back here together, and the house is finished…?" Her eyes were beginning to water as she turned to look at him. Ricky nodded his head silently. "And, it's all because of the hard work you did…" she added.

"Hey…" He walked up to her and pulled her gently into his arms. "Ricky just ended up in the right tavern on the right night with the right guys in the audience. You're the one who went and worked hard to get your degree."

"Yeah, but, you tried to keep your promise, and I didn't…" she said as a few tears began to roll down her eyes.

"If you had, we wouldn't be here," he replied. "If you were ready and waitin' when I showed up on my eighteenth birthday, we would have never gotten the house restored. We would have come home and started our own farm, and spent the rest of our lives underwater in debt." She raised her head and looked at him with a still guilty expression. "Ah' like this better," he said as he gazed back into her eyes. "It was worth waitin' for. You… were worth waitin' for," he said, leaning gently in towards her to give her a quick kiss. He turned and walked over to the other side of the room, grabbed a blanket that had been draped over a chest of drawers and pulled it off, revealing a shiny new record player on top. He opened one of the drawers and pulled out an old country record, and placed it carefully on the spindle inside and started it spinning.

> 456. "I Just Want to Dance with You" by George Strait *to play over this scene*

He walked back over to her and took her hands in his again, and they started to dance slowly across the room. As they did, a cracked window cast sunlight on them in strange patterns, creating the shadows of a young couple in love dancing across the back wall. It told two stories at the same time; one of times gone past, as well as one that was being written anew. The shadow couple danced alongside of them past the raised master bed on its two-step platform, past the stone lined fireplace at the foot of the bed, then out the door to explore the rest of the top floor. They made their way through the other bedrooms, starting in the bedroom that had an ornately carved wood fireplace, and French doors that led to a small Juliet balcony. Then, they moved to the one with rounded walls that oddly had a disembodied sink in the corner. Next was the strangely set up bathroom that had a door on each end, so it acted almost like a hallway between the two rooms when both doors were open. A stained-glass window adorned with pink and white Foxglove flowers was positioned over the clawfoot bathtub, and the pink light from the window brushed across them as they passed through.

They danced back down the stairwell to the main floor, and wove their way into the parlor room off of the kitchen. The parlor was also rounded with a bay window that had a built-in sitting bench below it, and over the window, small, individual squares of colored glass curved across the top like a pixelated rainbow. As they moved into the kitchen, the mint green cabinets shone like spring grass against the fresh white wallpaper, and the long, vintage trough sink that stretched for almost the entire length of the wall caught a few of the lost flowers from the entryway on its white enamel like shed petals on a still pond. The house had a number of odd quirks, including another staircase that was very narrow, and easily hidden behind a small door that would have made the standard person think it was a closet. This was likely a servant staircase. Between that hidden staircase, the dumbwaiter, and the fact that there were also two separate back doors to the outside, one grand and one unceremonious, this was likely once the home of a very rich family in the Victorian era. They wove their way carefully up the tiny second staircase back to the upper floor, and then up the next staircase to the grand stand-up attic. The attic ceiling was peaked with large beams that lined it's lengths like rib bones in the belly of a beast, and there was a smaller side room off of the main attic space. Likely servant or nanny quarters. The side room had a giant metal radiator right below the main window, and triangular shaped side windows that swiveled open on a metal center rod. As they took a quick break to open one, the gentle evening breeze sent the attic dust flying into the golden rays of the setting sun, so a thousand daylight stars parted in their wake as they danced back into the main room.

The shadow couple that had been dancing along side of them had come down off the wall and were at their feet now thanks to the setting sun. They swayed across the floor with Ricky and Melody until they completely faded away with the twilight, and all the tiny stars twinkled out with the last strands of the sunset.

> End Song 456

They ate a candlelight dinner of a frozen pizza cooked to perfection with a side of potato chips and strawberry popsicles for dessert, then spent a few hours sitting on the floor by the fireplace in the parlor playing Yahtzee before calling it a night.

As Melody was getting ready for bed, she heard something hit the bedroom window. She walked over to see if she could find what it was, but before she got to it, she saw a small, dark shape hit it again. She pushed the window up and found a pinecone on the outside window ledge.

"*Hey!*" a voice called up, and she looked down to see Ricky standing below. "*Is your dad asleep yet?*" he asked quietly.

"What?" she asked.

He looked around nervously, then asked again: "*Is… your… dad… asleep… yet?*"

"Um… yeah. I think… he passed out on the couch an hour ago?" she answered uncertainly.

"Okay…" he said, his voice becoming a little louder. He stepped forward and pulled an old blues guitar out of the bushes against the house. He threw the strap over his shoulder and strummed the strings across. "Ah've been tryin' to learn to play the guitar, and ah' kinda wrote you a song. Ah' hope you'll like it."

> 457. "I'll Have to Say I Love You in a Song" by Jim Croce

He started singing to her, and she set her elbows on the window sill, and cupped her chin in her hands as she listened. This was too cute. She did her best to fight back tears, he was going to make her cry again if she wasn't careful. The frogs and crickets kept a good rhythm in the background for him, and as he sang, a few small screech owls landed on nearby branches, a group of deer stepped out of the forest and walked up near him, and a raccoon and a few foxes also appeared out of the nearby bushes to take their place in the audience. If she didn't know better, this would be the point that she would have suspected she was dreaming about being in a Disney movie.

End Song 457

When he finished, he looked up at her and asked "Do… ya like it?"

"Do I like it!?" she said. "It was perfect! You keep playing like that and maybe someday your name will be in lights, saying: 'Ricky Raccoon Tonight.'"

"Well, now, ah' doubt that," Ricky replied.

She shook her head at him, then said: "Y'know, you could give any Disney princess a run for her money."

Ricky looked at her confused for a few seconds, but then glanced around him and noticed his audience. "Oh, right. Maybe. But, Ricky's hair ain't near fabulous enough," he replied, and they shared a quick laugh.

He set the guitar down so the bottom of it was on the ground while he leaned casually against the head, gazing at her drunkenly despite being perfectly sober, and she stared back for a few moments before saying: "So, this has been a nearly perfect day, but there's one thing wrong with this picture right now…"

"W'as that?" Ricky asked.

"You're down there, and I'm up here," she answered. Ricky pondered this for a few moments, then started running towards the front door.

## *Battle Creek, Michigan*

Hal entered the code on the keypad to the front door, then pulled it open. It was dusk, and he turned on the lights to the main room. The silver doorknobs and hinges shined as bright as chrome on a hot car, and the blond hardwood floors in the living room glowed like a layer of warm sand on a tropical beach. He walked into the kitchen and set the last box of stuff down on the counter. Flecks of abalone shell and quartz embedded in the black surface sparkled from the light coming in from the main room, making the counter look like a slab of starry sky harvested straight from the night above. His parents had helped him move most of the contents of his old room in over the weekend, and he'd just brought the last box in. It was official. The house was done, and he was staying his first night. He decided he'd put the last of the things away in the morning. The outside of the house was a very modern, urban-townhouse inspired design; painted in black, white, and mint green. Like mint-chocolate chip ice cream, except heavy on the chocolate, with the trim done in mint and white.

It was three stories high plus a basement, and a tower room that could technically be counted as a tiny fourth floor. The ground floor held the kitchen/living room/dining room plus a second living room or a 'sitting room' as it might have been called, plus a guest bathroom. The entire basement was a large gaming/media and theater room. The second floor had the recording studio and work space. The third floor was all the bedrooms plus a few bathrooms, and the tiny tower room was a lounging/sitting area.

He wanted to take another tour, and then go have a beer on the upper deck overlooking the lake before he went to bed. He started admiring right where he was in the kitchen. Aside from the counters, he had taken notes from Allen and had the whole kitchen done in a rock and roll theme, complete with all the little guitar spatulas, microphone tongs, drumstick end spoons, and a refrigerator, dishwasher and oven all done up to look like giant guitar amplifiers. The microwave was even painted up to look like a vintage radio. Framed records and other music art adorned the walls in the kitchen, plus the living room and dining room. In the media room with the giant TV screen, he had opted to go for more of a classic theater room design, and had giant framed posters of his favorite movies all along the walls. *Inception*, *Army of Darkness*, *Pirates of the Caribbean*, *The 5th Element*, *Toy Story*, *The Matrix*, and many others.

Going up two flights of stairs to the second floor, he inhaled the residual smell of fresh cut lumber as he turned the corner into the giant recording studio. Like downstairs, the walls were adorned with framed records, and the newest, highest quality equipment lined the room on three sides. The last side was an entire wall of floor-to-ceiling windows, with giant blackout curtains at either end that could be pulled shut if they were finding the outside world too distracting while they were trying to write. In the center of the room was a stand-alone gas fireplace with a 360 degree glass view of the inside, so they could write by firelight if it was one of those nights again. As he made his way up the next stairwell, the walls of the staircase were lined with beautifully painted custom guitars in all shapes and colors. All were functional, and could be removed from their mounts at will to be played. To the side of every stairwell in the house was also a tube slide from one floor to the next, at Ryan's request. It would certainly make going down the stairs easier for all of them if they were drunk. The third floor had two bathrooms and six large bedrooms. One for Hal, one for Ricky, one for Uli, one for Ryan, and two for guests. Hal had all their bedrooms themed and decorated to each of their likes. Uli's was painted black with black leather furniture, a black hardwood bed with black bedding, and various pieces of artwork depicting skulls and other assorted macabre things. Ryan's room had the hot tub and stripper pole he asked for, as well as a set of expensive, but 'distressed' looking furniture, and posters of various video games, punk bands, bikini-clad women, and other immature and irreverent things. Ricky's room was the hardest to figure out, and initially, Hal had half a mind to leave it bare to the studs to be funny, since Ricky had an aversion to anything new and upscale. But, he ultimately decided against doing that and gave it a simple, clean, rustic feel, leaning towards the 'vacation log cabin in the woods' style of decorating. It had a matching set of unvarnished cedar wood furniture, an actual hand-hewn log bed, and a few nice photo prints and oil paintings of wildlife and landscapes put on the walls. Then, there was his room. Hal did something a little different with his. He had always had a liking for the retro-futuristic mid-century modern design he had occasionally seen in old magazines. So, all his bedroom furniture had that 1950's/1960's 'land of tomorrow' space age look to it. Most of the furniture was white, and none of it had any right angles. Everything was rounded and streamlined. The center coffee table was in the shape of a boomerang, and he got a few egg chairs like the big white chairs from the *Men in Black* movies. The dresser had a rounded top with boomerang drawer pulls, and the matching side tables were asymmetric with bases that looked like giant blobs of goo reaching an arced arm up to hold an entirely glass-top table. The big bed was entirely round like a single-person UFO with a California King mattress in the middle, and he also had colorful abstract modern art on the walls. The art included a few prints from a *totally groovy* artist named Shag, who drew scenes of hip parties happening in very similarly decorated mod homes and living rooms. A stupid grin spread across Hal's face. This was too cool.

He went back out into the hallway to one of the bathrooms, and flipped on the lights. The raised glass bowl sink showed hints of rainbow color with its faceted cut as he moved his eyes across it, like the whole thing had been hewn from a single large crystal. He reached into the shower and turned the water on. He waited a few moments, and the black walls began to change color as the water warmed up. Heat reactive tiles. Where the water hit, they went from black to red, then orange, yellow, green, blue, purple. He put his hand on one of the tiles out of the water's range, then took it away, leaving a red handprint that slowly faded back to black. He was going to have way too much fun with that. He suddenly thought he heard muffled music start up down the hall, and he turned off the water and curiously poked his head out the door to see a band of light escaping out from under Ryan's bedroom door. He heard voices now as he approached, and he grabbed the doorknob and threw the door open.

458. "The Bad Touch" (The Discovery Channel Song) by The Bloodhound Gang *to play over this scene*

Inside, Ryan was chest deep in the hot tub with a beer bottle in his hand, and four bikini-clad girls around him. Two in the water, one sitting on the edge dipping her feet, and one trying her best to do spins on the pole, which was something she didn't appear to have any experience with.

"Dude! There you are!" Ryan said.

"Here *I* am!?" Hal asked.

"Yeah! I was wondering when you were going to show up!"

"You were wondering when *I* was going to show up!?" he repeated.

"Yeah, I was surprised you weren't here when I got in."

"You were… wait, how long have *you* been here!?"

"Like, three hours," Ryan answered. "You seem surprised."

"I am!" Hal said.

"Why?"

"I… I thought you were in Seattle."

"Well, I was," Ryan said. "But then I left and came here."

Hal stared at him for a moment. "Okay, I'm glad we cleared that up."

"Is there a problem?" Ryan asked.

"No, it's just… I sent out the emails with the door code to you guys this morning. I'm amazed you got here this fast."

"Well, I would have been here sooner, but the first flight here didn't leave until 3:00 p.m.," Ryan said.

"So… I take it the meeting with the family didn't go well?" Hal asked.

"Not so much," Ryan answered, then took another long gulp of beer. "Dude, this place is sick," he added afterwards.

"Yeah, it came out really good," Hal said proudly.

"I know Uli and Ricky aren't here, but why don't we give this place a proper christening tonight," Ryan said.

"What do you mean?" Hal asked.

"Well, as you can see, I brought company. And while I can take care of four at once, as you already know, that doesn't mean I'm not willing to share," he said, leaning halfway out of the hot tub, a devious smile on his face. "Let's have ourselves a little orgy."

"Oh… no, that's okay," Hal answered.

"Oh, come on! You've got the ultimate party pad here, let's do some partying in it!" Ryan insisted.

"Not tonight," Hal said.

"What, you have a headache or something?"

"No! It's just if we're going to *christen* this place somehow, we need to figure out a way to do it once all four of us are here."

"But if Ricky is here, we don't get to have an orgy!" Ryan complained.

"No, I don't imagine we do," Hal said. "But, feel free to christen your room any way you want tonight."

"Oh, I will," Ryan assured him. Hal was about to leave, then paused for a moment, and looked back. "Just don't get so drunk you drown in there. I don't want to clean that up."

"Not to worry. I've got four lifeguards here to give me mouth-to-mouth if necessary," Ryan said as he put his arm around one of the girls, and she giggled as he pulled her into an open-mouth kiss.

"Right. Well, have fun," Hal said as he walked out.

"Oh, I will," Ryan called back. And he would. He'd also make sure he didn't do any drowning in the hot tub. He'd drown his troubles in the usual way. Alcohol and sex. The standard methods to make himself forget. Though, he was trying to go a while without having a cigarette tonight...

End Song 458

After his newest failed attempt at a nice family visit, Ryan had found himself sitting alone in a bar down the street from his family's home in Seattle. He took another long drink of his beer. Why couldn't they patch this up? He swirled the liquid around in the mug and watched the foam rise and fall along the glass as he thought about it. A few minutes later, an older man took a seat on the stool next to him. "Well, hey there problem child," the man said. Ryan recognized the voice immediately and looked up to see the aged face of Dan. "D... Dan!?" he said.

"In the flesh," Dan replied. "Your mother said I would probably find you here."

"She told you I was home?"

"Yes, indeed. She asked me if I could talk to you."

"She did?"

"Yes. I've found myself a middleman in communication between people many times, and it seems today is no different."

"Okay, I mean... jeez, Dan, it's great to see you again! And I'm happy to sit here and talk to you about anything, but I don't know why she won't talk out our issues with me, like I just tried to do."

Dan looked at him sort of curiously, his expression slowly changing to something far more serious than Ryan had ever seen on his face. "You did?" he asked.

"Uh… yeah?" Ryan answered.

"Hmm. That's not what… I don't know how to explain this. That's not what she implied happened."

"What? What do you mean?" Ryan asked.

"Your mother made it sound like you showed up to make an appearance, I guess, and then argue with them and yell at them."

"She did!?" Ryan said.

"Yeah," Dan said. "But… you want to make things right with them?"

"Well, yeah," Ryan said.

"And that's what you told them when you showed up?"

"Yeah," Ryan said wearily. "But no matter what I do, it seems all we end up doing is fighting."

Dan sighed, then ordered himself a beer from the bartender. After he had taken the first small drink, he looked back at Ryan. "You know, I was always under the impression your family wanted the best for you. And that they genuinely wanted to try and work with you to improve your attitude in order to keep you from ending up in any bad situations in the future. But, seeing you did find success, it sounds like maybe it's them who need to be reminded about what it means to be able to forgive someone and love them unconditionally for who they are."

"Maybe. I don't know. I can't figure them out. If they don't want me around at all anymore, why did they send you to talk to me instead?"

"Well, I'm thinking maybe they want me to try and 'fix' you, like I used to do when you were younger. But, it sounds like they've fallen into a 'holier than thou' trap where they think theirs in the only opinion that is right. That mindset can be very blinding," he said quietly. "I know you've made some lifestyle choices that go against what they believe, but that shouldn't be allowed to break bonds between families."

"Well, they're probably right," Ryan said. "I've spent most of my life as a loser."

"What in the world are you talking about? You're playing in a successful band for heaven's sake! I'm sure you're making more money than both your parent's combined!" Dan replied.

"Alright, maybe loser was the wrong word, but I'm definitely a low-life dirtbag, and I can't seem to be anything else," Ryan lamented.

"Ryan, you're not a lowlife. Lowlifes take advantage of other people, and usually ruin their own lives in the process. From what I understand, you don't ever go out looking to hurt or manipulate anyone, correct?"

"Well, no," Ryan replied.

"And you're not actively hurting yourself in any way, are you?"

"No, well… not anymore," Ryan said quietly. "I was doing drugs for a bit, but I'm done with that now."

"Good! Good for you," Dan replied. "Okay, you're not hurting other people, and you're not hurting yourself at the present time, and hopefully won't ever again. So, I've got news for you. People may say there is no definition of 'normal,' but I did hear once there was something of a scientific/psychological definition for it, and that is a person that's not hurting themselves or others. So, Ryan, I'd like to congratulate you. You're actually normal," Dan announced. Ryan stared at him, mortified. "And, as far as what your family thinks of the way you live, all I can say is you're an adult now. You can make your own decisions. You already know what they consider right and wrong, and if you simply don't agree with parts of it, that's your prerogative. But, if there are other parts where you look inside yourself and genuinely see room for improvement, it's up to you now to make those changes. But don't let them telling you they don't like how you're living get you down. I'm pretty sure everyone on the planet has that issue with some people from time to time. Heck, look at me. I annoy my sweet wife to no end with my jokes and gags, but apparently she loves me enough that she is willing to stay with me. And you seem to have three dedicated friends who are going to tolerate you no matter what, so you're doing well for yourself," Dan announced.

Ryan seemed like he was trying to process all of this. "I suppose," he finally said. "I'm still a greedy jerk, though. I don't hurt other people, but I don't do anything good for them either. Everything I do is for me."

"Ryan, we're all sinners," Dan said. "And I'm sorry to inform you there are plenty of people out there far worse than you. Do what you can, but God is merciful and forgiving, despite what other people might scare you into believing. He loves us all like his children, the same way we're supposed to love each other. I'll tell you what, I'll try to talk to your mother and the rest of your family, and see if I can't remind them of that. I know you're about to head out to re-group with your bandmates, but hopefully next time you're in town, things will be different when you drop by to see them. How does that sound?" Dan asked.

Ryan shook his head slowly side to side. "Dan, you don't have to do that. But… I would really appreciate it if you did," Ryan said as he slowly raised his head to look at him.

Dan smiled. "Now, see? You've come a long way since we last met," he said.

Ryan smiled a little bit too. "So… have you taken on any other apprentices since I've been gone?" Ryan asked.

"Well, no. Not yet. But I have been noticing that a young man named Nathan, who has been going to the church with his family since he was an infant, has been becoming rather bratty and rude to his parents as of late. He's probably about six years old now. I already know his parents quite well, but I wasn't sure if I should go over there and talk to him or not. I know poor Cindy has had enough of me getting involved in other family's drama," Dan mused.

"Dan, can I give *you* some advice on the matter?" Ryan asked.

"Why yes, yes you can," Dan replied.

Ryan took the final gulp of his beer, then set the glass down on the counter. "Get him," Ryan said. It evicted a quick chuckle out of Dan.

"Alright, I'll keep that in mind," Dan said. "And I'll see what I can do about your family while I'm at it."

"Thanks, Dan," Ryan said.

"You're welcome. You take care of yourself, okay?" Dan said, holding his hand out to Ryan.

"I wi…" Ryan took his hand, and suddenly felt a massive, stinging jolt go up his arm. He shrieked as he fell off his barstool and hit the floor, then rolled over onto his back and looked up in shock.

"Oh, by the way, I finally made myself a proper hand buzzer. Everyone got so familiar with the pen, I figured I was never going to get anyone else with it ever again. What do you think?" Dan asked, looking down at him. Ryan didn't immediately answer him. "Well, thanks for testing it for me, regardless. At least I know it works. Let me know when you have a complete review drafted," Dan said with a smile. "Oh, by the way, I know you said you quit doing drugs, but I see that pack of cigarettes sticking out of your back pocket. Those aren't good for you, son. You should quit smoking."

"Will… do…" Ryan replied shakily.

After Hal left Ryan's room, he walked over to the spiral staircase at the end of the hall that led up the castle-like turret tower. At the top was a room capped with a large glass cone; the tiny fourth floor. It was a clear night, and he laid down on his back and marveled at the view. It was like being outside on the roof, minus the mosquitos. The moon was almost full, and it illuminated the room with blue light that cast shadows against the walls and on the ground. As he looked out, he could also see the lights of the other houses around the lake glimmer on the water's surface. Down in the back yard, a waterfall cascaded down into a lit swimming pool.

The house was a masterpiece. A giant work of art. And now, the four of them weren't together to enjoy it all at once. He lay on the floor for a while, thinking about it, trying to figure out what he would do now. He did have to ask himself why the idea of an orgy to break in the house didn't sound like a good idea. And while he didn't want to think it was because he was getting a little older, he couldn't quite dismiss the thought.

He looked down to the dark silhouette of the enormous cedar tree by the bank. The treehouse hadn't been built yet. He'd managed to find an actual treehouse master for the job, but they were still waiting for the permits to get approved by the county. Somehow, he'd imagined the 'christening' being them all taking a plunge into the lake from the treehouse deck with the giant swinging rope he was going to have tied on the highest branch. However, that could just be the christening for the treehouse. *What* was he doing? Ryan was partying with four beautiful women on the floor below, and he was sitting alone in the dark. He got up, and headed for the stairs, then hesitated to take the first step down. It hit him again. The feeling that he honestly didn't want to do it. It was depressing. But then, a different thought suddenly crossed his mind, and he ran downstairs to his room and turned on the computer. He went to a few websites, bought plane tickets for the next day, then went to bed for the night in his own personal UFO.

# CHAPTER 28

## (Any Way You Want It)

459. "Bad Romance" by Lady Gaga

460. "Mickey" by Toni Basil

461. "Fancy" by Reba McEntire

462. "Beautiful Life" by Ace of Base

463. "Love You Like a Love Song" by Selena Gomez & the Scene

464. "Edge of Seventeen" by Stevie Nicks

465. "I Want Candy" by Bow Wow Wow

466. "Where Have All the Cowboys Gone" by Paula Cole

467. "Stronger (What Doesn't Kill You)" by Kelly Clarkson

468. "Hands" by The Ting Tings

469. "Cruel Summer" by Bananarama

470. "I Hope You Dance" by Lee Ann Womack

471. "Blank Space" by Taylor Swift

472. "You're So Vain" by Carly Simon

473. "Heaven Is a Place on Earth" by Belinda Carlisle

474. "Can't Get You Out of My Head" by Kylie Minogue

475. "I Love You Always Forever" by Donna Lewis

476. "The Tide Is High" by Blondie

477. "Blood" by In This Moment

**The lights came on again** as fog poured onto the stage, and out of the mist, Lyrica rose slowly into the air, suspended by a back harness with translucent cords attached. She had on a two-piece outfit covered in dark emerald-turquoise sequins, as well as black gloves, black boots, a thick black choker necklace, and heavy black eyeliner. She looked all in the world like a beautiful, but pissed off little hummingbird rising out of a swamp. Hal leaned against the backstage wall, barely out of sight, and watched her sing to the screaming crowd. He could see the fire in her eyes and hear it in her voice. As much as she said it stressed her out, and claimed she was nothing more than a pawn in her own show, he couldn't quite believe it. She made too much of an effort for it to mean nothing to her. Flames shot up from the side of the stage, and an army of back-up dancers marched out to dance below her. She pointed to the people dramatically as she floated over them, and she let her hand hang down, though only to tease them. As high as they reached, she was just a little too far above for them to touch.

She floated back when the song was nearing its end, touching down gently amongst her back up dancers, and happened to look to the side and saw him. Their eyes met, and he took a few steps back. He hadn't meant to be seen, because he didn't want to distract her and cause her to lose her place. She didn't miss a beat. She kept her eyes on him for a few moments as she sang, then looked back out to the crowd. He stood further back through the entire rest of the show, until she made her grand exit backstage.

> End Songs 459 – 477

"Hi, Hal," she said casually as she strode by him.

"Hi. Hey, sorry about that. I wasn't trying to be a distraction or anything."

"Did I look like I was distracted?" she asked.

"No, not really," he said.

"If you want to be a distraction, you're going to have to try harder next time," she said, and he cringed, pretending the words hurt more than they did. "*Oooh...*"

"So, what? Am I getting dinner tonight?" she asked.

"That could easily be arranged," he said.

"Fine. Here..." She ripped a little piece of paper and quickly scribbled an address on it. "I'll be here for a bit finishing up, but you might as well go to the grocery store and get supplies until I'm done." She threw the paper at him as she marched past.

He took a quick look at it, then called back over his shoulder "See you in a bit!"

Later, in the hotel suite, he was humming to himself as he finished up frying something on the stovetop. Whatever it was smelled really good. She waited back in the living room area, where he was about knee-deep in her wine as she watched him through the glass. She swirled it slowly around his legs, then raised it a little until he was thigh-deep. Nice ass. No denying that. She'd been more stressed out and lonely than usual as of late, and she was starting to get the idea that later when he'd ultimately try to put the moves on her, she might consider not kicking him to the curb.

"Ta-da!" he announced as he turned around with two steaming plates of stir fry and brought them over to where she was sitting. He set them down on the table, and she felt the saliva filling in her mouth as she got a smell of it up close. She casually picked up her fork and started eating. "So, how have you been?" he asked.

"Same old, same old," she replied.

"Overworked and miserable?" he asked. She looked up from her plate for a second to see him with a genuine look of concern on his face, then looked backed down at her food.

"Same old, same old," she said, quieter.

"I'm sorry," he said.

"Why do you even care?"

"Because you're neat, and neat people shouldn't have to be sad," he answered.

"I'm not neat. I'm a perpetually angry bitch," she said.

"Now, look. You may have certain people convinced of that, you might have some of your road crew convinced of that, you might even have yourself convinced of that, but I'm sorry to inform you that you don't fool me."

She looked up again from her plate. "Fuck off."

"You can try as hard as you want, you're not going to change my mind," he said as he took a sip of his wine. They ate in silence for a few minutes after that, though what he said kept eating at her while she was having dinner. Why did he say crap like that? What did he know, anyways? She still couldn't figure out if he was a brilliant con artist, or if he was innocently stupid, and those are two things that aren't usually easy to confuse.

"Thanks for dinner," she said quietly. "This is really good. You're a good cook." He quit chewing mid-bite, and slowly looked up at her. "Don't let it go to your head," she quipped.

"Ooh! That reminds me!" he said as he pulled a small wad of brown wrapping paper out of his pocket, pulled the tape off, and unraveled it. Out of it appeared a small, glittering glass pendant on a black cord necklace. The pendant was in the shape of a large teardrop and was the exact same color as her hair. "I saw this in a little art shop in Vancouver. It reminded me of you, for obvious reasons."

"It's… burple!" she said.

"Burple?"

"Yeah, the color in my hair. Half of people would call it an indigo blue, and the other half would say it's royal purple. So, it's burple." She took the pendant from him and ran her fingers over it. Perfectly smooth, despite the multi-level look of the layered glass. "Thank you."

"You're welcome." He took another sip of his wine. "So, I know it's not really going out on a date to the movies, but I brought *Pirates of the Caribbean* if you're interested. Though, if you're tired and want to go to bed, I totally understand," he said.

"You brought *Pirates of the Caribbean?*" she asked in disbelief.

"Yes?" Hal replied, uncertainly.

Lyrica hesitated for a moment, then asked: "The first one?"

"Of course, poppet," he answered in a British accent.

"I haven't seen that movie in forever," she said.

"Well, shall we fix that?" Hal asked

"I guess I have enough energy left for a movie."

"Alright…" He got up, took the disc out of its case, and put it into the player. She went over and sat down on the couch, then he sat down beside her. Throughout the movie, she kept waiting for him to scoot closer and start groping her, or at least put his arm around her shoulder. But, he stayed planted about a foot and a half from her and didn't move. It started weirding her out. He had to be plotting something, but he remained like that all the way to the end.

The screen went back to the title menu, and he took the remote and shut it off. "Hey, thanks for watching a movie with me," he said.

"Sure. That was sort of fun, actually," she answered.

He got up from the couch with his empty wine glass and motioned at hers. "You want some more?'"

"Sure." She handed him her empty glass, and he took it to the kitchenette and filled it up, then sat back down next to her. "So, what have you been up to lately?" she asked.

"Me? Well, we finished up a tour a few months ago. So, not a whole lot as of late," he said. "It's kind of boring."

"Ha! I'm jealous."

"I know you are," he said. "And so am I."

"Well, I guess you were made for this. Me, not as much."

"Well, you're really good at it, for what it's worth. Though I think you need a nice, long vacation," he said.

"Wouldn't that be nice," she mumbled.

"You know, you really should consider firing your management team. You do have the power to do that."

"I have a contract," she said.

"It's not unbreakable. They just want you to think it is."

"Yeah, if I did anything like that my mom would kill me."

"Oh, tell your mom where to shove it," Hal said.

"You know, I'll go ahead and let you tell her that. Let me know how it goes," she replied.

Hal sighed. "Alright, look. This may sound weird, but my dad and grandfather were both in the mob. Like, for real. And if it's going to cause that much trouble, I'm sure through my connections I could find somebody who could make the whole thing look like an accident."

"OK, *now* you're talking," she laughed.

"Yeah, but, I am sorry you have to live the way you do. You shouldn't have to be miserable. And, I've realized lately how I sort of contributed to that for a while, and I wanted to apologize," he said, and she glanced up from her wine. "I've been living fast for so long, I sort of got used to getting everything I wanted, when I wanted it. But I should never have gone after you the way I did. That was me being a selfish ass." He was the one now looking into his wine as he swirled it, and she was about to agree with everything he said, but then she stopped and thought about it for a little longer.

"Well, yeah," she eventually replied. "But, I guess if you hadn't done what you did, I suppose I'd be sitting here alone right now, not having just watched *Pirates of the Caribbean* after having a great stir fry dinner. Though that time I pepper sprayed you, you totally deserved that."

"Yeah, I know," he admitted. "Thanks for humoring me, tonight. Been sort of lonely since our tour finished. Uli and Ricky went home, and Ryan, well, might still be in the hot tub at my house, but it's not the same without the other two there."

"Right," she said, then added: "Well, thanks again for dinner. I probably do need someone to talk to from time to time. You're okay, I guess," she said as she took the final sip of her wine. His eyes widened as he looked at her, stunned. Clearly the best compliment he had ever received. That look on his face was so goofy it was endearing, and she let a smile slip as she stopped herself from going as far as to laugh at him. That little smile knocked the wind out of him even more, and he huffed out a short breath as he felt the corners of his own mouth curling upwards. He stared at her for a few moments with his eyebrows raised in disbelief, and as she held his gaze with a genuine look of sincerity in her eyes, he found himself leaning in cautiously towards her. She began to lean in towards him as well, then felt the slightest flutter in her chest as their lips met. It startled her for a second, but then she closed her eyes slowly as she felt the warmth of his skin against her face. They stayed like that for a few seconds, then drew back slowly from it.

There were a few moments of silence as they gazed at each other dumbstruck, until he said: "Hey… we should… do this again some time."

"Um… yeah…" she replied reflexively.

"But, it's getting late and you're probably exhausted. I know how it is on a show night. I should probably let you go to bed," he said quietly. "Maybe I can drop by again some time and make you dinner?" he asked, and she nodded without thinking about it. "OK," he said, then started to get up. That snapped her out of her trance.

*Wait… seriously?* she thought to herself as she got up and followed him to the door.

"Thanks again for having me over. I enjoyed it," he said as he hesitated in the doorway. "I hope you get some good sleep tonight."

"Uh, yeah… thanks," she replied.

"Okay… have a good night," he said as he started to walk away, but she stepped out into the hall after him.

"Wait…" she blurted out, and he stopped and turned around. "I mean, you could stay a little longer tonight. You want to have one more glass of wine, at least?" she asked.

He raised one eyebrow, then said, "Sure" and she pulled the door shut behind them after he came back inside.

478. "S&M" by Rihanna *to play over this scene*

or

479. "Satisfaction" by Benny Benassi

Three glasses of wine later, she was tying his hands together with some cord, and then she tied them up to a thick metal air vent on the upper wall. His shirt was already off. "This is a nice belt…" she said as she reached around from behind him and started to take it off. "Real leather…" She pulled it through the loops, then held it taut between her hands. "Too bad we're going to ruin it." His heart was pounding as he heard her crack it mid-air. She noticed a few old scars on his back. Nothing too serious, though they were certainly visible with only the dim city lights filtering into the dark room. "Think you can just show up and be anybody's savior…" She lashed the belt hard across his back. The sharp pain went through him like a knife, but he held his breath and didn't cry out. "Like you're God's gift to woman…" She whipped him again with it. "You haven't lived my life…" She cracked it across his back harder this time, and he clenched his teeth as the stabbing pain went both directions along his spine. "I guess we'll see if you can at least hold up to your own words." She drew her arm back and gave it even more force.

"Aaa… hh…" He tried to stifle the cry the best he could.

"You asked for it, after all," she taunted. He felt a little warm run forming on his skin. That one was starting to bleed. Each crack of the belt added a little more fuel to the fire on his back. They were always so concentrated at first, he could trace every inch of the first strikes. But it would all eventually melt together into a single, throbbing burn; the feeling of his heart beating in his flesh as she tore into him. His knees started to buckle, and he let himself hang by his arms. A single tear went down his cheek. He licked it in with his tongue to keep it from dripping down. Now started the waiting game. The game to see who would cave first. Would she get bored, wear her arm out, and give up, or would he have to beg her to stop when he had enough. He always hoped for the latter. He nearly got there, too. Twenty minutes later, he was about two strikes away from it when she suddenly stopped. "Shit. You're tougher than you look," she said. "Never would have guessed."

> End Song 478 – 479

She dropped the belt on the floor and took a pocket knife and cut him loose from the vent. He collapsed back onto the floor with a loud thud, and it made him dizzy with pain. His hands were still tied together in front of him. She stepped on his chest with her stiletto. "OOOF!"

"You're lucky. If I hadn't done a show tonight, this would have ended differently," she said as she swung the other foot over and stepped off of him on the other side. She opened the closet door, took the shoes off, and threw them inside. That left her in only her bra and underwear. She had taken the rest of her clothes off after she had tied him to the vent, one piece at a time, barely out of reach of how far he could lean. He watched her walk upside down across the ceiling with his head bent back. He wasn't done with her yet. He wasn't anywhere near done. She hadn't made him beg.

"You were right, though. We should have done that a long time ago. That was very therapeutic," she said as she reached for her phone to check her messages. She started scrolling down the screen, but as she turned around, his bound hands suddenly slid down her back, pulling her tight against his body as he pinned her to the wall. The phone hit the floor. He was breathing hard, staring into her eyes, and she felt her heart start racing. That was quite the look he had. She had to wonder exactly how many women he had seduced with it in the past. He pressed his mouth firmly into hers, and she braced her hands on his chest as she licked the bottom of his tongue and found lingering hints of stir fry. His groin was pushing into hers, giving her a hot, tingling sensation as he moved to her neck and started sucking on her skin. She almost slapped him, but her hand didn't quite make it before she let it fall back down. He probably would have liked that, anyways. Whatever. She could cover up whatever damage he ended up doing with makeup in the morning. He licked her neck slowly from her collarbone up to her ear, then whispered: "*Your turn.*" That gave her a little start.

"Uh, getting whipped isn't how I roll," she replied.

He stopped moving for a second. "Let me re-phrase that. Your turn to get whatever you want."

"Pff," she grunted, then realized she didn't know what to say. No man had ever asked her that before.

"You tell me what we're going to do now, and if it's something I've never tried before, you're going to have to teach me," he whispered to her. "As you know, I'm good at following directions…" She could feel him smile as he said it, the flat fronts of his teeth touching down on her skin. What she wanted? She'd been put through so many different fetishes by various men over the years, but none of it really appealed to her. The honest truth was she wasn't as much of a freak as everyone assumed she was. She put on the show, but that's all it was, a show to entertain the crowd, not herself. He kissed her on the mouth again, and she got more of that warm tingling feeling. OK, there. Maybe that was it. That was what she wanted. That little feeling. Except, she didn't even really know what he was doing to cause it, so what was she supposed to say?

"Come on, there must be something…" he said after a few more moments of silence.

"You talk too much," she replied. He gave her a sideways glance. He could tell it was making her nervous.

"Gonna make me guess, huh? Fine, I can guess. We'll start with the classic treatment, and you give me clues where to go from there. Now it's just a matter of whether you want to give me my hands back or not," he said. "I'm told I'm pretty good with them, but if you'd rather watch me struggle, that works too."

"Hmmm," she mumbled dramatically. She led him on for a bit, looking like she was deep in thought trying to decide, but then she lifted his arms back over her and grabbed her pocket knife off the table and cut the cord apart. As soon as she had set the knife back down, he grabbed her from behind and tossed her sideways onto the bed. As she rolled onto her back to look up, he landed nearly on top of her.

---

480. "In the Dark" by Dev *to play over this scene*

481. "Breathe" by Telepopmusik

482. "Abracadabra" by Steve Miller Band

---

"Good choice," he said, grabbing her arms and pinning them down to the sheets over her head.

"We'll see," she said doubtingly as their lips met again, and his hands slowly slid up her arms to lace up with her fingers. He kissed her slowly to begin with, and slowed the pace even further from there, letting their lips linger together longer each time. It started a little fire in her that began to smolder, waiting for more fuel to start burning properly, but he kept it down low. It was actually very romantic. He had to be doing this on purpose just to torment her. He brought one hand down next to her head to stabilize himself as he kissed her a little harder, and she wrapped her arms around his shoulders, making him flinch as she touched his back. She lifted her hands off him in a sudden jerk movement, but then set them down on the back of his neck and ran her fingers up into his hair. She could feel his heart beating against her body as he slipped one hand behind her and started trying to undo her bra.

He worked the clasp loose, then pulled it off her in a quick motion and sent it flying across the room. He started kissing her down her neck, her chest, her stomach, then when he got to her hips, grabbed her underwear in his teeth and pulled them down as he crawled backwards off the end of the bed. Once he had them off her feet, he spit them sideways onto the floor, and started back along the same route he had just come. He kissed the tops of her feet, her ankles her legs, and she watched him with her best unimpressed expression, waiting for him to get on with it. But after he got over her knees, he started dragging his tongue up her thigh, and it actually took her a few moments to realize that her stomach isn't where he was heading next. She started to sit up, but fell right back down into the sheets again as she felt that hot tongue slide between her legs. She gasped in surprise, and grabbed onto his hair with both of her hands. He pushed her thighs wider apart, then kept a loose hold on them as he settled in and made himself at home. She was trying to not give in completely right away, but the warm tingling sensations were multiplying and swarming to the touch of his tongue. She let her head fall back on the pillow again as she shut her eyes. Every time she exhaled, a different sounding sigh escaped, and she couldn't stop it from happening. She loosened her grip on his hair a little, but kept her hands on the back of his head as she pressed him more firmly into her. *"Oohhh…,"* that tongue was getting everywhere, and she could barely handle it. She stole a glance down at him, and was terrified to find him looking right back at her, a maddeningly smug, triumphant smile on his face. She threw her head back again and clenched her teeth. *'I will slap that fucking smile right off your face you rotten asshole I swear to God…'* she thought to herself, and then let out a small, piercing scream as she went into a series of heavenly, gratifying spasms. She tightened her grip on his hair again, and he let out some sort of muffled grunt, but kept licking until her grip slowly began to loosen. She finally let go of him, and he looked up to find her breathing heavily, staring at the ceiling with a distant look on her face. He started to crawl up her, and as she glanced down she felt very much like some sort of stunned prey that had the predator moving in for the kill.

She waited until they were eye to eye, then shoved him forcefully sideways off the bed. He landed on his side, then struggled to get up. "Whoa, WHOA! Hey! I'm sorry! If you want to stop, we can stop!" He got to his feet and held his open hands out in front of him.

She stalked towards him, then grabbed him by his arms and slammed him up against the wall. "Will you just shut up for once!? You talk way too much!" she complained as she got down on her knees and started unbuttoning his fly. The terror on his face turned to disbelief faster than she could unzip the zipper. "I don't just do this for anyone, by the way. I hope you feel special," she muttered, and he felt his knees start to buckle as she took nearly all of him into her mouth at once. He grabbed onto the arm of the wall-mounted hotel room lamp next to him to keep from collapsing onto the floor, and found himself unable to do anything other than stand there and watch her with his mouth hanging open. This. Is. Happening. It's not everyday a guy gets to live out his wildest, most selfish fantasies. He slowly leaned his head back against the wall, and shut his eyes though his mouth remained hanging open.

"*Uuuugh…*" he grabbed tighter onto the lamp as the feeling really began to spread through him. She took the moments he had his eyes closed to examine him a bit better. Not a bad view from where she was observing. A nice, fit, body, with just the right amount of hair. Not one of those Sasquatch guys, nor the sort that can't manage to grow any at all. His ab muscles rolled smoothly into each other, a gentle pattern of three ups and downs on each side shining just slightly from the sweat rolling down his chest. She started rolling her tongue in circles around him, and he let go of the lamp and put both hands on her head as he bent over her reflexively, breathing harder and harder as the moments went by. Finally, he started tapping the side of her head gently with his fingers. She ignored him. He did it faster, more urgently. She still ignored him. "You might… want… to move…" he stammered out.

She took him out of her mouth briefly as she casually replied "Nah, go ahead," and then as she put her mouth back on him, he let out some sort of guttural yell, and she declined to mention that she had never done *that* for anyone before.

He gradually straightened back up, then slid down the wall until he was sitting in front of her. She slowly wiped one corner of her mouth on her bare arm as she kept an intense stare on him. He pushed himself up onto his haunches, then began crawling towards her on all fours. He backed her down so she was laying flat on the floor, then pulled a condom out of his back pocket and started getting settled between her legs. "Oh, god, not on the floor. My back gets enough strain from that harness they put me in during the concerts," she complained, and he immediately pushed himself back up onto his knees and gestured towards the bed. She got up on her feet in no particular hurry, and he took the opportunity to put the condom on as quick as he could. She started walking towards the bed, and right as she was about to get on it, he grabbed her from behind and bent her over the edge of it. Her open palms hit the bed with barely enough force to hold her up, and she felt his hand brush lightly down her butt crack as it moved inwards.

"*Any way you want it...*" he whispered, then spread her slowly but firmly with two of his fingers while holding a third one to the little sensitive spot right in front. She was really glad he couldn't see her face right then as she was the one now with the wide-eyed, open mouth look of shock. He put one leg to either side of her as he straddled her hips, then wrapped his arms around her stomach as he pulled her tight to himself and made the first few excruciating movements.

"*Uhh...*" she shut her eyes and rested her head down on the bed, some of the sweat on her forehead absorbing into the sheets as she started getting more of those little sensations. Her eyes rolled back into her head behind fluttering eyelids. Okay. Not bad. She could get used to this. She spread her legs a little wider and pushed her rear up harder against him, and he made a little choking noise as he started to hump harder. She dug her fingers into the bed and braced her feet to hold firm against his movements, then felt his hands come up underneath her and cup her breasts, gripping them tight enough that her flesh bulged through the spaces between his fingers, though not tight enough that it hurt. He started kissing her shoulder, then worked his way to her neck where he went back to sucking on the same spot he had been before. There was going to be quite a mark there in the morning, she had already relented to this, but she wasn't going to let him get away with it without giving him a matching one at some point tonight.

They went at it like that for quite a while, though eventually she wanted to not be bent over anymore, so she climbed up onto the bed and rolled over onto her back. He watched those two beautiful, round breasts slump gracefully down to either side of her chest, and he was all too willing to get in between them. He moved up over her, and she put her hands on his sides, low down by his waist, and felt the lean muscles stretching and moving underneath his skin as she grabbed his belt loops to pull him closer. She brought her feet up and hooked her big toes on either side of his pants, then pushed them down his legs to his ankles, his boxers going along with them. He kicked them the rest of the way off his feet, and his face was hovering right over hers and the surface of their lips began touching intermittently as he started to thrust into her again. She grabbed his head and turned it so she could start working on a spot of her own, and he let out a long breath as her teeth made contact with his skin. He quickly found, however, that she was gnawing away at far more than his neck. She wrapped her arms around him, and he didn't even flinch this time as her hands gripped his back. He could feel her body giving way, relaxing more, and, he started slowing down, though he wasn't moving any less forcefully. He began moaning lavishly in her ear, and even listening to him made her tingle. She hadn't felt this good in a long time. She'd nearly forgotten what it was like. She got a sudden, strong twinge between her legs that made her tighten up reflexively, and his breath hit her neck hard. *"Mmmm…"* she shut her eyes as the feeling rippled through her. A second one followed right behind it, and she bit her lip and tossed her head to the side on the pillow. A little rush of adrenaline went through him as he watched her. She started breathing harder, and he readied himself. The grand finales were always his favorite part, and the little smile growing on both ends of her lips made him ache with pride. Her eyes suddenly opened wide, her nails dug into him, and in a split second she scratched him hard across both sides of his back.

"AAAAGGGHH!" He did a fast push up over her and held still with his eyes wide open. "Aaaaagghh…" he said again, a little quieter. He was looking straight ahead and didn't notice her put both her hands over her mouth in horror. "Aaahh…" he clenched both his hands around the sheets and shuddered a little as he collapsed back down onto her. "*Aah…*"

She grabbed him by the back of his head and held him in shock as he started jerking against her, and her body followed suit, going into another series of small spasms that left her at the mercy of how long he could keep the feeling going.

End Songs 480 – 482

Once it ended, and both of them had a few moments to collect themselves, he rolled onto his back next to her, and she crossed her arms across her chest, as if trying to hold something in, and turned onto her side facing away from him. She felt his skin press to her back, and he started running his fingers through her hair as he said: "That wasn't fair."

"What?" she breathed in response.

"You made me break my number one rule."

"What's that?"

"Ladies first."

"I did go first," she reminded him.

"I meant for the second round."

She smiled. "Who in the hell ever told you I play fair?"

"I… I don't know what I was thinking," he admitted.

"Well, you're going to have to try harder next time."

"*Ouch*," he replied, then went back to playing with her hair. She laid still, feeling his touch along her head and neck, and he started humming quietly. She'd never had a guy start humming in her ear after sex before. She breathed in, then let it out slowly. That was nice. She felt happy. Calm, even. She shut her eyes. A stray thought entered her head right then. She tried to dismiss it, shoo it away, but it kept coming back. It swirled around in her brain for a bit, until she finally sighed and gave up. She reached her hand up behind her head and grabbed him tightly by the hair.

"GUH!" he uttered as she yanked his head forward, bringing it side by side with hers.

"I better not catch you with any other women from here on out, because you belong to me now," she said firmly.

She couldn't see his face from the angle they were pressed together, but, after a moment, he answered: "*Yes, honey…*" His voice sounded pleasured.

# CHAPTER 29

## (It Takes Two)

**Months went by. Hal split** his time three ways: visiting with his parents and playing with his little sister, travelling sporadically to spend time with Lyrica on her tour, and spending time working on bits and pieces of new songs. Anything that came to mind to have ready for them all to work on in the future. Ryan had planted himself in the house, and as far as Hal had seen, hadn't left for more than a few hours at a time since he first got there. They spent quite a few evenings playing video games together in the media room on the big screen. Down in Arkansas, Ricky was happily adjusting into his new, old life, and Uli had eventually gone back to Germany to visit his parents after a months-long stay in South Dakota. He flew back to see Claudia in late October so they could go out on Halloween together.

---

483. "Monster Mash" by Bobby 'Boris' Pickett and the Crypt Kickers *to play over this scene*

484. "Ghostbusters" by Ray Parker Jr.

485. "Grim Grinning Ghosts" by The Mellomen/Disney

486. "Mad Monster Party" by The Misfits

487. "This is Halloween" by The Citizens of Halloween Town/ Disney or Marilyn Manson

488. "Thriller" by Michael Jackson

489. "Dark Lady" by Cher

---

490. "Headless Horseman" by Bing Crosby/The Rhythmaires/
Disney

491. "Dig up Her Bones" by The Misfits

They went to a big Halloween party at a casino dressed as vampires. Not Count Dracula-style prim and polished vampires, but rather, as a couple of Victorian vampires. They had perhaps looked nice when the evening began, but then got hungry and staged a small massacre while dressed in their late 1800's finest. Their necks and the collars of their clothing were drenched in blood, and they had theatrical quality fangs and specialty contacts that turned their eyes red. They'd had their hair done meticulously, then took their hands and shook each other's hairdos up, so it had that 'I just left a fancy party and killed someone' look to it. They won third place in the couple's category of the costume contest.

After the party was over, they left in Claudia's black hearse, which had not only risen from the dead, but had acquired glittery purple flames on the hood. She had driven them to the party, but Uli was driving back so they both had a chance to get behind the wheel on All Hallows' Eve. Claudia had no idea he had more plans for them that evening until he turned down a different road than the one that led back to the house. She raised one eyebrow as she turned to look at him.

"Uh, oh. Where are we going?" she asked.

"You'll see," he answered with a smile. Uli had secretly done research to find something else other than the Halloween party for them to do that night. A few turns later, and they were off the pavement, heading down a gravel road into a thick grove of trees. It was about eleven forty-five in the evening, and the moon was full. It shone down with all its power and illuminated their way as they drove along the otherwise unlit road. The trees briefly blocked it out and left them in a few minutes of total darkness save for the headlights, until they reached a clearing again, and a sloping hill of headstones came into sight. He pulled to a stop in front of an old iron gate and turned off the car. The gate had been secured with chain and a rusted padlock, but previous visitors had bent part of the bars open wide enough that a determined adult body could make it through. He glanced over at her, and her look of child-like excitement was secondary only to the look of adult-like intrigue.

"Really, Uli? In a graveyard? On Halloween?" she asked.

He said nothing, but slowly searched her eyes with his. She slid closer on the bench seat. "*I like your style,*" she said quietly, and the smile on his face grew a little wider as she started to lean in towards him. He grabbed one of his fangs to pull it off, but she grabbed his hand and stopped him. "Wait." She leaned in a little closer. "*Leave them in.*" His hand sank back down to the seat as the breath he exhaled turned into a slight whistle, and a few seconds later, the hearse started rocking back and forth as they lunged at each other. The fangs rubbed together and left a few accidental scratches on lips, and as she started to crawl onto his lap, he leaned back against the door and caught the handle with the back of his coat. The next time he moved, the door popped open and dumped them backwards out onto the cold October ground.

There were a few moments of silence before Claudia said: "I think my hearse just told us to get a room."

Uli sat up, Claudia rising to a sitting position on his chest with him. "What about a tomb?" he suggested as he gestured towards the gate, and they both giggled like little kids as they got up and slipped through the bowed bars into the cemetery.

Like a perfect scene out of a horror movie, a low mist had formed along the ground, slowly swirling and wafting around the headstones. Right on cue, a coyote howled out in the night as they made their way deeper into the graveyard. As the mist parted around her feet, Claudia did a few spins to make her dress flare out and send the fog fleeing, then sat down on a headstone and looked around. "I didn't even know this place was here."

"It took some digging, if you will, to find it," Uli said, then had the unpleasant realization that he was starting to sound like Hal. Claudia groaned.

"*Booooo…*" she said, with a laugh.

"Another good word for tonight," Uli replied as he walked up to her.

"So. Did we come out here to wake the dead? Or what?" she asked slyly. Uli raised one eyebrow, and Claudia beckoned him closer with her pointer finger. He came over, set his hands down on the headstone to either side of her, and leaned in like he was going to kiss her, but then made a last second turn as he headed for her neck with ready fangs.

"*Aaaaaahhhh…*" he hissed, and she laughed as he bit her gently; certainly not hard enough to make her bleed. He came up to kiss her for real this time, but she grabbed his head and put him back against her neck.

"Harder," she commanded, and his grip tightened on the headstone as he obliged. She glanced down and noticed his bite wasn't the only thing getting harder as he sank the fangs into her. "*Mmmmm. Mmm. Little harder,*" she whispered, and as he increased the pressure further, she suddenly heard a little pop, and then only felt one fang in her skin. He stood back up straight, holding one of the teeth in his fingers. "Ah, damn," she said, and they both laughed. "We'll have to get some better ones at some point."

"Or maybe just better adhesive," he replied as he pressed the tooth back into his mouth.

"Oh, well, no matter…" she said as she reached up and draped her arms around his neck, and pulled him down into an open-mouth kiss. She sank her fingers into his long hair and massaged them into the back of his head, but as they kissed, something in his movements, something in his breathing, something in his reactions, or, lack thereof, tipped her off something wasn't quite right. He'd seemed a little off at times throughout that evening. She slowly broke away, drawing back until he was in focus, and looked into his eyes. "Hey, you all right?"

"What? Yes, I am fine. Why?"

"You've… seemed a little off tonight. Are you coming down with something?" She asked as she put her hand on his forehead.

"No, I feel fine," he said again.

"Something's up. What's going on?" she insisted.

"I have… had a lot on my mind," he admitted.

"Aww, babe, it's the happiest night of the year. What's bugging you?" she asked sweetly. She looked so cute with her little fangs sticking out and blood running down her chin. It was quite distracting.

"It is… hard to explain."

"Well, I think we're alone, and we've got all night," she said.

He sighed. "Claudia… the time I have spent with you over the last few months has been the happiest of my life, and, I think I'm falling in love with you," he said quietly, and she was obviously stunned.

"*That's* what's been bothering you!?" she said, distraught.

"NO! No. It is not that… it is… I am on break right now from the band, but eventually, the break is going to be over, and then we will go back to recording, and then back to touring again. When we go on tour, we are usually gone a long, long time, and I do not want…"

"Uli!" She cut him off, and the look in her eyes softened. "I'm not going anywhere," she said quietly and put her hand on his cheek. "I know you've got a demanding job, but you're living a dream most people only get to fantasize about. I would never want to take you away from that. I've enjoyed every moment we've spent together, too, and if that means I'll have to wait for a while sometimes to get more of those moments, that's something I'm ready to do."

"That would not be fair to you…" he said.

"Eh, life isn't fair," she shrugged. "But you're a part of life I'd like to keep having. Plus, I mean, I think I'm in love with you too…" she said softly. "So, I think at this point you wouldn't *get* to leave without promising to come back. No matter how long it takes." She leaned in closer. "*There's no escape now…*" she whispered.

This brought a smile out of him. "I just do not want to lose you if I am gone, because if I did, it would be my fault."

"Banish the thought," she said. "That's not going to happen."

"I will try," he replied. "You are not like anyone I have ever met before. You see the beauty in darkness."

"I don't understand why more people don't!" she replied. "Why would anyone want to live their life dealing with only the familiar when there's so many fun things hiding in the shadows?"

"Yes, yes… that is exactly it," Uli agreed.

"We speak the same language," Claudia said with a smile.

"We do," he agreed. She leaned in and kissed him again, and the stillness of the graveyard was oddly calming in that moment. No sound, no movement, nothing to distract, unlike if they had been in a nice restaurant, or out on a city street at night. It was a calm few people would ever be brave enough to embrace. As she drew back and opened her eyes again, he had a look of longing on his face that surprised her even in that moment. She stared back into his eyes, transfixed, for a few seconds until he said: "Claudia…"

"Yes?" she answered.

He reached into his back pocket and got down on one knee while she was still seated on the headstone. Both of their shadows in profile shown dark against the mist swirling around them from the light of the full moon. As the mist began to rise, the shadows rose as well, becoming their own vaporous, dark entities sitting and kneeling beside them in the graveyard. He brought forth a little black box and opened it. "Will you marry me?" Inside was a white gold ring crowned with a white gold skull holding a diamond tight in its teeth. Its eye sockets were filled with black onyx, and a few more small onyx gems lined the top of the band next to the skull. She looked at him for a moment, then collapsed onto the ground and hugged him.

"*Oh my God, yes!*" It was exactly midnight. He slipped the ring on her finger, and the dark eyes glistened under the light of the moon. The fog had risen barely enough to conceal two live bodies lying amongst the dead, and they stayed in the old graveyard long enough to see the first sunbeams of morning start to come over the horizon. It chased the shadows of Halloween back into the woods and under the grave markers for another year, and made the purple flames on the hearse glisten as they pulled back into the driveway. They trudged into the house to wash all the blood makeup off and then go to bed, since they had not exactly laid each other to rest in the old cemetery.

End Songs 483 – 491

It was only a few weeks later that three envelopes showed up at Hal's house, and one at his parent's. Each one of them contained the same thing, just addressed to different people. One for Hal, one for Uli, one for Ryan, and one for Cecilia & Harvey. Invitations to Ricky and Melody's wedding in the springtime of next year. Hal's came with a special note asking that he forward Ryan and Uli's to them if they weren't at the house. Hal scanned Uli's and emailed it to him, since he never actually got his parent's address in Germany. As Uli read it on his laptop screen, he realized he had his own announcement to make as well, though him and Claudia didn't have a date set or any firm plans yet. He still also had to break the news to his own parents. Hopefully it would be the nail in the coffin for them that he had his own life now, and he wasn't ever coming back to take over the family business.

When they all arrived in Battle Creek, Arkansas on the third of June, it was the first time they'd seen each other in over a year. Hal, Cecilia, Harvey, and Ryan all got out of the car in the grass parking lot of the little old church. They'd driven the long way around. Hal could see why Ricky had warned against it as it was a multi-hour detour compared to jumping off the train, but Hal wasn't about to put his mom and dad through that. Charlotte was being watched by a neighbor back home, as Cecilia was quite certain she didn't want to bring a toddler to a wedding.

"Hey! Look at this!" Hal said as they came up behind Uli and Claudia.

"Ah! Hello!" Uli said as they turned around.

"So, this fall you two are next, huh?" Hal said.

"Yes, guilty," Uli replied. He and Claudia had settled on the day before Halloween for the wedding. That way, Halloween itself could be the start of their honeymoon. "Everyone, this is Claudia."

Hal was the first to shake her hand. "Wonderful to meet you. I guess we sort of saw you at a distance at Burning Man, but good to finally make your acquaintance."

"Thank you, same," Claudia said. "It will be great to spend time with all of you today."

"Yeah! Hey, speaking of which, where is the man of the hour?"

"He is around back of the church. His mother and sisters are fussing over his tuxedo and boutonniere," Uli said.

"Is he wearing the hat during the wedding?" Hal asked.

"From what I understand he wanted to, but his mother has hidden it until the end of the ceremony."

"Ooh. He must be pissed," Hal said.

"Between that and being fussed over, I believe that is an accurate assessment," Uli said.

"Well, come on. Let's go save him," Ryan said as he started walking up the hill.

"Wait a sec!" Hal said, then ran behind the rental car and popped the trunk. He pulled out a box full of window paint, ribbons, and cans. "We have to get his car first before he sees us," Hal said, and they quickly slipped around the other side of the building to the gravel parking lot where a rusty hot rod was waiting.

Later inside the church, Ricky and Melody stood nervously at the altar; Ricky holding her hands in his. He had no second thoughts at all over marrying her, but instead of having an audience of strangers, he was stuck center stage in a tiny church surrounded by his family. He tried to imagine he was in a sold-out stadium instead to calm his nerves. Melody had a ring of fresh woven wildflowers and grass in her hair that Ricky's sisters had spent all morning making for her. She was also in Ricky's mother's wedding dress. Ruth had insisted she wear it, and it fit her very nicely. At one time, Ruth reminisced, she had been the same size as her. The best part, though, was what Melody had done with her hair. Since they had last seen her, she had dyed it black with two white stripes that ran down the center. She had it in a ponytail that went to the bottom of her neck, and so, it looked like she was wearing a skunk skin cap. She and Ricky must have been quite the sight when he had his hat on. Ricky was in a tuxedo with a red bow tie, wearing fancy black dress shoes. Ricky was actually wearing shoes. Hal and Ryan took ample pictures to prove it even happened.

"You will now exchange your vows," the minister said, then looked at Ricky. "Repeat after me… but look at her," he said, as Ricky had looked at him without thinking about it. Everyone in the church laughed a little, and Ricky turned a little red. Melody was giggling as he fixed his eyes on her.

"I…"

"Ah…" Ricky said.

"…Richard Ransom…" There was a pause after the minister said it. Ricky cringed.

"*Richard!?*" Ryan whispered to Hal and Uli. Hal clenched his mouth tight to keep from saying anything.

"… Richard… Ransom…" Ricky repeated painfully.

"…take you, Melody Gibson…"

"…take you, Melody Gibson… to be mah wedded wife… to have and to hold… for better or for worse… for richer… for poorer… in sickness and in health… to love and to cherish… from this day forward… until death do us part." Ricky finished his part, then Melody said her vows, and they put the rings on each other's fingers.

Finally, the minister said: "I now pronounce you husband and wife. You may kiss the bride!"

Ricky grabbed Melody and dipped her low for the kiss, and a flurry of camera flashes went off from among a huge cluster of Ricky's relatives. Minutes later, the two of them ran out the church doors, pelted with handfuls of rice from the same relatives. Once they reached the bottom of the church stairs, they turned towards the woods, and a few different people in the crowd shouted: "To the lake!"

"The lake? Are we having the reception on the lake shore?" Hal asked the minister, who happened to be walking right next to him.

"No, the reception will be back at the tent behind the church. The lake is a lil' tradition out here after a weddin'."

"They going to have their pictures taken by the water?" Hal asked.

"Well, people will take pictures, yes. But we're gonna shove 'em in."

"They're going to get shoved in the lake?" Hal asked in disbelief.

"Yep. They're gonna '*take the plunge*,'" he said.

"I see," Hal said. "Who gets to shove them in? His parents?"

"Well, it's often the parents, but it could be any number of people. We gotta decide who is most qualified and entitled to shove the two of them in."

"Well…" Hal said. "I do believe the three of us are probably quite well qualified to shove Ricky into a lake." Ryan and Uli agreed.

"And I do reckon you are probably right," the minister said. "Ron and Ruth already got to shove Robert in years ago, and they will have plenty of other chances to shove their other children in, I'm sure."

"Are we going to shove in Melody too?" Ryan asked. "I mean, she doesn't have any family here, does she?"

"No, poor girl doesn't. But this was already discussed amongst the town a few days ago, an' we've already settled on a qualified candidate for her," the minister said.

They all eventually made it to a part of the lake bank where there was a seven to eight foot ledge above the water, and Ricky and Melody walked up to it, then turned around facing the crowd. "Alright everyone, as y'all know, no couple gets married here in Battle Creek without 'taking the plunge' together," the minister said. "Because marriage is a messy business. You'll never keep it perfectly clean and presentable. But that doesn't mean it can't survive rough times as well as the good. So, your first test is to crawl out of the lake in your nice wedding clothes soaked in muck, your hair ruined, your makeup runnin', if you're wearin' makeup that is, and a smile on your face. Because now you don't have to crawl out of life's messes alone anymore." The crowd started clapping loudly. "Alright, shovers, take your places." Hal, Uli, and Ryan stepped forward in front of Ricky, and next to them, an elderly woman also stepped out. "Congratulations you two, on taking the plunge," the minister said, and Hal, Uli, and Ryan ran forward and shoved Ricky off the ledge. The older woman shoved Melody alongside them, and there was a loud splash as they hit the water. The woman suddenly turned around and threw her hands in the air with great excitement. "WOOO! I GET TO RETIRE NOW!" she yelled as she ran back into the crowd. "NO MORE BOVINE SUPPOSITORIES!" she added. A few moments later, Ricky and Melody came into view a few yards down the shore, where the hill sloped down to a sandy bank. They crawled out laughing as they picked water reeds out of each other's hair, and Melody escorted a frog off of Ricky's shoulder back into the water.

Back at the reception tent, the two of them sat at a table drying out while various people came and went, congratulating them. Hal, Uli, and Ryan were giving them a little space while talking to Ricky's father. "She won't stop. She just won't stop..." he rambled. "Even though Rob and Lily have one, she said we're going to keep havin' kids until she gets grandkids that live nearby. That was never part of the original deal," Ron said, looking more frazzled than last time they'd seen him. "Someday, I just want to get eight hours of sleep again, and get to use the bathroom alone, and, and not have to change any more diapers..."

"Well, I don't know how old Ruth is, and I'm totally not trying to be rude here or anything, but isn't she about at the age where she won't be able to have anymore kids soon?" Hal asked.

"Really, she should already be past it," Ron said. "Most women her age should have stopped bein' able to have kids years ago. I swear she's had so many it's like her body has gotten used to it to the point that she might just have them until she's old and grey."

"Well, not to get too personal, but have you thought about going and getting... tied?" Hal suggested.

"She'd kill me," Ron said flatly.

"Why does she want so many kids?" Claudia asked.

"I've tried to ask her that over the years, and she's never really given me a straight answer. But I'm startin' to think it's not having more kids per se as much as it is she likes bein' pregnant. Don't get me wrong, she loves all them kids and spends her whole day takin' care of them. But she did tell me once when she's not pregnant she feels empty inside," Ron said.

"Um... that's..." Hal started to say.

"Disgusting? Weird? Not normal?" Ron finished Hal's sentence.

"Yeah...?" Hal agreed.

"Dude, has your wife ever considered becoming a surrogate?" Ryan asked.

"A what?" Ron asked wearily.

"You know, one of those women who gets pregnant and gives birth to someone else's baby for them. Like, if there is an infertile couple that can't have a baby themselves, they go to a doctor and have their kid started in a lab or something, and then implanted in a surrogate mom?" Ryan said. Ron stared blankly at him. "I, uh, know you said Ruth is sort of religious, so I don't know how she'd feel about the idea, but I know surrogates get paid. I have no clue how much they make, but she'd get to be pregnant, the kid wouldn't be your problem, she'd get paid, and it'd make some other couple happy. So, I dunno, I figured I'd sugg..."

Ron suddenly stood up before Ryan finished. "RUTH! WE NEED TO TALK!" He said as he marched across the room towards her.

"...ggest it," Ryan said to himself.

"That poor man," Uli said quietly.

Hal looked at Ryan. "Dude, that was brilliant," he said. Ryan looked back at him awkwardly, then looked down at the drink in his hand, then held it out at arm's length and dumped it out in the grass.

After the reception, everyone moved from the tent to the gravel parking lot to see the newlyweds off. As Ricky came around the corner and caught sight of his car, it brought a smile to his face. All manner of ribbons were tied to the antenna, as well as some on the back bumper alongside strings tied to empty soup cans to drag behind the car. The windshield had been framed with little pink heart stickers along its edges, and a large patch of white fabric had been taped to the sloping trunk, on which "JUST MARRIED" had been hastily spray-painted. The look Ricky gave to Hal, Uli, and Ryan said it all. It was perfect.

> 492. "Carefree Highway" by Gordon Lightfoot *to play over this scene*

Ricky and Melody jumped in and waved to the crowd as they drove off into the sunset. It was like the perfect ending out of a sappy movie. Hal stood on the church lawn with his hands in his pockets watching them go. He stayed there even after they had disappeared in the distance. He half saw them leave, and half saw the last few years playing out again in his mind. The two visions lapping over one another like pictures falling to the ground and landing on top of each other. A gentle breeze picked up, running across the side of his face and blowing through his hair, and as he looked in the direction it was going, he saw Uli and Claudia sitting on a bench, talking and laughing together. He watched them for a few moments, then suddenly felt a hand on his shoulder. He turned around to see Ryan there.

"Hey…" Ryan said. "Don't worry, it's not the last we'll see of him." Hal looked at him quietly for a moment, then Ryan nodded towards the parking lot. "Come on," he said, and Hal turned to follow as they started walking back that way, looking back once or twice over his shoulder before they got to the car.

Back home, Hal leaned his head against the window pane, and watched the raindrops hit it, then roll down to the sill, splitting and becoming thinner as they went. He'd had another one of his 'bad singer' dreams. He was on stage, the first song had started, and then his voice wouldn't come out, and while the people stared at him struggling to sing, they would start to get up and leave, disappointed. That was last night's dream, anyways. Other nights it was all the instruments suddenly went out of tune, and the guys would put them down and walk off the stage, leaving him there all alone. Or maybe they were performing a new song that the crowd didn't like, and they started to boo. All things that didn't happen, and never would, but still the nightmares would come here and there to remind him of his greatest fears. Many years ago, when he was still a freelance DJ, he'd have similar 'Bad DJ' dreams. He'd hit the start button on a song, and it wouldn't play, and then all his equipment would short out and quit working completely. Or maybe all the good songs would disappear out of the music library, leaving only stupid, boring music that nobody liked, and he'd be forced to play it to keep there from being silence. It's not like he couldn't handle a few bad dreams, but he knew why they were happening more now that he was on break. He wasn't getting up on stage every other night to prove them wrong. He was bored and lonely. He wanted to get back out on the road. He wanted to get back on stage. Taking a break or waiting wouldn't have bothered him as much if there was an end in sight to it, but not knowing how long Ricky and Uli would want to break for was going to drive him crazy. He wasn't about to ruin their happiness by pestering them to get back to work, so he had been preparing a proposal for Lyrica. One that didn't involve a ring, or getting down on one knee.

"I've been thinking…" he said one night, lying in bed next to her. "We'd make an amazing duo act."

"Oh, Lord…" Lyrica mumbled.

"I'm serious. We'd make some bad-ass hits together. The crowds would love it."

"They probably would," she agreed.

"Look, it's been killing me staying at home and not putting on shows. I need to get back out there, but I'm no solo act."

"So, you wanna take over mine?"

"What? NO! No. Absolutely not. I'm just saying, with our powers combined, we could really be quite the force. It wouldn't be taking over your show. We'd become something totally new," he said. She looked at him skeptically. "Look… this probably does sound like I'm trying to take over your show, but that's not my intention. I've always dreamed of duetting with you, and you're second to none, so don't think I'm saying you're the next best thing next to my band. I was just sort of busy with them for years, and now that I'm not, this is the first chance I've had to ask you," he said. "If you wanna know the truth, I've never written a song entirely by myself. Ever. I've written big chunks of them, yes, but everything we have has all been a collaboration between the four of us. And all I'm asking is if you'd be willing to give song making a try *with* me. And if the answer is no, then we won't." She set her head back down on the pillow, facing away from him. "I'd never force you to, if you don't want to," he added. She sighed. "The worst thing about that whole idea is it's starting to sound tempting."

"Is… that a bad thing?" he asked.

She pondered it for a second, then answered: "I had fun once, it was awful."

"I see," Hal said with a smile. "Well, you could try it for a bit, and if it's *too* awful, then we can quit. There won't be any contracts required, I promise. Well, not until the album is set for production, I guess…" he added. "But you have a long trial period before that time."

"And what if I say yes?" she asked, pushing herself up so she was facing him again.

"Wait… what?"

"What happens if I say yes? Then what?" she asked.

"Uh… then… we… have a jam session? And do some songwriting? And go from there?"

She thought about it for a few moments, rapping her three center fingers along the top of the mattress, over and over, then said: "Alright."

"Wh… really!?" Hal said.

"Alright," she repeated. He smiled wide. "Sweet! So… I mean, what about tomorrow night? For having a jam session, that is. You doing anything tomorrow night?"

"No. Tomorrow night is my first night off in three weeks," she said.

His smile dropped. "You're going to make me suffer for this, aren't you?"

She leaned forward on her hands & knees, and crawled a few paces towards him, until she was nearly in his face. "*Isn't that how you like it?*" she asked quietly.

He raised both eyebrows as he looked into her eyes. "Yeah…"

"Well, then I don't see a problem. I am sleeping in tomorrow, though, and taking a long shower…" She took her pointer finger and gently prodded it into the tip of his nose. "So, don't show up until at least 4:00 p.m.," she said.

"Yes, dear…" he replied.

"Good," she said, then started picking her clothes back up from around the room and putting them back on to see him out the door for the night.

He showed up slightly after four in the afternoon the next day with a guitar, a small amplifier, and a little mix board with pre-tuned drum beats on it. His arms were totally full with the equipment, and he also had a notebook in his teeth, and a pencil sticking out of his back pocket. She reached forward and took the notebook out of his mouth. "Thank you!" he said, then shuffled past her and heaped all the equipment down in the middle of the room. "Okay, one more load," he said as he headed back for the door.

"There's more?" she asked.

"That's all the music equipment, but there's a few more supplies," he said. When he next appeared, he had two six packs of beer. One in each hand. "Okay. Now we're ready to write," he said, setting the beer down next to the pile on the floor. He sat down amongst the mess and beckoned her over. "Come, join me!"

"We're going to do this on the floor?" she asked.

"Oh, that's right. You're not a fan of doing it on the floor, are you?" he asked. She rolled her eyes and came over and sat down next to him.

"Songs are best written half drunk on the floor. I know from plenty of experience," he said as he popped the cap of the first bottle, handed it to her, and then started working on a second one for himself. "So, I figured we start with a beat, and see what develops from there," he said as he plugged in the little mix board. He turned it on and selected the first digital drum beat on it. "Let me know when you hear one you find interesting." He let the beat play for a few seconds, then hit the button to move to the next one. He made it to the sixth one before she told him to stop.

"There. That one," she said, then took the first drink of beer.

"Okay." He set it to keep repeating and turned the volume down a little. He took the guitar out of its case and plucked a few strings to make sure it was in tune. "So, I'm going to play anything that comes to me, as it comes, and if you think up any words, just start singing them out. We can always nix or edit later." He pulled the notebook between them. "And feel free to write stuff down too." He picked up his beer and took down about a third of the bottle. "And keep drinking. This gets much easier after you've had a few." He set the bottle down, then started strumming a few chords. He'd repeat the same pattern a few times before moving to another one, then another. For the first few minutes she sat there quietly and listened. He was like that little mix board, he just kept coming up with new combinations. He started another one that was sort of intriguing, and a few lines started coming into her head. She started thinking of more to match the first few, then he suddenly moved on again to another tune.

"No, wait, go back to that last one," she said. He looked up at her briefly, then grinned as he went back into the previous pattern. She listened to it through a few more times, then sang:

"Sitting on the floor on a Friday night, should be out partying, but it doesn't feel right…" She stopped. Hal kept playing, and as she tried to think of a second line, he suddenly added:

"Watching her watch me across the room, want to see what happens, right now it's too soon…"

"Keep telling myself I've got something better to do, but I'm starting to wonder if that's ever been true…" she sang back.

"If you're willing to give me a chance, I'll show you my world, we can make it a dance…" he replied. It was all a little cliché, but a lot of songs start that way. No matter how unique a house is built, they all have the same grey cement foundation. And as many adjustments as were necessary could be made from there, even if they ended up with something completely different from what they started with. Hours went by. They slowly got drunk, and verily, things got more interesting. Every time he got drunk with the guys back at his mom's house, the music always seemed to take a different turn. Sometimes they got metal drunk, or punk drunk, or country drunk, and it became a running joke that every time they drank they would end up adding a new genre to their act. Tonight, things ended up sounding a little hippie-ish/folk-ish, and, at some point, whistling started happening. Lots of whistling.

493. "Young Folks" by Peter, Bjorn & John

494. "Home" by Edward Sharpe and the Magnetic Zeroes

Hal started the beat over on the mix board and whistled a tune to start the song. Then he started singing to her, his face was flushed, but he had an oddly focused gleam in his eyes. He should have been about ready to fall over and pass out, but all he could see was her. As she started to sing back, she had the most content, genuine smile on her face. He knew it was only the alcohol talking, but he decided his new goal was to somehow make her smile like that more often when they were sober. For the chorus they sang together, and she had to admit, they sounded even better together than she thought they would.

End Songs 493 – 494

As they finished, she was giggling over nothing in particular as he drank down the last sip of beer. "I can't believe with as long as you've been in the industry, that you've never had a jam session with anyone," he said.

"Riiight!?" She laughed. "They hand me things…" she said as she held out one hand to the side. "I sing them." she added as she held out the other hand.

"That's kinda sad. Not that you sing things, but… that you've never jammed with anyone before."

"It's totally sad," she agreed as she let both hands drop to her sides.

"Well, we need to do this more often then," Hal said.

"Yeah, like *every night*!" she said. He was sitting on the floor leaning against the front of the couch to keep himself upright, and she crawled over and sat down beside him. "This was fun, but I think I'm out of words now," she said.

"Lyrica Wordsworth is out of words?" Hal asked.

"Lyrica Wordsworth is out of words!" she agreed with a laugh.

"Yeah, well, so am I!" Hal said, like it was a contest.

"What time is it?" she asked.

"Uh…" Hal looked at his watch. "It's either midnight or noon," he said, then stretched to look out the window behind them. It was dark. He looked back at her. "Midnight." He seemed mostly sure about the answer.

"That's good. If it was noon, that means I didn't get any sleep," she replied.

"Yeah. I should probably leave so you can go to bed," he added.

"You're gonna try to go back to your hotel like this?" she asked, doubtingly. Hal pondered this for a second, then turned to look at her.

"I'd eventually make it," he answered.

"Before or after pictures were taken for the tabloid covers?" she replied.

He pondered this too. "You're a real buzz kill sometimes, you know that?"

"I got drunk and hit the town once. The slime sheet covers were awful," she said.

"I think I rem'ber those…" he replied, his voice becoming a little more slurred.

"Come on…" she mumbled, starting to stand up. "Let's go to bed. And… you know, sleep."

Hal grabbed her before she was fully on her feet and pulled her back down into his lap. "I have a better idea. Let's stay up another six hours and go party." He didn't get anywhere near making it through the sentence with a straight face.

"I'm waaay too party to drunk," she protested.

"Yeah, well I'm rather party myself!" Hal said proudly. "But, not too party to not party."

"What the hell are you talking about?" she laughed.

"About how much more party you are than me?" he asked.

"I don't know what you just said. Let's go to bed," she said confidently, then tried to stand up, but didn't as he was still holding her arm gently, and it was enough to hold her down, apparently.

"Hey, that rhymed!" he said. "You're not out of words!" She sat still on his lap. She didn't have a comeback for that. She really was out of words now. He looked at her completely vacantly for a few seconds, then leaned in and kissed her. Despite being drunk, he did it very gently, and she closed her eyes and let his lips sink into hers. Then they slowly tipped over sideways, like two trees falling in slow motion, and hit the floor. They were so hung over the next morning, neither of them could remember if they made a sound when they fell.

495. "Little Talks" by Of Monsters and Men

She sang her first line, and then he sang his, looking straight across at each other from within their opposite recording booths. It went so smoothly, it was more like a beautiful, easy conversation instead of a recording take. They made it to the shared chorus, and as they sang in unison, she could see the passion on his face as he went through various expressions. His whole body bobbed up and down to the beat, starting down at his feet, tapping in rhythm to the song. It took her a few moments to notice she was doing the same thing. She'd never lived like this before. He never yelled at her, never told her what to do, never tried to control her life. And as much as her brain refused to accept it, her tapping feet were hard to deny. She was actually enjoying herself. It was totally weird. He had her thinking about music all the time now. Even though music had always been her life, now it was completely different. She was coming up with pieces of songs for herself, ones that she would make her own, instead of having them assigned to her. She'd show them to him, and he sometimes suggested changes and improvements, but he only ever added, never took away. He'd build things up bigger, never break them down, and he was always excited to see what new things she had come up with. As they approached the final chorus, their voices melded together again into a single, beautiful sound, and as she watched him singing his heart out to her, it suddenly all clicked. It was like a tiny little electric shock, a tiny shot of adrenaline, a brief heart palpitation. She'd never felt anything like it before, yet somehow knew exactly what it was.

> End Song 495

They finished the song, let it fade out, then he asked: "You like that run, or you wanna go again?"

"No, I think that was *the one*," she replied. "We'll have to listen to it over, but I think that was damn near perfection. Unless you didn't like it and want to go again."

"No, that one sounded good to me. Just wanted to run it by you," he said. "We should give it another listen to be sure, but I'm so hungry I can't even think. You want to go get some dinner first before we review it?"

"Yeah. I'm pretty hungry too. Let's," she answered.

"Alright. Let me shut a few things down," he said, turning around and closing out the mix screen on his laptop. The window disappeared and left only the desktop background on the screen. It was an image he had seen many times before, but he never got tired of looking at it. Their second album cover, with all four of them in skates out on the floor of an old roller rink. He was behind Ryan, pushing him forward while Ricky was skating backwards ahead of them, watching Ryan get pushed, and Uli was in back, struggling to remain on his feet as he crawled along the wall. He had to look at it again for a few moments before he turned the laptop off and laid the screen down. He walked out of his booth and met up with Lyrica across the room. "Ready?" he asked.

"Yes," she replied, and to his surprise, looped her arm through his as they went out the door.

# CHAPTER 30

## (My Way)

### ONE YEAR LATER

When the announcement of Hal and Lyrica's relationship, collaboration album, and combined tour was made public, it came with great fanfare. Every respectable and disrespectable entertainment news organization did stories on it for days, even weeks. When the tickets went on sale for the tour, they sold out fast. The two of them were hounded by cameras far more than usual after that, but they were both expecting it. Hal had signed on with Lyrica's management team for the collaboration, with the promise to her that he was going to figure out how to get a little revenge on them after he had studied their methods. They were unwittingly all too happy to have him, because they agreed Lyrica's and his collaboration would be a huge money-maker. Short of getting any real revenge on them yet, Hal would try to make Lyrica laugh after each concert by coming up with a new, creative and bizarre plan to irritate her manager. He suggested maybe they get a nice, rancid piece of roadkill off the highway and hide it in the ventilation system in his Manhattan office. Or perhaps nail him with little plastic bugs launched from a slingshot down dark hallways. Granted, it was all a little immature, but he got some giggles out of her none the less. The asshole had no sense of humor, so he made a great target.

Travelling with Hal made tours far more tolerable. Having someone, anyone, to talk to who wasn't ordering her around made a huge difference. But someone who suggested they put something dead in her manager's air ducts? This was the first tour she was actually looking forward to. There are people who might have been intimidated by the idea of working and living with the person they were in a relationship with 24/7 non-stop. But she had already pepper sprayed him, whipped him, thrown ceramic dishes at him, and left him tied naked to a bed for room service to rescue and he was still around. So, what the heck. They'd probably survive touring together.

The night of their first show came, and they stood backstage in the shadows, examining the crowd. It was almost go time. "You ready for this?" he asked her.

"Pshh. Are *you*?" she answered, and he smiled as he took her hand and squeezed it, and then the intro to the first song began.

> 496. "4 Minutes" by Madonna ft. Justin Timberlake
>
> 497. "Bring Me to Life" by Evanescence
>
> 498. "Moves Like Jagger" by Maroon 5 ft. Christina Aguilera

She ran to the other side of the stage behind the curtain, and then they crouched down and snuck out onto the stage behind two tall amplifiers on either side to make a surprise entrance. Their eyes met across the stage right before they walked out, and he looked so damn excited, it gave her second-hand butterflies. She was used to going out by herself and faking passion when all she was really feeling was exhaustion. But now, working with someone who actually had passion changed the whole experience. Watching him feed off the cheering and screams reminded her of a time long ago when she used to do the same. It was the first time in years she felt that rush again. They stepped out into view as they sang their first lines, and the crowd went wild with screams. She sauntered over to him, swinging her hips as she walked, and he met her eagerly in the middle of the stage. They walked in a tight circle facing each other for a few lines, then stopped, and reached out one arm and grabbed each other by the wrist. They had quite the special effects surprise in store for the audience. As the chorus hit, a power-ful white spotlight turned on from above and shined down on them. Their hair started blowing upwards, and they began to rise into the air. The gasps and cheers from the audience were deafening. They were initially upright, but quickly ended up horizontal with their feet out to the side like they were skydiving. The trick was done with some very strong fans underneath them, as well as powerful magnets strapped under their clothes. It rather looked like they were being abducted by aliens off the stage. The only problem with the stunt was with the fans running, they couldn't sing their lines because the blowing sound would be all that was heard through the microphones. So, for the few moments they were floating, there was some very precise, coordinated sound work going on. Right as the fans went on, the sound to their microphones would be cut, and pre-recorded lines were played through the speakers while they lip-synched the words. Then, once the fans went off a few moments later and they landed back on their feet, the sound to their mics would be turned back on. Hal was never, ever one to lip-sync, but he also thought this would be the coolest effect for a concert ever, so for a few seconds they decided to play along.

The recorded lines weren't off the final cut for the album. They were recorded in a large, empty stadium beforehand, so the echo would sound right, and no one would be any the wiser. He did sing his lines when they did this, even though no one would hear his voice, so that his throat would be moving to make it look right. As the fans turned off and they landed crouching, a wave of applause followed, and they stood up and kept going. He reveled in every second of that stunt. Floating in the air with Lyrica while singing to a sold-out stadium was, dare he use the word, magical? They set out to stun, and stun is what they did; night after night, city after city, state after state, across the country, and across the globe, for the next year and a half.

End Songs 496 – 498

Ricky and Uli were both secretly relieved when Hal announced he was planning to go on tour with Lyrica, and came to them to ask if it was okay? They both said of course, it was fine. They loved the band and travelling together, but they both needed a longer break to rest and recharge. Ricky had been especially nervous and torn about the idea of going back out to write and tour right after Melody and he got married, so Hal's announcement brought him a huge sigh of relief. He wanted to spend more time with her before it was back to work, and take time to try to catch up on all the years they had missed together. Melody was relieved as well. She had been working up to the conversation she didn't want to have with him about when he was going back to the group. The last thing she wanted to do was hold him back from them, or make him feel guilty about leaving for a while again. But at the same time, she was going to miss him terribly after being back together for only a short time. She was going to have a lot of veterinary work to do, but they both quickly realized that was no reason for them to have to be apart during the day.

"You're alright, you're alright!" Ricky reassured the screeching cat, gently turning its head back to face him as Melody worked on putting a cast around its broken leg. "You're going to be okay," he said, rubbing the cat's face. Within a few moments, it quit hissing and yowling, and then even began to purr gently.

"We are like, the greatest vet team ever," she said as she wrapped the plaster.

Yes!" he agreed. "You have the brains, and Ricky is a decent distraction."

"Ricky, honey, in both my personal opinion and the vast majority of public opinion, you are way better than a decent distraction. You're an *amazing* distraction," she said.

"Ah… nah!" he said, turning red. She certainly knew all the holds and other methods to restrain various animals for treatment, but the Ricky method made things much easier on both her and the animals. He got quite used to following her from site to site, patient to patient. After work, they'd go home and make dinner together, then maybe go for a walk out under an expansive sky of stars, or perhaps go for a sunset cruise in his car. Or, if it was Friday or Saturday, it was skating night at the nearest rink about an hour's drive away. The day's work went quickly, and their evenings were spent together. After many long years of chasing it, he'd finally caught what he thought might elude him forever. Once in a while, he'd pinch himself to see if it hurt. He figured if it hurt, and left a mark on his skin, that he wasn't dreaming. He was happy to find it kept hurting every time he checked.

Upon finding out about his extended break, Uli decided to go house hunting with Claudia. He told her to choose where she wanted to live. Anywhere, no limits. It was all the same to him, as he would eventually go travelling around the globe again. So, where did she want to be? Did she want to escape the countryside and move to L.A.? New York? Did she want to move to someplace warmer? Colder? North? South? Across the country? Across the ocean? Nearby? It was understandably an overwhelming question, so she took a few weeks to think about it. But when he checked back in, she still didn't have an answer. "I really don't know," she insisted. "Did you want to move back to Germany?"

"I don't have any major desire to," he said. "I can visit my parents as I wish, but I don't feel I need to move back. Unless Germany is where *you* want to move?"

"Oh, no, I don't have any reason to. I just wanted to check with you."

"As I said, do not worry about me. Wherever we settle, I will spend time both close and far away. Do you have any ideas at all?" he asked. The honest answer was she did, but she felt absolutely ridiculous over what it was.

"Honestly…" she started. "I've never had much of a desire to travel. Maybe a vacation here and there, but my family is here, and this has always been home, so…" She was too ashamed to say it.

"You want to stay here?" he said.

"Yeah…?" she answered sheepishly.

"OK," he replied.

"I mean, really? Living in nowheresville is alright with you?" she asked.

"It has been relaxing to be somewhere where nothing is happening instead of everything," he said. "When we are on the road, we are one place, and then somewhere else the next morning. One night is a party, then the next is a disaster, and everyone everywhere wants to talk to us all the time, and it is tiring, so this might be a nice balance to that," he said.

"Alright…" she said. "I mean, I don't want to move to another teeny tiny house…"

"Of course not," he agreed. "We will find something nice. And if nothing looks good, we can always have something built new."

"OK," she agreed, and there was a quick pause as she looked like she wanted to say something else. He waited for it. "Um… there is one extra little thing, well, maybe it's not little, I was hoping we could work in."

"Yes?" he asked curiously.

"I've always, sort of, wanted to have a bit of land, and a few horses," she said.

"Horses?" he asked.

"Horses…" she repeated timidly, and it was about three months later that they signed the closing paperwork on a very nice ranch house on thirteen lucky acres; pasture, corral, and stable included. The house was nice, but the flowered wallpaper and yellow appliances definitely had to go. It took another four months to take the whole thing a few shades darker, but new paint, black quartz counter tops, and a couple gothic flourishes later, it became a very comfortable lair. Once the house was done, it was time for the finishing touches: Thor and Freyja. Two giant, black, purebred Friesian Horses. Claudia had done riding lessons when she was younger and had occasionally gotten to ride one of her friend's horses more recently, so she was ready to teach Uli how to ride. He had only ridden a few ponies at the fair as a kid, so he had a lot of learning to do. Claudia and Freyja took right to each other and immediately formed a bond, while Uli and Thor had a rather healthy distrust of each other at first.

"Okay, put your left foot in the stirrup, then pull yourself up by the saddle horn and swing your right leg over," she said, and he carefully followed her instructions. Once he was seated, Thor took a few uncertain steps backwards. "Oh, where are you going?" She asked the horse sweetly, grabbing his bridle and pulling him gently back while rubbing him on the nose.

"It doesn't like me," Uli said nervously.

"You two are psyching each other out," she said. "He can tell you're nervous because you're so stiff, and he isn't quite sure what to do about it. And you're freaking out at every move he makes. Just try to relax," she said, and Uli did his best to loosen up. "Now, I'm going to walk him in a few circles around the corral, okay?"

"Alright," Uli said, and Claudia gently tugged on the lead rope to get Thor moving. They did a few slow laps, and Uli started to get more of a feel for it.

"Hey, pat him gently on the neck and rub right behind his ears," she suggested. Uli touched his neck gently to not startle him, and Thor's right ear rotated backwards like a little suspicious satellite dish, but after a few moments of stroking his neck, the ear went back forwards. "There, see? You two will get the feel for this in time," she said. And despite his doubts, Uli did pick up on horse riding more and more in the weeks to come. He and Claudia were riding together around the larger paddock within the first month, then they went on their first longer ride across the unfenced portion of the property after about three months. Before a year had fully passed, they were taking fast, sunset rides across the rolling hills on a daily basis. Getting those horses up to a full gallop was quite the experience; running to chase the sun down to the horizon through the dusty Dakota grass. Uli would sometimes even go out and work with Thor on his own. It was something Claudia could sit on the upper deck and watch for hours and hours while sipping on a glass of wine.

Ryan hung around the house. Hal was happy to let him since it meant some-one was around to keep an eye on the place, and he didn't have to bother his parents to go check in on it. Hal dropped in briefly a couple times during gaps between tour venues, but for the most part, Ryan was there alone. Alone, when he wasn't having wild parties with complete strangers. Knowing Hal would slaughter him if he wrecked the place, he got pretty good at cleaning up after himself and hiding the evidence.

During the year and a half Hal was on the road, Ryan pulled off some-thing he never thought possible. He actually partied hard enough that he got tired and had to take a break from it. He went six weeks without having sex. Six whole weeks. During that time, he did nothing but play video games and watch videos on YouTube. Toward the end of the sixth week, he got out of the shower one morning and caught a glimpse of himself in the mirror as he walked by. He stopped and backed up. He stared in disbelief for a few moments, and then a scream burst forth from the house. It echoed for miles, and remnants of it even made it all the way to a few nearby towns. He had developed a bit of a stomach. He was losing his stage body. Within an hour, he had a gym membership, and a new way to spend his free time. He went every other day. He worked out hard enough each time that he had to take the next day off to recover.

Within a few months, he was already seeing the stomach shrink, but he had been enjoying his workouts so much that he had no plans of quitting, even after the extra weight was completely gone. He was going to get ripped, goddammit. It was his new goal. He also hadn't realized until he had started working out just how much he really needed to get out of the house. He called up a few of his old friends from the hardware store, and spent a night here and there hanging out with them as well. Some nights they'd go out to the bar, and other nights they'd stay in, order pizza, and play video games. He feared no pizza, he'd burn it off the next day.

On top of the workouts and socializing, he took up something else in his spare time that he kept hidden from Hal, Ricky, and Uli. He knew if they ever found out, it'd be the end of his reputation. He went and volunteered a couple hours every week at a food bank. He worked mostly in the back, receiving the donation shipments, carrying the food into the warehouse, taking stock, and organizing it on the shelves. He always snuck in and out with his hoodie pulled tight over his head, hoping nobody would recognize him other than the few other people he worked with. It was his dirty little secret. He always needed to have something to hide to keep himself entertained, lest he should ever allow himself to grow boring and turn into an adult. He had set down his drumsticks for over a year, but a few months before the end of Hal and Lyrica's tour, he finally picked them up again. Beats radiated from the house through a single open window during the day and early evening, and anyone who knew who lived in that house took extra notice.

A young man went out of his house one day, out into the neighborhood road, and, pointing his cellphone towards the house, took a minute of video. He posted it online later. "This report coming to you from here in Battle Creek, MI. Look what I caught today by the lake!" he typed with the short video.

"Yes, YES! Praise the gods of rock for this most promising sign! The time may be drawing near that we will once again be fulfilled!" someone typed in response.

At about the same time many miles west, another unusual sound began to emanate from a ranch in the rolling hills of South Dakota. The pipe organ was finally together. Uli laughed maniacally to himself for a few moments as he gazed upon it. It took up nearly half the living room, rising all the way to the peak of the vaulted ceilings. He almost sat down to play, but then ran upstairs and returned with his long black leather trench coat. The christening of such an instrument wouldn't have been the same without it. Claudia was thankful at that moment that they had moved out onto acreage, because had they been close to any neighbors, they likely would have had noise complaints filed against them. And as arousing as it was to watch him laughing at the organ while wearing the coat, she could tell him and the organ clearly needed some alone time together. So, she went upstairs and watched ghost hunting videos until he finally wore himself out in the early hours of the morning. In the weeks that came, she convinced him to turn the sound down a little, and she would accompany him on the flute for a few pieces. They'd play for a couple hours each day before going riding, and the black plants on the shelves in the living room were looking healthier and fuller than ever before.

Down in Arkansas, Ricky lay in bed one night, watching the full moon rise over the hills in the distance. It hadn't been a very exciting day. Melody only had one cow to treat, and he just wasn't tired, even though she was sound asleep next to him. He got up quietly and crept to the window to get a better view. Moon shadows were forming behind the trees as the light crept down them, and it was something of a silent call. He snuck downstairs, got John's guitar out of its case, and wrote a note on a piece of scrap paper that he took upstairs and placed on his pillow; in case she awoke and wondered where he was.

Couldn't sleep.

Went to go hang out with the night animals for a bit.

Love you!

The sound of the door opening and closing gently downstairs did not wake her as he left. He held the guitar by its neck, slung over his shoulder as he made his way across the field into the woods. Once he was past the edge of the tree line, little sets of eyes started appearing around him, and followed behind like a flock of floating emeralds. He had been thinking he'd find a nice place to sit down and play, but the more he walked, the more he didn't want to stop. He pulled the guitar strap over his head and let the instrument swing down into his arms in front of him. He started to pick a few notes, strum a few chords, then played a few of their songs all the way through, acoustic style. As he made his way through patches of moonlight shining through the canopy, he looked back to see glimpses of various inhabitants of the woods trailing behind. Bats flitted between the trees and zipped directly in front of him, and a few owls followed overhead. They'd glide to a branch, sit for a bit and observe, and then take flight and glide to another once he had moved far enough ahead. It was a good feeling... being out in the woods with a small audience around, and his wife sleeping soundly back home. But at the same time, he was fighting back a small twinge of loneliness.

> 499. "House of the Rising Sun" by The Animals

He started to sing a bit. His voice carried for miles, though he didn't know it. The sound of the guitar and his words gently awoke Melody within a few minutes. She found the note and went and opened the window and listened for a while, resting on her knees with her arms folded over the windowsill. There was something mystical about hearing him play out of sight, hidden by the night. It was very much like the song of a coyote howling at the moon. He sang for her plenty, though she sensed tonight this was the song of a lonely coyote calling out for his pack, and it pained her to hear any animal suffering in its own loneliness.

> End Song 499

It was about three months after Hal and Lyrica's tour finished that the message finally came, showing up overnight in their email boxes and waiting to be discovered in the morning. It was short and simple:

> Hey all,
>
> As you probably know, me and Lyrica finished up our tour a few months ago, and now that I've had a nice long nap to recover, I was wondering if you guys wanted to come over sometime. We could maybe do some drinking, play a few games, and, I dunno, maybe do a bit of song writing if you're up for it? Let me know. You know where to find me and Ryan.
>
> -Hal

Uli responded that he needed about two weeks, then he'd be on his way. He told Claudia, and they spent as much time as they could together during that time. She ultimately decided she was going to go back to her old job as office coordinator at the real estate office once he left. Otherwise, she was just going to get bored during the day. In the evenings and on the weekends she would trade off riding Thor and Freyja to keep them up on their exercise. He assured her he wasn't going to disappear entirely for months on end, but he didn't know exactly when he'd get breaks long enough to fly out and see her. She told him it'd be a nice surprise she'd be on the lookout for. As she dropped him off at the airport, he picked her up and held her by her bottom, so they were perfectly eye to eye, and her feet were dangling right about at his knees as they kissed goodbye.

When Ricky read Uli's email that he was going to go in two weeks, Ricky responded that he'd do the same. He broke the news to Melody that night at dinner. They both knew it was coming since Hal had been back for a few months, but it still didn't make things any easier. When the day came that he was to leave, they walked up to the train tracks together a bit early, so they could walk slow. Ricky had his duffel bag packed full, as well as his original acoustic guitar in its duct tape case. He had the other three guitars (The Flaming Axe, the Four Piece Logo Guitar & John's Blues Guitar), shipped professionally a few days before.

When they got to the tracks, they turned to look at each other. Their expressions said most of what needed to be said. She hugged him tight. "I'm gonna miss you," she whispered.

"I'm going to miss you too," he replied. He looked at her longingly, then crouched down and put his hand on the ground. A little blue wildflower sprouted up between his fingers, and he picked it and handed it to her. She took it, and gently touched the petals. It would certainly be joining a very old, red wildflower she had dried in a book on her desk.

"That reminds me…" she said quietly. "I have something for you, too." She reached up and took his hat off and pulled her old pair of underwear out of the rip in the lining. She put them in her pocket, then pulled out a new pair of lilac underwear that were made entirely of thin lace. His eyes gradually widened as he looked at them. "I figured you could carry these around for a bit, and when you come back, I'll model them for you," she said as she stuffed them into the rip, and then replaced the hat on his head. He still looked like he was straining for something to say when they heard the first blast of the train horn in the distance. They looked and saw it turn the first corner into view down the line, which meant they had about one minute. He looked to her again.

"Ah' love you," he said as he hugged her again.

"Love you too."

"Be back as soon as ah' can," he said.

"Hey, enjoy your time with your friends. Don't feel bad about it," she said. "I've got plenty of work to do, and I'll be here, waiting. I won't disappear this time."

"Promise?" he asked.

"Promise," she replied.

He kissed her gently, holding onto it as long as they could before the train was entering the final few moments of its approach. Their hands gently slipped apart as he began to run. It came alongside them, and he jumped and grabbed onto the ladder. He held the rungs and turned so he was facing outwards, and they watched each other disappear into the distance. Once the train was out of sight, she turned slowly back towards the trail to town. They had been thinking about starting a family, but agreed it'd be best if they waited until this round of writing and touring was done. She didn't have the heart to tell him that those plans had been moved up. It's not like she was going to keep it secret from him, but if he found out before he left, she knew he wouldn't leave. And right now, he had some place else he needed to be. She figured she'd whisper it to him sweetly through the phone once he was in Michigan. If he had at least made it there, it'd be easier to convince him to stay. She wasn't going to let him give his career up. Considering they had survived the abuse and unintentional neglect that they had as kids, a child being raised by two loving parents who were perhaps a little busy should survive just fine. It would be a treat when they were all together, instead of something to be dreaded. Plus, she had a feeling she was going to have plenty of help, even when he was gone.

She made her way down the trail to his parent's farmhouse. They had invited her that night for dinner. It probably wouldn't be right for his mom to find out before he did, so she was going to have to hold onto the secret for a few more days. As the back of the house came into view, she was in time to see a young couple getting out of their car. Jack and Diane. She had met then once before. They were obviously here to visit the tummy again. Jack pulled the wheelchair out of the back of the trunk, and brought it around to the passenger side, where he helped his wife into it.

"Evenin." She greeted them as she walked by, and they said hi back. She walked up the stairs to the back porch and opened the door and leaned inside. "Hey! Y'all got company. Other than me."

"Oh! Thank you dear!" Ruth said from the living room. "Boys!" she yelled loudly. "Please come help Miss Diane inside!" No sooner had she said it, a flock of young men came down the stairs, and Melody moved to the side as they flooded out the back door. They surrounded the young woman in the wheelchair, then lifted her up, wheelchair and all, and carried her up the stairs and into the house over their shoulders like Cleopatra might have been carried through the streets of Egypt by her loyal servants. They set her down carefully inside.

"Thank you, all!" Diane said, then rolled into the living room where Ruth was sitting. Jack followed close behind. "Miss Ruth! How are you doing today?" she asked.

"Why, I am positively glowing! Thank you for asking!" she answered.

"And how is our little bun?"

"The little dear is coming along quite well, I think," Ruth said, and Melody saw the first look of relaxation on Ron's face she'd seen in years as he checked on a pot of beans simmering on the stovetop.

Ricky and Uli arrived at almost the same time, and Hal and Ryan were eagerly waiting. Ryan threw the door open, grabbed their luggage, and pulled them inside, saying it was about damn time. As much as both of them had promised they'd drop by, they hadn't actually made it up to see the house finished before now. The first order of business was the tour. Uli expressed his disbelief as they entered the glass top tower that Hal had actually gone through with the idea, to which Hal asked if he didn't like it. Uli said that wasn't what he said at all. Upon hearing that, Hal told him to wait for nightfall, when they could all go up and see the star show. The phrase 'star show' prompted Uli to ask how his tour with Lyrica went.

"Good, good," Hal said, a little too smugly. "You saw the floaty alien abduction trick clip I sent you guys, right?"

"Yes. That was impressive, even for you," Uli agreed.

"Are we all going to try it on our next tour?" Ryan asked.

"I think it's a distinct possibility," Hal replied.

"Okay, what else?" Uli asked.

"Oh jeez, it's going to take me days to tell all the stories. But I gotta say, that little slice of payback we dealt her manager right before the last concert is something I'm going to cherish for years to come."

"I heard bits and pieces of it on TV and in the news, but what exactly happened?" Ryan asked.

"So, a few minutes before we went on, her manager was chewing her out over some teeny tiny error she made during the last show, and I snuck up behind him with a hot mic. His tirade got projected to the whole stadium for a few moments before he heard it echoing and noticed something was wrong. That's when I hit the curtain motor button, and gave him a few, glowing moments in the spotlight in front of twenty thousand people. Everyone was a little confused at first, of course. But I explained to them in exceptionally sophisticated terms that this was Lyrica's asshole manager yelling at her, and that they should all boo him. There was a little delay, of course, while every-one was trying to figure out if it was a weird joke, but after a few moments, the booing started. Some of the people up front even started throwing water bottles and other stuff at him."

"Nice!" Ryan said.

"Oh god, it was amazing. He was cowering. Like, he actually started cowering. And, of course, a few people caught the entire thing on film because they were filming from the moment they came through the doors past the 'no filming' signs. So, once it had done a few million rounds through YouTube and the news, Lyrica was magically rid of that rotten management team that had tormented her for all those years," Hal said, and Uli held out a fist that Hal bumped his against.

"So, now what for Lyrica?" Ryan asked.

"She is going to take a well-deserved vacation, and then she said she was thinking about attempting to write an album entirely by herself," he said.

"Good for her!" Uli said.

"Yeah. And I asked Jim to find her the best manager in the whole industry."

"What did he say to that?" Ryan asked.

"He said he was too busy with us."

"Of course," Uli said.

"So, then I asked him to find her the second-best manager in the whole industry, to which he said no problem, and that he'd call his wife in the morning."

"His wife?" Uli asked.

"He's *married*!?" Ryan exclaimed.

"Yep. Apparently she just got done with a five-year contract with *Hate of the Union*, and they have stated they are definitely taking a multi-year break now to be with their families."

"Wait he's married, and his wife has been managing *HATE OF THE UNION*?" Ryan said, louder.

"Yeah. I was as surprised as you guys. Apparently the two of them see each other for about a combined twenty days every year."

"Poor Jim," Ricky said.

"Yeah, that was my first thought, too, but he told me the whole extended version of the story, and that's apparently about how long they can stand each other nowadays. He described it as 'keeping the relationship interesting,'" Hal explained, making quotation marks with his fingers.

"Oh," Ricky said.

"Yeah, anyways… she's going to be Lyrica's new manager, and Jim promises there will be absolutely no abuse. Even though the two of them have problems getting along, he had nothing but good things to say about her managing skills."

"Well, that is a good ending to the story, then," Uli said.

"So… when do we get to do a jam session with *Hate of the Union*?" Ryan interrupted.

"They all just went home. I think you can kiss that one goodbye for a while," Hal replied, then added: "Come on, we have a lot more house to see." He led them on a guided tour throughout the rest of the mansion, and then down the stairs to the back door. The grand finale came into sight as they made it halfway down the hill to the lake: The Treehouse. Two stories of log-cabin style glory dotted with artistic round windows and a tall wood ladder for access. At the top of the ladder, a round deck wrapped around the whole structure, and over the main door, a large sign with sloppily-carved script read: "No Gurlz Allowed." Ricky's eyes lit up like a kid's on Christmas. "Well?" Hal asked him, motioning towards the ladder. Ricky climbed up it as fast as he could, pausing at the top before going inside to admire the view of the lake through the tree branches. Once the other three made it up, he turned the handle, and the room materialized in its full splendor. A wide but low black table sat in the center, surrounded by four enormous bean bag chairs; a grey one, a red one, a black one, and a lime green one. Ryan had also already brought up a drum set piece by piece and assembled it off to the side of the green beanbag. Two of the walls were lined with empty bookcases and drawers, and a stainless-steel refrigerator sat in the corner. Hal reached to the side and turned on the overhead lights.

"There's 'lectricity?" Ricky was astounded.

"Yeah! How else are we supposed to keep the beer cold?" Ryan said.

"And keep us warm during the winter," Hal added, pointing to a forced air wall heater. "There's plumbing too." Hal walked to the corner of the room and opened a door to reveal a little half bathroom, sink and toilet. "And obviously, we need to do more decorating and bring some stuff up here to fill the shelves, and get band posters for the walls. It's a blank canvas ready to be worked on."

"What's upstairs?" Ricky asked.

"More hang out space," Hal said. "C'mon…" He started to climb the ladder to the second story, and the others followed. The second floor was a little smaller and circled the tree trunk in its center. Square windows lined the entire side facing the lake, but above the clear windows were four round stained-glass windows: one with the image of a microphone, one of a guitar, one of a piano and one of a drum set. The ceiling boards all angled into a sharp peak around the trunk above them, and the whole room had more of an unfinished look to it, making it feel like the lookout tower in a real, rustic treehouse. Ricky walked up to the window and put his hand on the edge of the frame as he admired the view. A little chickadee flew up to the window, grabbed onto the upper frame with its feet and hung upside down looking at Ricky for a moment. It cocked its head, then flew off and landed on one of the tree branches further away. As Ricky was looking at where it landed, he caught sight of the giant rope tied to the biggest, highest branch overhead. "Oh yeah, and there's that for the summertime," Hal said once he saw Ricky had noticed it, and they climbed back downstairs to inspect it. The huge rope was tied about twenty feet out from the deck, with a smaller lead rope that was tied to it and secured to the deck, ensuring they could always reel it back to the deck platform. The smaller rope had plenty of slack, so it didn't stop the big rope from swinging all the way out over the lake. "Have ya tried it yet?" Ricky asked.

"Nope. I figured you'd be the first to give it a go once summer rolls around," Hal said. Ricky looked at the rope, then out to the lake, then back at them. He took his hat off, hung it off a nearby tree branch, grabbed the rope, backed up a few steps, then ran off the edge of the deck. He dipped down in a fast arc as the rope swung, then once it reached its peak over the water, let go and plunged in. Hal, Uli, and Ryan were somewhat in shock, and just sort of quietly watched. It was early spring, and a bit too cold for any of them to want to follow. Ricky surfaced a few seconds later, shaking his hair out like a wet dog, and started making his way to the shore. It was then that Hal noticed a trail of green leaves right in the line of the rope. Leaves that had been barely opening buds a moment before, but were now displaying their full spring bodies in the gentle sunlight of the March afternoon.

# WE WILL ROCK YOU, AN EPILOGUE

**Many long nights were spent** in the treehouse. Procrastinating, drinking, messing around, and occasionally, even writing and composing. Stories were shared, announcements were made, and teasing followed those announcements being made. Then, somehow, in the early fall, through all the beautifully wasted time, enough new songs had come together that they had their next album. It went into production, but the release date was pushed out a few months to next spring, because *somebody* had to go home to be there for the birth of his daughter (as Ryan put it). Uli took the time to go home to see Claudia as well. After a few more months, when the first gentle rays of spring sunshine began to break through the clouds again, Ricky tearfully said goodbye again to Melody and his family. Ruth was rocking Harmony gently in her arms as she lifted the girl's little arm and helped her wave goodbye to her daddy.

Ruth ultimately forgave the two of them for naming the girl Harmony, even though that didn't start with an 'R'. Ricky and Melody named the son they had a few years later Rebel, just to make Ruth happy. And because Rebel Ransom is the most kick-ass name ever.

Uli and Claudia took one last early-spring sunset ride across the plains, then brought the horses back into the stable, brushed them, and gave them an apple each. Hal threw his little sister up in the air and caught her, and she giggled as he set her back down, then he hugged his parents goodbye. Later that night, he sent an email to Lyrica noting they'd be in the Miami area the same time she was going to be on vacation there, and that they should have dinner together one night. "*Oh, I suppose. If we have to*," she replied. Ryan spent a few hours at the house grudgingly draining and scrubbing the hot tub since he wouldn't be back to use it for a bit, and he didn't want it to be all moldy when he did return.

A few days later, the four of them found themselves standing out back of the arena in Detroit on the first night of their new tour, only a few minutes away from going on stage. Ryan was smoking a cigarette, his first one that day. He had been having success at waiting longer between them, but they were about to do a show and he needed to not be at the end of his nerves for the show. He inhaled the last draw, then spit the rest into the bucket out back designated for butts. Right as they were walking in, the opening band was walking out. They were an all-female punk band originally named 'Cunt Punt,' but, due to massive PR issues, started going by just 'Punt.' As Ryan and their lead singer, Delia (or 'Danger', as she was called), crossed paths, she suddenly stopped and grabbed him gently by the chin. She turned his head slightly side to side as if examining a piece of fruit at the grocery store; her long, lavender, claw-like fingernails gently resting against his skin. She had multiple piercings on her lip, nose and ears, and half of her head was shaved, while the other half sported bright blond hair hanging down slightly past her chin.

"Uh, hi. Can I help you?" Ryan asked politely as she examined him.

Sounding nearly bored, she responded: "You're cute. We should fuck after the show." Then let go of his face and continued on with her bandmates out the back door.

"Uh, oh... kay," Ryan said as he watched her go. He turned to look at the other three. "Sweet!" he said, then went inside to get into place. Uli and Ricky both looked out the back door at Danger, then back in Ryan's direction.

"I wouldn't hold your breath," Hal said, doubtingly.

The big, overhead lights went off, plunging the whole arena into darkness, and they snuck out onto stage to the thunderous roar of excited screams.

500. "Instant Karma! (We All Shine On)" by John Lennon/
Yoko Ono

Uli hit the first few notes on the shiny black grand piano that was travelling with them for this tour, and the cheering suddenly exploded. A multitude of stage lights came on all at once, casting hundreds of shadows of Hal all over the stage. Dark shadows, lighter ones, tall shadows that made him seem larger than life, some more the correct height, and all of them in a multitude of colors from the different colored lights. As he started to sing, he felt the excitement in his chest, and the chaos at his feet. A woman in the crowd held up a sign that said: 'Battle Creek is my anti-depression music!' Ricky caught sight of her, and pointed the head of his guitar in her direction and nodded, which brought a huge smile to her face. Ryan bobbed his head up and down to the beat, and the shadow of his mohawk appeared like half of a saw blade. Spiked high and rigid, it was a formidable line of defense above him. When they reached the first chorus, Hal raised his fist triumphantly into the air as he nearly screamed it out, and a multitude of hands flew up in response. Hands and arms were raised as far as they could see in the massive arena, waving back and forth in time with his. Thousands of people of all ages and walks of life, falling into sweet, synchronized rhythm with them.

End Song 500

# SONGS USED

1. "Ring of Fire" – Johnny Cash
2. "Thousand Miles from Nowhere' – Dwight Yoakam
3. "Country Roads Take Me Home" – John Denver
4. "Okie From Muskogee" – Merle Haggard
5. "Don't Rock the Jukebox" – Alan Jackson
6. "Achy Breaky Heart" – Billy Ray Cyrus
7. "It's the End of the World as We Know It (And I Feel Fine)" – R. E. M.
8. "Stayin' Alive" – The Bee Gees
9. "Starry Eyed Surprise" – Paul Oakenfold ft. Shifty Shellshock
10. "Uptown Funk" – Mark Ronson ft. Bruno Mars
11. "'Play that Funky Music White Boy" – Wild Cherry
12. "Electric Avenue" – Eddy Grant
13. "Macarena" – Los Del Rio
14. "Respect" – Aretha Franklin
15. "Video Killed the Radio Star" – The Buggles
16. "Jump in the Line" – Harry Belafonte
17. "U Can't Touch This" – MC Hammer
18. "Saturday Night" – The Bay City rollers
19. "Who Let the Dogs Out" – The Baha Men
20. "Whip It" – Devo
21. "Boys of Summer" – Don Henley

22.  "You Can Do Magic" – America
23.  "Life is a Highway" – Rascal Flatts
24.  "Rock You Like a Hurricane" – The Scorpions
25.  "Should I Stay or Should I Go?" – The Clash
26.  "I Want to Hold Your Hand" – The Beatles
27.  "Free Fallin'" – Tom Petty
28.  "All Summer Long" – Kid Rock
29.  "Alive" – P.O.D.
30.  "1985" – Bowling for Soup
31.  "American Pie" – Don McLean
32.  "16 Candles" – The Crests
33.  "Friends in Low Places" – Garth Brooks
34.  "Cemetery Gates" – Pantera
35.  "Peaches" – The Presidents of the United States of America
36.  "Absolutely (Story of a Girl)" – Nine Days
37.  "Riptide" – Vance Joy
38.  "Mr. Bojangles" – Nitty Gritty Dirt Band
39.  "Talk Dirty to Me" – Poison
40.  "What's My Age Again?" – Blink 182
41.  "Sunglasses at Night" – Corey Hart
42.  "Piano Man" – Billy Joel
43.  "Tutti Frutti" – Little Richard
44.  "Yakety Yak" – The Coasters
45.  "Clocks" – Coldplay
46.  "Leave the Night On" – Sam Hunt
47.  "Cum on Feel the Noize" – Quiet Riot
48.  "Lifestyles of the Rich and the Famous" – Good Charlotte
49.  "Rock this Town" – Stray Cats
50.  "Boot Scootin' Boogie" – Brooks & Dunn
51.  "We're Not Gonna Take It" – Twisted Sister
52.  "In Too Deep" – Sum 41

53. "Semi-Charmed Life" – Third Eye Blind
54. "How Country Feels" – Randy Houser
55. "I Don't Mind the Pain" – Danzig
56. "American Jesus" – Bad Religion
57. "Strangers in the Night" – Frank Sinatra
58. "Head Over Boots" – Jon Pardi
59. "Bat Country" – Avenged Sevenfold
60. "Paradise City" – Guns N Roses
61. "Dancing in the Dark" – Bruce Springsteen
62. "Time to Pretend" – MGMT
63. "Can I Play with Madness?" – Iron Maiden
64. "First Date" – Blink 182
65. "Rebel Rouser" – Duane Eddy
66. "Cake by the Ocean" – DNCE
67. "Fast Car" – Tracy Chapman
68. "The Way" – Fastball
69. "Don't Stop Believin'" – Journey
70. "18 and Life" – Skid Row
71. "Devil Inside" – INXS
72. "Down with the Sickness" – Disturbed
73. "The Rock Show" – Blink 182
74. "Thunder Rolls" – Garth Brooks
75. "Burnin' for You" – Blue Oyster Cult
76. "Born to Be Wild" – Steppenwolf
77. "Psychosocial" – Slipknot
78. "Bottoms Up" – Brantley Gilbert
79. "Smells Like Teen Spirit" – Nirvana
80. "Dirty Deeds Done Dirt Cheap" – AC/DC
81. "Rock Out" – Motorhead
82. "Smooth Criminal" – Alien Ant Farm
83. "Smoke Rings in the Dark" – Gary Allan

84. "Eve of Destruction" – The Turtles
85. "Send Me an Angel" – Real Life
86. "Jump Around" – House of Pain
87. 'We No Speak Americano" – Yolanda Be Cool Ft. D-Cup
88. "I Gotta Feeling" – The Black-Eyed Peas
89. "Around the World (La La La La La)" – ATC
90. "Dynamite" – Taio Cruz
91. "Hips Don't Lie" – Shakira ft. Wyclef Jean
92. "Intergalactic" – The Beastie Boys
93. "Party in My Head" – September
94. "I've Been Thinking About You" – Londonbeat
95. "Single Ladies (Put a Ring on It)" – Beyoncé
96. "Bailamos" – Enrique Iglesias
97. "Insane in the Brain" – Cypress Hill
98. "Mr. Vain" – Culture Beat
99. "Krazy" – Pitbull ft. Lil' Jon
100. "Don't Trust Me" – 3OH!3
101. "Honky Tonk Badonkadonk" –Trace Adkins
102. "Rise Above" – Black Flag
103. "Monster"- Skillet
104. "Power of Love" – Huey Lewis & the News
105. "Wake Me Up" – Avicci
106. "Johnny, I Hardly Knew Ya"- Dropkick Murphys
107. "Murmaider"- Dethklok
108. "Demons" – Imagine Dragons
109. "Dirt Road Anthem" – Jason Aldean
110. "I Predict a Riot" – Kaiser Chiefs
111. "One Shot at Glory" – Judas Priest
112. "Summer in the City" – The Lovin' Spoonful
113. "You Look Good in My Shirt" – Keith Urban
114. "American Idiot" – Green Day

115. "Sacrifice" – Danzig
116. "One Headlight" – The Wallflowers
117. "I Walk the Line" – Johnny Cash
118. "Why Don't You Get a Job?" – The Offspring
119. "Wrong Side of Heaven" – Five Finger Death Punch
120. "Up Around the Bend" – Creedence Clearwater Revival
121. "Gonna Make You Sweat (Everybody Dance Now)" – C+C Music Factory
122. "Sexy and I Know It" – LMFAO
123. "Dirrty" – Christina Aguilera
124. "I Like to Move It" – Reel 2 Real
125. "Livin La Vida Loca" – Ricky Martin
126. "Whine Up" – Kat Deluna ft. Elephant Man
127. "Sandstorm" – Darude
128. "The Power" – SNAP!
129. "Jumpin' Jumpin" – Destiny's Child
130. "Angel" – Shaggy ft. Rayvon
131. "Better Off Alone" – Alice Deejay
132. "Surfin' U.S.A." – The Beach Boys
133. "California Sun" – The Rivieras
134. "Surf City" – Jan & Dean
135. "Pipeline" – The Chantays
136. "Wipeout" –The Surfaris
137. "Miserlou" – Dick Dale and The Del-Tones
138. "Walk, Don't Run" – The Ventures
139. "Kokomo" – The Beach Boys
140. "Tubthumping" – Chumbawamba
141. "Sharp Dressed Man" – ZZ Top
142. "Punk Rock 101" – Bowling for Soup
143. "I Don't Want to Grow Up" – The Ramones
144. "Rock the Casbah" – The Clash

145. "The Wanderer" – Dion & The Del-Satins
146. "Desert Rose" – Sting
147. "Dragula" – Rob Zombie
148. "(s)AINT" – Marilyn Manson
149. "Through the Fire and Flames" – DragonForce
150. "Misery" – Maroon 5
151. "I Fought the Law" – Bobby Fuller Four
152. "Ticks" – Brad Paisley
153. "She Thinks My Tractor's Sexy" – Kenny Chesney
154. "Follow Me" – Uncle Kracker
155. "Summer of '69" – Bryan Adams
156. "Come with Me Now" – The Kongos
157. "Bad Reputation" – Joan Jett & The Blackhearts
158. "…Baby One More Time" – Britney Spears
159. "Before He Cheats" – Carrie Underwood
160. "Roar" – Kat Perry
161. "It's My Party" – Leslie Gore
162. "Hella Good" – No Doubt
163. "Mama's Broken Heart" – Miranda Lambert
164. "Crazy on You" – Heart
165. "U + UR Hand" – P!nk
166. "Girlfriend" – Avril Lavigne
167. "That Don't Impress Me Much" – Shania Twain
168. "Girls Just Want to Have Fun" – Cyndi Lauper
169. "Poker Face" – Lady Gaga
170. "Lovefool" – The Cardigans
171. "Sweet Dreams (Are Made of This)" – The Eurythmics
172. "Bad Guy" – Billie Eilish
173. "All About That Bass" – Meghan Trainor
174. "Building a Mystery" – Sarah McLachlan
175. "We Belong" – Pat Benatar

176. "Money for Nothing" – Dire Straits
177. "Joy to the World" – 3 Dog Night
178. "I Like It, I Love It" – Tim McGraw
179. "Wagon Wheel" – Darius Rucker
180. "The Gambler" – Kenny Rogers
181. "One Week" – Barenaked Ladies
182. "What Makes You Beautiful" – One Direction
183. "Blitzcreig Bop" – The Ramones
184. "Holiday" – Green Day
185. "Ring of Fire" – Social Distortion
186. "Pop" – NSYNC
187. "I'm a Believer" – The Monkees
188. "Crazy Train" – Ozzy Osbourne
189. "Land of Confusion" – Disturbed
190. "Chop Suey!" – System of a Down
191. "My Sharona" – The Knack
192. "Peace of Mind" – Boston
193. "I've Got a Name" – Jim Croce
194. "Let Your Love Flow" – The Bellamy Brothers
195. "Me and You and a Dog Named Boo" – Lobo
196. "End of the Line" – The Travelling Wilburys (Bob Dylan, George Harrison, Tom Petty, Roy Orbison, Jeff Lynne)
197. "Everybody's Talkin' at Me" – Harry Nillson
198. "Babylon" – David Grey
199. "Maybellene" – Chuck Berry
200. "(Sittin' On) The Dock of the Bay" – Otis Redding
201. "Build Me Up Buttercup" – The Foundations
202. "Stand by Me" – Ben E. King
203. "My Girl" – The Temptations
204. "Silhouettes on the Shade" – The Rays
205. "Hit the Road Jack" – Ray Charles

206.  "Mirrors" – Natalia Kills

207.  "Song Sung Blue" – Neil Diamond

208.  "Sexyback" – Justin Timberlake

209.  "Light My Fire" (Radio Edit) – The Doors

210.  "Burning Love" – Elvis Presley

211.  "Pour Some Sugar on Me" – Def Leppard

212.  "Do Ya Think I'm Sexy?" – Rod Stewart

213.  "Bitter Sweet Symphony" – The Verve

214.  "Cruise" – Florida Georgia Line

215.  "Enter Sandman" – Metallica

216.  "Anarchy in the UK"– The Sex Pistols

217.  "The Final Countdown" – Europe

218.  "One More Time" – Daft Punk

219.  "Twisted Transistor" – Korn

220.  "Amerika" – Rammstein

221.  "From Paris to Berlin" – Infernal

222.  "The Way I Are" – Timbaland ft. Keri Hilson

223.  "I See Right Through to You" – DJ Encore ft. Engelina

224.  "Whoomp! (There It Is)" – Tag Team

225.  "On the Floor" – Jennifer Lopez ft. Pitbull

226.  "Days Go By" – Dirty Vegas

227.  "We Found Love" – Rihanna

228.  "It Takes Two" – Robb Base & DJ E-Z Rock.

229.  "Whenever, Wherever" – Shakira

230.  "Summer Jam" – The Underdog Project

231.  "Scandalous" – Mis-Teeq

232.  "Music Sounds Better with You" – Stardust

233.  "Dancing Queen" – ABBA

234.  "Relax" – Frankie Goes to Hollywood

235.  "Y.M.C.A." – The Village People

236.  "Blue (Da Ba Dee)" – Eiffel 65

237. "Celebration" – Kool & The Gang
238. "One Night in Bangkok" – Murray Head
239. "MMMBop" – Hanson
240. "September" – Earth, Wind & Fire
241. "The Loco-Motion" – Little Eva
242. "Cotton Eye Joe" – The Rednex
243. "I Will Survive" – Gloria Gaynor
244. "Walk the Dinosaur" – Was (Not Was)
245. "You Sexy Thing" – Hot Chocolate
246. "Land Down Under" – Men at Work
247. "Under the Milky Way" – The Church
248. "It's My Life" – Bon Jovi
249. "Rehab" – Amy Winehouse
250. "Hey Brother" – Avicii
251. "Material Girl" – Madonna
252. "Teenage Dream" – Katy Perry
253. "Bitch" – Meredith Brooks
254. "Jolene" – Dolly Parton
255. "Black Horse & the Cherry Tree" – KT Tunstall
256. "We R Who We R" – Ke$ha
257. "Ironic" – Alanis Morissette
258. "My Boyfriend's Back" – The Angels
259. "Walk Like an Egyptian" – The Bangles
260. "Girl Next Door" – Brandy Clark
261. "Spice Up Your Life" – Spice Girls
262. "Get the Party Started" – P!nk
263. "That's the Way It Is" – Celine Dion
264. "Believe" – Cher
265. "Goodbye Earl" – Dixie Chicks
266. "Love Me Like You Do" – Ellie Goulding
267. "C'est La Vie" – B*Witched

268. "A Thousand Miles" – Vanessa Carlton

269. "Into You" – Ariana Grande

270. "Dream On" – Aerosmith

271. "Just Dropped in (To See What Condition My Condition Was In)" – The First Edition w/Kenny Rogers

272. "Clint Eastwood" – The Gorillaz

273. "In the End" – Linkin Park

274. "Bullet with Butterfly Wings" (Rat in a Cage) – The Smashing Pumpkins

275. "Working Class Hero" – Green Day

276. "Greenfields" – The Brothers Four

277. "Precious" – Depeche Mode

278. "Snap Your Fingers Snap Your Neck" – Prong

279. "Dust in the Wind" – Kansas

280. "Beds are Burning" – Midnight Oil

281. "Lonely People" – America

282. "Sound of Silence" – Simon & Garfunkel

283. "Lonesome Town" – Ricky Nelson

284. "Paint It Black" – The Rolling Stones

285. "Rhythm of the Rain" – The Cascades

286. "The One I Love" – R.E.M.

287. "Iris" – The Goo Goo Dolls

288. "Always on My Mind" – Willie Nelson

289. "Hey Mama" – David Guetta, Nicki Minaj, Bebe Rexha & Afrojack

290. "The Riddle" – Gigi D'Augustino

291. "Pet Sematary" – The Ramones

292. "The Greatest" – Sia

293. "The Mummer's Dance (Radio Edit)" – Loreena McKennitt

294. "Under a Violet Moon" – Blackmore's Night

295. "Only Teardrops" – Emmilie De Forest

296. "Only Time (Faster Radio Edit)" – Enya

297.  "Funkytown" – Lipps, Inc.
298.  "Mr. Sandman" – The Cordettes
299.  "Walk This Way" – Run DMC & Aerosmith
300.  "I'm Too Sexy" – Right Said Fred
301.  "Hot Stuff" – Donna Summer
302.  "Who Put the Bomp" – Barry Mann.
303.  "Love Shack" – The B-52's
304.  "Zuit Suit Riot" – Cherry Poppin' Daddies
305.  "Disco Inferno" – The Trammps
306.  "Eye of the Tiger" – Survivor
307.  "The Rockafeller Skank (Funk Soul Brother)" – Fatboy Slim
308.  "Car Wash" – Rose Royce
309.  "Larger Than Life" – The Backstreet Boys
310.  "Centerfold" – J. Geils Band
311.  "Devil with a Blue Dress" – Mitch Ryder & The Detroit Wheels
312.  "Roll to Me" – Del Amitri
313.  "Gimme Some Lovin" – Spencer Davis Group
314.  "What I like About You" – The Romantics
315.  "I've Been Everywhere" – Johnny Cash
316.  "Small Town Saturday Night" – Hal Ketchum
317.  "Chicken Fried" – Zac Brown Band
318.  "Danny's Song" – Loggins & Messina
319.  "Country Girl (Shake It for Me)" – Luke Bryan
320.  "The Cowboy in Me" – Tim McGraw
321.  "I Took a Pill in Ibiza" – Mike Posner
322.  "Smooth" – Santana ft. Rob Thomas
323.  "Baba O'Riley" – The Who
324.  "Jump" – Van Halen
325.  "Little Lion Man" – Mumford & Sons
326.  "Love Potion #9" – The Searchers
327.  "Self Esteem" – The Offspring

328. "Wild One" – Iggy Pop

329. "Ruby Soho" – Rancid

330. "Action" – Sweet

331. "Addicted" – Simple Plan

332. "Still Waiting" – Sum 41

333. "This Ain't a Scene, It's an Arm's Race" – Fall Out Boy

334. "Ob-La-Di, Ob-La-Da (Life Goes On)" – The Beatles

335. "China Grove" – The Doobie Brothers

336. "Your Woman" – White Town

337. "You Shook Me all Night Long" – AC/DC

338. "Great Balls of Fire" – Jerry Lee Lewis

339. "Hall of the Mountain King" – Apocalyptica

340. "Night on Bald Mountain" – Dead Rose Symphony

341. "Ace of Spades" – Motorhead

342. "Bodies (Let the Bodies Hit the Floor)" – Drowning Pool

343. "Resist & Bite" – Sabaton

344. "Last Resort" – Papa Roach

345. "Never Let You Go" – Third Eye Blind

346. "Daydream Believer" – The Monkees

347. "Bad to the Bone" – George Thorogood & The Destroyers

348. "Shelter from the Storm" – Bob Dylan

349. "Got My Mind Set on You" – George Harrison

350. "Counting Stars" – OneRepublic

351. "Thunder" – Imagine Dragons

352. "Fly" – Sugar Ray

353. "Shut Up and Dance" – Walk the Moon

354. "You Give Love a Bad Name" – Bon Jovi

355. "Kodachrome" – Paul Simon

356. "Runaround Sue" – Dion & The Belmonts

357. "Too Much Fun" – Daryle Singletary

358. "Honey, I'm Good" – Andy Grammer

359. "Bubba Shot the Jukebox" – Mark Chestnutt
360. "The Snakes Crawl at Night" – Charley Pride
361. "Theme from Rawhide" – Blues Brother's Movie Version: John Belushi & Dan Aykroyd
362. "Devil Went Down to Georgia" – Charlie Daniels Band
363. "Beautiful Day" – U2
364. "Rebel Yell" – Billy Idol
365. "Where Do You Go" – No Mercy
366. "Time of the Season" – The Zombies
367. "I'm Gonna Be (500 Miles)" – The Proclaimers
368. "She Drives Me Crazy" – Fine Young Cannibals
369. "Stacy's Mom" – Fountains of Wayne
370. "Pretty Fly for a White Guy" – The Offspring
371. "All the Small Things" – Blink 182
372. "London Dungeon" – The Misfits
373. "I Fought the Law" – The Clash
374. "Dirty Little Secret" – All-American Rejects
375. "Handclap" – Fitz and the Tantrums
376. "California Dreamin'" – The Mamas and the Papas
377. "Drops of Jupiter (Tell Me)" – Train
378. "Pretty Little Angel Eyes" – Curtis Lee
379. "How Bizarre" – OMC
380. "(I Just) Died in Your Arms" – Cutting Crew
381. "Feel So Numb" – Rob Zombie
382. "mOBSCENE" – Marilyn Manson
383. "I Stand Alone" – Godsmack
384. "Poison" – Alice Cooper
385. "Symphony of Destruction" – Megadeth
386. "Demons Are a Girl's Best Friend" – Powerwolf
387. "Californication" – Red Hot Chili Peppers
388. "Take Me Home Tonight" – Eddie Money

389. "Pop Muzik" – M
390. "Walkin' on the Sun" – Smash Mouth
391. "The Night Has a Thousand Eyes" – Bobby Vee
392. "Hanging by a Moment" – Lifehouse
393. "Sparks Fly" – Taylor Swift
394. "All I Want is You" – Barry Louis Polisar
395. "Shake, Rattle & Roll" – Bill Haley & His Comets
396. "Splish Splash" – Bobby Darin
397. "Do You Love Me?" – The Contours
398. "Tossin' & Turnin'" – Bobby Lewis
399. "Jailhouse Rock" – Elvis Presley
400. "Land of 1,000 Dances" – Wilson Pickett
401. "New Orleans" – Gary U.S. Bonds
402. "Oh, Boy!" – Buddy Holly and the Crickets
403. "Rockin' Robin" – Bobby Day
404. "The Twist" – Chubby Checker
405. "Earth Angel" – The Penguins
406. "Perfect (Dancing in the Dark)" – Ed Sheeran
407. "Will You Love Me Tomorrow" – The Shirelles
408. "I'd Love to Lay You Down" – Conway Twitty
409. "Forever Young" – Alphaville
410. "Night Moves" – Bob Seger
411. "Because the Night" – 10,000 Maniacs
412. "Let Her Go" – Passenger
413. "Twilight Time" – The Platters
414. "Hold Me, Thrill Me, Kiss Me" – Mel Carter
415. "Kiss Me" – Sixpence None the Richer
416. "Can't Help Falling in Love" – Elvis Presley
417. "I'm on Fire" – Bruce Springsteen
418. "Unchained Melody" – The Righteous Brothers
419. "I'm Not the Only One" – Sam Smith

420. "Blueberry Hill" – Fats Domino
421. "Save Tonight" – Eagle-Eye Cherry
422. "Airplanes" – B.O.B. ft. Hayley Williams
423. "Can't Fight the Moonlight" – LeAnn Rimes
424. "I Just Called to Say I Love You" – Stevie Wonder
425. "Cupid" – Sam Cooke
426. "If You Leave Me Now" – Chicago
427. "Nights in White Satin" – The Moody Blues
428. "Goodbye Stranger" – Supertramp
429. "What Becomes of the Broken Hearted?" – Jimmy Ruffin
430. "When a Man Loves a Woman" – Percy Sledge
431. "The Great Pretender" – The Platters
432. "Baby I Need Your Loving" – Four Tops
433. "Lean on Me" – Bill Withers
434. "I'm So Lonesome I Could Cry" – Hank Williams
435. "Dream Walkin" – Toby Keith
436. "Neon Moon" – Brooks & Dunn
437. "Juke Box Hero" – Foreigner
438. "Shout" – The Isley Brothers
439. "Hooked on a Feeling" – Blue Swede
440. "Come and Get Your Love" – Redbone
441. "Ice Ice Baby" – Vanilla Ice
442. "Stop in the Name of Love" – The Supremes
443. "Footloose" – Kenny Loggins
444. "Get Down Tonight" – KC and the Sunshine Band.
445. "Do Wah Diddy Diddy" – Manfred Mann
446. "Le Freak" – Chic
447. "Mambo #5" – Lou Bega
448. "You're the One I Want" – GREASE, John Travolta & Olivia Newton-John
449. "The Book of Love" – The Monotones

450.  "You Make Me Feel Like Dancing" – Leo Sayer

451.  "We Like to Party! (The Vengabus)" – The Vengaboys

452.  "You Spin Me Round (Like a Record)" – Dead or Alive

453.  "Turn the Beat Around" – Gloria Estefan

454.  "Stereo Hearts" – Gym Class Heroes ft. Adam Lavigne of Maroon 5

455.  "Hotel California" – The Eagles

456.  "I Just Want to Dance with You" – George Strait

457.  "I'll Have to Say I Love You in a Song" – Jim Croce

458.  "The Bad Touch (The Discovery Channel Song)" – The Bloodhound Gang

459.  "Bad Romance" – Lady Gaga

460.  "Mickey" – Toni Basil

461.  "Fancy" – Reba McEntire

462.  "Beautiful Life" – Ace of Base

463.  "Love You Like a Love Song" – Selena Gomez & the Scene

464.  "Edge of Seventeen" – Stevie Nicks

465.  "I Want Candy" – Bow Wow Wow

466.  "Where Have All the Cowboys Gone" – Paula Cole

467.  "Stronger (What Doesn't Kill You)" – Kelly Clarkson

468.  "Hands" – The Ting Tings

469.  "Cruel Summer" – Bananarama

470.  "I Hope You Dance" – Lee Ann Womack

471.  "Blank Space" – Taylor Swift

472.  "You're So Vain" – Carly Simon

473.  "Heaven Is a Place on Earth" – Belinda Carlisle

474.  "Can't Get You Out of My Head" – Kylie Minogue

475.  "I Love You Always Forever" – Donna Lewis

476.  "The Tide Is High" – Blondie

477.  "Blood" – In This Moment

478.  "S&M" – Rihanna

479.  "Satisfaction" – Benny Benassi

480. "In the Dark" – Dev
481. "Breathe" – Telepopmusik
482. "Abracadabra" – Steve Miller Band
483. "Monster Mash" – Bobby 'Boris' Pickett and the Crypt Kickers
484. "Ghostbusters" – Ray Parker Jr.
485. "Grim Grinning Ghosts" – The Mellomen
486. "Mad Monster Party" – The Misfits
487. "This is Halloween" – The Citizens of Halloween Town or Marilyn Manson
488. "Thriller" – Michael Jackson
489. "Dark Lady" – Cher
490. "Headless Horseman" – Bing Crosby/The Rhythmaires/Disney
491. "Dig up Her Bones" – The Misfits
492. "Carefree Highway" – Gordon Lightfoot
493. "Young Folks" – Peter, Bjorn & John
494. "Home" – Edward Sharpe and the Magnetic Zeroes
495. "Little Talks" – Of Monsters and Men
496. "4 Minutes" – Madonna ft. Justin Timberlake
497. "Bring Me to Life" – Evanescence
498. "Moves Like Jagger" – Maroon 5 ft. Christina Aguilera
499. "House of the Rising Sun" – The Animals
500. "Instant Karma! (We All Shine On)" – John Lennon/Yoko Ono

# SONGS CITED

Songwriters or 'additional' songwriters are mentioned if the individuals were not part of the band/group/artist named.

1. Johnny Cash. "Ring of Fire." Ring of Fire: The Best of Johnny Cash, Columbia Nashville, 1963. 12" Vinyl. Songwriters: June Carter, Merle Kilgore.

2. Dwight Yoakam. "A Thousand Miles from Nowhere." This Time, Reprise, 1993. CD Album.

3. John Denver. "Take Me Home, Country Roads." Poems, Prayers & Promises, RCA, 1971. 12" Vinyl Single. Additional Songwriters: Bill Danoff & Taffy Nivert.

4. Merle Haggard. "Okie from Muskogee." Okie from Muskogee, Capitol, 1969. 12" Vinyl. Additional Songwriter: Roy Edward Burris.

5. Alan Jackson. "Don't Rock the Jukebox." Don't Rock the Jukebox, 1991. CD Album.

6. Billy Ray Cyrus. "Achy Breaky Heart." Some Gave All, PolyGram, Mercury, 1992. CD Album. Songwriter: Don Von Tress.

7. R.E.M. "It's the End of the World as We Know It (and I Feel Fine)." Document, I.R.S., 1987. 12" Vinyl.

8. Bee Gees. "Stayin' Alive." Saturday Night Fever, RSO, 1977. 12" Vinyl.

9.  Paul Oakenfold ft. Shifty Shellshock. "Starry Eyed Surprise." Bunkka, Perfecto, Maverick, 2002. CD Single. Additional Songwriters: Seth Binzer, Andy Gray, Fred Neil.

10. Mark Ronson ft. Bruno Mars. "Uptown Funk." Uptown Special, Columbia, Sony, RCA, 2014. CD Album. Additional Songwriters: Philip Lawrence, Jeff Bhasker, Nicholas Williams, Devon Gallaspy, Charles Wilson, Robert Wilson, Ronnie Wilson, Rudolph Taylor, Lonnie Simmons.

11. Wild Cherry. "Play that Funky Music (White Boy)." Wild Cherry, Epic, 1976. 12" Vinyl.

12. Eddy Grant. "Electric Avenue." Killer on the Rampage, CBS, Portrait, Parlophone, EMI, 1983. 12" Vinyl.

13. Los del Rio. "Macarena." A mi me gusta, RCA, 1993. CD Album.

14. Aretha Franklin. "Respect." I Never Loved a Man the Way I Love You, Atlantic, 1967. 12" Vinyl. Songwriter: Otis Redding.

15. The Buggles. "Video Killed the Radio Star." The Age of Plastic, Island, 1979. 12" Vinyl. Songwriters: Geoff Downes, Trevor Horn, Bruce Woolley.

16. Harry Belafonte. "Jump in the Line (Shake Senora)." Jump Up Calypso, RCA Victor, 1961. 12" Vinyl. Songwriter: Lord Kitchener.

17. MC Hammer. "U Can't Touch This." Please Hammer Don't Hurt 'Em, Capitol, 1990. 12" Vinyl. Additional Songwriters: Rick James, Alonzo Miller.

18. Bay City Rollers. "Saturday Night." Rollin', Arista, 1973. 12" Vinyl. Songwriters: Bill Martin, Phil Coulter.

19. Baha Men. "Who Let the Dogs Out." Who Let the Dogs Out, S-Curve, 2000. CD Album.

20. Devo. "Whip It." Freedom of Choice, Warner Bros., 1980. 12" Vinyl.

21. Don Henley. "Boys of Summer." Building the Perfect Beast, Geffen, 1984. 12" Vinyl. Additional Songwriter: Mike Campbell.

22. America. "You Can Do Magic." View from the Ground, Capitol, 1982. 12" Vinyl. Songwriter: Russ Ballard.

23. Rascal Flatts. "Life is a Highway." Me and My Gang, Lyric Street, Walt Disney, 2006. CD Album. Song writer: Tom Cochrane.

24. Scorpions. "Hurricane." Love at First Sting, Harvest, Mercury, 1984. 12" Vinyl.

25. The Clash. "Should I Stay or Should I Go." Combat Rock, CBS, Epic, 1982. 12" Vinyl.

26. The Beatles. "I Want to Hold Your Hand." Single, Parlophone, Capitol, 1963. 12" Vinyl.

27. Tom Petty. "Free Fallin'." Full Moon Fever, MCA, 1989. 12" Vinyl. Additional Songwriter: Jeff Lynne.

28. Kid Rock. "All Summer Long." Rock n Roll Jesus, Atlantic, Top Dog, 2008. CD Album. Additional Songwriters: Edward King, Leroy Marinell, Gary Rossington, Matthew Shafer, Ronnie Van Zant, Waddy Wachtel, Warren Zevon.

29. P.O.D. "Alive." Satellite, Atlantic, 2001. CD Album.

30. Bowling for Soup. "1985." A Hangover You Don't Deserve, FFROE, Jive, Zomba, Silverstone, 2004. CD Album. Additional Songwriters: Mitch Allan, John Allen.

31. Don Mclean. "American Pie." American Pie, United Artists, 1971. 12" Vinyl.

32. The Crests. "16 Candles." Single, Coed, 1958. 7" Vinyl. Songwriters: Luther Dixon, Allyson R. Khent.

33. Garth Brooks. "Friends in Low Places." No Fences, Capitol Nashville, 1990. CD Album. Songwriters: Dewayne Blackwell, Earl Bud Lee.

34. Pantera. "Cemetery Gates." Cowboys from Hell, Atco, 1990. CD Album.

35. The Presidents of the Unites States of America. "Peaches." The Presidents of the United States of America, Columbia, PopLlama, 1996. CD Album.

36. Nine Days. "Absolutely (Story of a Girl)." The Madding Crowd, 550, Epic, 2000. CD Single.

37. Vance Joy. "Riptide." God Loves You When You're Dancing, Liberation, Infectious, Atlantic, 2013. CD Album.

38. Nitty Gritty Dirt Band. "Mr. Bojangles." Uncle Charlie & His Dog Teddy, Liberty, 1970. 12" Vinyl LP. Songwriter: Jerry Jeff Walker.

39. Poison. "Talk Dirty to Me." Look What the Cat Dragged In, Enigma, Capitol, 1987. 12" Vinyl.

40. Blink 182. "What's My Age Again?" Enema of the State, MCA, 1999. CD Album.

41. Corey Hart. "Sunglasses at Night." First Offense, EMI America, Aquarius, 1984. 12" Vinyl.

42. Billy Joel. "Piano Man." Piano Man, Columbia, 1973. 12" Vinyl.

43. Little Richard. "Tutti Frutti." Here's Little Richard, Specialty, 1955. 12" Vinyl. Additional Songwriter: Dorothy LaBostrie

44. The Coasters. "Yaket Yak." Single, Atco, 1958. 45 RPM Record. Songwriters: Jerry Leiber, Mike Stoller.

45. Coldplay. "Clocks." A Rush of Blood to the Head, Parlophone, Capitol, 2002. CD Album.

46. Sam Hunt. "Leave the Night On." Montevallo, MCA Nashville, 2014. CD Album. Additional Songwriters: Josh Osborne, Shane McAnally.

47. Quiet Riot. "Cum on Feel the Noize." Metal Health, Pasha, 1983. 12" Vinyl. Songwriters: Noddy Holder, Jim Lea.

48. Good Charlotte. "Lifestyles of the Rich and Famous." The Young and the Hopeless, Epic, 2002. CD Album. Additional Songwriter: Tim Armstrong.

49. Stray Cats. "Rock this Town." Stray Cats/Built for Speed, EMI America, Arista, 1982. 12" Vinyl.

50. Brooks & Dunn. "Boot Scootin' Boogie." Brand New Man, Arista Nashville, 1992. CD Single.

51. Twisted Sister. "We're Not Gonna Take It." Stay Hungry, Atlantic, 1984. 12" Vinyl.

52. Sum 41. "In Too Deep." All Killer No Filler, Aquarius, Island, Mercury, 2001. CD Album. Additional songwriter: Greig Nori.

53. Third Eye Blind. "Semi-Charmed Life." Third Eye Blind, Elektra, 1997. CD Album.

54. Randy Houser. "How Country Feels." How Country Feels, Stoney Creek, 2012. Songwriters: Vicky McGehee, Wendell Mobley, Neil Thrasher.

55. Danzig. "I Don't Mind the Pain." Danzig 4, American Recordings, 1994. CD Album.

56. Bad Religion. "American Jesus." Recipe for Hate, Atlantic, Sympathy for the Record Industry, Semaphore Records, 1993. CD Album.

57. Frank Sinatra. "Strangers in the Night." Strangers in the Night, Reprise, 1966. 12" Vinyl. Composer: Bert Kaempfert. Lyricists: Charles Singleton, Eddie Snyder.

58. Jon Pardi. "Head Over Boots." California Sunrise, Capitol Nashville, 2015. CD Album. Additional Songwriter: Luke Laird.

59. Avenged Sevenfold. "Bat Country." City of Evil, Warner, 2005. CD Album.

60. Guns N' Roses. "Paradise City." Appetite for Destruction, Geffen, 1989. 12" Vinyl.

61. Bruce Springsteen. "Dancing in the Dark." Born in the U.S.A., Columbia, 1984. 12" Vinyl.

62. MGMT. "Time to Pretend." Oracular Spectacular, Columbia, 2008. CD Album.

63. Iron Maiden. "Can I play with Madness?" Seventh Son of a Seventh Son, EMI, 1988. 12" Vinyl.

64. Blink 182. "First Date." Take Off Your Pants and Jacket, MCA, 2001. CD Album.

65. Duane Eddy. "Rebel Rouser." Have 'Twangy' Guitar Will Travel, Jamie, 1958. 12" Vinyl. Additional songwriter: Lee Hazlewood.

66. DNCE. "Cake by the Ocean." DNCE, Republic, 2015. Digital Download. Additional Songwriters: Robin Fredriksson, Mattias Larsson, Justin Tranter.

67. Tracy Chapman. "Fast Car." Tracy Chapman, Elektra, 1988. 12" Vinyl.

68. Fastball. "The Way." All the Pain Money Can Buy, Hollywood, 1998. CD Album.

69. Journey. "Don't Stop Believin'." Escape, Columbia, 1981. 12" Vinyl.

70. Skid Row. "18 and Life." Skid Row, Atlantic, 1989. 12" Vinyl.

71. INXS. "Devil Inside." Kick, Atlantic, 1988. 12" Vinyl.

72. Disturbed. "Down with the Sickness." The Sickness, Giant, 2000. CD Album.

73. Blink 182. "The Rock Show." Take Off Your Pants and Jacket, MCA, 2001. CD Album.

74. Garth Brooks. "Thunder Rolls." No Fences, Capitol Nashville, 1991. CD Album. Additional Songwriter: Pat Alger.

75. Blue Oyster Cult. "Burnin' for You." Fire of Unknown Origin, Columbia, 1981. 12" Vinyl. Songwriters: Donald Roeser, Richard Meltzer.

76. Steppenwolf. "Born to be Wild." Steppenwolf, Dunhill, RCA, 1968. 12" Vinyl. Songwriter: Mars Bonfire.

77. Slipknot. "Pyschosocial." All Hope is Gone, Roadrunner, 2008. CD Album.

78. Brantley Gilbert. "Bottoms Up." Just as I Am, Valory, 2013. CD Album. Additional Songwriters: Justin Weaver, Brett James.

79. Nirvana. "Smells Like Teen Spirit." Nevermind, DGC, 1991. CD Album.

80. AC/DC. "Dirty Deeds Done Dirt Cheap." Dirty Deeds Done Dirt Cheap, Albert Productions, 1976. 12" Vinyl.

81. Motorhead. "Rock Out." Motorizer, SPV/Steamhammer, 2008. CD Album.

82. Alien Ant Farm. "Smooth Criminal." Anthology, Dreamworks, 2001. CD Album. Songwriter: Michael Jackson.

83. Gary Allan. "Smoke Rings in the Dark." Smoke Rings in the Dark, MCA Nashville, 1999. Songwriters: Rivers Rutherford, Houston Robert.

84. The Turtles. "Eve of Destruction." It Ain't Me Babe, White Whale, 1965. 12" Vinyl. Songwriter: P. F. Sloan.

85. Real Life. "Send Me an Angel." Heartland, Wheatley, Curb, MCA, Intercord, Ariola, 1983. 12" Vinyl.

86. House of Pain. "Jump Around." House of Pain, Tommy Boy, 1992. CD Album. Songwriters: Lawrence Muggerud, Erik Schrody, Earl Nelson, Bobby Relf.

87. Yolanda Be Cool ft. D-Cup. "We No Speak Americano." Single, Sweat It Out!, 2010. CD Single. Songwriters: Johnson Peterson, Sylvester Martinez, Duncan Maclennan, Renato Carosone, Nicola Salerno.

88. The Black Eyed Peas. "I Gotta Feeling." The E.N.D., Interscope, 2009. CD Album. Additional Songwriters: David Guetta, Frederic Riesterer.

89. ATC. "Around the World (La La La La La)." Planet Pop, King Size, 2000. CD Album. Songwriters: Alexey Potekhin, Sergey Zhukov, Alex Christensen, Peter Konemann.

90. Taio Cruz. "Dynamite." Rokstarr, Island, 2010. CD Album. Additional songwriters: Dr. Luke, Max Martin, Benny Blanco, Bonnie McKee.

91.  Shakira ft. Wyclef Jean. "Hips Don't Lie." Oral Fixation, Vol. 2, Epic, Sony, 2006. CD Album. Additional Songwriters: Omar Alfanno, LaTavia Parker, Jerry Duplessis, Vinay Rao.

92.  Beastie Boys. "Intergalactic." Hello Nasty, Capitol, Grand Royal, 1998. CD Album. Additional Songwriter: Mario Caldato, Jr.

93.  September. "Party in My Head." Love CPR, Catchy Tunes, 2011. Digital Download. Songwriters: Wayne Hector, Lucas Secon, Daniel Davidsen, Peter Wallevik.

94.  Londonbeat. "I've Been Thinking About You." In the Blood, Radioactive, Anxious, 1990. CD Album.

95.  Beyoncé. "Single Ladies (Put a Ring on It)." I Am…Sasha Fierce, Columbia, 2008. CD Album. Additional Songwriters: Christopher "Tricky" Stewart, Terius "The-Dream" Nash, Thaddis Harrell.

96.  Enrique Iglesias. "Bailamos." Enrique, Fonovisa, Interscope, Overbrook, Universal, 1999. CD Album. Songwriters: Paul Barry, Mark Taylor.

97.  Cypress Hill. "Insane in the Brain." Black Sunday, Ruffhouse, Columbia, 1993. CD Album. Additional Songwriter: Jerry Corbitt.

98.  Culture Beat. "Mr. Vain." Serenity, Dance Pool, 1993. CD Album. Additional Songwriter: Steven Levis.

99.  Pitbull ft. Lil' Jon. "Krazy." Pitbull Starring in Rebelution, The Orchard, 2008. Digital Download. Additional songwriter: Jonathan Smith.

100.  3OH!3. "Don't Trust Me." Want, Photo Finish Records, 2008. CD Album. Additional Songwriter: Benjamin Levin.

101.  Trace Adkins. "Honky Tonk Badonkadonk." Songs About Me, Capitol Nashville, 2005. CD Album. Songwriters: Dallas Davidson, Randy Houser, Jamey Johnson.

102.  Black Flag. "Rise Above." Damaged, SST, 1981. 12" Vinyl.

103.  Skillet. "Monster." Awake, Lava, Ardent, Atlantic, 2009. CD Album. Additional Songwriter: Gavin Brown.

104. Huey Lewis & the News. "Power of Love." Back to the Future: Music from the Motion Picture Soundtrack, Chrysalis, 1985. 12" Vinyl.

105. Avicci. "Wake Me Up." True, PRMD, Island, 2013. Digital Download. Additional Songwriters: Egbert Nathaniel Dawkins III (Aloe Blacc), Mike Einziger.

106. Dropkick Murphys. "Johnny, I Hardly Knew Ya." The Meanest of Times, Born & Bred Records, Dew Process, 2007. CD Album. Songwriter: Joseph B. Geoghegan. Sung to the tune of "When Johnny Comes Marching Home" by Louis Lambert a.k.a. Patrick Gilmore.

107. Dethklok. "Murmaider." The Dethalbum, Williams Street, 2007. CD Album.

108. Imagine Dragons. "Demons." Night Visions, KIDinaKORNER, Interscope, 2013. Digital download. Additional Songwriters: Alexander Junior Grant (Alex da Kid), Josh Mosser.

109. Jason Aldean. "Dirt Road Anthem." My Kinda Party, Broken Bow, 2011. Songwriters: Brantley Gilbert, Colt Ford.

110. Kaiser Chiefs. "I Predict a Riot." Employment, B-Unique, Polydor, 2004. CD Album.

111. Judas Priest. "One Shot at Glory." Painkiller, Columbia, 1990. 12" Vinyl.

112. The Lovin' Spoonful. "Summer in the City." Hums of the Lovin' Spoonful, Kama Sutra, 1966. 12" Vinyl. Additional Songwriter: Mark Sebastian.

113. Keith Urban. "You Look Good in My Shirt." Golden Road, Capitol Nashville, 2008. CD Album. Songwriters: Mark Nesler, Tom Shapiro, Tony Martin.

114. Green Day. "American Idiot." American Idiot, Reprise, 2004. CD Album.

115. Danzig. "Sacrifice." Danzig 5: Blackaciddevil, Hollywood Records, 1996. CD Album.

116. The Wallflowers. "One Headlight." Bringing Down the Horse, Interscope, 1997. CD Album.

117. Johnny Cash. "I Walk the Line." Johnny Cash with His Hot and Blue Guitar, Sun, 1956. 12" Vinyl.

118. The Offspring. "Why Don't You Get a Job?" Americana, Columbia, 1999. CD Album.

119. Five Finger Death Punch. "Wrong Side of Heaven." The Wrong Side of Heaven and the Righteous Side of Hell, Volume 1, Prospect Park, 2014. CD Album. Additional Songwriter: Kevin Churko.

120. Creedence Clearwater Revival. "Up Around the Bend." Cosmo's Factory, Fantasy Records, 1970. 12" Vinyl.

121. C+C Music Factory. "Gonna Make You Sweat (Everybody Dance Now)." Gonna Make You Sweat, Columbia, 1990. CD Album.

122. LMFAO. "Sexy and I Know It." Sorry for Party Rocking, Interscope, 2011. Digital Download. Additional songwriters: David Jamahl Listenbee, Erin Beck, George M. Robertson, Kenneth Oliver.

123. Christina Aguilera ft. Redman. "Dirrty." Stripped, RCA, 2002. CD Album. Additional Songwriters: Dana Stinson, Balewa Muhammad, Reginald Noble.

124. Reel 2 Real. "I Like to Move It." Move It!, Strictly Rhythm, 1994. CD Single.

125. Ricky Martin. "Livin' La Vida Loca." Ricky Martin, Columbia, 1999. CD Album. Songwriters: Draco Rosa, Desmond Child.

126. Kat Deluna ft. Elephant Man. "Whine Up." 9 Lives, Epic, 2007. CD Album. Additional Songwriters: Nadir Khayat, Jane't Sewell-Ulepic, O'Neil Bryan, Tyrone Edmond.

127. Darude. "Sandstorm." Before the Storm, 16 Inch, Neo, Robbins, 1999. CD Album.

128. SNAP!. "The Power." World Power, Ariola, Arista, 1990. CD Album. Songwriters: Benito Benites, John "Virgo" Garrett III, Toni C.

129. Destiny's Child. "Jumpin', Jumpin'." The Writing's on the Wall, Columbia, 2000. CD Album. Additional Songwriters: Chad Elliot, Rufus Moore.

130. Shaggy ft. Rayvon. "Angel." Hot Shot. MCA, 2001. CD Album. Additional Songwriters: Rickardo Ducent, Nigel Staff, Dave Kelly, Shaun Pizzonia, Chip Taylor, Ahmet Ertegun, Eddie Curtis, Steve Miller.

131. Alice Deejay. "Better Off Alone." Who Needs Guitars Anyways?, Violent, 1999. CD Album.

132. The Beach Boys. "Surfin' U.S.A." Surfin' U.S.A., Capitol, 1963. 12" Vinyl. Additional songwriter: Chuck Berry.

133. The Rivieras. "California Sun." Single, Riviera, 1964. 7" Vinyl.

134. Jan & Dean. "Surf City." Surf City and Other Swingin' Cities, Liberty, 1963. 12" Single. Additional Songwriter: Brian Wilson.

135. The Chantays. "Pipeline." Pipeline, Downey, 1962. 12" Vinyl.

136. The Surfaris. "Wipe Out." Wipe Out, DFS, Princess, Dot, 1963. 12" Vinyl.

137. Dick Dale and The Del-Tones. "Miserlou." Surfer's Choice, Deltone Records, 1962. 12" Vinyl. Songwriters: Nick Roubanis, Fred Wise, Milton Leeds, Chaim Tauber. Adapted from an Eastern Mediterranean folk song of unknown authorship.

138. The Ventures. "Walk, Don't Run." Walk, Don't Run, Blue Horizon, Dolton, Reo, Top Rank, 1960. 12" Vinyl. Songwriter: Johnny Smith.

139. The Beach Boys. "Kokomo." Still Cruisin', Elektra, Capitol, 1988. 12" Vinyl. Songwriters: John Phillips, Scot McKenzie, Mike Love, Terry Melcher.

140. Chumbawamba. "Tubthumping." Tubthumper, EMI, Universal, Republic, 1997. CD Album.

141. ZZ Top. "Sharp Dressed Man." Eliminator, Warner Bros., 1983. 12" Vinyl.

142. Bowling for Soup. "Punk Rock 101." Drunk Enough to Dance, Zomba, Music for Nations, Jive, 2003. CD Album. Additional Songwriter: Butch Walker.

143. The Ramones. "I Don't Want to Grow Up." Adios Amigos!, Radioactive, 1995. CD Album. Songwriters: Tom Waits, Kathleen Brennan.

144. The Clash. "Rock the Casbah." Combat Rock, CBS, Epic, 1982. 12" Vinyl.

145. Dion & The Del-Satins. "The Wanderer." Runaround Sue, Laurie, 1961. 12" Vinyl. Songwriter: Ernie Maresca.

146. Sting ft. Cheb Mami. "Desert Rose." Brand New Day, A&M, 2000. CD Album.

147. Rob Zombie. "Dragula." Hellbilly Deluxe, Geffen, 1998. CD Album. Additional Songwriter: Scott Humphrey.

148. Marilyn Manson. '(s)AINT.' The Golden Age of Grotesque, Nothing, Interscope, 2003. CD Album. Additional Songwriters: John 5, Skold.

149. DragonForce. "Through the Fire and Flames." Inhuman Rampage, Sanctuary, Roadrunner, Universal, 2006.

150. Maroon 5. "Misery." Hands All Over, A&M Octone, 2010. CD Album.

151. Bobby Fuller Four. "I Fought the Law." I Fought the Law, Mustang, 1965. 12" Vinyl. Songwriter: Sonny Curtis.

152. Brad Paisley. "Ticks." 5th Gear, Arista Nashville, 2007. CD Album. Additional Songwriters: Kelley Lovelace, Tim Owens.

153. Kenny Chesney. "She Thinks My Tractor's Sexy." Everywhere We Go, BNA, 1999. CD Album. Songwriters: Jim Collins, Paul Overstreet.

154. Uncle Kracker. "Follow Me." Double Wide, Lava, Atlantic. Top Dog, 2000. CD Album. Additional Songwriter: Michael Bradford.

155. Bryan Adams. "Summer of 69." Reckless, A&M, 1985. 12" Vinyl. Additional Songwriter: Jim Vallance.

156. The Kongos. "Come with Me Now." Lunatic, Tokoloshe, Epic, Rock all Night Productions LLC, 2012. Digital Download.

157. Joan Jett & The Blackhearts. "Bad Reputation." Bad Reputation, Boardwalk, 1981. 12" Vinyl. Additional Songwriters: Ritchie Cordell, Kenny Laguna, Marty Joe Kupersmith.

158. Britney Spears. "…Baby One More Time." …Baby One More Time, Jive, 1998. CD Album. Songwriter: Max Martin.

159. Carrie Underwood. "Before He Cheats." Some Hearts, Arista, 2006. CD Album. Songwriters: Josh Kear, Chris Tompkins.

160. Katy Perry. "Roar." Prism, Capitol, 2013. CD Album. Additional Songwriters: Lukasz Gottwald, Max Martin, Bonnie McKee, Henry Walter.

161. Leslie Gore. "It's My Party." I'll Cry If I Want To, Mercury, 1963. 12" Vinyl. Songwriters: Walter Gold, John Gluck Jr., Herb Weiner, Seymour Gottlieb.

162. No Doubt. "Hella Good." Rock Steady, Interscope, 2002. CD Album. Additional Songwriters: Pharrell Williams, Chad Hugo.

163. Miranda Lambert. "Mama's Broken Heart." Four the Record, RCA Nashville, 2013. CD Album. Songwriters: Brandy Clark, Shane McAnally, Kacey Musgraves.

164. Heart. "Crazy on You." Dreamboat Annie, Mushroom, 1976. 12" Vinyl.

165. P!nk. "U + UR Hand." I'm Not Dead, LaFace, 2006. CD Album. Additional Songwriters: Max Martin, Lukasz Gottwald, Rami Yacoub.

166. Avril Lavigne. "Girlfriend." The Best Damn Thing, RCA, Columbia, 2007. CD Album. Additional Songwriter: Lukasz Gottwald.

167. Shania Twain. "That Don't Impress Me Much." Come on Over, Mercury, 1998. CD Album. Additional Songwriter: Robert John "Mutt" Lange.

168. Cyndi Lauper. "Girls Just Want to Have Fun." She's So Unusual, Portrait, 1983. Songwriter: Robert Hazard.

169. Lady Gaga. "Poker Face." The Fame, Streamline, KonLive, Cherrytree, Interscope, 2008. CD Album. Additional Songwriter: Nadir Khayat.

170. The Cardigans. "Lovefool." First Band on the Moon, Stockholm, Mercury, 1996. CD Album.

171. Eurythmics. "Sweet Dreams (Are Made of This)." Sweet Dreams (Are Made of This), RCA, 1983. 12" Vinyl.

172. Billie Eilish. "Bad Guy." When We All Fall Asleep, Where Do We Go?, Darkroom, Interscope, 2019. Digital Download. Additional Songwriter: Finneas O'Connell.

173. Meghan Trainor. "All About That Bass." Title, Epic, 2014. CD Album. Additional Songwriter: Kevin Kadish.

174. Sarah McLachlan. "Building a Mystery." Surfacing, Nettwerk, Arista, 1997. CD Album Additional Songwriter: Pierre Marchand.

175. Pat Benatar. "We Belong." Tropico, Chrysalis, 1984. 12" Vinyl. Songwriters: David Eric Lowen, Dan Navarro.

176. Dire Straits. "Money for Nothing." Brothers in Arms, Vertigo, 1985. 12" Vinyl. Additional Songwriter: Sting.

177. Three Dog Night. "Joy to the World." Naturally, Dunhill, 1971. 12" Vinyl. Songwriter: Hoyt Axton.

178. Tim McGraw. "I Like It, I Love It." All I Want, Curb, 1995. CD Album. Songwriters: Mark Hall, Jeb Stuart Anderson, Steve Dukes.

179. Darius Rucker ft. Lady Antebellum. "Wagon Wheel." True Believers, Capitol Nashville, 2013. CD Album. Songwriters: Bob Dylan, Ketch Secor.

180. Kenny Rogers. "The Gambler." The Gambler, United Artists, 1978. 12" Vinyl. Songwriter: Don Schiltz.

181. Barenaked Ladies. "One Week." Stunt, Reprise, 1998. CD Album.

182. One Direction. "What Makes You Beautiful." Up All Night, Syco, Columbia, 2011. CD Album. Songwriters: Savan Kotecha, Rami Yacoub, Carl Falk.

183. The Ramones. "Blitzkreig Bop." Ramones, Sire/ABC, 1976. 12" Vinyl.

184. Green Day. "Holiday." American Idiot, Reprise, WEA, 2005. CD Album.

185. Social Distortion. "Ring of Fire." Social Distortion, Epic, 1990. CD Album. Songwriters: June Carter Cash, Merle Kilgore.

186. NSYNC. "Pop." Celebrity, Jive, 2001. CD Album. Additional Songwriter: Wade Robson.

187. The Monkees. "I'm a Believer." More of the Monkees, Colgems, 1966. 12" Vinyl. Songwriter: Neil Diamond.

188. Ozzy Osbourne. "Crazy Train." Blizzard of Ozz, Jet, Epic, 1980. 12" Vinyl. Additional Songwriters: Bob Daisley, Randy Rhoads.

189. Disturbed. "Land of Confusion." Ten Thousand Fists, Reprise, 2006. CD Album. Songwriters: Mike Rutherford, Tony Banks, Phil Collins.

190. System of a Down. "Chop Suey!" Toxicity, American, Columbia, 2001. CD Album.

191. The Knack. "My Sharona." Get the Knack, Capitol, 1979. 12" Vinyl.

192. Boston. "Peace of Mind." Boston, Epic, 1977. 12" Vinyl.

193. Jim Croce. "I Got a Name." I Got a Name, ABC, 1973. 12" Vinyl. Songwriters: Charles Fox, Norman Gimbel.

194. The Bellamy Brothers. "Let Your Love Flow." Let Your Love Flow, Warner Bros., Curb, 1976. 12" Vinyl. Songwriter: Larry E. Williams.

195. Lobo. "Me and You and a Dog Named Boo." Introducing Lobo, Big Tree, 1971. 12" Vinyl.

196. The Travelling Wilburys (Bob Dylan, George Harrison, Tom Petty, Roy Orbison, Jeff Lynne). "End of the Line." Travelling Wilburys Vol. 1, Wilbury, 1989. 12" Vinyl.

197. Harry Nillson. "Everybody's Talkin'." Aerial Ballet, RCA/Victor, 1968. 12" Vinyl. Songwriter: Fred Neil.

198. David Grey. "Babylon." White Ladder, IHT, EastWest, RCA, 1999. CD Album.

199. Chuck Berry. "Maybellene." Chuck Berry is on Top, Chess, 1955. 12" Vinyl. Additional Songwriters: Russ Fratto, Alan Freed.

200. Otis Redding. "(Sittin' On) The Dock of the Bay." The Dock of the Bay, Volt, Atco, 1968. 12" Vinyl. Additional Songwriter: Steve Cropper.

201. The Foundations. "Build Me Up Buttercup." Build Me Up Buttercup, PYE, 1968. 12" Vinyl. Songwriters: Mike d'Abo, Tony Macaulay.

202. Ben E. King. "Stand by Me." Don't Play That Song!, Atco, 1961. 12" Vinyl. Additional songwriters: Jerry Leiber, Mike Stoller.

203. The Temptations. "My Girl." The Temptations Sing Smokey, Gordy, 1964. 12" Vinyl. Songwriters: Smokey Robinson, Ronald White.

204. The Rays. "Silhouettes." Single, XYZ, Cameo, 1957. 45 RPM Vinyl. Songwriters: Bob Crewe, Frank Slay.

205. Ray Charles. "Hit the Road Jack." Single, ABC, Paramount, 1961. 45 RPM Vinyl. Songwriter: Percy Mayfield.

206. Natalia Kills. "Mirrors." Perfectionist, will.i.am, Cherrytree, KonLive, Interscope, 2010. Digital Download. Additional Songwriters: Martin Kierszenbaum, Akon, Giorgio Tuinfort.

207. Neil Diamond. "Song Sung Blue." Moods, Uni, 1972. 12" Vinyl.

208. Justin Timberlake. "SexyBack." FutureSex/LoveSounds, Jive, Zomba, 2006. CD Album. Additional Songwriters: Tim Mosley, Nate "Danja" Hills.

209. The Doors. "Light My Fire." The Doors, Elektra, 1967. 12" Vinyl.

210. Elvis Presley. "Burning Love." Burning Love and Hits From His Movies, Volume 2, RCA Records, 1972. 12" Vinyl. Songwriter: Dennis Linde.

211. Def Leppard. "Pour Some Sugar on Me." Hysteria, Mercury, 1987. 12" Vinyl. Additional Songwriter: Robert John "Mutt" Lange.

212. Rod Stewart. "Do Ya Think I'm Sexy?" Blondes Have More Fun, Warner Bros., 1978. 12" Vinyl. Additional Songwriters: Carmine Appice, Duane Hitchings.

213. The Verve. "Bitter Sweet Symphony." Urban Hymns, Hut, Virgin, 1997. CD Album. Samples from the Andrew Oldham orchestral cover of "The Last Time" by The Rolling Stones.

214. Florida Georgia Line. "Cruise." Here's to the Good Times, Big Loud Mountain, Republic Nashville, 2012. Digital Download. Additional Songwriters: Joey Moi, Chase Rice, Jesse Rice.

215. Metallica. "Enter Sandman." Metallica, Elektra, 1991. CD Album.

216. The Sex Pistols. "Anarchy in the UK." Never Mind the Bollocks, Here's the Sex Pistols, EMI, 1976. 12" Vinyl.

217. Europe. "The Final Countdown." The Final Countdown, Epic, 1986. 12" Vinyl.

218. Daft Punk. "One More Time." Discovery, Virgin, 2000. CD Album. Additional  Songwriter: Anthony Moore.

219. Korn. "Twisted Transistor." See You on the Other Side, Virgin, 2005. CD Album. Additional Songwriters: Lauren Christy, Graham Edwards, Scott Spock.

220. Rammstein. "Amerika." Reise, Reise, Universal, 2004. CD Album.

221. Infernal. "From Paris to Berlin." From Paris to Berlin, Border Breakers, Central Station, 2004. CD Album. Additional Songwriter: Adam Powers.

222. Timbaland ft. Keri Hilson and D.O.E. "The Way I Are." Shock Value, Mosley, Blackground, Interscope, 2007. CD Album. Additional Songwriters: Nate Hills, The Clutch, Candice Nelson, John Maultsby.

223. DJ Encore ft. Engelina. "I See Right Through to You." Intuition, Universal, 2001. CD Album.

224. Tag Team. "Whoomp! (There It Is)." Whoomp! (There It Is), Life Records, 1993. CD Album.

225. Jennifer Lopez ft. Pitbull. "On the Floor." Love?, Island, 2011. CD Album. Songwriters: Nadir "RedOne" Khayat. Kinnda Hamid, AJ Junior, Teddy Sky, Bilal "The Chef", Armando Perez (Pitbull), Gonzalo Hermosa, Ulises Hermosa.

226. Dirty Vegas. "Days Go By." Dirty Vegas, Hydrogen, Credence. Parlophone, Capitol, 2001. CD Album. Additional Songwriter: Victoria Horn.

227. Rihanna. "We Found Love." Talk That Talk, Def Jam, SRP, 2011. CD Album. Songwriter: Calvin Harris.

228. Rob Base & DJ E-Z Rock. "It Takes Two." It Takes Two, Profile, 1988. 12" Vinyl. Additional songwriter: James Brown.

229. Shakira. "Whenever, Wherever." Laundry Service, Epic, 2001. CD Album. Additional Songwriters: Tim Mitchell, Gloria Estefan.

230. The Underdog Project. "Summer Jam." It Doesn't Matter, Polygram, 2000. CD Album. Additional Songwriters: Christoph Brux, Toni Cottura, Stephen Browarczyk, Shahin Moshirian.

231. Mis-Teeq. "Scandalous." Eye Candy, Telstar, Reprise, 2003. CD Album. Additional Songwriters: Tor Erik Hermansen, Mikkel S. Ericksen, Hallgeir Rustan.

232. Stardust. "Music Sounds Better with You." Single, Roule, Virgin, Because Music, 1998. CD Album. Additional Songwriters: Dominic King, Frank Musker.

233. ABBA. "Dancing Queen." Arrival, Polar, Epic, Atlantic, 1976. 12" Vinyl. Additional Songwriter: Stig Anderson.

234. Frankie Goes to Hollywood. "Relax." Welcome to the Pleasuredome, ZTT, 1983. 12" Vinyl.

235. The Village People. "Y.M.C.A." Cruisin', Casablanca, 1978. 12" Vinyl.

236. Eiffel 65. "Blue (Da Ba Dee)." Europop, Skooby, 1998. CD Album. Additional Songwriter: Massimo Gabutti.

237. Kool & The Gang. "Celebration." Celebrate! De-Lite, 1980. 12" Vinyl. Additional Songwriter: Eumir Deodato.

238. Murray Head. "One Night in Bangkok." Chess, RCA, 1984. 12" Vinyl. Songwriters: Tim Rice, Bjorn Ulvaeus, Benny Andersson.

239. Hanson. "MMMBop." Middle of Nowhere, Mercury, 1997. CD Album.

240. Earth, Wind & Fire. "September." The Best of Earth, Wind & Fire, Vol. 1, ARC/Columbia, 1978. 12" Vinyl. Additional Songwriter: Allee Willis.

241. Little Eva. "The Loco-Motion." The Loco-Motion, Dimension 1000, 1962. 12" Vinyl. Songwriters: Gerry Goffin, Carole King.

242. The Rednex. "Cotton Eye Joe." Sex & Violins, Internal Affairs, Battery, ZYX, 1994. CD Album. Songwriters: Janne Ericsson, Orjan Oban Oberg, Pat Reiniz, Patrik "The Hitmaker" Lindqvist.

243. Gloria Gaynor. "I Will Survive." Love Tracks, Polydor, 1978. 12" Vinyl. Songwriters: Freddie Perren, Dino Fekaris.

244. Was (Not Was). "Walk the Dinosaur." What Up, Dog? Chrysalis, Fontana, Phonogram, 1987. 12" Vinyl.

245. Hot Chocolate. "You Sexy Thing." Hot Chocolate, RAK, Big Tree (Atlantic), 1975. 12" Vinyl.

246. Men at Work. "Down Under." Business as Usual, Columbia, 1981. 12" Vinyl.

247. The Church. "Under the Milky Way." Starfish, Mushroom, Arista, 1988. 12" Vinyl. Additional Songwriter: Karin Jansson

248. Bon Jovi, "It's My Life." Crush, Island, 2000. CD Album. Additional Songwriter: Max Martin.

249. Amy Winehouse. "Rehab." Back to Black, Island, 2006. CD Album.

250. Avicci. "Hey Brother." True, PRMD, Universal, 2013. Digital Download. Additional songwriters: Salem Al Fakir, Veronica Maggio, Vincent Pontare, Ash Pournori. Sung by Dan Tyminski.

251. Madonna. "Material Girl." Like a Virgin, Sire, Warner Bros., 1985. 12" Vinyl. Songwriters: Peter Brown, Robert Rans.

252. Katy Perry. "Teenage Dream." Teenage Dream, Capitol, 2010. CD Album. Additional Songwriters: Lukasz Gottwald, Max Martin, Benjamin Levin, Bonnie McKee.

253. Meredith Brooks. "Bitch." Blurring the Edges, Capitol, 1997. CD Album. Additional Songwriter: Shelly Peiken.

254. Dolly Parton. "Jolene." Jolene, RCA Victor, 1973. 12" Vinyl.

255. KT Tunstall. "Black Horse and the Cherry Tree." Eye to the Telescope, Relentless, Virgin, 2005. CD Album.

256. Ke$ha. "We R Who We R." Cannibal, RCA, 2010. CD Album. Additional Songwriters: Joshua Coleman, Lukasz Gottwald, Jacob Kasher Hindlin, Benjamin Levin.

257. Alanis Morissette. "Ironic." Jagged Little Pill, Maverick, Warner Bros., 1996. CD Album. Additional Songwriter: Glen Ballard.

258. The Angels. "My Boyfriend's Back." My Boyfriend's Back, Smash, 1963. 12" Vinyl. Songwriters: Bob Feldman, Jerry Goldstein, Richard Gottehrer.

259. The Bangles. "Walk Like an Egyptian." Different Light, Columbia, Bangle-a-lang Music, 1986. 12" Vinyl. Songwriter: Liam Sternberg.

260. Brandy Clark. "Girl Next Door." Big Day in a Small Town, Warner Bros., 2016. Digital Download. Additional Songwriters: Jessie Jo Dillon, Shane McAnally.

261. Spice Girls. "Spice Up Your Life." Spiceworld, Virgin, 1997. CD Album. Additional Songwriters: Richard Stannard, Matt Rowe.

262. P!nk. "Get the Party Started." Missundaztood, LaFace, Arista, 2001. CD Album. Songwriter: Linda Perry.

263. Celine Dion. "That's the Way It Is." All the Way…A Decade of Song, Columbia, Epic, 1999. CD Album. Songwriters: Max Martin, Kristian Lundin, Andreas Carlsson.

264. Cher. "Believe." Believe, Warner Bros., 1998. CD Album. Additional Songwriters: Brian Higgins, Stuart McLennen, Paul Barry, Steven Torch, Matthew Gray, Timothy Powell.

265. Dixie Chicks. "Goodbye Earl." Fly, Monument, 2000. CD Album. Songwriter: Dennis Linde.

266. Ellie Goulding. "Love Me Like You Do." Fifty Shades of Grey: Original Motion Picture Soundtrack, Cherrytree, Interscope, Republic, 2015. Digital Download. Songwriters: Max Martin, Savan Kotecha, Ilya Salmanzadeh, Ali Payami, Tove Nilsson.

267. B*Witched. "C'est La Vie." B*Witched, Epic, Glowworm, 1998. CD Album. Additional Songwriters: Ray "Madman" Hedges, Martin Brannigan, Tracy Ackerman.

268. Vanessa Carlton. "A Thousand Miles." Be Not Nobody, A&M, 2002. CD Album.

269. Ariana Grande. "Into You." Dangerous Woman, Republic, 2016. Digital Download. Additional Songwriters: Max Martin, Savan Kotecha, Alexander Kronlund, Ilya Salmanzadeh.

270. Aerosmith. "Dream On." Aerosmith, Columbia, 1973. 12" Vinyl.

271. The First Edition w/Kenny Rogers. "Just Dropped in (To See What Condition My Condition Was In)." The First Edition, Reprise, 1967. 12" Vinyl. Songwriter: Mickey Newbury.

272. Gorillaz. "Clint Eastwood." Gorillaz, Parlophone, Virgin, EMI, 2001. CD Album. Additional Songwriter: Del the Funky Homosapien (Teren Delvon Jones).

273. Linkin Park. "In the End." Hybrid Theory, Warner Bros., 2001. CD Album.

274. The Smashing Pumpkins. "Bullet with Butterfly Wings (Rat in a Cage)." Mellon Collie and the Infinite Sadness, Virgin, 1995. CD Album.

275. Green Day. "Working Class Hero." Instant Karma: The Amnesty International Campaign to Save Darfur, Warner Bros. Amnesty International, 2007. CD Album. Songwriter: John Lennon.

276. The Brothers Four. "Greenfields." The Brothers Four, Columbia, 1960. 12" Vinyl. Songwriters: Richard Dehr, Frank Miller, Terry Gilkyson.

277. Depeche Mode. "Precious." Playing the Angel, Mute, Sire, Reprise, 2005. CD Album.

278. Prong. "Snap Your Fingers Snap Your Neck." Cleansing, Epic, 1994. CD Album.

279. Kansas. "Dust in the Wind." Point of Know Return, Kirshner, 1978. 12" Vinyl.

280. Midnight Oil. "Beds are Burning." Diesel and Dust, Columbia, 1987. 12" Vinyl.

281. America. "Lonely People." Holiday, Warner Bros., 1974. 12" Vinyl. Additional Songwriter: Catherine Peek.

282. Simon & Garfunkel. "Sound of Silence." Sounds of Silence, Columbia, 1965. 12" Vinyl.

283. Ricky Nelson. "Lonesome Town." Ricky Sings Again, Imperial, 1958. 12" Vinyl. Songwriter: Baker Knight.

284. The Rolling Stones. "Paint It Black." Aftermath, Decca, London, 1966. 12" Vinyl.

285. The Cascades. "Rhythm of the Rain." Rhythm of the Rain, Valiant Records, 1962. 12" Vinyl.

286. R.E.M. "The One I Love." Document, I.R.S., 1987. 12" Vinyl.

287. The Goo Goo Dolls. "Iris." Dizzy up the Girl, Reprise, Warner Bros. 1998. CD Album.

288. Willie Nelson. "Always on My Mind." Always on My Mind, Columbia, 1982. 12" Vinyl. Songwriters: Johnny Christopher, Wayne Carson Thompson, Mark James.

289. David Guetta ft. Nicki Minaj, Bebe Rexha & Afrojack. "Hey Mama." Listen, Parlophone, Atlantic, 2015. Digital Download. Additional Songwriters: Ester Dean, Sean Douglas, Giorgio Tuinfort, Nick van de Wall, Alan Lomax.
290. Gigi D'Augustino. "The Riddle." L'Amour Toujours, ZYX, EMI Music, 1999. CD Album. Songwriter: Nik Kershaw.
291. The Ramones. "Pet Sematary." Brain Drain, Sire, Chrysalis, 1989. 12" Vinyl. Additional Songwriter: Daniel Rey.
292. Sia. "The Greatest." This is Acting, Monkey Puzzle, RCA, 2016. Digital Download. Additional Songwriters: Greg Kurstin, Kendrick Duckworth, Blair MacKichan.
293. Loreena McKennitt. "The Mummer's Dance (Radio Edit)." The Book of Secrets, Quinlan Road, Warner Bros., 1997. CD Album.
294. Blackmore's Night. "Under a Violet Moon." Under a Violet Moon, Edel, Platinum Entertainment, 1999. CD Album.
295. Emmilie De Forest. "Only Teardrops." Only Teardrops, Sony Music, 2013. CD Album. Songwriters: Lise Cabble, Julia Fabrin Jakobsen, Thomas Stengaard.
296. Enya. "Only Time (Radio Edit)." A Day Without Rain, WEA, Reprise, 2000. CD Album. Additional Songwriter: Roma Ryan.
297. Lipps, Inc. "Funkytown." Mouth to Mouth, Casablanca, 1980. 12" Vinyl. Songwriter: Steven Greenberg.
298. The Chordettes. "Mr. Sandman." Single, Cadence, 1954. 12" Vinyl. Songwriter: Pat Ballard.
299. Run DMC & Aerosmith. "Walk This Way." Raising Hell, Profile, Geffen, 1986. 12" Vinyl.
300. Right Said Fred. "I'm Too Sexy." Up, Tug, Charisma, 1991. CD Album.
301. Donna Summer. "Hot Stuff." Bad Girls, Casablanca, 1979. 12" Vinyl. Songwriters: Pete Bellotte, Harold Faltermeyer, Keith Forsey.

302. Barry Mann. "Who Put the Bomp (in the Bomp, Bomp, Bomp.)" Who Put the Bomp, ABC-Paramount, 1961. 12" Vinyl. Additional Songwriter: Gerry Goffin.

303. The B-52's. "Love Shack." Cosmic Thing, Reprise, 1989. 12" Vinyl.

304. Cherry Poppin' Daddies. "Zoot Suit Riot." Zoot Suit Riot: The Swingin' Hits of the Cherry Poppin' Daddies, Space Age Bachelor Pad, Mojo Records, 1997. CD Album.

305. The Trammps. "Disco Inferno." Disco Inferno, Atlantic, 1976. 12" Vinyl. Additional Songwriter: Leroy Green.

306. Survivor. "Eye of the Tiger." Eye of the Tiger, EMI, Scotti Brothers, 1982. 12" Vinyl.

307. Fatboy Slim. "The Rockafeller Skank (Funk Soul Brother)." You've Come a Long Way, Baby, Skint, 1998. CD Album. Additional Songwriters: John Barry, Winford Terry.

308. Rose Royce. "Car Wash." Car Wash: Original Motion Picture Soundtrack, MCA, 1976. 12" Vinyl. Songwriter: Norman Whitfield.

309. The Backstreet Boys. "Larger Than Life." Millennium, Jive, 1999. CD Album. Additional Songwriters: Max Martin, Kristian Lundin.

310. J. Geils Band. "Centerfold." Freeze Frame, EMI America, 1981. 12" Vinyl. Songwriter: Seth Justman.

311. Mitch Ryder and The Detroit Wheels. "Devil with a Blue Dress." Breakout! New Voice, 1966. 12" Vinyl. Songwriters: Frederick Long, William Stevenson.

312. Del Amitri. "Roll to Me." Twisted, A&M, 1995. CD Album.

313. The Spencer Davis Group. "Gimme Some Lovin.'" Single, Fontana, United Artists, 1966. 12" Vinyl.

314. The Romantics. "What I like About You." The Romantics, Nemperor, Epic. 1979. 12" Vinyl.

315. Johnny Cash. "I've Been Everywhere." Unchained, American, 1996. CD Album. Songwriter: Geoff Mack.

316. Hal Ketchum. "Small Town Saturday Night." Past the Point of Rescue, Curb, 1991. CD Album. Songwriters: Pat Alger, Hank DeVito.

317. Zac Brown Band. "Chicken Fried." The Foundation, Live Nation, Home Grown, Atlantic, 2008. CD Album. Additional Songwriter: Wyatt Durrette.

318. Loggins & Messina. "Danny's Song." Sittin' In, Columbia, 1971. 12" Vinyl.

319. Luke Bryan. "Country Girl (Shake It for Me)." Tailgates & Tanlines, Capitol Nashville, 2011. CD Album. Additional Songwriter: Dallas Davidson.

320. Tim McGraw. "The Cowboy in Me." Set This Circus Down, Curb, 2001. CD Album. Songwriters: Al Anderson, Craig Wiseman, Jeffrey Steele.

321. Mike Posner. "I Took a Pill in Ibiza." At Night, Alone, Island, 2015. Digital Download.

322. Santana ft. Rob Thomas. "Smooth." Supernatural, Arista, BMG, 1999. CD Album. Additional Songwriter: Itaal Shur.

323. The Who. "Baba O'Riley (Teenage Wasteland)." Who's Next, Polydor, 1971. 12" Vinyl.

324. Van Halen. "Jump." 1984, Warner Bros., 1983. 12" Vinyl.

325. Mumford & Sons. "Little Lion Man." Sigh No More, Island, Glassnote, 2009. CD Album.

326. The Searchers. "Love Potion #9." Meet The Searchers, Kapp, KJB-27, 1964. 12" Vinyl. Songwriters: Jerry Leiber, Mike Stoller.

327. The Offspring. "Self Esteem." Smash, Epitaph, 1994. CD Album.

328. Iggy Pop. "Real Wild Child (Wild One)." Blah-Blah-Blah, A&M, 1986. 12" Vinyl. Songwriters: Johnny Greenan, Johnny O'Keefe, Dave Owens, Tony Withers.

329. Rancid. "Ruby Soho." ...And Out Come the Wolves, Epitaph, 1995. CD Album.

330. Sweet. "Action." Strung Up, RCA, Capitol, 1975. 12" Vinyl.

331. Simple Plan. "Addicted." No Pads, No Helmets…Just Balls, Lava, 2003. CD Album. Additional Songwriter: Arnold Lanni.

332. Sum 41. "Still Waiting." Does This Look Infected?, Island, 2002. CD Album.

333. Fall Out Boy. "This Ain't a Scene, It's an Arm's Race." Infinity on High, Island, 2006. CD Album.

334. The Beatles. "Ob-La-Di, Ob-La-Da (Life Goes On)." The Beatles, Apple, 1968. 12" Vinyl.

335. The Doobie Brothers. "China Grove." The Captain and Me, Warner Brothers, 1973. 12" Vinyl.

336. White Town. "Your Woman." Women in Technology, Chrysalis, Brilliant!, EMI, 1997. CD Album. Additional songwriters: Bing Crosby, Max Wartell, Irving Walkman.

337. AC/DC. "You Shook Me all Night Long." Back in Black, Atlantic, 1980. 12" Vinyl.

338. Jerry Lee Lewis. "Great Balls of Fire." Single, Sun 281, 1957. 12" Vinyl. Songwriters: Otis Blackwell, Jack Hammer.

339. Apocalyptica. "Hall of the Mountain King." Cult, Mercury, Universal, 2000. CD Album. Composer: Edvard Grieg.

340. Dead Rose Symphony. "Night on Bald Mountain." The Dark Gift, CD Baby, 2009. CD Album. Composer: Modest Mussorgsky.

341. Motorhead. "Ace of Spades." Ace of Spades, Bronze, 1980. 12" Vinyl.

342. Drowning Pool. "Bodies (Let the Bodies Hit the Floor)." Sinner, Wind-up, 2001. CD Album.

343. Sabaton. "Resist & Bite." Heroes, Nuclear Blast, 2014. Digital Download.

344. Papa Roach. "Last Resort." Infest, DreamWorks, 2000. CD Album.

345. Third Eye Blind. "Never Let You Go." Blue, Elektra, Eastwest, 2000. CD Album.

346. The Monkees. "Daydream Believer." The Birds, The Bees & The Monkees, Colgems #1012, 1967. 12" Vinyl. Songwriter: John Stewart.

347. George Thorogood & The Destroyers. "Bad to the Bone." Bad to the Bone, Emi America, 1982. 12" Vinyl.

348. Bob Dylan. "Shelter from the Storm." Blood on the Tracks, Columbia, 1975. 12" Vinyl.

349. George Harrison. "Got My Mind Set on You." Cloud Nine, Dark Horse, 1987. CD Album. Songwriter: Rudy Clark.

350. OneRepublic. "Counting Stars." Native, Mosley, Interscope, 2013. CD Album.

351. Imagine Dragons. "Thunder." Evolve, Interscope, Kidinakorner, 2017. Digital download. Additional Songwriters: Alexander Grant, Jayson DeZuzio.

352. Sugar Ray. "Fly." Floored, Atlantic, Lava, 1997. CD Album.

353. Walk the Moon. "Shut Up and Dance." Talking is Hard, RCA, 2014. Digital download. Additional Songwriters: Ben Berger, Ryan McMahon.

354. Bon Jovi. "You Give Love a Bad Name." Slippery When Wet, Mercury, 1986. 12" Vinyl. Additional Songwriter: Desmond Child.

355. Paul Simon. "Kodachrome." There Goes Rhymin' Simon, Columbia, 1973. 12" Vinyl.

356. Dion & The Belmonts. "Runaround Sue." Runaround Sue, Laurie, 1961. 12" Vinyl. Additional Songwriter: Ernie Maresca.

357. Daryle Singletary. "Too Much Fun." Daryle Singletary, Giant, 1995. CD Album. Songwriters: Curtis Wright, Jeff Knight.

358. Andy Grammer. "Honey, I'm Good." Magazines or Novels, S-Curve, 2014. Digital Download. Additional Songwriter: Nolan Sipe.

359. Mark Chestnutt. "Bubba Shot the Jukebox." Longnecks & Short Stories, MCA, 1992. CD Album. Songwriter: Dennis Linde.

360. Charley Pride. "The Snakes Crawl at Night." Country Charley Pride, RCA 1966. 12" Vinyl. Songwriters: Mel Tillis, Fred Burch.

361. John Belushi & Dan Aykroyd (Elwood, Jake & The Blues Brother's Band). "Theme from Rawhide (Blues Brothers Movie Version)." The Blues Brothers: Original Soundtrack Recording, Atlantic, 1980. 12" Vinyl. Songwriters: Dimitri Tiomkin, Ned Washington.

362. Charlie Daniels Band. "Devil Went Down to Georgia." Million Mile Reflections, Epic, 1979. 12" Vinyl.

363. U2. "Beautiful Day." All That You Can't Leave Behind, Island, Interscope, 2000. CD Album.

364. Billy Idol. "Rebel Yell." Rebel Yell, Chrysalis, 1983. 12" Vinyl. Additional Songwriter: Steve Stevens.

365. No Mercy. "Where Do You Go." My Promise, MCI, BMG, Arista, 1996. CD Album. Songwriters: Peter Bischof, Franz Reuther.

366. The Zombies. "Time of the Season." Odessey and Oracle, CBS, 1968. 12" Vinyl.

367. The Proclaimers. "I'm Gonna Be (500 Miles)." Sunshine on Leith, Chrysalis, 1988. 12" Vinyl.

368. Fine Young Cannibals. "She Drives Me Crazy." The Raw & The Cooked, London Records, 1988. 12" Vinyl.

369. Fountains of Wayne. "Stacy's Mom." Welcome Interstate Managers, S-Curve, Virgin, 2003. CD Album.

370. The Offspring. "Pretty Fly (for a White Guy)." Americana, Columbia, 1998. CD Album. Additional Songwriters: Steve Clark, Joe Elliot, Robert John "Mutt" Lange.

371. Blink 182. "All the Small Things." Enema of the State, MCA, 2000. CD Album.

372. The Misfits. "London Dungeon." 3 Hits from Hell, Plan 9, 1981. 12" Vinyl.

373. The Clash. "I Fought the Law." The Cost of Living, CBS, 1979. 12" Vinyl. Songwriter: Sonny Curtis.

374. The All-American Rejects. "Dirty Little Secret." Move Along, Doghouse, Interscope, 2005. CD Album.

375. Fitz and the Tantrums. "Handclap." Fitz and The Tantrums, Elektra, 2016. CD Album. Additional Songwriters: Eric Frederic, Sam Hollander.

376. The Mamas and the Papas. "California Dreamin'." If You Can Believe Your Eyes and Ears, Dunhill Records, RCA Victor, 1965. 12" Vinyl.

377. Train. "Drops of Jupiter (Tell Me)." Drops of Jupiter, Columbia, 2001. CD Album.

378. Curtis Lee. "Pretty Little Angel Eyes." Single, Dune Records, 1961. 12" Vinyl. Additional Songwriter: Tommy Boyce.

379. OMC. "How Bizarre." How Bizarre, Huh!, Polydor, Mercury, 1995. CD Album.

380. Cutting Crew. "(I Just) Died in Your Arms." Broadcast, Virgin, 1986. 12" Vinyl.

381. Rob Zombie. "Feel So Numb." The Sinister Urge, Geffen, 2001. CD Album. Additional Songwriter: Scott Humphrey.

382. Marilyn Manson. "mOBSCENE." The Golden Age of Grotesque, Nothing, Interscope, 2003. CD Album. Additional Songwriter: John 5.

383. Godsmack. "I Stand Alone." Faceless, Universal, 2002. CD Album.

384. Alice Cooper. "Poison." Trash, Epic, 1989. 12" Vinyl. Additional Songwriters: Desmond Child, John McCurry.

385. Megadeth. "Symphony of Destruction." Countdown to Extinction, Capitol, 1992. CD Album.

386. Powerwolf. "Demons Are a Girl's Best Friend." The Sacrament of Sin, Napalm Records, 2018. CD Album.

387. Red Hot Chili Peppers. "Californication." Californication, Warner Bros., 2000. CD Album.

388. Eddie Money. "Take Me Home Tonight." Can't Hold Back, Columbia, 1986. 12" Vinyl. Songwriters: Mike Leeson, Peter Vale, Ellie Greenwich, Jeff Barry, Phil Spector.

389. M. "Pop Muzik." New York * London * Paris * Munich, MCA, EMI, Sire, 1979. 12" Vinyl.

390. Smash Mouth. "Walkin' on the Sun." Fush Yu Mang, Interscope, 1997. CD Album.

391. Bobby Vee. "The Night Has a Thousand Eyes." The Night Has a Thousand Eyes, Liberty, 1962. 12" Vinyl. Songwriters: Benjamin Weisman, Dorothy Wayne, Marilyn Garrett.

392. Lifehouse. "Hanging by a Moment." No Name Face, DreamWorks, 2000. CD Album.

393. Taylor Swift. "Sparks Fly." Speak Now, Big Machine, 2011. CD Album.

394. Barry Louis Polisar. "All I Want is You." Music from the Motion Picture Juno, Rhino Entertainment, 2007. CD Album.

395. Bill Haley & His Comets. "Shake, Rattle & Roll." Shake, Rattle & Roll, Decca Records, 1954. 12" Vinyl. Songwriter: Jesse Stone aka Charles E. Calhoun.

396. Bobby Darin. "Splish Splash." Single, Atco 6117, 1958. 12" Vinyl. Additional Songwriter: Murray Kaufman.

397. The Contours. "Do You Love Me?" Do You Love Me (Now That I Can Dance), Gordy, 1962. 12" Vinyl. Songwriter: Berry Gordy Jr.

398. Bobby Lewis. "Tossin' & Turnin'." Tossin' & Turnin', Beltone, 1961. 12" Vinyl. Songwriters: Ritchie Adams, Malou Rene.

399. Elvis Presley. "Jailhouse Rock." Jailhouse Rock, RCA Victor, 1957. 12" Vinyl. Songwriters: Jerry Leiber, Mike Stoller.

400. Wilson Pickett. "Land of 1,000 Dances." The Exciting Wilson Pickett, Atlantic, 1966. 12" Vinyl. Songwriter: Chris Kenner.

401. Gary U.S. Bonds. "New Orleans." Dance 'Til Quarter to Three with U.S. Bonds, Legrand, 1960. 12" Vinyl. Songwriters: Frank Guida, Joseph Royster.

402. Buddy Holly and the Crickets. "Oh, Boy!" The "Chirping" Crickets, Brunswick, 1957. 12" Vinyl. Songwriters: Sonny West, Bill Tilghman, Norman Petty.

403. Bobby Day. "Rockin' Robin." Rockin' with Robin, Class, 1958. 12" Vinyl. Songwriter: Leon Rene.

404. Chubby Checker. "The Twist." Twist with Chubby Checker, Parkway, 1960. 12" Vinyl. Songwriter: Hank Ballard.

405. The Penguins. "Earth Angel." Single, Dootone, 1954. 12" Vinyl. Additional Songwriters: Jesse Belvin, Gaynel Hodge.

406. Ed Sheeran. "Perfect (Dancing in the Dark)." Divide, Asylum, Atlantic, 2017. Digital Download.

407. The Shirelles. "Will You Love Me Tomorrow." Tonight's the Night, Scepter, 1960. 12" Vinyl. Songwriters: Gerry Goffin, Carole King.

408. Conway Twitty. "I'd Love to Lay You Down." Heart & Soul, MCA, 1980. 12" Vinyl. Songwriter: Johnny MacRae.

409. Alphaville. "Forever Young." Forever Young, WEA, 1984. 12" Vinyl.

410. Bob Seger & The Silver Bullet Band. "Night Moves." Night Moves, Capitol, 1976. 12" Vinyl.

411. 10,000 Maniacs. "Because the Night." MTV Unplugged, Elektra, MTV Networks, 1993. CD Album. Songwriters: Bruce Springsteen, Patti Smith.

412. Passenger. "Let Her Go." All the Little Lights, Embassy of Music, Black Crow Records, Nettwerk, 2012. Digital Download.

413. The Platters. "Twilight Time." Single, Mercury Records, 1958. 12" Vinyl. Songwriters: Buck Ram, Morty Nevins, Al Nevins, Artie Dunn.

414. Mel Carter. "Hold Me, Thrill Me, Kiss Me." Hold Me, Thrill Me, Kiss Me, Imperial, 1965. 12" Vinyl. Songwriter: Harry Noble.

415. Sixpence None the Richer. "Kiss Me." Sixpence None the Richer, Squint, Columbia, Elektra, 1998. CD Album.

416. Elvis Presley. "Can't Help Falling in Love." Blue Hawaii, RCA Victor, 1961. 12" Vinyl. Songwriters: Hugo Peretti, Luigi Creatore, George Davis Weiss.

417. Bruce Springsteen. "I'm on Fire." Born in the U.S.A., Columbia, 1985. 12" Vinyl.

418. The Righteous Brothers. "Unchained Melody." Just Once in My Life, Phillies, Verve, 1965. 12" Vinyl. Songwriters: Alex North, Hy Zaret.

419. Sam Smith. "I'm Not the Only One." In the Lonely Hour, Capitol, 2014. Digital Download. Additional Songwriter: James Napier.

420. Fats Domino. "Blueberry Hill." This Is Fats Domino!, Imperial, 1956. 12" Vinyl. Songwriters: Vincent Rose, Larry Stock, Al Lewis.

421. Eagle-Eye Cherry. "Save Tonight." Desireless, Superstudio Bla, Polydor, Work, 1997. CD Album.

422. B.O.B. ft. Hayley Williams. "Airplanes." B.O.B. Presents: The Adventures of Bobby Ray, Grand Hustle, Rebel Rock, Atlantic, A&M/Octone, 2010. CD Album. Additional Songwriters: Jeremy "Kinetics" Dussolliet, Tim "One Love" Sommers, Justin Franks, Alexander Grant, Christine Dominguez.

423. LeAnn Rimes. "Can't Fight the Moonlight." Coyote Ugly Soundtrack, Curb, London, 2000. CD Album. Songwriter: Diane Warren.

424. Stevie Wonder. "I Just Called to Say I Love You." The Woman in Red, Motown, 1984. 12" Vinyl.

425. Sam Cooke. "Cupid." Single, RCA Victor, 1961. 45 RPM Vinyl.

426. Chicago. "If You Leave Me Now." Chicago X, Columbia, 1976. 12" Vinyl.

427. The Moody Blues. "Nights in White Satin." Days of Future Passed, Deram, 1967. 12" Vinyl.

428. Supertramp. "Goodbye Stranger." Breakfast in America, A&M, 1979. 12" Vinyl.

429. Jimmy Ruffin. "What Becomes of the Broken Hearted?" Jimmy Ruffin Sings Top Ten, Soul, 1966. 12" Vinyl. Songwriters: William Weatherspoon, Paul Riser, James Dean.

430. Percy Sledge. "When a Man Loves a Woman." When a Man Loves a Woman, Atlantic, 1966. 12" Vinyl. Songwriters: Calvin Lewis, Andrew Wright.

431. The Platters. "The Great Pretender." Single, Mercury, 1955. 45 RPM Vinyl. Songwriter: Buck Ram.

432. Four Tops. "Baby I Need Your Loving." Four Tops, Motown, 1964. 12" Vinyl. Songwriters: Holland-Dozier-Holland.

433. Bill Withers. "Lean on Me." Still Bill, Sussex, 1972. 12" Vinyl.

434. Hank Williams. "I'm So Lonesome I Could Cry." Single, MGM, 1949. 45 RPM Vinyl.

435. Toby Keith. "Dream Walkin'." Dream Walkin', Mercury Nashville, 1998. CD Album. Additional Songwriter: Chuck Cannon.

436. Brooks & Dunn. "Neon Moon." Brand New Man, Arista, 1992. CD Album.

437. Foreigner. "Juke Box Hero." 4, Atlantic, 1982. 12" Vinyl.

438. The Isley Brothers. "Shout." Shout! RCA Victor, 1959. 12" Vinyl.

439. Blue Swede. "Hooked on a Feeling." Hooked on a Feeling, EMI Svenska, 1974. 12" Vinyl. Songwriter: Mark James.

440. Redbone. "Come and Get Your Love." Epic, 1974. 12" Vinyl.

441. Vanilla Ice "Ice Ice Baby." To the Extreme, SBK, 1990. CD Album. Additional Songwriters: Floyd Brown, Mario Johnson, Brian May, David Bowie, Freddie Mercury, John Deacon, Roger Taylor.

442. The Supremes. "Stop in the Name of Love." More Hits by The Supremes, Motown, 1965. 12" Vinyl. Songwriters: Holland-Dozier-Holland.

443. Kenny Loggins. "Footloose." Footloose: Original Soundtrack of the Paramount Motion Picture, Columbia, 1984. 12" Vinyl. Additional Songwriter: Dean Pitchford.

444. KC and the Sunshine Band. "Get Down Tonight." KC and the Sunshine Band, TK, 1975. 12" Vinyl.

445. Manfred Mann. "Do Wah Diddy Diddy." The Manfred Mann Album, HMV POP, Ascot, Capitol, 1964. 12" Vinyl. Songwriters: Jeff Berry, Ellie Greenwich.

446. Chic. "Le Freak." C'est Chic, Atlantic, 1978. 12" Vinyl. Additional Songwriter: Bernard Edwards.

447. Lou Bega. "Mambo No.5 (A Little Bit of…)." A Little Bit of Mambo, Ariola, RCA, 1999. CD Album. Additional Songwriters: Damaso Perez Prado, Zippy Davids.

448. John Travolta & Olivia Newton-John. "You're the One That I Want." Grease: The Original Soundtrack from the Motion Picture, RSO, 1978. 12" Vinyl. Songwriter: John Farrar.

449. The Monotones. "The Book of Love." Who Wrote The Book Of Love, Mascot, Argo, 1958. 12" Vinyl.

450. Leo Sayer. "You Make Me Feel Like Dancing." Endless Flight, Chrysalis, Warner Bros., 1976. 12" Vinyl. Additional Songwriter: Vini Poncia.

451. The Vengaboys. "We Like to Party! (The Vengabus)." The Party Album, Groovilicious/S.R., 1998. CD Album. Songwriters: Danski, DJ Delmundo.

452. Dead or Alive. "You Spin Me Round (Like a Record)." Youthquake, Epic, 1984. 12" Vinyl.

453. Gloria Estefan. "Turn the Beat Around." Hold Me, Thrill Me, Kiss Me, Epic, 1994. CD Album. Songwriters: Gerald Jackson, Peter Jackson.

454. Gym Class Heroes ft. Adam Lavigne of Maroon 5. "Stereo Hearts." The Papercut Chronicles II, Decaydance, Fueled by Ramen, 2011.

CD Album. Additional Songwriters: Benjamin Levin, Sterling Fox, Ammar Malik, Dan Omelio.

455. The Eagles. "Hotel California." Hotel California, Asylum, 1977. 12" Vinyl.

456. George Strait. "I Just Want to Dance with You." One Step at a Time, MCA Nashville, 1998. CD Album. Songwriters: Roger Cook, John Prine.

457. Jim Croce. "I'll Have to Say I Love You in a Song." I Got a Name, ABC Records, 1974. 12" Vinyl.

458. The Bloodhound Gang. "The Bad Touch (The Discovery Channel Song)." Hooray for Boobies, Jimmy Franks, Geffen, 1999. CD Album.

459. Lady Gaga. "Bad Romance." The Fame Monster, Streamline, KonLive, Cherrytree, Interscope, 2009. CD Album. Additional Songwriter: Nadir Khayat.

460. Toni Basil. "Mickey." Word of Mouth, Chrysalis, Radialchoice/Virgin, 1982. 12" Vinyl. Songwriters: Mike Chapman, Nicky Chinn.

461. Reba McEntire. "Fancy." Rumor Has It, MCA, 1991. CD Album. Songwriter: Bobbie Gentry.

462. Ace of Base. "Beautiful Life." The Bridge, Mega, 1995. CD Album. Additional Songwriter: John Ballard.

463. Selena Gomez & the Scene. "Love You Like a Love Song." When the Sun Goes Down, Hollywood, 2011. CD Album. Songwriters: Antonina Armato, Tim James, Adam Schmalholz.

464. Stevie Nicks. "Edge of Seventeen." Bella Donna, Modern, 1982. 12" Vinyl.

465. Bow Wow Wow. "I Want Candy." The Last of the Mohicans, RCA, 1982. 12" Vinyl. Songwriters: Bert Berns, Bob Feldman, Jerry Goldstein, Richard Gottehrer.

466. Paula Cole. "Where Have All the Cowboys Gone." This Fire, Warner Bros., Imago, 1997. CD Album.

467. Kelly Clarkson. "Stronger (What Doesn't Kill You)." Stronger, RCA, 2012. Digital Download. Songwriters: Jorgen Elofsson, Ali Tamposi, David Gamson, Greg Kurstin.

468. The Ting Tings. "Hands." Single, Columbia, 2010. CD Album.

469. Bananarama. "Cruel Summer." Bananarama, London, 1983. 12" Vinyl. Additional Songwriters: Steve Jolley, Tony Swain.

470. Lee Ann Womack. "I Hope You Dance." I Hope You Dance, MCA Nashville, 2000. CD Album. Songwriters: Mark D. Sanders, Tia Sillers.

471. Taylor Swift. "Blank Space." 1989, Big Machine, Republic, 2014. Digital Download. Additional Songwriters: Max Martin, Shellback.

472. Carly Simon. "You're So Vain." No Secrets, Elektra, 1972. 12" Vinyl.

473. Belinda Carlisle. "Heaven Is a Place on Earth." Heaven on Earth, MCA, 1987. 12" Vinyl. Songwriters: Rick Nowels, Ellen Shipley.

474. Kylie Minogue. "Can't Get You Out of My Head." Fever, Parlophone, 2001. CD Album. Songwriters: Cathy Dennis, Rob Davis.

475. Donna Lewis. "I Love You Always Forever." Now in a Minute, Atlantic, 1996. CD Album.

476. Blondie. "The Tide Is High." Autoamerican, Chrysalis, 1980. 12" Vinyl. Songwriter: John Holt.

477. In This Moment. "Blood." Blood, Century Media, 2012. Digital Download.

478. Rihanna. "S&M." Loud, Def Jam, SRP, 2011. CD Album. Songwriters: Mikkel S. Ericksen, Tor Erik Hermansen, Sandy Wilhelm, Ester Dean.

479. Benny Benassi. "Satisfaction." Hypnotica, D:vision, 2002. CD Album. Songwriter: Alle Benassi.

480. Dev. "In the Dark." The Night the Sun Came Up, Universal Motown, 2011. CD Album. Additional Songwriters: Niles Hollowell-Dhar, David Singer-Vine.

481. Telepopmusik. "Breathe." Genetic World, Catalogue, Chrysalis, Capitol, 2002. CD Album. Additional Songwriter: Angela McCluskey.

482. Steve Miller Band. "Abracadabra." Abracadabra, Capitol, Mercury, 1982. 12" Vinyl.

483. Bobby 'Boris' Pickett and the Crypt Kickers. "Monster Mash." The Original Monster Mash, Garpax, London, 1962. 12" Vinyl. Additional Songwriter: Leonard Capizzi.

484. Ray Parker Jr. "Ghostbusters." Ghostbusters: Original Soundtrack Album, Arista, 1984. 12" Vinyl.

485. The Mellomen. "Grim Grinning Ghosts." A Musical Tour: Treasures of the Walt Disney Archives at The Reagan Library, Walt Disney Records, 2012 (CD Release). Original Song Release: 1969. CD Album. Songwriters: Buddy Baker, X. Atencio.

486. The Misfits. "Mad Monster Party." Friday The 13th, Misfits Records, 2016. Vinyl E.P.

487. The Citizens of Halloween Town (A) or Marilyn Manson (B). "This is Halloween." A. Citizens of Halloween Town (The Cast of The Nightmare Before Christmas). "This is Halloween." The Nightmare Before Christmas: Original Motion Picture Soundtrack, Walt Disney, 1993. CD Album. Songwriter: Danny Elfman. B. Marilyn Manson. "This is Halloween." Nightmare Revisited, Walt Disney, 2008. CD Album. Songwriter: Danny Elfman.

488. Michael Jackson. "Thriller." Thriller, Epic, CBS, 1984. 12" Vinyl. Songwriter: Rod Temperton.

489. Cher. "Dark Lady." Dark Lady, MCA, 1974. 12" Vinyl. Songwriter: Johnny Durrill.

490. Bing Crosby & Jud Conlon's Rhythmaires. "Headless Horseman Song." The Adventures of Ichabod and Mr. Toad, Walt Disney, 1949. Digital Download. Songwriters: Don Raye, Gene de Paul.

491. The Misfits. "Dig up Her Bones." American Psycho, Geffen, 1997. CD Album.

492. Gordon Lightfoot. "Carefree Highway." Sundown, Reprise, 1974. 12" Vinyl.

493. Peter, Bjorn & John ft. Victoria Bergsman. "Young Folks." Writer's Block, Wichita, P B and J, 2006. CD Album.

494. Edward Sharpe and the Magnetic Zeroes. "Home." Up from Below, Rough Trade, Community, 2010. CD Album.

495. Of Monsters and Men. "Little Talks." My Head Is an Animal, Universal Republic, 2011. CD Album.

496. Madonna ft. Justin Timberlake. "4 Minutes." Hard Candy, Warner Bros., 2008. CD Album. Additional Songwriters: Tim Mosley, Nate Hills.

497. Evanescence. "Bring Me to Life." Fallen, Wind-up, 2003. CD Album.

498. Maroon 5 ft. Christina Aguilera. "Moves like Jagger." Hands All Over, A&M Octone, 2011. CD Album. Additional Songwriters: Benny Blanco, Ammar Malik, Shellback.

499. The Animals. "House of the Rising Sun." The Animals, Columbia, MGM, 1964. 12" Vinyl. Adapted from a traditional folk song of unknown authorship.

500. John Lennon/Yoko Ono with the Plastic Ono Band. "Instant Karma! (We All Shine On)." Single, Apple, 1970. 12" Vinyl.